# Baen Books by Mercedes Lackey

**BARDIC VOICES**
*The Lark and the Wren*
*The Robin and the Kestrel*
*The Eagle and the Nightingales*
*The Free Bards*
*Four & Twenty Blackbirds*
*Bardic Choices: A Cast of Corbies*
(with Josepha Sherman)

*The Fire Rose*

*The Wizard of Karres* (with
Eric Flint & Dave Freer)

*Werehunter*

*Fiddler Fair*

*Dragon's Teeth* (omnibus)

*Brain Ships* (with Anne
McCaffrey & Margaret Ball)
*The Sword of Knowledge* (with
C.J. Cherryh, Leslie Fish &
Nancy Asire)
*The Ship Who Searched 20th
Anniversary Edition* (with
Anne McCaffrey)

*Bedlam's Bard* (with Ellen
Guon)
*Beyond World's End* (with
Rosemary Edghill)
*Spirits White as Lightning* (with
Rosemary Edghill)
*A Host of Furious Fancies*
(omnibus, with Rosemary
Edghill)
*Mad Maudlin* (with Rosemary
Edghill)
*Music to my Sorrow* (with
Rosemary Edghill)

*Bedlam's Edge* (ed. with
Rosemary Edghill)

**THE SERRATED EDGE**
*Chrome Circle* (with Larry
Dixon)
*The Chrome Borne* (with Larry
Dixon)
*The Otherworld* (with Larry
Dixon & Mark Shepherd)

**HISTORICAL FANTASIES
WITH ROBERTA GELLIS**
*This Scepter'd Isle*
*Ill Met by Moonlight*
*By Slanderous Tongues*
*And Less Than Kind*

**HEIRS OF ALEXANDRIA
SERIES**
by Mercedes Lackey,
Eric Flint & Dave Freer
*The Shadow of the Lion*
*This Rough Magic*
*Much Fall of Blood*
*Burdens of the Dead*

**THE SECRET WORLD
CHRONICLE**
*Invasion: Book One of the Secret
World Chronicle* (with Steve
Libbey, Cody Martin
& Dennis Lee)
*World Divided: Book Two of the
Secret World Chronicle* (with
Cody Martin, Dennis Lee &
Veronica Giguere)
*Revolution: Book Three of the
Secret World Chronicle* (with
Cody Martin, Dennis Lee
& Veronica Giguere,
forthcoming)

# DRAGON'S TEETH

MERCEDES LACKEY

DRAGON'S TEETH

*Fiddler Fair* copyright © 1998 by Mercedes Lackey. "Fiddler Fair," in *Magic in Ithkar 3* (Tor 1989); "Balance" and "Dragon's Teeth," in *Bardic Voices One* (Hypatia Press 1988) (HC), in *Spellsingers* (DAW 1988) (PB); "Dance Track," in *Alternate Heroes*, Mike Resnick, ed. (Bantam Spectra 1989); "Last Rights," in *Dinosaur Fantastic*, Martin Greenberg, ed. (DAW 1993); "Jihad," in *Alternate Warriors*, Mike Resnick, ed. (Tor 1993); "Dumb Feast," in *Christmas Ghosts*, Mike Resnick, ed. (DAW 1993); "Small Print" in *Deals with the Devil*, Mike Resnick, ed. (DAW 1994); "The Cup and the Caldron," in *Grails of Light* (DAW); "Once and Future," in *Excalibur!*, Martin Greenberg, ed. (Warner Aspect 1995); "Enemy of My Enemy," *Friends of the Horseclans*, Robert Adams, ed. (NAL 1989)

*Werehunter* copyright © 1999 by Mercedes Lackey. "Werehunter" copyright © 1989 (*Tales of the Witch World*); "SKitty" copyright © 1991 (*Catfantastic*, Andre Norton, ed.); "A Tail of Two SKitties" copyright © 1994 (*Catfantastic 3*, Andre Norton & Martin Greenberg, eds.); "SCat" copyright © 1996 (*Catfantastic 4*, Andre Norton & Martin Greenberg, eds.); "A Better Mousetrap" copyright © 1999 (*Werehunter*, Baen Books); "The Last of the Season" copyright © *American Fantasy Magazine*; "Satanic, Versus . . ." copyright © 1990 (*Marion Zimmer Bradley's Fantasy Magazine*, Fall 1990); "Nightside" copyright © 1990 (*Marion Zimmer Bradley's Fantasy Magazine*, Spring 1990); "Wet Wings" copyright © 1995 (*Sisters of Fantasy 2*, Susan Shwartz & Martin Greenberg, ed.); "Stolen Silver" copyright © 1991 (*Horse Fantastic*); "Roadkill" copyright © 1990 (*Marion Zimmer Bradley's Fantasy Magazine*, Summer 1990); "Operation Desert Fox" copyright © 1993 (*Honor of the Regiment: Bolos, Book I*, eds. Keith Laumer & Bill Fawcett); "Grey" copyright © 1997 (*Sally Blanchard's Pet Bird Report* October 1997); "Grey's Ghost" copyright © 1999 (*Werehunter*, Baen Books)

"For Those About to Rock" copyright © 2013 by Mercedes Lackey & Dennis Lee. "John Murdock's Journal" copyright © 2013 by Mercedes Lackey & Cody Martin. "Valse Triste" copyright © 2013 by Mercedes Lackey. "White Bird" copyright © 2013 by Mercedes Lackey. "Sgian Dubh" copyright © 2013 by Mercedes Lackey.

A Baen Book

Baen Publishing Enterprises
P.O. Box 1403
Riverdale, NY 10471
www.baen.com

ISBN: 978-1-4516-3943-8

Cover art by Eric Williams

First Baen printing, December 2013

Distributed by Simon & Schuster
1230 Avenue of the Americas
New York, NY 10020

Library of Congress Cataloging-in-Publication Data

Lackey, Mercedes.
 [Short stories. Selections]
 Dragon's teeth / Mercedes Lackey.
   pages cm
 Summary: "Fiddler Fair and Werehunter in one novel. Stories set in Mercedes Lackey's Heralds of Valdemar universe, Bardic fantasy series, Diana Tregarde occult series and many others"-- Provided by publisher.
 ISBN 978-1-4516-3943-8 (pbk.)
 I. Title.
 PS3562.A246D83 2014
 813'.54--dc23

                          2013035074

Printed in the United States of America

10  9  8  7  6  5  4  3  2

# Table of Contents

## PART I

### FIDDLER FAIR

How I Spent My Summer Vacation ............................. 5
Aliens Ate My Pickup ........................................ 13
Small Print ................................................. 19
Last Rights ................................................. 31
Dumb Feast .................................................. 41
Dance Track ................................................. 51
Jihad ....................................................... 67
Balance ..................................................... 83
Dragon's Teeth .............................................. 105
The Cup and the Cauldron .................................... 139
Once and Future ............................................. 157
Fiddler Fair ................................................ 169
The Enemy of My Enemy ....................................... 189
Bibliography ................................................ 231

### WEREHUNTER

Introduction ................................................ 235
Werehunter .................................................. 245
SKitty ...................................................... 271
A Tail of Two SKitties ...................................... 287
SCat ........................................................ 301
A Better Mousetrap .......................................... 319
The Last of the Season ...................................... 335
Satanic, Versus ............................................. 349
Nightside ................................................... 365
Wet Wings ................................................... 383
Stolen Silver ............................................... 389
Roadkill .................................................... 403
Operation Desert Fox ........................................ 411
Grey ........................................................ 437
Grey's Ghost ................................................ 451

# Table of Contents

## PART II

For Those About to Rock .......................................................... 487

Haunt You ........................................................................... 503

Valse Triste ......................................................................... 527

White Bird ........................................................................... 539

Sgian Dubh .......................................................................... 549

# PART
## ✳ I ✳

# FIDDLER FAIR

*✳✳✳*

## Mercedes Lackey

# How I Spent My Summer Vacation

## And every other free minute for five straight years

After any number of requests to put all our short stories together in one place, the idea began to take on some merit.

When Larry and I looked into the idea we discovered that we had a lot of other short fiction; about ten years' worth.

*Ten years?* Unbelievable as it seemed at the time, I found the very first story I ever had published (I had sold one story before that, but it wasn't published until the following month). *Fantasy Book* magazine, September 1985. The story was "Turnabout" which was a Tarma and Kethry story, which is going into another collection. For the record, the first story I ever *sold* was for Marion Zimmer Bradley's *Free Amazons of Darkover* "Friends of Darkover" anthology, which was published in December of that year. The story was "A Different Kind of Courage."

Some of these stories are a little gray around the edges, but I include them as a kind of object lesson in writing. Some of the things in them I winced at when I read again—I had no idea of how to write a well-viewpointed story, for instance, and someone should have locked my thesaurus away and not given it back to me for a while! And insofar as the march of technology goes—the earliest were written on my very first computer, which had *no* hard-drive, a whopping four kilobytes—(that's *kilo*bytes, not megabytes)—of RAM, and had two *single* sided *single* density disk drives. I wrote five whole books and many short stories on that machine, which did not have a spell-check function, either. On the other hand, if ewe sea watt effect modern spell-checkers halve on righting, perhaps it that was knot a bad thing. It's just as well; if it had, it would have taken half a day to spell-check twenty pages. So for those of you who are wailing that you can't *possibly* try to write because you only have an ancient

286 with a 40-meg hard-drive . . . forgive me if I raise a sardonic eyebrow. Feh, I say! Feh!

I held down a job as a computer programmer for American Airlines during seven of those ten years, and every minute that I wasn't working, I was writing. I gave up hobbies, I stopped going to movies, I didn't watch television; I wrote. Not less than five hours every day, all day on Saturday and Sunday. I wanted to be able to write for a living, and the only way to get better at writing is to do it. I managed to slow down a bit after being able to quit that job, but I still generally write every day, not less than ten pages a day. And that is the answer to the often-asked question, "How do you become a writer?" You *write.* You write a great deal. You give up everything else so that you can concentrate on writing.

There are many fine books out there (the title usually begins with "How to Write . . .") to teach you the mechanics of writing. Ray Bradbury has also written an excellent book on the subject. You only learn the soul of writing with practice. Practice will make you better— or it will convince you that maybe what you really want to do is go into furniture restoration and get your own television show on The Learning Channel.

Here are the answers to a few more frequently asked questions:

*How do you develop an idea?*

Mostly what we do is to look at what we have done in the past and try to do something different. As for finding ideas, I can only say that finding them is easy; they come all the time. Deciding which ones are worth developing is the difficult part. To find an idea, you simply never accept that there are absolute answers for anything, and as Theodore Sturgeon said, "You ask the next question" continuously. For example: one story evolved from seeing a piece of paper blowing across the highway in an uncannily lifelike manner, and asking myself, "What if that was a real, living creature *disguised* as a piece of paper?" The next questions were, "Why would it be in disguise?" and "What would it be?" and "What would happen if someone found out what it really was ?"

*Do you ever get "writer's block" and what do you do about it?*

When I get stalled on something, I do one of two things. I either work on another project (I always have one book in the outline stage and two in the writing stage, and I will also work on short stories at the same time) or I discuss the situation with Larry. Working with another person—sometimes even simply verbalizing a snag—always gets the book unstuck. There is a perfectly good reason for this: when you speak about something you actually move it from one side of the brain to the other, and often that alone shakes creativity loose.

*How do you do revisions?*

I may revise the ending of the book between outlining and actual writing, but that is only because a more logical and satisfying conclusion presents itself. I am really not thinking of anything other than that. The only other revisions are at the request of the publisher, and may vary from none to clarifying minor points or further elaborating a minor point. In the case of clarification, this amounts to less than 1,000 words in a book of 120,000 or more. In the case of elaboration this usually amounts to the addition of 5,000 words to 10,000 words, generally less.

*Would you call your books "character driven?"*

I think that is quite correct, my books are character-driven. To me, how people react to a given situation is what makes a story interesting. History is nothing more than a series of people's reactions, after all, and many "alternate history" stories have been written about "what would have happened if." The idea—the situation—is only half the story. What the characters do about it is the other.

*Do you base your characters on people you know?*

With very rare exceptions I don't base my characters on anyone I know—those exceptions are minor ones, where I'll ask permission to write a friend into a walk-on role. They do come out of my observation of people in general.

*When did you know you wanted to write?*

I knew I wanted to tell stories from a very early age—in fact, I told them to the kids I babysat for, then wrote them in letters to friends and pen-pals. It was only when I "graduated" from amateur fiction to being paid for what I wrote that I realized I did have a talent for writing—and I had the will to pursue it. That was some thirty years later.

*Where do you start?*

Plotting is usually done with Larry, and one of the first things we do is determine what the characters will be like, then what the major conflict of the book will be. Then we figure out the minor conflicts, the ways that those characters will deal with those conflicts, and ways we can make their lives even more complicated. The resolution generally comes at that point, but not always; sometimes it doesn't come to us until we are actually writing the book, and we change the way it ended in the outline.

*When did you start reading science fiction?*

I started reading sf/f when I was about eight or nine. As I recall, it was the "Space Cat" books, followed by something called *The City Under the Back Steps*, a kind of ant-version of "Honey, I Shrank The Kids," followed immediately by a leap into Andre Norton, Heinlein, and my father's adult sf. *Daybreak 2250 AD* by Norton was one of the first things I read, James Schmidt's *Agent of Vega* was another. Mostly I read Norton, all the Norton I could get my hands on, saving my allowance to order them directly from Ace. Little did I guess I would one day be working for Andre's editor (Donald A. Wollheim)!

*Who were your influences?*

In order of influence: Andre Norton, J.R.R. Tolkien, Robert Heinlein, Theodore Sturgeon, Thomas Burnett Swann, Anne McCaffrey, C.J. Cherryh, Marion Zimmer Bradley. As for editors, I learn something from every editor I have. My three main editors, Elizabeth Wollheim, Melissa Singer, and Jim Baen, have been incredibly helpful.

*What do you choose to write?*

I write what I would like to read, with a caveat—after thirteen years in the marketplace, I am beginning to get a feeling for things that will sell, so obviously I do tailor what I would like to write to the marketplace. I never wrote intentionally for any particular audience, but I seem to have hit on a number of things that are archetypal in nature, which may account for the appeal. The other possibility is that I tend to write about people who are misunderstood, outsiders . . . people who read tend to think of themselves that way, particularly sf/f readers, so they can identify with the characters.

*Do you answer fan-mail?*

When possible, we do. We *always* read it. When mail comes without a self-addressed stamped envelope for a reply, we assume the writer doesn't want a reply; it is only courteous not to waste the time of someone you supposedly like by including a self-addressed, stamped envelope if you want an answer. We don't answer abusive mail, but it does get filed in a special file for future reference. We return manuscripts unread; after some trouble Marion Zimmer Bradley had with a fan-writer, our agent has advised both of us that we can't read unsolicited manuscripts anymore. This is an awful pity, but life is complicated enough without going out and finding ways to add trouble!

*How do you work with a collaborator?*

Working with collaborators depends on the collaborator. If possible, we work on the outline together until we're both happy with it, then one of us starts, passes it off to the other when s/he gets stuck, and gets it passed back under the same circumstances. It goes incredibly fast that way, and it is the way Larry and I always work, even though he is not always on the cover as a co-writer.

*Have you ever encountered any censorship?*

I haven't encountered any censorship at the publisher/editor level on any of my books. I have heard rumors of fundamentalist groups causing problems with the Herald Mage series because of the gay characters, but I have never had any of those rumors substantiated. There are always going to be people who have trouble with characters who don't fit their narrow ideas of what is appropriate: I have perfectly good advice for them. Don't read the books. Nobody is forcing you to march into the bookstore and buy it. Actually, I have been considering borrowing the disclaimer from the game *Stalking the Night Fantastic* by Richard Tucholka—"If anything in this book offends you, please feel free to buy and burn as many copies as you like. Volume discounts are available."

*What's Larry like?*
I'll let him answer for himself!

Misty and I met on a television interview just before a convention in Mississippi; we were both Guests of Honor there. By the end of that weekend, we had plotted our first book together *(Ties Never Binding,* which later became *Winds of Fate),* and have been together ever since.

I am an alumnus of the North Carolina School of the Arts, and while there I made some fairly respectable inroads into the world of Fine Arts. However, my basic trouble with galleries was that regardless of the content of my work, it would only reach that segment of the population that went to galleries. I was "preaching to the converted." Couple that distressing truth with an irrepressible irreverence, and my days of wearing black and being morose for my art were limited. I needed giggles, I needed money, and I needed to *accomplish* something. I had been an sf and fantasy fan for years. When I saw the other people who were also fans, I knew that here was a place to be welcomed, serve an audience, and make a difference through entertainment. Ever since, it has been a matter of matching the message to the medium. Some lend themselves well to text, others to paintings, others to satire or dialogues.

I have been introduced to folks as "The other half of Mercedes Lackey," and there's a bit to that. I've been working with Misty on prose since and including *Magic's Price,* which I co-plotted and alpha-edited. Incidentally, it was accepted by DAW exactly as it is printed; there were no revisions or mispe . . . misspel.., uhm.., words spelled wrong. Since then I've worked on them all, with heavier co-writing on the subsequent trilogies. I'm not about to steal any of Misty's thunder, though—she is a mighty fine writer without me! Our styles, skills, and areas of knowledge happen to complement each others'. I also get a kick out of hearing old-fogy writers grousing about female fantasy writers, when I've been one for years now. *The Black Gryphon* was about my fourth or fifth co-written book (silently, with Misty), but was one of the first with a cover credit. Go figure. My future is inextricably linked to Misty, and I would want it no other way. High Flight Arts and Letters is flying strongly, and the best is yet to come.

You may have noticed that there is not a lot of really personal information in all of this, and that's on purpose.

Larry and I tend to be very private, and frankly, we find all the self-aggrandizing, highly personal "I love this" and "I hate that" in some Author's Notes kind of distasteful. We've included some historical notes on the various stories, and while I will be the last person to claim I'm not opinionated (see the note to "Last Rights" for instance) just because *I* think something, that doesn't mean you should. Go out, read and experience everything you can, and form your own opinions; don't get life second-hand from a curmudgeon like me!

*I thought it might be fun to start this off on a light note.*

*This is an entirely new story, never before seen, and was supposed to be in Esther Friesner's anthology,* Alien Pregnant By Elvis *(Hey, don't blame me, this is the same lady who brought you the title of* Chicks In Chainmail *by Another Company). For some reason it never got printed, and none of us understand why. Must have dropped into the same black hole that eats alternate socks and the pair of scissors you're looking for at the time the anthology was put together.*

*Anyway, here it is now. Any resemblance to the writer is purely coincidental.*

# Aliens Ate My Pickup

## Mercedes Lackey

Yes'm, I'm serious. Aliens ate my pickup. Only it weren't really aliens, jest one, even though it was my Chevy four-ton, and he was a little bitty feller, not like some Japanese giant thing . . . an' he didn't really *eat* it, he just kinda chewed it up a little, look, you can see the teeth-marks on the bumper here an' . . .

Oh, start at the beginin'? Well, all right, I guess.

My name? It's Jed, Jed Pryor. I was born an' raised on this farm outsida Claremore, been here all my life. Well, 'cept for when I went t' OU.

What? Well, heck fire, sure I graduated!

What? Well, what makes you thank Okies tawk funny?

Degree? You bet I gotta degree! I gotta Batchler in Land Management right there on the wall of m'livingroom and—

Oh, the alien. Yeah, well, it was dark of the moon, middle of this June, when I was out doin' some night-fishin' on m'pond. Stocked it about five years ago with black an' stripy bass, just let 'em be, started fishin' it this year. I'm tellin' you, I got a five pounder on m'third cast this spring an'—

Right, the alien. Well, I was out there drownin' a coupla lures about midnight, makin' the fish laugh, when *wham!* all of a sudden the sky lights up like Riverparks on Fourth of July. I mean t'tell you, I haven't seen nothin' like that in all my born days! I 'bout thought them scifi writers lives over on the next farm had gone an' bought out one'a them fireworks factories in Tennessee again, like they did just before New Years. Boy howdy, that was a night! I swan, it looked like the sky over ol' Baghdad, let me tell you! Good thing they warned us they was gonna set off some doozies, or—

Right, the night'a them aliens. Well, anyway, the sky lit up, but it was all over in lessn' a minute, so I figgered it couldn't be them writers. Now, we get us some weird stuff ev'ry now an' again, y'know, what with MacDac—that's MacDonald-Douglas t'you—bein' right over the county line an' all, well I just figgered they was testin' somethin' that I wasn't supposed t' know about an' I went back t' drownin' worms.

What? Why didn' I think it was a UFO? Ma'am, what makes you thank Okies got hayseeds in their haids? I got a satylite dish on m'front lawn, I watch NASA channel an' PBS an' science shows all the *time,* an' I got me a subscription t' *Skeptical* Inquirer, an' I ain't never seen nothin' t'make me think there was such a thang as UFOs. Nope, I purely don't believe in 'em. Or I didn't, anyway.

So, like I was sayin' I went back t' murderin' worms an' makin' the bass laugh, an' finally got tired'a bein' the main course fer the skeeters an' chiggers an' headed back home. I fell inta bed an' didn' think nothin' about it till I walked out next mornin'.

An' *dang* if there ain't a big ol' mess in the middle'a my best hayfield! What? Oh heckfire, ma'am, it was one'a them crop circle things, like on the cover'a that Led Zeppelin record. Purely ruint m'hay. You cain't let hay get flattened down like that, spoils it right quick 'round here if they's been any dew, an' it was plenty damp that mornin'.

How'd I feel? Ma'am, I was *hot*. I figgered it was them scifi writers, foolin' with me; them city folk, they dunno you cain't do that t'hay. But they didn' have no cause t'fool with me like that, we bin pretty good neighbors so far, I even bought their books an' liked 'em pretty much too, 'cept for the stuff 'bout the horses. Ev'body knows a white horse's deaf as a post, like as not, less'n' it's one'a them Lippyzaners. Ain't no horse gonna go read yer mind, or go ridin' through fire an' all like that an'—

Oh, yeah. Well, I got on th' phone, gonna give 'em what for, an' turns out they're gone! One'a them scifi *con*ventions. So it cain't be them.

Well, shoot, now I dunno what t'think. That's when I heerd it, under th' porch. Somethin' whimperin', like.

Now y'know what happens when you live out in the country. People dump their dang-blasted strays all th' time, thinkin' some farmer'll take care of 'em. Then like as not they hook up with one'a the dog packs an' go wild an' start runnin' stock. Well, I guess I gotta soft heart t'match my soft head, I take 'em in, most times. Get 'em fixed, let 'em run th' rabbits outa my garden. Coyotes get 'em sooner or later, but I figger while they're with me, they at least got t'eat and gotta place t'sleep. So I figgered it was 'nother dang stray, an' I better get 'im out from under th' porch 'fore he messes under there an' it starts t'smell.

So I got down on m'hands an' knees like a pure durn fool, an' I whistled an' coaxed, an' carried on like some kinda dim bulb, an' finally that stray come out. But ma'am, what come outa that porch weren't no dog.

It *was* about the ugliest thing on six legs I ever seen in my life. Ma'am, that critter looked like somebody done beat out a fire on its face with a ugly stick. Looked like five miles 'a bad road. Like the reason first cousins hadn't ought t'get married. Two liddle, squinchy eyes that wuz all pupil, nose like a burnt pancake, jaws like a bear-trap. Hide all mangy and patchy, part scales and part fur, an' all of it putrid green. No ears that I could see. Six legs, like I said, an' three tails, two of 'em whippy and ratty, an' one sorta like a club. It drooled, an' its nose ran. Id'a been afraid of it, 'cept it crawled outa there with its three tails 'tween its legs, whimperin' an' wheezin' an' lookin' up at me like it was 'fraid I was gonna beat it. I figgered, hell, poor critter's scarder of me than I am of it—an' if *it* looks ugly *t'me,* reckon I must look just's ugly right back.

So I petted it, an' it rolled over on its back an' stuck all six legs in th'air, an' just acted about like any other pup. I went off t' the barn an' got Thang—I ended up callin' it Thang fer's long as I had it—I got Thang a big ol' bowl'a dog food, didn' know what else t'give it. Well, he looked pretty pleased, an' he ate it right up—but then he sicked it right back up too. I shoulda figgered, I guess, he bein' from someplace else an' all, but it was worth a try.

But 'fore I could try somethin' else, he started off fer m'bushes. I figgered he was gonna use 'em fer the usual—

But heckfire if he didn't munch down m' junipers, an' then sick *them* up! Boy howdy, was *that* a mess! Look, you can see the place right there—

Yes'm, I know. I got th' stuff tested later, after it was all over. Chemist said th' closest thang he'd ever seen to't was somethin' he called *Aquia Rega* or somethin' like—kind've a mix a' all kinda acids together, real nasty stuff, etches glass an' everthang.

Anyhow, I reckon gettin' fed an' then sickin' it all back up agin jest made the poor critter 'bout half crazy bein' hungry. But next I know, Thang's took off like a shot, a headin' fer one'a my chickens!

Well, he caught it, an he ate it down, beak an' feathers, an' he sicked it right back up agin' 'fore I could stop 'im.

That made me hot all over agin'. Some dang idjut makes a mess'a my hayfield, then this Thang makes messes all over m'yard, an' then it eats one'a my chickens. Now I'm a soft man, but there's one thing I don't stand for, an' that's critters messin' with the stock. I won't have no dog that runs cows, sucks eggs, or kills chickens. So I just grabbed me the first thang that I could and I went after that Thang t'lay inta him good. Happens it was a shovel, an' I whanged him a *good* one right upside th' haid 'fore he'd even finished bein' sick. Well, it seemed t'hurt him 'bout as much as a rolled-up paper'll hurt a pup, so I kept whangin' him an' he kept cowerin' an' whimperin' an' then he grabbed the shovel, the metal end.

An' he ate it.

He didn't sick that up, neither.

Well, we looked at each other, an' he kinda wagged his tails, an' I kinda forgave 'im, an' we went lookin' fer some more stuff he could eat.

I tell you, I was a pretty happy man 'fore the day was over. I reckoned I had me th' answer to one of m'bills. See, I c'n compost 'bout ev'thang organic, an' I can turn them aluminum cans in, but the rest of th' trash I gotta pay for pickup, an' on a farm, they's a lot of it what they call hazardous, an' thats extra. What? Oh, you know, barrels what had chemicals in 'em, bug-killer, weed-killer, fertilizer. That an' there's just junk that kinda accumulates. An' people are always dumpin' their dang old cars out here, like they dump their dang dogs. Lotsa trash that I cain't get rid of an' gotta pay someone t'haul.

But ol' Thang, he just ate it right up. Plastic an' metal, yes'm, that was what he et. Didn' matter how nasty, neither. Fed 'im them chemical barrels, fed 'im ol' spray-paint cans, fed 'im th' cans from chargin' the air-conditioner, he just kept waggin' his tails an' lookin' fer more. That's how he come t' chew on my Chevy; I was lookin' fer somethin' else t'feed him, an' he started chawin' on the bumpers. Look, see them teethmarks? Yes'm, he had him one good set of choppers all right. Naw, I never took thought t'be afraid of him, he was just a big puppy.

Well, like I said, by sundown I was one happy man. I figgered I not only had my trash problem licked, I could purt-near take care of the whole dang county. You know how much them fellers get t'take care'a hazardous waste? Heckfire, all I had t'do was feed it t'ol' Thang, an' what came out 'tother end looked pretty much like ash. I had me a goldmine, that's how I figgered.

Yeah, I tied ol' Thang up with what was left of a couch t'chew on an' a happy grin on his ugly face, an' I went t'sleep with m'accountin' program dancin' magic numbers an m'head.

An' I woke up with a big, bright light in m'eyes, an' not able t'move. I kinda passed out, an' when I came to, Thang was gone, an' all that was left was the leash an' collar. All I can figger is that whoever messed up m'hayfield was havin' a picnic or somethin' an' left their doggie by accident. But I reckon they figger I took pretty good care of 'im, since I 'spect he weighed 'bout forty, fifty pounds more when they got 'im back.

But I 'spose it ain't all bad. I gotta friend got a plane, an' he's been chargin' a hunnert bucks t'take people over th' field, an' splittin' it with me after he pays fer the gas. And folks that comes by here, well, I tell 'em, the story, they get kinda excited an. . . .

What ma'am? Pictures? Samples? Well sure. It'll cost you fifty bucks fer a sample'a where Thang got sick, an' seventy-five fer a picture of the bumper of my Chevy.

Why ma'am, what made you thank Okies was dumb?

*This story appeared in* Deals With The Devil, *edited by Mike Resnick. Larry and I live near Tulsa, Oklahoma, home of Oral Roberts University and widely termed "The Buckle of the Bible Belt." We have more televangelists per square mile here in this part of the country than I really care to think about. Maybe somebody out there will figure out how to spray for them.*

# Small Print

## Mercedes Lackey and Larry Dixon

Lester Parker checked the lock on the door of his cheap motel room for the fifth time; once again, it held. He checked the drapes where he had clothes-pinned them together; there were no cracks or gaps. He couldn't afford to be careless, couldn't possibly be too careful. If anyone from any of the local churches saw him—

He'd picked this motel because he knew it, frequented it when he had "personal business," and knew that for an extra ten bucks left on the bed, the room would be cleaned *completely* with no awkward questions asked. Like, was that blood on the carpet, or, why was there black candlewax on the bureau? Although he hadn't checked in under his own name, he couldn't afford awkward questions the next time he returned. They knew his face, even if they didn't know his name.

Unless, of course, this actually worked. Then it wouldn't matter. Such little irregularities would be taken care of.

His hands trembled with excitement as he opened his briefcase on the bed and removed the two sets of papers from it. One set was handwritten, in fading pen on yellowed paper torn from an old spiral-bound notebook. These pages were encased in plastic page-protectors to preserve them. The other was a brand-new contract, carefully typed and carefully checked.

He had obtained—been given—the first set of papers less than a week ago, here in this very motel.

He'd just completed a little "soul-searching" with Honey Butter, one of the strippers down at Lady G's and a girl he'd "counseled" plenty of times before. He'd been making sure that he had left nothing incriminating behind—it had become habit—when there was a knock on the door.

Reflexively he'd opened it, only realizing when he had it partly open just where he was, and that it could have been the cops.

But it hadn't been. It was one of Honey's coworkers with whom he also had an arrangement; she knew who and what he really was and she could be counted on to keep her mouth shut. Little Star DeLite looked at him from under her fringe of thick, coarse peroxide-blonde hair, a look of absolute panic on her face, her heavily made-up eyes blank with fear. Without a word, she had seized his hand and dragged him into the room next door.

On the bed, gasping in pain and clutching his chest, was a man he recognized; anyone who watched religious broadcasting would have recognized that used-car-salesman profile. Brother Lee Willford, a fellow preacher, but a man who was to Lester what a whale is to a sardine. Brother Lee was a televangelist, with his own studio, his own TV shows, and a take of easily a quarter million a month. Lester had known that Brother Lee had come to town for a televised revival, of course; that was why he himself had taken the night off. No one would be coming to his little storefront church as long as Brother Lee was in town, filling the football stadium with his followers.

He had not expected to see the preacher here—although he wasn't particularly surprised to see him with Star. She had a weakness for men of the cloth, and practically begged to be "ministered to." Besides, rumor said that Brother Lee had a weakness for blonds.

Lester had taken in the situation in a glance, and acted accordingly.

He knew enough to recognize a heart attack when he saw one, and he had also known what would happen if Brother Lee was taken to a hospital from this particular motel. People would put two and two together—and come up with an answer that would leave Brother Lee in the same shape as Jim Bakker. Ruined and disgraced, and certainly not fluid enough to pay blackmail.

First things first; Brother Lee's wallet had been lying on the stand beside the bed. Lester grabbed it, pulled some bills out of it and shoved them at Star. The little blond grabbed them and fled without a word.

Now one complication had been dealt with. Star wouldn't say anything to anyone; a hooker whose clients died didn't get much business.

Then, he had helped Brother Lee back into his pants; shoved the wallet into his coat-pocket (a small part of his mind writhing with envy to see that the suit was Armani and the fabric was silk) and draped the coat over Brother Lee's shoulders. He could not be found here; he had to be found somewhere neutral and safe.

There were car keys on the nightstand too; Lester had assumed they were for the vehicle outside. He had hoped there was a car-phone in it, but even if there hadn't been he could still have worked something out.

But there had been a phone, a portable; Lester dialed the emergency number, returned to the motel room, got Brother Lee into the car and got the car down into the street moments before the ambulance arrived. There was, after all, no harm in being rescued from the street—only in being taken from a motel room in a state of undress. He had followed the ambulance in Brother Lee's car, and claiming to be a relative, set himself up in the waiting room.

The reporters came before the doctors did. He had told them a carefully constructed but simple story; that he had met Brother Lee just that day, that the great man had offered his advice and help out of the kindness of his heart, and that they had been driving to Lester's little storefront church when Brother Lee began complaining of chest pains, and then had collapsed. Smiling modestly, Lester credited the Lord with helping him get the car safely to the side of the road. He'd also spewed buckets of buzzwords about God calling the man home and how abundant life was to believers. The reporters accepted the story without a qualm.

He had made certain that Brother Lee found out exactly what he had told the reporters.

He bided his time, checking with the hospital twice a day, until Lee was receiving visitors. Finally Brother Lee asked to see him.

He had gone up to the private room to be greeted effusively and thanked for his "quick thinking." Lester had expected more than thanks, however.

He was already framing his discreet demand, when Brother Lee startled him by offering to give him his heart's desire.

"I'm going to give you the secret of my success," the preacher had said, in a confidential whisper. "I used to be a Man of God; now I just run a nice scam. You just watch that spot there."

Lester had been skeptical, expecting some kind of stunt; but when the quiet, darkly handsome man in the blue business suit appeared in a ring of fire at the foot of Brother Lee's hospital bed, he had nearly had a heart-attack himself. It wasn't until Brother Lee introduced the—being—as "My colleague, Mister Lightman" that Lester began to understand what was going on.

Brother Lee had made a compact with the Devil. The "number one saver of souls" on the airwaves was dealing with the Unholy Adversary.

And yet—it made sense. How else could Brother Lee's career have skyrocketed the way it had without some kind of supernatural help? Lester had assumed it was because of Mafia connections, or even help from—Him—but it had never occurred to him that Brother Lee had gone over to the Other Side for aid. And Brother Lee and his "colleague" had made it very clear to Lester that such aid was available to him as well.

Still, there was such a thing as high-tech trickery. But Mr. Lightman was ready for that suspicion.

"I will give you three requests," the creature said. "They must be small—but they should be things that would have *no* chance of occurring otherwise." He had smiled, and when Lester had a glimpse of those strange, savagely pointed teeth, he had not thought "trickery," he had shuddered. "When all three of those requests have been fulfilled, you may call upon me for a more complete contract, if you are convinced."

Lester had nodded, and had made his requests. First, that the transmission of his car, which he had already had inspected and knew was about to go, be "healed."

Lightman had agreed to that one, readily enough.

Second, that his rather tiresome wife should be removed permanently from his life.

Lightman had frowned. "No deaths," he had said. "That is not within the scope of a 'small' request."

Lester had shrugged. "Just get her out. You can make me look stupid," he said. "Just make me sympathetic." Lightman agreed.

And third, that the sum of ten thousand, two hundred and fifty three dollars end up in Lester's bank account. Why that sum, Lester had no idea; it was picked arbitrarily, and Lightman agreed to that, as well.

He had vanished the same way he had arrived, in a ring of fire that left no marks on the hospital linoleum. That was when Brother Lee had given him the battered pages, encased in plastic sleeves.

"This is yours, now," Brother Lee had said. "When you want Lightman to bring you a contract, you follow these directions." He grimaced a little. "I know they're kind of unpleasant, but Lightman says they prove that you are sincere."

Lester had snorted at the idea of the Devil relying on sincerity, but he had taken the sheets anyway, and had returned to his car to wait out the fulfillment of the requests.

The very first thing that he noticed was that the transmission, which had been grinding and becoming harder to shift, was now as smooth as if it was brand new. Now, it might have been possible for Lightman to know that Lester's tranny was about to go—certainly it was no secret down at the garage—but for him to have gotten a mechanic and a new transmission into the parking lot at the hospital, performed the switch, and gotten out before Lester came down from the hospital—well, that was practically impossible.

But there were other explanations. The men at the garage might have been lying. They might have doctored his transmission the last time he was in, to make him think it needed work that it didn't. Something could have been "fixed" with, he didn't know, a turn of a screw.

Then two days later, he came home to find a process-server waiting for him. The papers were faxed from his wife, who was filing for divorce in Mexico. He found out from a neighbor that she had left that morning, with no explanations. He found out from a sniggering "friend" that she had run off with a male stripper. As he had himself specified; she was gone, he had been made to look stupid, but among his followers, he also was garnering sympathy for having been chained to "that kind" of woman for so long.

She had cleaned out the savings account, but had left the checking account alone.

But that left him in some very dire straits; there were bills to pay, and her secretarial job had been the steady income in the household. With that gone—well, he was going to *need* that ten grand. If it came through.

Late that Wednesday night, as he was driving back from the storefront church and contemplating a collection of less than twenty dollars, the back of an armored car in front of him had popped open and a bag had fallen out. The armored car rolled on, the door swinging shut again under its own momentum as the car turned a corner. There was no one else on the street. No witnesses, either walking or driving by.

He stopped, and picked up the bag.

It was full of money; old worn bills of varying denominations; exactly the kind of bills people put into the collection plate at a church. There were several thousand bills in the bag.

They totaled exactly ten thousand, two hundred, and fifty three dollars. Not a copper penny more.

He drove straight to the bank, and deposited it all in his savings account. Then he drove straight home, took out the papers Brother Lee had given him and began to read.

Before he was finished, his mind was made up.

The ritual called for some nasty things—not impossible to obtain or perform, but unpleasant for a squeamish man to handle and do. Dancing around in the nude was embarrassing, even if there was no one there to see him. And although he was certain that this motel room had seen worse perversions than the ones he was performing, he felt indescribably filthy when he was through.

Still; if this really worked, it would be worth it all.

If . . .

"Now how could you possibly doubt me?" asked a genteel voice from behind him.

Lester jumped a foot, and whirled. Mr. Lightman sat comfortably at his ease in the uncomfortable green plastic chair beneath the swag-lamp at the window. Lester thought absently that only a demonic fiend could have been comfortable in that torture-device disguised as a chair.

He was flushing red with acute shame, and terribly aware of his own physical inadequacies. Mr. Lightman cocked his head to one side, and frowned.

"Shame?" he said. "I think not. We'll have none of that here."

He gestured—not with his index finger, but with the second. Suddenly Lester's shame vanished, as if the emotion had been surgically removed. And as he looked down bemusedly at himself, he realized that his physical endowments had grown to remarkable adequacy.

"A taste of things to come," Lightman said easily. "You must be a perfect specimen, you know. People trust those who are handsome; those who are sexy. Think how many criminals are convicted who are plain, or even ugly—and how few who are handsome. People want to believe in the beautiful. They want to believe in the powerful. Above all, they want to believe."

Lester nodded, and lowered himself down onto the scratchy bedspread. "As you can see, I'm ready to deal," he told the fiend calmly.

"So I do see." Lightman snapped his fingers, and the neatly-typed pages of Lester's contract appeared in his hand. He leafed through them, his mouth pursed. "Yes," he murmured, and, "Interesting." Then he looked up. "You seem to have thought this through very carefully. Brother Lee was not quite so—thorough. The late Brother Lee."

Lester nodded; then took in the rest of the sentence. "The—late?"

Lightman nodded. "His contract ran out," the fiend said, simply. "Perhaps he had been planning to gain some extra years by bringing you into the flock, but he had not written any such provision into his contract—and a bargain is a bargain, after all. The usual limit for a contract is seven years. I rarely make exceptions to that rule."

Lester thought back frantically, and could recall no such provision in his own contract.

But then he calmed himself with the remembrance of his loophole. The very worst that would happen would be that he would live a fabulous life and then die. That prospect no longer held such terror for him with the hard evidence of an afterlife before him. With the Devil so real, God was just as real, right?

That beautiful loophole; so long as he repented, merciful God would forgive his sins. The Adversary would not have him. And he would repent, most truly and sincerely, every sin he committed as *soon as* he committed them. It was all there in the Bible, in unambiguous terms. If you repented, you were forgiven. That was the mistake everyone else who made these bargains seemed to make; they waited until the last minute, and before they could repent, *wham.* He wouldn't be so stupid.

But Mr. Lightman seemed blithely unconcerned by any of this. "I'd like to make a slight change in this contract, if I might," he said instead. "Since Brother Lee's empire is going begging, I would like to install you in his place. Conservation of effort, don't you know, and it will make his flock so much more comfortable."

Lester nodded cautiously; the fiend waved his hand and the change appeared in fiery letters that glowed for a moment.

"And now, for my articles." Lightman handed the contract back, and there was an additional page among the rest. He scanned them carefully, including all the fine print. He had expected trouble there, but to his surprise, it seemed to be mostly verses from the Bible itself, including the Lord's Prayer, with commentaries. It looked, in fact, like a page from a Bible-studies course. He looked up from his perusal to see Lightman gazing at him sardonically.

"What, have you never heard that the Devil can quote Scripture?" The fiend chuckled. "It's simply the usual stuff. So that you know that I know all the things people usually count on for loopholes."

That gave him pause for a moment, but he dismissed his doubts. "I'm ready to sign," he said firmly.

Lightman nodded, and handed him a pen filled with thick, red fluid. He doubted it was ink.

He was the most popular televangelist ever to grace the home screen; surpassing Brother Lee's popularity and eclipsing it. His message was a simple one, although he never phrased it bluntly: *buy your way into heaven, and into heaven on earth.* Send Lester Parker money, and Lester will not only see that God puts a "reserved" placard on your seat in the heavenly choir, he'll see to it that God makes your life on earth a comfortable and happy one. He told people what they wanted to hear, no uncomfortable truths. And there were always plenty of letters he could show, which told stories of how the loyal sheep of his flock had found Jesus, peace of mind, and material prosperity as soon as they sent Lester their check.

Of course, some of those same people would have been happy to ascribe a miraculous reversal of fortune to their "personal psychic" if they'd called the Psychic Hotline number instead of Lester's. Above all else, people wanted to believe—wasn't that what both sides said?

He had a computerized answering service for all his mail; no dumping letters into the trash at the bank for him, no sir! He had a fanatically loyal bunch of part-time housewives read the things, enter the letter's key words into the computer, and have an answer full of homey, sensible advice and religious homilies tailored to the individual run up by the machine in about the time it took to enter the address. Every letter came out a little different; every letter sounded like one of his sermons. Every letter looked like a personal answer from Lester. The computer was a wonderful thing.

They could have gotten the same advice from Dear Abby—in fact, a good part of the advice tendered *was* gleaned from the back issues of Dear Abby's compiled columns. But Abby didn't claim to speak for God, and Lester did.

He also preached another sort of comfort—that hatred was no sin. It was no accident that his viewers were nearly one hundred percent white; white people had money, and black, yellow, and red ones didn't, or if they did, they generally weren't going to part with it. That's what his Daddy had taught him. He sprinkled his sermons with Bible quotations *proving* that it was no sin to hate unbelievers— or to act on that hatred. After all, *those* people had placed themselves beyond the pale of God's forgiveness. They had not and would not repent. They should be purged from the body of mankind. "If thine eye offends thee, pluck it out!" he stormed, and his legions of followers went out looking for offending eyes, their own blind to mirrors.

Most of his prosperity he owed to his own cleverness, but there were times when he needed that little helping hand—just as he had thought he might. Like the time when his network of informers let him know that *Newsweek* had found his ex-wife, and she was going to spill some embarrassing things about him. Or that one of his many ex-mistresses was going to write a tell-all biography. Or that the IRS was planning an audit.

All he had to do was whisper Lightman's name, and his request, and by midnight, it was taken care of.

By twelve-oh-one, he was truly, sincerely, repenting that he had ordered his wife's murder—or whatever other little thing he had requested. Truly, sincerely, and deeply, confessing himself to God and showing that repentance in concrete sacrifices of tears and cash. From the beginning, he had told himself that he *was* acting on God's behalf, spitting in the face of Satan by tricking the Great Trickster. He told himself every time he prayed that he *was* working for God.

It was a foolproof scheme, and the seven years flew by. During the last year, he was cautious, but resigned. He knew that Lightman would arrange for his death, so there was no point in trying to avoid it. And, indeed, on the very instant of the seventh-year anniversary of the contract, he had a heart attack. As he prayed before his video-congregation. Just like Brother Lee.

Lester stood beside the body in the expensive hospital bed and stared down at it. The monitors were mostly flatlined; the only ones showing any activity were those reporting functions that had been taken over by machines. *Strange,* he thought. The man in the bed looked so healthy.

"Ah, Lester, you're right on time," Lightman said genially, stepping around from behind a curtain.

Lester shrugged. "Is there any reason why I shouldn't be?" he asked, just as genially. He could afford to be genial; after all, he wasn't going to be leaving with Lightman.

"What, no screaming, no crying, no begging?" Lightman seemed genuinely surprised. "Normally your kind are the worst—"

Lester only chuckled. "Why should I be worried?" he replied. "You only *think* you have me. But I repented of every single one of those crimes I asked you to commit. Every death, every blackmail scheme, every disgrace—I even repented the small things, repented every time I accepted someone's Social Security check—every time I arranged a special-effects miracle or convinced someone to leave me everything in their will—"

But he stopped as Lightman began laughing. "Oh yes, you did," Lightman told him merrily. "And my Opponent has forgiven you for those sins. But *you* didn't read the fine print." He handed Lester the copy of his contract, and pointed to the last page. "Read the commentary, dear boy. Carefully, this time."

The words leapt off the page at him.

*Sins repented will* be *forgiven by the Opposition, but forgiveness does not imply repayment. All sins committed by the party* of *the first part must* be *repaid to the party of the second part regardless of whether or not forgiveness has been obtained.*

"These are the sins you'll be repaying, my boy," Lightman said pleasantly, waving his hand. A stack of computer forms as tall as Lester appeared beside him. "But that is not why I am truly pleased to have you among us—"

Another stack of computer forms appeared, impossibly high, reaching up as far as Lester could see, millions of them.

"This stack—" Lightman placed his hand on the first pile "—represents all the sins you committed directly. But *this* pile represents all those you encouraged others to commit, with your doctrine of salvation through donation and hate-thy-neighbor. And those, dear boy, you did not repent of. You are a credit to our side! And we will be so happy to have you with us!"

The floor opened up, and Lightman stood in midair. "Learn to enjoy it, dear Lester," he chuckled, as the demons drew the false prophet down among them. "You'll reach your depth soon enough."

Lightman smiled as the mountain of sin forms buried Lester Parker. "So I believe."

*Larry and I are members of the North American Falconry Association and federally licensed raptor (bird of prey) rehabilitators. We have to be pragmatic and scientific—when you take care of predatory birds, they eat meat, and when you teach them to hunt so that they can be released, they have to learn how to make kills on their own. There is no shortcut for that process, and no way to "fake" making a kill. Needless to say, we Do Not Do Politically Correct, although we have not (yet) suffered harassment at the hands of people with Way Too Much Spare Time On Their Hands that some other rehabbers and fellow falconers have. Nevertheless, we've gotten very tired of seeing people who have never lived next to a field of cattle claim that cows are gentle, harmless, and intelligent—or try to raise their dogs on a vegetarian diet. So when Mike Resnick asked us for a story for* Dinosaur Fantastic, *we knew immediately what we were going to write for him.*

# Last Rights

## Mercedes Lackey and Larry Dixon

Two men and a woman huddled in the wet bushes surrounding the GenTech Engineering facility in Los Lobos, California. Across the darkened expanse of expensive GenTech Grasite lay their goal; the GenTech Large Animal Development Project. It was "Grasite," not "grass"; this first product of GenTech's researches was a plant that was drought-resistant, seldom needed mowing, and remained green even when dry; perfect for Southern California. Sadly, it also attracted grasshoppers who seemed to be fooled by its verdant appearance; they would remain on a Grasite lawn, hordes of them, trying valiantly to extract nourishment from something the texture and consistency of Astroturf, all during the worst droughts. Anyone holding a garden party in Hollywood had better plan on scheduling CritterVac to come in and sweep the premises clean or his guests would find every step they took crunching into a dozen insects, lending the soiree all the elegance of the wrath of Moses.

But Grasite was not the target tonight; these three had no argument with gene-tailored plantlife. In fact, they strongly supported many of GenTech's products—RealSkin, which reacted to allergens and irritants exactly the way human skin did, or Steak'N'Taters, a tuber with the consistency and taste of a cross between beef and baked potato. But all three of them were outraged by this assault upon helpless animals that GenTech was perpetrating in their new development lab—

Mary Lang, Howard Emory, and Ken Jacobs were self-styled "guerrillas" in defense of helpless beasties everywhere, charter members of Persons In Defense of Animo-beings; P.I.D.A. for short. There was nothing they would not do to secure the rights of exploited and abused animals. This year alone they, personally, had already chalked up the release of several hundred prisoner-rats from a lab in Lisle, Illinois. It was too bad about the mutated bubonic plague spreading through Chicago afterwards, but as Ken said, people had choices, the rats didn't. Tonight, they were after bigger game.

DinoSaurians. Patent Pending.

Real, living, breathing dinosaurs—slated to become P.O.Z.s (Prisoners of Zoos) the world over. And all because some corporate MBA on the Board of the San Diego Zoo had seen the attendance numbers soar when the Dunn traveling animated dinosaur exhibit had been booked there for a month. He had put that together with the discovery that common chickens and other creatures could be regressed to their saurian ancestors—the pioneering work had already been done on the eohippus and aurochs—and had seen a goldmine waiting for both the zoos and GenTech.

"How could they do this to me?" Mary whined. "They had such a promising record! I was going to ask them for a corporate donation! And now—this—"

"Money," Ken hissed. "They're all money-grubbing bastards, who don't care if they sell poor animals into a life of penal servitude. Just wait; next thing you'll be seeing is DinoBurgers."

Howard winced, and pulled the collar of his unbleached cotton jacket higher. "So, what have we got?" he asked. "What's the plan?"

Ken consulted the layout of the facility and the outdoor pens. It had been ridiculously easy to get them; for all the furor over the DinoSaurians, there was remarkably little security on this facility. Only signs, hundreds of them, warning of "DANGEROUS ANIMALS." Ridiculous. As if members of P.I.D.A. would be taken in by such blatant nonsense! There was no such thing as a dangerous animal; only an animal forced to act outside of its peaceful nature. "There are only three dino-animopersons at the moment, and if we can release all three of them, it will represent such a huge loss to GenTech that I doubt they'll ever want to create more. There's a BrontoSaurian here—" He pointed at a tiny pen on the far northern corner of the map. "It's inside a special pen with heavy-duty electric fences and alarms around it, so that will be your target, Howard. You're the alarms expert."

Howard looked over Ken's shoulder, and winced again. "That pen isn't even big enough for a horse to move around in!" he exclaimed. "This is inhuman! It's veal calves all over again!"

Ken tilted the map towards Mary. "There's something here called a 'Dinonychus' that's supposed to be going to the San Diego Zoo. It looks like they've put it in some kind of a bare corral. You worked with turning loose the rodeo horses and bulls last year, so you take this one, Mary."

Mary Lang nodded, and tried not to show her relief. The corral didn't look too difficult to get into, and from the plans, all she'd have to do would be to open the corral gate and the animal would run for freedom. "Very active" was the note photocopied along with the map. That was fine; the rodeo horses hadn't wanted to leave their pens, and it had taken *forever* to get them to move. And she'd gotten horsecrap all over her expensive synthetic suede pants.

"That leaves the Tricerotops in the big pasture to me." Ken folded the map once they had all memorized the way in. "Meet you here in an hour. Those poor exploited victims of corporate humanocentrism are already halfway to freedom. We'll show the corporate fat cats that they can't live off the misery of tortured, helpless animals!"

Howard had never seen so many alarms and electric shock devices in his life. He thought at first that they were meant to keep people out—but all the detectors pointed inward, not outward, so they had all been intended to keep this pathetic BrontoSaurian trapped inside his little box.

Howard's blood-pressure rose by at least ten points when he saw the victim; they were keeping it inside a bare concrete pen, with no educational toys, nothing to look at, no variation in its environment at all. It looked like the way they used to pen "killer" elephants in the bad old days; the only difference was that this BrontoSaurian wasn't chained by one ankle. There was barely enough room for the creature to turn around; no room at all for it to lie down. There was nothing else in the pen but a huge pile of green vegetation at one end and an equally large pile of droppings at the other.

*Good God,* he thought, appalled, *Don't they even clean the cage?*

As he watched, the BrontoSaurian dropped its tiny head, curved its long, flexible neck, and helped itself to a mouthful of greenery. As the head rose, jaws chewing placidly, another barrel of droppings added itself to the pile from the other end of the beast.

The BrontoSaurian seemed to be perfect for making fertilizer, if nothing else.

Well, soon he would be fertilizing the acreage of the Los Lobos National Park, free and happy, and the memory of this dank, cramped prison would be a thing of the past.

Howard disabled the last of the alarms and shock fences, pulled open the gates, and stepped aside, proudly waiting for the magnificent creature to take its first steps into freedom.

The magnificent creature dropped its head, curved its neck, and helped itself to another mouthful of greenery. As the head rose, jaws chewing placidly, it took no note of the open gates just past its nose.

"Come on, big boy!" Howard shouted, waving at it.

It ignored him.

He dared to venture into the pen.

It continued to ignore him. Periodically it would take another mouthful and drop a pile, but except for that, it could just as well have been one of the mechanical dinosaurs it was supposed to replace.

Howard spent the next half-hour trying, with diminishing patience, to get the BrontoSaurian to leave. It didn't even *look* at him, or the open door, or anything at all except the pile of juicy banana leaves and green hay in front of it. Finally, Howard couldn't take it any longer.

His blood-pressure rising, he seized the electric cattle prod on the back wall, and let the stupid beast have a good one, right in the backside.

As soon as he jolted the poor thing, his conscience struck him a blow that was nearly as hard. He dropped the prod as if it had shocked *him,* and wrapped his arms around the beast's huge leg, babbling apologies.

Approximately one minute later, while Howard was still crying into the leathery skin of the Bronto's leg, it noticed that it had been stung. Irritating, but irritation was easy to avoid. It shifted its weight, as it had been taught, and stepped a single pace sideways.

Its left hind foot met a little resistance, and something made a shrieking sound—but there had been something shrieking for some time, and it ignored the sound as it had all the rest. After all, the food was still here.

Presently, it finished the pile of food before it and waited patiently. There was a buzzing noise, and a hole opened in the wall a little to its right. That was the signal to shift around, which it did.

A new load of fresh vegetation dropped down with a rattle and a dull thud, as the automatic cleaning system flushed the pile of droppings and the rather flat mortal remains of her savior Howard down into the sewage system.

Mary approached the corral carefully, on the alert for guards and prepared to act like a stupid, lost bimbo if she were sighted. But there were no guards; only a high metal fence of welded slats, centered with a similar gate. There was something stirring restlessly inside the corral; she couldn't see what it was, for the slats were set too closely together. But as she neared the gate, she heard it pacing back and forth in a way that made her heart ache.

Poor thing—it needed to run loose! How could these monsters keep a wild, noble creature like this penned up in such an unnaturally barren environment?

There were alarms on the gate and on the fence; she didn't have Howard's expertise in dealing with such things, but these were easy, even a child could have taken them off-line. As she worked, she talked to the poor beast trapped on the other side of the gate, and it paused in its pacing at the sound of her voice.

"Hang in there, baby," she crooned to it. "There's a whole big National Park on the other side of the lab fence—as soon as we get you loose, we'll take that big BrontoSaurian through it, and that will leave a hole big enough for a hundred animopersons to run through! Then you'll be free! You'll be able to play in the sunshine, and roll in the grass—eat all the flowers you want—we'll make sure they never catch you, don't you worry."

The beast drew nearer, until she felt the warmth of its breath on her coat sleeve as she worked. It snuffled a little, and she wrinkled her nose at the smell.

Poor thing! What were they feeding it, anyway? Didn't they ever give it a chance to bathe? Her resentment grew as it sniffed at the gap between the metal slats. Why, it was lonely! The poor thing was as lonely as some of those rodeo horses had been! Didn't anyone ever come to pet and play with it?

Finally she disabled the last of the alarms. The creature inside the corral seemed to sense her excitement and anticipation as she worked at the lock on the gate. She heard it shifting its weight from foot to foot in a kind of dance that reminded her of her pet parakeet when he wanted out of his cage, before she'd grown wiser and freed it into the abundant outdoors.

"Don't worry little fellow," she crooned at it. "I'll have you out of here in no time—"

With a feeling of complete triumph, she popped the lock, flipped open the hasp on the gate, and swung it wide, eager for the first sight of her newly freed friend.

The first thing she saw was a huge-headed lizard, about six feet tall, that stood on two legs, balancing itself with its tail. It was poised to leap through the gate. The last thing she saw was a grinning mouth like a bear-trap, full of sharp, carnivorous teeth, closing over her head.

Hank threw his rope over a chair in the employee lounge and sank into the one next to it, feeling sweat cool all over his body. He pulled his hat down over his eyes. This had not been the most disastrous morning of his life, but it was right up there. Somehow the Dino had gotten into Gertie's pen—and whoever had left the gate open last night was going to catch hell. The little carnivore couldn't hurt the Bronto, but he had already eaten all the Dobermans that were supposed to be guarding the complex, and he was perfectly ready to add a lab tech or lab hand to the menu. You couldn't trank the Saurians; their metabolism was too weird. You couldn't drive a Dino; there wasn't anything he was afraid of. The only safe way to handle the little bastard was to get two ropes on him and haul him along, a technique Hank had learned roping rhinos in Africa. It had taken him and Buford half the morning to get the Dino roped and hauled back to his corral. They'd had to work on foot since none of the horses would come anywhere near the Dino. All he needed was one more thing—"Hank!" someone yelled from the door.

"What, dammit?" Hank Sayer snapped. "I'm tired! Unless you've got the chowderhead that left Dino and Gertie's pens open"

"They weren't *left* open, they were opened last night," said the tech, his voice betraying both anger and excitement. "Some animal-rights yoyos got in last night, the security guys found them on one of the tapes. *And* the cleanup crews found what was left of two of them in the pit under Gertie's pen and just inside Dino's doghouse!"

That was more than enough to make Hank sit up and push his hat back. "What the hell—how come—"

The tech sighed. "These bozos think every animal is just like the bunny-wunnies they had as kids. I don't think one of them has been closer to a real bull than videotape. They sure as hell didn't research the Saurians, else they'd have known the Dino's a land-shark, and it takes Gertie a full minute to process any sensation and act on it. We found what was left of the cattle-prod in the pit."

Hank pushed his hat back on his head and scratched his chin. "Holy shit. So the bozos just got in the way of Gertie after they shocked her, and opened Dino's pen to let him out?"

"After disabling the alarms and popping the locks," the tech agreed. "Shoot, Dino must have had fifteen or twenty minutes to get a good whiff and recognize fresh meat . . . ."

"He must've thought the pizza truck had arrived—" Suddenly another thought occurred to him. "Man, we've got three Saurians in here—did anybody think to check Tricky's pen?"

Alarm filled the tech's face. "I don't think so—"

"Well, come *on* then," Hank yelled, grabbing his lariat and shooting for the door like Dino leaping for a side of beef. "Call it in and meet me there!"

Tricky's pen was the largest, more of an enclosure than a pen; it had been the home of their herd of aurochs before the St. Louis zoo had taken delivery. Tricky was perfectly placid, so long as you stayed on your side of the fence. Triceratops, it seemed, had a very strong territorial instinct. Or at least, the GenTech reproductions did. It was completely safe to come within three feet of the fence. Just don't come any closer . . . .

Hank saw with a glance that the alarms and cameras had been disabled here, too. And the gate stood closed—but it was not locked anymore.

Tricky was nowhere in sight.

"He wouldn't go outside the fence," Hank muttered to himself, scanning the pasture with his brow furrowed with worry. "Not unless someone dragged him—"

"Listen!" the tech panted. Hank held his breath, and strained his ears.

*"Help!"* came a thin, faint voice, from beyond the start of the trees shading the back half of Tricky's enclosure. *"Help!"*

"Oh boy." Hank grinned, and peered in the direction of the shouts. "This time we got one."

Sure enough, just through the trees, he could make out the huge brown bulk of the Tricerotops standing in what Hank recognized as a belligerent aggression-pose. The limbs of the tree moved a little, shaking beneath the weight of whoever Tricky had treed.

*"Help!"* came the faint, pathetic cry.

"Reckon he didn't read the sign," said Buford, ambling up with both their horses, and indicating the sign posted on the fence that read, "IF YOU CROSS THIS FIELD, DO IT IN 9.9 SECONDS; TRICKY THE TRICERATOPS DOES IT IN 10."

"Reckon not," Hank agreed, taking the reins of Smoky from his old pal and swinging into the saddle. He looked over at the tech, who hastened to hold open the gate for both of them. "You'd better go get security, the cops, the medics and the lawyers in that order," he said, and the tech nodded.

Hank looked back into the enclosure. Tricky hadn't moved.

"Reckon that'un's the lucky'un," Buford said, sending Pete through the gate at a sedate walk.

"Oh, I dunno," Hank replied, as Smoky followed, just as eager for a good roping and riding session as Hank wasn't. Smoky was an overachiever; best horse Hank had ever partnered, but a definite workaholic.

"Why you say that?" Buford asked.

Hank shook his head. "Simple enough. Gettin' treed by Tricky's gonna be the best part of his day. By the time the lawyers get done with 'im—well, I reckon he's likely to wish Gertie'd stepped on him, too. They ain't gonna leave him anything but shredded underwear. If he thought Tricky was bad—"

*"Uh-huh,"* Buford agreed, his weathered face splitting with a malicious grin. Both of them had been top rodeo riders before the animal-rights activists succeeded in truncating the rodeo-circuit. They'd been lucky to get this job. "You know, I reckon we had oughta take our time about this. Exercise'd do Tricky some good."

Hank laughed, and held Smoky to a walk. "Buford, old pal, I

reckon you're readin' my mind. You don't suppose the damn fools hurt Tricky, do ya?"

Faint and far, came a snort; Hank could just barely make out Tricky as he backed up a little and charged the tree. A thud carried across the enclosure, and the tree shook. "Naw, I think Tricky's healthy as always."

*"Help!"* came the wail from the leaves. Hank pulled Smoky up just a little more.

And grinned fit to split his face.

This wasn't the best day of his life, but damn if it wasn't right up there.

*Mike Resnick is one of my favorite anthology editors, and he got us to do a number of stories at the same time; when he first said the book this story was slated for was to be called* Christmas Ghosts, *the concept was so weird I knew I had to contribute!*

*Warning: this is not a nice story, but then I'm not always a nice person.*

# Dumb Feast

## Mercedes Lackey

Aaron Brubaker considered himself a rational man, a logical man, a modern man of the enlightened nineteenth century. He was a prosperous lawyer in the City, he had a new house in the suburbs, and he cultivated other men like himself, including a few friends in Parliament. He believed in the modern; he had gas laid on in his house, had indoor bathrooms with the best flushing toilets (not that a polite man would discuss such things in polite company), and had a library filled with the writings of the best minds of his time. Superstition and old wives' tales had no place in his cosmos. So what he was about to do was all the more extraordinary.

If his friends could see him, he would have died of shame. And yet—and yet he would have gone right on with his plans.

Nevertheless, he had made certain that there was no chance he might be seen; the servants had been dismissed after dinner, and would not return until tomorrow after church services. They were

41

grateful for the half-day off, to spend Christmas Eve and morning with their own families, and as a consequence had not questioned their employer's generosity. Aaron's daughter, Rebecca, was at a properly chaperoned party for young people which would end in midnight services at the Presbyterian Church, and she would not return home until well after one in the morning. And by then, Aaron's work would be done, whether it bore fruit, or not.

The oak-paneled dining room with its ornately carved table and chairs was strangely silent, without the sounds of servants or conversation. And he had not lit the gaslights of which he was so proud; there must only be two candles tonight to light the proceedings, one for him, one for Elizabeth. Carefully, he laid out the plates, the silver; arranged Elizabeth's favorite winter flowers in the centerpiece. One setting for himself, one for his wife. His dear, and very dead, wife.

His marriage had not precisely been an *arranged* affair, but it had been made in accordance with Aaron's nature. He had met Elizabeth in church; had approved of what he saw. He had courted her, in proper fashion; gained consent of her parents, and married her. He had seen to it that she made the proper friends for his position; had joined the appropriate societies, supported the correct charities. She had cared for his home, entertained his friends in the expected manner, and produced his child. In that, she had been something of a disappointment, since it should have been "children," including at least one son. There was only Rebecca, a daughter rather than a son, but he had forgiven her for her inability to do better. Romance did not precisely enter into the equation. He had expected to feel a certain amount of modest grief when Elizabeth died—

But not the depth of loss he had uncovered. He had mourned unceasingly, confounding himself as well as his friends. There simply was no way of replacing her, the little things she did. There had been an artistry about the house that was gone now; a life that was no longer there. His house was a home no longer, and his life a barren, empty thing.

In the months since her death, the need to see her again became an obsession. Visits to the cemetery were not satisfactory, and his desultory attempt to interest himself in the young widows of the parish came to nothing. And that was when the old tales from his childhood, and the stories his grandmother told, came back to—literally—haunt him.

He surveyed the table; everything was precisely in place, just as it had been when he and Elizabeth dined alone together. The two candles flickered in a draft; they were in no way as satisfactory as the gaslights, but his grandmother, and the old lady he had consulted from the Spiritualist Society, had been adamant about that—there must be two candles, and only two. No gaslights, no candelabra.

From a chafing dish on the sideboard he took the first course: Elizabeth's favorite soup. Tomato. A pedestrian dish, almost lower-class, and not the clear consummes or lobster bisques that one would serve to impress—but he was not impressing anyone tonight. These must be *Elizabeth's* favorites, and not his own choices. A row of chafing dishes held his choices ready: tomato soup, spinach salad, green peas, mashed potatoes, fried chicken, apple cobbler. No wine, only coffee. All depressingly middle-class . . .

That was not the point. The point was that they were the bait that would bring Elizabeth back to him, for an hour, at least.

He tossed the packet of herbs and what-not on the fire, a packet that the old woman from the Spiritualists had given him for just that purpose. He was not certain what was in it; only that she had asked for some of Elizabeth's hair. He'd had to abstract it from the lock Rebecca kept, along with the picture of her mother, in a little shrine-like arrangement on her dresser. When Rebecca had first created it, he had been tempted to order her to put it all away, for the display seemed very pagan. Now, however, he thought he understood her motivations.

This little drama he was creating was something that his grandmother—who had been born in Devonshire—called a "dumb feast." By creating a setting in which all of the deceased's favorite foods and drink were presented, and a place laid for her—by the burning of certain substances—and by doing all this at a certain time of the year—the spirit of the loved one could be lured back for an hour or two.

The times this might be accomplished were four. May Eve, Midsummer, Halloween, and Christmas Eve.

By the time his need for Elizabeth had become an obsession, the Spring Equinox and Midsummer had already passed. Halloween seemed far too pagan for Aaron's taste—and besides, he had not yet screwed his courage up to the point where he was willing to deal with his own embarrassment that he was resorting to such humbug.

What did all four of these nights have in common? According to the Spiritualist woman, it was that they were nights when the "vibrations of the Earth Plane were in harmony with the Higher Planes." According to his grandmother, those were the nights when the boundary between the spirit world and this world thinned, and many kinds of creatures, both good and evil, could manifest. According to her, that was why Jesus had been born on that night—

Well, that was superstitious drivel. But the Spiritualist had an explanation that made sense at the time; something about vibrations and currents, magnetic attractions. Setting up the meal, with himself, and all of Elizabeth's favorite things, was supposed to set up a magnetic attraction between him and her. The packet she had given him to burn was supposed to increase that magnetic attraction, and set up an electrical current that would strengthen the spirit. Then, because of the alignment of the planets on this evening, the two Planes came into close contact, or conjunction, or—something.

It didn't matter. All that mattered was that he see Elizabeth again. It had become a hunger that nothing else could satisfy. No one he knew could ever understand such a hunger, such an overpowering desire.

The hunger carried him through the otherwise unpalatable meal, a meal he had timed carefully to end at the stroke of midnight, a meal that must be carried out in absolute silence. There must be no conversation, no clinking of silverware. Then, at midnight, it must end. There again, both the Spiritualist and his grandmother had agreed. The "dumb feast" should end at midnight, and then the spirit would appear.

He spooned up the last bite of too-sweet, sticky cobbler just as the bells from every church in town rang out, calling the faithful to Christmas services. Perhaps he would have taken time to feel gratitude for the Nickleson's party, and the fact that Rebecca was well out of the way—

Except that, as the last bell ceased to peal, *she* appeared. There was no fanfare, no clamoring chorus of ectoplasmic trumpets—one moment there was no one in the room except himself, and the next, Elizabeth sat across from him in her accustomed chair. She looked exactly as she had when they had laid her to rest; every auburn hair in place in a neat and modest French Braid, her body swathed from chin to toe in an exquisite lace gown.

A wild exultation filled his heart. He leapt to his feet, words of welcome on his lips—

Tried to, rather. But he found himself bound to his chair, his voice, his lips paralyzed, unable to move or to speak.

The same paralysis did not hold Elizabeth, however. She smiled, but not the smile he loved, the polite, welcoming smile—no, it was another smile altogether, one he did not recognize, and did not understand.

"So, Aaron," she said, her voice no more than a whisper. "At last our positions are reversed. You, silent and submissive; and myself the master of the table."

He almost did not understand the words, so bizarre were they. Was this Elizabeth, his dear wife? Had he somehow conjured a vindictive demon in her place?

She seemed to read his thoughts, and laughed. Wildly, he thought. She reached behind her neck and let down her hair; brushed her hand over her gown and it turned to some kind of medievalist costume, such as the artists wore. The ones calling themselves "Pre-Raphelites," or some such idiocy. He gaped to see her attired so, or would have, if he had been in control of his body.

"I am no demon, Aaron," she replied, narrowing her green eyes. "I am still Elizabeth. But I am no longer 'your' Elizabeth, you see. Death freed me from you, from the narrow constraints you placed on me. If I had known this was what would happen, I would have died years ago!"

He stared, his mind reeled. What did she mean? How could she say those things?

"Easily, Aaron," Elizabeth replied, reclining a little in the chair, one elbow on the armrest, hand supporting her chin. "I can say them very, very easily. Or don't you remember all those broken promises?"

Broken—

"Broken promises, Aaron," she continued, her tone even, but filled with bitterness. "They began when you courted me. You promised me that you did not want me to change—yet the moment the ring was on my finger, you broke that promise, and began forcing me into the mold *you* chose. You promised me that I could continue my art—but you gave me no place to work, no money for materials, and no time to paint or draw."

But that was simply a childish fancy—

"It was my *life,* Aaron!" she cried passionately. "It was my life, and you took it from me! And I believed all those promises, that in a year you would give me time and space—after the child was born—after she began school. I believed it right up until the moment when the promise was 'after she finishes school.' Then I knew that it would become 'after she is married,' and then there would be some other, distant time—" Again she laughed, a wild peal of laughter than held no humor at all. "Cakes yesterday, cakes tomorrow, but never cakes today! Did you think I would never see through that?"

But why did she have to paint? Why could she not have turned her artistic sensibilities to proper lady's—

"What? Embroidery? Knitting? Lace-making? I was a *painter,* Aaron, and I was a good one! Burne-Jones himself said so! Do you know how rare that is, that someone would tell a girl that she must paint, must be an artist?" She tossed her head, and her wild mane of red hair—now as bright as it had been when he had first met her—flew over her shoulder in a tumbled tangle. And now he remembered where he had seen that dress before. She had been wearing it as she painted, for she had been—

"Painting a self-portrait of myself as the Lady of Shallot," she said, with an expression that he could not read. "Both you and my father conspired together to break me of my nasty artistic habits. 'Take me out of my dream-world,' I believe he said. Oh, I can hear you both—" her voice took on a pompous tone, and it took him a moment to realize that she was imitating him, " 'don't worry, sir, once she has a child she'll have no time for that nonsense—' And you saw to it that I had no time for it, didn't you? Scheduling ladies' teas and endless dinner parties, with women who bored me to death and men who wouldn't know a Rembrandt from an El Greco! Enrolling me without my knowledge or consent in group after group of other useless women, doing utterly useless things! And when I *wanted* to do something—anything!—that might serve a useful purpose, you forbade it! Forbade me to work with the Salvation Army, forbade me to help with the Wayward Girls—oh no, *your* wife couldn't do that, it wasn't *suitable!* Do you know how much I came to hate that word, 'suitable'? Almost as much as the words 'my good wife.' "

*But I gave you everything—*

"You gave me nothing!" she cried, rising now to her feet. "You gave me jewelry, gowns ordered by *you* to *your* specifications, furniture, useless trinkets! You gave me nothing that mattered! No freedom, no authority, no responsibility!"

Authority? He flushed with guilt when he recalled how he had forbidden the servants to obey her orders without first asking him— how he had ordered her maid to report any out-of-the-ordinary thing she might do. How he had given the cook the monthly budget money, so that she could not buy a cheaper cut of roast and use the savings to buy paint and brushes.

"Did you think I didn't know?" she snarled, her eyes ablaze with anger as she leaned over the table. "Did you think I wasn't aware that I was a prisoner in my own home? And the law supported *you*, Aaron! I was well aware of that, thanks to the little amount of work I did before you forbade it on the grounds of 'suitability.' One woman told me I should be grateful that you didn't beat me, for the law permits that as well!"

He was only doing it for her own good . . . .

"You were only doing it to be the master, Aaron," she spat. "What I wanted did not matter. You proved that by your lovemaking, such as it was."

Now he flushed so fiercely that he felt as if he had just stuck his head in a fire. How could she be so—

"Indelicate? Oh I was more than indelicate, Aaron, I was passionate! And you killed that passion, just as you broke my spirit, with your cruelty, your indifference to me. What should have been joyful was shameful, and you made it that way. You hurt me, constantly, and never once apologized. Sometimes I wondered if you made me wear those damned gowns just to hide the bruises from the world!"

All at once, her fury ran out, and she sagged back down into her chair. She pulled the hair back from her temples with both hands, and gathered it in a thick bunch behind her head for a moment. Aaron was still flushing from the last onslaught. He hadn't known—

"You didn't care," she said, bluntly. "You knew; you knew it every time you saw my face fall when you broke another promise, every time you forbade me to dispose my leisure time where it would do some good. You knew. But all of that, I could have forgiven, if you had simply let Rebecca alone."

This time, indignation overcame every other feeling. How could she say something like that? When he had given the child everything a girl could want?

"Because you gave her nothing that *she* wanted, Aaron. You never forgave her for not being a boy. Every time she brought something to you—a good grade, a school prize, a picture she had done—you belittled her instead of giving her the praise her soul thirsted for!" Elizabeth's eyes darkened, and the expression on her face was positively demonic.

"Nothing she did was good enough—or was as good as a boy would have done."

But children needed correction—

"Children need *direction*. But that wasn't all, oh no. You played the same trick on her that you did on me. She wanted a pony, and riding lessons. But that wasn't suitable; she got a piano and piano lessons. Then, when her teacher told you she had real talent, and could become a concert artist, you took both away, and substituted *French* lessons!" Again, she stood up, her magnificent hair flowing free, looking like some kind of ancient Celtic goddess from one of her old paintings, paintings that had been filled with such pagan images that he had been proud to have weaned her away from art and back to the path of a true Christian woman. She stood over him with the firelight gleaming on her face, and her lips twisted with disgust. "You still don't see, do you? Or rather, you are so *sure,* so *certain* that you could know better than any foolish woman what is best for her, that you still think you were right in crushing my soul, and trying to do the same to my daughter!"

He expected her to launch into another diatribe, but instead, she smiled. And for some reason, that smile sent cold chills down his back.

"You didn't even guess that all this was my idea, did you?" she asked, silkily. "You had no idea that I had been touching your mind, prodding you toward this moment. You forgot what your grandmother told you, because I made you forget—that the dumb feast puts the living in the power of the dead."

She moved around the end of the table, and stood beside him. He would have shrunk away from her if he could have—but he still could not move a single muscle. "There is a gas leak in this room, Aaron," she said, in the sweet, conversational tone he remembered so well. "You never could smell it, because you have no sense of smell. What those awful cigars of yours didn't ruin, the port you drank after dinner killed. I must have told you about the leak a hundred times, but you never listened. I was only a woman, how could I know about such things?"

But why hadn't someone else noticed it?

"It was right at the lamp, so it never mattered as long as you kept the gaslights lit; since you wouldn't believe me and I didn't want the house to explode, I kept them lit day and night, all winter long. Remember? I told you I was afraid of the dark, and you laughed, and permitted me my little indulgence. And of course, in the summer, the windows were open. But you turned the lights off for this dumb feast, didn't you, Aaron. You sealed the room, just as the old woman told you. And the room has been filling with gas, slowly, all night."

Was she joking? No, one look into her eyes convinced him that she was not. Frantic now, he tried to break the hold she had over his body, and found that he still could not move.

"In a few minutes, there will be enough gas in this room for the candles to set it off—or perhaps the chafing dish—or even the fire. There will be a terrible explosion. And Rebecca will be free—free to follow her dream and become a concert pianist. Oh, Aaron, I managed to thwart you in that much. The French teacher and the piano teacher are very dear friends. The lessons continued, even though you tried to stop them. And you never guessed." She looked up, as if at an unseen signal, and smiled. And now he smelled the gas.

"It will be a terrible tragedy—but I expect Rebecca will get over her grief in a remarkably short time. The young are so resilient." The smell of gas was stronger now.

She wiggled her fingers at him, like a child. "Goodbye, Aaron," she said, cheerfully. "Merry Christmas. See you soon—"

*This story was for one of Mike Resnick's "Alternate" anthologies, Alternate Celebrities, I believe. The wonderful thing about the alternate-history books is that you can take someone in history that you really like but who may not have . . . made some of the wisest choices in the world . . . and make him (or her) into something a little better.*

*Since Larry and I decided to do this one together, we combined our two passions—his for cars and mine for dance. Although . . . I am coming to share that passion for cars, and even took a High-Performance Racing school at Stevens Racing at Hallet Raceway (enjoying it very much, thank you). That, by the way, is the same track Mark Shepherd and I set Wheels of Fire at. We're currently thinking about getting a Catterham Seven, which is a new old Lotus Seven, and doing vintage racing and autocross—but I digress.*

*In this case, we took the Mother of Modern Dance, Isadora Duncan, and gave her a little more common sense. We also had her born about 25 years later than she actually was, so that she participated in World War Two rather than World War One. But yes, in WWI, she did drive an ambulance for the Allies. As for her protégé Jimmy, well, we made his fate a lot kinder, too.*

# Dance Track

## Mercedes Lackey and Larry Dixon

Dora blew her hair out of her eyes with an impatient snort and wiped sweat off her forehead. And simultaneously adjusted the timing on

51

the engine, yelled a correction on tire selection to her tire man, and took a quick look out of the corner of her eye for her driver.

He wasn't late—yet. He liked to give her these little heart attacks by showing up literally at the last possible moment. She would, of course, give him hell, trying to sound like the crew chief that she was, and not like his mother, which she was old enough to be—

—And most certainly not like an aging lover, which half the Bugatti team and every other team assumed she was.

The fact that they *weren't* had no bearing on the situation. Dora had been well aware from the moment she joined Bugatti at the end of the war that her position in this part of Man's World would always be difficult. That was all right; when had she ever had an easy life?

"All right!" She pulled clear of the engine compartment, hands up and in plain sight, as she had taught all her mechanics to do. Too many men in Grand Prix racing had missing fingers from being caught in the wrong place when an engine started—but not on her team. The powerful Bugatti engine roared to life; she nodded to the mechanic in Jimmy's seat, and he floored the pedal.

She cocked her head to one side, frowning a little; then grinned and gave the mech a thumbs-up. He killed the engine, answering her grin, and popped out of the cockpit—just as Jimmy himself came swaggering up through the chaotic tangle of men and machines in the pits.

She knew he was there by the way the men's eyes suddenly moved to a point just behind and to one side of her. They never learned—or else, they never guessed how they gave themselves away. Probably the latter; they *were* mostly Italian, steeped in generations of presumed male superiority, and they would never even think that a woman could be more observant than they, no matter how often she proved it to them.

She pivoted before Jimmy could slap her butt, and gave him The Look. She didn't even have to say anything, it was all there in The Look.

He stopped, standing hip-shot as if he were posing for one of his famous publicity shots, his born-charmer grin countering her Look. The blue eyes that made millions of teenage girls suffer heart-palpitations peered cheerfully at Dora through his unruly blond hair. He'd grown a thatch over his eyes for his last movie, and hadn't cut it yet. He probably wouldn't, Dora reflected. His image as a rebel wasn't just an image, it was the real Jimmy.

She pulled her eyes away from his, and The Look turned to a real frown as she took in the dark ankle-length trenchcoat and the flamboyant, long silk scarf he wore.

"Out," she ordered, and watched his grin fade in surprise. "You heard me," she said when he hesitated. "You know the pit-rules. *Nothing* that can get caught in machinery! God help us, that scarf could get your neck broken! I told you once, and I meant it; I don't care how many movies you've made, in here you're the Bugatti rookie-driver, you're here on probation, even if you *are* the best damn driver I've ever seen, and you toe the line and act like a professional. And if you think you're going to make me break my promise not to compete again by getting yourself strangled, you can think again! Now get out of here and come back when you're dressed like a driver and not some Hollywood gigolo."

She turned her back on him, and went back to the crew changing the tires, but she did not miss his surprised—and suddenly respectful—"*Yes ma'am!*" She also didn't miss the surprised and respectful looks on the faces of her mechanics and pit-crew. *So, they didn't expect me to chew him out in public.* She couldn't help but see the little nods, and the satisfaction on the men's faces. And she hid a grin of her own, as she realized what that meant. The last rumors of her protege being her lover had just gone up in smoke. No lovelorn, aging female would lay into her young lover that way in public. And no young stud would put up with that kind of treatment from a woman, young or old, unless the only position she held in his life was as respected mentor.

She raised her chin aggressively, and raked her crew with her stern gaze. "Come on, come on, pick it up," she said, echoing every other crew chief here in the pits. "We're running a race here, not an ice cream social! *Move it!*"

"Ready, Miz Duncan," said a sober voice at her shoulder. She turned to see Jimmy was back already, having ditched the coat and scarf for the racing suit of her own design. His helmet tucked under one arm, he waited while she looked him over critically. "Nothing binding?" she asked, inspecting every visible seam and wrinkle. It was as fireproof as modern technology could make it, asbestos fabric over cotton, covering the driver from neck to ankle. Thick asbestos boots covered his feet, which would be under the engine compartment. It would be hotter than all the fires of hell in there, but Jimmy would be cooler than most of the other drivers, who shunned her innovations in favor of jerseys and heavy canvas pants.

And he would be safer than she had been, who'd won the French Grand Prix in '48 in a leotard and tights.

And if she could have put an air-conditioner in there, she would have. Temperatures in the cockpit ran over 120 degrees Fahrenheit while the car was moving—worse when it idled. In the summer, and at those temperatures, strange things started to happen to a driver's brain. Heat exhaustion and the dangerous state leading up to it had probably caused more crashes than anyone wanted to admit.

She finished her inspection and gave him the nod; he clapped his helmet on—a full head helmet, not just an elaborate leather cap, but one with a faceplate—and strolled over to his car, beginning his own inspection.

Just as she had taught him.

While the mechanics briefed him on the Bugatti's latest quirks—and Grand Prix racers always developed new quirks, at least a dozen for each race, not counting intended modifications—she took a moment to survey the nearest crews. To her right, Ferrari and Lola; to her left, Porsche and Mercedes.

Nothing to show that this was Wisconsin and not Italy or Monte Carlo. Nothing here at the track, that is. She had to admit that it was a relief being back in the U.S.; not even the passing of a decade had erased all the scars the War had put on the face of Europe. And there were those who thought that reviving the Grand Prix circuit in '46 had been both frivolous and ill-considered in light of all that Europe had suffered.

Well, those people didn't have to invest their money, their time, or their expertise in racing. The announcement that the Indianapolis

500 would be held in 1946 had given those behind the project the incentive they needed to get the plans off the drawing board and into action. The Prince in Monaco had helped immeasurably by offering to host the first race. Monte Carlo had not suffered as much damage as some of the other capitals, and it was a neutral enough spot to lure even the Germans there.

She shook herself mentally. Woolgathering again; it was a good thing she was out of the cockpit and on the sidelines, if she was going to let her thoughts drift like that.

Jimmy nodded understanding as the steering-specialist made little wiggling motions with his hand. Dora cast another glance up and down pit row, then looked down at the hands of her watch. Time.

She signaled to the crew, who began to push the car into its appointed slot in line. This would be a true Le Mans start; drivers sprinting to their cars on foot and bullying through the pack, jockeying for position right from the beginning. In a way, she would miss it if they went to an Indy-type start; with so little momentum, crashes at the beginning of the race were seldom serious—but when they were, they were devastating. And there were plenty of promising contenders taken out right there in the first four or five hundred yards.

She trotted alongside Jimmy as they made their way to the starting line. "All right, now listen to me: save the engine, save the tires. You have a long race ahead of you. We've got a double whammy on us," she warned. "Remember, a lot of drivers have it in for Bugatti because of me—and the Europeans aren't really thrilled with the Bugatti preference for Yankee drivers. The other thing: this is Ford country; Ford is fielding six cars in the factory team alone. None of the other chiefs I've talked to know any of the drivers personally, which tells me they're in Ford's back pocket."

"Which means they might drive as a team instead of solo?" Jimmy hazarded shrewdly. "Huh. That could be trouble. Three cars could run a rolling roadblock."

"We've worked on the engine since the trials, and there's another twenty horse there," she added. "It's just the way you like it: light, fast, and all the power you need. If I were you, I'd use that moxie early, get yourself placed up in the pack, then lay off and see what the rest do."

She slowed as they neared driver-only territory; he waved acknowledgment that he had heard her, and trotted on alone. She went back to the pits; the beginning of the race really mattered only in that he made it through the crush at the beginning, and got in a little ahead of the pack. That was one reason why she had given over the cockpit to a younger driver; she was getting too old for those sprints and leaps. Places where she'd hurt herself as a dancer were starting to remind her that she was forty-five years old now. Let Jimmy race to the car and fling himself into it, he was only twenty-five.

The view from her end of pit-row wasn't very good, but she *could* see the start if she stood on the concrete fire-wall. One of the men steadied her; Tonio, who had been with her since *she* was the driver. She handed her clipboard down to him, then noticed a stranger in their pit, wearing the appropriate pass around his neck. She was going to say something, but just then the drivers on the line crouched in preparation for the starting gun, and her attention went back to them.

The gun went off; Jimmy leapt for his car like an Olympic racer, vaulting into it in a way that made her simultaneously sigh with envy and wince. The Bugatti kicked over like a champ; Jimmy used every horse under that hood to bully his way through the exhaust-choked air to the front of the pack, taking an outside position. Just like she'd taught him.

The cars pulled out of sight, and she jumped down off the wall. The stranger was still there—and the pits were for the first time today, quiet. They would not be that way for long, as damaged or empty cars staggered into the hands of their keepers, but they were for the moment, and the silence impacted the ears as the silence between incoming artillery barrages had—

She headed for the stranger—but he was heading for her. "Miss Duncan?" he said quickly. "Jim got me this pit-pass—he came over to see us do *Death of a Salesman* last night and when he came backstage and found out I race too, he got me the pass and told me to check in with you."

"What kind of racing?" she asked cautiously. It would be just like Jimmy to pal around with some kid just because he was an up-and-coming actor and saddle her with someone who didn't know when to get the hell out of the way.

"Dirt-track, mostly," he said modestly, then quoted her credentials that made her raise her eyebrow. "I'll stay out of the way."

The kid had an open, handsome face, and another set of killer blue eyes—and the hand that shook hers was firm and confident. She decided in his favor.

"Do that," she told him. "Unless there's a fire—tell you what, you think you can put up with hauling one of those around for the rest of the race?" She pointed at the rack of heavy fire-bottles behind the fire-wall, and he nodded. "All right; get yourself one of those and watch our pit, Porsche, and Ferrari. That's the cost of you being in here. If there's a fire in any of 'em, deal with it." Since the crews had other things on their minds—and couldn't afford to hang extinguishers around their necks—this kid might be the first one on the spot.

"Think you can handle that—what is your name, anyway?"

"Paul," he said, diffidently. "Yeah, I can handle that. Thanks, Miss Duncan."

"Dora," she replied automatically, as she caught the whine of approaching engines. She lost all interest in the kid for a moment as she strained to see who was in front.

It was Lola, but the car was already in trouble. She heard a tell-tale rattle deep in, and winced as the leaders roared by—

Jimmy was in the first ten; that was all that mattered, that, and his first-lap time. She glanced at Fillipe, who had the stop-watch; he gave her a thumbs-up and bent to his clipboard to make notes, as he would for almost every lap. She let out her breath in a sigh.

"Miss Duncan, how did you get into racing?"

She had forgotten the kid but he was still there—as he had promised, out of the way, but still within talking distance.

She shook her head, a rueful smile on her lips. "Glory. How fleeting fame. Retire, and no one's ever heard of you—"

"Oh, I know all about the Grand Prix wins," the kid said hastily.

"I just wanted to know why you stopped dancing. Jimmy told me you were kind of a—big thing in Europe. It doesn't seem like a natural approach to racing. I mean, Josephine Baker didn't go into racing."

She chuckled at being compared to the infamous cabaret dancer, but no one had ever asked her the question in quite that way. "A couple of reasons," she replied, thoughtfully. "The biggest one is that my dingbat brother was a better dancer than I ever was. I figured that the world only needed one crazy dancing Duncan preaching Greek revival and naturalism. And really, Ruth St. Denis and Agnes de Mille were doing what I would have been doing. Agnes was doing more; she was putting decent dancing into motion pictures, where millions of little children would see it. When I think about it, I don't think Isadora Duncan would have made any earthshaking contributions to dancing." Then she gave him her famous impish smile, the one that peeled twenty years off of her. "On the other hand, every Grand Prix driver out there does the 'Duncan Dive' to hit the cockpit. And they are starting to wear the driving suits I've been working on. So I've done that much for racing."

The kid nodded; he started to ask something else, but the scream of approaching engines made him shake his head before she held up her hand.

Jimmy was still there, still within striking distance of the leaders. But there was trouble developing—because the Ford drivers were doing just what Dora had feared they would do. They were driving as a team—in two formations of three cars each. Quite enough to block. Illegal as hell, but only if the race officials caught on and they could get someone on the Ford team to spill the beans. Obvious as it might be, the worst the drivers would get would be fines, unless someone fessed up that it was premeditated—then the whole team could be disqualified.

Illegal as hell, and more than illegal—dangerous. Dora bit her lip, wondering if they really knew just how dangerous.

Halfway through the race, and already the kid had more than earned his pit-pass. Porsche was out, bullied into the wall by the Ford flying-wedge, in a crash that sent the driver to the hospital. Ferrari was out too, victim of the same crash; both their LMCs had taken shrapnel that had nicked fuel-lines. Thank God Paul'd been close to the pits when the leaking fuel caught fire. The Ferrari had come in trailing a tail of fire and smoke and the kid was right in there, the first one on the scene with his fire-bottle, foaming the driver down first then going under the car with the nozzle. He'd probably prevented a worse fire—And now the alliances in the pits had undergone an abrupt shift. It was now the Europeans and the independents against the Ford monolith. Porsche and Ferrari had just come to her—her, who Porsche had never been willing to give the time of day!—offering whatever they had left. "Somehow" the race officials were being incredibly blind to the illegal moves Ford was pulling.

Then again . . . how close was Detroit to Wisconsin?

It had happened before, and would happen again, for as long as businessmen made money on sport. All the post-race sanctions in the world weren't going to help that driver in the hospital, and no fines would change the outcome of the inevitable crashes.

The sad, charred hulk of the Ferrari had been towed, its once-proud red paint blistered and cracked; the pit-crew was dejectedly cleaning up the oil and foam.

On the track, Jimmy still held his position, despite two attempts by one of the Ford wedges to shove him out of the way. That was the advantage of a vehicle like the Bugatti, as she and the engineers had designed it for him. The handling left something to be desired, at least so far as she was concerned, but it was Jimmy's kind of car. Like the 550 Porsche he drove for pleasure now, that he used to drive in races, she'd built it for speed. "Point and squirt," was how she often put it, dryly. Point it in the direction you wanted to go, and let the horses do the work.

The same thing seemed to be passing through Paul's mind, as he watched Jimmy scream by, accelerating out of another attempt by Ford to pin him behind their wedge. He shook his head, and Dora elbowed him.

"You don't approve?" she asked.

"It's not that," he said, as if carefully choosing his words. "It's just not my kind of driving. I like handling; I like to slip through the pack like—like I was a fish and they were the water. Or I was dancing on the track—"

She had to smile. "Are you quoting that, or did you not know that was how they described my French and Monte Carlo Grand Prix wins?"

His eyes widened. "I didn't know—" he stammered, blushing. "Honest! I—"

She patted his shoulder, maternally. "That's fine, Paul. It's a natural analogy. Although I bet you don't know where I got my training."

He grinned. "Bet I do! Dodging bombs! I read you were an ambulance driver in Italy during the war. Is that when you met Ettore Bugatti?"

She nodded, absently, her attention on the cars roaring by. Was there a faint sound of strain in her engine? For a moment her nerves chilled.

But no, it was just another acceleration; a little one, just enough to blow Jimmy around the curve ahead of the Mercedes.

Her immediate reaction was annoyance; he shouldn't have had to power his way out of that, he should have been able to *drive* his way out. He was putting more stress on the engine than she was happy with.

Then she mentally slapped her own hand. *She* wasn't the driver, he was.

But now she knew how Ettore Bugatti felt when she took the wheel in that first Monte Carlo Grand Prix.

"You know, Bugatti was one of my passengers," she said, thinking aloud, without looking to see if Paul was listening. "He was with the Resistance in the Italian Alps. You had to be as much a mechanic as a driver, those ambulances were falling apart half the time, and he saw me doing both before I got him to the field hospital."

Sometimes, she woke up in the middle of the night, hearing the bombs falling, the screams of the attack-fighters strafing the road— Seeing the road disintegrate in a flash of fire and smoke behind her, in front of her; hearing the moans of the wounded in her battered converted bread-truck.

All too well, she remembered those frantic moments when

getting the ambulance moving meant getting herself and her wounded passengers out of there before the fighter-planes came back. And for a moment, she heard those planes—No, it was the cars returning. She shook her head to free it of unwanted memories. She had never lost a passenger, or a truck, although it had been a near thing more times than she cared to count. Whenever the memories came between her and a quiet sleep, she told herself that—and reminded herself why she had volunteered in the first place.

Because her brother, the darling of the Metaphysical set, was hiding from the draft at home by remaining in England among the blue-haired old ladies and balletomanes who he charmed. Because, since they would not accept her as a combatant, she enlisted as a noncombatant.

*Some noncombatant.* She had seen more fire than most who were on the front lines.

Bugatti had been sufficiently impressed by her pluck and skill to make her an offer.

*"When this is over, if you want a job, come to me."*

Perhaps he had meant a secretarial job. She had shown up at the decimated Bugatti works, with its "EB" sign in front cracked down the middle, and offered herself as a mechanic. And Bugatti, faced with a dearth of men who were able-bodied, never mind experienced, had taken her on out of desperation.

"It was kind of a fluke, getting to be Bugatti's driver," she continued, noting absently that Paul was listening intently. "The driver for that first Grand Prix had broken an ankle, right at starting-lineup, and I was the only one on the team that could make the sprint for the car!"

Paul chuckled, and it had been funny. Everyone else was either too old, or had war injuries that would slow them down. So she had grabbed the racing-helmet before anyone could think to object and had taken the man's place. In her anonymous coverall, it was entirely possible none of the officials had even noticed her sex.

She had made the first of her famous "Duncan Dives" into the cockpit; a modified *grand jete* that landed her on the seat, with a twist and bounce down into the cockpit itself.

"I can still hear that fellow on the bullhorn—there was no announcer's booth, no loudspeaker system—" She chuckled again. *"And coming in third—Isadora Duncan?"*

The next race, there had been no doubt at all of her sex. She had nearly died of heat-stroke behind that powerful engine, and she had been shocked at what that had done to her judgment and reflexes. So this time, she had worn one of her old dancing costumes, a thick cotton leotard and tights—worn inside-out, so that the seams would not rub or abrade her.

The other drivers had been so astounded that she had gotten nearly a two-second lead on the rest of them in the sprint—and two seconds in a race meant a quarter mile.

For her third race, she had been forbidden to wear the leotard, but by then she had come up with an alternative; almost as form-fitting, and enough to cause a stir. And that had been in France, of course, and the French had been amused by her audacity. "La Belle Isadora" had her own impromptu fanclub, who showed up at the race with noisemakers and banners.

Perhaps that had been the incentive she needed, for that had been her first win. She had routinely placed in the first three, and had taken home to Bugatti a fair share of first-place trophies. The other drivers might have been displeased, but they could not argue with success.

Bugatti had been overjoyed, and he had continuously modified his racing vehicles to Isadora's specifications: lighter, a little smaller than the norm, with superb handling. And as a result of Isadora's win, the Bugatti reputation had made for many, many sales of sportscars in the speed-hungry, currency-rich American market. And it did not hurt that his prize driver was an attractive, *American* lady.

But in 1953 she had known that she would have to retire, and soon. She was slowing down—and more importantly, so were her reflexes. That was when she had begun searching for a protege, someone she could groom to take her place when she took over the retiring crew-chief's position.

She had found it in an unlikely place: Hollywood. And in an unlikely person, a teenage heartthrob, a young, hard-living actor. But she had not seen him first on the silver screen; she had seen him racing, behind the wheel of his treasured silver Porsche.

He had been torn by indecision, although he made time for her coaching and logged a fair amount of time in Bugatti racing machines. She and the retiring crew chief worked on design changes to suit his style of driving to help lure him. But it was Hollywood itself that forced his choice.

When a near-fatality on a lonely California highway left his Porsche a wreck, his studio issued an ultimatum. *Quit driving, or tear up your contract. We don't cast corpses.*

He tore up his contract, took the exec's pipe from his mouth, stuffed the scraps in the pipe, slammed it down on the desk and said "Smoke it." He bought a ticket for Italy the same day.

"Miss Duncan?" Paul broke into her thoughts. "We have company."

She turned, to see the crew chiefs of Ferrari, Mercedes, Lola, and a dozen more approaching. Her first thought was—*What have we done now?*

But it was not what she had done, nor her crew, nor even Jimmy. It was what Ford had done.

"Isadora," said Paul LeMond, the Ferrari crew chief, who had evidently been appointed spokesman, "we need your help."

Ten years of fighting her way through this man's world, with no support from anyone except Bugatti and a few of her crew had left her unprepared for such a statement.

She simply stared at them, while they laid out their idea.

This would be the last pit-stop before the finish, and Dora was frankly not certain how Jimmy was going to take this. But she leaned down into the cockpit where she would not be overheard and shouted the unthinkable into his ear over the roar of his engine. How the crews of every other team still on the track were fed up with the performance of the Ford drivers—and well they should be, with ten multi-car wrecks leaving behind ruined vehicles and drivers in hospital. The fact that one of those wrecks had included one of the Ford three-car flying wedges had not been good enough.

"So if Ford is going to play footsie with the rules, so are we," she shouted. "They think you're the best driver on the track, Jimmy. The only one good enough to beat cheaters. So every other driver on the track's been given orders to block for you, or let you pass."

She couldn't see Jimmy's expression behind the faceplate, but she did see the muscles in his jaw tense. "So they're going to just give me the win?" he shouted back.

That was not how Jimmy wanted his first Grand Prix to end— and she didn't blame him.

"Jimmy—they decided you're the best out there! Not only your peers, but *mine!* Are you going to throw that kind of vote away?" It was the only way she would win this argument, she sensed it. And she sensed as his mood turned to grudging agreement.

"All right," he said finally. "But you tell them this—"

She rapped him on the top of the helmet. "No, you listen. They said to tell *you* that if you get by Ford early enough, they're going to do the same for Giorgio with the old Ferrari and Peter for Citroen. And as many more as they can squeeze by."

She sensed his mood lighten again, although he didn't answer. But by then the crew was done, and she stood back as he roared back out onto the track.

When he took the track, there were ten laps to go—but five went by without anyone being able to force a break for Jimmy, not even when the Ford wedge lapped slower cars. She had to admit that she had seldom seen smoother driving, but it was making her blood boil to watch Jimmy coming up behind them, and being forced to hold his place.

Three laps to go, and there were two more cars wrecked, one of them from Citroen. Two laps. One.

Flag lap.

Suddenly, on the backstretch, an opening, as one of the Ford drivers tired and backed off a little. And Jimmy went straight for it.

Dora was on the top of the fire-wall, without realizing she had jumped up there, screaming at the top of her lungs, with half the crew beside her. Ford tried to close up the wedge, but it was too late.

Now it was just Jimmy and the lead Ford, neck and neck—down

the backstretch, through the chicane, then on the home run for the finish line.

Dora heard his engine howling; heard strain that hadn't been there before. Surely if she heard it, so would he. He should have saved the engine early on—if he pushed it, he'd blow the engine, he had to know that—

He pushed it. She heard him drop a gear, heard the engine scream in protest—

And watched the narrow-bodied, lithe steel Bugatti surge across the finish-line a bare nose ahead of the Ford, engine afire and trailing a stream of flame and smoke that looked for all the world like a victory banner.

Dora was the first to reach him, before he'd even gotten out of the car. While firefighters doused the vehicle with impartial generosity, she reached down and yanked off his helmet.

She seized both his ears and gave him the kind of kiss only the notorious Isadora Duncan, toast of two continents, could have delivered—a kiss with every year of her considerable amatory experience behind it.

"That's for the win," she said, as he sat there, breathless, mouth agape and for once completely without any kind of response.

Then she grasped his shoulders and shook him until his teeth rattled.

"And *that's* for blowing up my engine, you idiot!" she screamed into his face.

By then, the crowd was on him, hauling him bodily out of the car and hoisting him up on their shoulders to ride to the winner's circle.

Dora saw to it that young Paul was part of that privileged party, as a reward for his fire-fighting and his listening. And when the trophy had been presented and the pictures were all taken, she made sure he got up to the front.

Jimmy recognized him, as Jimmy would, being the kind of man he was. "Hey!" he said, as the Race Queen hung on his arm and people thrust champagne bottles at him. "You made it!"

Paul grinned, shyly. Dora felt pleased for him, as he shoved the pass and a pen at Jimmy. "Listen, I know it's awful being asked—"

"Awful? Hell no!" Jimmy grabbed the pen and pass. "Have you made up your mind about what you want to do yet? Acting, or whatever?"

Paul shook his head, and Dora noticed then what she should have noticed earlier—that his bright blue eyes and Jimmy's were very similar. *And if he isn't a heartbreaker yet,* she thought wryly, *he will be.*

"I still don't know," he said.

"Tell you what," Jimmy said, pausing a moment to kiss another beauty queen for the camera, "you make a pile of money in the movies, *then* go into racing. Get a good mentor like Dora."

And then he finished the autograph with a flourish—and handed it back to the young man.

*To Paul Newman, who can be my driver when I take over the chief mechanic slot from Dora, best* of *luck.*

And the familiar autograph, *James Dean.*

NOTE:

Just as a postscript—yes, Paul Newman *was* doing dinner-theater and summer-stock in the Midwest in the 1950s. He did drive dirt-track, as well as going into professional auto racing. And James Dean was considered by his peers to be an excellent race-driver with great potential in the sport.

And in case you don't happen to be a dance-buff, Isadora Duncan was killed when the long, trailing scarf she wore (about twelve feet worth of silk) was caught in the wheel-spokes of a Bugatti sportscar in which she was riding, breaking her neck.

*This story was for Mike Resnick's* Alternate Heroes. *While T. E. Lawrence (aka Lawrence of Arabia, another historical favorite of mine) was* really *a hero, I wondered what would have happened if a certain life-shattering experience he had at Deraa had come out a bit differently . . . .*

*Due to the actual historical details this story is rather a stiff one at the beginning, and definitely NC-17.*

# Jihad

## Mercedes Lackey

Pain was a curtain between Lawrence and the world; pain *was* his world, there was nothing else that mattered. "Take him out of here, you fools! You've spoiled him!" Lawrence heard Bey Nahi's exclamation of disgust dimly; and it took his pain-shattered mind a moment to translate it from Turkish to English.

Spoiled him; as if he was a piece of meat. Well, now he was something less than that.

He could not reply; he could only retch and sob for mercy. There was no part of him that was not in excruciating pain.

Pain. All his life, since he had been a boy, pain had been his secret terror and obsession. Now he was drugged with it, a too-great force against which he could not retain even a shred of dignity.

As he groveled and wept, conversation continued on above his head. There were remonstrations on the part of the soldiers, but the

Bey was adamant—and angry. Most of the words were lost in the pain, but he caught the sense of a few. "Take him out—" and "Leave him for the jackals."

So, the Bey was not to keep him until he healed. Odd. After Nahi's pawing and fondling, and swearing of desire, Lawrence would have thought—

"You stay." That, petulantly, to the corporal, the youngest and best-looking of the lot. Coincidentally, he was the one who had been the chiefest and most inventive of the torturers. He had certainly been the one that had enjoyed his role the most. "Take that out," the Bey told the others. Lawrence assumed that Nahi meant him.

If he had been capable of appreciating anything, he would have appreciated that—the man who had wrought the worst on his flesh, should take his place in the Bey's bed.

The remaining two soldiers seized him by the arms. Waves of pain rolled up his spine and into his brain, where they crashed together, obliterating thought. He couldn't stand up; he couldn't even get his feet under him. His own limbs no longer obeyed him.

They dragged him outside; the cold air on his burning flesh made him cry out again, but this time no one laughed or struck him. Once outside, his captors were a little gentler with him; they draped his arms over their shoulders, and half-carried him, letting him rest most of his weight on them. The nightmarish journey seemed to last a lifetime, yet it was only to the edge of the town.

Deraa. The edge of Deraa. The edge of the universe. He noted, foggily, that he did not recognize the street or the buildings as they passed; they must have brought him to the opposite side of the town. There was that much more distance now between himself and his friends and allies. Distance controlled and watched by the enemy.

Assuming he wanted to reach them. Assuming he wanted them to find him, see him—see what had been done to him, guess at the lacerations that were not visible.

*No.*

His captors let him down onto the muddy ground at the side of the road. Gently, which was surprising. One of them leaned over, and muttered something—Lawrence lost the sense of it in the pain. He closed his eyes and snuggled down into the mud, panting for breath. Every breath was an agony, as something, probably a broken bone, made each movement of his ribs stab him sharply.

He heard footsteps retreating, quickly, as if his erstwhile captors could not leave his presence quickly enough.

Tears of despair, shameful, shamed tears, trickled down his cheeks. The unmoved stars burned down on him, and the taste of blood and bile was bitter in his mouth.

Slowly, as the pain ebbed to something he could think through, he itemized and cataloged his injuries to regain control of his mind, as he had tried to count the blows of the whip on his back. The bones in his foot, fractured during the chaos of the last sabotage-raid, had been shattered again. The broken rib made breathing a new torture. Somewhere in the background of everything, the dull pain of his head spoke of a concussion, which had probably happened when they kicked him to the head of the stairs. The lashes that had bit into his groin had left their own burning tracks behind.

His back was one shapeless weight of pain. He had thought to feel every separate, bleeding welt, but he could only feel the accumulated agony of all of them in a mass. But as he lay in the mud, the cold of the night numbed him, leaving only that final injury still as sharp and unbearable as ever, the one that was not visible. The laceration of his soul.

Now he knew how women felt; to be the helpless plaything of others, stronger or more powerful. To be forced to give of their bodies whether or not they willed or wanted it. To be handled and used— *like a piece of meat*—And worst of all, at one level, the certainty that he had somehow deserved it all. That he had earned his punishment. That he had asked for his own violation. After all, wasn't that what they said of women, too? It was this final blow that had cracked the shell of his will and brought down the walls of the citadel of his integrity.

How could he face them, his followers, now? They would watch him, stare at him, and murmur to one another—no matter how silent he kept, they would know, surely they would know. And knowing, how could they trust him?

They would not, of course. He no longer trusted himself. His nerve was broken, his will, his soul broken across that guardroom bench. There was nothing left but despair. He literally had nothing left to live for; the Revolt had become his life, and without it, he had no will to live. The best thing he could do for the Revolt would be to die. Perhaps Feisal would take it upon himself to avenge his strange English friend, Aurens; certainly Auda, that robber, would use Aurens' death as an excuse to further raid the Turks. And Ali, Ali ibn el Hussein; he would surely exact revenge. But could they hold the Revolt together?

*Inshallah.* As God wills it. Here, in his extremity, he had at last come to the fatalism of the Moslem. It was no longer his concern. Life was no longer his concern. Only death, and the best way to meet it, without further torment, to drown his shame in its dark waters where no one would guess what those waters hid.

This would not be the place to die. Not here, where his beaten and brutalized body would draw attention—where his anxious followers might even come upon it and guess the foulness into which he had fallen. Let him crawl away somewhere; let him disappear into the waste and die where he would not be found, and let his death become a mystery to be wondered at.

Then he would be a martyr, if the Revolt could have such a thing. It might even be thought that he vanished, like one of the old prophets, into the desert, to return at some vague future date. His death would become a clean and shining thing. They would remember him as the confident leader, not the battered, bloody rag of humanity he was now.

He lay in a sick stupor, his head and body aching and growing slowly numb with cold. Finally a raging thirst brought him to life—and spurred him to rise.

He struggled to his feet, and rocked in place, moaning, his shaking hands gathering his torn clothing about him. He might have thought that this was a nightmare, save for the newly-wakened pain. Somewhere he heard someone laughing, and the sound shocked him like cold water. Deraa felt inhuman with vice and cruelty; he could not die here.

The desert. The desert was clean. The desert would purge him, as it had so many times before.

He stopped at a trough by the wells; scooped a little water into his hands and rubbed it over his face, then drank. He looked up at the stars, which would not notice if there was one half-Arab Englishman less on the earth, and set off, one stumbling step at a time, for the clean waste beyond this vile pit of humanity. He walked for a long time, he thought. The sounds of humanity faded, replaced by the howling of dogs or jackals, off in the middle distance. Tears of pain blurred his sight; he hoped he could find some hole to hide himself away before dawn, a grave that he might fall into, and falling, fall out of life.

He stumbled, jarring every injury into renewed agony, and a white light of pain blinded him. He thought he would die then, dropping in his tracks; then he thought that the blackness of unconsciousness would claim him.

But the light did not fade; it grew brighter. It burned away the pain, burned away thought, burned away everything but a vague sense of self. It engulfed him, conquered him, enveloped him. He floated in a sea of light, dazzled, sure that he had dropped dead on the road. But if that were true, where was he? And what was this?

Even as he wondered that, he became aware of a Presence within the light. Even as he recognized it, it spoke.

*I AM I.*

On the bank of the Palestine Railway above the huddle of Deraa they waited; Sherif Ali ibn el Hussein, together with the two men that Aurens had designated as his bodyguards, Halim and Faris, and the sheik of Tafas, Talal el Hareidhin. "Tell me again," Ali said fiercely. "Tell me what it was you did."

Faris, old and of peasant stock, did not hesitate, although this was the fifth time in as many hours that Ali had asked the question. Talal hissed through his teeth, but did not interrupt.

"We came into Deraa by the road, openly," Faris recounted, as patient as the sand. "There was wire, and trenches, some flying machines in the sheds; some men about, but they took no note of us.

We walked on, into Deraa. A Syrian asked after our villages, and whether the Turks were there; I think he meant to desert. We left him and walked on again; someone called after us in Turkish, which we feigned not to understand. Then another man, in a better uniform, ran after us. He took Aurens by the arm, saying 'The Bey wants you.' He took Aurens away, through the tall fence, into their compound. This was when I saw him no more. I hung about, but there was no sign of him although I watched until well after nightfall. The Turks became restless, and looked evilly at me, so I left before they could take me too."

Talal shook his head. "This is pointless," he said. "Aurens is either dead or a prisoner, and in neither case can we help him. If the former, it is the will of Allah; if the latter, we must think of how long he will deceive them, and where we must go when he does."

"Into the desert, whence we came," Ali said glumly. "The Revolt is finished. There is no man of us who can do as he has done, for there is no man of us who has not a feud with another tribe; there is not a one of us who has no tribe to answer to. There is no one we may trust to whom the English will listen, much less give gold and guns to. We are finished."

Talal widened his eyes at that, but did not speak. Ali took a last look at Deraa, and the death of their hopes, and turned resolutely away.

"Where do we go, lord?" asked Faris, humbly, the peasant still.

"To Azrak," Ali replied. "We must collect ourselves, and then scatter ourselves. If Aurens has been taken and betrayed us, we must think to take ourselves where the Turks cannot find us."

The others nodded at this gloomy wisdom, as the rains began again, falling down impartially upon Turks and Bedouin alike.

The ride to the old fortress of Azrak, which Aurens and his followers had taken for the winter, was made longer by their gloom. There was not one among them who doubted the truth of Ali's words; and Ali thought perhaps that there was not one among them who was not trying to concoct some heroic scheme, either to rescue Aurens, or to avenge him. But a thousand unconnected raids of vengeance would not have a quarter of the power of the planned and coordinated raids Aurens had led them in. And there was still the matter of gold and guns—gold, to buy the loyalty of the wilder tribes, to make Suni fight beside Shia, half-pagan desert tribesman beside devout Meccan. Guns, because there were never enough guns, never enough ammunition, and because there were those who would fight for the promise of guns who would not be moved for anything else. Swords would not prevail against the Turkish guns, no matter how earnest the wielder. They must gather their people, each his own, and scatter. Ali would take it upon himself to bear the evil news to Feisal, who would, doubtless, take it to his father and the English.

More ill thoughts; how long would King Hussein, ever jealous of his son's popularity and inclined to mistrust him, permit Feisal even so much as a bodyguard? Without Aurens to speak to the English, and the English to temper the father, the son could not rally the Revolt either.

It was truly the death of their hopes.

The fortress loomed in the distance, dark and dismal in the rain. Ali did not think he could bear to listen to the spectral wailings of the ghost-dogs of Beni Hillal about the walls tonight. He would gather his people and return to his tribe—What was that noise?

He raised his eyes from contemplating the neck of his camel, just as a shaft of golden light, as bright as the words of the Koran, broke through the clouds. Where it struck the ground, on the road between them and the fortress, there was a stark white figure, that seemed to take in the golden light and transmute it to his own brightness.

Ali squinted against the light. Who was this? Was it mounted?

Yes, as it drew nearer, strangely bringing the beam of sunlight with it, he saw that it was mounted. Not upon a camel, but upon a horse of a whiteness surpassing anything Ali had ever seen. Not even the stud reft away from the Turks was of so noble a color—

Now he saw what the noise was; behind the rider came every man of the fortress, cheering and firing into the air—

Ali goaded his mount into a loping canter, his heart in his throat. It could not be, could it?

From the canter he urged the camel into a gallop. The size was right; the shape—but whence the robes, the headcloth, even the headropes, of such dazzling whiteness? They had been mired in mud for months, he had not thought ever to see white robes until spring.

It was. His heart leapt with joy. It was! The figure was near enough to see features now; and it was not to be mistaken for any other. Aurens!

He reined his camel in beside the white stallion, and the beast did not even shy, it simply halted, though Aurens made no move to stop it. He raised his hand, and the mob at his back fell respectfully silent.

Ali looked down at his friend; Aurens looked up, and there was a strange fire in those blue eyes, a burning that made Ali rein his camel back a pace. There was something there that Ali had never seen before, something that raised the hair on the back of his neck and left him trembling between the wish to flee and the wish to fall from his camel's back and grovel at the Englishman's feet.

"Lawrence?" Ali said, using the English name, rather than the one they all called him. As if by using that name, he could drive that strangeness from Aurens' eyes. "Lawrence? How did you escape from the Turks?"

The blue eyes burned brighter, and the robes he wore seemed to glow. "Lawrence is dead," he said. "The Turks slew him. There is only Aurens. Aurens, and the will of Allah."

Ali's blood ran hot and cold by turns as he stared down into those strange, unhuman blue eyes. "And what," he whispered, as he would whisper in a mosque, "is the will of Allah?"

At last the eyes released him, leaving him shivering with reaction, and with the feeling that he had gazed into something he could not, and would never, understand.

"The will of Allah," said Aurens, gazing toward Deraa, toward Damascus, and beyond, "is this."

Silence, in which not even the camels stirred.

"There will be *jihad.*"

General Allenby swore, losing the last of his composure. "He's *where*?" the commander of the British forces in the Middle East shouted, as his aides winced and the messenger kept his upper lip appropriately stiff in the face of the general's anger.

"Outside of Damascus, sir," he repeated. "I caught up with him there." He paused for a moment, for if this much of the message had the general in a rage, the rest of it would send him through the roof. He was sweatingly grateful that it was no longer the custom to slay the bearer of bad news. "He sent me to tell you, sir, that if you wish to witness the taking of Damascus, you had best find yourself an aeroplane."

The general did, indeed, go through the roof. Fortunately, early on in the tirade, Allenby said something that the messenger could take as a dismissal, and he took himself out.

There was a mob lying in wait for him in the officers' mess.

"What did he say?" "What did he do?" "Is it true he's gone native?" "Is it—"

The messenger held up his hands. "Chaps! One at a time! Or else, let me tell it once, from the beginning."

The hubbub cooled then, and he was allowed to take a seat, a throne, rather, while the rest of them gathered around him, as attentive as students upon a Greek philosopher.

*Or as Aurens' men upon his word.* The similarity did not escape him. What he wondered now, was how he had escaped that powerful personality. Or had he been *permitted* to escape, because it suited Aurens' will to have him take those words back to Jerusalem?

First must come how he had found Aurens—he could no more think of the man as "T. E. Lawrence" than he could think of the Pope as "Binky." There was nothing of Britain in the man he had spoken to, save only the perfect English, and the clipped, precise accent. Not even the blue eyes—they had held something more alien than all the mysteries of the east.

"I was told he had last been seen at Deraa, so that was where I went to look for him. He wasn't there; but his garrison was."

"His garrison! These wogs couldn't garrison a stable!" There was an avalanche of comments about that particular term; most disparaging. Kirkbride waited until the comments had subsided.

"I tell, you, it was a *garrison.*" He shook his head. "I can't explain it. As wild as you like, tribesmen riding like devils in their games outside, the Turkish headquarters wrecked and looted—but everything outside that, untouched. The Turks, prisoners, housed and fed and clean—the guards on the town, as disciplined as—" He lacked words. The contrast had been so great, he could hardly believe it. But more than that, the town had been held by men from a dozen different tribes, or more—and yet there was no serious quarreling, no feuding. When he ventured to ask questions, it had been "Aurens said," and "Aurens commanded," as though Aurens spoke for Allah.

Aurens, it appeared, was on the road to Damascus, sweeping all before him.

"They gave me a guide, and sent me off camel-back, and what was the oddest, I would have sworn that they knew I was coming and were only waiting for me." That had been totally uncanny. The moment he had appeared, he had been escorted to the head of the garrison, some Sheik or other, then sent immediately out to the waiting guide and saddled camel. And the only answer to his question of "Where are you taking me?" was "Aurens commands."

Deraa had been amazing. The situation outside Damascus was beyond imagination.

As he described it for his listeners, he could not fault them for their expressions of disbelief. He would not have believed it, if he had not seen it. Massed before Damascus was the greatest Arab army the world had ever seen. Kirkbride had been an Oxford scholar in History, and he could not imagine that such a gathering had ever occurred even at the height of the Crusades. Tribe after feuding tribe was gathered there, together, in the full strength of fighters. Boys as young as their early teens, and scarred old graybeards. There was order; there was discipline. Not the "discipline" of the British regulars, of drill and salute, of uniforms and ranks—a discipline of a peculiarly Eastern kind, in which individual and tribal differences were forgotten, submerged in favor of a goal that engaged every mind gathered here in a kind of white-hot fervor. Kirkbride had recognized Bedouins that were known to be half-pagan alongside Druses, alongside King Hussein's own devout guard from Mecca—

That had brought him up short, and in answer to his stammered question, his guide had only smiled whitely. "You shall see," he said only. "When we reach Aurens."

Reach Aurens they did, and he was brought into the tent as though into the Presence. He was announced, and the figure in the spotlessly white robes turned his eyes on the messenger.

His listeners stilled, as some of his own awe communicated itself to them. He had no doubt, at that moment, that Aurens *was* a Presence. The blue eyes were unhuman; something burned in them that Kirkbride had never seen in all of his life. The face was as still as marble, but stronger than tempered steel. There was no weakness in this man, anywhere.

Aurens would have terrified him at that moment, except that he remembered the garrison holding Deraa. The Turks there were cared for, honorably. Their wounded were getting better treatment than their own commanders gave them. Somewhere, behind the burning eyes, there was mercy as well.

It took him a moment to realize that the men clustered about Aurens, as disciples about a master, included King Hussein, side-by-side, and apparently reconciled, with his son Feisal. King Hussein, pried out of Mecca at last—

Clearly taking a subservient role to Aurens, a foreigner, a Christian.

Kirkbride had meant to stammer out his errand then—except that at that moment, there came the call to prayer. Wild and wailing, it rang out across the camp.

Someone had translated it for Kirkbride once, imperfectly, or so he said. *God alone is great; I testify that there are no Gods but God, and Mohammed is his Prophet. Come to prayer; come to security. God alone is great; there is no God but God.*

And Aurens, the Englishman, the Christian, unrolled his carpet, faced Mecca with the rest, and fell upon his face.

That kept Kirkbride open-mouthed and speechless until the moment of prayer was over, and all rose again, taking their former places.

"He did *what?*" The officers were as dumbfounded as he had been.

Once again, Kirkbride was back in that tent, under the burning, blue gaze of those eyes. "He said to tell Allenby that if he wanted to see the taking of Damascus, he should find an aeroplane, else it would happen before he got there." Kirkbride swallowed, as the mess erupted in a dozen shouted conversations at once.

Some of those involved other encounters with Aurens over the past few weeks. How he had been in a dozen places at once, always riding a white Arabian stallion or a pure white racing camel of incredible endurance. How he had rallied the men of every tribe. How he had emptied Mecca of its fighting men.

How he had appeared, impeccably uniformed, with apparently genuine requisition orders for guns, ammunition, explosives, supplies. How he had vanished into the desert with laden camels— and only later, were the orders proved forgeries so perfect that even Allenby could not be completely sure he had not signed them.

How, incredibly, all those incidents had taken place in the same day, at supply depots spread miles apart.

It was possible—barely. Such a feat could have been performed by a man with access to a high-powered motorcar. No one could prove Aurens had such access—but Hussein did; he owned several. And Hussein was now with Aurens—

It would still have taken incredible nerve and endurance. Kirkbride did not think *he* had the stamina to carry it off.

No one was paying any attention to him; he slipped out of the officers' mess with his own head spinning. There was only one thing of which he was certain now.

He wanted to be in at the kill. But to do that, he had to get himself attached to Allenby's staff within the next hour.

Impossible? Perhaps. But then again, had Aurens not said, as he took his leave, "We will meet again in Damascus"?


Kirkbride sat attentively at the general's side; they had not come by aeroplane after all, but by staff car, and so they had missed the battle.

All six hours of it.

Six hours! He could scarcely credit it. Even the Germans had fled in terror at the news of the army camped outside their strongholds; they had not even waited to destroy their own supplies. The general would not have believed it, had not French observers confirmed it. Allenby had mustered all of the General Staff of the Allied forces, and a convoy of staff cars had pushed engines to the breaking-point to convey them all to the city, but Kirkbride had the feeling that this was the mountain come to Mohammed, and not the other way around. He had been listening to the natives, and the word in their mouths, spoken cautiously, but fervently, was that Aurens *was* Mohammed, or something very like him. The victories that Allah had granted were due entirely to his holiness, and not to his strategy. Strangest of all, this was agreed upon by Suni and Shiite, by Kurd and Afghani, by purest Circassian and darkest Egyptian, by Bedouin wanderer and Lebanese shopkeeper. There had been no such accord upon a prophet since the very days of Mohammed himself.

Allenby had convinced himself somehow that Aurens was going to simply, meekly, hand over his conquests to his rightful leader.

Kirkbride had the feeling that Allenby was not going to get what he expected.

Damascus was another Deraa, writ large. Only the Turkish holdings had been looted; the rest remained unmolested. There were no fires, no riots. High-spirited young warriors gamed and sported outside the city walls; inside, a stern and austere martial order prevailed. Even the hospital holding the wounded and sick Turkish prisoners was in as good order as might be expected, for a place that had been foul when the city was in Turkish hands. There was government; there was order. It was not an English order; organization was along tribal lines, rather than rank, to each tribe, a duty, and if they failed it, another was appointed to take it, to their eternal shame. But it was an order, and at the heart of it was the new Arab Government.

Allenby had laughed to hear that, at the gates of the city. As they were ushered into that government's heart, he was no longer laughing. There were fire brigades, a police force; the destitute were being fed by the holy men from out of the looted German stores, and the sick tended by the Turkish doctors out of those same stores. There were scavenger-gangs to clear away the dead, with rights to loot the bodies to make up for the noisome work. British gold became the new currency; there was a market already, with barter encouraged. Everywhere Kirkbride looked, there was strange, yet logical, order. And Allenby's face grew more and more grave.

Aurens permitted him, and the envoys of the other foreign powers, into his office, commandeered from the former governor. The aides remained behind. "My people will see to us, and to them," Aurens said, with quiet authority. A look about the room, at the men in a rainbow of robes, with hands on knife-hilts, dissuaded arguments.

The door closed.

Kirkbride did not join with the others, drinking coffee and making sly comments about their guardians. He had the feeling, garnered from glances shared between dark faces, and the occasional tightening of a hand on a hilt, that all of these "barbarians" knew English quite well. Instead, he kept to himself, and simply watched and waited.

The hour of prayer came, and the call went up. All the men but one guarding them fell to praying; Kirkbride drew nearer to that one, a Circassian as blond as Aurens himself.

"You do not pray?" he asked, expecting that the man would understand.

And so he did. He shrugged. "I am Christian, for now." He cast his glance towards the closed door, and his eyes grew bright and thoughtful. "But—perhaps I shall convert."

Kirkbride blinked in surprise; not the least of the surprises of this day. "What was it that the caller added to the end of the chant?" he asked, for he had noted an extra sentence, called in a tone deeper than the rest.

The man's gaze returned to Kirkbride's face. "He said, 'God alone is good, God alone is great, and He is very good to us this day, Oh people of Damascus.' "

At that moment, the door opened, and a much subdued delegation filed out of the door. Allenby turned, as Aurens followed a little into the antechamber, and stopped. His white robes seemed to glow in the growing dusk, and Kirkbride was astonished to see a hint of a smile on the thin, ascetic lips.

"You can't keep this going, you know," Allenby said, more weary than angry. "This isn't natural. It's going to fall apart."

"Not while I live, I think," Aurens said, in his crisp, precise English.

"Well, when you die, then," Allenby retorted savagely. "And the moment you're dead, we'll be waiting—just like the vultures you called us in there."

If anything, the smile only grew a trifle. "Perhaps. Perhaps not. There is wealth here, and wealth can purchase educations. In a few years, there will be men of the tribes who can play the politicians' game with the best of them. Years more, and there will be men of the tribes who look farther than the next spring, into the next century. We need not change, you know—we need only adopt the tools and weapons, and turn them to our own use. I would not look to cut up the East too soon, if I were you." Now he chuckled, something that surprised Kirkbride so much that his jaw dropped. "And in any event," Aurens concluded carelessly, "I intend to live a very long time."

Allenby swore under his breath, and turned on his heel. The rest, all but Kirkbride, followed.

He could not, for Aurens had turned that luminous blue gaze upon him again.

"Oxford, I think," the rich voice said.

He nodded, unable to speak.

The gaze released him, and turned to look out one of the windows; after a moment, Kirkbride recognized the direction. East.

Baghdad.

"I shall have need of Oxford men, to train my people in the English way of deception," the voice said, carelessly. "And the French way of double-dealing, and the German way of ruthlessness. To train them so that they understand, but do not become these things."

Kirkbride found his voice. "You aren't trying to claim that 'your people' aren't double-dealing, deceitful, and ruthless, I hope?" he said, letting sarcasm color his words. "I think that would be a little much, even from you."

The eyes turned back to recapture his, and somewhere, behind the blue fire, there was a hint of humor.

"Oh, no," Aurens said, with gentle warmth. "But those are *Arab* deceptions, double-dealings, and ruthlessness. Clever, but predictable to another Arab; these things are understood all around. They have not yet learned the ways of men who call themselves civilized. I should like to see them well-armored, before Allah calls me again."

Kirkbride raised an eyebrow at that. "You haven't done anything any clever man couldn't replicate," he replied, half in accusation. "Without the help of Allah."

"Have I ever said differently?" Aurens traded him look for ironic look.

"I heard what happened before the battle." Aurens, they said, had ridden his snow-white stallion before them all. "In whose name do you ride?" he had called. "Like a trumpet," Kirkbride's informant had told him, as awed as if he had spoken of the Archangel Gabriel.

And the answer, every man joined in one roar of response. *"In the name of Allah, and of Aurens."*

Aurens only looked amused. "Ride with me to Baghdad." This had less the sound of a request than a command. "Ride with me to Yemen. Help me shape the world." Again, the touch of humor, softening it all. "Or at least, so much of it as we can. *Inshallah.* I have Stirling, I have some others, I should like you."

Kirkbride weighed the possibilities, the gains, the losses. Then weighed them against the intangible; the fire in the eyes, the look of eagles.

Then, once again, he looked Aurens full in the eyes; was caught in the blue fire of them, and felt that fire catch hold in his soul, outweighing any other thoughts or considerations.

Slowly, knowing that he wagered all on a single cast of the dice, he drew himself up to attention. Then he saluted; slowly, gravely, to the approval of every one of the robed men in that room.

"To Baghdad, and Yemen, Aurens," he said. *"Inshallah."*

*This story first appeared in* Fantasy Book *magazine; it was later combined with the following story, "Dragon's Teeth," and stories by Marion Zimmer Bradley and Jennifer Roberson for a volume originally called* Bardic Voices, *later published by DAW as* Spell Singers.

*Martis is very close to being a soul-sister to Tarma and Kethry.*

# Balance

## Mercedes Lackey

*"You're* my bodyguard?"

The swordsman standing in the door to Martis' cluttered quarters blinked in startled surprise. He'd been warned that the sorceress was not easy to work with, but he hadn't expected her to be quite so rude. He tried not to stare at the tall, disheveled mage who stood, hands on hips, amid the wreckage she'd made of her own quarters. The woman's square features, made harsher by nervous tension, reflected her impatience as the mercenary groped for the proper response to make.

Martis was a little embarrassed by her own ill manners, but really, this—child—must surely be aware that his appearance was hardly likely to invoke any confidence in his fighting ability!

For one thing, he was slim and undersized; he didn't even boast the inches Martis had. For another, the way he dressed was absurd; almost as if he were a dancer got up as a swordsman for some theatrical production. He was too clean, too fastidious; that costume

83

wasn't even the least worn-looking—and silk, for Kevreth's sake! Blue-green silk at that! He carried two swords, and whoever had heard of anyone able to use two swords at once outside of a legend? His light brown hair was worn longer than any other fighter Martis had ever seen—too long, Martis thought with disapproval, and likely to get in the way despite the headband he wore to keep it out of his eyes. He even moved more like a dancer than a fighter.

This was supposed to guard her back? It looked more like she'd be guarding *him*. It was difficult to imagine anything that looked less like a warrior.

"The Guard-serjant did send this one for that purpose, Mage-lady, but since this one does not please, he shall return that another may be assigned."

Before Martis could say anything to stop him, he had whirled about and vanished from the doorway without a sound. Martis sighed in exasperation and turned back to her packing. At this moment in time she was not about to start worrying about the tender feelings of a hire-sword!

She hadn't gotten much farther along when she was interrupted again—this time by a bestial roar from the bottom of the stair.

"MARTIS!" the walls shook with each step as Trebenth, Guard-serjant to the Mage Guild, climbed the staircase to Martis' rooms. Most floors and stairs in the Guild-hold shook when Trebenth was about. He was anything but fat—but compared to the lean mages he worked for, he was just so—massive. Outside of the Guards' quarters, most of the Guild-hold wasn't designed to cope with his bulk. Martis could hear him rumbling under his breath as he ascended; the far-off mutterings of a volcano soon to erupt. She flinched and steeled herself for the inevitable outburst.

He practically filled the doorframe; as he glared at Martis, she half-expected steam to shoot from his nostrils. It didn't help that he *looked* like a volcano, dressed in Mage-hireling red, from his tunic to his boots; it matched the red of his hair and beard, and the angry flush suffusing his features. "Martis, what in the name of the Seven is your *problem?*"

"My *problem*, as you call it, is the fact that I need a bodyguard, not a temple dancer!" Martis matched him, glare for glare, her flat gray eyes mirroring his impatience. "What are you trying to push on me, Ben? Zaila's toenails, if it weren't for the fact that Guild law prevents a mage from carrying weapons, I'd take sword myself rather than trust my safety to *that* toy!"

"Dammit, Martis, you've complained about every guard I've ever assigned to you! *This* one was too sullen, *that* one was too talkative, *t'other* one *snored* at night—" he snorted contemptuously. "Mother of the Gods, Martis, snored?"

"You ought to know by now that a mage needs undisturbed sleep more than food—besides, anyone stalking us would have been able to locate our campsite by ear alone!" she replied, pushing a lock of blond hair—just beginning to show signs of gray—out of her eyes. The gesture showed both her annoyance and her impatience; and pulling her robe a bit straighter could not conceal the fact that her hands trembled a little.

He lost a portion of his exasperation; after all, he and Martis were old friends, and she *did* have a point. "Look, when have I ever sent you a guard that couldn't do the job? I think this time I've really found the perfect match for you—he's quiet, half the time you don't even know he's there, in fact—and Mart, the lad's *good.*"

"*Him?* Ben, have you lost what little mind you ever had? Who told you he was good?"

"Nobody," he replied, affronted. "I don't take anyone's word on the guards I hire. I tested him myself. The boy moves so fast he doesn't *need* armor, and as for those two toy swords of his, well—he's good. He came within a hair of taking *me* down."

Martis raised an eyebrow in surprise. To her certain knowledge, it had been years since anyone could boast of taking Trebenth down—or even coming close.

"Why's he dress himself up like a friggin' faggot, then?"

"I don't know, Mart. Ask him yourself. I don't care if my guards wear battleplate or paint themselves green, so long as they can do the job. Mart, what's bothering you? You're not usually so damn picky. You generally save your complaining till the job's over."

Martis collapsed tiredly into a chair, shoving aside a box of tagged herbs and a pile of wrinkled clothing. Trebenth saw with sudden concern the lines of worry crossing her forehead and her puffy, bruised-looking eyelids.

"It's the job. Guild business—internal problems."

"Somebody need disciplining?"

"Worse. Gone renegade—and he's raising power with blood-magic. He was very good before he started this; I've no doubt he's gotten better. If we can't do something about him now, we'll have another Sable Mage-King on our hands."

Trebenth whistled through his teeth. "A black adept in the making, eh? No wonder they're sending you."

Martis sighed. "Just when I'd begun to think the Guild would never set me to anything but teaching again. But that's not what's troubling me, old friend. I knew him—a long and close association. He was one of my best students."

Trebenth winced. To set Martis out after one of her old students was a cruel thing to do. The powers manipulated by mages gifted them with much that lesser folk could envy—but those powers took as well as gave. Use of magic for any length of time rendered the user sterile. In many ways Martis' students took the place of the children she'd never have.

They often took the place of friends, too. She'd served the Guild since she'd attained Masterclass, and her barely past what for the unTalented would have been marriageable age. There were few sorcerers among her contemporaries, male or female, that didn't secretly fear and envy the Masterclass mages. There were no mages of her own rank interested in taking a lover whose powers equaled their own. They preferred their women pliant, pretty, and not too bright. Martis's relations with her own kind were cordial, but barren.

Trebenth himself had been one of the few lovers she'd had—and she hadn't taken another since he'd toppled like a felled tree for his little Margwynwy, and she'd severed that side of their relationship herself. It was times like this one, with her loneliness standing bare in her eyes, that he pitied her with all his heart.

Martis caught his glance, and smiled thinly. "The Council did their level best to spare me this, I'll give them that much. The fact is, we don't know for certain how deeply he's gotten himself in yet; we know he's been sacrificing animals, but so far rumors of *human* deaths are just that—rumors. They want to give him every chance to get himself out of the hole he's digging for himself. Frankly, he's got too much Talent to waste. One of the factors in deciding to send me is that they hope he'll give me a chance to reason with him. If reason doesn't work, well, I'm one of the few sorcerers around with a chance of defeating him. After all, I taught him. I know all his strengths and weaknesses."

*"Knew,"* Trebenth reminded her. "Can I assign Lyran to your service, now that I've vouched for his ability, or are you still wanting someone else?"

"Who? Oh—the boy. All right, Ben, you know what you're doing. You've been hiring guards as long as I've been training mages. Tell him to get the horses ready, I want to make a start before noon."

When Martis had finished ransacking her room for what she wanted, she slung her packed saddlebags over her shoulder and slammed the door on the entire mess. By the time she returned—*if* she returned—the Guild servants would have put everything back in order again. That was one of the few benefits of being a Masterclass sorceress. The Guild provided comfortable, safe quarters and reliable servants who never complained—at least not to her. Those benefits were paid for, though; a Masterclass mage lived and died in service to the Guild. No one with that rating was ever permitted to take service independently.

Martis had a liking for heights and a peculiar phobia about having people living above her, so her room was at the top of the staircase that linked all four floors of the Masters' quarters. As she descended the stairs, she found that a certain reluctant curiosity was beginning to emerge concerning this unlikely swordsman, Lyran. The order she'd given Trebenth, to have the lad ready the horses, was in itself a test. Martis' personal saddlebeast was an irascible bay gelding of indeterminant age and vile temper, the possessor of a number of bad habits. He'd been the cause of several grooms ending in the Healer's hands before this. Martis kept him for two reasons—the first was that his gait was as sweet as his temper was foul; the second that he could be trusted to carry a babe safely through Hell once it was securely in the saddle. To Martis, as to any other mage, these traits far outweighed any other considerations. If this Lyran could handle old Tosspot, there was definitely hope for him.

It was Martis' turn to blink in surprise when she emerged into the dusty, sunlit courtyard. Waiting for her was the swordsman, the reins of his own beast in one hand and those of Tosspot in the other. Tosspot was not trying to bite, kick, or otherwise mutilate either the young man or his horse. His saddle was in place, and Martis could tell by his disgruntled expression that he hadn't managed to get away with his usual trick of "blowing" so that his saddle girth would be loose. More amazing still, the swordsman didn't appear to be damaged in any way, didn't even seem out of breath.

"Did he give you any trouble?" she asked, fastening her saddlebags to Tosspot's harness, and adroitly avoiding his attempt to step on her foot.

"He is troublesome, yes, Mage-lady, but this one has dealt with a troublesome beast before," Lyran replied seriously. At just that moment the swordsman's dust-brown mare lashed out with a wicked hoof, which the young man dodged with reflexive agility. He reached up and seized one of the mare's ears and twisted it once, hard. The mare immediately resumed her good behavior. "Sometimes it would seem that the best animals are also the vilest of temper," he continued as though he hadn't been interrupted. "It then is of regrettable necessity to prove, that though they are stronger, this one has more knowledge."

Martis mounted Tosspot, and nodded with satisfaction when his girth proved to be as tight as it looked. "I don't think this old boy will be giving you any more trouble. From the sour look he's wearing, I'd say he learned his lesson quite thoroughly."

The swordsman seemed to glide into his saddle and gracefully inclined his head in thanks for the compliment. "Truly he must have more intelligence than Jesalis," he replied, reining in his mare so that the sorceress could take the lead, "for this one must prove the truth of the lesson to her at least once a day."

"Jesalis?" Martis asked incredulously; for the jesalis was a fragile blossom of rare perfume, and nothing about the ugly little mare could remind anyone of a flower.

"Balance, Mage-lady," Lyran replied, so earnestly that Martis had to hide a smile. "So foul a temper has she, that it is necessary to give her a sweet name to leaven her nature."

They rode out of the Guild-hold in single file with Martis riding in the lead, since protocol demanded that the "hireling" ride behind the "mistress" while they were inside the town wall. Once they'd passed the gates, they reversed position. Lyran would lead the way as well as providing a guard, for all of Martis' attention must be taken up by her preparations to meet with her wayward former student. Tosspot would obey his training and follow wherever the rider of Jesalis led.

This was the reason that Tosspot's gait and reliability were worth more than gold pieces. Most of Martis' time in the saddle would be spent in a trancelike state as she gradually gathered power to her. It was this ability to garner and store power that made her a Master-class sorceress—for after all, the most elaborate spell is useless without the power to set it in motion.

There were many ways to accumulate power. Martis' was to gather the little aimless threads of it given off by living creatures in their daily lives. Normally this went unused, gradually dissipating, like dye poured into a river. Martis could take these little tag-ends of energy, spin them out and weave them into a fabric that was totally unlike what they had been before. This required total concentration, and there was no room in her calculations for mistake.

Martis was grateful that Lyran was neither sullen nor inclined to chatter. She was able to sink into her magic gathering-trance undistracted by babble and undisturbed by a muddy, surly aura riding in front of her. Perhaps Ben had been right after all. The boy was so unobtrusive that she might have been riding alone. She spared one scant moment to regret faintly that she would not be able to enjoy the beauties of the summer woods and meadows they were to ride through. It was so seldom that she came this way . . .

****

The atmosphere was so peaceful that it wasn't until she sensed—more than felt—the touch of the bodyguard's hand on her leg that she roused up again. The sun was westering, and before her was a small clearing, with Lyran's horse contentedly grazing and a small, neat camp already set up. Martis' tent was to the west of the clearing, a cluster of boulders behind it, and the tent-flap open to the cheerful fire. Lyran's bedroll lay on the opposite side. Jesalis was unsaddled, and her tack laid beside the bedroll. From what Martis could see, all of her own belongings had been placed unopened just inside the tent. And all had been accomplished without Martis being even remotely aware of it.

"Your pardon, Mage-lady," Lyran said apologetically, "but your horse must be unsaddled."

"And you can't do that with me still sitting on him," Martis finished for him, highly amused. "Why didn't you wake me earlier? I'm perfectly capable of helping make camp."

"The Guard-serjant made it plain to this one that you must be allowed to work your magics without distraction. Will you come down?"

"Just one moment—" There was something subtly wrong, but Martis couldn't pinpoint what it was. Before she could say anything, however, Lyran suddenly seized her wrist and pulled her down from her saddle, just as an arrow arced through the air where she had been. Lyran gave a shrill whistle, and Jesalis threw up her head, sniffed the breeze, and charged into the trees to their left. Martis quickly sought cover in some nearby bushes, as Lyran hit the ground and rolled up into a wary crouch.

A scream from where the mare had vanished told that the horse had removed the obstacle of the archer, but he had not been alone. From under the cover of the trees stepped not one, but three swordsmen. Lyran regained his feet in one swift motion, drew the swords he wore slung across his back, and faced them in a stance that was not of any fighting style Martis recognized. He placed himself so that they would have to pass him to reach her.

The first of the assassins—Martis was reasonably sure that this was what they were—laughed and swatted at Lyran with the flat of his blade in a careless, backhanded stroke, aiming negligently for his head.

"This little butterfly is mine—we will see if he likes to play the woman he apes—" he began.

Lyran moved, lithe as a ferret. The speaker stared stupidly at the sword blade impaling his chest. Lyran had ducked and come up inside his guard, taking him out before he'd even begun to realize what the bodyguard was about.

Lyran pulled his blade free of the new-made corpse while the assassin still stood. He whirled to face the other two before the first fell to the ground.

They moved in on him with far more caution than their companion had, circling him warily to attack him from opposite sides. He fended off their assault easily, his two swords blurring, they moved so fast, his movement dancelike. But despite his skill he could seem to find no opening to make a counterattack. For the moment all three were deadlocked. Martis chafed angrily at her feeling of helplessness—the combative magics she'd prepared were all meant to be used against another mage. To use any of the spells she knew that would work against a fighter, she'd have to reach her supplies in her saddlebags—now rather hopelessly out of reach. She found that she was sharply aware of the incongruous scent of the crushed blossoms that lay beneath the dead man's body.

The deadlock was broken before Martis could do more than curse at her own helplessness.

Within the space of a breath, Lyran feinted at the third of the assassins, drawing the second to attack. He caught his opponent's blade in a bind, and disarmed him with practiced ease. Then the third lunged at him, and he moved aside just enough for his blade to skim past his chest. Lyran's left-hand blade licked out and cut his throat with the recovery of the stroke that had disarmed the second. Before Martis could blink, he continued the flow of movement before the third could fall to cut the second nearly in half with the sword in his right.

And behind him, the first dead man rose, sword in hand, and hacked savagely at the unsuspecting Lyran's blind side. Lyran got one blade up in time to deflect the blow, but the power behind it forced him to one knee. The Undead hammered at the bodyguard, showing sorcerous strength that far exceeded his abilities in life. Lyran was forced down and back, until the Undead managed to penetrate his defenses with an under-and-over strike at his left arm.

The slice cut Lyran's arm and shoulder nearly to the bone. The sword dropped from his fingers and he tried to fend off the liche with the right alone.

The Undead continued to press the attack, its blows coming even faster than before. Lyran was sent sprawling helplessly when it caught him across the temple with the flat of its blade.

Martis could see—almost as if time had slowed—that he would be unable to deflect the liche's next strike.

She, Lyran, and the Undead all made their moves simultaneously.

Martis destroyed the magic that animated the corpse, but not before it had made a two-handed stab at the bodyguard.

But Lyran had managed another of those ferret-quick squirms. As the liche struck, he threw himself sideways—a move Martis would have thought impossible, and wound up avoiding impalement by inches. The Undead collapsed then, as the magic supporting it dissolved.

Freed from having to defend himself, Lyran dropped his second blade, groped for the wound, and sagged to his knees in pain.

Martis sprinted from out of hiding, reaching the swordsman's side in five long strides. Given the amount of damage done his arm, it was Lyran's good fortune that his charge was Masterclass! In her mind she was gathering up the strands of power she'd accumulated during the day, and reweaving them into a spell of healing; a spell she knew so well she needed nothing but her memory to create.

Even in that short period of time, Lyran had had the presence of mind to tear off the headband that had kept his long hair out of his eyes and tie it tightly about his upper arm, slowing the bleeding. As Martis reached for the wounded arm, Lyran tried feebly to push her away.

"There is—no need—Mage-lady," he gasped, his eyes pouring tears of pain.

Martis muttered an obscenity and cast the spell. "No guard in *my* service stays wounded," she growled. "I don't care what or who you've served before; I take care of my own."

Having said her say and worked her magics, she went to look at the bodies while the spell did its work.

What she found was very interesting indeed, so interesting that at first she didn't notice that Lyran had come to stand beside her where she knelt. When she did notice, it was with some surprise that she saw the slightly greenish cast to the guard's face, and realized that Lyran was striving valiantly not to be sick. Lyran must have seen her surprise written clear in her expression, for he said almost defensively, "This one makes his living by the sword, Mage-lady, but it does not follow that he enjoys viewing the consequences of his labor."

Martis made a noncommittal sound and rose. "Well, you needn't think your scoutcraft's at fault, young man. These men—the archer, too, I'd judge—were brought here by magic just a few moments before they attacked us. I wish you could have taken one alive. He could have told us a lot."

"It is this one's humble opinion that one need not look far for the author of the attack," Lyran said, looking askance at Martis.

"Oh, no doubt it's Kelven's work, all right. He knows what my aura looks like well enough to track me from a distance and pinpoint my location with very little trouble, and I'm sure he knows that it's me the Guild would send after him. And he knows the nearest Gate-point, and that I'd be heading there. No, what I wish I knew were the orders he gave this bunch. Were they to kill—or to disable and capture?" She dusted her hands, aware that the sun was almost gone and the air was cooling. "Well, I'm no necromancer, so the knowledge is gone beyond my retrieval."

"Shall this one remove them?" Lyran still looked a little sick.

"No, the healing-spell I set on you isn't done yet, and I don't want you tearing that wound open again. Go take care of Tosspot and find your mare, wherever she's gotten herself to. I'll get rid of them."

Martis piled the bodies together and burned them to ash with mage-fire. It was a bit of a waste of power, but the energy liberated by the deaths of the assassins would more than make up for the loss—though Martis felt just a little guilty at using that power. Violent death always released a great deal of energy—it was a short-cut to gaining vast quantities of it—which was why blood-magic was proscribed by the Guild. Making use of what was released when you had to kill in self-defense was one thing—cold-blooded killing to gain power was something else.

When Martis returned to the campsite, she discovered that not only had Lyran located his mare and unharnessed and tethered Tosspot, but that he'd made dinner as well. Browning over the pocket-sized fire was a brace of rabbits.

"Two?" she asked quizzically. "I can't eat more than half of one. And where did you get them?"

"This one has modest skill with a sling, and there were many opportunities as we rode," Lyran replied. "And the second one is for breakfast in the morning."

Lyran had placed Tosspot's saddle on the opposite side of the fire from his own, just in front of the open tent. Martis settled herself on her saddle to enjoy her dinner. The night air was pleasantly cool, night creatures made sounds around them that were reassuring because it meant that no one was disturbing them. The insects of the daylight hours were gone, those of the night had not yet appeared. And the contradictions in her guard's appearance and behavior made a pleasant puzzle to mull over.

"I give up," she said at last, breaking the silence between them, silence that had been punctuated by the crackle of the fire. "You are the strangest guard I have ever had."

Lyran looked up, and the fire revealed his enigmatic expression. He had eaten his half of the rabbit, but had done so as if it were a duty rather than a pleasure. He still looked a bit sickly.

"Why does this one seem strange to you, Mage-lady?"

"You dress like a dancer playing at being a warrior, you fight like a friggin' guard-troop all by yourself—then you get sick afterwards because you killed someone. You wear silks that would do a harlot proud, but you ride a mare that's a damn trained killer. What *are* you, boy? What land spawned something like you?"

"This one comes from far—a great distance to the west and south. It is not likely that you have ever heard of the People, Mage-lady. The Guard-serjant had not. As for why this one is the way he is—this one follows A Way."

"*The* Way?"

"No, Mage-lady, 'A Way.' The People believe that there are many such Ways, and ours is of no more merit than any other. Our way is the Way of Balance."

"You said something about 'Balance' before—" Now Martis' curiosity was truly aroused. "Just what does this Way entail?"

"It is simplicity. One must strive to achieve Balance in all things in one's life. This one—is on a kind of pilgrimage to find such Balance, to find a place where this one may fit within the pattern of All. Because this one's nature is such that he does well to live by the sword, he must strive to counter this by using that sword in the service of peace—and to cultivate peace in other aspects of his life. And, in part, it must be admitted that this one fosters a helpless outer aspect," Lyran smiled wryly. "The Mage-lady will agree that appearing ineffectual does much to throw the opponent off his guard. So—that is the *what* of this one. As to the why—the People believe that the better one achieves Balance, the better one will be reborn."

"I certainly hope you don't include good and evil in your Balance—either that, or I'll do the cooking from now on." Lyran laughed.

"No Mage-lady, for how could one weigh 'good' and 'evil'? Assuredly, it was 'good' that this one slew your foes, but was it not 'evil' to them? Sometimes things are plainly one or the other, but too often it depends upon where one stands one's own self. A primary tenet of our Way is to do no harm when at all possible—to wound, rather than kill, subdue rather than wound, reason rather than subdue, and recall when reasoning that the other may have the right of it."

"Simple to state, but—"

"Ai, difficult to live by. It would seem that most things worth having are wrapped in difficulty. Have you not spent your life in magecraft, and yet still learn? And does this not set you farther apart from others—sacrificing knowledge for the common ties of life?"

Martis scrutinized her companion across the flames. Not so young, after all. Not nearly so young as she had thought—nor so simple. It was only the slight build, the guileless eyes, the innocence of the heart-shaped face that made you think "child." And attractive too. Damned attractive . . . *"Don't be a fool,"* she scolded herself. *"You haven't the time or energy to waste—besides, he's young enough to be your son. Well, maybe not your son. But too damned young for the likes of you! Hellfires! You have more to think about than a sweet-faced hireling! Get your mind back to business."*

"Before we sleep, I'm intending to gather power as I was doing on the road," she stretched a little. "I want you to rouse me when the moon rises."

"Mage-lady—would quiet chanting disturb you?" Lyran asked anxiously. "This one would offer words for those slain."

"Whatever for? They wouldn't have mourned *you!*" Once again, Lyran had surprised her.

"That is their Way, not this one's. If one does not mourn that one has slain, the heart soon dies. Under other circumstances, might they not have been comrades?"

"I suppose you're right," Martis replied thoughtfully. "No, chanting isn't going to disturb me any. Just make sure you also keep a good watch out for any more surprises."

"Of a certainty, Mage-lady." Lyran didn't even seem annoyed at the needless admonition, a fact that made Martis even more thoughtful. Professional mercenaries she'd known in the past tended to get a bit touchy about mages giving them "orders" like she'd just given him. Nothing much seemed to ruffle that serene exterior. How long, she wondered, had it taken him to achieve that kind of mind-set? And what kind of discipline had produced it? A puzzle; truly a puzzle.

The next day brought them to a ring of standing stones—the Gate-site. The inherent magic residing in this place made it possible to use it as a kind of bridge to almost any other place on the earth's surface. Martis had been to Kelven's tower once, and with mage-habit had memorized the lay of the land surrounding it. They would be able to ride straight from *here* to *there* once the proper spell was set into motion. This would have another benefit, besides saving them a long and tiring journey; Kelven would "lose" them if he had been tracking them, and without knowing exactly where to look for them, would not know how many of them had survived his attack. They rested undisturbed that evening, with Martis quickly regaining from the place the energy she spent in shielding their presence there.

The Gate spell took the better part of the next morning to set up. Martis had no intentions of bringing them in very near, for she had other notions as to how she wanted this confrontation to be played out. After a light noon meal, she activated the Gate.

The standing stones began to glow, not from within, but as if an unquenchable fire burned along their surfaces. The fire from each reached out to join with the fires of the stones on either side. Before an hour had passed, the ring was a near-solid thing of pulsating orange light.

Martis waited until the power-flux built to an internal drawing that was well-nigh unendurable—then led them at a gallop between two of the stones. They rode in through one side—but not out the other.

They emerged in the vicinity of Kelven's tower—and the confrontation Martis had been dreading was at hand.

She wasn't sure whether the fact that there had been no attempt to block them at the Gate was good or bad. It could be that Kelven was having second thoughts about the situation, and would be ready to be persuaded to amend his ways. It also could be that he was taking no further chances on the skills of underlings or working at a distance, and was planning to eliminate her himself in a sorcerers' duel.

They rode through country that was fairly wild and heavily wooded, but Kelven's tower lay beyond where the woods ended, at the edge of a grass-plain. Martis described the situation to Lyran, who listened attentively, then fell silent. Martis was not inclined to break that silence, lost in her own contemplations.

"Mage-lady—" Lyran broke into Martis' thoughts not long before they were to reach Kelven's stronghold. "—is it possible that the Mage-lord may not know about the continued survival of this one?"

"It's more than possible, it's likely," Martis told him. "I've been shielding our movements ever since the attack."

"But would you have gone on if this one had fallen? Would it not have been more likely that you would return to the Guild Hall to seek other guards?"

They had stopped on the crest of a ridge. Below them lay grasslands and scrub forest that stretched for furlongs in all directions but the one they had come.

Kelven's tower was easily seen from here, and about an hour's distance away. The sun beat down on their heads, and insects droned lazily. The scene seemed ridiculously incongruous as a site of imminent conflict.

Martis laughed—a sound that held no trace of humor. "Anybody else but me *would* do just that. But I'm stubborn, and I've got a rotten temper. Kelven knows that. He watched me drag myself and two pupils—he was one of them—through a stinking, bug-infested bog once, with no guides and no bodyguards. The guides had been killed and the guards were in no shape to follow us, y'see; we'd been attacked by a Nightmare. I was, by-Zaila, not going to let it get away back to its lair! By the time we found it I was so mad that I fried the entire herd at the lair by myself. If you'd been killed back there, I'd be out for blood—or at least a *damn* convincing show of repentance. And I wouldn't let a little thing like having no other guard stand in my way."

"Then let this one propose a plan, Mage-lady. The land below is much like this one's homeland. It would be possible to slip away from you and make one's way hidden in the tall grass—and this one has another weapon than a sling." From his saddlebag Lyran took a small, but obviously strong bow, unstrung, and a quiverful of short arrows. "The weapon is too powerful to use for hunting, Mage-lady, unless one were hunting larger creatures than rabbits and birds. This one could remain within bow-shot, but unknown to the Mage-lord, if you wished."

"I'm glad you thought of that, and I think it's more than a good idea," Martis said, gazing at the tower. Several new thoughts had occurred to her, none of them pleasant. It was entirely possible that Kelven wanted her here, had allowed them to walk into a trap. "If nothing else—this is an order. If Kelven takes me captive—shoot *me*. Shoot to kill. Get him too, if you can, but make sure you kill me. There's too many ways he could use me, and anyone can be broken, if the mage has time enough. I can bind my own death-energy before he can use it—I think."

Lyran nodded, and slipped off his mare. He rearranged saddle-pad and pack to make it appear that Martis was using the ill-tempered beast as a pack animal. In the time it took for Martis to gather up the mare's reins, he had vanished into the grassland without a trace.

Martis rode towards the tower as slowly as she could, giving Lyran plenty of time to keep up with the horses and still remain hidden.

She could see as she came closer to the tower that there was at least one uncertainty that was out of the way. She'd not have to call challenge to bring Kelven out of his tower—he was already waiting for her. Perhaps, she thought with a brightening of hope, this meant he *was* willing to cooperate.

When Lyran saw, after taking cover in a stand of scrub, that the mage Kelven had come out of his tower to wait for Martis, he lost no time in getting himself positioned within bowshot. He actually beat the sorceress' arrival by several moments. The spot he'd chosen, beneath a bush just at the edge of the mowed area that surrounded the tower, was ideal in all respects but one—since it was upwind of where the mage stood, he would be unable to hear them speak. He only hoped he'd be able to read the mage's intentions from his actions.

There were small things to alert a watcher to the intent of a mage to attack—provided the onlooker knew exactly what to look for. Before leaving, Trebenth had briefed him carefully on the signs to watch for warning of an attack by magic without proper challenge being issued. Lyran only hoped that his own eyes and instincts would be quick enough.

****

"Greetings, Martis," Kelven said evenly, his voice giving no clue as to his mindset.

Martis was a little uneasy to see that he'd taken to dressing in stark, unrelieved black. The Kelven she remembered had taken an innocent pleasure in dressing like a peacock. For the rest, he didn't look much different from when he'd been her student—he'd grown a beard and moustache, whose black hue did not quite match his dark brown hair. His narrow face still reminded her of a hawk's, with sharp eyes that missed nothing. She looked closer at him, and was alarmed to see that his pupils were dilated such that there was very little to be seen of the brown irises. Drugs sometimes produced that effect— particularly the drugs associated with blood-magic.

"Greetings, Kelven. The tales we hear of you are not good these days," she said carefully, dismounting and approaching him, trying to look stern and angry.

"Tales. Yes, those old women on the Council are fond of tales. I gather they've sent you to bring the erring sheep back into the fold?" he said. She couldn't tell if he was sneering.

"Kelven, the course you're set on can do no one any good," she faltered a little, a recollection of Kelven seated contentedly at her feet suddenly springing to mind. He'd been so like a son—this new Kelven *must* be some kind of aberration! "Please—you were a good student; one of my best. There must be a lot of good in you still, and you have the potential to reach Masterclass if you put your mind to it." She was uncomfortably aware that she was pleading, and an odd corner of her mind noted the buzzing drone of the insects in the grass behind her. "I was very fond of you, you know I was—I'll speak for you, if you want. You can 'come back to the fold,' as you put it, with no one to hold the past against you. But you must also know that no matter how far you go, there's only one end for a practitioner of blood-magic. And you must know that if I can't persuade you, I have to stop you."

There was a coldness about him that made her recoil a little from him—the ice of one who had divorced himself from humankind. She found herself longing to see just a hint of the old Kelven; one tiny glimpse to prove he wasn't as far gone as she feared he must be. But it seemed no such remnant existed.

"Really?" he smiled. "I never would have guessed."

Any weapon of magic she would have been prepared for. The last thing she ever would have expected was the dagger in his hand. She stared at the flash of light off the steel as he lifted it, too dumbfounded to do more than raise her hands against it in an ineffectual attempt at defense.

His attack was completed before she'd done more than register the fact that he was making it.

"First you have to beat me, *teacher,*" he said viciously, as he took the single step between them and plunged it into her breast.

She staggered back from the shock and pain, all breath and thought driven from her.

"I'm no match for you in a sorcerer's duel—" he said, a cruel smile curving his lips as his hands moved in the spell to steal her dying power from her, "—not yet—but I'll be the match of *any* of you with all I shall gain from your death!"

Incredibly, he had moved like a striking snake, his every movement preplanned—all this had taken place in the space of a few eyeblinks. She crumpled to the ground with a gasp of agony, both hands clutching ineffectually at the hilt. The pain and shock ripped away her ability to think, even to set into motion the spell she'd set to lock her dying energy away from his use. Blood trickled hotly between her fingers, as her throat closed against the words she had meant to speak to set a death-binding against him. She could only endure the hot agony, and the knowledge that she had failed—and then looked up in time to see three arrows strike him almost simultaneously, two in the chest, the third in the throat. Her hands clenched on the dagger hilt as he collapsed on top of her with a strangling gurgle. Agony drove her down into darkness.

Her last conscious thought was of gratitude to Lyran.

There were frogs and insects singing, which seemed odd to Martis. No one mentioned frogs or insects in any version of the afterlife that she'd ever heard. As her hearing improved, she could hear nightbirds in the distance, and close at hand, the sound of a fire and the stirring of nearby horses. That definitely did not fit in with the afterlife—unless one counted Hellfires, and this certainly didn't sound big enough to be one of those. Her eyes opened slowly, gritty and sore, and not focusing well.

Lyran sat by her side, anxiety lining his brow and exhaustion graying his face.

"Either I'm alive," Martis coughed, "or you're dead—and I don't remember you being dead."

"You live, Mage-lady—but it was a very near thing. Almost, I did not reach you in time. You are fortunate that sorcerers are not weapons-trained—no swordsman would have missed your heart as he did."

"Martis. My name is Martis—you've earned the right to use it." Martis coughed again, amazed that there was so little pain—that the worst she felt was a vague ache in her lungs, a dreamy lassitude and profound weakness. "Why am I still alive? Even if he missed the heart, that blow was enough to kill. You're no Healer—" she paused, all that Lyran had told her about his "Way" running through her mind, "—are you?"

"As my hands deal death, so they must also preserve life," Lyran replied. "Yes, among my People, all who live by weapons are also trained as Healers, even as Healers must learn to use weapons, if only to defend themselves and the wounded upon the field of battle."

He rubbed eyes that looked as red and sore as her own felt. "Since I am not Healer-born, it was hard, very hard. I am nearly as weak as you as a consequence. It will be many days before I regain my former competence, my energy, or my strength. It is well you have no more enemies that I must face, for I would do so, I fear, on my hands and knees!"

Martis frowned. "You aren't talking the way you used to."

Lyran chuckled. "It is said that even when at the point of death the Mage will observe and record—and question. Yes, I use familiar speech with you, my Mage-lady. The Healing for one not born to the Gift is not like yours—I sent my soul into your body to heal it; for a time we were one. That is why I am so wearied. You are part of myself as a consequence—and I now speak to you as one of my People.'"

"Thank the gods. I was getting very tired of your everlasting 'this one's.'" They laughed weakly together, before Martis broke off with another fit of coughing.

"What happens to you when we get back to the Guild-hold?" Martis asked presently.

"My continued employment by the Guild was dependent on your satisfaction with my performance," Lyran replied. "Since I assume that you are satisfied—"

"I'm alive, aren't I? The mission succeeded. I'm a good bit more than merely 'satisfied' with the outcome."

"Then I believe I am to become part of the regular staff, to be assigned to whatever mage happens to need a guard. And—I think here I have found what I sought; the place where my sword may serve peace, the place the Way has designed for me." Despite his contented words, his eyes looked wistful.

Martis was feeling unwontedly sensitive to the nuances in his expression. There was something behind those words she had not expected—hope—longing? And—directed at *her*?

And—under the weariness, was there actually *desire*?

"Would that I could continue in your service, Mage—Martis. I think perhaps we deal well together."

"Hmm," Martis began tentatively, not sure she was reading him correctly; not daring to believe what she thought she saw. "I'm entitled to a permanent hireling as a Master, I just never exercised the privilege. Would you be interested?"

"As a hireling—alone? Or, could I hope you would have more of me than bought-service?"

Dear gods, was he asking what she *thought* he was asking? "Lyran, you surely can't be seriously propositioning me?"

"We have been one," he sighed, touching her cheek lightly. "As you have felt a tie to me, so have I felt drawn to you. There is that in each of us that satisfies a need in the other, I think. I—care for you. I would gladly be a friend; more than friend, if you choose."

"But I'm old enough to be your mother!"

"Ah, lady," he smiled, his eyes old in his young face, "what are years? Illusion. Do each of us not know the folly of illusion?" And he cupped one hand gently beneath her cheek to touch his lips to hers. As her mouth opened beneath his, she was amazed at the stirring of passion—it was impossible, but it was plainly there, despite years, wounds, and weariness. Maybe—maybe there was something to this after all.

"I—" she began, then chuckled.

"So?" he cocked his head to one side, and waited for enlightenment.

"Well—my friends will think I'm insane, but this certainly fits your Way of Balance—my gray hairs against your youth."

"So—" the smile warmed his eyes in a way Martis found fascinating, and totally delightful, "—then we shall confound your friends, who lack your clear sight. We shall seek Balance together. Yes?"

She stretched out her hand a little to touch his, already feeling some of her years dissolving before that smile. "Oh, yes."

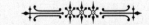

# Dragon's Teeth

## Mercedes Lackey

Trebenth, broad of shoulder and red of hair and beard, was Guard-serjant to the Mage Guild. Not to put too fine a point on it, he was Guard-serjant at High Ridings, *the* chief citadel of the Mage Guild, and site of the Academe Arcanum, *the* institution of Highest Magicks. As such, *he* was the warrior responsible for the safety and well-being of the mages he served.

This was hardly the soft post that the uninformed thought it to be. Mages had many enemies—and were terribly vulnerable to physical attack. It only took one knife in the dark to kill a mage—Trebenth's concern was to circumvent that vulnerability; by overseeing their collective safety in High Ridings, or their individual safety by means of the bodyguards he picked and trained to stand watchdog over them.

And there were times when his concern for their well-being slid over into areas that had nothing to do with arms and assassinations.

This was looking—to his worried eyes, at least—like one of those times.

He was standing on the cold granite of the landing at the top of a set of spiraling tower stairs, outside a particular tower apartment in the Guildmembers Hall, the highest apartment in a tower reserved for the Masterclass Mages. Sunlight poured through a skylight above him, reflecting off the pale wooden paneling of the wall he faced. There was no door at the head of this helical staircase; there *had* been one, but the occupant of the apartment had spelled it away, presumably so that her privacy *could not* be violated. But although Trebenth could not enter, he *could* hear something of what was going on beyond that featureless paneled wall.

Masterclass Sorceress Martis Orleva Kiriste of High Ridings, a chief instructress of the Academe, and a woman of an age *at least* equal to Trebenth's middle years was—giggling. Giggling like a giddy adolescent.

*Mart hasn't been the same since she faced down Kelven,* Ben gloomed, shifting his weight restlessly from his left foot to his right. *I thought at first it was just because she hadn't recovered yet from that stab-wound. Losing that much blood—gods, it would be enough to fuddle anyone's mind for a while. Then I thought it was emotional backlash from having been forced to kill somebody that was almost a substitute child for her. But then—she started acting odder instead of saner. First she requisitioned that outlander as her own, and then installed him in her quarters—and is making no secret that she's installed him in her bed as well. It's like she's lost whatever sense of proportion she had.*

Behind the honey-colored paneling Trebenth heard another muffled giggle, and his spirits slipped another notch. *I thought I'd finally found her the perfect bodyguard with that outlander Lyran; one that wouldn't get in her way. He was so quiet, so—so humble. Was it all a trick to worm his way into some woman's confidence? What the hell did I really bring in? What did I let latch onto her soul?*

He shifted his weight again, sweating with indecision. Finally he couldn't bear it any longer, and tapped with one knuckle, uncharacteristically hesitant, in the area where the door *had* been. "Go away," Martis called, the acid tone of her low voice clearly evident even through the muffling of the wood. "I am *not* on call. Go pester Uthedre."

"Mart?" Ben replied unhappily. "It's Ben. It isn't—" There was a shimmer of golden light, and the door popped into existence under his knuckles, in the fleeting instant between one tap and the next.

Then it swung open so unexpectedly that he was left stupidly tapping empty air.

Beyond the door was Martis' sitting room; a tiny room, mostly taken up by a huge brown couch with overstuffed cushions. Two people were curled close together there, half-disappearing into the soft pillows. One was a middle-aged, square-faced woman, graying blond hair twined into long braids that kept coming undone. Beside her was a slender young man, his shoulder-length hair nearly the color of dark amber, his obliquely slanted eyes black and unfathomable. He looked—to Trebenth's mind—fully young enough to be Martis' son. In point of fact, he was her hireling bodyguard—and her lover.

"Ben, you old goat!" Martis exclaimed from her seat on the couch, "Why didn't you say it was you in the first place? I'd never lock you out, no matter what, but you *know* I'm no damn good at aura-reading."

To Trebenth's relief, Martis was fully and decently clothed, as was the young outland fighter Lyran seated beside her. She lowered the hand she'd used to gesture the door back into reality and turned the final flourish into a beckoning crook of her finger. With no little reluctance Trebenth sidled into the sun-flooded outermost room of her suite. She cocked her head to one side, her gray eyes looking suspiciously mischievous and bright, her generous mouth quirked in an expectant half-smile.

"Well?" she asked. "I'm waiting to hear what you came all the way up my tower to ask."

Trebenth flushed. "It's—about—"

"Oh my, you sound embarrassed. Bet I can guess. Myself and my far-too-young lover, hmm?"

"Mart!" Ben exclaimed, blushing even harder. "I—didn't—"

"Don't bother, Ben," she replied, lounging back against the cushions, as Lyran watched his superior with a disconcertingly serene and thoughtful expression on his lean face. "I figured it was all over High Ridings by now. Zaila's Toenails! Why is it that when some old goat of a *man* takes a young wench to his bed everyone chuckles and considers it a credit to his virility, but when an old *woman*—"

"You are *not* old," Lyran interrupted her softly, in an almost musical tenor.

"Flatterer," she said, shaking her head at him. "I know better. So, why is it when an *older* woman does the same, everyone figures her mind is going?"

Trebenth was rather at a loss to answer that far-too-direct question.

"Never mind, let it go. I suspect, though, that you're worried about what I've let leech onto me. Let me ask you a countering question. Is Lyran causing trouble? Acting up? Flaunting status—spending my gold like water? Boasting about his connections or—his 'conquest'?"

"Well," Ben admitted slowly, "no. He acts just like he did before; so quiet you hardly know he's there. Except—"

"Except what?"

"Some of the others have been goin' for *him*. At practice, mostly."

"And?" Beside her, Lyran shifted, and laid his right hand unobtrusively—but protectively—over the one of hers resting on the brown couch cushion between them.

"Everything stayed under control until this morning. Harverth turned the dirty side of his tongue on you 'stead of Lyran, seeing as he wasn't gettin' anywhere baiting the boy. Harverth was armed, Lyran wasn't."

Martis raised one eyebrow. "So? What happened?"

"I was gonna mix in, but they finished it before I could get involved. It didn't take long. Harverth's with the Healers. They tell me he *might* walk without limping in a year or so, but they won't promise. Hard to Heal shattered kneecaps."

Martis turned a reproachful gaze on the young, long-haired man beside her. Lyran flushed. "Pardon," he murmured. "This one was angered for your sake more than this one knew. This one lost both Balance and temper."

"You lost more'n that, boy," Ben growled. "You lost me a trained—"

"Blowhard," Martis interrupted him. "You forget that you assigned that dunderhead to me once—he's damned near useless, and he's a pain in the aura to a mage like me. You know damned well you've been on the verge of kicking that idiot out on his rear a half-dozen times—you've told me so yourself! Well, now you've got an excuse to pension him off—it was *my* hireling and *my* so-called honor involved; deduct the bloodprice from my account and throw the bastard out of High Ridings. There, are you satisfied?"

Ben wasn't. "Mart," he said pleadingly, "it's not just that—"

"What is it? The puppies in your kennel still likely to go for Lyran?"

"No, not after this morning."

"What is it then? Afraid I'm going to become a laughingstock? Got news for you, Ben, I already *am,* and I don't give a damn. Or are you afraid *for* me, afraid that I'm making a fool of myself?"

Since that was exactly what Trebenth *had* been thinking, he flushed again, and averted *his* eyes from the pair on the sofa.

"Ben," Martis said softly, "when have you ever seen us acting as anything other than mage and hireling outside of my quarters? Haven't we at least kept the appearance of respectability?"

"I guess," he mumbled, hot with embarrassment.

"People would be talking even if there was *nothing* between us. They've talked about me ever since I got my Mastery. There were years at the beginning when everybody was *certain* I'd earned it in bed, not in the circles. And when you and I—they talked about that, too, didn't they? The only difference now is that I'm about half-again older than Lyran. People just don't seem to like that, much. But my position is in no danger. When the push comes, it's my power the Guild cares about, not what damage I do to an already dubious reputation. And *I* don't care. I'm happy, maybe for the first time in years. Maybe in my life."

He looked up sharply. "Are you? Really? Are you sure?"

"I'm sure," she replied with absolute candor, as Lyran raised his chin slightly, and his eyes silently dared his superior to challenge the statement.

Trebenth sighed, and felt a tiny, irrational twinge of jealousy. After all, *he* had Margwynwy—but *he'd* never been able to bring that particular shine to Martis' eyes—not even at the height of their love affair. "All right, then," he said, resigned. "As long as you don't care about the gossip—"

"Not in the slightest."

"I guess I was out of line."

"No Ben," Martis replied fondly. "You're a friend. Friends worry about friends; I'm glad you care enough to worry. My wits haven't gone south, honestly."

"Then—I guess I'll go see about paying a certain slacker off and pitching him out."

Martis gestured the door closed behind the towering Guard-serjant, then removed the door with another gesture, and turned back to her seatmate with frustration in her eyes. "Why didn't you tell me that you were being harassed?" Lyran shook his head; his light brown hair shimmered in the warm sun pouring through the skylight above his head.

"It didn't matter. Words are only as worthy as the speaker."

"It got beyond words."

"I am better than anyone except the Guild-serjant." It wasn't a boast, Martis knew, but a plain statement of fact. "What did I have to fear from harassment? It was only—" It was Lyran's turn to flush, although he continued to hold her gaze with his own eyes. "I could not bear to hear you insulted."

Something rather atavistic deep down inside glowed with pleasure at his words. "So you leapt to my defense, hmm?"

"How could I not? Martis—lady—love—" His eyes warmed to her unspoken approval.

She laughed, and leaned into the soft cushion behind her. "I suppose I'm expected to reward my defender now, hmm? Now that you've fought for my honor?"

He chuckled, and shook his head. "Silly and primitive of us, doubtless, but it does rouse up certain instinctive responses, no?"

She slid a little closer on the couch, and reached up to lace the fingers of both hands behind his neck, under his long hair. Not even the silk of his tunic was as soft as that wonderful hair . . . .

"You know good and well how I feel." The healing-magic of his

People that he had used to save her life had bound their souls together; that was the reason why Lyran did *not* refer to himself in the third person when they were alone together. And it was why each tended to know now a little of what the other felt. It would have been rather futile to deny her feelings even if she'd wanted to . . . which she didn't.

"*Are* you happy, my Mage-lady?" She felt an unmistakable twinge of anxiety from him. "*Do* the words of fools hurt you? If they do—"

"They don't," she reassured him, coming nearer to him so that she could hold him closer and bury her face in that wonderful, magical hair. She wondered now how she could ever have thought it too long, and untidy, or why she had thought him effeminate. She breathed in the special scent of him; a hint of sunlight and spicy grasses. And she felt the tension of anxiety inside him turn to tension of another kind. His hands, strong, yet gentle, slid around her waist and drew her closer still.


But a few hours later there came a summons she could not ignore; a mage-message from the Council. And the moment the two of them passed her threshold it would have been impossible for anyone to have told that they were lovers from their demeanor. Martis was no mean actress—she was diplomat and teacher as well as sorceress, and both those professions often required the ability to play a part. And Lyran, with his incredible *mental* discipline, and a degree of training in control that matched and was in fact incorporated in his physical training, could have passed for an ice-sculpture. Only Martis could know for certain that his chill went no deeper than the surface.

He was her bodyguard; he was almost literally her possession until and unless he chose not to serve her. And as such he went with her everywhere—even into the hallows of the Council chamber. Just as the bodyguards of the five Councilors did.

The carved double doors of a wood so ancient as to have turned black swung open without a hand touching them, and she and Lyran entered the windowless Council Chamber. It was lit entirely by mage-lights as ancient as the doors, all still burning with bright yellow incandescence high up on the walls of white marble. The room was perfectly circular and rimmed with a circle of malachite; in the center was a second circle inlaid in porphyry in the white marble of the floor. Behind that circle was the half-circle of the Council table, of black-lacquered wood, and the five matching thronelike chairs behind it. All five of those chairs were occupied by mages in the purple robes of the Mage Guild Council.

Only one of the Councilors, the cadaverous Masterclass Mage Ronethar Gethry, gave Lyran so much as a glance; and from the way Ronethar's eyes flickered from Lyran to Martis and back, the sorceress rather guessed that it was because of the gossip that he noticed her guard at all.

The rest ignored the swordsman, as they ignored their own hirelings, each standing impassively behind his master's chair, garbed from head to toe, as was Lyran, in Mage Guild hireling red: red leathers, red linen—even one, like Lyran, in red silk.

The Councilors were worried; even Martis could read that much behind their impassive masks. They wasted no time on petty nonsense about her private life. What brought them all to the Council Chamber was serious business, not accusations about with whom she was dallying.

Not that they'd dare take *her* to task over it. She was the equal of any of the mages in those five seats; she could sit there behind the Council table any time she chose. She simply had never chosen to do so. They knew it, and she knew it, and they knew she knew. She was not accountable to them, or anything but her conscience, for her behavior. Only for her actions as the representative of the Guild.

The fact was that she didn't *want* a Council seat; as a Masterclass mage she had little enough freedom as it was. Sitting on the Council would restrict it still further. The Masterclass mage served only the Guild, the powers of the Masterclass being deemed too dangerous to be put at hire.

"Martis." Rotund old Dabrel was serving as Chief this month; he was something less of an old stick than the others.

"Councilor," she responded. "How may I serve my Guild?"

"By solving a mystery," he replied. "The people of Lyosten have been acting in a most peculiar and disturbing fashion—"

"He means they've been finding excuses to put off a Guild inspection," sour-faced and acid-voiced Liavel interrupted. "First there was a fever—so they say—then a drought, then the road was blocked by a flood. It doesn't ring true; nobody else around Lyosten is having any similar troubles. We believe they're hiding something."

"Lyosten is a Free City, isn't it?" Martis asked. "Who's in charge?"

"The Citymaster—a man called Bolger Freedman."

"Not a Guildsman. A pity. That means we can't put pressure on him through his own Guild," Martis mused. "You're right, obviously; they must be covering up *something,* so what's the guess?"

"We think," Dabrel said, leaning over the table and steepling his fingertips together, "That their local mage has gone renegade in collusion with the townsfolk; that he's considering violating the Compacts against using magecraft in offensive manner against nonmages. They've been feuding off and on with Portravus for decades; we think they may be deciding to end the feud."

"And Portravus has no mage—" said mousy Herjes, looking as much frightened as worried. "Just a couple of hedge-wizards and some assorted Low Magick practitioners. And not a lot of money to spare to hire one."

Martis snorted. *"Just* what I wanted to hear. Why me?"

"You're known." replied Dabrel. "They don't dare cause you any overt magical harm. You're one of the best at offensive and defensive magics. Furthermore, you can activate the Gates to get in fairly close to the town *before* they can think up another excuse. We'll inform them that you're coming about a day before you're due to arrive."

"And there's another factor," creaked ancient Cetallas. "Your hireling. The boy is good; damned good. Best I've seen in—can't remember when. No Free City scum is going to get past *him* to take you out. He's a healer of sorts, so Ben tells us. That's no bad thing to have about, a healer you can trust just in case some physical accident happens. And you must admit he's got a pretty powerful incentive to keep you alive." The old man wheezed a little, and quirked an amused eyebrow at the two of them. Martis couldn't help but notice the twinkle of laughter in his eyes. She bit her lip to keep from smiling.

So the old bird still had some juice in him—and wasn't going to grudge her *her* own pleasures!

"You have a point," she admitted. "And yes, Lyran does have something more at stake with me than just his contract." She was rather surprised to see the rest of the Councilors nod soberly.

*Well. Well, well! They may not* like *it—they may think I'm some kind of fool, or worse—but they've got to admit that what Lyran and I have can be pretty useful to the Guild.* "How soon do you want us to leave?"

"Are you completely recovered from—"

"Dealing with Kelven? Physically, yes. Mentally, emotionally— to be honest, only time will tell. Betrayal; gods, that's not an easy thing to deal with."

"Admitted—and we're setting you up to deal with another traitor." Dabrel had the grace to look guilty.

"At least this one isn't one of my former favorite pupils," she replied, grimacing crookedly. "I don't even think I know him."

"You don't," Herjes said. "I trained him. He also is not anywhere near Kelven's potential, and he *isn't* dabbling in blood-magic. Speaking of which—have you recovered arcanely as well as physically?"

"I'm at full power. I can go any time."

"In the morning, then?"

"In the morning." She inclined her head slightly; felt the faintest whisper of magic brush her by.

*Show-offs,* she thought, as she heard the doors behind her open. *Two can play that game.*

"We will be on our way at dawn, Councilors," she said, carefully setting up the *rolibera* spell in her mind, and wrapping it carefully about both herself *and* Lyran. There weren't too many mages even at Masterclass level that could translate two people at once. She braced herself, formed the energy into a tightly coiled spring with her mind, then spoke one word as she inclined her head again—There was a flash of light behind her eyes, and a fluttery feeling in her stomach as if she had suddenly dropped the height of a man.

And she and Lyran stood side-by-side within the circle carved into the floor of her private workroom.

She turned to see the mask of indifference drop from him, and his thin, narrow face come alive with mingled humor and chiding.

"Must you always be challenging them, beloved?"

She set her mouth stubbornly. He shook his head. "Alas," he chuckled, "I fear if you stopped, I would no longer know you. Challenge and avoidance—" He held out his arms, and she flowed into them. "Truly, beloved," he murmured into her ear, as she pressed her cheek into the silk of his tunic shoulder, "we Balance each other."

They would not be riding Jesalis and Tosspot, those beasts of foul temper and fiercely protective instincts. This was a mission which would depend as much on the impression they would give as their capabilities, and Tosspot and Jesalis would be unlikely to impress anyone. Instead, when they descended the tower stairs in the pale, pearly light of dawn, Martis found the grooms in the stone-paved courtyard holding the reins of two showy palfreys, a gray and a bay. Tethered behind the bay on a lead rope was a glossy mule loaded with packs. The harness of the gray was dyed a rich purple, and that of the bay was scarlet. Lyran approached the horses with care, for the eyes of the bay rolled with alarm at the sight of the stranger. He ran his hands over their legs once he could get near them, and walked slowly back to Martis' side with his arms folded, shaking his head a little.

"Hmm?" she asked.

"Worthless," he replied. "I hope we will not be needing to entrust our lives to them. No strength, no stamina—and worst of all, no sense."

"They're just for show," Martis frowned, feeling a little dubious herself. "We aren't supposed to have to do any hard riding, or long, except for the gallop to take us through the Gates. A day's ride to the first Gate, half a day to the second. In and out of both Gates, then a ride of less than half a day to the city."

"If all goes well. And what if all does not go well?"

"I—" Martis fell silent. "Well, that's why you're along."

Lyran looked back over his shoulder at the horses, and grimaced. "This one will do the best one can, Mage-lady," he said formally. "Will the Mage-lady mount?"

Martis had been doing more with Lyran's aid than her colleagues suspected. A few moons ago she would not have been able to mount unaided—now she swung into her saddle with at least some of the grace of her lover. The exercises he had been insisting she practice had improved her strength, her wind, her flexibility—she was nearly as physically fit as she'd been twenty-odd years ago, when she'd first come to the Academe.

Lyran mounted at nearly the same moment, and his bay tried to shy sideways. It jerked the reins out of the groom's hands, and danced backwards, then reared. Lyran's mouth compressed, but that was the only sign that he was disturbed that Martis could see. The scarlet silk of his breeches rippled as he clamped his legs around the bay gelding's barrel, and the reins seemed to tighten of themselves as he forced the gelding back down to the ground, and fought him to a standstill. As the horse stood, sweating, sides heaving, Lyran looked up at her.

"This one will do what this one can, Mage-lady," he repeated soberly.

The gray palfrey Martis rode was of a more placid disposition, for which she was profoundly grateful. She signed to the groom to release his hold and turned its head to face the open wooden gate set into the stone walls of the court. At Lyran's nod she nudged it with her heels and sent it ambling out beneath the portcullis.

They rode in single file through the city, Lyran trailing the mule at a respectful distance from "his employer." Four times the bay started and shied at inconsequential commonplaces; each time Lyran had to fight the beast back onto all four hooves and into sweating good behavior. The last time seemed to convince it that there was no unseating its rider, for it did not make another attempt. Once outside the city walls, they reversed their positions, with Lyran and the mule going first. Ordinarily Martis would now be spending her time in half-trance, gathering power from the living things around her. But her mount was *not* her faithful Tosspot, who could be relied upon to keep a falling-down drunk in the saddle—and Lyran's beast was all too likely to shy or dance again, and perhaps send her gelding off as well. So instead of gathering always-useful energy, she fumed and fretted, and was too annoyed even to watch the passing landscape.

****

They reached the Gate at sunset. The ring of standing stones in the center of the meadow stood out black against the flaming glow of the declining sun. The wide, weed-grown fields around them were otherwise empty; not even sheep cared to graze this near a Gate. The evening wind carried a foretaste of autumnal chill as it sighed through the grasses around them. Martis squinted against the bloody light and considered their options.

Lyran had finally decided to exhaust his misbehaving mount by trotting it in circles around her as they traveled down the road until it was too tired to fuss. Now it was docile, but plainly only because it was weary. It still rolled its eyes whenever a leaf stirred. The sorceress urged her gelding up beside his.

"Can you get one last run out of him?" Martis asked anxiously.

"Probably," Lyran replied. "Why?"

"I'd like to take this Gate now, if we can, while that misbegotten horse of yours is too tired to bolt."

He looked at her in that silent, blank-faced way he had when he was thinking. "What if he did bolt?"

"The gods only know where you'd end up," she told him frankly. "If he got out of my influence—I can't predict what point beyond the Gate you'd come out at, or even what direction it would be in."

"And if I can't get him to a gallop?"

"Almost the same—if you didn't keep within my aura you'd come out somewhere between here and where I'd land."

He reached out and touched her face with the tips of his fingers. "You seem tired, beloved."

"I *am* tired," she admitted, confessing to him what she would admit to no other living person. "But I'm not too tired to Gate-spell, and I think it's safer to do it now than it will be later."

"Then I will force this bundle of contrariness disguised as a horse into keeping up with you."

"Hold butter-brains here, would you?" she passed him the reins of her mount, not trusting it to stand firm on its own. She drew entirely into herself, centering all her concentration on the hoarded power within herself, drawing it gradually to the surface with unspoken words and careful mental probes. Her eyes were closed, but she could feel the energy stirring, flowing, coming up from—elsewhere—and beginning to trickle along the nerves of her spine. At first it was barely a tingle, but the power built up quickly until she was vibrating to its silent song.

At that point she opened the channels to her hands, raising her arms out in front of her and holding her hands out with the open palms facing the ring of standing stones.

The power surged along her arms and leapt for the ring of the Gate with an eagerness that was almost an emotion. She sang the words of the Gate-spell now, sang it in a barely audible whisper. Her eyes were half-open, but she really wasn't paying a great deal of attention to anything but the flow of power from her to the Gate.

The ring of stones began to glow, glowing as if they were stealing the last of the sun's fire and allowing it to run upon their surfaces. The color of the fire began to lighten, turning from deep red to scarlet to a fiery orange. Then the auras surrounding each Gate-stone extended; reaching for, then touching, the auras beside it, until the circle became one pulsating ring of golden-orange light.

Martis felt the proper moment approaching, and signed to Lyran to hand her back her reins. She waited, weighing, judging—then suddenly spurred her mount into one of the gaps between the stones, with Lyran's gelding practically on top of her horse's tail.

They emerged into a forest clearing beneath a moon already high, exactly five leagues from the next Gate.

"Gods, I wish I had Tosspot under me," Martis muttered, facing the second Gate under a bright noontide sun. This one stood in the heart of the forest, and the stones were dwarfed by the stand of enormous pine trees that towered all about them. The sorceress was feeling depleted, and she had not been able to recuperate the energy she'd spent on the last spell.

"We could wait," Lyran suggested. "We could rest here, and continue on in the morning."

Martis shook her head with regret. "I only wish we could. But it isn't healthy to camp near a Gate—look at the way the magic's twisted those bushes over there, the ones growing up against the stones! And besides, we need to come as close to surprising our hosts as we can."

She coughed; there was a tickle in the back of her throat that threatened to turn into a cold. Lyran noted that cough, too, and tightened his mouth in unvoiced disapproval, but made no further objections. Martis handed him her reins, and began the second spell— But they emerged, not into a sunlit clearing as she'd expected, but into the teeth of the worst storm she'd ever seen.

Rain, cold as the rains of winter, lashed at them, soaking them to the skin in moments. It would have been too dark to see, except that lightning struck so often that the road was clearly lit most of the time. Lyran spurred his horse up beside the sorceress as she gasped for breath beneath the onslaught of the icy water. He'd pulled his cloak loose from the lashings that held it to his saddle and was throwing it over her shoulders before she even had recovered the wit to *think* about the fact that she needed it. The cloak was sodden in seconds, but it was wool—warm enough, even though wet. She stopped shivering a little, but the shock of chill coming on top of the strain of the spells had unbalanced her a little. She fumbled after her reins, but her mind wouldn't quite work; she couldn't seem to think where they should be going.

Lyran put his hand under her chin, and turned her face toward his. She blinked at him, at his searching expression as revealed by the flickers of lightning. Some rational little bit of her that hadn't been stunned hoped idly that he remembered what she'd told him once, about how mages sometimes went into spell-shock when they were low on energy and hit with unexpected physical conditions. This happened most frequently when they were ungrounded and uncentered—and the Gate-spell demanded that she be both when taking them in transit.

Evidently he did, for he took the reins out of her unresisting fingers and nudged his gelding into a nervy, shuddering walk, leaving her to cling to the saddle as best she could while he led her mount.

It was impossible to hear or be heard over the nearly continuous roar of the thunder, so she didn't even try to speak to him. She just closed her eyes and concentrated on getting herself centered and grounded again. So it was that she never noticed when the road approached the brink of a river—once peaceful, now swollen and angry with flood water. She knew that there *was* such a road, and such a river—she knew that they were to cross it before reaching Lyosten. She knew that there was a narrow, aged bridge that was still nonetheless sound, but she was too deeply sunk within herself to see it, as Lyran urged the horses onto its span.

But she *felt* the lightning-strike, so close it scorched the wood of the bridge not ten paces in front of them.

And as her eyes snapped open, she saw Lyran's horse rearing above her in complete panic—a darkly writhing shape that reared and thrashed—and toppled over onto *hers*. She had no time to react; she felt herself go numb and open-mouthed in fear, and then pain as all of them, horses, humans, and mule, crashed through the railing of the bridge to plunge into the churning water below. She flailed wildly with unfocused energy trying to form up something to catch them—and lost spell and all in the shock of hitting the raging water.

Martis pulled herself up onto the muddy bank, scraping herself across the rocks and tree-roots protruding from it, and dragging Lyran with her by the shoulder-fabric of his tunic. She collapsed, half-in, half-out of the water, too spent to go any farther. The swordsman pulled himself, coughing, up onto the bank beside her. A child of open plains, *he* couldn't swim.

Fortunately for both of them, Martis could. And equally fortunately, he'd had the wit to go limp when he felt her grabbing his tunic. The storm—now that the damage was done—was slackening.

"Are you all right?" she panted, turning her head and raising herself on her arms enough to be able to see him, while her teeth chattered like temple rattles.

Lyran had dragged himself up into a sitting position, and was clutching a sapling as if it were a lover. His eyes were bruised and swollen, one of them almost shut, and there was a nasty welt along the side of his face. He coughed, swallowed, nodded. "I think—yes."

"Good." She fell back onto the bank, cheek pressed into the mud, trying to keep from coughing herself. If she did—it felt as if she might well cough her aching lungs out. She fought the cough with closed eyes, the rain plastering hair and clothing flat to her skin.

*This is witched weather; the power is everywhere, wild, undisciplined. How could that Lyosten mage have let himself get so out of control?* But that was just a passing thought, unimportant. The important thing was the cold, the aching weariness. She was so cold now that she had gone beyond feeling it—

"Martis—"

She was drifting, drifting away, being carried off to somewhere where there was sun and warmth. In fact, she was actually beginning to feel warm, not cold. She felt Lyran shake her shoulder, and didn't care. All she wanted to do was sleep. She'd never realized how soft mud could be.

*"Martis!"* It was the sharp-edged fear in his voice as much as the stinging slap he gave her that woke her. She got her eyes open with difficulty.

"What?" she asked stupidly, unable to think.

"Beloved, *thena,* you are afire with fever," he said, pulling her into his arms and chafing her limbs to get the blood flowing. "I cannot heal disease, only wounds. Fight this—you must fight this, or you will surely die!"

"Ah—" she groaned, and tried to pummel the fog that clouded her mind away. But it was a battle doomed to be lost; she felt the fog take her, and drifted away again.

Lyran half-carried, half-dragged the mage up the last few feet of the road to the gates of Lyosten. The horses were gone, and the mule, and with them everything except what they had carried on their persons that had not been ripped away by the flood waters. His two swords were gone; he had only his knife, his clothing, and the money belt beneath his tunic. Martis had only her robes; no implements of magic or healing, no cloak to keep her warm—

At least she had not succumbed to shock or the cold-death; she was intermittently conscious, if not coherent. But she was ill—very ill, and like to become worse.

The last few furlongs of road had been a waking nightmare;

the rain stopped as if it had been shut off, but the breeze that had sprung up had chilled them even as it had dried their clothing. Once past the thin screen of trees lining the river, there had been nothing to buffer it. It hadn't helped that Lyran could see the bulk of Lyosten looming in the distance, dark gray against a lighter gray sky. He'd forced himself and Martis into motion, but more often than not he was supporting her; sheer exhaustion made them stagger along the muddy road like a pair of drunks, getting mired to the knees in the process. It was nearly sunset when they reached the gates of the city.

He left Martis leaning against the wood of the wall and went to pound on the closed gates themselves, while she slid slowly down to crouch in a miserable huddle, fruitlessly seeking shelter from the wind.

A man-sized door opened in the greater gate, and a surly, bearded fighter blocked it.

"What's the ruckus?" he growled.

Lyran drew himself up and tried not to shiver. "This one is guard to Martis, Master Sorceress and envoy of the Mage Guild," he replied, his voice hoarse, his throat rasping. "There has been an accident—"

"Sure, tell me another one," the guard jeered, looking from Lyran to the bedraggled huddle that was Martis, and back again. He started to close the portal. "You think I've never heard *that* one before? Go around to th' Beggar's Gate."

"Wait!" Lyran blocked the door with his foot, but before he could get another word out, the guard unexpectedly lashed out with the butt of his pike, catching him with a painful blow to the stomach. It knocked the wind out of him and caused him to land on his rump in the mud of the road. The door in the gate slammed shut.

Lyran lowered Martis down onto the pallet, and knelt beside her. He covered her with every scrap of ragged blanket or quilt that he could find. She was half out of her mind with fever now, and coughing almost constantly. The cheap lamp of rock-oil gave off almost as much smoke as light, which probably didn't help the coughing any.

"Martis?" he whispered, hoping against hope for a sane response.

This time he finally got one. Her eyes opened, and there was sense in them. "Lyr—" she went into a coughing fit. He helped her to sit up, and held a mug of water to her mouth. She drank, her hand pressed against his, and the hand was so hot it frightened him. *"Thena,"* he said urgently. "You are ill, very ill. I cannot heal sickness, only hurts. Tell me what I must do."

"Take me—to the Citymaster—" He shook his head. "I tried; they will not let me near. I cannot prove that I am what I say—"

"Gods. And I can't—magic to prove it."

"You haven't even been answering me." He put the cup on the floor and wedged himself in behind her, supporting her. She closed her eyes as if even the dim light of the lamp hurt them. Her skin was hot and dry, and tight-feeling, as he stroked her forehead. "The storm—witched."

"You said as much in raving, so I guessed it better to avoid looking for the city wizard. Tell me what I must do!"

"Is there—money—?"

"A little. A very little."

"Get—trevaine-root. Make tea."

He started. "And poison you? Gods and demons—!"

"Not poison." She coughed again. "It'll put me—where I can trance. Heal myself. Only way."

"But—"

"Only way I know," she repeated, and closed her eyes. Within moments the slackness of her muscles told him she'd drifted off into delirium again.

He lowered her back down to the pallet, and levered himself to his feet. The bed and the lamp were all the furnishings this hole of a room had; Martis had bigger closets back at High Ridings. And he'd been lucky to find the room in the first place. The old woman who rented it to him had been the first person he'd accosted that had "felt" honest.

He blew out the lamp and made his way down to the street. Getting directions from his hostess, he headed for the marketplace. The ragged and threadbare folk who jostled him roused his anxiety to a fever-pitch. He sensed that many of them would willingly knife him from behind for little or no reason. He withdrew into himself, shivering mentally, and put on an icy shell of outward calm.

The streets were crowded; Lyran moved carefully within the flow of traffic, being cautious to draw no attention to himself. He was wearing a threadbare tunic and breeches nearly identical to a dozen others around him; his own mage-hireling silk was currently adorning Martis' limbs beneath her mage-robes. The silk was one more layer of covering against the chill—and he didn't like the notion of appearing in even stained mage-hireling red in public; not around here. He closed his mind to the babble and his nose to the stench of unwashed bodies, uncleaned privies, and garbage that thickened the air about him. But these people worried him; he had only his knife for defense. What if some of this street-scum should learn about Martis, and decide she was worth killing and robbing? If he had his swords, or even just a single sword of the right reach and weight, he could hold off an army—but he didn't, nor could he afford one. The only blades he'd seen yet within his scanty resources were not much better than cheap metal clubs.

Finally he reached the marketplace. Trevaine-root was easy enough to find, being a common rat-poison. He chose a stall whose owner "felt" reasonably honest and whose wares looked properly preserved, and began haggling.

A few moments later he slid his hand inside his tunic to extract the single coin he required from the heart-breakingly light money-belt, separating it from the others by feel. The herbalist handed over the scrap of root bound up in a bit of old paper without a second glance; Lyran hadn't bought enough to seem suspicious. But then, it didn't take much to make a single cup of strong tea.

Lyran turned, and narrowly avoided colliding with a scarred man, a man who walked with the air of a tiger, and whose eyes were more than a little mad. Lyran ducked his head, and willed himself invisible with all his strength. If only he had a *sword*! The need was beginning to be more than an itch—it was becoming an ache.

Lyran was heading out of the market and back to the boarding-house when he felt an unmistakable mental "pull," not unlike the calling he had felt when he first was moved to take up the Way of the sword, the pull he had felt when he had chosen his Teacher. It did not "feel" wrong, or unbalanced. Rather, it was as if Something was sensing the need in him for a means to protect Martis, and was answering that need.

Hardly thinking, he followed that pull, trusting to it as he had trusted to the pull that led him to the doorstep of the woman destined to be his Teacher, and as he had followed the pull that had led him ultimately to the Mage Guild at High Ridings and to Martis. This time it led him down the twisting, crooked path of a strangely silent street, a street hemmed by tall buildings so that it scarcely saw the sun; a narrow street that was wide enough only for two people to pass abreast. And at the end of it—for it proved to be a dead-end street, which accounted in part for the silence—was an odd little junk shop.

There were the expected bins of rags, cracked pottery pieces, the scavenged flotsam of a thousand lives. Nothing ever went to waste in this quarter. Rags could be patched together into clothing or quilts like those now covering Martis; bits of crockery were destined to be fitted and cemented into a crazy-paving that would pass as a tiled floor. Old papers went to wrap parcels, or to eke out a thinning shoe-sole. No, nothing was ever thrown away here; but there was more to this shop than junk, Lyran could sense it. People could find what they *needed* here.

"You require something, lad," said a soft voice at his elbow.

Lyran jumped—he hadn't sensed *any* presence at his side—yet there was a strange little man, scarcely half Lyran's height; a dwarf, with short legs, and blunt, clever hands, and bright, birdlike eyes. And a kindness like that of the widow who had rented them her extra room, then brought every bit of covering she had to spare to keep Martis warm. "A sword," Lyran said hesitantly. "This one needs a sword."

"I should think you do," replied the little man, after a long moment of sizing Lyran up. "A swordsman generally does need a sword. And it can't be an ill-balanced bludgeon, either—that would be worse than nothing, eh, lad?"

Lyran nodded, slowly. "But this one—has but little—" The man barked rather than laughed, but his good humor sounded far more genuine than anything coming from the main street and marketplace. "Lad, if you had money, you wouldn't be *here*, now, would you? Let me see what I can do for you."

He waddled into the shop door, past the bins of rags and whatnot; Lyran's eyes followed him into the darkness of the doorway, but couldn't penetrate the gloom. In a moment, the shopkeeper was back, a long, slim shape wrapped in oily rags in both his hands. He handed the burden to Lyran with a kind of courtly flourish.

"Here you be, lad," he said. "I think that may have been what was calling you."

The rags fell away, and the little man caught them before they hit the paving stones—

At first Lyran was conscious only of disappointment. The hilt of this weapon had once been ornamented, wrapped in gold wire, perhaps—but there were empty sockets where the gems had been, and all traces of gold had been stripped away.

"Left in pawn to me, but the owner never came back, poor man," the shopkeeper said, shaking his head. "A good man fallen on hard times—unsheath it, lad."

The blade was awkward in his hand for a moment, the hilt hard to hold with the rough metal bare in his palm—but as he pulled it from its sheath, it seemed to come almost alive; he suddenly found the balancing of it, and as the point cleared the sheath it had turned from a piece of dead metal to an extension of his arm.

He had feared that it was another of the useless dress-swords, the ones he had seen too many times, worthless mild steel done up in long-gone jewels and plating. This sword—this blade had belonged to a fighter, had been made for a swordsman. The balance, the temper were almost too good to be true. It more than equaled his lost twin blades, it surpassed them. With this one blade in hand he could easily have bested a twin-Lyran armed with his old sword-pair; that was the extent of the "edge" this blade could give him.

"How—how much?" he asked, mouth dry.

"First you must answer me true," the little man said softly. "You be the lad with the sick lady, no? The one that claimed the lady to be from the Mage Guild?"

Lyran whirled, stance proclaiming that he was on his guard. The dwarf simply held out empty hands. "No harm to you, lad. No harm meant. Tell me true, and the blade's yours for three copper bits. Tell me not, or tell me lie—I won't sell it. Flat."

"What if this one is not that person?" Lyran hedged.

"So long as the answer be true, the bargain be true."

Lyran swallowed hard, and followed the promptings of his inner guides. "This one—is," he admitted with reluctance. "This one and the lady are what this one claims—but none will heed."

The dwarf held out his hand, "Three copper bits," he said mildly. "And some advice for free."

Lyran fumbled out the coins, hardly able to believe his luck. The worst pieces of pot-metal pounded into the shape of a sword were selling for a silver—yet this strange little man had sold him a blade worth a hundred times that for the price of a round of cheese! "This one never rejects advice."

"But you may or may not heed it, eh?" The man smiled, showing a fine set of startlingly white teeth. "Right enough; you get your lady to tell you the story of the dragon's teeth. Then tell her that Bolger Freedman has sown them, but can't harvest them."

Lyran nodded, though without understanding. "There's some of us that never agreed with him. There's some of us would pay dearly to get shut of what we've managed to get into. Tell your lady that— and watch your backs. I'm not the only one who's guessed."

Lyran learned the truth of the little man's words long before he reached the widow's boarding-house.

The gang of street-toughs lying in ambush for him were probably considered canny, crafty and subtle by the standards of the area. But Lyran knew that they were there as he entered the side-street; and he knew *where* they were moments before they attacked him.

The new sword was in his hands and moving as the first of them struck him from behind. It sliced across the thug's midsection as easily as if Lyran had been cutting bread, not flesh, and with just about as much resistance. While the bully was still falling, Lyran took out the one dropping on him from the wall beside him with a graceful continuation of that cut, and kicked a third rushing him from out of an alley, delivering a blow to his knee that shattered the kneecap, and then forced the knee to bend in the direction opposite to that which nature had intended for a human.

He couldn't get the blade around in time to deal with the fourth, so he ducked under the blow and brought the pommel up into the man's nose, shattering the bone and driving the splinters into the brain.

And while the fifth man stared in open-mouthed stupefication, Lyran separated his body from his head.

Before anyone could poke a curious nose into the street to see what all the noise was about, Lyran vaulted to the top of the wall to his left, and from there to the roof of the building it surrounded. He scampered quickly over the roof and down again on the other side, taking the time to clean and sheath the sword and put it away before dropping down into the next street.

After all, he hadn't spent his childhood as a thief without learning something about finding unconventional escape routes.

About the time he had taken a half a dozen paces, alarm was raised in the next street. Rather than running away, Lyran joined the crowd that gathered about the five bodies, craning his neck like any of the people around him, wandering off when he "couldn't get a look."

A childhood of thieving had taught him the truth of what his People often said: "If you would be taken for a crow, join the flock and caw."


Lyran took the cracked mug of hot water from his hostess, then shooed her gently out. He didn't want her to see—and perhaps recognize—what he was going to drop into it. She probably wouldn't understand. For that matter, he didn't understand; he just trusted Martis.

His lover tossed her head on the bundle of rags that passed for a pillow and muttered, her face sweat-streaked, her hair lank and sodden. He soothed her as best he could, feeling oddly helpless.

When the water was lukewarm and nearly black, he went into a half-trance and soul-called her until she woke. Again—to his relief—when he finally brought her to consciousness, there was foggy sense in her gray eyes.

"I have the tea, *thena,*" he said, helping her into a sitting position. She nodded, stifling a coughing fit, and made a weak motion with her hand. Interpreting it correctly, he held the mug to her lips. She clutched at it with both hands, but her hands shook so that he did not release the mug, only let her guide it.

He lowered her again to the pallet when she had finished the foul stuff, sitting beside her and holding her hands in his afterwards.

"How long will this take?"

She shook her head. "A bit of time before the drug takes; after that, I don't know." She coughed, doubling over; he supported her.

"Have you ever known any story about 'dragon's teeth,' my lady?" he asked, reluctantly. "I—was advised to tell you that Bolger has sown the dragon's teeth, but cannot harvest them."

She shook her head slightly, a puzzled frown creasing her forehead—then her eyes widened. "Harvest! Gods! I—"

The drug chose that moment to take her; between one word and the next her eyes glazed, then closed. Lyran swore, in three languages, fluently and creatively. It was some time before he ran out of invective.

"*I* know 'bout dragon's teeth," said a high, young voice from the half-open door behind him. Lyran jumped in startlement for the second time that day. Truly, anxiety for Martis was dulling his edge!

He turned slowly, to see the widow's youngest son peeking around the doorframe.

"And would you tell this one of dragon's teeth?" he asked the dirty-faced urchin as politely as he could manage.

Encouraged, the youngster pushed the door open a little more. "You ain't never seen a dragon?" he asked.

Lyran shook his head, and crooked his finger. The boy sidled into the room, clasping his hands behind his back. To the widow's credit, only the child's face was dirty—the cut-down tunic he wore was threadbare, but reasonably clean. "There are no dragons in this one's homeland."

"Be there mages?" the boy asked, and at Lyran's negative headshake, the child nodded. "That be why. Dragons ain't natural beasts, they be mage-made. Don't breed, neither. You want 'nother dragon, you take tooth from a live dragon an' plant it. Only thing is, baby dragons come up hungry an' mean. Takes a tamed dragon to harvest 'em, else they go out killin' an feedin' an' get the taste fer fear. Then their brains go bad, an' they gotta be killed thesselves."

"This one thanks you," Lyran replied formally. The child grinned, and vanished.

Well, now he knew about dragon's teeth. The only problem was that the information made no sense—at least not to him! It had evidently meant something to Martis, though. She must have some bit of information that *he* didn't have.

He stroked the mage's damp forehead and sighed. At least the stuff hadn't killed her outright—he'd been half-afraid that it would. And she *did* seem to be going into a proper trance; her breathing had become more regular, her pulse had slowed—Suddenly it was far too quiet in the street outside. Lyran was on his feet with his new sword in his hands at nearly the same moment that he noted the absence of sound. He slipped out the door, closing it carefully behind him once he knew that the musty hallway was "safe." The stairs that led downwards were at the end of that hall—but he had no intention of taking them.

Instead he glided soundlessly to the window at the other end of the hall; the one that overlooked the scrap of back yard. The shutters were open, and a careful glance around showed that the yard itself was empty. He sheathed the sword and adjusted the makeshift baldric so that it hung at his back, then climbed out onto the ledge, balancing there while he assessed his best path.

There was a cornice with a crossbeam just within reach; he got a good grip on it, and pulled himself up, chinning himself on the wood of the beam—his arms screamed at him, but he dared not make a sound. Bracing himself, he let go with his right hand and swung himself up until he caught the edge of the roof. Holding onto it with a death-grip he let go of the cornice entirely, got his other hand on the roof-edge, and half-pulled, half-scrambled up onto the roof itself. He lay there for one long moment, biting his lip to keep from moaning, and willing his arms back into their sockets.

When he thought he could move again, he slid over the roof across the splintery, sunwarmed shingles to the street-side, and peered over the edge.

Below him, as he had suspected, were a half-dozen armed men, all facing the door. Except for them, the street below was deserted.

There was one waiting at the blind side of the door. Lyran pulled his knife from the sheath in his boot and dropped on him.

The *crack* as the man's skull hit the pavement—he hadn't been wearing a helm—told Lyran that he wouldn't have to worry about slitting the fighter's throat.

Lyran tumbled and rolled as he landed, throwing the knife as he came up at the man he judged to be the leader. His aim was off—instead of hitting the throat it glanced off the fighter's chest-armor. But the move distracted all of them enough to give Lyran the chance to get his sword out and into his hands.

There was something wrong with these men; he knew that as soon as he faced them. They moved oddly; their eyes were not quite focused. And even in the heat of the day, when they must have been standing out in the sun for a good long time setting up their ambush, with one exception they weren't sweating.

Then Lyran noticed that, except for the man he'd thrown the dagger at—the man who *was* sweating—they weren't casting any shadows. Which meant that they were illusions. They could only harm him if he believed in them.

So he ignored them, and concentrated his attention on the leader. He went into a purely defensive stance and waited for the man to act.

The fighter, a rugged, stocky man with a wary look to his eyes, sized him up carefully—and looked as if he wasn't happy with what he saw. Neither of them moved for a long, silent moment. Finally Lyran cleared his throat, and spoke.

"This one has no quarrel with any here, nor does this one's lady. You have done your best; this one has sprung the trap. There is no dishonor in retreat. Hireling to hireling, there is no contract violation."

The man straightened, looked relieved. "You—"

"*No!*"

The voice was high, cracking a little, and came from Lyran's left, a little distance up the street. It was a young voice; a breath later the owner emerged from the shadow of a doorway, and the speaker matched the voice. It was a white-blond boy, barely adolescent, dressed in gaudy silks; from behind him stepped two more children, then another pair. All of them were under the age of fifteen, all were dressed in rainbow hues—and all of them had wild, wide eyes that looked more than a little mad.

The man facing Lyran swallowed hard; *now* he was sweating even harder. Lyran looked at him curiously. It almost seemed as if he were *afraid* of these children! Lyran decided to act.

He stepped out into the street and placed himself between the man and the group of youngsters. "There has been no contract violation," he said levelly, meeting their crazed eyes, blue and green and brown, with his own. "The man has fulfilled what was asked." Behind him, he heard the fighter take to his heels once the attention of the children had switched from himself to Lyran. Lyran sighed with relief; that was one death, at least, that he would not have to Balance. "This one has no quarrel with you," he continued. "Why seek you this one?"

The children stared at him, a kind of insane affrontery in their faces, as if they could not believe that he would defy them. Lyran stood easily, blade held loosely in both hands, waiting for their response.

The blond, nearest and tallest, raised his hands; a dagger of light darted from his outstretched palms and headed straight for Lyran's throat—

But this was something a Mage Guild fighter was trained to defend against; fire daggers could not survive the touch of cold steel—

Lyran's blade licked out, and intercepted the dagger before it reached its target. It vanished when the steel touched it.

The child snarled, his mouth twisted into a grimace of rage ill-suited to the young face. Another dagger flew from his hands, and another; his companions sent darts of light of their own. Within moments Lyran was moving as he'd never moved in his life, dancing along the street, his swordblade blurring as he deflected dagger after dagger.

And still the fire-daggers kept coming, faster and faster—yet—

The air was growing chill, the sunlight thinning, and the faces of the children losing what little color they had possessed. Lyran realized then that they were draining themselves and everything about them for the energy to create the daggers. Even as the realization occurred to him, one of them made a choking sound and collapsed to the pavement, to lie there white and still.

If he could just hold out long enough, he *might* be able to outlast them! But the eldest of the group snarled when his confederate collapsed, and redoubled his efforts. Lyran found himself being pressed back, the light-daggers coming closer and closer before he was able to intercept them, his arms becoming leaden and weary—

He knew then that he would fail before they did.

And he saw, as he deflected a blade heading for his heart, another heading for his throat—and he knew he would not be able to intercept this one.

He had an instant to wonder if it would hurt very much. Then there was a blinding flash of light.

He wasn't dead—only half-blind for a long and heart-stopping moment. And when his eyes cleared—

Martis stood in the doorway of the house that had sheltered them, bracing herself against the frame, her left palm facing him, her right, the children. Both he and the youngsters were surrounded by a haze of light; his was silver, theirs was golden.

Martis gestured, and the haze around him vanished. He dropped to the pavement, so weak with weariness that his legs could no longer hold him. She staggered over to his side, weaving a little.

"Are you going to be all right?" she asked. He nodded, panting. Her hair was out of its braids, and stringy with sweat, her robes limp with it. She knelt beside him for a moment; placed both her hands on his shoulders and looked long and deeply into his eyes. "Gods, love—that was close. Too close. Did they hurt you?"

He shook his head, and she stared at him as he'd sometimes seen her examine something for magic taint. Evidently satisfied by what she saw, she kissed him briefly and levered herself back up onto her feet.

His eyes blurred for a moment; when they refocused, he saw that the haze around the remaining four children had vanished, and that they had collapsed in a heap, crying, eyes no longer crazed. Martis stood, shoulders sagging just a little, a few paces away from them.

She cleared her throat. The eldest looked up, face full of fear—

But she held out her arms to them. "It wasn't your fault," she said, in a voice so soft only the children and Lyran could have heard the words, and so full of compassion Lyran scarcely recognized it. "I know it wasn't your fault—and I'll help you, if you let me."

The children froze—then stumbled to their feet and surrounded her, clinging to her sweat-sodden robes, and crying as if their hearts had been broken, then miraculously remended.

"—so Bolger decided that he had had enough of the Mage Guild dictating what mages could and could not do. He waited until the Lyosten wizard had tagged the year's crop of mage-Talented younglings, then had the old man poisoned."

The speaker was the dwarf—who Lyran now knew was one of the local earth-witches, a cheerful man called Kasten Ythres. They were enjoying the hospitality of his home while the Mage Guild dealt with the former Citymaster and the clutch of half-trained children he'd suborned.

Martis was lying back against Lyran's chest, wearily at ease within the protective circle of his arms. They were both sitting on the floor, in one corner by the fireplace in the earth-witch's common room; there were no furnishings here, just piles of flat pillows. Martis had found it odd, but it had reminded Lyran strongly of home.

It was an oddly charming house, like its owner: brown and warm and sunny; utterly unpretentious. Kasten had insisted that they relax and put off their mage-hireling act. "It's my damned house," he'd said, "and you're my guests. To the nether hells with so-called propriety!"

"How on earth did he think he was going to get them trained?" Martis asked.

Kasten snorted. "He thought he could do it out of books—and if that didn't work, he'd get one of us half-mages to do it for him. Fool."

"He sowed the dragon's teeth," Martis replied acidly, "he shouldn't have been surprised to get dragons."

"Lady—dragon's teeth?" Lyran said plaintively, still at a loss to understand.

Martis chuckled, and settled a little more comfortably against Lyran's shoulder. "I was puzzled for a moment, too, until I remembered that the storm that met us had been witched—and that the power that created it was out of control. Magic power has some odd effects on the mind, love—if you *aren't* being watched over and guided properly, it can possess you. That's why the tales about demonic possession; you get a Talented youngling or one who blooms late, who comes to power with no training—they go mad. Worst of all, they *know* they're going mad. It's bad—and you only hope you can save them before any real damage is done."

"Aye," Kasten agreed. "I suspect that's where the dragon's teeth tale comes from too—which is why I told your man there to remind you of it. The analogy being that the younglings are the teeth, the trained mage is the dragon. What I'd like to know is what's to do about this? You can't take the younglings to the Academe—and I surely couldn't handle them!"

"No, they're too powerful," Martis agreed. "They need someone around to train them *and* keep them drained, until they've gotten control over their powers instead of having the powers control them. We have a possible solution, though. The Guild has given me a proposition, but I haven't had a chance to discuss it with Lyran yet." She craned her head around to look at him. "How would you like to be a father for the next half-year or so?"

"Me?" he replied, too startled to refer to himself in third person.

She nodded. "The Council wants them to have training, but feels that they would be best handled in a stable, homelike setting. But their blood-parents are frightened witless of them. But you—you stood up to them, you aren't afraid of them—and you're kind, love. You have a wonderful warm heart. And you know how I feel about youngsters. The Council feels that we would be the best parental surrogates they're ever likely to find. If you're willing, that is."

Lyran could only nod speechlessly.

"And they said," Martis continued with great satisfaction in her voice, "that if you'd agree, they'd give you anything you wanted."

"Anything?"

"They didn't put any kind of limitation on it. They're worried; these are *very* Talented children. All five of the Councilors are convinced you and I are their only possible salvation."

Lyran tightened his arms around her. "Would they—would they give this one rank to equal a Masterclass mage?"

"Undoubtedly. You certainly qualify for Swordmaster—only Ben could better you, and he's a full Weaponsmaster. If you weren't an outlander, you'd *have* that rank already."

"Would they then allow this one to wed as he pleased?"

He felt Martis tense, and knew without asking why she had done so. She feared losing him so much—and feared that this was just exactly what was about to happen. But they were interrupted before he could say anything. "That and more!" said a voice from the door. It was the Chief Councilor, Dabrel, purple robes straining over his stomach. "Swordmaster Lyran, do you wish to be the young fool that I think you do?"

"If by that, the Mastermage asks if this one would wed the Master Sorceress Martis, then the Mastermage is undoubtedly correct," Lyran replied demurely, a smile straining at the corners of his mouth as he heard Martis gasp.

"Take her with our blessings, Swordmaster," the portly mage chuckled. "Maybe you'll be able to mellow that tongue of hers with your sweet temper!"

"Don't I get any say in this?" Martis spluttered.

"Assuredly." Lyran let her go, and putting both hands on her shoulders, turned so that she could face him. "Martis, *thena,* lady of my heart and Balance of my soul, would you deign to share your life with me?"

She looked deeply and soberly into his eyes. "Do you mean that?" she whispered. "Do you really mean that?"

He nodded, slowly.

"Then—" she swallowed, and her eyes misted briefly. Then the sparkle of mischief that he loved came back to them, and she grinned. "Will you bloody well *stop* calling yourself 'this one' if I say yes?"

He sighed, and nodded again.

"Then that is an offer I will *definitely* not refuse!"

*This story was written for the Grail anthology that was to be presented at the World Fantasy convention in Atlanta. Richard Gilliam approached me and asked me if I would contribute. We discussed this idea, which I had almost immediately, and he loved it, so I wrote it. The book was later broken into two volumes and published as* Grails of Light *and* Grails of Darkness.

# The Cup and the Caldron

## Mercedes Lackey

Rain leaked through the thatch of the hen-house; the same dank, cold rain that had been falling for weeks, ever since the snow melted. It dripped on the back of her neck and down her back under her smock. Though it was nearly dusk, Elfrida checked the nests one more time, hoping that one of the scrawny, ill-tempered hens might have been persuaded, by a miracle or sheer perversity, to drop an egg. But as she had expected, the nests were empty, and the hens resisted her attempts at investigation with nasty jabs of their beaks. They'd gotten quite adept at fighting, competing with and chasing away the crows who came to steal their scant feed over the winter. She came away from the hen-house with an empty apron and scratched and bleeding hands.

Nor was there remedy waiting for her in the cottage, even for that. The little salve they had must be hoarded against greater need than hers.

Old Mag, the village healer and Elfrida's teacher, looked up from the tiny fire burning in the pit in the center of the dirt-floored cottage's single room. At least the thatch here was sound, though rain dripped in through the smoke-hole, and the fire didn't seem to be warming the place any. Elfrida coughed on the smoke, which persisted in staying inside, rather than rising through the smoke-hole as it should.

Mag's eyes had gotten worse over the winter, and the cottage was very dark with the shutters closed. "No eggs?" she asked, peering across the room, as Elfrida let the cowhide down across the cottage door.

"None," Elfrida replied, sighing. "This spring—if it's this bad now, what will summer be like?"

She squatted down beside Mag, and took the share of barley-bread the old woman offered, with a crude wooden cup of bitter-tasting herb tea dipped out of the kettle beside the fire.

"I don't know," Mag replied, rubbing her eyes—Mag, who had been tall and straight with health last summer, who was now bent and aching, with swollen joints and rheumy eyes. Neither willow-bark nor eyebright helped her much. "Lady bless, darling, I don't know. First that killing frost, then nothing but rain—seems like what seedlings the frost didn't get, must've rotted in the fields by now. Hens aren't laying, lambs are born dead, pigs lay on their own young . . . what we're going to do for food come winter, I've no notion."

When Mag said "we," she meant the whole village. She was not only their healer, but their priestess of the Old Way. Garth might be hetman, but she was the village's heart and soul—as Elfrida expected to be one day. This was something she had chosen, knowing the work and self-sacrifice involved, knowing that the enmity of the priests of the White Christ might fall upon her. But not for a long time—Lady grant.

That was what she had always thought, but now the heart and soul of the village was sickening, as the village around her sickened. But why?

"We made the proper sacrifices," Elfrida said, finally. "Didn't we? What've we done or not done that the land turns against us?"

Mag didn't answer, but there was a quality in her silence that made Elfrida think that the old woman knew something—something important. Something that she hadn't yet told her pupil.

Finally, as darkness fell, and the fire burned down to coals, Mag spoke.

"We made the sacrifices," she said. "But there was one—who didn't."

"Who?" Elfrida asked, surprised. The entire village followed the Old Way—never mind the High King and his religion of the White Christ. That was for knights and nobles and suchlike. Her people stuck by what they knew best, the turning of the seasons, the dance of the Maiden, Mother and Crone, the rule of the Horned Lord. And if anyone in the village had neglected their sacrifices, surely she or Mag would have known!

"It isn't just our village that's sickening," Mag said, her voice a hoarse, harsh whisper out of the dark. "Nor the county alone. I've talked to the other Wise Ones, to the peddlers—I talked to the crows and the owls and ravens. It's the whole land that's sickening, failing—and there's only one sacrifice can save the land."

Elfrida felt her mouth go dry, and took a sip of her cold, bitter tea to wet it. "The blood of the High King," she whispered.

"Which he will not shed, come as he is to the feet of the White Christ." Mag shook her head. "My dear, my darling girl, I'd hoped the Lady wouldn't lay this on us . . . I'd prayed she wouldn't punish us for his neglect. But 'tisn't punishment, not really, and I should've known better than to hope it wouldn't come. Whether he believes it or not, the High King is tied to the land, and Arthur is old and failing. As he fails, the land fails—"

"But—surely there's something we can do?" Elfrida said timidly into the darkness.

Mag stirred. "If there is, I haven't been granted the answer," she said, after another long pause. "But perhaps—you've had Lady-dreams before, 'twas what led you to me . . . ."

"You want me to try for a vision?" Elfrida's mouth dried again, but this time no amount of tea would soothe it, for it was dry from fear. For all that she had true visions, when she sought them, the experience frightened her. And no amount of soothing on Mag's part, or encouragement that the—things—she saw in the dark waiting for her soul's protection to waver could not touch her, could ever ease that fear.

But weighed against her fear was the very real possibility that the village might not survive the next winter. If she was worthy to be Mag's successor, she must dare her fear, and dare the dreams, and see if the Lady had an answer for them since High King Arthur did not. The land and the people needed her and she must answer that need.

"I'll try," she whispered, and Mag touched her lightly on the arm.

"That's my good and brave girl," she said. "I knew you wouldn't fail us." Something on Mag's side of the fire rustled, and she handed Elfrida a folded leaf full of dried herbs.

They weren't what the ignorant thought, herbs to bring visions. The visions came when Elfrida asked for them—these were to strengthen and guard her while her spirit rode the night winds, in search of answers. Foxglove to strengthen her heart, moly to shield her soul, a dozen others, a scant pinch of each. Obediently, she placed them under her tongue, and while Mag chanted the names of the Goddess, Elfrida closed her eyes, and released her all-too-fragile hold on her body.

The convent garden was sodden, the ground turning to mush, and unless someone did something about it, there would be nothing to eat this summer but what the tithes brought and the King's Grace granted them. Outside the convent walls, the fields were just as sodden; so, as the Mother Superior said, "A tithe of nothing is still nothing, and we must prepare to feed ourselves." Leonie sighed, and leaned a little harder on the spade, being careful where she put each spadeful of earth. Behind the spade, the drainage trench she was digging between each row of drooping pea-seedlings filled with water. Hopefully, this would be enough to keep them from rotting. Hopefully, there would be enough to share. Already the eyes of the children stared at her from faces pinched and hungry when they came to the convent for Mass, and she hid the bread that was half her meal to give to them.

Her gown was as sodden as the ground; cold and heavy with

water, and only the fact that it was made of good wool kept it from chilling her. Her bare feet, ankle-deep in mud, felt like blocks of stone, they were so cold. She had kirtled her gown high to keep the hem from getting muddied, but that only let the wind get at her legs. Her hair was so soaked that she had not even bothered with the linen veil of a novice; it would only have flapped around without protecting her head and neck any. Her hands hurt; she wasn't used to this.

The other novices, gently-born and not, were desperately doing the same in other parts of the garden. Those that could, rather; some of the gently-born were too ill to come out into the soaking, cold rain. The sisters, as many as were able, were outside the walls, helping a few of the local peasants dig a larger ditch down to the swollen stream. The trenches in the convent garden would lead to it—and so would the trenches being dug in the peasants' gardens, on the other side of the high stone wall.

"We must work together," Mother Superior had said firmly, and so here they were, knight's daughter and villien's son, robes and tunics kirtled up above the knee, wielding shovels with a will. Leonie had never thought to see it.

But the threat of hunger made strange bedfellows. Already the convent had turned out to help the villagers trench their kitchen gardens. Leonie wondered what the village folk would do about the fields too large to trench, or fields of hay? It would be a cold summer, and a lean winter.

What had gone wrong with the land? It was said that the weather had been unseasonable—and miserable—all over the kingdom. Nor was the weather all that had gone wrong; it was said there was quarreling at High King Arthur's court; that the knights were moved to fighting for its own sake, and had brought their leman openly to many court gatherings, to the shame of the ladies. It was said that the Queen herself—

But Leonie did not want to hear such things, or even think of them. It was all of a piece, anyway; knights fighting among themselves, killing frosts and rain that wouldn't end, the threat of war at the borders, raiders and bandits within, and starvation and plague hovering over all.

Something was deeply, terribly wrong.

She considered that, as she dug her little trenches, as she returned to the convent to wash her dirty hands and feet and change into a drier gown, as she nibbled her meager supper, trying to make it last, and as she went in to Vespers with the rest.

Something was terribly, deeply wrong.

When Mother Superior approached her after Vespers, she somehow knew that her feeling of *wrongness* and what the head of the convent was about to ask were linked.

"Leonie," Mother Superior said, once the other novices had filed away, back to their beds, "when your family sent you here, they told me it was because you had visions."

Leonie ducked her head and stared at her sandals. "Yes, Mother Magdalene."

"And I asked you not to talk about those visions in any way," the nun persisted. "Not to any of the other novices, not to any of the sister, not to Father Peregrine."

"Yes, Mother Magdalene—I mean, no Mother Magdalene—" Leonie looked up, flushing with anger. "I mean, I haven't—"

She knew why the nun had ordered her to keep silence on the subject; she'd heard the lecture to her parents through the door. The Mother Superior didn't believe in Leonie's visions—or rather, she was not convinced that they were really visions. "This could simply be a young woman's hysteria," she'd said sternly, "or an attempt to get attention. If the former, the peace of the convent and the meditation and prayer will cure her quickly enough—if the latter, well, she'll lose such notions of self-importance when she has no one to prate to."

"I know you haven't, child," Mother Magdalene said wearily, and Leonie saw how the nun's hands were blistered from the spade she herself had wielded today, how her knuckles were swollen, and her cheekbones cast into a prominence that had nothing to do with the dim lighting in the chapel. "I wanted to know if you still have them."

"Sometimes," Leonie said hesitantly. "That was how—I mean, that was why I woke last winter, when Sister Maria was elf-shot—"

"Sister Maria was not elf-shot," Mother Magdalene said

automatically. "Elves could do no harm to one who trusts in God. It was simply something that happens to the very old, now and again, it is a kind of sudden brain-fever. But that isn't the point. You're still having the visions—but can you still see things that you want to see?"

"Sometimes," Leonie said cautiously. "If God and the Blessed Virgin permit."

"Well, if God is ever going to permit it, I suspect He'd do so during Holy Week," Mother Magdalene sighed. "Leonie, I am going to ask you a favor. I'd like you to make a vigil tonight."

"And ask for a vision?" Leonie said, raising her head in sudden interest.

"Precisely." The nun shook her head, and picked up her beads, telling them through her fingers as she often did when nervous. "There is something wrong with us, with the land, with the kingdom—I want you to see if God will grant you a vision of *what*." As Leonie felt a sudden upsurge of pride, Mother Magdalene added hastily, "You aren't the only one being asked to do this—every order from one end of the kingdom to the other has been asked for visions from their members. I thought long and hard about asking this. But you are the only one in my convent who has ever—had a tendency to visions."

The Mother Superior had been about to say something else, Leonie was sure, for the practical and pragmatic Mother Magdalene had made her feelings on the subject of mysticism quite clear over the years. But that didn't matter—what did matter was that she was finally going to be able to release that pent-up power again, to soar on the angels' wings. Never mind that there were as many devils "out there" as angels; her angels would protect her, for they always had, and always would.

Without another word, she knelt on the cold stone before the altar, fixed her eyes on the bright little gilded cross above it, and released her soul's hold on her body.

"What did you see?" Mag asked, as Elfrida came back, shivering and spent, to consciousness. Her body was lying on the ground beside the fire, and it felt too tight, like a garment that didn't fit anymore—but she was glad enough to be in it again, for there had been *thousands* of those evil creatures waiting for her, trying to prevent her from reaching—

"The Cauldron," she murmured, sitting up slowly, one hand on her aching head. "There was a Cauldron"

"Of course!" Mag breathed. "The Cauldron of the Goddess! But—" It was too dark for Elfrida to see Mag, other than as a shadow in the darkness, but she somehow felt Mag's searching eyes. "What about the Cauldron? When is it coming back? Who's to have it? Not the High King, surely—"

"I'm—supposed to go look for it—" Elfrida said, vaguely. "That's what They said—I'm supposed to go look for it."

Mag's sharp intake of breath indicated her shock. "But—no, I know you, when you come out of this," she muttered, almost as if to herself. "You can't lie. If you say They said for you to go, then go you must."

Elfrida wanted to say something else, to ask what it all meant, but she couldn't. The vision had taken too much out of her, and she was whirled away a second time, but this time it was not on the winds of vision, but into the arms of exhausted sleep.

"What did you see?" Mother Superior asked urgently. Leonie found herself lying on the cold stone before the altar, wrapped in someone's cloak, with something pillowed under her head. She felt very peaceful, as she always did when the visions released her, and very, very tired. There had been many demons out there, but as always, her angels had protected her. Still, she was glad to be back. There had never been quite so many of the evil things there before, and they had frightened her.

She had to blink a few times, as she gathered her memories and tried to make sense of them. "A cup," she said, hesitantly—then her eyes fell upon the Communion chalice on the altar, and they widened as she realized just what she truly *had* seen. "No—not a cup, *the* Cup! We're to seek the Grail! That's what They told me!"

"The Grail?" Mother Magdalene's eyes widened a little herself, and she crossed herself hastily. "Just before you—you dropped over, you reached out. I thought I saw—I thought I saw something faint, like a ghost of a glowing cup in your hands—"

Leonie nodded, her cheek against the rough homespun of the habit bundled under her head. "They said that to save the kingdom, we have to seek the Grail."

"We?" Mother Magdalene said, doubtfully. "Surely you don't mean—"

"The High King's knights and squires, some of the clergy—and—me—" Leonie's voice trailed off, as she realized what she was saying. "They said the knights will know already and that when you hear about it from Camelot, you'll know I was speaking the truth. But I don't *want* to go!" she wailed. "I don't! I—"

"I'm convinced of the truth now," the nun said. "Just by the fact that you don't want to go. If this had been a sham, to get attention, you'd have demanded special treatment, to be cosseted and made much of, not to be sent off on your own."

"But—" Leonie protested frantically, trying to hold off unconsciousness long enough to save herself from this exile.

"Never mind," the Mother Superior said firmly. "We'll wait for word from Camelot. When we hear it, then you'll go."

Leonie would have protested further, but Mother Magdalene laid a cool hand across her hot eyes, and sleep came up and took her.

Elfrida had never been this far from her home village before. The great forest through which she had been walking for most of the day did not look in the least familiar. In fact, it did not look like anything anyone from the village had ever described.

And why hadn't Mag brought her here to gather healing herbs and mushrooms?

The answer seemed clear enough; she was no longer in lands Mag or any of the villagers had ever seen.

She had not known which way to go, so she had followed the raven she saw flying away from the village. The raven had led her to the edge of the woods, which at the time had seemed quite ordinary. But the oaks and beeches had turned to a thick growth of fir; the deeper she went, the older the trees became, until at last she was walking on a tiny path between huge trunks that rose far over her head before properly branching out. Beneath those spreading branches, thin, twiggy growth reached out skeletal fingers like blackened bones, while the upper branches cut off most of the light, leaving the trail beneath shrouded in a twilight gloom, though it was midday.

Though she was on a quest of sorts, that did not mean she had left her good sense behind. While she was within the beech and oak forest, she had gleaned what she could on either side of the track. Her pack now held two double-handfuls each of acorns and beechnuts, still sound, and a few mushrooms. Two here, three or four there, they added up.

It was just as well, for the meager supply of journey-bread she had with her had been all given away by the end of the first day of her quest. A piece at a time, to a child here, a nursing mother there . . . but she had the freedom of the road and the forest; the people she encountered were tied to their land and could not leave it. Not while there was any chance they might coax a crop from it.

They feared the forest, though they could not tell Elfrida why. They would only enter the fringes of it, to feed their pigs on acorns, to pick up deadfall. Further than that, they would not go.

Elfrida had known for a long time that she was not as magical as Mag. She had her visions, but that was all; she could not see the power rising in the circles, although she knew it was there, and could sometimes feel it. She could not see the halos of light around people that told Mag if they were sick or well. She had no knowledge of the future outside of her visions, and could not talk to the birds and animals as Mag could.

So she was not in the least surprised to find that she could sense nothing about the forest that indicated either good or ill. If there was something here, she could not sense it. Of course, the gloom of the fir-forest was more than enough to frighten anyone with any imagination. And while nobles often claimed that peasants had no more imagination than a block of wood—well, Elfrida often thought that nobles had no more sense than one of their high-bred, high-strung horses, that would break legs, shying at shadows. Witless, useless—and irresponsible. How many of them were on their lands, helping their liegemen and peasants to save their crops? Few enough; most were idling their time away at the High King's Court, gambling, drinking, wenching, playing at tourneys and other useless pastimes. And she would wager that the High King's table was not empty; that the nobles' children were not going pinch-faced and hungry to bed. The religion of the White Christ had divorced master from man, noble from villager, making the former into a master in truth, and the latter into an income-producing slave. The villager was told by his priest to trust in God and receive his reward in heaven. The lord need feel no responsibility for any evils he did or caused, for once they had been confessed and paid for—usually by a generous gift to the priest—his God counted them as erased. The balance of duty and responsibility between the vassal and his lord was gone.

She shook off her bitter thoughts as nightfall approached. Without Mag's extra abilities Elfrida knew she would have to be twice as careful about spending the night in this place. If there were supernatural terrors about, she would never know until they were on her. So when she made her little camp, she cast circles around her with salt and iron, betony and rue, writing the runes as clear as she could, before she lit her fire to roast her nuts.

But in the end, when terror came upon her, it was of a perfectly natural sort.

Leonie cowered, and tried to hide in the folds of her robe. Her bruised face ached, and her bound wrists were cut and swollen around the thin twine the man who had caught her had used to bind her.

She had not gotten more than two days away from the convent— distributing most of her food to children and the sick as she walked—when she had reached the edge of the forest, and her vague visions had directed her to follow the path through it. She had seen no signs of people, nor had she sensed anything about the place that would have caused folk to avoid it. That had puzzled her, so she had dropped into a walking trance to try and sort out what kind of a place the forest was.

That was when someone had come up behind her and hit her on the head.

Now she knew why ordinary folk avoided the forest; it was the home of bandits. And she knew what her fate was going to be. Only the strength of the hold the chieftain had over his men had kept her from that fate until now. He had decreed that they would wait until all the men were back from their errands—and then they would draw lots for their turns at her . . . .

Leonie was so terrified that she was beyond thought; she huddled like a witless rabbit inside her robe and prayed for death.

"What's *this?*" the bandit chief said, loudly, startling her so that she raised her head out of the folds of her sleeves. She saw nothing at first; only the dark bulking shapes of men against the fire in their midst. He laughed, long and hard, as another of his men entered their little clearing, shoving someone in front of him. "By Satan's arse! The woods are sprouting wenches!"

Elfrida caught her breath at the curse; so, these men were not "just" bandits—they were the worst kind of bandit, nobles gone beyond the law. Only one who was once a follower of the White Christ would have used his adversary's name as an exclamation. No follower of the Old Way, either Moon- or Blood-path would have done so.

The brigand who had captured her shoved her over to land beside another girl—and once again she caught her breath, as her talisman-bag swung loose on its cord, and the other girl shrunk away, revealing the wooden beads and cross at the rope that served her as a belt. Worse and worse—the girl wore the robes of one who had vowed herself to the White Christ! There would be no help there . . . if she were not witless before she had been caught, she was probably frightened witless now. Even if she would accept help from the hands of a "pagan."

Leonie tried not to show her hope. Another girl! Perhaps between the two of them, they could manage to win free!

But as the girl was shoved forward, to drop to the needles beside

Leonie, something swung free of her robe to dangle over her chest. It was a little bag, on a rawhide thong.

And the bandit chief roared again, this time with disapproval, seizing the bag and breaking the thong with a single, cruelly hard tug of his hand. He tossed it out into the darkness and backhanded the outlaw who had brought the girl in.

"You witless bastard!" he roared. "You brought in a witch!" A *witch?*

Leonie shrunk away from her fellow captive. A witch? Blessed Jesu—this young woman would be just as pleased to see Leonie raped to death! She would probably call up one of her demons to help!

As the brigand who had been struck shouted and went for his chief's throat, and the others gathered around, yelling encouragement and placing bets, she closed her eyes, bowed her head, and prayed. *Blessed Mother of God! hear me. Angels of grace, defend us. Make them forget us for just a moment . . . .*

As the brainless child started in fear, then pulled away, bowed her head, and began praying, Elfrida kept a heavy hand on her temper. Bad enough that she was going to die—and in a particularly horrible way—but to have to do it in such company!

But—suddenly the outlaws were fighting. One of them appeared to be the chief; the other the one who had caught her. And they were ignoring the two girls as if they had somehow forgotten their existence . . . .

*Blessed Mother, hear me. Make it so.*

The man had only tied her with a bit of leather, no stronger than the thong that had held her herb-bag. If she wriggled just right, bracing her tied hands against her feet, she could probably snap it.

She prayed, and pulled. And was rewarded with the welcome release of pressure as the thong snapped.

She brought her hands in front of her, hiding them in her tunic, and looked up quickly; the fight had involved a couple more of the bandits. She and the other girl were in the shadows now, for the fire had been obscured by the men standing or scuffling around it. If she crept away quickly and quietly—

No sooner thought than done. She started to crawl away, got as far as the edge of the firelight, then looked back.

The other girl was still huddled where she had been left, eyes closed. Too stupid or too frightened to take advantage of the opportunity to escape.

If Elfrida left her there, they probably wouldn't try to recapture her. They'd have one girl still, and wouldn't go hunting in the dark for the one that had gotten away . . . .

Elfrida muttered an oath, and crawled back.

Leonie huddled with the witch-girl under the shelter of a fallen tree, and they listened for the sounds of pursuit. She had been praying as hard as she could, eyes closed, when a painful tug on the twine binding her wrists had made her open her eyes.

"Well, come *on!*" the girl had said, tugging again. Leonie had not bothered to think about what the girl might be pulling her into, she had simply followed, crawling as best she could with her hands tied, then getting up and running when the girl did.

They had splashed through a stream, running along a moonlit path, until Leonie's sides ached. Finally the girl had pulled her off the path and shoved her under the bulk of a fallen tree, into a little dug-out den she would never have guessed was there. From the musky smell, it had probably been made by a fox or badger. Leonie huddled in the dark, trying not to sob, concentrating on the pain in her side and not on the various fates the witch-girl could have planned for her.

Before too long, they heard shouts in the distance, but they never came very close. Leonie strained her ears, holding her breath, to try and judge how close their pursuers were, and jumped when the witch-girl put a hand on her.

"Don't," the girl whispered sharply. "You won't be going far with your hands tied like that. Hold still! I'm not going to hurt you."

Leonie stuttered something about demons, without thinking. The girl laughed.

"If I had a demon to come when I called, do you think I would have let a bastard like that lay hands on me?" Since there was no logical answer to that question, Leonie wisely kept quiet. The girl touched her hands, and then seized them; Leonie kept herself from pulling away, and a moment later, felt the girl sawing at her bonds with a bit of sharp rock. Every so often the rock cut into Leonie instead of the twine, but she bit her lip and kept quiet, gratitude increasing as each strand parted. "What were you doing out here, anyway?" the girl asked. "I thought they kept your kind mewed up like prize lambs."

"I had a vision—" Leonie began, wondering if by her words and the retelling of her holy revelation, the witch-girl might actually be converted to Christianity. It happened that way all the time in the tales of the saints, after all . . . .

So while the girl sawed patiently at the bonds with the sharp end of the rock, Leonie told her everything, from the time she realized that something was wrong, to the moment the bandit took her captive. The girl stayed silent through all of it, and Leonie began to hope that she *might* bring the witch-girl to the Light and Life of Christ.

The girl waited until she had obviously come to the end, then laughed, unpleasantly. "Suppose, just suppose," she said, "I were to tell you that the *exact same* vision was given to me? Only it isn't some mystical cup that this land needs, it's the Cauldron of Cerridwen, the ever-renewing, for the High King refuses to sacrifice himself to save his kingdom as the Holy Bargain demands and only the Cauldron can give the land the blessing of the Goddess."

The last of the twine snapped as she finished, and Leonie pulled her hands away. "Then I would say that your vision is wrong, evil," she retorted. "There is no goddess, only the Blessed Virgin—"

"Who is one face of the Goddess, who is Maiden, Mother and Wise One," the girl interrupted, her words dripping acid. "Only a fool would fail to see that. And your White Christ is no more than the Sacrificed One in one of *His* many guises—it is the Cauldron the land needs, not your apocryphal Cup—"

"Your cauldron is some demon-thing," Leonie replied, angrily. "Only the Grail—"

Whatever else she was going to say was lost, as the tree-trunk above them was riven into splinters by a bolt of lightning that blinded and deafened them both for a moment.

When they looked up, tears streaming from their eyes, it was to see something they both recognized as The Enemy.

Standing over them was a shape, outlined in a glow of its own. It was three times the height of a man, black and hairy like a bear, with the tips of its outstretched claws etched in fire. But it was not a bear, for it wore a leather corselet, and its head had the horns of a bull, the snout and tusks of a boar, dripping foam and saliva, and its eyes, glowing an evil red, were slitted like a goat's.

Leonie screamed and froze. The witch-girl seized her bloody wrist, hauled her to her feet, and ran with her stumbling along behind.

The beast roared and followed after. They had not gotten more than forty paces down the road, when the witch-girl fell to the ground with a cry of pain, her hand slipping from Leonie's wrist.

*Her ankle*—Leonie thought, but no more, for the beast was shambling towards them. She grabbed the girl's arm and hauled her to her feet; draped her arm over her own shoulders, and dragged her erect. Up ahead there was moonlight shining down on something— perhaps a clearing, and perhaps the beast might fear the light—

She half-dragged, half-guided the witch-girl towards that promise of light, with the beast bellowing behind them. The thought crossed her mind that if she dropped the girl and left her, the beast would probably be content with the witch and would not chase after Leonie . . . .

*No,* she told herself, and stumbled onward.

They broke into the light, and Leonie looked up—

And sank to her knees in wonder.


Elfrida fell beside the other girl, half-blinded by tears of pain, and tried to get to her feet. The beast—she had to help Leonie up, they had to run—

Then she looked up.

And fell again to her knees, this time stricken not with pain, but with awe. And though she had never felt *power* before, she felt it now;

humming through her, blood and bone, saw it in the vibration of the air, in the purity of the light streaming from the Cup—

The Cup held in the hand of a man, whose gentle, sad eyes told of the pain, not only of His own, but of the world's, that for the sake of the world, He carried on His own shoulders.

Leonie wept, tears of mingled joy and fear—joy to be in the Presence of One who was all of Light and Love, and fear, that this One was She and not He—and the thing that she held, spilling over the Light of Love and Healing was Cauldron and not Cup.

*I was wrong*—she thought, helplessly.

*Wrong?* said a loving, laughing Voice. *Or simply—limited in vision?*

And in that moment, the Cauldron became a Cup, and the Lady became the Lord, Jesu—then changed again, to a man of strange, draped robes and slanted eyes, who held neither Cup nor Cauldron, but a cup-shaped Flower with a jeweled heart—a hawk-headed creature with a glowing stone in His hand—a black-skinned Woman with a bright Bird—

And then to another shape, and another, until her eyes were dazzled and her spirit dizzied, and she looked away, into the eyes of Elfrida. *The witch-girl—Wise Girl* whispered the Voice in her mind, *and Quest-Companion*—looked similarly dazzled, but the joy in her face must surely mirror Leonie's. The girl offered her hand, and Leonie took it, and they turned again to face—

A Being of light, neither male nor female, and a dazzling Cup as large as a Cauldron, the veil covering it barely dimming its brilliance.

*Come,* the Being said, *you have proved yourselves worthy.*

Hand in hand, the two newest Grail Maidens rose, and followed the shining beacon into the Light.

*It was inevitable that the Holy Grail anthology would spawn an Excalibur anthology. I kept promising to write the story and things got in the way . . . like other deadlines! But bless their hearts, they held a place for me, and here is the story itself. It's not at all like the Grail story; in fact, it's not a very heroic story, which may surprise some people.*

# Once and Future

## Mercedes Lackey

Michael O'Murphy woke with the mother of all hangovers splitting his head in half, churning up his stomach like a winter storm off the Orkneys, and a companion in his bed.

*What in Jaysus did I do last night?*

The pain in his head began just above his eyes, wrapped around the sides, and met in the back. His stomach did not bear thinking about. His companion was long, cold, and unmoving, but very heavy.

*I took a board to bed? Was I that hard up for a sheila? Michael, you're slipping!*

He was lying on his side, as always. The unknown object was at his back. At the moment it was no more identifiable than a hard presence along his spine, uncomfortable and unyielding. He wasn't entirely certain he wanted to find out exactly what it was until he mentally retraced his steps of the previous evening. Granted, this was

157

irrational, but a man with the mother of all hangovers is not a rational being.

The reason for his monumental drunk was clear enough in his mind; the pink slip from his job at the docks, presented to him by the foreman at the end of the day. *That would be yesterday, Friday, if I haven't slept the weekend through.*

He wasn't the only bloke cashiered yesterday; they'd laid off half the men at the shipyard. *So it's back on the dole, and thank God Almighty I didn't get serious with that little bird I met on holiday. Last thing I need is a woman nagging at me for losing me job and it wasn't even me own fault.* Depression piled atop the splitting head and the foul stomach. Michael O'Murphy was not the sort of man who accepted the dole with any kind of grace other than ill.

He cracked his right eye open, winced at the stab of light that penetrated into his cranium, and squinted at the floor beside his bed.

Yes, there was the pink slip, crumpled into a wad, beside his boots—and two bottles of Jameson's, one empty, the other half-full and frugally corked.

*Holy Mary Mother of God. I don't remember sharing out that often, so I must've drunk most of it myself. No wonder I feel like a walk through Purgatory.*

He closed his eye again, and allowed the whiskey bottle to jog a few more memories loose. So, he'd been sacked, and half the boys with him. And they'd all decided to drown their sorrows together.

*But not at a pub, and not at pub prices. You can't get royally, roaring drunk at a pub unless you've got a royal allowance to match. So we all bought our bottles and met at Tommy's place.*

There'd been a half-formed notion to get shellacked there, but Tommy had a car, and Tommy had an idea. He'd seen some nonsense on the telly about "Iron Johns" or some such idiocy, over in America—

*Said we was all downtrodden and "needed to get in touch with our inner selves"; swore that we had to get "empowered" to get back on our feet, and wanted to head out into the country—*There'd been some talk about "male bonding" ceremonies, pounding drums, carrying on like a lot of Red Indians—and drinking of course. Tommy went on like it was some kind of communion; the rest of them had already started on their bottles before they got to Tommy's, and at that point, a lot of pounding and dancing half-naked and drinking sounded like a fine idea. So off they went, crammed into Tommy's aging Morris Minor with just enough room to get their bottles to their lips.

At some point they stopped and all piled out; Michael vaguely recalled a forest, which might well have been National Trust lands and it was a mercy they hadn't been caught and hauled off to gaol. Tommy had gotten hold of a drum somewhere; it was in the boot with the rest of the booze. They all grabbed bottles and Tommy got the drum, and off they went into the trees like a daft May Day parade, howling and carrying on like bleeding loonies.

How Tommy made the fire—and why it hadn't been seen, more to the point!—Michael had not a clue. He remembered a great deal of pounding on the drum, more howling, shouting and swearing at the bosses of the world, a lot of drinking, and some of the lads stripping off their shirts and capering about like so many monkeys. *About then was when I got an itch for some quiet.* He and his bottles had stumbled off into the trees, following an elusive moonbeam, or so he thought he remembered. The singing and pounding had faded behind him, and in his memory the trees loomed the way they had when he was a nipper and everything seemed huge. *They were like trees out of the old tales, as big* as *the one they call Robin Hood's Oak in Sherwood.* There was only one way to go since he didn't even consider turning back, and that was to follow the path between them, and the fey bit of moonlight that lured him on.

*Was there a mist? I think there was. Wait! That was when the real path appeared.* There had been mist, a curious, blue mist. It had muffled everything, from the sounds of his own footsteps to the sounds of his mates back by the fire. Before too very long, he might have been the only human being alive in a forest as old as time and full of portentous silence.

He remembered that the trees thinned out at just about the point where he was going to give up his ramble and turn back. He had found himself on the shores of a lake. It was probably an ordinary enough pond by daylight, but last night, with the mist drifting over it and obscuring the farther shore, the utter and complete silence of the place, and the moonlight pouring down over everything and touching everything with silver, it had seemed . . . uncanny, a bit frightening, and not entirely in the real world at all.

He had stood there with a bottle in each hand, a monument to inebriation, held there more by inertia than anything else, he suspected. He could still see the place as he squeezed his eyes shut, as vividly as if he stood there at that moment. The water was like a sheet of plate glass over a dark and unimaginable void; the full moon hung just above the dark mass of the trees behind him, a great round Chinese lantern of a moon, and blue-white mist floated everywhere in wisps and thin scarves and great opaque billows. A curious boat rested by the bank not a meter from him, a rough-hewn thing apparently made from a whole tree-trunk and shaped with an axe. Not even the reeds around the boat at his feet moved in the breathless quiet.

Then, breaking the quiet, a sound; a single splash in the middle of the lake. Startled, he had seen an arm rise up out of the water, beckoning.

He thought, of course, that someone had fallen in, or been swimming and took a cramp. One of his mates, even, who'd come round to the other side and taken a fancy for a dip. It never occurred to him to go back to the others for help, just as it never occurred to him not to rush out there to save whoever it was.

He dropped his bottles into the boat at his feet, and followed them in. He looked about for the tether to cast off, but there wasn't one—looked for the oars to row out to the swimmer, but there weren't any of those, either. Nevertheless, the boat was moving, and heading straight for that beckoning arm as if he was willing it there. And it didn't seem at all strange to him that it was doing so, at least, not at the time.

He remembered that he'd been thinking that whoever this was, she'd fallen in fully clothed, for the arm had a long sleeve of some heavy white stuff. And it had to be a she—the arm was too white and soft to be a man's. It wasn't until he got up close, though, that he realized there was nothing showing *but* the arm, that the woman had been under an awfully long time—and that the arm sticking up out of the water was holding something.

*Still, daft as it was, it wasn't important*—He'd ignored everything but the arm, ignored things that didn't make any sense. As the boat got within range of the woman, he'd leaned over the bow so far that *he* almost fell in, and made a grab for that upraised arm.

But the hand and wrist slid through his grasp somehow, although he was *sure* he'd taken a good, firm hold on them, and he fell back into the boat, knocking himself silly against the hard wooden bottom, his hands clasped tight around whatever it was she'd been holding. He saw stars, and more than stars, and when he came to again, the boat was back against the bank, and there was no sign of the woman.

But he had her sword.

*Her sword? I had her sword?*

Now he reached behind him to feel the long, hard length of it at his back.

*By God—it is a sword!*

He had no real recollection of what happened after that; he must have gotten back to the lads, and they all must have gotten back to town in Tommy's car, because here he was.

In bed with a sword.

*I've heard of being in bed with* a *battle-axe, but never a sword.*

Slowly, carefully, he sat up. Slowly, carefully, he reached into the tumble of blankets and extracted the drowning woman's sword.

It was real, it looked old, and it was damned heavy. He hefted it in both hands, and grunted with surprise. If this was the kind of weapon those old bastards used to hack at one another with in the long-ago days that they made films of; there must have been as much harm done by breaking bones as by whacking bits off.

It wasn't anything fancy, though, not like you saw in the flicks or the comics; a plain, black, leather-wrapped hilt, with what looked like brass bits as the cross-piece and a plain, black leather-bound sheath. Probably weighed about as much as four pry-bars of the same length put together.

He put his hand to the hilt experimentally, and pulled a little, taking it out of the sheath with the vague notion of having a look at the blade itself.

*PENDRAGON!*

The voice shouted in his head, an orchestra of nothing but trumpets, and all of them played at top volume.

He dropped the sword, which landed on his toes. He shouted with pain, and jerked his feet up reflexively, and the sword dropped to the floor, half out of its sheath. "What the *hell* was that?" he howled, grabbing his abused toes in both hands, and rocking back and forth a little. He was hardly expecting an answer, but he got one anyway.

*It was I, Pendragon.*

He felt his eyes bugging out, and he cast his gaze frantically around the room, looking for the joker who'd snuck inside while he was sleeping. But there wasn't anyone, and there was nowhere to hide. The rented room contained four pieces of furniture—his iron-framed bed, a cheap deal bureau and nightstand, and a chair. He bent over and took a peek under the bed, feeling like a frightened old aunty, but there was nothing there, either.

*You're looking in the wrong place.*

"I left the radio on," he muttered, "that's it. It's some daft drama. Gawd, I hate those BBC buggers!" He reached over to the radio on the nightstand and felt for the knob. But the radio was already off, and cold, which meant it hadn't *been* on with the knob broken.

*Pendragon, I am on the floor, where you dropped me.*

He looked down at the floor. The only things besides his boots were the whiskey bottles and the sword.

"I never heard of no Jameson bottles talking in a bloke's head before," he muttered to himself, as he massaged his toes, "and me boots never struck up no conversations before."

*Don't be absurd,* said the voice, tartly. *You know what I am, as you know what you are.*

The sword. It had to be the sword. "And just what am I, then?" he asked it, wondering when the boys from the Home were going to come romping through the door to take him off for a spot of rest. *This is daft. I must have gone loopy. I'm talking to a piece of metal, and it's talking back to me.*

*You are the Pendragon,* the sword said patiently, and waited. When he failed to respond except with an uncomprehending shrug, it went on—but with far less patience. *You are the Once and Future King. The Warrior Against the Darkness.* It waited, and he still had no notion what it was talking about.

*You are ARTHUR,* it shouted, making him wince. *You are King Arthur, Warleader and Hero!*

"Now it's *you* that's loopy," he told it sternly. "I don't bloody well think! King Arthur indeed!"

The only recollection of King Arthur he had were things out of his childhood—stories in the schoolbooks, a Disney flick, Christmas pantomimes. Vague images of crowns and red-felt robes, of tin swords and papier-mache armor flitted through his mind—and talking owls and daft magicians. "King Arthur! Not likely!"

*You are!* the sword said, sounding desperate now. *You are the Pendragon! You have been reborn into this world to be its Hero! Don't you remember?*

He only snorted. "I'm Michael O'Murphy, I work at the docks, I'll be on the dole on Monday, and I don't bloody think anybody needs any bloody more Kings these days! They've got enough troubles with the ones they've—*Gawd!*"

He fell back into the bed as the sword bombarded his mind with a barrage of images, more vivid than the flicks, for he was *in* them. Battles and feasts, triumph and tragedy, success and failure—a grim stand against the powers of darkness that held for the short space of one man's lifetime.

It all poured into his brain in the time it took for him to breathe twice. And when he sat up again, he remembered.

All of it.

He blinked, and rubbed his mistreated head. "Gawd!" he complained. "You might warn a lad first!"

*Now do you believe?* The sword sounded smug.

Just like the nuns at his school, when they'd gotten done whapping him "for his own good."

"I believe you're damn good at shoving a lot of rubbish into a man's head and making him think it's his," he said stubbornly, staring down at the shining expanse of blade, about ten-centimeter's worth, that protruded out of the sheath. "I still don't see where all this makes any difference, even if I *do* believe it."

If the sword could have spluttered, it probably would have. *You don't—you're Arthur! I'm Excalibur! You're supposed to take me up and use me!*

"For what?" he asked, snickering at the mental image of prying open tins of beans with the thing. "You don't make a good pry-bar, I can't cut wood with you even if I had a wood stove, which I don't, nobody's going to believe you're a fancy saw-blade, and there's laws about walking around with something like you strapped to me hip. What do I do, fasten a sign to you, and go on a protest march?"

*You—you—*Bereft of words, the sword resorted to another flood of images. Forewarned by the last one, Michael stood his ground.

But this time the images were harder to ignore.

He saw himself taking the sword and gathering his fighters to his side—all of his friends from the docks, the ones who'd bitched along with him about what a mess the world was in. He watched himself making an army out of them, and sending them out into the streets to clean up the filth there. He saw himself as the leader of a new corps of vigilantes who tracked down the pushers, the perverts, the thugs and the punks and gave them all a taste of what they had coming to them.

He saw his army making the city safe for people to live in, saw them taking back the night from the Powers of Evil.

He saw more people flocking to his banner and his cause, saw him carrying his crusade from city to city, until a joyous public threw the House of Hanover out of Buckingham Palace and installed him on the throne, and a ten-year-old child could carry a gold bar across the length of the island and never fear a robber or a molester.

*Or try this one, if that doesn't suit you!*

This time he saw himself crossing to Ireland, confronting the leadership of every feuding party there, and defeating them, one by one, in challenge-combat. He saw himself bringing peace to a land that had been torn by strife for so long that there wasn't an Irish child alive that didn't know what a knee-capper was. He saw the last British

Tommy leaving the island with a smile on his face and a shamrock in his lapel, withdrawing in good order since order itself had been restored. He saw plenty coming back to the land, prosperity, saw Ireland taking a major role in the nations of the world, and "Irish honor" becoming a byword for "trust." Oh, this was cruel, throwing a vision like that in his face! He wasn't for British Rule, but the IRA was as bad as the PLO by his lights—and there wasn't anything he could do about either.

Until now.

*Or here—widen your horizons, lift your eyes beyond your own sordid universe!*

This time he started as before, carried the sword to Ireland and restored peace there, and went on—on to the Continent, to Eastern Europe, taking command of the UN forces there and forcing a real and lasting peace by the strength of his arm. Oh, there was slaughter, but it wasn't a slaughter of the innocents but of the bastards that drove the fights, and in the end that same ten-year-old child could start in Galway and end in Saraejevo, and no one would so much as dirty the lace on her collar or offer her an unkind word.

The sword released him, then, and he sat blinking on his shabby second-hand bed, in his dingy rented room, still holding his aching toes in both hands. It all seemed so tawdry, this little world of his, and all he had to do to earn a greater and brighter one was to reach out his hand.

He looked down at the sword at the side of his bed, and the metal winked smugly up at him. "You really think you have me now, don't you," he said bitterly to it.

It said nothing. It didn't have to answer.

But he had answers enough for all the temptations in his own mind. Because now he *remembered* Arthur—and Guinevere, and Lancelot and Agravaine and Morgaine.

And Mordred.

Oh yes. He had no doubt that there would be a Mordred out there, somewhere, waiting for him the moment he took up the sword. He hadn't been any too careful, AIDS notwithstanding, and there could be any number of bastards scattered from his seed. Hell, there would be a Mordred even if it *wasn't* his son. For every Warrior of the Light there was a Warrior of the Dark; he'd seen that quite, quite clearly. For every Great Friend there was always the Great Betrayer—hadn't Peter betrayed Christ by denying him? For every Great Love there was the Great Loss.

It would *not* be the easy parade of victories the sword showed him; he was older and far, far wiser than the boy-Arthur who'd taken Excalibur the last time. He was not to be dazzled by dreams. The *most* likely of the scenarios to succeed was the first—some bloke in New York had done something like that, called his lads the "Guardian Angels"—and even *he* hadn't succeeded in cleaning up more than a drop or two of the filth in one city, let alone hundreds.

That scenario would only last as long as it took some punk's parents to sue him. What good would a sword be in court, eh? What would he do, slice the judge's head off?

And this was the age of the tabloids, of smut-papers. They'd love him for a while, then they'd decide to bring him down. If they'd had a time with Charles and Di, what would they do with him—and Guinevere, and Lancelot—and Mordred?

For Mordred and Morgaine were surely here, and they might even have got a head start on him. They could be waiting for him to appear, waiting with hired thugs to take him out.

For that matter, Mordred might be a lawyer, ready for him at this very moment with briefs and briefcase, and he'd wind up committed to the loony asylum before he got two steps! Or he might be a smut-reporter, good at digging up dirt. His own, real past wouldn't make a pretty sight on paper.

Oh no. Oh, no.

"I don't think so, my lad," he said, and before the sword could pull any clever tricks, he reached down, and slammed it home in the sheath.

Three hours and six aspirins later, he walked into the nearest pawn shop with a long bundle wrapped in old newspapers under his arm. He handed it across the counter to the wizened old East Indian who kept the place.

The old boy unwrapped the papers, and peered at the sword

without a hint of surprise. God alone knew he'd probably seen stranger things pass across his counter. He slid it out of its sheath and examined the steel before slamming it back home. Only then did he squint through the grill at Michael.

"It's mild steel. Maybe antique, maybe not, no way of telling. Five quid," he said. "Take it or leave it."

"I'll take it," said the Pendragon.

*This is one of those fun ones. I submitted this to Andre Norton for her* Magic in Ithkar *braided anthology for Another Company; this was during that time when braided anthologies (otherwise known as "shared worlds") were Hot Stuff. I didn't know if I had a hope of getting in, but I tried—and she accepted it! Later, since* Magic in Ithkar *only made it to volume two, and I really liked the concept of the Free Bards, this became the basis for the "Bardic Voices" series I do for Baen. This is a case where I was able to "file the serial numbers off" and do a rewrite to fit the story into an entirely original world; you can't always do that, but sometimes it works.*

# Fiddler Fair

## Mercedes Lackey

All the world comes to Ithkar Fair.

That's what they said, anyway—and it certainly seemed that way to Rune, as she traveled the Trade Road down from her home near the Galzar Pass. She wasn't walking on the dusty, hard-packed road itself; she'd likely have been trampled by the press of beasts, then run over by the carts into the bargain. Instead, she walked with the rest of the foot-travelers on the road's verge. It was no less dusty, what grass there had been had long since been trampled into powder by all the feet of the pilgrims and fairgoers, but at least a traveler was able to move along without risk of acquiring hoofprints on his anatomy.

Rune was close enough now to see the gates of the Fair itself, and the Fair-ward beside them. This seemed like a good moment to separate herself from the rest of the throng, rest her tired feet, and plan her next moves before entering the grounds of the Fair.

She elbowed her way out of the line of people, some of whom complained and elbowed back, and moved away from the road to a place where she had a good view of the Fair and a rock to sit on. The sun beat down with enough heat to be felt through her soft leather hat as she plopped herself down on the rock and began massaging her tired feet while she looked the Fair over.

It was a bit overwhelming. Certainly it was much bigger than she'd imagined it would be. It was equally certain that there would be nothing dispensed for free behind those log palings, and the few coppers Rune had left would have to serve to feed her through the three days of trials for admission to the Bardic Guild. After that—

Well, after that, she should be an apprentice, and food and shelter would be for her master to worry about. If not—

She refused to admit the possibility of failing the trials. She couldn't—the Three surely *wouldn't* let her fail. Not after getting this far.

But for now, she needed somewhere to get herself cleaned of the road-dust, and a place to sleep, both with no price tags attached. Right now, she was the same gray-brown from head to toe, the darker brown of her hair completely camouflaged by the dust, or at least it felt that way. Even her eyes felt dusty.

She strolled down to the river, her lute thumping her shoulder softly on one side, her pack doing the same on the other. Close to the docks the water was muddy and roiled; there was too much traffic on the river to make an undisturbed bath a viable possibility, and too many wharf-rats about to make leaving one's belongings a wise move. She backtracked upstream a bit, while the noise of the Fair faded behind her, crossed over the canal and went hunting the rapids that the canal bypassed. The bank of the river was wilder here, and overgrown, not like the carefully tended area of the canalside. Finally she found a place where the river had cut a tiny cove into the bank. It was secluded; trees overhung the water, their branches making a good thick screen that touched the water, the ground beneath them bare of growth, and hollows between some of the roots just big enough to cradle her sleeping roll. Camp, bath, and water, all together, and within climbing distance on one of the trees was a hollow big enough to hide her bedroll and those belongings she didn't want to carry into the Fair.

She waited until dusk fell before venturing into the river and kept her eyes and ears open while she scrubbed herself down. Once clean, she debated whether or not to change into the special clothing she'd brought tonight; it might be better to save it—then the thought of donning the sweat-soaked, dusty traveling gear became too distasteful, and she rejected it out of hand.

She felt strange and altogether different once she'd put the new costume on. Part of that was due to the materials—except for when she'd tried the clothing on for fit, this was the first time she'd ever worn silk and velvet. Granted, the materials were all old; bought from a second-hand vendor and cut down from much larger garments. The velvet of the breeches wasn't *too* rubbed; the ribbons on the sleeves of the shirt and the embroidery should cover the faded places, and the vest should cover the stain on the back panel completely. Her hat, once the dust was beaten out of it and the plumes she'd snatched from the tails of several disgruntled roosters were tucked into the band, looked brave enough. Her boots, at least, were new, and when the dust was brushed from them, looked quite well. She tucked her remaining changes of clothing and her bedroll into her pack, hid the lot in the tree-hollow, and felt ready to face the Fair.

The Fair-ward at the gate eyed her carefully. "Minstrel?" he asked suspiciously, looking at the lute and fiddle she carried in their cases, slung from her shoulders.

She shook her head. "Here for the trials, m'lord."

"Ah," he appeared satisfied. "You come in good time, boy. The trials begin tomorrow. The Guild has its tent pitched hard by the main gate of the Temple; you should have no trouble finding it."

The wizard of the gate looked bored, ignoring her. Rune did not correct the Fair-ward's assumption that she was a boy; it was her intent to pass as male until she'd safely passed the trials. She'd never heard of the Bardic Guild admitting a girl, but so far as she'd been able to determine, there was nothing in the rules and Charter of the Guild preventing it. So once she'd been accepted, once the trials were safely passed, she'd reveal her sex, but until then, she'd play the safe course.

She thanked him, but he had already turned his attention to the next in line. She passed inside the log walls and entered the Fair itself.

The first impressions she had were of noise and light; torches burned all along the aisle she traversed; the booths to either side were lit by lanterns, candles, or other, more arcane methods. The crowd was noisy; so were the merchants. Even by torchlight it was plain that these were the booths featuring shoddier goods; secondhand finery, brass jewelry, flash and tinsel. The entertainers here were—surprising. She averted her eyes from a set of dancers. It wasn't so much that they wore little but imagination, but the *way* they were dancing embarrassed even her; and a tavern-bred child has seen a great deal in its life.

She kept a tight grip on her pouch and instruments, tried to ignore the crush, and let the flow of fairgoers carry her along.

Eventually the crowd thinned out a bit (though not before she'd felt a ghostly hand or two try for her pouch and give it up as a bad cause). She followed her nose then, looking for the row that held the cookshop tents and the ale-sellers. She hadn't eaten since this morning, and her stomach was lying in uncomfortably close proximity to her spine.

She learned that the merchants of tavern-row were shrewd judges of clothing; hers wasn't fine enough to be offered a free taste, but wasn't poor enough to be shooed away. Sternly admonishing her stomach to be less impatient, she strolled the length of the row twice, carefully comparing prices and quantities, before settling on a humble tent that offered meat pasties (best not ask what beast the meat came from, not at these prices) and fruit juice or milk as well as ale and wine. Best of all, it offered seating at rough trestle-tables as well. Rune took her flaky pastry and her mug of juice (no wine or ale for her; not even had she the coppers to spare for it. She dared not be the least muddle-headed, not with a secret to keep and a competition on the morn), and found herself a spot at an empty table where she could eat and watch the crowd passing by. The pie was more crust than meat, but it was filling and well-made and fresh; that counted for a great deal. She noted with amusement that there were two sorts of the clumsy, crude clay mugs. One sort, the kind they served the milk and juice in, was ugly and shapeless (too ugly to be worth stealing) but was just as capacious as the exterior promised. The other, for wine and ale, was just the same ugly shape and size on the *outside* (though a different shade of toad-back green), but had a far thicker bottom, effectively reducing the interior capacity by at least a third.

"Come for the trials, lad?" asked a quiet voice in her ear. Rune jumped, nearly knocking her mug over, and snatching at it just in time to save the contents from drenching her shopworn finery (and however would she have gotten it clean again in time for the morrow's competition?). There hadn't been a sound or a hint of movement or even the shifting of the bench to warn her, but now there was a man sitting beside her.

He was of middle years, red hair going to gray, smile-wrinkles around his mouth and gray-green eyes, with a candid, triangular face. Well, that said nothing; Rune had known highwaymen with equally friendly and open faces. His dress was similar to her own; leather breeches instead of velvet, good linen instead of worn silk, a vest and a leather hat that could have been twin to hers, knots of ribbon on the sleeves of his shirt—and the neck of a lute peeking over his shoulder. A Minstrel!

Of the Guild? Rune rechecked the ribbons on his sleeves, and was disappointed. Blue and scarlet and green, not the purple and silver of a Guild Minstrel, nor the purple and gold of a Guild Bard. This was only a common songster, a mere street-player. Still, he'd bespoken her kindly enough, and the Three knew not everyone with the music-passion had the skill or the talent to pass the trials—

"Aye, sir," she replied politely. "I've hopes to pass; I think I've the talent, and others have said as much."

His eyes measured her keenly, and she had the disquieting feeling that her boy-ruse was fooling *him* not at all. "Ah well," he replied, "There's a-many before you have thought the same, and failed."

"That may be," she answered the challenge in his eyes, "but I'd bet fair coin that none of *them* fiddled for a murdering ghost, and not only came out by the grace of their skill but were rewarded by that same spirit for amusing him!"

"Oh, so?" a lifted eyebrow was all the indication he gave of being impressed, but somehow that lifted brow conveyed volumes. "You've made a song of it, surely?"

"Have I not! It's to be my entry for the third day of testing."

"Well then—" He said no more than that, but his wordless attitude of waiting compelled Rune to unsling her fiddlecase, extract her instrument, and tune it without further prompting.

"It's the fiddle that's my first instrument," she said apologetically, "And since 'twas the fiddle that made the tale—"

"Never apologize for a song, child," he admonished, interrupting her. "Let it speak out for itself. Now let's hear this ghost-tale."

It wasn't easy to sing while fiddling, but Rune had managed the trick of it some time ago. She closed her eyes a half-moment, fixing in her mind the necessary changes she'd made to the lyrics— for unchanged, the song would have given her sex away—and began.

> "I sit here on a rock, and curse
> my stupid, bragging tongue,
> And curse the pride that would not let
> me back down from a boast
> And wonder where my wits went,
> when I took that challenge up
> And swore that I would go
> and fiddle for the Skull Hill Ghost!"

Oh, aye, that had been a damn fool move—to let those idiots who patronized the tavern where her mother worked goad her into boasting that there wasn't anyone, living or dead, that she couldn't cozen with her fiddling. Too much ale, Rune, and too little sense. And too tender a pride, as well, to let them rub salt in the wound of being the tavern wench's bastard.

"It's midnight, and there's not a sound
up here upon Skull Hill
Then comes a wind that chills my blood
and makes the leaves blow wild"

Not a good word choice, but a change that had to be made—that was one of the giveaway verses.

"And rising up in front of me,
a thing like shrouded Death.
A voice says, 'Give me reason why
I shouldn't kill you, child.'"

Holy Three, that thing had been ghastly; cold and old and totally heartless; it had smelled of Death and the grave, and had shaken her right down to her toenails. She made the fiddle sing about what words alone could never convey, and saw her audience of one actually shiver.

The next verse described Rune's answer to the spirit, and the fiddle wailed of fear and determination and things that didn't rightly belong on earth. Then came the description of that night-long, lightless ordeal she'd passed through, and the fiddle shook with the weariness she'd felt, playing the whole night long, and the tune rose with dawning triumph when the thing not only didn't kill her outright, but began to warm to the music she'd made. Now she had an audience of more than one, though she was only half-aware of the fact.

"At last the dawnlight strikes my eyes;
I stop, and see the sun.
The light begins to chase away
the dark and midnight cold—
And then the light strikes something more—
I stare in dumb surprise—
For where the ghost had stood
there is a heap of shining gold!"

The fiddle laughed at Death cheated, thumbed its nose at spirits, and chortled over the revelation that even the dead could be impressed and forced to reward courage and talent.

Rune stopped, and shook back brown locks dark with sweat, and looked about her in astonishment at the applauding patrons of the cook-tent. She was even more astonished when they began to toss coppers in her open fiddlecase, and the cook-tent's owner brought her over a full pitcher of juice and a second pie.

"I'd'a brought ye wine, laddie, but Master Talaysen there says ye go to trials and mustna be a-muddled," she whispered as she hurried back to her counter.

"I hadn't meant—"

"Surely this isn't the first time you've played for your supper, child?" the minstrel's eyes were full of amused irony.

"Well, no, but—"

"So take your well-earned reward and don't go arguing with folk who have a bit of copper to fling at you, and who recognize the Gift when they hear it. No mistake, youngling, you *have* the Gift. And sit and eat; you've more bones than flesh. A good tale, that."

"Well," Rune blushed, "I did exaggerate a bit at the end. 'Twasn't gold, it was silver. But silver won't rhyme. And it was that silver that got me here—bought me my second instrument, paid for lessoning, kept me fed while I was learning. I'd be just another tavern-musician, otherwise—"

"Like me, you are too polite to say?" the minstrel smiled, then the smile faded. "There are worse things, child, than to be a free musician. I don't think there's much doubt your Gift will get you past the trials—but you might not find the Guild to be all you think it to be."

Rune shook her head stubbornly, wondering briefly why she'd told this stranger so much, and why she so badly wanted his good opinion. "Only a Guild Minstrel would be able to earn a place in a noble's train. Only a Guild Bard would have the chance to sing for royalty. I'm sorry to contradict you, sir, but I've had my taste of wandering, singing my songs out only to know they'll be forgotten in the next drink, wondering where my next meal is coming from. I'll never get a secure life except through the Guild, and I'll never see my songs live beyond me without their patronage."

He sighed. "I hope you never regret your decision, child. But if you should—or if you need help, ever—well, just ask for Talaysen. I'll stand your friend."

With those surprising words, he rose soundlessly, as gracefully as a bird in flight, and slipped out of the tent. Just before he passed out of sight among the press of people, Rune saw him pull his lute around and begin to strum it. She managed to hear the first few notes of a love-song, the words rising golden and glorious from his throat, before the crowd hid him from view and the babble of voices obscured the music.

Rune was waiting impatiently outside the Guild tent the next morning, long before there was anyone there to take her name for the trials. It was, as the Fair-ward had said, hard to miss; purple in the main, with pennons and edgings of silver and gilt. Almost—*too* much; almost gaudy. She was joined shortly by three more striplings, one well-dressed and confident, two sweating and nervous. More trickled in as the sun rose higher, until there was a line of twenty or thirty waiting when the Guild Registrar, an old and sour-looking scribe, raised the tent-flap to let them file inside. He wasn't wearing Guild colors, but rather a robe of dusty brown velvet; a hireling therefore.

He took his time, sharpening his quill until Rune was ready to scream with impatience, before looking her up and down and asking her name.

"Rune, child of Lista Jesaril, tavernkeeper." That sounded a trifle better than her mother's *real* position, serving wench.

"From whence?"

"Karthar, East and North—below Galzar Pass."

"Primary instrument?"

"Fiddle."

"Secondary?"

"Lute."

He raised an eyebrow; the usual order was lute, primary; fiddle, secondary. For that matter, fiddle wasn't all that common even as a secondary instrument.

"And you will perform—?"

"First day, primary, 'Lament Of The Maiden Esme.' Second day, secondary, 'The Unkind Lover.' Third day, original, 'The Skull Hill Ghost.' " An awful title, but she could hardly use the *real* name of "Fiddler Girl." "Accompanied on primary, fiddle."

"Take your place."

She sat on the backless wooden bench trying to keep herself calm. Before her was the raised wooden platform on which they would all perform; to either side of it were the backless benches like the one she warmed, for the aspirants to the Guild. The back of the tent made the third side, and the fourth faced the row of well-padded chairs for the Guild Judges. Although she was first here, it was inevitable that they would let others have the preferred first few slots; there would be those with fathers already in the Guild, or those who had coins for bribes. Still, she shouldn't have to wait too long—rising with the dawn would give her that much of an edge, at least.

She got to play by midmorning. The "Lament" was perfect for fiddle, the words were simple and few, and the wailing melody gave her lots of scope for improvisation. The row of Guild Judges, solemn in their tunics or robes of purple, white silk shirts trimmed with gold or silver ribbon depending on whether they were Minstrels or Bards, were a formidable audience. Their faces were much alike: well-fed and very conscious of their own importance; you could see it in their eyes. As they sat below the platform and took unobtrusive notes, they seemed at least mildly impressed. Even more heartening, several of the boys yet to perform looked satisfyingly worried when she'd finished.

She packed up her fiddle and betook herself briskly out—to find herself a corner of Temple Wall to lean against as her knees sagged when the excitement that had sustained her wore off. It was several long moments before she could get her legs to bear her weight and her hands to stop shaking. It was then that she realized that she hadn't eaten since the night before—and that she was suddenly ravenous. Before she'd played, the very thought of food had been revolting.

The same cookshop tent as before seemed like a reasonable

proposition. She paid for her breakfast with some of the windfall-coppers of the night before; this morning the tent was crowded and she was lucky to get a scant corner of a bench to herself. She ate hurriedly and joined the strollers through the Fair.

Once or twice she thought she glimpsed the red hair of Talaysen, but if it was he, he was gone by the time she reached the spot where she had thought he'd been. There were plenty of other street-singers, though. She thought wistfully of the harvest of coin she'd garnered the night before as she noted that none of them seemed to be lacking for patronage. But now that she was a duly registered entrant in the trials, it would be going against custom, if not the rules, to set herself up among them.

So instead she strolled, and listened, and made mental notes for further songs. There was many a tale she overheard that would have worked well in song-form; many a glimpse of silk-bedecked lady, strangely sad or hectically gay, or velvet-clad lord, sly and foxlike or bold and pompous, that brought snatches of rhyme to mind. By early evening her head was crammed full—and it was time to see how the Guild had ranked the aspirants of the morning.

The list was posted outside the closed tent-flaps, and Rune wasn't the only one interested in the outcome of the first day's trials. It took a bit of time to work her way in to look, but when she did—

By the Three! There she was, "Rune of Karthar"— listed *third*.

She all but floated back to her riverside tree-roost.

The second day of the trials was worse than the first; the aspirants performed in order, lowest ranking to highest. That meant that Rune had to spend most of the day sitting on the hard wooden bench, clutching the neck of her lute in nervous fingers, listening to contestant after contestant and sure that each one was *much* better on his secondary instrument than she was. She'd only had a year of training on it, after all. Still, the song she'd chosen was picked deliberately to play up her voice and de-emphasize her lute-strumming. It was going to be pretty difficult for any of these others to match her high contralto (a truly cunning imitation of a boy's soprano), since most of them had passed puberty.

At long last her turn came. She swallowed her nervousness as best she could, took the platform, and began.

Privately she thought it was a pretty silly song. Why on earth any man would put up with the things that lady did to him, and all for the sake of a "kiss on her cold, quiet hand" was beyond her. Still, she put all the acting ability she had into it, and was rewarded by a murmur of approval when she'd finished.

"That voice—I've seldom heard one so pure at that late an age!" she overheard as she packed up her instrument. "If he passes the third day—you don't suppose he'd agree to become castrati, do you? I can think of half a dozen courts that would pay red gold to have him."

She smothered a smile—imagine their surprise to discover that it would *not* be necessary to eunuch her to preserve her voice!

She lingered to listen to the last of the entrants, then waited outside for the posting of the results.

She nearly fainted to discover that she'd moved up to second place.

"I told you," said a quiet voice in her ear. "But are you still sure you want to go through with this?"

She whirled, to find the minstrel Talaysen standing behind her, the sunset brightening his hair and the soft shadows on his face making him appear scarcely older than she.

"I'm sure," she replied firmly. "One of the judges said today that he could think of half a dozen courts that would pay red gold to have my voice."

"Bought and sold like so much mutton? Where's the living in that? Caged behind high stone walls and never let out of the sight of m'lord's guards, lest you take a notion to sell your services elsewhere? Is *that* the life you want to lead?"

"Trudging down roads in the pouring cold rain, frightened half to death that you'll take sickness and ruin your voice—maybe for good? Singing with your stomach growling so loud it drowns out the song? Watching some idiot with half your talent being clad in silk and velvet and eating at the high table, while you try and please some brutes of guardsmen in the kitchen in hopes of a few scraps and a corner by the fire?" she countered. "No thank you. I'll take my chances with the Guild. Besides, where else would I be able to *learn?* I've got no more silver to spend on instruments or teaching."

"There are those who would teach you for the love of it—welladay, you've made up your mind. As you will, child," he replied, but his eyes were sad as he turned away and vanished into the crowd again.

Once again she sat the hard bench for most of the day, while those of lesser ranking performed. This time it was a little easier to bear; it was obvious from a great many of these performances that few, if any, of the boys had the Gift to create. By the time it was Rune's turn to perform, she judged that, counting herself and the first-place holder, there could only be five real contestants for the three open Bardic apprentice slots. The rest would be suitable only as Minstrels; singing someone else's songs, unable to compose their own.

She took her place before the critical eyes of the Judges, and began.

She realized with a surge of panic as she finished the first verse that they did *not* approve. While she improvised, she mentally reviewed the verse, trying to determine what it was that had set those slight frowns on the Judicial faces.

Then she realized; *boasting.* Guild Bards simply did not admit to being boastful. Nor did they demean themselves by reacting to the taunts of lesser beings. Oh, Holy Three—

Quickly she improvised a verse on the folly of youth; of how, had she been older and wiser, she'd never have gotten herself into such a predicament. She heaved an invisible sigh of relief as the frowns disappeared.

By the last chorus, they were actually nodding and smiling, and one of them was tapping a finger in time to the tune. She finished with a flourish worthy of a Master, and waited, breathlessly. And they *applauded.* Dropped their dignity and *applauded.*

The performance of the final contestant was an anticlimax.

None of them had left the tent since this last trial began. Instead of a list, the final results would be announced, and they waited in breathless anticipation to hear what they would be. Several of the boys had already approached Rune, offering smiling congratulations on her presumed first-place slot. A hush fell over them all as the chief of the Judges took the platform, a list in his hand.

"First place, and first apprenticeship as Bard—Rune, son of Lista Jesaril of Karthar—"

"Pardon, my lord—" Rune called out clearly, bubbling over with happiness and unable to hold back the secret any longer."—but it's not son—it's *daughter.*"

She had only a split second to take in the rage on their faces before the first staff descended on her head.

They flung her into the dust outside the tent, half-senseless, and her smashed instruments beside her. The passersby avoided even looking at her as she tried to get to her feet, and fell three times. Her right arm dangled uselessly; it hurt so badly that she was certain that it must be broken, but it hadn't hurt half as badly when they'd cracked it as it had when they'd smashed her fiddle; that had broken her heart. All she wanted to do now was to get to the river and throw herself in. With any luck at all, she'd drown.

But she couldn't even manage to stand.

"Gently, lass," firm hands took her and supported her on both sides. "Lady be my witness, if ever I thought they'd have gone this far, I'd never have let you go through with this farce."

She turned her head, trying to see through tears of pain, both of heart and body, with eyes that had sparks dancing before them. The man supporting her on her left she didn't recognize, but the one on the right—

"T-Talaysen?" she faltered.

"I told you I'd help if you needed it, did I not? I think you have more than a little need at the moment—"

"Th-they broke my fiddle, Talaysen. And my lute. They broke them, and they broke my arm."

"Oh, Rune, lass—" There were tears in *his* eyes, and yet he almost seemed to be laughing as well. "If *ever* I doubted you'd the makings of a Bard, you just dispelled those doubts. *First* the fiddle, *then* the lute—and only *then* do you think of your own hurts. Ah, come away lass, come where people can care for such a treasure as you—"

Stumbling through darkness, wrenched with pain, carefully supported and guided on either side, Rune was in no position to judge where or how far they went. After some unknown interval however, she found herself in a many-colored tent, lit with dozens of lanterns, partitioned off with curtains hung on wires that criss-crossed the entire dwelling. Just now most of these were pushed back, and a mixed crowd of men and women greeted their entrance with cries of welcome that turned to dismay at the sight of her condition.

She was pushed down into an improvised bed of soft wool blankets and huge, fat pillows, while a thin, dark girl dressed like a gypsy bathed her cuts and bruises with something that stung, then numbed them, and a gray-bearded man *tsk*'d over her arm, prodded it once or twice, then, without warning, pulled it into alignment. When he did that, the pain was so incredible that Rune nearly fainted.

By the time the multi-colored fire-flashing cleared from her eyes, he was binding her arm up tightly with thin strips of wood, while the girl was urging her to drink something that smelled of herbs and wine.

Before she had a chance to panic, Talaysen reappeared as if conjured at her side.

"Where—"

"You're with the Free Bards—the *real* Bards, not those pompous pufftoads with the Guild," he said. "Dear child, I thought that all that would happen to you was that those inflated bladders of self-importance would give you a tongue-lashing and throw you out on your backside. If I'd had the slightest notion that they'd do *this* to you, I'd have kidnapped you away and had you drunk insensible till the trials were over. I may never forgive myself. Now, drink your medicine."

"But how—why—who *are* you?" Rune managed between gulps.

" 'What are you?' I think might be the better place to start. Tell her, will you, Erdric?"

"We're the Free Bards," said the gray-bearded man. "As Master Talaysen told you—he's the one who banded us together, when he found that there were those who, like himself, had the Gift and the Talent but were disinclined to put up with the self-aggrandizement and politics and foolish slavishness to form of Guild nonsense. We go where we wish and serve—or not serve—who we will, and sing as we damn well please and no foolishness about who'll be offended. We also keep a sharp eye out for youngsters like you, with the Gift, and with the spirit to fight the Guild. We've had our eye on you these three years now."

"You—but how?"

"Myself, for one," said a new voice, and a bony fellow with hair that kept falling into his eyes joined the group around her. "You likely don't remember me, but I remember you—I heard you fiddle in your tavern when I was passing through Karthar, and I passed the word."

"And I'm another." This one, Rune recognized; he was the man that sold her her lute, who had seemed to have been a gypsy peddler selling new and used instruments. He had also unaccountably stayed long enough to teach her the rudiments of playing it.

"You see, we keep an eye out for all the likely lads and lasses we've marked, knowing that soon or late, they'd come to the trials. Usually, though, they're not so stubborn as you." Talaysen smiled.

"I should hope to live!" the lanky fellow agreed. "They made the same remark my first day about wanting to have me stay a liltin' soprano the rest of me days. That was enough for me!"

"And they wouldn't even give *me* the same notice they'd have given a flea," the dark girl laughed. "Though I hadn't the wit to think of passing myself off as a boy for the trials."

"But—why are you—together?" Rune asked, bewildered.

"We band together to give each other help; a spot of silver to tide you over an empty month, a place to go when you're hurt or ill, someone to care for you when you're not as young as you used to be," the gray-haired Erdric said. "And to teach, and to learn. And we have more and better patronage than you, or even the Guild suspect; not everyone finds the precious style of the Guild songsters to their taste, especially the farther you get from the large cities. Out in the countryside, away from the decadence of courts, they like their songs, like their food, substantial and heartening."

"But why does the Guild let you get away with this, if you're taking patronage from them?" Rune's apprehension, given her recent treatment, was real and understandable.

"Bless you, child, they couldn't do without us!" Talaysen laughed. "No matter what you think, there isn't an original, creative Master among 'em! Gwena, my heart, sing her 'The Unkind Lover'—your version, I mean, the real and original."

Gwena, the dark girl, flashed dazzling white teeth in a vulpine grin, plucked a gittern from somewhere behind her, and began.

Well, it was the same melody that Rune had sung, and some of the words—the best phrases—were the same as well. But this was no ice-cold princess taunting her poor knightly admirerer with what he'd never touch; no, this was a teasing shepherdess seeing how far she could harass her cowherd lover, and the teasing was kindly meant. And what the cowherd claimed at the end was a good deal more than a "kiss on her cold, quiet hand." In fact, you might say with justice that the proceedings got downright heated!

"That 'Lament' you did the first day's another song they've twisted and tormented; most of the popular ballads the Guild touts as their own are ours," Talaysen told her with a grin.

"As you should know, seeing as you've written at least half of them!" Gwena snorted.

"But what would you have done if they had accepted me anyway?" Rune wanted to know.

"Oh, you wouldn't have lasted long; can a caged thrush sing? Soon or late, you'd have done what I did—escaped your gilded cage, and we'd have been waiting."

"Then, *you* were a Guild Bard?" Somehow she felt she'd known that all along. "But I never hear of one called Talaysen, and if the 'Lament' is yours—"

"Well, I changed my name when I took my freedom. Likely though, you wouldn't recognize it—"

"Oh she wouldn't, you think? Or are you playing mock-modest with us again?" Gwena shook back her abundant black hair. "I'll make it known to you that you're having your bruises tended by Master Bard Merridon, himself."

"Merridon?" Rune's eyes went wide as she stared at the man, who coughed, deprecatingly. "But—but—I thought Master Merridon was supposed to have gone into seclusion—"

"The Guild would hardly want it known that their pride had rejected 'em for a pack of gypsy jonglers, now would they?" the lanky fellow pointed out.

"So, can I tempt you to join with us, Rune, lass?" the man she'd known as Talaysen asked gently.

"I'd like—but I can't," she replied despairingly. "How could I keep myself? It'll take months for my arm to heal. And—my instruments are splinters, anyway." She shook her head, tears in her eyes. "They weren't much, but they were all I had. I'll have to go home; they'll take me in the tavern. I can still turn a spit and fill a glass one-handed."

"Ah lass, didn't you hear Erdric? We take care of each other— we'll care for you till you're whole again—" The old man patted her shoulder, then hastily found her a rag when scanning their faces brought her belief—and tears.

"As for the instruments—" Talaysen vanished and returned again as her sobs quieted, "—I'll admit to relief at your words. I was half-afraid you'd a real attachment to your poor, departed friends. 'They're splinters, and I loved them' can't be mended, but 'They're splinters and they were all I had' is a different tune altogether. What think you of these twain?"

The fiddle and lute he laid in her lap weren't new, nor were they the kind of gilded, carved and ornamented dainties Guild musicians boasted, but they held their own kind of quiet beauty, a beauty of mellow wood and clean lines. Rune plucked a string on each, experimentally, and burst into tears again. The tone was lovely, smooth and golden, and these were the kind of instruments she'd never dreamed of touching, much less owning.

When the tears had been soothed away, the various medicines been applied both internally and externally, and introductions made all around, Rune found herself once again alone with Talaysen—or Merridon, though on reflection, she liked the name she'd first known him by better. The rest had drawn curtains on their wires close in about her little corner, making an alcove of privacy. "If you'll let me join you—" she said, shyly.

"Let!" he laughed. "Haven't we made it plain enough we've been trying to lure you like coney-catchers? Oh, you're one of us, Rune, lass. You'll not escape us now!"

"Then—what am I supposed to do?"

"You heal, that's the first thing. The second, well, we don't have formal apprenticeships amongst us. By the Three, there's no few things you could serve as Master in, and no question about it! You could teach most of us a bit about fiddling, for one—"

"But—" she looked and felt dismayed, "—one of the reasons I wanted to join the Guild was to *learn!* I can't read nor write music; there's so many instruments I can't play—" her voice rose to a soft wail "—how am I going to learn if a Master won't take me as an apprentice?"

"Enough! Enough! No more weeping and wailing, my heart's oversoft as it is!" he said hastily. "If you're going to insist on being an apprentice, I suppose there's nothing for it. Will I do as a Master to you?"

Rune was driven to speechlessness, and could only nod.

"Holy Three, lass, you make a liar out of me, who swore never to take an apprentice! Wait a moment." He vanished around the curtain for a moment, then returned. "Here—" He set down a tiny harp. "This can be played one-handed, and learning the ways of her will keep you too busy to bedew me with any more tears while your arm mends. Treat her gently—she's my own very first instrument, and she deserves respect."

Rune cradled the harp in her good arm, too awe-stricken to reply.

"We'll send someone in the morning for your things, wherever it is you've cached 'em. Lean back there—oh, it's a proper nursemaid I am—" He made her comfortable on her pillows, covering her with blankets and moving her two—no, three—new instruments to a place of safety, but still within sight. He seemed to understand how seeing them made her feel. "We'll find you clothing and the like as well. That sleepy-juice they gave you should have you nodding shortly. Just remember one thing before you doze off. I'm not going to be an easy Master to serve; you won't be spending your days lazing about, you know! Come morning, I'll set you your very first task. You'll teach *me*—" his eyes lighted with unfeigned eagerness "—that ghost-song!"

Not long after I was accepted into the Magic in Ithkar *anthology,* the late Robert Adams who was the co-editor asked me to participate in his Friends of the Horseclans *anthologies as well. I was happy to, since I liked Robert a great deal, and this was the result, which appeared in Volume Two.*

*Robert was an odd duck; you either liked him and chuckled over his eccentricities, or you passionately hated him. His most popular books, the "Horseclans" series, have not weathered the change in political climate well. For some background, they are set in a distant future following a nuclear war in which (apparently) the U.S. and the Soviet Union both bombed each other back to the Stone Age. The hero of the earliest books is immortal and telepathic, having evidently stood in the right place at the wrong time as one of the nukes hit. He decides to single-handedly bring civilization in the U.S. back up to par, mostly by uniting the remains of the population with the Native Americans who, being on remote reservations, survived intact. The villains of the books are the Greeks, who sustained very little damage, since it seems that none of the greater powers thought they were worth bombing back to the Stone Age. They proceed to flourish and conquer in the tradition of Alexander, eventually moving on to the North American continent. However, thanks to better living through radiation, there are telepathic horses and mutated, large cats in North America, both of which have teamed up with the Horseclans-folk.*

*In those more innocent times, no one raised the objection that all that long-term radiation would probably render the population sterile rather than producing beneficial mutations; the concept of Nuclear Winter hadn't even occurred to anyone. But the possibility of a Third World/First Nuclear War was very real.*

*One of the obsessions of the more devoted of Horseclans fans was to try and figure out just what the real place-names and proper names were of the locations and characters; Robert had some formula by which he took English names and places, distorted and then phonetically respelled them. Some of them I never could figure out.*

*At any rate, it occurred to me that there was another, highly* mobile ethnic group that could have survived Robert's WWIII by being outside the cities; the gypsies, who would have strenuously resisted being absorbed into the Horseclans as they have strenuously resisted being absorbed into every other culture they have come into contact with.

✛══✶✶✶══✛

# The Enemy of My Enemy

## Mercedes Lackey

The fierce heat radiating from the forge was enough to deaden the senses all by itself, never mind the creaking and moaning of the bellows and the steady tap-tapping of Kevin's youngest apprentice out in the yard working at his assigned horseshoe. The stoutly built stone shell was pure hell to work in from May to October; you could open windows and doors to the fullest, but heat soon built up to the point where thought ceased, the mind went numb, and the world narrowed to the task at hand.

But Kevin Floyd was used to it, and he was alive enough to what was going on about him that he sensed someone had entered his smithy, although he dared not interrupt his work to see who it was. This was a commissioned piece—and one that could cost him dearly if he did a less-than-perfect job of completing it. Even under the best of circumstances the tempering of a swordblade was always a touchy bit of business. The threat of his overlord's wrath—and the implied loss of his shop—did not make it less so.

So he dismissed the feeling of eyes on the back of his neck, and went on with the work stolidly. For the moment he would ignore the visitor as he ignored the heat, the noise, and the stink of scorched leather and many long summers' worth of sweat—horse-sweat and man-sweat—that permeated the forge. Only when the blade was safely quenched and lying on the anvil for the next step did he turn to see who his visitor was.

He almost overlooked her entirely, she was so small, and was tucked up so invisibly in the shadowy corner where he kept oddments of harness and a pile of leather scraps. Dark, nearly black eyes peered up shyly at him from under a tangled mop of curling black hair as she perched atop his heap of leather bits, hugging her thin knees to her chest. Kevin didn't recognize her.

That, since he knew every man, woman and child in Northfork by name, was cause for certain alarm.

He made one step toward her. She shrank back into the darkness of the corner, eyes going wide with fright. He sighed. "Kid, I ain't gonna hurt you—"

She looked terrified. Unfortunately, Kevin frequently had that effect on children, much as he liked them. He looked like a red-faced, hairy ogre, and his voice, rough and harsh from years of smoke and shouting over the forge-noise, didn't improve the impression he made. He tried again.

"Where you from, huh? Who's your kin?"

She stared at him, mouth set. He couldn't tell if it was from fear or stubbornness, but was beginning to suspect the latter. So he persisted, and when she made an abortive attempt to flee, shot out an arm to bar her way. He continued to question her, more harshly now, but she just shook her head at him, frantically, and plastered herself against the wall. She was either too scared now to answer, or wouldn't talk out of pure cussedness.

"Jack," he finally shouted in exasperation, calling for his helper, who was around the corner outside the forge, manning the bellows. "Leave it for a minute and c'mere."

A brawny adolescent sauntered in the door from the back, scratching at his mouse-colored hair. "What—" he began.

"Where's this come from?" Kevin demanded. "She ain't one of ours, an' I misdoubt she came with the King."

Jack snorted derision. "King, my left—"

Kevin shared his derision, but cautioned—"When he's here, you call him what he wants. No matter he's King of only about as far as he can see, he's paid for mercs enough to pound you inta the ground like a tent-peg if you make him mad. Or there's worse he could do. What the hell good is my journeyman gonna be with only one hand?"

Jack twisted his face in a grimace of distaste. He looked about as intelligent as a brick wall, but his sleepy blue eyes hid the fact that he missed very little. HRH King Robert the Third of Trihtown had *not* impressed him. "Shit. Ah hell; King, then. Naw, she ain't with his bunch. I reckon that youngun' came with them trader jippos this mornin'. She's got that look."

"What jippos?" Kevin demanded. "Nobody told me about no jippos—"

"Thass cause you was in here, poundin' away at His Highass' sword when they rode in. It's them same bunch as was in Five Point last month. Ain't no wants posted on 'em, so I figgered they was safe to let be for a bit."

"Aw hell—" Kevin glanced at the waiting blade, then at the door, torn by duty and duty. There hadn't been any news about traders from Five Points, and bad news *usually* traveled faster than good— but—dammit, he had responsibility. As the duly appointed Mayor, it was his job to cast his eye over any strangers to Northfork, apprise them of the town laws, see that they knew troublemakers got short shrift. And he knew damn well what Willum Innkeeper would have to say about his dealing with them so tardily as it was—pissant fool kept toadying up to King Robert, trying to get himself appointed Mayor.

*Dammit,* he thought furiously. *I didn't want the damn job, but I'll be sheep-dipped if I'll let that suckass take it away from me with his rumor-mongering and back-stabbing. Hell, I have to go deal with these jippos, and quick, or he'll be on my case again—*

On the other hand, to leave King Robert's sword three-quarters finished—

Fortunately, before he could make up his mind, his dilemma was solved for him.

A thin, wiry man, as dark as the child, appeared almost magically, hardly more than a shadow in the doorway; a man so lean he barely blocked the strong sunlight. He could have been handsome but for the black eyepatch and the ugly keloid scar that marred the right half of his face. For the rest, he was obviously no native of any town in King Robert's territory; he wore soft riding boots, baggy pants of a wild scarlet, embroidered shirt and vest of blue and black, and a scarlet scarf around his neck that matched the pants. Kevin was surprised he hadn't scared every horse in town with an outfit like that.

"Your pardon—" the man said, with so thick an accent that Kevin could hardly understand him "—but I believe something of ours has strayed here, and was too frightened to leave."

Before Kevin could reply, he had turned with the swift suddenness of a lizard and held out his hand to the girl, beckoning her to his side. She flitted to him with the same lithe grace he had displayed, and half-hid behind him. Kevin saw now that she wasn't as young as he'd thought; in late adolescence—it was her slight build and lack of height that had given him the impression that she was a child.

"I sent Chali aseeing where there be the smithy," the man continued, keeping his one eye on Kevin and his arm about the girl's shoulders. "For we were atold to seek the Townman there. And dear she loves the forgework, so she stayed to be awatching. She meant no harm, God's truth."

"Well neither did I," Kevin protested. "I was just trying to ask her some questions, an' she wouldn't answer me. I'm the Mayor here, I gotta know about strangers—"

"Again, your pardon," the man interrupted, "but she *could not* give answers. Chali has been mute for long since—show, mouse—"

At the man's urging the girl lifted the curls away from her left temple to show the unmistakable scar of a hoofmark.

*Aw, hellfire. Big man, Kevin, bullying a little cripple.* Kevin felt about as high as a horseshoe nail. "Shit," he said awkwardly. "Look, I'm sorry—hell, how was *I* to know?"

Now the man smiled, a wide flash of pearly white teeth in his dark face. "You could not. Petro, I am. I lead the Rom."

"Kevin Floyd; I'm Mayor here."

The men shook hands; Kevin noticed that this Petro's grip was as firm as his own. The girl had relaxed noticeably since her clansman's arrival, and now smiled brightly at Kevin, another flash of white against dusky skin. She was dressed much the same as her leader, but in colors far more muted; Kevin was grateful, as he wasn't sure how much more of that screaming scarlet his eyes could take.

He gave the man a quick rundown of the rules; Petro nodded acceptance. "What of your faiths?" he asked, when Kevin had finished. "Are there things we must or must not be adoing? Is there Church about?"

Kevin caught the flash of a gold cross at the man's throat. Well, hey—no wonder he said "Church" like it was poison. A fellow Christer—not like those damn Ehleen priests. This was a simple one-barred cross, not the Ehleen two-barred. "Live and let be" was a Christer's motto; "a godly man converts by example, not words nor force"—which might well be why there were so few of them. Kevin and his family were one of only three Christer families in town, and Christer traders weren't that common, either. "Nothing much," he replied. "King Robert, he didn't go in for religion last I heard. So, what's your business here?"

"We live, what else?" Petro answered matter-of-factly. "We have livestock for trading. Horses, mules, donkeys—also metalwork."

"Don't know as I care for that last," Kevin said dubiously, scratching his sweaty beard.

"Na, na, not ironwork," the trader protested. "Light metals. Copper, brass—ornament, mostly. A few kettles, pans."

"Now *that* sounds a bit more like! Tell you—you got conshos, harness-studs, that kinda thing? You willin' to work a swap for shoein'?"

"The shoes, not the shoeing. Our beasts prefer the hands they know."

"Done." Kevin grinned. He was good enough at tools or weaponwork, but had no talent at ornament, and knew it. He could make good use of a stock of pretty bits for harnesses and the like. Only one frippery could he make, and that was more by accident than anything else. And since these people were fellow Christers and he was short a peace-offering—He usually had one in his apron pocket; he felt around among the horseshoe nails until his hand encountered a shape that wasn't a nail, and pulled it out.

"Here, missy—" he said apologetically. "Little somethin' fer scarin' you."

The girl took the cross made of flawed horseshoe nails into strong, supple fingers, with a flash of delight in her expressive eyes.

"Hah! A generous apology!" Petro grinned. "And you cannot know how well comes the fit."

"How so?"

"It is said of my people, when the Christ was to be killed, His enemies meant to silence Him lest He rouse His followers against them. The evil ones made four nails—the fourth for His heart. But one of the Rom was there, and stole the fourth nail. So God blessed us in gratitude to awander wherever we would."

"Well, hey." Kevin returned the grin, and a thought occurred to him. Ehrik was getting about the right size to learn riding. "Say, you got any ponies, maybe a liddle horse gettin' on an' gentle? I'm lookin' for somethin' like that for m'boy."

The jippo regarded him thoughtfully. "I think, perhaps yes."

"Then you just may see me later on when I finish this."

Chali skipped to keep up with the wiry man as they headed down the dusty street toward the *tsera* of their *kumpania.* The town, of gray wood-and-stone buildings enclosed inside its shaggy log palisade depressed her and made her feel trapped—she was glad to be heading out to where the *kumpania* had made their camp. Her eyes were flashing at Petro with the only laughter she could show. *You did not tell him the rest of the tale, Elder Brother,* she mindspoke. *The part that tells how the good God then granted us the right to steal whatever we needed to live.*

"There is such a thing as telling more truth than a man wishes to hear," Petro replied. "Especially to *Gaje.*"

*Huh. But not all Gaje. I have heard a different tale from you every time we come to a new holding. You tell us to always tell the whole of the truth to the Horseclans folk, no matter how bitter.*

"They are not *Gaje*. They are not *o phral*, either, but they are not *Gaje*. I do not know what they are, but one does not lie to them."

*But why the rule? We have not seen Horseclans since before I can remember*, she objected.

"They are like the Wind they call upon—they go where they will. But they have the *dook*. So it is wise to be prepared for meeting them at all times."

I *would like to see them, one day*.

He regarded her out of the corner of his eye. "If I am still *rom baro*, you will be hidden if we meet them. If I am not, I hope you will be wise and hide yourself. They have *dook*, I tell you—and I am not certain that I wish them to know that we also have it."

She nodded, thoughtfully. The Rom had not survived this long by giving away secrets. *Do you think my* dook *is greater than theirs? Or that they would seek me out if they knew of it?*

"It could be. I know they value such gifts greatly. I am not minded to have you stolen from us for the sake of the children you could bear to one of them."

She clasped her hands behind her, eyes looking downward at the dusty, trampled grass as they passed through the open town gate. This was the first time Petro had ever said anything indicating that he thought her a woman and not a child. Most of the *kumpania*, including Petro's wife Sara and their boy Tibo, treated her as an odd mixture of child and *phuri dai*. Granted, she *was* tiny; perhaps the same injury that had taken her voice had kept her small. But she was nearly sixteen winters—and still they reacted to her body as to that of a child's, and to her mind as to that of a *drabarni* of sixty. As she frowned a little, she pondered Petro's words, and concluded they were wise. Very wise. That the Rom possessed *draban* was not a thing to be bandied about. That her own *dook* was as strong as it was should rightly be kept secret as well.

*Yes*, rom baro, I *will do* as *you advise*, she replied.

Although he did not mindspeak her in return, she knew he had heard everything she had told him perfectly well. She had so much *draban* that any human and most beasts could hear her when she chose. Petro could hear and understand her perfectly, for though his mindspeech was not as strong as hers, he would have heard her even had he been mind-deaf.

That he had no strong *dook* was not unusual; among the Rom, since the Evil Days, it was the women that tended to have more *draban* than the men. That was one reason why females had come to enjoy all the freedoms of a man since that time—when his wife could make a man feel every blow, he tended to be less inclined to beat her . . . when his own eyes burned with every tear his daughter shed, he was less inclined to sell her into a marriage with someone she feared or hated.

And when she could blast you with her own pain, she tended to be safe from rape.

As she skipped along beside Petro on the worn ruts that led out of the palisade gate and away from town, she was vaguely aware of every mind about her. She and everyone else in the *kumpania* had known for a very long time that her *dook* was growing stronger every year, perhaps to compensate for her muteness. Even the herd-guard horses, those wise old mares, had been impressed, and it took a great deal to impress *them!*

Petro sighed, rubbing the back of his neck absently, and she could read his surface thoughts easily. *That was an evil day, when ill-luck led us to the settlement of the Chosen. A day that ended with poor Chali senseless—her brother dead, and Chali's parents captured and burned as witches. And every other able-bodied, weapons-handy member of the* kumpania *either wounded or too busy making sure the rest got away alive to avenge the fallen.* She winced as guilt flooded him as always.

*You gave your eye to save me, Elder Brother. That was more than enough.*

"I could have done more. I could have sent others with your mama and papa. I could have taken everyone away from that sty of pigs, that nest of—I will *not* call them Chosen of God. Chosen of *o Beng* perhaps—"

*And* o Beng *claims his own, Elder Brother. Are we not* o phral? *We have more patience than all the* Gaje *in the world. We will see the day when* o Beng *takes them.* Chali was as certain of that as she was of the sun overhead and the grass beside the track.

Petro's only reply was another sigh. He had less faith than she. He changed the subject that was making him increasingly uncomfortable. "So, when you stopped being a frighted *tawnie juva*, did you touch the *qajo*, the Townsman's heart? Should we sell him old Pika for his little son?"

I *think yes. He is* a *good one, for* Gaje. *Pika will like him; also, it is nearly fall, and another winter wandering would be hard on his bones.*

They had made their camp up against a stand of tangled woodland, and a good long way off from the palisaded town. The camp itself could only be seen from the top of the walls, not from the ground. That was the way the Rom liked things—they preferred to be apart from the *Gaje*.

The *tsera* was within shouting distance by now, and Petro sent her off with a pat to her backside. The *vurdon*, those neatly built wooden wagons, were arranged in a precise circle under the wilderness of trees at the edge of the grasslands, with the common fire neatly laid in a pit in the center. Seven wagons, seven families—Chali shared Petro's. Some thirty seven Rom in all—and for all they knew, the last Rom in the world, the only Rom to have survived the Evil Days.

But then, not a great deal had survived the Evil Days. Those trees, for instance, showed signs of having once been a purposeful planting, but so many generations had passed since the Evil Days they were now as wild as any forest.

Chali headed, not for the camp, but for the unpicketed string of horses grazing beyond. She wanted to sound out Pika. If he was willing to stay here, this Mayor Kevin would have his gentle old pony for his son, and cheap at the price. Chali knew Pika would guard any child in his charge with all the care he would give one of his own foals. Pika was a stallion, but Chali would have trusted a tiny baby to his care.

Petro trusted her judgment in matters of finding their horses homes; a few months ago she had allowed him to sell one of their saddlebred stallions and a clutch of mares to mutual satisfaction on the part of horses, Rom, and buyers. Then it had been a series of sales of mules and donkeys to folk who wound up treating them with good sense and more consideration than they gave to their own well-being. And in Five Points she had similarly placed an aging mare Petro had raised from a filly, and when Chali had helped the *rom baro* strain his meager *dook* to bid her farewell, Lisa had been nearly incoherent with gratitude for the fine stable, the good feeding, the easy work.

Horses were bred into Chali's blood, for like the rest of this *kumpania,* she was of the *Lowara natsiyi*—and the Lowara were the Horsedealers. Mostly, anyway, though there had been some Kalderash, or Coppersmiths, among them in the first years. By now the Kalderash blood was spread thinly through the whole *kumpania.* Once or twice in each generation there were artificers, but most of *rom baro* Petro's people danced to Lowara music.

She called to Pika without even thinking his name, and the middle-aged pony separated himself from a knot of his friends and ambled to her side. He rubbed his chestnut nose against her vest and tickled her cheek with his whiskers. His thoughts were full of the hope of apples.

*No apples, greedy pig! Do you like this place? Would you want to stay?*

He stopped teasing her and stood considering, breeze blowing wisps of mane and forelock into his eyes and sunlight picking out the white hairs on his nose. She scratched behind his ears, letting him take his own time about it.

*The grass is good,* he said, finally. *The* Gaje *horses are not ill-treated. And my bones ache on cold winter mornings, lately. A warm stable would be pleasant.*

*The blacksmith has a small son*—she let him see the picture she had stolen from the *qajo's* mind, of a blond-haired, sturdily built bundle of energy. *The gajo seems kind.*

*The horses here like him,* came the surprising answer. *He fits the shoe to the hoof, not the hoof to the shoe. I think I will stay. Do not sell me cheaply.*

If Chali could have laughed aloud, she would have. Pika had been Romano's in the rearing—and he shared more than a little with that canny trader. *I will tell Romano—not that I need to. And don't forget, prala, if you are unhappy—*

*Ha!* the pony snorted with contempt. *If I am unhappy, I shall not leave so much as a hair behind me!*

Chali fished a breadcrust out of her pocket and gave it to him, then strolled in the direction of Romano's *vurdon.* When this *kumpania* had found itself gifted with *dook,* with more *draban* than they ever dreamed existed, it had not surprised them that they could speak with their horses; Lowara Rom had practically been able to do that before. But *draban* had granted them advantages they had never *dared* hope for—

Lowara had been good at horsestealing; now only the Horseclans could better them at it. All they needed to do was to sell one of their four-legged brothers into the hands of the one they wished to . . . relieve of the burdens of wealth. All the Lowara horses knew how to lift latches, unbar gates, or find the weak spot in any fence. And Lowara horses were as glib at persuasion as any of their two-legged friends. Ninety-nine times out of a hundred, the Lowara would return to the *kumpania* trailing a string of converts.

And if the *kumpania* came across horses that *were* being mistreated . . .

Chali's jaw tightened. That was what had set the Chosen at their throats.

She remembered that day and night, remembered it far too well. Remembered the pain of the galled beasts that had nearly driven her insane; remembered how she and Toby had gone to act as decoys while her mother and father freed the animals from their stifling barn.

Remembered the anger and fear, the terror in the night, and the madness of the poor horse that had been literally goaded into running her and Toby down.

It was just as well that she had been comatose when the "Chosen of God" had burned her parents at the stake—*that* might well have driven her completely mad.

That anger made her sight mist with red, and she fought it down, lest she broadcast it to the herd. When she had it under control again, she scuffed her way slowly through the dusty, flattened grass, willing it out of her and into the ground. She was so intent on controlling herself that it was not until she had come within touching distance of Romano's brightly painted *vurdon* that she dared to look up from the earth.

Romano had an audience of children, all gathered about him where he sat on the tail of his wooden wagon. She tucked up against the worn side of it, and waited in the shade without drawing attention to herself, for he was telling them the story of the Evil Days.

"So old Simza, the *drabarni,* she spoke to the *rom baro* of her fear, and a little of what she had seen. Giorgi was her son, and he had *dook* enough that he believed her."

"Why shouldn't he have believed her?" tiny Ami wanted to know.

"Because in those days *draban* was weak, and even the *o phral* did not always believe in it. We were different, even among Rom. We were one of the smallest and least of *kumpania* then; one of the last to leave the old ways—perhaps that is why Simza saw what she saw. Perhaps the steel carriages the Rom had taken to, and the stone buildings they lived in, would not let *draban* through."

"Steel carriages? *Rom chal,* how would such a thing move? What horse could pull it?" That was Tomy, skeptical as always.

"I do not know—I only know that the memories were passed from Simza to Yanni, to Tibo, to Melalo, and so on down to me. If you would see, look."

As he had to Chali when she was small, as he did to every child, Romano the Storyteller opened his mind to the children, and they saw, with their *dook,* the dim visions of what had been. And wondered.

"Well, though there were those who laughed at him, and others of his own *kumpania* that left to join those who would keep to the cities of the *Gaje,* there were enough of them convinced to hold to the *kumpania.* They gave over their *Gaje* ways and returned to the old wooden *vurdon,* pulled by horses, practicing their old trades of horsebreeding and metal work, staying strictly away from the cities. And the irony is that it was the *Gaje* who made this possible, for they had become mad with fascination for the ancient days and had begun creating festivals that the Yanfi *kumpania* followed about."

Again came the dim sights—half-remembered music, laughter, people in wilder garments than ever the Rom sported.

"Like now?" asked one of the girls. "Like markets and trade-days?"

"No, not like now; these were special things, just for amusement, not really for trade. I am not certain I understand it; they were all a little mad in those times. Well, then the Evil Days came . . ."

Fire, and red death; thunder and fear—more people than Chali had ever seen alive, fleeing mindlessly the wreckage of their cities and their lives.

"But the *kumpania* was safely traveling out in the countryside, with nothing needed that they could not make themselves. Some others of the Rom remembered us and lived to reach us; Kalderash, mostly."

"And we were safe from *Gaje* and their mad ways?"

"When have the Rom ever been safe?" he scoffed. "No, if anything, we were in more danger yet. The *Gaje* wanted our horses, our *vurdon,* and *Gaje* law was not there to protect us. And there was disease, terrible disease that killed more folk than the Night of Fire had. One sickly *gajo* could have killed us all. No, we hid at first, traveling only by night and keeping off the roads, living where man had fled or died out."

These memories were clearer, perhaps because they were so much closer to the way the *kumpania* lived now. Hard years, though, and fear-filled—until the Rom learned again the weapons they had forgotten. The bow. The knife. And learned to use weapons they had never known like the sharp hooves of their four-legged brothers.

"We lived that way until the old weapons were all exhausted. Then it was safe to travel openly, and to trade; we began traveling as we do now—and now life is easier. For true God made the *Gaje* to live so that we might borrow from them what we need. And that is the tale."

Chali watched with her *dook* as Romano reached out with his mind to all the children seated about him; and found what he had been looking for. Chali felt his exultation; of all the children to whom Romano had given his memories and his stories, there was one in whose mind the memories were still as clear as they were when they had come from Romano's. Tomy had the *draban* of the Storyteller; Romano had found his successor.

Chali decided that it was wiser not to disturb them for now, and slipped away so quietly that they never knew she had been there.

The scout for Clan Skaht slipped into the encampment with the evening breeze and went straight to the gathering about Chief's fire. His prairiecat had long since reported their impending arrival, so the raidleaders had had ample time to gather to hear him.

"Well, I have good news and bad news," Daiv Mahrtun of Skaht announced, sinking wearily to the bare earth across the fire from his Chief. "The good news is that these Dirtmen look lazy and ripe for the picking—the bad news is that they've got traders with 'em, so the peace-banners are up. And I mean to tell you, they're the weirdest damn traders I ever saw. Darker than any Ehleenee—dress like no clan I know—and—" He stopped, not certain of how much more he wanted to say—and if he'd be believed.

Tohnee Skaht snorted in disgust, and spat into the fire. "Dammit anyway—if we break trade-peace—"

"Word spreads fast," agreed his cousin Jahn. "We may have trouble getting other traders to deal with us if we mount a raid while this lot's got the peace-banners up."

There were nearly a dozen clustered about the firepit; men and a pair of women, old and young—but all of them were seasoned raiders, regardless of age. And all of them were profoundly disappointed by the results of Daiv's scouting foray.

"Which traders?" Tohnee asked after a long moment of thought. "Anybody mention a name or a clan you recognized?"

Daiv shook his head emphatically. "I tell you, they're not like any lot I've ever seen *or* heard tell of. They got painted wagons, and they ain't the big tradewagons; more, they got whole families, not just the menfolk—and they're Horsetraders."

Tohnee's head snapped up. "Horse—"

"Before you ask, I mindspoke their horses." This was a perfect opening for the most disturbing of Daiv's discoveries. "*This* oughta curl your hair. *The horses wouldn't talk to me.* It wasn't 'cause they couldn't, and it wasn't 'cause they was afraid to. It was like I was maybe an enemy—was surely an outsider, and maybe not to be trusted. Whoever, whatever these folks are, they got the same kind of alliance with their horses as we have with ours. And *that's* plainly strange."

"Wind and sun—dammit Daiv, if I didn't know you, I'd be tempted to call you a liar!" That was Dik Krooguh, whose jaw was hanging loose with total astonishment.

"Do the traders mindspeak?" Tohnee asked at nearly the same instant.

"I dunno," Daiv replied, shaking his head, "I didn't catch any of 'em at it, but that don't mean much. My guess would be they do, but I can't swear to it."

"I think maybe we need more facts—" interrupted Alis Skaht. "If they've got Horsebrothers, I'd be inclined to say they're not likely to be a danger to us—but we can't count on that. Tohnee?"

"Mm," he nodded. "Question is, how?"

"I took some thought to that," Daiv replied. "How about just mosey in openlike? Dahnah and I could come in like you'd sent us to trade with 'em." Dahnah was Daiv's twin sister; an archer with no peer in the clan, and a strong mindspeaker. "We could hang around for a couple of days without making 'em too suspicious. And a pair of Horseclan kids doin' a little dickerin ain't gonna make the Dirtmen *too* nervous. Not while the peace-banners are up."

Tohnee thought that over a while, as the fire cast weird shadows on his stony face. "You've got the sense to call for help if you end up needing it—and you've got Brighttooth and Stubtail backing you."

The two young prairiecats lounging at Daiv's side purred agreement.

"All right—it sounds a good enough plan to me," Tohnee concluded, while the rest of the sobered clansfolk nodded, slowly. "You two go in at first morning light and see what you can find. And I know I don't need to tell you to be careful, but I'm telling you anyway."

Howard Thomson, son of "King" Robert Thomson, was distinctly angered. His narrow face was flushed, always a bad sign, and he'd been drinking, which was worse. When Howard drank, he thought he owned the world. Trouble was, he was almost right, at least in this little corner of it. His two swarthy merc-bodyguards were between Kevin and the doors.

*Just what I didn't need,* Kevin thought bleakly, taking care that nothing but respect showed on his face, *a damn-fool touchy idiot with a brat's disposition tryin' to put me between a rock and a hard place.*

"I tell you, my father sent me expressly to fetch him that blade, *boy.*" Howard's face was getting redder by the minute, matching his long, fiery hair. "You'd better hand it over *now,* before you find yourself lacking a hand."

*I'll just bet he sent you,* Kevin growled to himself. *Sure he did. You just decided to help yourself, more like—and leave me to explain to your father where his piece went, while you deny you ever saw me before.*

But his outwardly cool expression didn't change as he replied, stolidly, "Your pardon, but His Highness gave *me* orders that I was to put it into no one's hands but his. And he hasn't sent me written word telling me any different."

Howard's face enpurpled as Kevin obliquely reminded him that the Heir *couldn't* read or write. Kevin waited for the inevitable lightning to fall. Better he should get beaten to a pulp than that King Robert's wrath fall on Ehrik and Keegan, which it would if he gave in to Howard. What with Keegan being pregnant—better a beating. He tensed himself and waited for the order.

Except that, just at the moment when Howard was actually beginning to splutter orders to his two merc-bodyguards to take the blacksmith apart, salvation, in the form of Petro and a half-dozen strapping jippos came strolling through the door to the smithy. They were technically unarmed, but the long knives at their waists were a reminder that this was only a technicality.

"*Sarishan, gajo,*" he said cheerfully. "We have brought you your pony—"

Only then did he seem to notice the Heir and his two bodyguards.

"Why, what is this?" he asked with obviously feigned surprise. "Do we interrupt some business?"

Howard growled something obscene—if he started something *now* he would be breaking trade-peace, and no trader would deal with him *or* his family again without an extortionate bond being posted. For one moment Kevin feared that his temper might get the better of him anyway, but then the young man pushed past the jippos at the door and stalked into the street, leaving his bodyguards to follow as they would.

Kevin sagged against his cold forge, only now breaking into a sweat. "By all that's holy, man," he told Petro earnestly, "your timing couldn't have been better! You saved me from a beatin', and that's for damn sure!"

"Something more than a beating," the jippo replied, slowly, "— or I misread that one. I do not think we will sell any of our beasts *there*, no. But—" he grinned suddenly "—we lied, I fear. We did not bring the pony—we brought our other wares."

"You needed six men to carry a bit of copperwork?" Kevin asked incredulously, firmly telling himself that he would *not* begin laughing hysterically out of relief.

"Oh no—but I was *not* of a mind to carry back horseshoes for every beast in our herd by myself! I am *rom baro*, not a packmule!"

Kevin began laughing after all, laughing until his sides hurt.

Out of gratitude for their timely appearance, he let them drive a harder bargain with him than he normally would have allowed, trading shoes and nails for their whole equippage for about three pounds of brass and copper trinkets and a set of copper pots he knew Keegan would lust after the moment she saw them. And a very pretty little set of copper jewelry to brighten her spirit; she was beginning to show, and subject to bouts of depression in which she was certain her pregnancy made her ugly in his eyes. This bit of frippery might help remind her that she was anything but. He agreed to come by and look at the pony as soon as he finished a delivery of his own. He was going to take no chances on Howard's return; he was going to deliver that sword himself, now, and straight into Robert's palsied hands!

"So if that one comes, see that he gets no beast nor thing of ours,"

Petro concluded. "Chali, you speak to the horses. Most like, he will want the king stallion, if any."

Chali nodded. *We could say Bakro is none* of *ours—that he's* a *wild one that follows our mares.*

Petro grinned approval. "Ha, a good idea! That way nothing of blame comes on us. For the rest—we wish to leave only Pika, is that not so?" The others gathered about him in the shade of his *vurdon* murmured agreement. They had done well enough with their copper and brass jewelry, ornaments and pots and with the odd hen or vegetable or sack of grain that had found a mysterious way into a Rom kettle or a *vurdon.*

"Well then, let us see what we can do to make them unattractive."

Within the half-hour the Rom horses, mules and donkeys little resembled the sleek beasts that had come to the call of their two-legged allies. Coats were dirty, with patches that looked suspiciously like mange; hocks were poulticed, and looked swollen; several of the wise old mares were ostentatiously practicing their limps, and there wasn't a hide of an attractive color among them.

And anyone touching them would be kicked at, or *nearly* bitten—the horses were not minded to have their two-legged brothers punished for *their* actions. Narrowed eyes and laid-back ears gave the lie to the hilarity within. No one really knowledgeable about horses would want to come near this lot.

And just in time, for Howard Thomson rode into the camp on an oversized, dun-colored dullard of a gelding only a few moments after the tools of their deceptions had been cleaned up and put away. Chali briefly touched the beast's mind to see if it was being mistreated, only to find it nearly as stupid as one of the mongrels that infested the village.

He surveyed the copper trinkets with scorn, and the sorry herd of horses with disdain. Then his eye lit upon the king stallion.

"You there—trader—" he waved his hand at the proud bay stallion, who looked back at this arrogant two-legs with the same disdain. "How much for that beast there?"

"The noble prince must forgive us," Petro fawned, while Chali was glad, for once, of her muteness; she did not have to choke on her giggles as some of the others were doing. "But that one is none of ours. He is a wild one; he follows our mares, which we permit in hopes of foals like him."

"Out of nags like *those?* You hope for a miracle, man!" Howard laughed, as close to being in good humor as Petro had yet seen him. "Well, since he's none of yours, you won't mind if my men take him—"

Hours later, their beasts were ready to founder, the king stallion was still frisking like a colt, and none of them had come any closer to roping him than they had been when they started. The Rom were nearly bursting, trying to contain their laughter, and Howard was purple again.

Finally he called off the futile hunt, wrenched at the head of his foolish gelding, and spurred it back down the road to town . . .

And the suppressed laughter died, as little Ami's youngest brother toddled into the path of the lumbering monster—and Howard grinned and spurred the gelding at him—hard.

Kevin was nearly to the trader's camp when he saw the baby wander into the path of Howard's horse—and his heart nearly stopped when he saw the look on the Heir's face as he dug his spurs savagely into his gelding's flanks.

The smith didn't even think—he just *moved*. He frequently fooled folk into thinking he was slow and clumsy because of his size; now he threw himself at the child with every bit of speed and agility he possessed.

He snatched the toddler, curled protectively around it, and turned his dive into a frantic roll. As if everything had been slowed by a magic spell, he saw the horse charging at him and every move horse and rider made. Howard sawed savagely at the gelding's mouth, trying to keep it on the path. But the gelding shied despite the bite of the bit; foam-flecks showered from its lips, and the foam was spotted with blood at the corners of its mouth. It half-reared, and managed to avoid the smith and his precious burden by a hair—one hoof barely scraped Kevin's leg—then the beast was past, thundering wildly toward town.

****

Kevin didn't get back home until after dark—and he was not entirely steady on his feet. The stuff the Rom drank was a bit more potent than the beer and wine from the tavern, or even his own home-brew. Pacing along beside him, lending a supporting shoulder and triumphantly groomed to within an inch of his life and adorned with red ribbons, was the pony, Pika.

Pika was a gift—Romano wouldn't accept a single clipped coin for him. Kevin was on a first-name basis with all of the Rom now, even had a mastered a bit of their tongue. Not surprising, that— seeing as they'd sworn brotherhood with him.

He'd eaten and drunk with them, heard their tales, listened to their wild, blood-stirring music—felt as if he'd come home for the first time. Rom, that was what they called themselves, not "jippos"— and "o phral," which meant "the people," sort of. They danced for him—and he didn't wonder that they wouldn't sing or dance before outsiders. It would be far too easy for dullard *gajo* to get the wrong idea from some of those dances—the women and girls danced with the freedom of the wind and the wildness of the storm—and to too many men, "wild" and "free" meant "loose." Kevin had just been entranced by a way of life he'd never dreamed existed.

Pika rolled a not-unsympathetic eye at him as he stumbled, and leaned in a little closer to him. Funny about the Rom and their horses—you'd swear they could read each other's minds. They had an affinity that was bordering on witchcraft—

Like that poor little mute child, Chali. Kevin had seen with his own eyes how wild the maverick stallion had been—at least when Howard and his men had been chasing it. But he'd also seen Chali walk up to him, pull his forelock, and hop aboard his bare back as if he were no more than a gentle, middle-aged pony like Pika. And then watched the two of them pull some trick riding stunts that damn near pulled the eyes out of his sockets. It was riding he'd remember for a long time, and he was right glad he'd seen it. But he devoutly hoped Howard hadn't.

Howard hadn't but one of his men had.

****

Daiv and Dahnah rode up to the trader's camp in the early morning, leaving Brighttooth and Stubtail behind them as eyes to the rear. The camp appeared little different from any other they'd seen— at first glance. Then you noticed that the wagons were small, shaped almost like little houses on wheels, and painted like rainbows. They were almost distracting enough to keep you from noticing that there wasn't a beast around the encampment, not donkey nor horse, that was hobbled or picketed.

*I almost didn't believe you, Daivie,* his sister said into his mind, wonderingly.

His mare snorted; so did he. *Huh. Thanks a lot, sis. You catch any broad-beaming?*

She shook her head, almost imperceptibly, as her mount shifted a little. *Not so much as a stray thought*—her own thought faded for a moment, and she bit her lip. *Now that I think of it, that's damned odd. These people are buttoned up as tight as a yurt in a windstorm.*

*Which means what?* He signaled Windstorm to move up beside Snowdancer.

*Either they're naturally shielded as well as the best mindspeaker I ever met, or they do have the gift. And the first is about as likely as Brighttooth sitting down to dinner with an Ehleenee priest.*

*Only if the priest was my dinner, sister,* came the mischievous reply from the grassland behind them. With the reply came the mock disgust and nausea from Stubtail that his littermate would even *contemplate* such a notion as eating vile-tasting Ehleenee flesh.

*So where does that leave us?* Daiv asked.

*We go in, do a little dickering, and see if we can eavesdrop. And I'll see if I can get any more out of the horses that you did.*

*Fat chance!* he replied scornfully, but followed in the wake of her mare as she urged her into the camp itself.

The fire on the hearth that was the only source of light in Howard's room crackled. Howard lounged in his thronelike chair in the room's center. His back was to the fire, which made him little more than a dark blot to a petitioner, and cast all the available light on a petitioner's face.

Howard eyed the lanky tavernkeeper who was now kneeling before him with intense speculation. "You say the smith's been consorting with the heathen traders?"

"More than traders, m'lord," Willum replied humbly. "For the past two days there's been a brace of horse barbarians with the traders as well. I fear this means no good for the town."

"I knew about the barbarians," Howard replied, leaning back in his padded chair and staring at the flickering shadows on the wall behind Willum thoughtfully. Indeed he did know about the barbarians—twins they were, with hair like a summer sun; he'd spotted the girl riding her beast with careless grace, and his loins had ached ever since.

"I fear he grows far too friendly with them, m'lord. His wife and child spend much of the day at the trader's camp. I think that, unlike those of us who are loyal, he has forgotten where his duties lie."

"And you haven't, I take it?" Howard almost smiled.

"M'lord knows I am but an honest tavernkeeper—"

"And has the honest tavernkeeper informed my father of this possibly treacherous behavior?"

"I tried," Willum replied, his eyes not quite concealing his bitterness. "I have *been* trying for some time now. King Robert will not hear a word against the man."

"King Robert is a senile old fool!" Howard snapped viciously, jerking upright where he sat so that the chair rocked and Willum sat back on his heels in startlement. "King Robert is far too readily distracted by pretty toys and pliant wenches." His own mouth turned down with a bitterness to equal Willum's—for the talented flame-haired local lovely that had been gracing *his* bed had deserted it last night for his father's. Willum's eyes narrowed, and he crept forward on his knees until he almost touched Howard's leg. "Perhaps," he whispered, so softly that Howard could barely hear him, "it is time for a change of rulers—"

Chali had been banished to the forest as soon as the bright golden heads of the Horseclan twins had been spotted in the grasslands beyond the camp. She was not altogether unhappy with her banishment—she had caught an unwary thought from one of them, and had shivered at the strength of it. Now she did not doubt the *rom baro's* wisdom in hiding her. *Dook* that strong would surely ferret out her own, and she had rather not betray the secret gifts of her people until they knew more about the intent of these two. So into the forest she had gone, with cloak and firestarter and sack of food and necessaries.

Nor was she alone in her exile; Petro had deemed it wiser not to leave temptation within Howard's reach, and sent Bakro, the king stallion, with her. They had decided to explore the woods—and had wandered far from the encampment. To their delight and surprise, they had discovered the remains of an apple orchard deep in the heart of the forest—the place had gone wild and reseeded itself several times over, and the apples themselves were far smaller than those from a cultivated orchard, hardly larger than crabapples. But they were still sweet—and most of them were ripe. They both gorged themselves as much as they dared on the crisp, succulent fruits, until night had fallen. Now both were drowsing beneath a tree in Chali's camp, sharing the warmth of her fire, and thinking of nothing in particular—

—when the attack on the Rom *tsera* came.

Chali was awake on the instant, her head ringing with the mental anguish of the injured—and God, oh God, the dying! Bakro wasn't much behind her in picking up the waves of torment. He screamed, a trumpeting of defiance and rage. She grabbed a handful of mane and pulled herself up onto his back without being consciously aware she had done so, and they crashed off into the darkness to the source of that agony.

But the underbrush they had threaded by day was a series of maddening tangles by night; Bakro's headlong dash ended ignominiously in a tangle of vine, and when they extricated themselves from the clawing branches, they found their pace slowed to a fumbling crawl. The slower they went, the more frantic they felt, for it was obvious from what they were being bombarded with that the Rom were fighting a losing battle. And one by one the voices in their heads lost strength. Then faded.

Until finally there was nothing.

They stopped fighting their way through the brush, then, and stood, lost in shock, in the blackness of the midnight forest—utterly, completely alone.

Dawn found Chali on her knees, exhausted, face tear-streaked, hands bruised from where she'd been pounding them on the ground, over and over. Bakro stood over her, trembling; not from fear or sorrow, but from raw, red hatred. *His* herd had survived, though most had been captured by the enemy two-legs. But his two-leg herd—Chali was all he had left.

He wanted *vengeance*—and he wanted it now.

Slowly the hot rage of the stallion penetrated Chali's grief.

*I hear you,* prala, *I do hear you,* she sent slowly, fumbling her way out of the haze of loss that had fogged her mind. *Kill!* the stallion trumpeted with mind and voice. *Kill them all!*

She clutched her hands at her throat, and encountered the thong that held the little iron cross. She pulled it over her head, and stared at it, dully. What good was a God of forgiveness in the light of this slaughter? She cast the cross—and all it implied—from her, violently.

She rose slowly to her feet, and put a restraining hand on the stallion's neck. He ceased his fidgeting and stood absolutely still, a great bay statue.

*We will have revenge,* prala, *I swear it,* she told him, her own hatred burning as high as his, *but we shall have it wisely.*

Kevin was shoved and kicked down the darkened corridor of the King's manorhouse with brutal indifference, smashing up against the hard stone of the walls only to be shoved onward again. His head was near to splitting, and he'd had at least one tooth knocked out, the flat, sweet taste of blood in his mouth seemed somehow unreal.

He was angry, frightened—and bewildered. He'd awakened to distant shouts and screams, run outside to see a red glow in the direction of the Rom camp—then he'd been set upon from behind. Whoever it was that had attacked him clubbed him into apparent submission. Then he had his hands bound behind him—and his control broke; he began fighting again, and was dragged, kicking and

Willum smiled, his eyes cast humbly down. From his vantage point on the floor, Kevin saw the balefire he thought he'd glimpsed leap into a blaze before being quenched. "I always intended to, my lord."

Chali crept in to the remains of the camp in the gray light before dawn and collected what she could. The wagons were charred ruins; there were no bodies. She supposed, with a dull ache in her soul, that the murderers had dragged the bodies off to be looted and burned. She hoped that the *mule* would haunt their killers to the end of their days—

There wasn't much left, a few bits of foodstuff, of clothing, other oddments—certainly not enough to keep her through the winter— but then, she would let the winter take care of itself. She had something more to concern her.

Scrabbling through the burned wood into the secret compartments built into the floor of every *vurdon,* she came up with less of use than she had hoped. She had prayed for weapons. What she mostly found was coin; useless to her.

After searching until the top of the sun was a finger's length above the horizon and dangerously near to betraying her, she gave up the search. She *did* manage to collect a bow and several quivers' worth of arrows—which was what she wanted most. Chali had been one of the best shots in the *kumpania.* Now the *Gaje* would learn to dread her skill.

She began her one-person reign of terror when the gates opened in late morning.

She stood hidden in the trees, obscured by the foliage, but well within bowshot of the gates, an arrow nocked, a second loose in her fingers, and two more in her teeth. The stallion stood motionless at her side. She had managed to convince the creatures of the woods about her that she was nothing to fear—so a blackbird sang within an arm's length of her head, and rabbits and squirrels hopped about in the grass at the verge of the forest, unafraid. Everything looked perfectly normal. The two men opening the gates died with shafts in their throats before anyone realized that there was something distinctly out of the ordinary this morning.

When they *did* realize that there was something wrong, the stupid *Gaje* did exactly the wrong thing; instead of ducking into cover, they ran to the bodies. Chali dropped two more who trotted out to look.

*Then* they realized that they were in danger, and scrambled to close the gates again. She managed to get a fifth before the gates closed fully and the bar on the opposite side dropped with a *thud* that rang across the plain, as they sealed themselves inside.

Now she mounted on Bakro, and arrowed out of cover. Someone on the walls shouted, but she was out of range before they even had time to realize that she was the source of the attack. She clung to Bakro's back with knees clenched tightly around his barrel, pulling two more arrows from the quiver slung at her belt. He ran like the wind itself, past the walls and around to the back postern-gate before anyone could warn the sleepy townsman guarding it that something was amiss.

She got him, too, before someone slammed the postern shut, and picked off three more injudicious enough to poke their heads over the walls.

Now they were sending arrows of their own after her, but they were poor marksmen, and their shafts fell short. She decided that they were bad enough shots that she dared risk retrieving *their* arrows to augment her own before sending Bakro back under the cover of the forest. She snatched at least a dozen sticking up out of the grass where they'd landed, leaning down as Bakro ran, and shook them defiantly at her enemies on the walls as they vanished into the underbrush.

Chali's vengeance had begun.

Kevin was barely conscious; only the support of Pika on one side and Keegan on the other kept him upright. Ehrik was uncharacteristically silent, terribly frightened at the sight of his big, strong father reduced to such a state.

King Howard and his minions had been "generous"; piling as much of the family's goods on the pony's back as he could stand before sending the little group out the gates. In cold fact that had been Willum's work, and it hadn't been done out of kindness; it had been done to make them a more tempting target for the horse barbarians or whatever strange menace it was that now had them hiding behind their stout wooden walls. That much Kevin could remember; and he waited in dull agony for arrows to come at them from out of the forest.

But no arrows came; and the pathetic little group, led by a little boy who was doing his best to be brave, slowly made their way up the road and into the grasslands.

Chali mindspoke Pika and ascertained that the smith had had nothing to do with last night's slaughter—that in fact, he was being cast out for objecting to it. So she let him be—besides, she had other notions in mind.

She couldn't keep them besieged forever—but she could make their lives pure hell with a little work.

She found hornets' nests in the orchard; she smoked the insects into slumberous stupefication, then took the nests down, carefully. With the help of a scrap of netting and two springy young saplings, she soon had an improvised catapult. It wasn't very accurate, but it didn't have to be. All it had to do was get those nests over the palisade.

Which it did.

The howls from within the walls made her smile for the first time that day.

Next she stampeded the village cattle by beaming pure fear into their minds, sending them pounding against the fence of their corral until they broke it down, then continuing to build their fear until they ran headlong into the grasslands. They might come back; they might not. The villagers would have to send men out to get them.

They did—and she killed one and wounded five more before their fire drove her back deeper into the forest.

They brought the cattle inside with them—barely half of the herd she had sent thundering away. That made Chali smile again. With the cattle would come vermin, noise, muck—and perhaps disease.

And she might be able to add madness to that—

*Bakro?* she broadbeamed, unafraid now of being overheard. *Have you found the mind-sick weed yet?*

But to her shock, it was not Bakro who answered her.

Daiv struggled up out of a darkness shot across with lances of red agony. It hurt even to think—and it felt as if every bone in his body had been cracked in at least three places. For a very long time he lay without even attempting to move, trying to assess his real condition and whereabouts through a haze of pain. Opening his eyes did not lessen the darkness, but an exploratory hand to his face told him that although the flesh was puffed and tender, his eyes were probably not damaged. And his nose told him of damp earth. So he was probably being held in a pit of some kind, one with a cover that let in no light. Either that, or it was still dark—

Faint clanks as he moved and his exploring fingers told him that chains encircled his wrists and ankles. He tried to lever himself up into a sitting position, and quickly gave up the idea; his head nearly split in two when he moved it, and the bones of his right arm grated a little.

He started then to mindcall to Dahnah—then he remembered.

Hot, helpless tears burned his eyes; scalded along the raw skin of his face. He didn't care. *Wind—oh Wind.*

For he remembered that Dahnah was dead, killed defending two of the trader's tiny children. And uselessly, for the children had been spitted seconds after she had gone down. She'd taken one of the bastards with her though—and Stubtail had accounted for another before they'd gotten him as well.

But Daiv couldn't remember seeing Brighttooth's body—perhaps the other cat had gotten away!

He husbanded his strength for a wide-beam call, opened his mind—

And heard the stranger.

*Bakro?* came the voice within his mind, strong and clear as any of his kin could send. *Have you found the mind-sick weed yet?*

He was so startled that he didn't think—he just answered. *Who are you?* he beamed. *Please—who are you?*

Chali stood, frozen, when the stranger's mind touched her own—

then shut down the channel between them with a ruthless, and somewhat frightened haste. She kept herself shut down, and worked her way deeper into the concealment of the forest, worming her way into thickets so thick that a rabbit might have had difficulty in getting through. There she sat, curled up in a ball, shivering with reaction.

Until Bakro roused her from her stupor with his own insistent thought.

*I have found the mind-sick weed,* drabarni, *and something else as well.* She still felt dazed and confused. *What,* she replied, raising her head from her knees. And found herself looking into a pair of large, golden eyes.

Kevin had expected that the Horseclan folk would find them, eventually. What he had not expected was that they would be kind to him and his family.

He had a moment of dazed recognition of what and who it was that was approaching them across the waving grass. He pushed himself away from the pony, prepared to die defending his loved ones—

And fell over on his face in a dead faint.

When he woke again he was lying on something soft, staring up at blue sky, and there were two attentive striplings carefully binding up his head. When they saw he was awake, one of them frowned in concentration, and a Horseclan warrior strolled up in the next moment.

"You're damn lucky we found you," he said, speaking slowly so that Kevin could understand him. He spoke Merikan, but with an odd accent, the words slurring and blurring together. "Your mate was about t' fall on her nose, and your little one had heat-sick. Not to mention the shape *you* were in."

Kevin started to open his mouth, but the man shook his head. "Don't bother; what the pony didn't tell us, your mate did." His face darkened with anger. "I knew Dirtmen were rotten—but this! Only one thing she didn't know—there were two of ours with the traders—"

The nightmare confrontation with Howard popped into Kevin's

mind, and he felt himself blanch, fearing that this friendly barbarian would slit his throat the moment he knew the truth.

But the moment the memory surfaced, the man went absolutely rigid; then leapt to his feet, shouting. The camp boiled up like a nest of angry wasps—Kevin tried to rise as his two attendants sprang to *their* feet.

Only to pass into oblivion again.

Chali stared into the eyes of the great cat, mesmerized.

*My brother is within those walls,* the cat said to her, *and I am hurt. You must help us.* True, the cat was hurt; a long cut along one shoulder, more on her flanks.

Chali felt anger stirring within her at the cat's imperious tone. *Why should I help you?* she replied. *Your quarrel is nothing to me!*

The cat licked her injured shoulder a moment, then caught her gaze again. *We have the same enemy,* she said shortly.

Chali pondered that for a moment. *And the enemy of my enemy— is my friend?*

The cat looked at her with approval. *That,* she said, purring despite the pain of her wounds, *is wisdom.*

Daiv had just about decided that the mind-call he'd caught had been a hallucination born of pain, when the stranger touched him again.

He snatched at the tentatively proffered thought-thread with near-desperation. *Who are you?* he gasped. *Please—*

*Gently, brother*—came a weaker mind-voice, joining the first. And that was one he knew!

*Brighttooth!*

*The same.* Her voice strengthened now, and carried an odd other-flavor with it, as if the first was somehow supporting her. *How is it with you?*

He steadied himself, willing his heart to stop pounding. *Not good. They've put chains on my arms and legs; my right arm's broken, I think—where are you? Who's with you?*

*A friend. Two friends. We are going to try and free you. No-Voice says that she is picking up the thoughts of those Dirteaters regarding you, and they are not pleasant.*

He shuddered. He'd had a taste of those thoughts himself, and he rather thought he'd prefer being sent to the Wind.

*We are going to free you, my brother,* Brighttooth continued. *I cannot tell you how, for certain—but it will be soon; probably tonight. Be ready.*

It was well past dark. Chali, aided by Bakro, reached for the mind of Yula, the cleverest mare of the Rom herd. Within a few moments she had a good idea of the general lay of things inside the stockaded village, at least within the mare's line-of-sight—and she knew *exactly* where the Horseclans boy was being kept. They'd put him in an unused grain pit a few feet from the corral where the horses had been put. Yula told Chali that they had all been staying very docile, hoping to put their captors off their guard.

*Well done!* Chali applauded. *Now, are you ready for freedom?*

*More than ready,* came the reply. *Do we free the boy as well?* There was a definite overtone to the mare's mind-voice that hinted at rebellion if Chali answered in the negative.

*Soft heart for hurt colts, hmm, elder sister? Na, we free him. How is your gate fastened?*

Contempt was plain. *One single loop of rawhide! Fools! It is not even a challenqe!*

*Then here is the plan . . . .*

About an hour after full dark, when the nervous guards had begun settling down, the mare ambled up to the villager who'd been set to guard the grain pit.

"Hey old girl," he said, surprised at the pale shape looming up out of the darkness, like a ghost in the moonlight. "How in hell did *you* get . . . . "

He did not see the other, darker shape coming in behind him. The hooves of a second mare lashing into the back of his head ended his sentence and his life.

At nearly the same moment, Brighttooth was going over the back wall of the stockade. She made a run at the stallion standing rock-steady beneath the wall, boosting herself off the scavenged saddle Bakro wore. There was a brief sound of a scuffle; then the cat's thoughts touched Chali's.

*The guard is dead. He tasted awful.*

Chali used Bakro's back as the cat had, and clawed her own way over the palisade. She let herself drop into the dust of the other side, landing as quietly as she could, and searched the immediate area with mind touch.

Nothing and no one.

She slid the bar of the gate back, and let Bakro in, and the two of them headed for the stockade and the grain-pits. The cat was already there.

If it had not been for the cat's superior night-sight, Chali would not have been able to find the latch holding it. The wooden cover of the pit was heavy; Chali barely managed to get it raised. Below her she could see the boy's white face peering up at her, just touched by the moonlight.

*Can you climb?* she asked.

*Hell, no,* he answered ruefully.

*Then I must come down to you.*

She had come prepared for this; there was a coil of scavenged rope on Bakro's saddle. She tied one end of it to the pommel and dropped the other down into the pit, sliding down to land beside the boy.

Once beside him, she made an abrupt reassessment. *Not a boy.* A young man; one who might be rather handsome under the dirt and dried blood and bruises. She tied the rope around his waist as he tried, awkwardly, to help.

From above came an urgent mind-call. *Hurry,* Brighttooth fidgeted. *The guards are due to report and have not. They sense something amiss.*

*We're ready,* she answered shortly. Bakro began backing, slowly. She had her left arm around the young man's waist, holding him steady and guiding him, and held to the rope with the other, while they "walked" up the side of the pit. It was hardly graceful—and Chali was grateful that the pit was not too deep—but at length they reached the top. Her shoulders were screaming in agony, but she let go of him and caught the edge with that hand, then let go of the rope and hung for a perilous moment on the verge before hauling herself up. She wanted to lie there and recover, but there was no time—

*They have found the dead one! Texal o rako lengo gortiano!* she spat. The young man was trying to get himself onto the rim; she grabbed his shoulders while he hissed softly in pain and pulled him up beside her. *What?* he asked, having sensed something.

*No time!* she replied, grabbing his shoulder and shoving him at Bakro. She threw herself into the saddle, and wasted another precious moment while Bakro knelt and she pulled at the young man again, catching him off-balance and forcing him to fall face-down across her saddle-bow like a sack of grain. *NOW, my wise ones! NOW!*

The last was broad-beamed to all the herd—and even as the perimeter guards began shouting their discovery, and torches began flaring all over the town, the Rom horses began their stampede to freedom.

The cat was already ahead of them, clearing the way with teeth and flashing claws; her task was to hold the gate against someone trying to close it. Chali clung to Bakro's back with aching legs—she was having her hands full trying to keep the young man from falling off. He was in mortal agony, every step the stallion took jarring his hurts without mercy, but he was fastened to her leg and stirrup-iron like a leech.

The herd was in full gallop now—sweeping everything and everyone aside. There was only one thing to stop them.

The narrowness of the postern gate—only three horses could squeeze through at any one time. If there was anyone with a bow and good sense, he would have stationed himself there.

Chali heard the first arrow. She felt the second hit her arm. She shuddered with pain, ducked, and spread herself over the body in front of her, trying to protect her passenger from further shots.

Bakro hesitated for a moment, then shouldered aside two mules and a donkey to bully his own way through the gate.

But not before Chali had taken a second wound, and a third, and a fourth.

\*\*\*\*

"I'll say this much for you, Dirtman, you're stubborn." The Horseclan warrior's voice held grudging admiration as it filtered out of the darkness beside Kevin. He had been detailed to ride at the smith's left hand and keep him from falling out of his saddle. He had obviously considered this duty something of an embarrassing ordeal. Evidently he didn't think it was anymore.

Kevin's face was white with pain, and he was nearly blind to everything around him, but he kept his seat. "Don't call me that. I told you—after what they did to my blood-brothers, *I'm not one of them*. I'm with you—all the way. If that means fighting, I'll fight. Those oathbreaking, child-murdering bastards don't deserve anything but a grave. They ain't even human anymore, not by my way of thinking."

That was a long speech for him, made longer still by the fact that he had to gasp bits of it out between flashes of pain. But he meant it, every word—and the Horseclansman took it at face value, simply nodding, slowly.

"I just—" A shout from the forward scout stopped them all dead in their tracks. The full moon was nearly as bright as day—and what it revealed had Kevin's jaw dropping.

It was a mixed herd of horses, mules and donkeys—all bone-weary and covered with froth and sweat, heads hanging as they walked. And something slumped over the back of one in the center that gradually revealed itself to be two near-comatose people, seated one before the other and clinging to each other to keep from falling of the horse's saddle. The clan chief recognized the one in front, and slid from his horses's back with a shout. The herd approaching them stopped coming, the beasts moving only enough to part and let him through.

Then Kevin recognized the other, and tumbled off *his* horse's back, all injuries forgotten. While the clan chief and another took the semi-conscious boy from the front of the saddle, cursing at the sight of the chains on his wrists and ankles, it was into Kevin's arms that Chali slumped, and *he* cursed to see the three feathered shafts protruding from her leg and arm.

\*\*\*\*

Chali wanted to stay down in the soft darkness, where she could forget—but They wouldn't let her stay there. Against her own will she swam slowly up to wakefulness, and to full and aching knowledge of how completely alone she was.

The *kumpania* was gone, and no amount of vengeance would bring it back. She was left with nowhere to go and nothing to do with her life—and no one who wanted her.

*No-Voice is a fool,* came the sharp voice in her head.

She opened her eyes, slowly. There was Brighttooth, lying beside her, carefully grooming her paw. The cat was stretched out along a beautifully tanned fur of dark brown; fabric walls stretched above her, and Chali recognized absently that they must be in a tent.

*How,* a *fool?* asked a second mind-voice; Chali saw the tent-wall move out of the corner of her eye—the wall opened and became a door, and the young man she had helped to rescue bent down to enter. He sat himself down beside the cat, and began scratching her ears; she closed her eyes in delight and purred loudly enough to shake the walls of the tent. Chali closed her eyes in a spasm of pain and loss; their brotherhood only reminded her of what she no longer had.

*I asked you, lazy one, how a fool?*

Chali longed to be able to turn her back on them, but the wounds in her side made that impossible. She could only turn her face away, while tears slid slowly down her cheeks—as always, soundlessly.

A firm, but gentle hand cupped her chin and turned her head back toward her visitors. She squeezed her eyes shut, not wanting these *Gaje* to see her loss and her shame at showing it.

"It's no shame to mourn," said the young man aloud, startling her into opening her eyes. She had been right about him—with his hurts neatly bandaged and cleaned up, he *was* quite handsome. And his gray eyes were very kind—and very sad.

*I mourn, too,* he reminded her.

Now she was even more ashamed, and bit her lip. How could she have forgotten what the cat had told her, that he had lost his twin—lost her in defending *her* people. *For the third time, how a fool?*

Brighttooth stretched, and moved over beside her, and began cleaning the tears from her cheeks with a raspy tongue. *Because No-Voice forgets what she herself told me.*

*Which is?*

*The enemy of my enemy is my brother.*

*My* friend. *I said, the enemy of my enemy is my friend,* Chali corrected hesitantly, entering the conversation at last.

*Friend, brother, all the same,* the cat replied, finishing off her work with a last swipe of her tongue. *Friends are the family you choose, not so? I—*

"You're not gonna be alone, not unless you want to," the young man said, aloud. "Brighttooth is right. You can join us, join any family in the clan you want. There ain't a one of them that wouldn't reckon themselves proud to have you as a daughter and a sister."

There was a certain hesitation in the way he said "sister." Something about that hesitation broke Chali's bleak mood.

*What of you?* she asked. *Would you welcome me as a sister?*

*Something*—he sent, shyly,—*maybe*—*something closer than sister?*

She was so astonished that she could only stare at him. She saw that he was looking at her in a way that made her very conscious that she *was* sixteen winters old—in a way that no member of the *kumpania* had ever looked at her. She continued to stare as he gently took one of her hands in his good one. It took Brighttooth to break the spell.

*Pah—two-legs!* she sent in disgust. *Everything is complicated with you! You need clan; here is clan for the taking. What could be simpler?*

The young man dropped her hand as if it had burned him, then began to laugh. Chali smiled, shyly, not entirely certain she had truly seen that admiration in his eyes—

"Brighttooth has a pretty direct way of seein' things," he said, finally. "Look, let's just take this in easy steps, right? *One,* you get better. *Two,* we deal with when you're in shape t' think about."

Chali nodded.

*Three—you'll never be alone again,* he said in her mind, taking her hand in his again. *Not while I'm around to have a say in it. Friend, brother—whatever. I won't let you be lonely.*

Chali nodded again, feeling the aching void inside her filling. Yes, she would mourn her dead—

But she would rejoin the living to do so.

# Bibliography

*Arrows of the Queen* (DAW)
*Arrow's Flight* (DAW)
*Arrow's Fall* (DAW)
*Oathbound* (DAW)
*Oathbreakers* (DAW)
*Magic's Pawn* (DAW)
*Magic's Promise* (DAW)
*Magic's Price* (DAW)
*Reap the Whirlwind,* with C. J. Cherryh (Baen)
*Knight of Ghosts and Shadows,* with Ellen Guon (Baen)
*By the Sword* (DAW)
*Summoned to Tourney,* with Ellen Guon, (Baen)
*Winds of Fate* (DAW)
*Winds of Change* (DAW)
*Winds of Fury* (DAW)
*The Elvenbane,* with Andre Norton (TOR)
*Bardic Voices One: The Lark and the Wren* (Baen)
*Bardic Voices Two: The Robin and the Kestrel* (Baen)
*The Eagle and the Nightingales* (Baen)
*Cast of Corbies, with Josepha Sherman* (Baen)
*Born to Run, with Larry Dixon* (Baen)
*Wheels of Fire, with Mark Shepherd* (Baen)
*When the Bough Breaks, with Holly Lisle* (Baen)
*Chrome Circle, with Larry Dixon* (Baen)
*The Ship Who Searched, with Anne McCaffrey* (Baen)
*Castle of Deception, with Josepha Sherman* (Baen)
*Fortress of Frost and Fire, with Ru Emerson* (Baen)

*Prison of Souls,* with Mark Shepherd (Baen)
*Wing Commander: Freedom Flight,* with Ellen Guon (Baen)
*If I Pay Thee Not In Gold,* with Piers Anthony (Baen)
*The Black Gryphon,* with Larry Dixon (DAW)
*The White Gryphon,* with Larry Dixon (DAW)
*The Silver Gryphon,* with Larry Dixon (DAW)
*Sacred Ground* (TOR)
*Burning Water* (TOR)
*Children of the Night* (TOR)
*Jinx High* (TOR)
*Darkover Rediscovery,* with Marion Zimmer Bradley (DAW)
*Storm Warning* (DAW)
*Storm Rising* (DAW)
*Storm Breaking* (DAW)
*Elvenblood,* with Andre Norton (TOR)
*Tiger Burning Bright,* with Marion Zimmer Bradley
    and Andre Norton (Avonova)
*The Fire Rose* (Baen)
*The Firebird* (TOR)
*Four and Twenty Blackbirds* (Baen)

# WEREHUNTER

✳✳✳

## Mercedes Lackey

# Introduction

Those of you who are more interested in the stories than in some chatty author stuff should just skip this part, since it will be mostly about the things people used to ask us about at science fiction conventions.

For those of you who have never heard of SF conventions (or "cons" as they are usually called), these are gatherings of people who are quite fanatical about their interest in one or more of the various fantasy and science fiction media. There are talks and panel discussions on such wildly disparate topics as costuming, prop-making, themes in SF/F literature, *Star Wars*, *Star Trek*, *Babylon 5*, *X-Files*, SF/F art, medieval fighting, horse-training, dancing, and the world of fans in general. There are workshops on writing and performance arts. Guests featured in panels and question and answer sessions are often featured performers from television and movies along with various authors and the occasional professional propmaker. Larry and I no longer attend conventions for a number of reasons, not the least of which is that we have a great many responsibilities that require us to be home.

Some of those responsibilities are that we are volunteers for our local fire department. Larry is a driver and outside man; I am learning to do dispatch, and hopefully will be able to take over the night shift, since we are awake long after most of the rest of the county has gone to sleep. Our local department is strictly volunteer and works on a very tight budget. Our equipment is old and needs frequent repair, we get what we can afford, and what we can afford is generally third or fourth-hand, having passed through a large metropolitan department or the military to a small municipal department to the Forestry Service and finally to us. In summer I am a water-carrier at grass-fires, meaning that I bring drinking-water to the overheated firefighters so they don't collapse in the 100-plus-degree heat.

Another duty is with the EOC (formerly called the Civil Defense Office). When we are under severe weather conditions, the firefighters are called in to wait at the station in case of emergency, so Larry is there. I go in to the EOC office to read weather-radar for the storm-watchers in the field. Eventually I hope to get my radio license so I can also join the ranks of the storm-watchers. We don't "chase" as such, although there are so few of the storm-watchers that they may move to active areas rather than staying put. Doppler radar can only give an indication of where there is rotation in the clouds; rotation may not produce a tornado. You have to have people on the ground in the area to know if there is a funnel or a tornado (technically, it isn't a tornado until it touches the ground; until then it is a funnel-cloud). Our area of Oklahoma is not quite as active as the area of the Panhandle or around Oklahoma City and Norman (which is why the National Severe Storms Laboratory is located there) but we get plenty of severe, tornado-producing storms.

In addition, we have our raptor rehabilitation duties.

Larry and I are raptor rehabilitators; this means that we are licensed by both the state and the federal government to collect, care for, and release birds of prey that are injured or ill. Occasionally we are asked to bring one of our "patients" for a talk to a group of adults or children, often under the auspices of our local game wardens.

I'm sure this sounds very exciting and glamorous, and it certainly impresses the heck out of people when we bring in a big hawk riding on a gloved hand, but there are times when I wonder how we managed to get ourselves into this.

We have three main "seasons"—baby season, stupid fledgling season, and inexpert hunter season.

Now, injuries—and victims of idiots with guns—can come at any time. We haven't had too many shooting victims in our area, thank heavens, in part because the cattle-farmers around our area know that shooting a raptor only adds field rats and mice to their property. But another rehabber gave up entirely a few years ago, completely burned out, because she got the same redtail hawk back *three times*, shot out of the sky. Injuries that we see in our area are most often the case of collision—literally—with man's environmental changes. Birds hit windows that seem to them to be sky, Great Blue Herons collide with power-lines, raptors get electrocuted by those same lines. But most often, we get birds hit by cars. Owls will chase prey across the road, oblivious to the fact that something is approaching, and get hit. Raptors are creatures of opportunity and will quite readily come down to feed on roadkill and get hit. Great Horned Owls, often called the "tigers of the sky," are top predators, known to chase even eagles off nests to claim the nest for themselves—if a Great Horned is eating roadkill and sees a car approaching, it will stand its ground, certain that it will get the better of anything daring to try to snatch its dinner! After all, they have been developing and evolving for millions of years, and swiftly moving vehicles have only been around for about seventy-five years; they haven't had nearly enough time to adapt to the situation as a species. Individuals *do* learn, though, often to take advantage of the situation. Kestrels and redtails are known to hang around fields being harvested to snatch the field-rats running from the machinery, or suddenly exposed after the harvesters have passed. Redtails are also known to hang about railway right-of-ways, waiting for trains to spook out rabbits!

Our current education bird, a big female redtail we call Cinnamon, is one such victim; struck in the head by a CB whip-antenna, she has only one working eye and just enough brain damage to render her partially paralyzed on one side and make her accepting and calm in our presence. This makes her a great education-bird, as nothing alarms her and children can safely touch her, giving them a new connection with wild things that they had never experienced before.

But back to the three "seasons" of a raptor rehabber, and the different kinds of work they involve.

First is "baby season," which actually extends from late February to July, beginning with Great Horned Owl babies and ending when the second round of American Kestrels (sparrowhawks, or "spawks" as falconers affectionately call them) begins to push their siblings out of nests. The first rule of baby season is—try to get the baby back into the nest, or something like the nest. Mother birds are infinitely better at taking care of their youngsters than any human, so when wind or weather send babies (eyases, is the correct term) tumbling, that is our first priority. This almost always involves climbing, which means that poor Larry puts on his climbing gear and dangles from trees. When nest and all have come down, we supply a substitute, in as close to the same place as possible; raptor mothers are far more fixated on the kids than the house, and a box filled with branches will do nicely, thank you.

Sometimes, though, it's not possible to put the eyases back. Youngsters are found with no nest in sight, or the nest is literally unreachable (a Barn Owl roost in the roof of an institution for the criminally insane, for instance), or worst of all, the parents are known to be dead.

Young raptors eat a lot. Kestrels need feeding every hour or so, bigger birds every two to three, and that's from dawn to dusk. We've taken eyases with us to doctor's appointments, on vacation, on shopping expeditions, and even to racing school! And we're not talking Gerber' here; "mom" (us) gets to take the mousie, dissect the mousie, and feed the mousie parts to baby. By hand. Yummy! Barred Owl eyases are the easiest of the lot; they'll take minnows, which are of a size to slip down their little throats easily, but not the rest. There's no use thinking you can get by with a little chicken, either—growing babies need a lot of calcium for those wonderful hollow bones that they're growing so fast, so they need the whole animal.

Fortunately, babies do grow up, and eventually they'll feed themselves. Then it's just a matter of helping them learn to fly (which involves a little game we call "Hawk Tossing") and teaching them to hunt. The instincts are there; they just need to connect instinct with practice. But this is *not* for the squeamish or the tender-hearted; for the youngsters to grow up and have the skills to make them successful, they have to learn to kill.

The second season can stretch from late April to August, and we call it "silly fledgling season." That's when the eyases, having learned to fly at last, get lost. Raptor mothers—with the exception of Barn Owls—continue to feed the youngsters and teach them to hunt after they've fledged, but sometimes wind and weather again carry the kids off beyond finding their way back to mom. Being inexperienced flyers and not hunters at all yet, they usually end up helpless on the ground, which is where we come in.

These guys are actually the easiest and most rewarding; they know the basics of flying and hunting, and all we have to do is put some meat back on their bones and give them a bit more experience. We usually have anywhere from six to two dozen kestrels at this stage every year, which is when *we* get a fair amount of exercise, catching grasshoppers for them to hunt.

Then comes the "inexpert hunter" season, and I'm not referring to the ones with guns. Some raptors are the victims of a bad winter, or the fact that they concentrated on those easy-to-kill grasshoppers while their siblings had graduated to more difficult prey. Along about December, we start to get the ones that nothing much is wrong with except starvation. Sometimes starvation has gone too far for them to make it; frustrating and disappointing for us.

We've gotten all sorts of birds over the years; our wonderful vet, Dr. Paul Welch (on whom may blessings be heaped!) treats wildlife for free, and knows that we're always suckers for a challenge, so he has gotten some of the odder things to us. We've had two Great Blue Herons, for instance. One was an adult that had collided with a powerline. It had a dreadful fracture, and we weren't certain if it would be able to fly again (it did) but since we have a pond, we figured we could support a land-bound heron. In our ignorance, we had no idea that Great Blues are terrible challenges to keep alive because they are so shy; we just waded right in, force-feeding it minnows when it refused to eat, and stuffing the minnows right back down when it tossed them up. This may not sound so difficult, but remember that a Great Blue has a two-foot sword on the end of its head, a spring-loaded neck to put some force behind the stab, and the beak-eye coordination to impale a minnow in a foot of water. It has *no* trouble targeting your eye.

We fed it wearing welding-masks.

We believe very strongly in force-feeding; our experience has been that if you force-feed a bird for two to three days, it gives up trying to die of starvation and begins eating on its own. Once again, mind you, this is not always an easy proposition; we're usually dealing with fully adult birds who want nothing whatsoever to do with us, and have the equipment to enforce their preferences. We very seldom get a bird that is so injured that it gives us no resistance. Great Horned Owls can exert pressure of 400 ft/lbs per talon, which can easily penetrate a Kevlar-lined welding glove, as I know personally and painfully.

That is yet another aspect of rehabbing that most people don't think about—injury. Yours, not the bird's. We've been "footed" (stabbed with talons), bitten, pooped on (okay, so that's not an injury, but it's not pleasant), gouged, and beak-slashed. And we have to stand there and continue doing whatever it was that earned us those injuries, because it certainly isn't the *bird's* fault that he doesn't recognize the fact that you're trying to help him.

We also have to know when we're out of our depth, or when the injury is *so* bad that the bird isn't releasable, and do the kind and responsible thing. Unless a bird is *so* endangered that it can go into a captive breeding project, or is the rare, calm, quiet case like Cinnamon who will be a perfect education bird, there is no point in keeping one that can't fly or hunt again. You learn how to let go and move on very quickly, and just put your energy into the next one.

On the other hand, we have personal experience that raptors are a great deal tougher than it might appear. We've successfully released one-eyed hawks, who learn to compensate for their lack of binocular vision very well. Birds with one "bad" leg learn to strike only with the good one. One-eyed owls are routine for us now; owls mostly hunt by sound anyway and don't actually need both eyes. But the most amazing is that another rehabber in our area has routinely gotten successful releases with owls that are minus a wingtip; evidently owls are such strong fliers that they don't need their entire wingspan to prosper, and *that* is quite amazing and heartening.

We've learned other things, too; one of the oddest is that owls by-and-large don't show gradual recovery from head injuries. They will go on, day after day, with nothing changing—then, suddenly, one morning you have an owl fighting to get out of the box you've put him in to keep him quiet and contained! We've learned that once birds learn to hunt, they prefer fresh-caught dinner to the frozen stuff we offer; we haven't had a single freeloader keep coming back long after he should be independent. We've learned that "our" birds learn quickly not to generalize about humans feeding them—once they are free-flying (but still supplementing their hunting with handouts) they don't bother begging for food from anyone but those who give them the proper "come'n'get it" signal, and even then they are unlikely to get close to anyone they don't actually recognize.

We already knew that eyases in the "downy" stage, when their juvenile plumage hasn't come in and they look like little white puffballs, will imprint very easily, so we quickly turn potentially dangerous babies (like Great Horned Owls) over to rehabbers who have "foster moms"—non-releasable birds of the right species who will at least provide the right role model for the youngsters. Tempting as the little things are, so fuzzy and big-eyed, none of us wants an imprinted Great Horned coming back in four or five years when sexual maturity hits, looking for love in all the wrong places! Remember those talons?

For us, though, all the work is worth the moment of release, when we take the bird that couldn't fly, or the now-grown-up and self-sufficient baby, and turn him loose. For some, we just open the cage door and step back; for others, there's a slow process called "hacking out," where the adolescent comes back for food until he's hunting completely on his own. In either case, we've performed a little surgery on the fragile ecosystem, and it's a good feeling to see the patient thriving.

Those who have caught the raptor bug seem like family; we associate with both rehabber and falconers. If you are interested in falconry—and bear in mind, it is an extremely labor-intensive hobby—contact your local Fish and Wildlife Department for a list of local falconers, and see if you can find one willing to take you as an apprentice. If you want to get into rehab, contact Fish and Wildlife for other rehabbers who are generally quite happy to help you get started.

Here are some basic facts about birds of prey. Faloners call the young in the nest an eyas; rehabbers and falconers call the very small ones, covered only in fluff, "downies." In the downy stage, they are very susceptible to imprinting; if we have to see babies we would rather they were at least in the second stage, when the body feathers start to come in. That is the only time that the feathers are not molted; the down feathers are actually attached to the juvenile feathers, and have to be picked off, either by the parent or the youngster. Body feathers come in first, and when they are about half-grown, the adults can stop brooding the babies, for they can retain their body heat on their own, and more importantly, the juvenile feathers have a limited ability to shed water, which the down will not do. If a rainstorm starts, for instance, the downies will be wet through quickly before a parent can return to the nest to cover them, they'll be hypothermic in seconds and might die; babies in juvenile plumage are safe until a parent gets back to cover them.

If eyases don't fight in the nest over food this means both that their environmeent provides a wealth of prey and that their parents are excellent hunters. If they are hungry, the youngest of the eyases often dies or is pushed out of the nest to die.

Redtails can have up to four offspring; two is usual. Although it is rare, they have been known to double-clutch if a summer is exceptionally long and warm. They may also double-clutch if the first batch is infertile.

Redtails in captivity can live up to twenty-five years; half that is usual in the wild. They can breed at four years old, though they have been known to breed as young as two. In their first year they do not have red tails and their body plumage is more mottled than in older birds; this is called "juvenile plumage" and is a signal to older birds that these youngsters are no threat to them. Kestrels do not have juvenile plumage, nor do most owls, and eagles hold their juvenile plumage for four years. Kestrels for live about five years in the wild, up to fifteen in captivity; eagles live fifty years in captivity and up to twenty-five in the wild.

Should you find an injured bird of prey, you need three things for a rescue: a heavy blanket or jacket, cohesive bandage (the kind of athletic wrap that sticks to itself), and a heavy, dark-colored sock. Throw the blanket over the victim, locate and free the head and pull the sock over it. Locate the feet, and wrap the feet together with the bandage; keep hold of the feet, remove the blanket, get the wings folded in the "resting" position and wrap the body in cohesive bandage to hold the wings in place. Make a ring of a towel in the bottom of a cardboard box just big enough to hold the bird, and put the bird in the box as if it was sitting in a nest. Take the sock off and quickly close up the box and get the victim to a rehabber, a local game warden or Fish and Wildlife official, or a vet that treats injured wildlife. Diurnal raptors are very dependent on their sight; take it away and they "shut down"—which is the reason behind the traditional falconhood. By putting the sock over the head, you take away the chief source of stress—the sight of enormous two-legged predators bearing down on it.

*Andre Norton, who (as by now you must be aware) I have admired for ages, was doing a "Friends of the Witch World" anthology, and asked me if I would mind doing a story for her.*

*Would I mind? I flashed back to when I was thirteen or fourteen years old, and I read Witch World and fell completely and totally into this wonderful new cosmos. I had already been a fan of Andre's since I was nine or ten and my father (who was a science fiction reader) loaned me Beast Master because it had a horse in it and I was horse-mad. But this was something different, science fiction that didn't involve thud and blunder and iron-thewed barbarians. I was in love.*

*Oh—back in "the old days" it was all called "science fiction." There was no category for "fantasy," and as for "hard s/f," "sword and sorcery," "urban fantasy," "high fantasy," "cyberpunk," "horror," "space-opera"—none of those categories existed. You'd find Clark Ashton Smith right next to E. E. "Doc" Smith, and Andre Norton and Fritz Leiber wrote gothic horror, high fantasy, and science fiction all without anyone wondering what to call it. Readers of imaginative literature read everything, and neither readers nor writers were compelled by marketing considerations to read or write in only a single category.*

*At any rate, many years later, my idol Andre Norton asked me for a story set in one of my favorite science-fiction worlds. Somehow I managed to tell Andre that I would be very happy to write a story. This is it. In fact, this is the longer version; she asked me to cut some, not because she didn't like it the way it was, but because she was only allowed stories of 5,000 words or less; here it is as I originally wrote it.*

# Werehunter

## Mercedes Lackey

It had been raining all day, a cold, dismal rain that penetrated through clothing and chilled the heart to numbness. Glenda trudged through it, sneakers soaked; beneath her cheap plastic raincoat her jeans were soggy to the knees. It was several hours past sunset now, and still raining, and the city streets were deserted by all but the most hardy, the most desperate, and the faded few with nothing to lose.

Glenda was numbered among those last. This morning she'd spent her last change getting a bus to the welfare office, only to be told that she hadn't been a resident long enough to qualify for aid. That wasn't true—but she couldn't have known that. The supercilious clerk had taken in her age and inexperience at a glance, and assumed "student." If he had begun processing her, he'd have been late for lunch. He guessed she wouldn't know enough to contradict him, and he'd been right. And years of her aunt's browbeating ("Isn't one 'no' good enough for you?") had drummed into her the lesson that there were no second chances. He'd gone off to his lunch date; she'd trudged back home in the rain. This afternoon she'd eaten the last packet of cheese and crackers and had made "soup" from the stolen packages of fast-food ketchup—there was nothing left in her larder that even resembled food. Hunger had been with her for so long now that the ache in her stomach had become as much a part of her as her hands

247

and feet. There were three days left in the month; three days of shelter, then she'd be kicked out of her shoddy efficiency and into the street.

When her Social Security orphan's benefits had run out when she'd turned eighteen, her aunt had "suggested" she find a job and support herself—elsewhere. The suggestion had come in the form of finding her belongings in boxes on the front porch with a letter to that effect on top of them.

So she'd tried, moving across town to this place, near the university; a marginal neighborhood surrounded by bad blocks on three sides. But there were no jobs if you had no experience—and how did you get experience without a job? The only experience she'd ever had was at shoveling snow, raking leaves, mowing and gardening which was the only ways she could earn money for college, since her aunt had never let her apply for a job that would have been beyond walking distance of her house. Besides that, there were at least forty university students competing with her for every job that opened up anywhere around here. Her meager savings (meant, at one time, to pay for college tuition) would be soon gone.

She rubbed the ring on her left hand, a gesture she was completely unaware of. That ring was all she had of the mother her aunt would never discuss—the woman her brother had married over her own strong disapproval. It was silver, and heavy; made in the shape of a crouching cat with tiny glints of topaz for eyes. Much as she treasured it, she would gladly have sold it—but she couldn't get it off her finger, she'd worn it for so long.

She splashed through the puddles, peering listlessly out from under the hood of her raincoat. Her lank, mouse-brown hair straggled into her eyes as she squinted against the glare of headlights on rain-glazed pavement. Despair had driven her into the street; despair kept her here. It was easier to keep the tears and hysterics at bay out here, where the cold numbed mind as well as body, and the rain washed all her thoughts until they were thin and lifeless. She could see no way out of this trap—except maybe by killing herself.

But her body had other ideas. *It* wanted to survive, even if Glenda wasn't sure *she* did.

A chill of fear trickled down her backbone like a drop of icy rain, driving all thoughts of suicide from her, as behind her she recognized the sounds of footsteps.

She didn't have to turn around to know she was being followed, and by more than one. On a night like tonight, there was no one on the street but the fools and the hunters. She knew which she was.

It wasn't much of an alley—a crack between buildings, scarcely wide enough for her to pass. *They* might not know it was there—even if they did, they couldn't know what lay at the end of it. She did. She dodged inside, feeling her way along the narrow defile, until one of the two buildings gave way to a seven-foot privacy fence.

She came to the apparent deadend, building on the right, a high board fence on the left, building in front. She listened, stretching her ears for sounds behind her, taut with fear. Nothing; they had either passed this place by, or hadn't reached it yet.

Quickly, before they could find the entrance, she ran her hand along the boards of the fence, counting them from the dead-end. Four, five—when she touched the sixth one, she gave it a shove sideways, getting a handful of splinters for her pains. But the board moved, pivoting on the one nail that held it, and she squeezed through the gap into the yard beyond, pulling the board back in place behind her.

Just in time; echoing off the stone and brick of the alley were harsh young male voices. She leaned against the fence and shook from head to toe, clenching her teeth to keep them from chattering, as they searched the alley, found nothing, and finally (after hours, it seemed) went away.

"Well, you've got yourself in a fine mess," she said dully. "Now what? You don't dare leave, not yet—they might have left someone in the street, watching. Idiot! Home may not be much, but it's dry, and there's a bed. Fool, fool, fool! So now you get to spend the rest of the night in the back yard of a spookhouse. You'd just better hope the spook isn't home."

She peered through the dark at the shapeless bulk of the tristory townhouse, relic of a previous century, hoping *not* to see any signs of life. The place had an uncanny reputation; even the gangs left it alone. People had vanished here—some of them important people, with good reasons to want to disappear, some who had been uninvited visitors. But the police had been over the house and grounds more than once, and never found anything. No bodies were buried in the back yard—the ground was as hard as cement under the inch-deep layer of soft sand that covered it. There was nothing at all in the yard but the sand and the rocks; the crazy woman that lived here told the police it was a "Zen garden." But when Glenda had first peeked through the boards at the back yard, it didn't look like any Zen garden *she* had ever read about. The sand wasn't groomed into wave-patterns, and the rocks looked more like something out of a mini-Stonehenge than islands or mountain-peaks.

There were four of those rocks—one like a garden bench, that stood before three that formed a primitive arch. Glenda felt her way towards them in the dark, trusting to the memory of how the place had looked by daylight to find them. She barked her shin painfully on the "benchrock," and her legs gave out, so that she sprawled ungracefully over it. Tears of pain mingled with the rain, and she swore under her breath.

She sat huddled on the top of it in the dark, trying to remember what time it was the last time she'd seen a clock. Dawn couldn't be too far off. When dawn came, and there were more people in the street, she could probably get safely back to her apartment.

For all the good it would do her.

Her stomach cramped with hunger, and despair clamped down on her again. She shouldn't have run—she was only delaying the inevitable. In two days she'd be out on the street, and this time with nowhere to hide, easy prey for them, or those like them.

"So wouldn't you like to escape altogether?"

The soft voice out of the darkness nearly caused Glenda's heart to stop. She jumped, and clenched the side of the bench-rock as the voice laughed. Oddly enough, the laughter seemed to make her fright wash out of her. There was nothing malicious about it—it was kind-sounding, gentle. Not crazy.

"Oh, I like to make people think I'm crazy; they leave me alone that way." The speaker was a dim shape against the lighter background of the fence.

"Who—"

"I am the keeper of this house—and this place; not the first, certainly not the last. So there is nothing in this city—in this world—to hold you here anymore?"

"How—did you know *that*?" Glenda tried to see the speaker in the dim light reflected off the clouds, to see if it really was the woman that lived in the house, but there were no details to be seen, just a human-shaped outline. Her eyes blurred. Reaction to her narrow escape, the cold, hunger; all three were conspiring to make her light-headed.

"The only ones who come to me are those who have no will to live *here*, yet who still have the will to live. Tell me, if another world opened before you, would you walk into it, not knowing what it held?"

This whole conversation was so surreal, Glenda began to think she was hallucinating the whole thing. Well, if it was a hallucination, why not go along with it?

"Sure, why not? It couldn't be any worse than here. It might be better."

"Then turn, and look behind you—and choose."

Glenda hesitated, then swung her legs over the bench-stone. The sky was lighter in that direction—dawn was breaking. Before her loomed the stone arch—

Now she *knew* she was hallucinating—for framed within the arch was no shadowy glimpse of board fence and rain-soaked sand, but a patch of reddening sky, and another dawn—

A dawn that broke over rolling hills covered with waving grass, grass stirred by a breeze that carried the scent of flowers, not the exhaust-tainted air of the city.

Glenda stood, unaware that she had done so. She reached forward with one hand, yearningly. The place seemed to call to something buried deep in her heart—and she wanted to answer.

"Here—or there? Choose now, child."

With an inarticulate cry, she stumbled toward the stones—

And found herself standing alone on a grassy hill.

※※※※

After several hours of walking in wet, soggy tennis shoes, growing more spacey by the minute from hunger, she was beginning to think she'd made a mistake. Somewhere back behind her she'd lost her raincoat; she couldn't remember when she'd taken it off. There was no sign of people anywhere—there were animals; even sheep, once, but nothing like "civilization." It was frustrating, maddening; there was food all around her, on four feet, on wings—surely even some of the plants were edible—but it was totally inaccessible to a city-bred girl who'd never gotten food from anywhere but a grocery or restaurant. She might just as well be on the moon.

Just as she thought that, she topped another rise to find herself looking at a strange, weatherbeaten man standing beside a rough pounded-dirt road.

She blinked in dumb amazement. He looked like something out of a movie, a peasant from a King Arthur epic. He was stocky, blond-haired; he wore a shabby brown tunic and patched, shapeless trousers tucked into equally patched boots. He was also holding a strung bow, with an arrow nocked to it, and frowning—a most unfriendly expression.

He gabbled something at her. She blinked again. She knew a little Spanish (you had to, in her neighborhood); she'd taken German and French in high school. This didn't sound like any of those.

He repeated himself, a distinct edge to his voice. To emphasize his words, he jerked the point of the arrow off back the way she had come. It was pretty obvious he was telling her to be on her way.

"No, wait—please—" she stepped toward him, her hands outstretched pleadingly. The only reaction she got was that he raised the arrow to point at her chest, and drew it back.

"Look—I haven't got any weapons! I'm lost, I'm *hungry*—"

He drew the arrow a bit farther.

Suddenly it was all too much. She'd spent all her life being pushed and pushed—first her aunt, then at school, then out on the streets. This was the last time *anybody* was going to back her into a corner— this time she was going to fight!

A white-hot rage like nothing she'd ever experienced before in her life took over.

"Damn you!" she was so angry she could hardly think. "You stupid clod! *I need help!*" she screamed at him, as red flashes interfered with her vision, her ears began to buzz, and her hands crooked into involuntary claws. *"Damn you and everybody that looks like you!"*

He backed up a pace, his blue eyes wide with surprise at her rage.

She was so filled with fury that grew past controlling—she couldn't see, couldn't think; it was like being possessed. Suddenly she gasped as pain lanced from the top of her head to her toes, pain like a bolt of lightning—

—her vision blacked out; she fell to her hands and knees on the grass, her legs unable to hold her, convulsing with surges of pain in her arms and legs. Her feet, her hands felt like she'd shoved them in a fire—her face felt as if someone were stretching it out of shape. And the ring finger of her left hand—it burned with more agony than both hands and feet put together! She shook her head, trying to clear it, but it spun around in dizzying circles. Her ears rang, hard to hear over the ringing, but there was a sound of cloth tearing—

Her sight cleared and returned, but distorted. She looked up at the man, who had dropped his bow, and was backing away from her, slowly, his face white with terror. She started to say something to him—

—and it came out a snarl.

With that, the man screeched, turned his back on her, and ran.

And she caught sight of her hand. It wasn't a hand anymore. It was a paw. Judging by the spotted pelt of the leg, a leopard's paw. Scattered around her were the ragged scraps of cloth that had once been her clothing.

Glenda lay in the sun on top of a rock, warm and drowsy with full-bellied content. Idly she washed one paw with her tongue, cleaning the last taint of blood from it. Before she'd had a chance to panic or go crazy back there when she'd realized what had happened to her, a rabbitlike creature had broken cover practically beneath her nose. Semi-starvation and confusion had kept her dazed long enough for leopard-instincts to take over. She'd caught and killed the thing and had half-eaten it before the reality of what she'd done and become broke through her shock. Raw rabbit-thing tasted *fine* to leopard-Glenda; when she realized that, she finished it, nose to tail. Now for the first time in weeks she was warm and content. And for the first time in years *she* was something to be afraid of. She gazed about her from her vantage-point on the warm boulder, taking in the grassy hills and breathing in the warm, hay-scented air with a growing contentment.

Becoming a leopard might not be a bad transformation.

Ears keener than a human's picked up the sound of dogs in the distance; she became aware that the man she'd frightened might have gone back home for help. They just *might* be hunting her.

Time to go.

She leapt down from her rock, setting off at a right angle to the direction the sound of the baying was coming from. Her sense of smell, so heightened now that it might have been a new sense altogether, had picked up the coolth of running water off this way, dimmed by the green odor of the grass. And running water was a good way to break a trail; she knew that from reading.

Reveling in the power of the muscles beneath her sleek coat, she ran lightly over the slopes, moving through the grass that had been such a waist-high tangle to girl-Glenda with no impediment whatsoever. In almost no time at all, it seemed, she was pacing the side of the stream that she had scented.

It was quite wide, twenty feet or so, and seemed fairly deep in the middle. Sunlight danced on the surface, giving her a hint that the current might be stiffish beneath the surface. She waded into it, up to her stomach, hissing a little at the cold and the feel of the water on her fur. She trotted upstream a bit until she found a place where the course had narrowed a little. It was still over her head, but she found she could swim it with nothing other than discomfort. The stream wound between the grassy hills, the banks never getting very high, but there rarely being any more cover along them than a few scattered bushes. Something told her that she would be no match for the endurance of the hunting pack if she tried to escape across the grasslands. She stayed in the watercourse until she came to a wider valley than anything she had yet encountered. There were trees here;

she waded onward until she found one leaning well over the streambed. Gathering herself and eying the broad branch that arced at least six feet above the watercourse, she leaped for it, landing awkwardly, and having to scrabble with her claws fully extended to keep her balance.

She sprawled over it for a moment, panting, hearing the dogs nearing—belling in triumph as they caught her trail, then yelping in confusion when they lost it at the stream.

Time to move again. She climbed the tree up into the higher branches, finding a wide perch at least fifty or sixty feet off the ground. It was high enough that it was unlikely that anyone would spot her hide among the dappled leaf-shadows, wide enough that she could recline, balanced, at her ease, yet it afforded to leopard-eyes a good view of the ground and the stream.

As she'd expected, the humans with the dogs had figured out her scent-breaking ploy, and had split the pack, taking half along each side of the stream to try and pick up where she'd exited. She spotted the man who had stopped her easily, and filed his scent away in her memory for the future. The others with him were dressed much the same as he, and carried nothing more sophisticated than bows. They looked angry, confused; their voices held notes of fear. They looked into and under the trees with noticeable apprehension, evidently fearing what might dwell under their shade. Finally they gave up, and pulled the hounds off the fruitless quest, leaving her smiling catwise, invisible above them in her tree, purring.

Several weeks later Glenda had found a place to lair up; a cave amid a tumble of boulders in the heart of the forest at the streamside. She had also discovered why the hunters hadn't wanted to pursue her into the forest itself. There was a—thing—an evil presence, malicious, but invisible, that lurked in a circle of standing stones that glowed at night with a sickly yellow color. Fortunately it seemed unable to go beyond the bounds of the stones themselves. Glenda had been chasing a half-grown deer-beast that had run straight into the middle of the circle, forgetting the danger before it because of the danger pursuing it. She had nearly been caught there herself, and only the thing's preoccupation with the first prey had saved her. She had hidden in her lair, nearly paralyzed with fear, for a day and a night until hunger and thirst had driven her out again.

Other than that peril, easily avoided, the forest seemed safe enough. She'd found the village the man had come from by following the dirt road; she'd spent long hours when she wasn't hunting lurking within range of sight and hearing of the place. Aided by some new sense she wasn't sure that she understood—the one that had alerted her to the danger of the stone circle as she'd blundered in—she was beginning to make some sense of their language. She understood at least two-thirds of what was being said now, and could usually guess the rest.

These people seemed to be stuck at some kind of feudal level—had been overrun by some higher-tech invaders the generation before, and were only now recovering from that. The hereditary rulers had mostly been killed in that war, and the population decimated; the memories of that time were still strong. The man who'd stopped her had been on guard-duty and had mistrusted her appearance out of what they called "the Waste" and her strange clothing. When she'd transformed in front of his eyes, he must have decided she was some kind of witch.

Glenda had soon hunted the more easily caught game out; now when hunger drove her, she supplemented her diet with raids on the villager's livestock. She was getting better at hunting, but she still was far from being an expert, and letting leopard-instincts take over involved surrendering herself to those instincts. She was beginning to have the uneasy feeling that every time she did that she lost a little more of her humanity. Life as leopard-Glenda was much easier than as girl-Glenda, but it might be getting to be time to think about trying to regain her former shape—before she was lost to the leopard entirely.

She'd never been one for horror or fantasy stories, so her only guide was vague recollections of fairy-tales and late-night werewolf movies. She didn't think the latter would be much help here—after all, she'd transformed into a leopard, not a wolf, and by the light of day, not the full moon.

But—maybe the light of the full moon would help.

She waited until full dark before setting off for her goal, a still pond in the far edge of the forest, well away from the stone circle, in a clearing that never seemed to become overgrown. It held a stone, too; a single pillar of some kind of blueish rock. That pillar had never "glowed" at night before, at least not while Glenda had been there, but the pond and the clearing seemed to form a little pocket of peace. Whatever evil might lurk in the rest of the forest, she was somehow sure it would find no place there.

The moon was well up by the time she reached it. White flowers had opened to the light of it, and a faint, crisp scent came from them. Glenda paced to the poolside, and looked down into the dark, still water. She could see her leopard form reflected clearly, and over her right shoulder, the full moon.

Well, anger had gotten her into this shape, maybe anger would get her out. She closed her eyes for a moment, then began summoning all the force of that emotion she could—*willing* herself back into the form she'd always worn. She stared at her reflection in the water, forcing it, angrily, to be *her*. Whatever power was playing games with her was *not* going to find her clay to be molded at will!

As nothing happened, her frustration mounted; soon she was at the boiling point. Damn everything! She—would—not—be—played—with—

The same incoherent fury that had seized her when she first changed washed over her a second time—and the same agonizing pain sent blackness in front of her eyes and flung her to lie twitching helplessly beside the pool. Her left forepaw felt like it was afire—

In moments it was over, and she found herself sprawling beside the pond, shivering with cold and reaction, and totally naked. Naked, that is, except for the silver cat-ring, whose topaz eyes glowed hotly at her for a long moment before the light left them.

The second time she transformed to leopard was much easier; the pain was less, the amount of time less. She decided against being human—after finding herself without a stitch on, in a perilously vulnerable and helpless form, leopard-Glenda seemed a much more viable alternative.

But the ability to switch back and forth proved to be very handy. The villagers had taken note of her raids on their stock; they began mounting a series of systematic hunts for her, even penetrating into the forest so long as it was by daylight. She learned or remembered from reading countless tricks to throw the hunters off, and being able to change from human to leopard and back again made more than one of those possible. There *were* places girl-Glenda could climb and hide that leopard-Glenda couldn't, and the switch in scents when she changed confused and frightened the dog-pack. She began feeling an amused sort of contempt for the villagers, often leading individual hunters on wild-goose chases for the fun of it when she became bored.

But on the whole, it was better to be leopard; leopard-Glenda was comfortable and content sleeping on rocks or on the dried leaves of her lair—girl-Glenda shivered and ached and wished for her roach-infested efficiency. Leopard-Glenda was perfectly happy on a diet of raw fish, flesh and fowl—girl-Glenda wanted to throw up when she thought about it. Leopard-Glenda was content with nothing to do but tease the villagers and sleep in the sun when she wasn't hunting—girl-Glenda fretted, and longed for a book, and wondered if what she was doing was right . . .

So matters stood until Midsummer.

Glenda woke, shivering, with a mouth gone dry with panic. The dream—

It wasn't just a nightmare. This dream had been so real she'd expected to wake with an arrow in her ribs. She was still panting with fright even now.

There had been a man—he hadn't looked much like any of the villagers; they were mostly blond or brown-haired, and of the kind of hefty build her aunt used to call "peasant-stock" in a tone of contempt. No, he had resembled her in a way—as if she were a kind of washed-out copy of the template from which his kind had been cut. Where her hair was a dark mousy-brown, his was just as dark, but the color was more intense. They had the same general build: thin, tall, with prominent cheekbones. His eyes—

Her aunt had called her "cat-eyed," for she didn't have eyes of a normal brown, but more of a vague yellow, as washed-out as her hair. But *his* had been truly and intensely gold, with a greenish back-reflection like the eyes of a wild animal at night.

And those eyes had been filled with hunter-awareness; the eyes of a predator. And *she* had been his quarry!

The dream came back to her with extraordinary vividness; it had begun as she'd reached the edge of the forest, with him hot on her trail. She had a vague recollection of having begun the chase in human form, and having switched to leopard as she reached the trees. He had no dogs, no aid but his own senses—yet nothing she'd done had confused him for more than a second. She'd even laid a false trail into the stone circle, something she'd never done to another hunter, but she was beginning to panic—he'd avoided the trap neatly. The hunt had begun near mid-morning; by false dawn he'd brought her to bay and trapped her—

And that was when she'd awakened.

She spent the early hours of the morning pacing beside the pond; feeling almost impelled to go into the village, yet afraid to do so. Finally the need to *see* grew too great; she crept to the edge of the village past the guards, and slipped into the maze of whole and half-ruined buildings that was the village-proper.

There was a larger than usual market-crowd today; the usual market stalls had been augmented by strangers with more luxurious goods, foodstuffs, and even a couple of ragged entertainers. Evidently this was some sort of fair. With so many strangers about, Glenda was able to remain unseen. Her courage came back as she skirted the edge of the marketplace, keeping to shadows and sheltering within half-tumbled walls, and the terror of the night seemed to become just one more shadow.

Finally she found an ideal perch—hiding in the shadow just under the eaves of a half-ruined building that had evidently once belonged to the local lordling, and in whose courtyard the market was usually held. From here she could see the entire court and yet remain unseen by humans and unscented by any of the livestock.

She had begun to think her fears were entirely groundless—when she caught sight of a stranger coming out of the door of what passed for an inn here, speaking earnestly with the village headman. Her blood chilled, for the man was tall, dark-haired, and lean, and dressed entirely in dark leathers just like the man in her dream.

He was too far away for her to see his face clearly, and she froze in place, following him intently without moving a muscle. The headman left him with a satisfied air, and the man gazed about him, as if looking for something—

He finally turned in her direction, and Glenda nearly died of fright—for the face was that of the man in her dream, and he was staring directly at her hiding place as though he knew exactly where and what she was!

She broke every rule she'd ever made for herself—broke cover, in full sight of the entire village. In the panicked, screaming mob, the hunter could only curse—for the milling, terror-struck villagers were only interested in fleeing in the opposite direction from where Glenda stood, tail lashing and snarling with fear.

She took advantage of the confusion to leap the wall of the courtyard and sprint for the safety of the forest. Halfway there she changed into human for a short run—there was no one to see her, and it might throw him off the track. Then at forest edge, once on the springy moss that would hold no tracks, she changed back to leopard. She paused in the shade for a moment, to get a quick drink from the stream, and to rest, for the full-out run from the village had tired her badly—only to look up, to see him standing directly across the stream from her. He was shading his eyes with one hand against the sun that beat down on him, and it seemed to her that he was smiling in triumph.

She choked on the water, and fled.

She called upon every trick she'd ever learned, laying false trails by the dozen; fording the stream as it threaded through the forest not once but several times; breaking her trail entirely by taking to the treetops on an area where she could cross several hundred feet without once having to set foot to the ground. She even drove a chance-met herd of deer-creatures across her back-trail, muddling the tracks past following. She didn't remember doing any of this in her dream—in her dream she had only run, too fearful to do much that was complicated—or so she remembered. At last, panting with weariness, she doubled back to lair-up in the crotch of a huge tree, looking back down the way she had passed, certain that she would see him give up in frustration.

He walked so softly that even *her* keen ears couldn't detect his tread; she was only aware that he was there when she saw him. She froze in place—she hadn't really expected he'd get *this* far! But surely, surely when he came to the place she'd taken to the branches, he would be baffled, for she'd first climbed as girl-Glenda, and there wasn't any place where the claw-marks of the leopard scored the trunks within sight of the ground.

He came to the place where her tracks ended—and closed his eyes, a frown-line between his brows. Late afternoon sun filtered through the branches and touched his face; Glenda thought with growing confidence that he had been totally fooled by her trick. He carried a strung bow, black as his clothing and highly polished, and wore a sword and dagger, which none of the villagers ever did. As her fear ebbed, she had time to think (with a tiny twinge) that he couldn't have been much older than she—and was very, very attractive.

As if that thought had touched something that signaled him, his eyes snapped open—and he looked straight through the branches that concealed her to rivet his own gaze on *her* eyes.

With a mew of terror she leapt out of the tree and ran in mindless panic as fast as she could set paw to ground.

The sun was reddening everything; she cringed and thought of blood. Then she thought of her dream, and the dweller-in-the-circle. If, instead of a false trail, she laid a *true* one—waiting for him at the end of it—

If she rushed him suddenly, she could probably startle him into the power of the thing that lived within the shelter of those stones. Once in the throes of its mental grip, she doubted he'd be able to escape.

It seemed a heaven-sent plan; relief made her light-headed as she ran, leaving a clear trail behind her, to the place of the circle. By the time she reached its vicinity it was full dark—and she knew the power of the dweller was at its height in darkness. Yet, the closer she drew to those glowing stones, the slower her paws moved; and a building reluctance to do this thing weighed heavily on her. Soon she could see the stones shining ahead of her; in her mind she pictured the man's capture—his terror—his inevitable end.

Leopard-Glenda urged—kill!

Girl-Glenda wailed in fear of him, but stubbornly refused to put him in the power of *that*.

The two sides of her struggled, nearly tearing her physically in two as she half-shifted from one to the other, her outward form paralleling the struggle within.

At last, with a pathetic cry, the leopard turned in her tracks and ran from the circle. The will of girl-Glenda had won.

Whenever she paused to rest, she could hear him coming long before she'd even caught her breath. The stamina of a leopard is no match for that of a human; they are built for the short chase, not the long. And the stamina of girl-Glenda was no match for that of he who hunted her; in either form now, she was exhausted. He had driven her through the moon-lit clearings of the forest she knew out beyond the territory she had ranged before. This forest must extend deep into the Waste, and this was the direction he had driven her. Now she stumbled as she ran, no longer capable of clever tricks, just fear-prodded running. Her eyes were glazed with weariness; her mind numb with terror. Her sides heaved as she panted, and her mouth was dry, her thirst a raging fire inside her.

She fled from bush to tangled stand of undergrowth, at all times avoiding the patches of moonlight, but it seemed as if her foe knew this section of the wilderness as well or better than she knew her own territory. She could not rid herself of the feeling that she was being driven to some goal only he knew.

Suddenly, as rock-cliff loomed before her, she realized that her worst fears were correct. He had herded her into a deadend ravine, and there was no escape for her, at least not in leopard-form.

The rock before her was sheer; to either side it slanted inward. The stone itself was brittle shale; almost impassable—yet she began shifting into her human form to make that attempt. Then a sound from behind her told her that she had misjudged his nearness—and it was too late.

She whirled at bay, half-human, half-leopard, flanks heaving as she sucked in pain-filled gasps of air. He blocked the way out; dark and grim on the path, nocked bow in hand. She thought she saw his eyes shine with fierce joy even in the darkness of the ravine. She had no doubts that he could see her as easily as she saw him. There was nowhere to hide on either side of her.

Again leopard-instinct urged—kill!

Her claws extended, and she growled deep in her throat, half in fear, half in warning. He paced one step closer.

She could—she could fight him. She could dodge the arrow—at this range he could never get off the second. If she closed with him, she could kill him! His blood would run hot between her teeth—

Kill!

*No!* Never, never had she harmed another human being, not even the man who had denied her succor. No!

Kill!

She fought the leopard within, knowing that if it won, there would never be a girl-Glenda again; only the predator, the beast. And that would be the death of her—a death as real as that which any arrow could bring her.

And he watched from the shadows; terrible, dark, and menacing, his bow half-drawn. And yet—he did not move, not so much as a single muscle. If he had, perhaps the leopard would have won; fear triumphing over will. But he stirred not, and it was the human side of her that conquered.

And she waited, eyes fixed on his, for death.

:*Gentle, lady.*:

She started as the voice spoke in her head—then shook it wildly, certain that she had been driven mad at last.

:*Be easy—do not fear me.*:

Again that voice! She stared at him, wild-eyed—was he some kind of magician, to speak in her very thoughts?

And as if that were not startlement enough, she watched, dumbfounded, as he knelt, slowly—slowly eased the arrow off the string of his bow—and just as slowly laid them to one side. He held out hands now empty, his face fully in the moonlight—and *smiled*.

And rose—and—

At first she thought it was the moonlight that made him seem to writhe and blur. Then she thought that certainly her senses were deceiving her as her mind had—for his body *was* blurring, shifting, changing before her eyes, like a figure made of clay softening and blurring and becoming another shape altogether—

Until, where the hunter had stood, was a black leopard, half-again her size.

Glenda stared into the flames of the campfire, sipping at the warm wine, wrapped in a fur cloak, and held by a drowsy contentment. The wine, the cloak and the campfire were all Harwin's.

For that was the name of the hunter—Harwin. He had coaxed her into her following him; then, once his camp had been reached, coaxed her into human form again. He had given her no time to be shamed by her nakedness, for he had shrouded her in the cloak almost before the transformation was complete. Then he had built this warming fire from the banked coals of the old, and fed her the first cooked meal she'd had in months, then pressed the wine on her. And all with slow, reassuring movements, as if he was quite well aware how readily she could be startled into transforming back again, and fleeing into the forest. And all without speaking much besides telling her his name; his silence not unfriendly, not in the least, but as if he were waiting with patient courtesy for her to speak first.

She cleared her throat, and tentatively spoke her first words in this alien tongue, her own voice sounding strange in her ears.

"Who—are you? *What* are you?"

He cocked his head to one side, his eyes narrowing in concentration, as he listened to her halting words.

"You speak the speech of the Dales as one who knows it only indifferently, lady," he replied, his words measured, slow, and pronounced with care, as if he guessed she needed slow speech to understand clearly. "Yet you do not have the accent of Arvon—and I do not think you are one of the Old Ones. If I tell you who and what I am, will you do me like courtesy?"

"I—my name is Glenda. I couldn't do—this—at home. Wherever home is. I—I'm not sure what I am."

"Then your home is not of this world?"

"There was—" it all seemed so vague, like a dream now, "a city. I—lived there, but not well. I was hunted—I found a place—a woman. I thought she was crazy, but—she said something, and I saw this place—and I had to come—"

"A Gate, I think, and a Gate-Keeper," he nodded, as if to himself. "That explains much. So you found yourself here?"

"In the Waste. Though I didn't know that was what it was. I met a man—I was tired, starving, and he tried to drive me away. I got mad."

"The rest I know," he said. "For Elvath himself told me of how you went *were* before his eyes. Poor lady—how bewildered you must have been, with no one to tell you what was happening to you! And then?"

Haltingly, with much encouragement, she told him of her life in the forest; her learning to control her changes—and her side of the night's hunt.

"And the woman won over the beast," he finished. "And well for you that it did." His gold eyes were very somber, and he spoke with emphasis heavy in his words. "Had you turned on me, I doubt that you would ever have been able to find your human self again."

She shuddered. "What am I?" she asked at last, her eyes fixed pleadingly on his. "And where am I? And why has all this been happening to me?"

"I cannot answer the last for you, save only that I think you are here because your spirit never fit truly in that strange world from which you came. As for where—you are in the Dale lands of High Halleck, on the edge of the Waste—which tells you nothing, I know. And what you are—like me, you are plainly of some far-off strain of Wereblood. Well, perhaps not quite like me; among my kind the females are not known for being able to shape-change, and I myself am of half-blood only. My mother is Kildas of the Dales; my father Harl of the Wereriders. And I—I am Harwin," he smiled, ruefully, "of no place in particular."

"Why—why did you hunt me?" she asked. "Why did they want *you* to hunt me?"

"Because they had no notion of my Wereblood," he replied frankly. "They only know of my reputation as a hunter—shall I begin at the beginning? Perhaps it will give you some understanding of this world you have fallen into."

She nodded eagerly.

"Well—you may have learned that in my father's time the Dales were overrun by the Hounds of Alizon?" At her nod, he continued. "They had strange weapons at their disposal, and came very close to destroying all who opposed them. At that time my father and his brother-kin lived in the Waste, in exile for certain actions in the past from the land of Arvon, which lies to the north of the Waste. They—as I, as you—have the power of shape-change, and other powers as well. It came to the defenders of the Dales that one must battle strangeness with strangeness, and power with power; they made a pact with the Wereriders. In exchange for aid, they would send to them at the end of the war in the Year of the Unicorn twelve brides and one. You see, if all went well, the Wererider's exile was to end then—but if all was not well, they would have remained in exile, and they did not wish their kind to die away. The war ended, the brides came—the exile ended. But one of the bridegrooms was—like me—of half-blood. And one of the brides was a maiden of Power. There was much trouble for them; when the trouble was at an end they left Arvon together, and I know nothing more of their tale. Now we come to my part of the tale. My mother Kildas has gifted my father with three children, of which two are a pleasure to his heart and of like mind with him. I am the third."

"The misfit? The rebel?" she guessed shrewdly.

"If by that you mean the one who seems destined always to anger his kin with all he says and does—aye. We cannot agree, my father and I. One day in his anger, he swore that I was another such as Herrel. Well, that was the first that *I* had ever heard of one of Wereblood who was like-minded with me—I plagued my mother and father both until they gave me the tale of Herrel Half-blood and his Witch-bride. And from that moment, I had no peace until I set out to find them. For surely, I thought, I would find true kin-feeling with them, the which I lacked with those truly of my blood."

"And did you find them?"

"Not yet," he admitted. "At my mother's request I came here first, to give word to her kin that she was well, and happy, and greatly honored by her lord. Which is the entire truth. My father—loves her dearly; grants her every wish before she has a chance to voice it. I could wish to find a lady with whom—well, that was one of the reasons that I sought Herrel and his lady."

He was silent for so long, staring broodingly into the flames, that Glenda ventured to prompt him.

"So—you came here?"

"Eh? Oh, aye. And understandably enough, earned no small reputation among my mother-kin for hunting, though they little guessed in what form I did my tracking!" He grinned at her, and she found herself grinning back. "So when there were rumors of another Were here at the edge of the Waste—and a Were that thoughtlessly preyed on the beasts of these people as well as its rightful game—understandably enough, I came to hear of it. I thought at first that it must be Herrel, or a son. Imagine my surprise on coming here to learn that the Were was female! My reputation preceded me—the headman begged me to rid the village of their 'monster'—" He spread his hands wide. "The rest, you know."

"What—what will you do with me now?" she asked in a small, fearful voice.

"Do with you?" he seemed surprised. "Nothing—nothing not of your own will, lady. I am not going to harm you—and I am not like my father and brother, to force a one in my hand into anything against her wishes. I—I go forward as I had intended—to find Herrel. You, now that you know what your actions should *not* be, lest you arouse the anger of ordinary folk against you, may remain here—"

"And?"

"And I shall tell them I have killed the monster. You shall be safe enough—only remember that you must *never* let the leopard control you, or you are lost. Truly, you should have someone to guide and teach you, though—"

"I—know that, now," she replied, very much aware of how attractive he was, gold eyes fixed on the fire, a lock of dark hair falling over his forehead. But no man had ever found her to be company to be sought-after. There was no reason to think that he might be hinting—

No reason, that is, until he looked full into her eyes, and she saw the wistful loneliness there, and a touch of pleading.

"I would be glad to teach you, lady," he said softly. "Forgive me if I am over-forward, and clumsy in my speech. But—I think you and I could companion well together on this quest of mine—and—I—" he dropped his eyes to the flames again, and blushed hotly "—I think you very fair."

"Me?" she squeaked, more startled than she had been since he transformed before her.

"Can you doubt it?" he replied softly, looking up eagerly. He held out one hand to her. "Can I hope—you *will* come with me?"

She touched his fingers with the hesitation of one who fears to break something. "You mean you really want me with you?"

"Since I touched your mind—lady, more than you could dream! Not only are you kin-kind, but—mind-kin, I think."

She smiled suddenly, feeling almost light-headed with the revelations of the past few hours—then giggled, as an irrelevant though came to her. "Harwin—what happens to your clothes?"

"My *what*?" he stared at her for a moment as if she had broken into a foreign tongue—then looked at her, and back at himself—and blushed, then grinned.

"Well? I mean, I left bits of jeans and t-shirt all over the Waste when *I* changed—"

"What happens to your ring, lady?"

"It—" her forehead furrowed in thought. "I don't know, really. It's gone when I change, it's back when I change back." She regarded the tiny beast thoughtfully, and it seemed as if one of its topaz eyes closed in a slow wink. But—no. That could only have been a trick of the firelight.

"Were-magic, lady. And magic I think I shall let you avail yourself of, seeing as I can hardly let you take a chill if you are to accompany me—" He rummaged briefly in his pack and came up with a shirt and breeches, both far too large for her, but that was soon remedied with a belt and much rolling of sleeves and cuffs. She changed quickly under the shelter of his cloak.

"They'll really change with me?" she looked down at herself doubtfully.

"Why not try them?" He stood, and held out his hand—then blurred in that disconcerting way. The black leopard looked across the fire at her with eyes that glowed with warmth and approval.

*:The night still has time to run, Glenda-my-lady. Will you not run with it, and me?:*

The eyes of the cat-ring glowed with equal warmth, and Glenda found herself filled with a feeling of joy and freedom—and of *belonging*—that she tossed back her head and laughed aloud as she had never in her life done before. She stretched her own arms to the stars, and called on the power within her for the first time with joy instead of anger—

And there was no pain—only peace—as she transformed into a slim, lithe she-leopard, whose eyes met that of the he with a happiness that was heart-filling.

*:Oh yes, Harwin-my-lord! Let us run the night to dawn!:*

*The four SKitty stories appeared in "Cat Fantastic" Anthologies edited by Andre Norton. I'm very, very fond of SKitty; it might seem odd for a bird person to be fond of cats, but I am, so there it is. I was actually a cat person before I was a bird mother, and I do have two cats, both Siamese-mix, both rather old and very slow. Just, if the other local cats poach too often at my bird feeders, they can expect to get a surprise from the garden hose.*

# SKitty

## Mercedes Lackey

:*Nasty,*: SKitty complained in Dick's head. She wrapped herself a little closer around his shoulders and licked drops of oily fog from her fur with a faint mew of distaste. :*Smelly.*:

Dick White had to agree. The portside district of Lacu'un was pretty unsavory; the dismal, foggy weather made it look even worse. Shabby, cheap, and ill-used.

Every building here—all twenty of them!—was off-world design; shoddy prefab, mostly painted in shades of peeling gray and industrial green, with garish neon-bright holosigns that were (thank the Spirits of Space!) mostly tuned down to faintly colored ghosts in the daytime. There were six bars, two gambling-joints, one chapel run by the neo-Jesuits, one flophouse run by the Reformed Salvation Army, five government buildings, four stores, and once place better left unnamed. They had all sprung up, like diseased fungus, in the

271

year since the planet and people of Lacu'un had been declared Open for trade. There was nothing native here; for that you had to go outside the Fence—

*And to go outside the Fence,* Dick reminded himself, *you have to get permits signed by everybody and his dog.*

:*Cat,*: corrected SKitty.

*Okay, okay,* he thought back with wry amusement. *Everybody and his cat. Except they don't have cats here, except on the ships.*

SKitty sniffed disdainfully. :*Fools.*: she replied, smoothing down an errant bit of damp fur with her tongue, thus dismissing an entire culture that currently had most of the companies on their collective knees begging for trading concessions.

*Well, we've seen about everything there is to see,* Dick thought back at SKitty, reaching up to scratch her ears as she purred in contentment. *Are you quite satisfied?*

:*Hunt now?*: she countered hopefully.

*No, you can't hunt. You know that very well. This is a Class Four world; you have to have permission from the local sapients to hunt, and they haven't given us permission to even sneeze outside the Fence. And inside the Fence you are valuable merchandise subject to catnapping, as you very well know. I played shining knight for you once, furball, and I don't want to repeat the experience.*

SKitty sniffed again. :*Not love me.*:

*Love you too much, pest. Don't want you ending up in the hold of some tramp freighter.*

SKitty turned up the volume on her purr, and rearranged her coil on Dick's shoulders until she resembled a lumpy black fur collar on his gray shipsuit. When she left the ship—and often when she was in the ship—that was SKitty's perch of choice. Dick had finally prevailed on the purser to put shoulderpads on all his shipsuits—sometimes SKitty got a little careless with her claws.

When man had gone to space, cats had followed; they were quickly proven to be a necessity. For not only did man's old pests, rats and mice, accompany his trade—there seemed to be equivalent pests on every new world. But the shipscats were considerably different from their Earthbound ancestors. The cold reality was that a spacer couldn't afford a pet that had to be cared for—he needed something closer to a partner.

Hence SKitty and her kind; gene-tailored into something more than animals. SKitty was BioTech Type F-021; forepaws like that of a raccoon, more like stubby little hands than paws. Smooth, short hair with no undercoat to shed and clog up air filters. Hunter second to none. Middle-ear tuning so that not only was she not bothered by hyperspace shifts and freefall, she actually enjoyed them. And last, but by no means least, the enlarged head showing the boosting of her intelligence.

BioTech released the shipscats for adoption when they reached about six months old; when they'd not only been weaned, but trained. Training included maneuvering in freefall, use of the same sanitary facilities as the crew, and knowledge of emergency procedures. SKitty had her vacuum suit, just like any other crew member; a transparent hard plex ball rather like a tiny lifeslip, with a simple panel of controls inside to seal and pressurize it. She was positively paranoid about having it *with* her; she'd haul it along on its tether, if need be, so that it was always in the same compartment that she was. Dick respected her paranoia; any good spacer would.

Officially she was "Lady Sundancer of Greenfields"; Greenfields being BioTech Station NA-73. In actuality, she was SKitty to the entire crew, and only Dick remembered her real name.

Dick had signed on to the CatsEye Company ship *Brightwing* just after they'd retired their last shipscat to spend his final days with other creaky retirees from the spacetrade in the Tau Epsilon Old Spacers Station. As junior officer Dick had been sent off to pick up the replacement. SOP was for a BioTech technician to give you two or three candidates to choose among—in actuality, Dick hadn't had any choice. "Lady Sundancer" had taken one look at him and launched herself like a little black rocket from the arms of the tech straight for him; she'd landed on his shoulders, purring at the top of her lungs. When they couldn't pry her off, not without injuring her, the "choice" became moot. And Dick was elevated to the position of Designated Handler.

For the first few days she was "Dick White's Kitty"—the rest of his fellow crewmembers being vastly amused that she had so thoroughly attached herself to him. After a time that was shortened first to "Dick's Kitty" and then to "SKitty," which name finally stuck.

Since telepathy was *not* one of the traits BioTech was supposedly breeding and genesplicing for, Dick had been more than a little startled when she'd started speaking to him. And since none of the others ever mentioned hearing her, he had long ago come to the conclusion that he was the only one who could. He kept that a secret; at the least, should BioTech come to hear of it, it would mean losing her. BioTech would want to know where *that* particular mutation came from, for fair.

"Pretty gamy," he told Erica Makumba, Legal and Security Officer, who was the current on-watch at the airlock. The dusky woman lounged in her jumpseat with deceptive casualness, both hands behind her curly head—but there was a stun-bracelet on one wrist, and Erica just happened to be the *Brightwing*'s current karate champ.

"Eyeah," she replied with a grimace. "Had a look out there last night. Talk about your low-class dives! I'm not real surprised the Lacu'un threw the Fence up around it. Damn if *I'd* want that for neighbors! Hey, we may be getting a break, though; invitation's gone out to about three cap'ns to come make trade-talk. Seems the Lacu'un got themselves a lawyer—"

"So much for the 'unsophisticated primitives,'" Dick laughed. "I thought TriStar was riding for a fall, taking that line."

Erica grinned; a former TriStar employee, she had no great love for her previous employer. "Eyeah. So, lawyer goes and calls up the records on every Company making bids, goes over 'em with a fine-tooth. Seems only three of us came up clean; us, SolarQuest, and UVN. We got invites, rest got bye-byes. Be hearing a buncha ships clearing for space in the next few hours."

"My heart bleeds," Dick replied. "Any chance they can fight it?"

"Ha! Didn't tell you *who* they got for their mouthpiece. Lan Ventris."

Dick whistled. "*Somebody's* been looking out for them!"

"Terran Consul; she was the scout that made first contact. They wouldn't have anybody else, adopted her into the ruling sept, keep her at the Palace. Nice lady, shared a beer or three with her. She likes these people, obviously, takes their welfare real personal. Now—you want the quick low-down on the invites?"

Dick leaned up against the bulkhead, arms folded, taking care not to disturb SKitty. "Say on."

"One—" she held up a solemn finger, "Vena—that's the Consul—says that these folk have a long martial tradition; they're warriors, and admire warriors—but they admire honor and honesty even more. The trappings of primitivism are there, but it's a veneer for considerable sophistication. So whoever goes needs to walk a line between pride and honorable behavior that will be a *lot* like the old Japanese courts of Terra. Two, they are very serious about religion—they give us a certain amount of leeway for being ignorant outlanders, but if you transgress too far, Vena's not sure what the penalties may be. So you want to watch for signals, body-language from the priest-caste; that could warn you that you're on dangerous ground. Three—and this is what may give us an edge over the other two—they are very big on their totem animals; the sept totems are actually an important part of sept pride and the religion. So the Cap'n intends to make you and Her Highness there part of the delegation. Vena says that the Lacu'un intend to issue three contracts, so we're all gonna get one, but the folks that impress them the most will be getting first choice."

If Dick hadn't been leaning against the metal of the bulkhead he might well have staggered. As most junior on the crew, the likelihood that he was going to even go beyond the Fence had been staggeringly low—but that he would be included in the first trade delegation was mind-melting!

SKitty caroled her own excitement all the way back to his cabin, launching herself from his shoulder to land in her own little shock-bunk, bolted to the wall above his.

Dick began digging through his catch-all bin for his dress-insignia; the half-lidded topaz eye for CatsEye Company, the gold wings of the ship's insignia that went beneath it, the three tiny stars signifying the three missions he'd been on so far . . . .

He caught flickers of SKitty's private thoughts then; thoughts of pleasure, thoughts of nesting—

*Nesting!*

Oh *no!*

He spun around to meet her wide yellow eyes, to see her treading out her shock-bunk.

*SKitty,* he pled, *Please don't tell me you're pregnant—*

:Kittens,: she affirmed, very pleased with herself.

*You swore to me that you weren't in heat when I let you out to hunt!*

She gave the equivalent of a mental shrug. *:I lie.:*

He sat heavily down on his own bunk, all his earlier excitement evaporated. BioTech shipscats were supposed to be sterile—about one in a hundred weren't. And you had to sign an agreement with BioTech that you wouldn't neuter yours if it proved out fertile; they wanted the kittens, wanted the results that came from outbreeding. Or you could sell the kittens to other ships yourself, or keep them; provided a BioTech station wasn't within your ship's current itinerary. But of course, only BioTech would take them before they were six months old and trained . . . .

That was the rub. Dick sighed. SKitty had already had one litter on him—only two, but it had seemed like twenty-two. There was this problem with kittens in a spaceship; there was a period of time between when they were mobile and when they were about four months old that they had exactly two neurons in those cute, fluffy little heads. One neuron to keep the body moving at warp speed, and one neuron to pick out the situation guaranteed to cause the most trouble.

Everyone in the crew was willing to play with them—but no one was willing to keep them out of trouble. And since SKitty was Dick's responsibility, it was *Dick* who got to clean up the messes, and *Dick* who got to fish the little fluffbrains out of the bridge console, and *Dick* who got to have the anachronistic litter pan in his cabin until SKitty got her babies properly toilet trained.

Securing a litter pan for freefall was not something he had wanted to have to do again. Ever.

*How could you do this to me?* he asked SKitty reproachfully. She just curled her head over the edge of her bunk and trilled prettily.

He sighed. Too late to do anything about it now.

" . . . and you can see the carvings adorn every flat surface," Vena Ferducci, the small, dark-haired woman who was the Terran Consul, said, waving her hand gracefully at the walls. Dick wanted to stand and gawk; this was *incredible!*

The Fence was actually an opaque forcefield, and only *one* of the reasons the companies wanted to trade with the Lacu'un. Though they did not have spaceflight, there were certain applications of forcefield technologies they *did* have that seemed to be beyond the Terran's abilities. On the other side of the Fence was literally another world.

These people built to last, in limestone, alabaster, and marble, in the wealthy district, and in cast stone in the outer city. The streets were carefully poured sections of concrete, cleverly given stress-joints to avoid temperature-cracking, and kept clean enough to eat from by a small army of street-sweepers. No animals were allowed on the streets themselves, except for housetrained pets. The only vehicles permitted were single- or double-being electric carts, that could move no faster than a man could walk. The Lacu'un dressed either in filmy, silken robes, or in more practical, shorter versions of the same garments. They were a handsome race, upright bipeds, skin tones in varying shades of browns and dark golds, faces vaguely avian, with a frill like an iguana's running from the base of the neck to a point between and just above the eyes.

As Vena had pointed out, every wall within sight was heavily carved, the carvings all having to do with the Lacu'un religion.

Most of the carvings were depictions of various processions or ceremonies, and no two were exactly alike.

"That's the Harvest-Gladness," Vena said, pointing, as they walked, to one elaborate wall that ran for yards. "It's particularly appropriate for Kla'dera; he made all his money in agriculture. Most Lacu'un try to have something carved that reflects on their gratitude for 'favors granted.'"

"I think I can guess that one," the Captain, Reginald Singh, said with a smile that showed startlingly white teeth in his dark face. The carving he nodded to was a series of panels; first a celebration involving a veritable kindergarten full of children, then those children—now sex-differentiated and seen to be all female— worshiping at the alter of a very fecund-looking Lacu'un female, and finally the now-maidens looking sweet and demure, each holding various religious objects.

Vena laughed, her brown eyes sparkling with amusement. "No, that one isn't hard. There's a saying, 'as fertile as Gel'vadera's wife.' Every child was a female, too, that made it even better. Between the bride-prices he got for the ones that wanted to wed, and the officer's price he got for the ones that went into the armed services, Gel'vadera was a rich man. His First Daughter owns the house now."

"Ah—that brings up a question," Captain Singh replied. "Would you explain exactly who and what we'll be meeting? I read the briefing, but I still don't quite understand who fits in where with the government."

"It will help if you think of it as a kind of unholy mating of the British Parliamentary system and the medieval Japanese Shogunates," Vena replied. "You'll be meeting with the 'king'—that's the Lacu'ara—his consort, who has equal powers and represents the priesthood—that's the Lacu'teveras—and his three advisors, who are elected. The advisors represent the military, the bureaucracy, and the economic sector. The military advisor is always female; all officers in the military are female, because the Lacu'un believe that females will not seek glory for themselves, and so will not issue reckless orders. The other two can be either sex. 'Advisor' is not altogether an accurate term to use for them; the Lacu'ara and Lacu'teveras rarely act counter to their advice."

Dick was paying scant attention to this monologue; he'd already picked all this up from the faxes he'd called out of the local library after he'd read the briefing. He was more interested in the carvings, for there was something about them that puzzled him.

All of them featured strange little six-legged creatures scampering about under the feet of the carved Lacu'un. They were about the size of a large mouse, and seemed to Dick to be wearing very smug expressions . . . though of course, he was surely misinterpreting.

"Excuse me Consul," he said, when Vena had finished explaining the intricacies of Lacu'un government to Captain Singh's satisfaction. "I can't help wondering what those little lizardlike things are."

"Kreshta," she said. "*I* would call them pests; you don't see them out on the streets much, but they are the reason the streets are kept so clean. You'll see them soon enough once we get inside. They're like mice, only worse; fast as lightning—they'll steal food right off your plate. The Lacu'un either can't or won't get rid of them, I can't tell you which. When I asked about them once, my host just rolled his eyes heavenward and said what translates to 'it's the will of the gods.'"

"Insh'allah?" Captain Singh asked.

"Very like that, yes. I can't tell if they tolerate the pests because it is the gods' will that they must, or if they tolerate them because the gods favor the little monsters. Inside the Fence we have to close the government buildings down once a month, seal them up, and fumigate. We're just lucky they don't breed very fast."

*:Hunt?:* SKitty asked hopefully from her perch on Dick's shoulders.

*No!* Dick replied hastily. *Just look, don't hunt!*

The cat was gaining startled—and Dick thought, appreciatively—looks from passersby.

"Just what is the status value of a totemic animal?" Erica asked curiously.

"It's the fact that the animal can be tamed at all. Aside from a handful of domestic herbivores, most animal life on Lacu'un has never been tamed. To be able to take a carnivore and train it to the hand implies that the gods are with you in a very powerful way." Vena dimpled. "I'll let you in on a big secret; frankly, Lan and I preferred the record of the *Brightwing* over the other two ships; you seemed to be more sympathetic to the Lacu'un. That's why we told you about the totemic animals, and why we left you until last."

"It wouldn't have worked without Dick," Captain Singh told her. "SKitty has really bonded to him in a remarkable way; I don't think this presentation would come off half so impressively if he had to keep her on a lead."

"It wouldn't," Vena replied, directing them around a corner. At the end of a short street was a fifteen-foot wall—carved, of course—pierced by an arching entranceway.

"The Palace," she said, rather needlessly.

Vena had been right. The kreshta were *everywhere*.

Dick could feel SKitty trembling with the eagerness to hunt, but she was managing to keep herself under control. Only the lashing of her tail betrayed her agitation.

He waited at parade rest, trying not to give in to the temptation to stare, as the Captain and the Negotiator, Grace Vixen, were presented to the five rulers of the Lacu'un in an elaborate ceremony that resembled a stately dance. Behind the low platform holding the five dignitaries in their iridescent robes were five soberly clad retainers, each with one of the "totemic animals." Dick could see now what Vena had meant; the handlers had their creatures under control, but only barely. There was something like a bird; something resembling a small crocodile; something like a snake, but with six very tiny legs; a creature vaguely catlike, but with a feathery coat, and a beast resembling a teddybear with scales. None of the handlers was actually holding his beast, except the bird-handler. All of the animals were on short chains, and all of them punctuated the ceremony with soft growls and hisses.

So SKitty, perched freely on Dick's shoulders, had drawn no few murmurs of awe from the crowd of Lacu'un in the Audience Hall.

The presentation glided to a conclusion, and the Lacu'teveras whispered something to Vena behind her fan.

"With your permission, Captain, the Lacu'teveras would like to know if your totemic beast is actually as tame as she appears?"

"She is," the Captain replied, speaking directly to the consort, and bowing, exhibiting a charm that had crossed species barriers many times before this.

It worked its magic again. The Lacu'teveras fluttered her fan and trilled something else at Vena. The audience of courtiers gasped.

"Would it be possible, she asks, for her to touch it?"

*SKitty?* Dick asked quickly, knowing that she was getting the sense of what was going on from his thoughts.

*:Nice,:* the cat replied, her attention momentarily distracted from the scurrying hints of movement that were all that could be seen of the kreshta. *:Nice lady. Feels good in head, like Dick.:*

*Feels good in head?* he thought, startled.

"I don't think that there will be any problem, Captain," Dirk murmured to Singh, deciding that he could worry about it later. "SKitty seems to like the Lacu'un. Maybe they smell right."

SKitty flowed down off his shoulder and into his arms as he stepped forward to present the cat to the Lacu'teveras. He showed the Lacu'un the cat's favorite spot to be scratched, under the chin. The long talons sported by all Lacu'un were admirably suited to the job of cat-scratching.

The Lacu'teveras reached forward with one lilac-tipped finger, and hesitantly followed Dick's example. The Audience Hall was utterly silent as she did so, as if the entire assemblage was holding its breath, waiting for disaster to strike. The courtiers gasped at her temerity when the cat stretched out her neck—then gasped again, this time with delight, as SKitty's rumbling purr became audible.

SKitty's eyes were almost completely closed in sensual delight; Dick glanced up to see that the Lacu'teveras' amber, slit-pupiled eyes were widened with what he judged was an equal delight. She let her other six fingers join the first, tentative one beneath the cat's chin.

"Such soft—" she said shyly, in musically accented Standard. "—such nice!"

"Thank you, High Lady," Dick replied with a smile. "We think so."

*:Verrry nice,:* SKitty seconded. *:Not head-talk like Dick, but feel good in head, like Dick. Nice lady have kitten soon, too.:*

The Lacu'teveras took her hand away with some reluctance, and signed that Dick should return to his place. SKitty slid back up onto his shoulders and started to settle herself.

It was then that everything fell apart.

The next stage in the ceremony called for the rulers to take their seats in their five thrones, and the Captain, Vena, and Grace to assume theirs on stools before the thrones so that each party could present what it wanted out of a possible relationship.

But the Lacu'teveras, her eyes still wistfully on SKitty, was not looking where she placed her hand. And on the armrest of the throne was a kreshta, frozen into an atypical immobility.

The Lacu'teveras put her hand—with all of her weight on it—right on top of the kreshta. The evil-looking thing squealed, squirmed, and bit her as hard as it could.

The Lacu'teveras cried out in pain—the courtiers gasped, the Advisors made warding gestures—and SKitty, roused to sudden and protective rage at this attack by *vermin* on the nice lady who was *with kitten*—leapt.

The kreshta saw her coming, and blurred with speed—but it was not fast enough to evade SKitty, gene-tailored product of one of BioTech's finest labs. Before it could cover even half the distance between it and safety, SKitty had it. There was a crunch audible all over the Audience Chamber, and the ugly little thing was hanging limp from SKitty's jaws.

Tail high, in a silence that could have been cut into bricks and used to build a wall, she carried her prize to the feet of the injured one Lacu'un and laid it there.

*:Fix him!:* Dick heard in his mind. *:Not hurt nice-one-with-kitten!:*

The Lacu'ara stepped forward, face rigid, every muscle tense.

*Spirits of Space!* Dick thought, steeling himself for the worst. *That's bloody well torn it—*

But the Lacu'ara, instead of ordering the guards to seize the Terrans, went to one knee and picked up the broken-backed kreshta as if it were a fine jewel.

Then he brandished it over his head while the entire assemblage of Lacu'un burst into cheers—and the Terrans looked at one another in bewilderment.

SKitty preened, accepting the caresses of every Lacu'un that could reach her with the air of one to whom adulation is long due.

Whenever an unfortunate kreshta happened to attempt to skitter by, she would turn into a bolt of black lightning, reenacting her kill to the redoubled applause of the Lacu'un.

Vena was translating as fast as she could, with the three Advisors all speaking at once. The Lacu'ara was tenderly bandaging the hand of his consort, but occasionally one or the other of them would put in a word too.

"Apparently they've never been able to exterminate the kreshta; the natural predators on them *can't* be domesticated and generally take pieces out of anyone trying, traps and poisoned baits don't work because the kreshta won't take them. The only thing they've *ever* been able to do is what we were doing behind the Fence: close up the building and fumigate periodically. And even that has problems—the Lacu'teveras, for instance, is violently allergic to the residue left when the fumigation is done."

Vena paused for breath.

"I take it they'd like to have SKitty around on a permanent basis?" the Captain said, with heavy irony.

"Spirits of Space, Captain—they think SKitty is a sign from the gods, incarnate! I'm not sure they'll let her leave!"

Dick heard that with alarm—in a lot of ways, SKitty was the best friend he had—

To leave her—the thought wasn't bearable!

SKitty whipped about with alarm when she picked up what he was thinking. With an anguished yowl, she scampered across the slippery stone floor and flung herself through the air to land on Dick's shoulders. There she clung, howling her objections at the idea of being separated at top of her lungs.

"What in—" Captain Singh exclaimed, turning to see what could be screaming like a damned soul.

"She doesn't want to leave me, Captain," Dick said defiantly. "And I don't think you're going to be able to get her off my shoulder without breaking her legs or tranking her."

Captain Singh looked stormy. "Damn it then, get a trank—"

"I'm afraid I'll have to veto that one, Captain," Erica interrupted apologetically. "The contract with BioTech clearly states that only the

designated handler—and that's Dick—or a BioTech representative
can treat a shipscat. And furthermore—" she continued, halting the
Captain before he could interrupt, "—it also states that to leave a
shipscat without its designated handler will force BioTech to refuse
anymore shipscats to *Brightwing* for as long as you are the Captain.
Now I don't want to sound like a troublemaker, Captain, but I for
one will flatly refuse to serve on a ship with no cat. Periodic vacuum
purges to kill the vermin do *not* appeal to me."

"Well then, I'll order the boy to—"

"Sir, I *am* the *Brightwing*'s legal advisor—I hate to say this, but
to order Dick to ground is a clear violation of *his* contract. He
hasn't got enough hours spacing yet to qualify him for a ground
position."

The Lacu'teveras had taken Vena aside, Dick saw, and was
chattering at her at top speed, waving her bandaged hand in the air.

"Captain Singh," she said, turning away from the Lacu'un and
tugging at his sleeve, "the Lacu'teveras has figured out that something
you said or did is upsetting the cat, and she's not very happy with
that—"

Captain Singh looked just about ready to swallow a bucket of
heated nails. "Spacer, *will* you get that feline calmed down before they
throw me in the local brig?"

"I'll—try sir—"

*Come on, old girl—they won't take you away. Erica and the nice
lady won't let them,* he coaxed. *You're making the nice lady unhappy,
and that might hurt her kitten—*

SKitty subsided, slowly, but continued to cling to Dick's shoulder
as if he was the only rock in a flood. :*Not take Dick.*:

*Erica won't let them.*

:*Nice Erica.*:

A sudden thought occurred to him. *SKitty-love, how long would
it take before you had your new kittens trained to hunt?*

She pondered the question. :*From wean? Three heats,*: she said
finally.

About a year, then, from birth to full hunter. "Captain, I may
have a solution for you—"

"I would be overjoyed to hear one," the Captain replied dryly.

"SKitty's pregnant again—I'm sorry, sir, I just found out today and I didn't have time to report it—but sir, this is going to be to our advantage! If the Lacu'un insisted, *we* could handle the whole trade deal, couldn't we, Erica? And it should take something like a year to get everything negotiated and set up, shouldn't it?"

"Up to a year and a half, Standard, yes," she confirmed. "And basically, whatever the Lacu'un want, they get, so far as the Company is concerned."

"Once the kittens are a year old, they'll be hunters just as good as SKitty is—so if you could see your way clear to doing all the set up—and sort of wait around for us to get done rearing the kittens—"

Captain Singh burst into laughter. "Boy, do you have any notion just how *many* credits handling the entire trade negotiations would put in *Brightwing*'s account? Do you have any idea what that would do for *my* status?"

"No sir," he admitted.

"Suffice it to say I *could* retire if I chose. And—Spirits of Space—kittens? Kittens we *could* legally sell to the Lacu'un? I don't suppose you have any notion of how many kittens we can expect this time?"

He sent an inquiring tendril of thought to SKitty. "Uh—I think four, sir."

"Four! And they were offering us *what* for just her?" the Captain asked Vena.

"A more-than-considerable amount," she said dryly. "Exclusive contract on the forcefield applications."

"How would they feel about bargaining for four to be turned over in about a year?"

Vena turned to the rulers and translated. The excited answer she got left no doubts in anyone's mind that the Lacu'un were overjoyed at the prospect.

"Basically, Captain, you've just convinced the Lacu'un that you hung the moon."

"Well—why don't we settle down to a little serious negotiation, hmm?" the Captain said, nobly refraining from rubbing his hands together with glee. "I think that all our problems for the future are about to be solved in one fell swoop! Get over here, Spacer. You and that cat have just received a promotion to Junior Negotiator."

:*Okay?*: SKitty asked anxiously.

*Yes, love,* Dick replied, taking Erica's place on a negotiator's stool. *Very okay!*

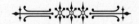

# A Tail of Two SKittys

## Mercedes Lackey

The howls coming from inside the special animal shipping crate sounded impatient, and had been enough to seriously alarm the cargo handlers. Dick White, Spaceman First Class, Supercargo on the CatsEye Company ship *Brightwing,* put his hand on the outside of the plastile crate, just above the word "Property." From within the crate the muffled voice continued to yowl general unhappiness with the world.

*Tell her that it's all right, SKitty,* he thought at the black form that lay over his shoulders like a living fur collar. *Tell her I'll have her out in a minute. I don't want her to come bolting out of there and hide the minute I crack the crate.*

SKitty raised her head. Yellow eyes blinked once, sleepily. Abruptly, the yowling stopped.

:*She fine,*: SKitty said, and yawned, showing a full mouth of needle-pointed teeth. :*Only young, scared. I think she make good mate for Furrball.*:

Dick shook his head; the kittens were not even a year old, and already their mother was matchmaking. Then again, that *was* the tendency of mothers the universe over.

At least now he'd be able to uncrate this would-be "mate" with a minimum of fuss.

The full legend imprinted on the crate read "Female Shipscat Astra Stardancer of Englewood, Property of BioTech Interstellar, leased to CatsEye Company. Do not open under penalty of law." Theoretically, Astra was, like SKitty, a bio-engineered shipscat, fully capable of handling freefall, alien vermin, conditions that would poison, paralyze, or terrify her remote Terran ancestors, and all without turning a hair. In actuality, Astra, like the nineteen other shipscats Dick had uncrated, was a failure. The genetic engineering of her middle-ear and other balancing organs had failed. She could not tolerate freefall, and while most ships operated under grav-generators, there were always equipment malfunctions and accidents.

That made her and her fellows failures by BioTech standards. A shipscat that could not handle freefall was not a shipscat.

Normally, kittens that washed out in training were adopted out to carefully selected planet- or stationbound families of BioTech employees. However, this was not a "normal" circumstance by any stretch of the imagination.

The world of the Lacu'un, graceful, bipedal humanoids with a remarkably sophisticated, if planetbound, civilization, was infested with a pest called a "kreshta." Erica Makumba, the Legal Advisor and Security Chief of Dick's ship described them as "six-legged crosses between cockroaches and mice." SKitty described them only as "nasty," but she hunted them gleefully anyway. The Lacu'un opened their world to trade just over a year ago, and some of their artifacts and technologies made them a desirable trade ally indeed. The *Brightwing* had been one of the three ships invited to negotiate, in part because of SKitty, for the Lacu'un valued totemic animals highly.

And that was what had led to Captain Singh of the *Brightwing* conducting the entire trade negotiations with the Lacu'un—and had kept *Brightwing* ground-bound for the past year. SKitty had done the—to the Lacu'un—impossible. She had killed kreshta. She had already been assumed to be *Brightwing*'s totemic animal; that act elevated her to the status of "god-touched miracle," and had given the captain and crew of her ship unprecedented control and access to the rulers here.

SKitty had been newly pregnant at the time; part of the price for the power Captain Singh now wielded had been her kittens. But Dick had gotten another idea, and had used his own share of the profits *Brightwing* was taking in to purchase the leases of twenty more "failed" cats to supplement SKitty's four kittens. BioTech cats released for leases were generally sterile, SKitty being a rare exception. If these twenty worked out, the Lacu'un would be very grateful, and more importantly, so would Vena Ferducci, the attractive, petite Terran Consul assigned to the new embassy here. In the past few months, Dick had gotten to know Vena very well—and he hoped to get to know her better. Vena had originally been a Survey Scout, and she was getting rather restless in her ground-based position as Consul. And in truth, the Lacu'un lawyer, Lan Ventris, was much better suited to such a job than Vena. She had hinted that as soon as the Lacu'un felt they could trust Ventris, she would like to resign and go back to space. Dick rather hoped she might be persuaded to take a position with the *Brightwing*. It was too soon to call this little dance a "romance," but he had hopes . . . .

Hopes which could be solidified by this experiment. If the twenty young cats he had imported worked out as well as SKitty's four half-grown kittens, the Lacu'un would be able to import their intelligent pest-killers at a fraction of what the lease on a shipscat would be. This would make Vena happy; anything that benefited her Lacu'un made her happy. And if Dick was the cause of that happiness . . .

:*Dick go courting?*: SKitty asked innocently, salting her query with decidedly *not*-innocent images of her own "courting."

Dick blushed. *No courting,* he thought firmly. *Not yet, anyway.*

:*Silly,*: SKitty replied scornfully. The overtones of her thoughts were—why waste such a golden opportunity? Dick did not answer her.

Instead, he thumbed the lock on the crate, a lock keyed to his DNA only. A tiny prickle was the only indication that the lock had taken a sample of his skin for comparison, but a moment later a hairline-thin crack appeared around the front end of the crate, and Dick carefully opened the door and looked inside.

A pair of big green eyes in a pointed gray face looked out at him from the shadows. "Meowrrrr?" said a tentative voice.

*Tell her it's all right, SKitty,* he thought, extending a hand for Astra to sniff. It was too bad that his telepathic connection with SKitty did not extend to these other cats, but she seemed to be able to relay everything he needed to tell them.

Astra sniffed his fingers daintily, and oozed out of the crate, belly to the floor. After a moment though, a moment during which SKitty stared at her so hard that Dick was fairly certain his little friend was communicating any number of things to the newcomer, Astra stood up and looked around, her ears coming up and her muscles relaxing. Finally she looked up at Dick and blinked.

"Prrow," she said. He didn't need SKitty's translation to read that. He held out his arms and the young cat leapt into them, to be carried in regal dignity out of the quarantine area.

As he turned away from the crate, he thought he caught a hint of movement in the shadows at the back. But when he turned to look, there was nothing there, and he dismissed it as nothing more than his imagination. If there *had* been anything else in Astra's crate, the manifest would have listed it—and Astra was definitely sterile, so it could not have been an unlicensed kitten.

Erica Makumba and Vena were waiting for him in the corridor outside. Vena offered her fingers to the newcomer; much more secure now, Astra sniffed them and purred. "She's lovely," Vena said in admiration. Dick had to agree; Astra was a velvety blue-gray from head to tail, and her slim, clean lines clearly showed her descent from Russian Blue ancestors.

*:She for Furrball,:* SKitty insisted, gently nipping at his neck.

*Is this your idea or hers?* Dick retorted.

*:Sees Furrball in head; likes Furrball.:* That seemed to finish it as far as SKitty was concerned. *:Good hunter, too.:* Dick gave in to the inevitable.

"Didn't we promise one of these new cats to the Lacu'teveras?" Dick asked. "This one seems very gentle; she'd probably do very well as a companion for Furrball." SKitty's kittens all had names as fancy as Astra's—or as SKitty's official name, for that matter. Furrball was "Andreas Widefarer of Lacu'un"; Nuisance was "Misty Snowspirit of Lacu'un"; Rags was "Lady Flamebringer of Lacu'un"; and Trey was

"Garrison Starshadow of Lacu'un." But they had, as cats always do, acquired their own nicknames that had nothing to do with the registered names. Astra would without a doubt do the same.

Each of the most prominent families of the Lacu'un had been granted one cat, but the Royal Family had three: two of SKitty's original kittens, and one of the newcomers. Astra would bring that number up to four, a sacred number to the Lacu'un and very propitious.

"We did," Vena replied absently, scratching a pleased Astra beneath her chin. "And I agree with you; I think this one would please the Lacu'teveras very much." She laughed a little. "I'm beginning to think you're psychic or something, Dick; you haven't been wrong with your selections yet."

"Me?" he said ingenuously. "Psychic? Spirits of Space, Vena, the way these people are treating the cats, it doesn't matter anyway. Any 'match' I made would be a good one, so far as the cat is concerned. They couldn't be pampered more if they were Lacu'un girl-babies!"

"True," she agreed, and reluctantly took her hand away. "Well, four cats should be just about right to keep the Palace vermin-free. It's really kind of funny how they've divided the place up among them with no bickering. They almost act as if they were humans dividing up patrols!" Erica shot him an unreadable glance; did she remember how he had sat down with the original three and SKitty— and a floor-plan of the place—when he first brought them all to the Palace?

"They are bred for high intelligence," he reminded both of them hastily. "No one really knows how bright they are. They're bright enough to use their life-support pods in an emergency, and bright enough to learn how to use the human facilities in the ships. They seem to have ways of communicating with each other, or so the people at BioTech tell me, so maybe they did establish patrols."

"Well, maybe they did," Erica said after a long moment. He heaved a mental sigh of relief. The last thing he needed was to have someone suspect SKitty's telepathic link with him. BioTech was not breeding for telepathy, but if such a useful trait ever showed up in a *fertile* female, they would surely cancel *Brightwing*'s lease and haul SKitty back to their nearest cattery to become a breeding queen. SKitty was his best friend; to lose her like that would be terrible.

:*No breeding*,: SKitty said firmly. :*Love Dick, love ship. No breeding; breeding dull, kittens a pain. Not leave ship ever.*:

Well, at least SKitty agreed.

For now, anyway, now that her kittens were weaned. Whenever she came into season, she seemed to change her mind, at least about the part that resulted in breeding, if not the breeding itself.

The Lacu'teveras, the Ruling Consort of her people, accepted Astra into the household with soft cries of welcome and gladness. Erica was right, the Lacu'un could not possibly have pampered their cats more. Whenever a cat wanted a lap or a scratch, one was immediately provided, whether or not the object of feline affection was in the middle of negotiations or a session of Council or not. Whenever one wished to play—although with the number of kreshta about, there was very little energy left over for playing—everything else was set aside for that moment. And when one brought in a trophy kreshta, tail and ears held high with pride, the entire court applauded. Astra was introduced to Furrball at SKitty's insistence. Noses were sniffed, and the two rubbed cheeks. It appeared that Mama's matchmaking was going to work.

The three humans and the pleased feline headed back across the city to the spaceport and the Fence around it. The city of the Lacu'un was incredibly attractive, much more so than any other similar city Dick had ever visited. Because of the rapidity with which the kreshta multiplied given any food and shelter, the streets were kept absolutely spotless, and the buildings clean and in repair. Most had walls about them, giving the inhabitants little islands of privacy. The walls of the wealthy were of carved stone; those of the poor of cast concrete. In all cases, ornamentation was the rule, not the exception.

The Lacu'un themselves walked the streets of their city garbed in delicate, flowing robes, or shorter more practical versions of the same garments. Graceful and handsome, they resembled avians rather than reptiles; their skin varied in shade from a dark brown to a golden tan, and their heads bore a kind of frill like an iguana's, that ran from the base of the neck to a point just above and between the eyes.

Their faces were capable of something like a smile, and the expression meant the same for them as it did for humans. Most of them smiled when they saw Dick and SKitty; although the kreshta-destroying abilities of the cat were not something any of them would personally feel the impact of for many years, perhaps generations, they still appreciated what the cats Dick had introduced could do. The kreshta had been a plague upon them for as long as their history recorded, even being so bold as to steal the food from plates and injure unguarded infants. For as long as that history, it had seemed that there would never be a solution to the depredations of the little beasts. But now—the most pious claimed the advent of the cats was a sign of the gods' direct intervention and blessing, and even the skeptics were thrilled at the thought that an end to the plague was in sight. It was unlikely that, even with a cat in every household, the kreshta would ever be destroyed—but such things as setting a guard on sleeping babies and locking meals in metal containers set into the tables could probably be eliminated.

When they crossed the Fence into Terran territory, however, the surroundings dropped in quality by a magnitude or two. Dick felt obscurely ashamed of his world whenever he looked at the shabby, garish spaceport "facilities" that comprised most of the Terran spaceport area. At least the headquarters that Captain Singh and CatsEye had established were handsome; adaptations of the natives' own architecture, in cast concrete with walls decorated with stylized stars, spaceships, and suggestions of slit-pupiled eyes. SolarQuest and UVN, the other two Companies that had been given Trade permits, were following CatsEye's lead, and had hired the same local architects and contractors to build their own headquarters. It looked from the half-finished buildings as if SolarQuest was going with a motif taken from their own logo of a stylized sunburst; UVN was going for geometrics in their wall-decor.

There were four ships here at the moment rather than the authorized three; for some reason, the independent freighter that had brought in the twenty shipscats was still here on the landing field.

Dick wondered about that for a moment, then shrugged mentally. Independents often ran on shoestring budgets; probably they had only loaded enough fuel to get them here, and refueling was taking more time than they had thought it would.

Suddenly, just as they passed through the doors of the building, SKitty howled, hissed, and leapt from Dick's shoulders, vanishing through the rapidly closing door.

He uttered a muffled curse and turned to run after her. What had gotten into her, anyway?

He found himself looking into the muzzle of a weapon held by a large man in the nondescript coveralls favored by the crew of that independent freighter. The man was as nondescript as his clothing, with ash-blond hair cut short and his very ordinary face—with the exception of that weapon, and the cold, calculating look in his iron-gray eyes. Dick put up his hands, slowly. He had the feeling this was a very bad time to play hero.


"Where's the damn cat?" snapped the one Dick was coming to think of as "the Gray Man." One of his underlings shrugged.

"Gone," the man replied shortly. "She got away when we rounded up these three, and she just vanished somewhere. Forget the cat. How much damage could a cat do?"

The Gray Man shrugged. "The natives might get suspicious if they don't see her with our man."

"She probably wouldn't have cooperated with our man," the underling pointed out. "Not like she did with this one. It doesn't matter—White got the new cats installed, and we don't need an animal that was likely to be a handful anyway."

The Gray Man nodded after a while and went back to securing the latest of his prisoners. The offices in the new CatsEye building had been turned into impromptu cells; Dick had gotten a glimpse of Captain Singh in one of them as he had been frog-marched past. He didn't know what these people had done with the rest of the crew or with Vena and Erica, since Vena had been taken off somewhere separately and Erica had been stunned and dragged away without waiting for her surrender.

The Gray Man watched him with his weapon trained on him as two more underlings installed a tangle-field generator across the doorway. With no windows, these little offices made perfect holding-pens. Most of them didn't have furniture yet, those that did didn't really contain anything that could be used as a weapon. The desks were simple slabs of native wood on metal supports, the chairs molded plastile, and both were bolted to the floor. There was nothing in Dick's little cubicle that could even be thrown.

Dick was still trying to figure out who and what these people were, when something finally clicked. He looked up at the Gray Man. "You're from TriStar, aren't you?" he asked.

If the Gray Man was startled by this, he didn't show it. "Yes," the man replied, gun-muzzle never wavering. "How did you figure that out?"

"BioTech never ships with anyone other than TriStar if they can help it," Dick said flatly. "I wondered why they had hired a tramp-freighter to bring out their cats; it didn't seem like them, but then I thought maybe that was all they could get."

"You're clever, White," the Gray Man replied, expressionlessly. "Too clever for your own good, maybe. We might just have to make you disappear. You and the Makumba woman; she'll probably know some of us as soon as she wakes up, and we don't have the time or the equipment to brain-wipe you."

Dick felt a chill going down his back, as the men at the door finished installing the field and left, quickly. "BioTech is going to wonder if one of their designated handlers just vanished. And without me, you're never going to get SKitty back; BioTech isn't going to care for that, either. They might start asking questions that you can't answer."

The Gray Man stared at him for a long moment; his expression did not vary in the least, but at least he didn't make any move to shoot. "I'll think about it," he said finally. He might have said more, but there was a shout from the corridor outside.

"*The cat!*" someone yelled, and the Gray Man was out of the door before Dick could blink. Unfortunately, he paused long enough to trigger the tangle-field before he ran off in pursuit of what could only have been SKitty.

Dick slumped down into the chair, and buried his face in his hands, but not in despair. He was thinking furiously.

*TriStar didn't like getting cut out of the negotiations; what they can't get legally, they'll get any way they can. Probably they intend to use us as hostages against Vena's good behavior, getting her to put them up as the new negotiators. I solved the problem of getting the cats for them; now there's no reason they couldn't just step in. But that can't go on forever, sooner or later Vena is going to get to a comm-unit or send some kind of message off-world. So what would these people do then?*

TriStar had a reputation as being ruthless, and he'd heard from Erica that it was justified. So how do you get rid of an entire crew of a spaceship *and* the Terran Consul? And maybe the crews of the other two ships into the bargain?

Well, there was always one answer to that, especially on a newly opened world. Plague.

The chill threaded his backbone again as he realized just what a good answer that was. These TriStar goons could use sickness as the excuse for why the CatsEye people weren't in evidence. A rumor of plague might well drive the other two ships off-world before *they* came down with it. The TriStar people could even claim to be taking care of the *Brightwing*'s crew.

*Then, after a couple of weeks, they all succumb to the disease, the Terran Consul with them . . . .*

It was a story that would work, not only with the Terran authorities, but with the Lacu'un. The Fence was a very effective barrier to help from the natives; the Lacu'un would not cross it to find out the truth, even if they were suspicious.

*I have to get to a comm-set,* he thought desperately. His own usefulness would last only so long as it took them to trap SKitty and find some way of caging her. No one else, so far as he knew, could hear her thoughts. All they needed to do would be to catch her and ship her back to BioTech, with the message that the designated handler was dead of plague and the cat had become unmanageable. It wouldn't have been the first time.

A soft hiss made him look up, and he strangled a cry of mingled joy and apprehension. It was SKitty! She was right outside the door, and she seemed to be trying to do something with the tangle-field generator.

*SKitty!* he thought at her as hard as he could. *SKitty, you have to get away from here, they're trying to catch you—*

There was no way SKitty was going to be able to deal with those controls; they were deliberately made difficult to handle, just precisely because shipscats were known to be curious. And how could she know what complicated series of things to do to take down the field anyway?

But SKitty ignored him, using her stubby raccoonlike hands on the controls of the generator and hissing in frustration when the controls would not cooperate.

Finally, with a muffled yowl of triumph, she managed to twist the dial into the "off" position and the field went down. Dick was out the door in a moment, but SKitty was uncharacteristically running off ahead of him instead of waiting for him. Not that he minded! She was safer on the ground in case someone spotted him and stunned him; she was small and quick, and if they caught him again, she would still have a chance to hide and get away. But there was something odd about her bounding run; as if her body was a little longer than usual. And her tail seemed to be a lot longer than he remembered—

*Never mind that, get moving!* he scolded himself, trying to recall where they'd set up all the comms and if any of them were translight. SKitty whisked ahead of him, around a corner; when he caught up with her, she was already at work on the tangle-field generator in front of another door.

Practice must have made perfect; she got the field down just before he reached the doorway, and shot down the hall like a streak of black lightning. Dick stopped; inside was someone lying down on a cot, arm over her dark mahogany head. Erica!

"Erica!" he hissed at her. She sat bolt upright, wincing as she did so, and he felt a twinge of sympathy. A stun-migraine was no picnic.

She saw who was at the door, saw at the same moment that there was no tangle-field shimmer between them, and was on her feet and out in a fraction of a second. "How?" she demanded, scanning the corridor and finding it as curiously empty as Dick had.

"SKitty took the generator offline," he said. "She got yours, too, and she headed off that way—" He pointed towards the heart of the building. "Do you remember where the translight comms are?"

"Eyeah," she said. "In the basement, if we can get there. That's the emergency unit and I don't think they know we've got it."

She cocked her head to one side, as if she had suddenly heard something. He strained his ears—and there was a clamor, off in the distance beyond the walls of the building. It sounded as if several people were chasing something. But it couldn't have been SKitty; she was still in the building.

"It sounds like they're busy," Erica said, and grinned. "Let's go while we have the chance!"

But before they reached the basement comm room, they were joined by most of the crew of the *Brightwing,* some of whom had armed themselves with whatever might serve as a weapon. All of them told the same story, about how the shipscat had taken down their tangle-fields and fled. Once in the basement of the building— after scattering the multiple nests of kreshta that had moved right in—the Com Officer took over while the rest of them found whatever they could to make a barricade and Dick related what he had learned and what his surmises were. Power controls were all down here; there would be no way short of blowing the building up for the TriStar goons to cut power to the com. Now all they needed was time—time to get their message out, and wait for the Patrol to answer.

*But time just might be in very short supply,* Dick told himself as he grabbed a sheet of reflective insulation to use as a crude stun-shield. And as if in answer to that, just as the Com Officer got the link warmed up and began to send, Erica called out from the staircase.

"Front and center—here they come!"

Dick slumped down so that the tiny medic could reach his head to bandage it. He knew he looked like he'd been through a war, but either the feeling of elated triumph or the medic's drugs or both prevented him from really feeling any of his injuries. In the end, it had come down to the crudest of hand-to-hand combat on the staircase, as the Com Officer resent the message as many times as he could and the rest of them held off the TriStar bullies. He could only thank the Spirits of Space that they had no weapons stronger than stunners—or at least, they hadn't wanted to use them down in the basement where so many circuits lay bare. Eventually, of course, they had been overwhelmed, but by then it was too late. The Com Officer had gotten a reply from the Patrol. Help was on the way. Faced with the collapse of their plan, the TriStar people had done the only wise thing. They had retreated.

With them, they had taken all evidence that they *were* from TriStar; there was no way of proving who and what they were, unless the Patrol corvette now on the way in could intercept them and capture them. Contrary to what the Gray Man had thought, Erica had recognized none of her captors.

But right now, none of that mattered. What did matter was that *they* had come through this—and that SKitty had finally reappeared as soon as the TriStar ship blasted out, to take her accustomed place on Dick's shoulders, purring for all she was worth and interfering with the medic's work.

"Dick—" Vena called from the door to the medic's office, "I found your—"

Dick looked up. Vena was cradling SKitty in her arms.

But SKitty was already on his shoulders.

She must have looked just as stunned as he did, but he recovered first, doing a double-take. *His* SKitty was the one on her usual perch—Vena's SKitty was a little thinner, a little taller—

And most *definitely* had a lot longer tail!

:Is Prrreet,: SKitty said with satisfaction. :Handsome, no? Is bred for being Patrol-cat, war-cat.:

"Vena, what's the tattoo inside that cat's ear?" he asked, urgently. She checked.

"FX-003," she said, "and a serial number. But the X designation is for experimental, isn't it?"

"Uh—yeah." He got up, ignoring the medic, and came to look at the new cat. Vena's stranger also had much more humanlike hands than his SKitty; suddenly the mystery of how the cat had managed to manipulate the tangle-field controls was solved.

*Shoot, he might even have been trained to do that!*

:*Yes,*: SKitty said simply. :*I go play catch-me-stupid, he open human-cages. He hear of me on station, come to see me, be mate. I think I keep him.*:

Dick closed his eyes for a moment. Somewhere, there was a frantic BioTech station trying to figure out where one of their experimentals had gone. He *should* turn the cat over to them!

:*No,*: SKitty said positively. :*No look. Is deaf one ear; is pet. Run away, find me.*:

"He uh—must have come in as an extra with that shipment," Dick improvised quickly. "I found an extra invoice, I just thought they'd made a mistake. He's deaf in one ear, that's why they washed him out. I uh—I suppose *Brightwing* could keep him."

"I was kind of hoping I could—" Vena began, and flushed, lowering her eyes. "I suppose I still could . . . after this, the embassy is going to have to have a full staff with Patrol guards and a real Consul. They won't need me anymore."

Dick began to grin, as he realized what Vena was saying. "Well, he will need a handler. And I have all I can do to take care of *this* SKitty."

:*Courting?*: SKitty asked slyly, reaching out to lick one of Prrreet's ears.

This time Dick did not bother to deny it.

# SCat

## Mercedes Lackey

"NoooOOOWOWOWOW!"

The metal walls of Dick's tiny cabin vibrated with the howl. Dick White ignored it, as he injected the last of the four contraception-beads into SKitty's left hind leg. The black-coated shipscat did not move, but she did continue her vocal and mental protest.

:*Mean,*: she complained, as Dick held the scanner over the right spot to make certain that he *had* gotten the bead placed where it was supposed to go. :*Mean, mean Dick.*:

Indignation showing in every line of her, she sat up on his fold-down desk and licked the injection site. It hadn't hurt; he *knew* it hadn't hurt, for he'd tried it on himself with a neutral bead before he injected her.

*Nice, nice Dick, you should be saying,* he chided her. *One more unauthorized litter and BioTech would be coming to take you away for their breeding program. You're too fertile for your own good.*

SKitty's token whine turned into a real yowl of protest, and her mate, now dubbed "SCat", joined her in the wail from his seat on Dick's bunk.

:*Not leave Dick!*: SKitty shrilled in his head. :*Not leave ship!*:

*Then no more kittens—at least not for a while!* he responded. *No more kittens means SKitty and SCat stay with Dick.*

SKitty leapt to join her mate on the bunk, where both of them began washing each other to demonstrate their distress over the idea of leaving Dick. SKitty's real name was "Lady Sundancer of Greenfields," and she was the proud product of BioTech's masterful genesplicing. Shipscats, those sturdy, valiant hunters of vermin of every species, betrayed their differences from Terran felines in a number of ways. BioTech had given them the "hands" of a raccoon, the speed of a mongoose, the ability to adjust to rapid changes in gravity or no gravity at all, and greatly enhanced mental capacity. What they did not know was that "Lady Sundancer"—aka "Dick White's Kitty," or "SKitty" for short—had another, invisible enhancement. She was telepathic—at least with Dick.

Thanks to SKitty and to her last litter, the CatsEye Company trading ship *Brightwing* was one of the most prosperous in this end of the Galaxy. That was due entirely to SKitty's hunting ability; she had taken swift vengeance when a persistent pest native to the newly opened world of Lacu'un had bitten the consort of the ruler, killing with a single blow a creature the natives had *never* been able to exterminate. That, and her own charming personality, had made her kittens-to-be *most* desirable acquisitions, so precious that not even the leaders of Lacu'un "owned" them; they were held in trust for the world. Thanks to the existence of that litter and the need to get them appropriately pedigreed BioTech mates, SKitty's own mate—called "Prrreet" by SKitty and unsurprisingly dubbed "SCat" by the crew, for his ability to vanish—had made his own way to SKitty, stowing aboard with the crates containing more BioTech kittens for Lacu'un.

Where *he* came from, only he knew, although he was definitely a shipscat. His tattoo didn't match anything in the BioTech register. Too dignified to be called a "kitty," this handsome male was "Dick White's Cat."

And thanks to SCat's timely arrival and intervention, an attempt to kill the entire crew of the *Brightwing* and the Terran Consul to Lacu'un in order to take over the trading concession had been unsuccessful. SCat had disabled critical equipment holding them all imprisoned, so that they were able to get to a comm station to call for help from the Patrol, while SKitty had distracted the guards.

SCat had never demonstrated telepathic powers with Dick, for which Dick was grateful, but he certainly possessed something of the sort with SKitty, and he was odd in other ways. Dick would have been willing to take an oath that SCat's forepaws were even more handlike than SKitty's, and that his tail showed some signs of being prehensile. There were other secrets locked in that wide black-furred skull, and Dick only wished he had access to them.

Dick was worried, for the *Brightwing* was in space again and heading towards one of the major stations with the results of their year-long trading endeavor with the beings of Lacu'un in their hold. Shipscats simply did not come out of nowhere; BioTech kept very tight control over them, denying them to ships or captains with a record of even the slightest abuse or neglect, and keeping track of where every one of them was, from birth to death. They were expensive—traders running on the edge could not afford them, and had to rid themselves of vermin with periodic vacuum-purges. SKitty claimed that her mate had "heard about her" and had come specifically to find her—but she would not say from where. SCat had to come from *somewhere,* and wherever that was, someone from there was probably looking for him. They would very likely take a dim view of their four-legged Romeo heading off on his own in search of his Juliet.

Any attempt to question the tom through SKitty was useless. SCat would simply stare at him with those luminous yellow eyes, then yawn, and SKitty would soon grow bored with the proceedings. After all, to her, the important thing was that SCat was *here,* not where he had come from.

Behind Dick, in the open door of the cabin, someone coughed. He turned to find Captain Singh regarding Dick and the cats with a jaundiced eye. Dick saluted hastily.

"Sir—contraceptive devices in place and verified sir!" he affirmed, holding up the injector to prove it.

The Captain, a darkly handsome gentleman as popular with the females of his own species as SCat undoubtably was with felines, merely nodded. "We have a problem, White," he pointed out. "The *Brightwing*'s manifest shows *one* shipscat, not two. And we still don't know where number two came from. I know what will happen if we try to take SKitty's mate away from her, but I also know what will happen if anyone finds out we have a second cat, origin unknown. BioTech will take a dim view of this."

Dick had been thinking at least part of this through. "We *can* hide him, sir," he offered. "At least until I can find out where he came from."

"Oh?" Captain Singh's eyebrows rose. "Just how do you propose to hide him, and where?"

Dick grinned. "In plain sight, sir. Look at them—unless you have them side-by-side, you wouldn't be able to tell which one you had in front of you. They're both black with yellow eyes, and it's only when you can see the size difference and the longer tail on SCat that you can tell them apart."

"So we simply make sure they're never in the same compartment while strangers are aboard?" the Captain hazarded. "That actually has some merit; the Spirits of Space know that people are always claiming shipscats can teleport. No one will even notice the difference if we don't say anything, and they'll just think she's getting around by way of the access tubes. How do you intend to find out where this one came from without making people wonder why you're asking about a stray cat?"

Dick was rather pleased with himself, for he had actually thought of this solution first. "SKitty is fertile—unlike nine-tenths of the shipscats. That is why we had kittens to offer the Lacu'un in the first place, and was why we have the profit we do, even after buying the contracts of the other young cats for groundside duty as the kittens' mates."

The Captain made a faint grimace. "You're stating the obvious."

"Humor me, sir. Did you know that BioTech routinely offers their breeding cats free choice in mates? That otherwise, they don't breed well?" As the Captain shook his head, Dick pulled out his trump card. "I am—ostensibly—going to do the same for SKitty. As long as we 'find' her a BioTech mate that she approves of, BioTech will be happy. And we need more kittens for the Lacu'un; we have no reason to *buy* them when we have a potential breeder of our own."

"But we got mates for her kittens," the Captain protested. "Won't BioTech think there's something odd going on?"

Dick shook his head. "You're thinking of housecats. Shipscats aren't fertile until they're four or five. At that rate, the kittens won't be old enough to breed for four years, and the Lacu'un are going to want more cats before then. So I'll be searching the BioTech breeding records for a tom of the right age and appearance. Solid black is recessive—there can't be *that* many black toms of the right age."

"And once you've found your group of candidates—?" Singh asked, both eyebrows arching. "You look for the one that's missing?" He did not ask how Dick was supposed to have found out that SKitty "preferred" a black tom; shipscats were more than intelligent enough to choose a color from a set of holos.

Dick shrugged. "The information may be in the records. Once I know where SCat's from, we can open negotiations to add him to our manifest with BioTech's backing. *They* won't pass up a chance to make SKitty half of a breeding pair, and I don't think there's a captain willing to go on BioTech's record as opposing a shipscat's choice of mate."

"I won't ask how you intend to make that particular project work," Singh said hastily. "Just remember, no more kittens in freefall."

Dick held up the now-empty injector as a silent promise.

"I'll brief the crew to refer to both cats as 'SKitty'—most of the time they do anyway," the Captain said. "Carry on, White. You seem to have the situation well in-hand."

Dick was nowhere near that certain, but he put on a confident expression for the Captain. He saluted Singh's retreating back, then sat down on the bunk beside the pair of purring cats. As usual, they were wound around each other in a knot of happiness.

*I wish my love-life was going that well.* He'd hit it off with the Terran Consul well enough, but she had elected to remain in her ground-bound position, and his life was with the ship. Once again, romance took a second place to careers. Which in his case, meant no romance. There wasn't a single female in this crew that had shown anything other than strictly platonic interest in him.

If he *wanted* a career in space, he had to be very careful about what he did and said. As most junior officer on the *Brightwing,* he was the one usually chosen for whatever unpleasant duty no one else wanted to handle. And although he could actually *retire,* thanks to the prosperity that the Lacu'un contract had brought the whole crew, he didn't want to. That would mean leaving space, leaving the ship— and leaving SKitty and SCat.

He could also transfer within the company, but why change from a crew full of people he liked and respected, with a good Captain like Singh, to one about which he knew nothing? That would be stupid. And he couldn't leave SKitty, no matter what. She was his best friend, even if she did get him into trouble sometimes.

He also didn't have the experience to be anything other than the most junior officer in any ship, so transferring wouldn't have any benefits.

Unless, of course, he parlayed his profit-share into a small fortune and bought his own ship. Then he could be Captain, and he might even be able to buy SKitty's contract—but he lacked the experience that made the difference between prosperity and bankruptcy in the shaky world of the Free Traders. He was wise enough to know this.

As for the breeding project—he had some ideas. The *Brightwing* would be visiting Lacu'un for a minimum of three weeks on every round of their trading route. Surely something could be worked out. Things didn't get chancy until after the kittens were mobile and before SKitty potty-trained them to use crew facilities. Before they were able to leave the nest-box, SKitty took care of the unpleasant details. If they could arrange things so that the period of mobility-to-weaning took place while they were on Lacu'un . . .

Well, he'd make that Jump when the coordinates came up. Right now, he had to keep outsiders from discovering that there was feline contraband on board, and find out where that contraband came from.

:*Dick smart,*: SKitty purred proudly. :*Dick fix everything.*:

*Well,* he thought wryly, *at least I have* her *confidence, if no one else's!*

It had been a long time since the *Brightwing* had been docked at a major port, and predictably, everyone wanted shore leave. Everyone except Dick, that is. He had no intentions of leaving the console in cargo where he was doing his "mate-hunting" unless and until he found his match. The fact that there was nothing but a skeleton crew aboard, once the inspectors left, only made it easier for Dick to run his searches through the BioTech database available through the station. This database was part of the public records kept on every station, and updated weekly by BioTech. Dick had a notion that he'd get his "hit" within a few hours of initiating his search.

He was pleasantly surprised to discover that there were portraits available for every entry. It might even be possible to identify SCat just from the portraits, once he had all of the black males of the appropriate age sorted out. That would give him even more rationale for the claim that SKitty had "chosen" her mate herself.

With an interested feline perching on each arm of the chair, he logged into the station's databases, identified himself and gave the station his billing information, then began his run.

There was nothing to do at that point but sit back and wait.

"I hope you realize all of the difficulties I'm going through for you," he told the tom, who was grooming his face thoughtfully. "I'm doing without shore-leave to help you here. I wouldn't do this for a fellow human!"

SCat paused in his grooming long enough to rasp Dick's hand with his damp-sandpaper tongue.

The computer *beeped* just at that moment to let him know it was done. He was running all this through the cargo dumb-set; he could have used the *Brightwing*'s Expert-System AI, but he didn't want the AI to get curious, and he didn't want someone wondering why he was using a Mega-Brain to access feline family trees. What he *did* want was the appearance that this was a brainstorm of his own, an attempt to boost his standing with his Captain by providing further negotiable items for the Lacu'un contract. There was something odd about all of this, something that he couldn't put his finger on, but something that just felt wrong and made him want to be extra-cautious. Why, he didn't know. He only knew that he didn't want to set off any tell-tales by acting as if this mate-search was a priority item.

The computer asked if he wanted to use the holo-table, a tiny square platform built into the upper right-hand corner of the desk. He cleared off a stack of hard-copy manifests, and told it "yes." Then the first of his feline biographies came in.

He'd made a guess that SCat was between five and ten years old; shipscats lived to be fifty or more, but their useful lifespan was about twenty or thirty years. All too often their job was hazardous; alien vermin had poisonous fangs or stings, sharp claws and teeth. Cats suffered disabling injuries more often than their human crewmates, and would be retired with honors to the homes of retired spacers, or to the big assisted-living stations holding the very aged and those with disabling injuries of their own. Shipscats were always welcome, anywhere in space.

*And I can think of worse fates than spending my old age watching the stars with SKitty on my lap.* Dick gazed down fondly at his furred friend, and rubbed her ears.

SKitty purred and butted her head into his hand. She paid very little attention to the holos as they passed slowly in review. SCat was right up on the desk, however, not only staring intently at the holos, but splitting his attention between the holos and the screen.

*You don't suppose he can read . . . ?*

Suddenly, SCat let out a yowl, and swatted the holoplate. Dick froze the image and the screen-biography that accompanied it.

He looked first at the holo—and it certainly looked more like SCat than any of the others had. But SCat's attention was on the screen, not the holo, and he stared fixedly at the modest insignia in the bottom right corner.

*Patrol?*

He looked down at SCat, dumbfounded. "You were with the Patrol?" He whispered it; you did not invoke the Patrol's name aloud unless you wanted a visit from them.

Yellow eyes met his for a moment, then the paw tapped the screen. He read further.

*Type MF-025, designation Lightfoot of Sun Meadow. Patrol ID FX-003. Standard Military genotype, standard Military training.* Well, that explained how he had known how to shut down the "pirate" equipment. Now Dick wondered how much else the cat had done, outside of his sight. And a military genotype? He hadn't even known there *was* such a thing.

*Assigned to Patrol ship DIA-9502, out of Oklahoma Station, designated handler Major Logan Greene.*

Oklahoma Station—that was *this* station. Drug Interdiction? He whistled softly.

Then a date, followed by the ominous words, *Ship missing, all aboard presumed dead.*

All aboard—except the shipscat.

The cat himself gave a mournful yowl, and SKitty jumped up on the desk to press herself against him comfortingly. He looked back down at SCat. "Did you jump ship before they went missing?"

He wasn't certain he would get an answer, but he had lived with SKitty for too long to underestimate shipscat intelligence. The cat shook his head, slowly and deliberately—in the negative.

His mouth went dry. "Are you saying—you got away?"

A definite nod.

"Your ship was boarded, and you got away?" He was astonished. "But how?"

For an answer, the cat jumped down off the desk and walked over to the little escape pod that neither he nor SKitty ever forgot to drag with them. He seized the tether in his teeth and dragged it over to an access tube. It barely fit; he wedged it down out of sight, then pawed open the door, and dropped down, hidden, and now completely protected from what must have happened.

He popped back out again, and walked to Dick's feet. Dick was thinking furiously. There had been rumors that drug smugglers were using captured Patrol ships; this more or less confirmed those rumors. Disable the ship, take the exterior airlock and blow it. Whoever wasn't suited up would die. Then they board and finish off whoever was suited up. They patch the lock, restore the air, and weld enough junk to the outside of the ship to disguise it completely. Then they can bring it in to any port they care to—even the ship's home port.

*This station. Which is where SCat escaped.*

"Can you identify the attackers?" he asked SCat. The cat slowly nodded.

*:They know he gone. He run, they chase. He try get home, they stop. He hear of me on dock, go hide in ship bringing mates. They kill he, get chance,:* SKitty put in helpfully.

He could picture it easily enough: SCat being pursued, cut off from the Patrol section of the station—hiding out on the docks— catching the scent of the mates being shipped for SKitty's kittens and deciding to seek safety offworld. Cats, even shipscats, did not tend to grasp the concept of "duty"; he knew from dealing with SKitty that she took her bonds of personal affection seriously, but little else. So once "his" people were dead, SCat's personal allegiance to the Patrol was nonexistent, and his primary drive would be self-preservation. *Wonderful. I wonder if they—whoever they are—figured out he got away on another ship.* Another, more alarming thought occurred to him. *I wonder if my fishing about in the BioTech database touched off any tell-tales!*

No matter. There was only one place to go now—straight to Erica Makumba, the Legal and Security Officer.

He dumped a copy of the pertinent datafile to a memory cube, then scooped up both cats and pried their life-support ball out of its hiding place. Then he *ran* for Erica's cabin, praying that she had not gone off on shore-leave.

The Spirits of Space were with him; the indicator outside her cabin door indicated that she was in there, but did not want to be disturbed. He pounded on the door anyway. Erica *might* kill him— but there were people after SCat who had murdered an entire Patrol DIA squad.

After a moment, the door cracked open a centimeter.

"White." Erica's flat, expressionless voice boded extreme violence. "This had better be an emergency."

He said the one word that would guarantee her attention. "Hijackers."

The door snapped open; she grabbed him and pulled him inside, cats, support-ball and all, and slammed the door shut behind him. She was wearing a short robe, tying it hastily around herself, and she wasn't alone. But the man watching them both alertly from the disheveled bed wasn't one of the *Brightwing*'s crew, so Dick flushed, but tried to ignore him.

"I found out where SCat's from," he babbled, dropping one cat to hand the memory-cube to her. "Read that—quick!"

She punched up the console at her elbow and dropped the cube in the receiver. The BioTech file, minus the holo, scrolled up on the screen. The man in the bed leaned forward to read it too, and whistled.

Erica swiveled to glare at him. "You keep this to yourself, Jay!" she snapped. Then she turned back to Dick. "Spill it!" she ordered.

"SCat's ship was hijacked, probably by smugglers," he said quickly. "He hid his support-ball in an access tube, and he was in it when they blew the lock. They missed him in the sweep, and when they brought their prize in here, he got away. But they know he's gone, and they know he can ID them."

"And they'll be giving the hairy eyeball to every ship with a black cat on it." She bit her knuckle—and Jay added his own two credits' worth.

"I hate to say this, but they've probably got a tell-tale on the BioTech data files, so they know whenever anyone accesses them. It's not restricted data, so anyone could leave a tell-tale." The man's face was pale beneath his normally dusky skin-tone. "If they don't know you've gone looking by now, they will shortly."

They all looked at each other. "Who's still on board?" Dick asked, and gulped.

Erica's mouth formed a tight, thin line. "You, me, Jay and the cats. The cargo's off-loaded, and regs say you don't need more than two crew on board in-station. *Theoretically*, no one can get past the security at the lock."

Jay barked a laugh, and tossed long, dark hair out of his eyes.

"Honey, I'm a comptech. Trust me, you can get past the security. You just hack into the system, tell it the ship in the bay is bigger than it really is, and upload whoever you want as additional personnel."

Erica swore—but Jay stood up, wrapping the sheet around himself like a toga, and pushed her gently aside. "What can be hacked can be unhacked—or at least I can make it a lot more difficult for them to get in and make those alterations stick. Give me your code to the AI."

Erica hesitated. He turned to stare into her eyes. "I need the AI's help. *You* two and the cats are going to get out of here—get over to the Patrol side of the station. I'm going to hold them off as long as I can, and play stupid when they do get in, but I need the speed of the AI to help me lay traps. You've known me for three years. You trusted me enough to bring me here, didn't you?"

She swore again, then reached past him to key in her code. He sat down, ignoring them and plunging straight into a trance of concentration.

"Come on!" Erica grabbed Dick's arm, and put the support-ball on the floor. SKitty and SCat must have been reading *her* mind, for they both squirmed into the ball, which was big enough for more than one cat. They'd upgraded the ball after SKitty had proved to be so—fertile. Erica shoved the ball at Dick, and kept hold of his arm, pulling him out into the corridor.

"Where are we going?" he asked.

"To get our suits, then to the emergency lock," she replied crisply. "If we try to go out the main lock into the station, they'll get us for certain. So we're going outside for a little walk."

*A little walk? All the way around the station? Outside?*

He could only hope that "they" hadn't thought of that as well. They reached the suiting-up room in seconds flat.

He averted his eyes and climbed into his own suit as Erica shed her robe and squirmed into hers. "How far is it to the Patrol section?" he asked.

"Not as far as you think," she told him. "And there's a maintenance lock just this side of it. What I want to know is how *you* got all this detailed information about the hijacking."

He turned, and saw that she was suited up, with her faceplate still open, staring at him with a calculating expression.

*This is probably not the time to hold out on her.*

He swallowed, and sealed his suit up, leaving his own faceplate open. Inside the ball, the cats were watching both of them, heads swiveling to look from one face to the other, as if they were watching a tennis match.

"SKitty's telepathic with me," he admitted. "I think SCat's telepathic with her. She seems to be able to talk with him, anyway."

He waited for Erica to react, either with disbelief or with revulsion. Telepaths of any species were not always popular among humankind . . . .

But Erica just pursed her lips and nodded. "Eyeah. I thought she might be. And telepathy's one of the traits BioTech doesn't talk about, but security people have know for a while that the MF type cats are bred for it. Maybe SKitty's momma did a little wandering over on the miltech side of the cattery, hmm?"

SKitty made a "silent" meow, and he just shrugged, relieved that Erica wasn't phobic about it. And equally relieved to learn that telepathy was already a trait that BioTech had established in their shipscat lines. *So they won't be coming to take SKitty away from me when they find out that she's a 'path . . . .*

But right now, he'd better be worrying about making a successful escape. He pulled his faceplate down and sealed it, fastening the tether-line of the ball to a snaplink on his waistband. He warmed up his suit-radio, and she did the same. "I hope you know what you're getting us into," he said, as Erica sealed her own plate shut and led the way to the emergency lock.

She looked back over her shoulder at him.

"So do I," she replied soberly.

The trip was a nightmare.

Dick had never done a spacewalk on the exterior of a station before. It wasn't at all like going out on the hull of a ship. There were hundreds of obstacles to avoid—windows, antenna, instrument-packages, maintenance robots. Any time an inspection drone came along, they had to hide to avoid being picked up on camera. It was work, hard work, to inch their way along the station in this way, and Dick was sweating freely before a half an hour was up.

It seemed like longer. Every time he glanced up at the chronometer in his faceplate HUD, he was shocked to see how little time had passed. The suit-fans whined in his ears, as the life-support system alternately fought to warm him up when they hid in the shade, or cool him down when they paused in full sunlight. Stars burned down on them, silent points of light in a depth of darkness that made him dizzy whenever he glanced out at it. The knowledge that he could be lost forever out there if he just made one small mistake chilled his heart.

Finally, Erica pointed, and he saw the outline of a maintenance lock just ahead. The two of them pulled themselves hand-over-hand toward it, reaching it at the same instant. But it was Erica who opened it, while Dick reeled the cats in on their tether.

With all four of them inside, Erica sealed the lock from the inside and initiated pressurization. Within moments, they were both able to pop their faceplates and breathe station-air again.

Something prompted Dick to release the cats from their ball before Erica unsealed the inner hatch. He unsnapped the tether and was actually straightening up, empty ball in both hands, when Erica opened the door to a hallway—

—and dropped to the floor, as the shrill squeal of a stun-gun pierced the quiet of the lock.

"Erica!" Without thinking, he ran forward, and found himself facing the business-end of a powerful stunner, held by a nondescript man who held it as if he was quite used to employing it. He was *not* wearing a station uniform.

The man looked startled to see him, and Dick did the only thing he could think of. He threw the support-ball at the man, as hard as he could.

It hit cleanly, knocking the man to the floor as it impacted with his chest. He clearly was not aware that the support-balls were as massy as they were. The two cats flashed past him, heading for freedom, and Dick tried to follow their example. But the man was quick to recover, and as Dick tried to jump over his prone body, the fellow grabbed his ankle and tripped him up.

Then it turned into a brawl, with Dick the definite underdog. Even in the suit, the stranger still outweighed him.

Within a few seconds, Dick was on his back on the floor, and the stranger held him down, easily. The stun-gun was no longer in his hands, but it didn't look to Dick as if he really needed it.

In fact, as the man's heavy fist pounded into Dick's face, he was quickly convinced that he didn't need it. Pain lanced through his jaw as the man's fist smashed into it; his vision filled with stars and red and white flashes of light. More agony burst into his skull as the blows continued. He flailed his arms and legs, but there was nothing he could do—he was trapped in the suit, and he couldn't even get enough leverage to defend himself. He tasted blood in his mouth— he couldn't see—

*:BAD MAN!:*

There was a terrible battle-screech from somewhere out in the corridor, and the blows stopped. Then the weight lifted from his body, as the man howled in pain.

Dick managed to roll to one side, and stagger blindly to his feet with the aid of the corridor bulkhead—he still couldn't see. He dashed blood out of his eyes with one hand, and shook his head to clear it, staring blindly in the direction of the unholy row.

"*Get it off! Get it off me!*" Human screams mixed with feline battle-cries, telling him that whichever of the cats had attacked, they were giving a good accounting of themselves.

But there were other sounds—the sounds of running feet approaching, and Dick tried frantically to get his vision to clear. A heavy body crashed into him, knocking him into the bulkhead with enough force to drive all the breath from his body, as the *zing* of an illegal neuro-gun went off somewhere near him.

*SKitty!*

But whoever was firing swore, and the cat-wail faded into the distance.

"It got away!" said one voice, over the sobbing of another.

A third swore, as Dick fought for air. "You. Go after it," the third man said, and there was the sound of running feet. Meanwhile, footsteps neared where Dick lay curled in a fetal bundle on the floor.

"What about this?" the second voice asked.

The third voice, cold and unemotional, wrote Dick's death warrant. "Get rid of it, and the woman, too."

And Dick could not even move. He heard someone breathing heavily just above him; sensed the man taking aim—

Then—

"Patrol! Freeze! Drop your weapons now!"

Something clattered to the deck beside him, as more running feet approached; and with a sob of relief, Dick finally drew a full breath. There was a scuffle just beside him, then someone helped him to stand, and he heard the hiss of a hypospray and felt the tell-tale sting against the side of his neck. A moment later, his eyes cleared—just in time for him to catch SKitty as she launched herself from the arms of a uniformed DIA officer into his embrace.

"So, the bottom line is, you'll let us take SCat's contract?" Captain Singh sat back in his chair while Dick rubbed SKitty's ears. She and SCat both burdened Dick's lap, as they had since SCat, the Captain, the DIA negotiator, and Erica had all walked into the sickbay where Dick was still recovering. Erica was clearly nursing a stun-headache; the Captain looked a little frazzled. The DIA man, as most of his ilk, looked as unemotional as an android. The DIA had spent many hours with a human-feline telepathic specialist debriefing SCat. Apparently SCat was naturally only a receptive telepath; it took a human who was also a telepath to "talk" to him.

"There's no reason why not," the DIA agent said. "You civilians have helped materially in this case; both you and he are entitled to certain compensation, and if that's what you all want, then he's yours with our blessing—the fact that he is only a receptive telepath makes him less than optimal for further Patrol duties." The agent shrugged. "We can always get other shipscats with full abilities. According to the records, the only reason we kept him was because Major Logan selected him."

SKitty bristled, and Dick sent soothing thoughts at her.

Then the agent smiled, making his face look more human. "Major Logan was a good agent, but he didn't particularly care for having a cat talking to him. I gather that Lightfoot and he got along all right, but there wasn't the strong bond between them that we would have preferred. It would have been just a matter of time before that squad and ship got a new cat-agent team. Besides, we aren't completely inhuman. If your SKitty and this boy here are happily mated, who and what in the Patrol can possibly want to separate them?"

"Judging by the furrows SKitty left in that 'jacker's face and scalp, it isn't a good idea to get between her and someone she loves," Captain Singh said dryly. "He's lucky she left him one eye."

The agent's gaze dropped briefly to the swath of black fur draped over Dick's lap. "Believe me," he said fervently, "that *is* a consideration we had taken into account. Your little lady there is a warrior for fair, and we have no intention of denying her anything her heart is set on. If she wants Lightfoot, and he wants her, then she's got him. We'll see his contract is transferred over to *Brightwing* within the hour." His eyes rose to meet Dick's. "You're a lucky man to have a friend like her, young man. She put herself between you and certain death. Don't you ever forget it."

SKitty's purr deepened, and SCat's joined with hers as Dick's hands dropped protectively on their backs. "I know that, sir," he replied, through swollen lips. "I knew it before any of this happened."

SKitty turned her head, and he gazed into amused yellow eyes. :*Smart Dick*,: she purred, then lowered her head to her paws. :*Smart man. Mate happy here, mate stay. Everything good. Love you.*:

And that, as far as SKitty was concerned, was the end of it. The rest were simply "minor human matters."

He chuckled, and turned his own attention to dealing with those "minor human matters," while his best friend and her mate drifted into well-earned sleep.

# A Better Mousetrap

## Mercedes Lackey

If there was one thing that Dick White had learned in all his time as SuperCargo of the CatsEye Company Free Trader *Brightwing,* it was that having a cat purring in your ear practically forced you to relax. The extremely comfortable form-molding chair he sat in made it impossible to feel anything but comfortable, and warm black fur muffled both of Dick White's ears, a steady vibration massaging his neck. "Build a better mousetrap, and the world will beat a path to your door," Dick said idly, as SCat poured himself like a second fluid, black rug over the blue-gray of his lap. It was SKitty who was curled up around his shoulders, vibrating contentedly in what Dick called her "subsonic purr-mode," while her mate took it as his responsibility to make sure there was plenty of hair shed on the legs of his gray shipsuit uniform.

"What?" asked Terran Ambassador Vena Ferducci, looking up from the list of Lacu'un nobles petitioning for one of SKitty's latest litter. The petite, dark-haired woman sat in a less comfortable, metal chair behind a stone desk, which stood next to a metal rack stuffed with archaic rolled paper documents. The Lacu'un had not yet devised the science of filing paperwork in multiples yet, which made them ultra-civilized in Vena's opinion. This, her office in the Palace of the Lacu'ara and Lacu'teveras, was not often used for that very reason. When she dealt with *Terran* bureaucracy, she needed every electronic helper she could get.

The list she perused was very long, and made rather cumbersome due to the Lacu'un custom of presenting all official court documents in the form of a massively ornamented yellow-parchment scroll, with case and end caps of engraved bronze and illuminated capital-initials. Dick had a notion that somewhere in the universe there probably was a collector of handwritten documents who would pay a small fortune for it, but when every petitioner on the list had been satisfied, it would probably be sent to the underclerks, scraped clean, and reused.

"It's an old Terran folk saying," Dick elaborated, and gestured to the list by way of explanation. "One which certainly seems to be borne out by our present situation."

"Yes, well, given the length of this list we're doubly fortunate that SKitty and SCat are so—ah—*fertile*, and that BioTech is willing to send us their shipscat washouts." Vena stretched out her hand towards SCat's head, and the huge black tom cooperated by craning his neck towards her. Even before her fingers contacted his fur, SCat was purring loudly, giving Dick an uncannily similar sensation to being strapped in while the ship he served was under full power.

Dick White could well be one of the wealthiest supercargoes in the history of space-trade—his share of the profits from CatsEye Company's lucrative trade with the Lacu'un amounted to quite a tidy sum. It wasn't enough to buy and outfit his own ship—yet—but if trade progressed as it had begun, there was the promise that one day it would be.

*Not that I want my own ship yet!* he told himself. *Not until I know as much as Captain Singh. There are easier ways to commit suicide than pretending I know enough to command a starship when all I really know is how to run the cargo hold!*

Not that Captain Singh would *let* him take his profit-share and do something so stupid. Dick grinned to himself, imagining the Captain's face if he showed up in the office with *that* kind of harebrained proposal. Captain Singh's expression would be one to behold—following which, Dick would probably find himself stunned unconscious and wake under the solicitous attentions of a concerned head-shrinker!

The Captain *had* been willing, even more than willing, to let Dick stay on-planet for few Terran-months though, after SKitty and SCat announced the advent of a litter-to-be. One of her last litter was co-opted to serve as shipscat pro tem, while Dick and his two charges waited out the delivery, maturation, and weaning of eight little black furballs who were, if that was possible, even cuter than the last batch. It was a good thing that they all *were* on-planet, too, because the Octet managed to get themselves into a hundred times more mischief than the previous lot.

The trouble is, they have a lot of energy, absolutely no sense, and no fear at all at this age. Brainless kitten antics rapidly begin to pall when you've fished a wailing fuzz-mote out of the comconsole for the fifteenth time in a single shift.

But every Lacu'un in the palace, from the Lacu'teveras down to the lowliest scullery-lad, was thrilled to the toes—or rather, claws—to play with, rescue, and cuddle the bratlings. If SKitty and SCat had not taken their duties as parents, palace guardians, and role models so seriously, they wouldn't have had to do anything but lie about and wait for the kittens to be carried in to them for feeding.

Fortunately for all concerned, their parents had powerful senses of responsibility towards their offspring. Both cats were born and bred—literally—for duty. Yes, they were cats, with a cat's sense of independence and contrariness, but they took duty very, very seriously. And their duty was vermin control.

This was a duty that went back centuries to the very beginnings of the association of man and cat, but until BioTech developed shipscats, never had a feline been better suited to or more cooperative in the execution of that duty. Furthermore, Dick now knew what few others did—that the shipscats so necessary to the safety of traders and their ships were actually a highly profitable byproduct of other research, secret research, designed to give the men and women of the Patrol uniquely clever comrades-in-arms.

These genetically altered cats were not just clever, it was not just that they had forepaws modeled after the forepaws of raccoons—oh no. That was not enough. Patrol cats were telepaths.

SCat had been a Patrol cat—but although he could understand the thoughts of humans, he couldn't speak to them. This was a flaw, so far as the Patrol was concerned, though not an insurmountable flaw. However, when criminals took over the ship he served on and killed all of those aboard, SCat was the only survivor and the only witness—unable to call for help or relate what he had witnessed, he had sought for help from his own kind and found it in SKitty. When the same criminals learned SCat was still alive and tried to eliminate him and the crew of the Free Trader ship *Brightwing,* for good measure, it had been Dick's research and deductive reasoning that had learned the truth in time, and with SCat's and SKitty's help he had foiled the plot.

As for SKitty, she was something of an aberration herself— ordinary shipscats were not supposed to be telepathic *or* fertile; she was both.

As far as Dick could tell, she was telepathic only with him— though, given that she was all cat, with a cat's puckish sense of humor, she might well choose not to let him know she could "speak" to others. Everyone on the ship knew she was fertile, though—when they had first come to the world of the Lacu'un, she'd already had one litter and was pregnant with another. That first litter—born and raised in the ship—had shown just what kind of a nightmare two loose kittens could be within the close confines of a spaceship. Dick had not been looking forward to telling Captain Singh of the second litter, when SKitty had solved the problem for them.

The Lacu'un, a race of golden-skinned, vaguely reptilian anthropoids, suffered from the depredations of a particularly voracious, fast, and apparently indestructible pest called *kreshta.* The only way to keep them from taking over completely was to lock anything edible (and the creature could eat practically anything) in airtight containers of metal, glass, ceramic, or stone, and build only in materials the pest couldn't eat. The pests did keep the streets so clean that they sparkled and there was no such thing as a trash problem, but those were the only benefits to the plague.

The Lacu'un had just opened their planet to trade from outside, and the *Brightwing* was one of several ships that had arrived to represent either themselves or one of the large companies. Only Captain Singh had the foresight to include SKitty in their delegation, however, for only he had bothered to research the Lacu'un thoroughly enough to learn that they placed great value on totemic animals and had virtually *nothing* in the way of domesticated predators themselves. He reckoned that a tame predator would be very impressive to them, and he was right.

SKitty had been on her best behavior, charming them all, and taking to this alien race immediately. The Lacu'teveras, the female co-ruler, had been particularly charmed, so much so that she had missed the presence of one of the little pests, which had bitten her. Enraged at this attack on someone she favored, SKitty had killed the creature.

For the Lacu'un, this was nothing short of a miracle, the end of a scourge that had been with them since the beginning of their civilization. After that moment, there was no question of anyone else getting most-favored trading status with the Lacu'un, ever.

CatsEye got the plum contract, SKitty's kittens-to-be got immediate homes, and Dick White's life became incredibly complicated.

Since then, he was no longer just an apprentice supercargo and Designated Shipscat Handler on a small Free Trader ship. He'd been imprisoned by Company goons, stalked and beaten within an inch of his life by cold-blooded murderous hijackers, and had to face the Patrol itself to bargain for SCat's freedom. He'd had enough adventure in two short Standard years to last most people for the rest of their lives.

But all that was in the past. Or so he hoped.

*For a while, anyway, it would be nice if the most difficult decision I had to make would be which of the Lacu'un nobles get SKitty-babies and which have to make do with shipscat washouts.*

Those "washouts" were mature cats that for one reason or another couldn't adapt to ship life. Gengineering wasn't perfect, even now; there were cats that couldn't handle freefall, cats that were claustrophobes, cats that were shy or anti-social. Those had the opportunity to come here, to join the vermin-hunting crew. Thus far, thirty had made the trip, some to become mates for the first litter, others to take up solitary residence with a noble family. There were other washouts, who didn't pass the intelligence tests, but those were never offered to the Lacu'un—they already filled a steady need for companions in children's hospitals and retirement homes, where the high shipscat intelligence wasn't needed, just a loving friend smart enough to understand what not to do around someone sick or in pain.

There were still far more Lacu'un who urgently craved the boon of a cat than there were cats to fill the need. Thus far, none of SKitty's female offspring had carried that rare gene for fertility—when one did, that one would go back to BioTech, to be treated like the precious object she was, pampered and amused, asked to breed only so often as *she* chose. There was always a trade-off in any gengineering effort; lack of fertility was a small price to pay in a species as notoriously prolific as cats.

Meanwhile, the proud parents were in the last stages of educating their current offspring. There was a pile of the dead vermin just in front of Vena's desk; every so often, one of the half-grown kittens would bring another to add to the pile, then sit politely and wait for his parents to approve. Sometimes, when the pest was particularly large, SCat would descend from Dick's lap with immense dignity, inspect the kill, and bestow a rough lick by way of special reward.

Dick couldn't keep track of how many pests each of the kittens had destroyed, but from the size of the pile so far, the parents had reason to be proud of their offspring.

The kittens certainly inherited their parents' telepathic skills as well as their hunting skills, for just as it occurred to Dick that it was about time for them to be fed, they scampered in from all available doorways. In a moment, they were neatly lined up, eight identical pairs of yellow eyes staring avidly from eight little black faces beneath sixteen enormous ears. At this age, they seemed to consist mainly of eyes, ears, paws and tails.

The Lacu'un servant whose proud duty it was to feed the

weanlings arrived with a bowl heaping with their imported food. She was clothed in the simple, silky draped tunic in the deep gold of the royal household. The frilled crest running from the back of her neck to just above her eye-ridge stood totally erect and was flushed to a deep salmon color with pleasure and pride. She started to put the bowl on the floor, and the kittens leapt to their feet and ran for the food—

But suddenly SCat sprang from Dick's lap, every hair on end, spitting and yowling. He landed at the startled servant's feet and did a complete flip over, so that he faced his kittens. As they skidded on the slick stone, he growled and batted at them, sending them flying.

"*SCat!*" Vena shouted, as she jumped to her feet, horrified and angry. "What are you doing? Bad cat!"

"No he's not!" Dick replied, making a leap of his own for the food bowl and jerking it from the frightened servant's hands. He had already heard SKitty's frantic mental screech of *:Bad food!:* as she followed her mate off of Dick's shoulders to keep the kittens from the deadly bowl.

"The food's poisoned," Dick added, sniffing the puffy brown nodules suspiciously, as the servant backed away, the slits in her golden-brown eyes so wide he could scarcely see the iris. "SCat must have scented it—that's probably one of the things Patrol cats are trained in. *I* can't tell the difference, but—" as SKitty held the kittens at bay, he held the bowl down to SCat, who took a delicate sniff and backed away, growling. "See?"

Vena's expression darkened, and she turned to the servant. "The food has been poisoned," she said flatly. "Who had access to it?" They both knew that Shivari, the servant, was trustworthy; she would sooner have thrown herself between the kittens and a ravening monster than see any hurt come to them. She proved that now by her behavior; her crest-frill flattened, she turned bright yellow—the Lacu'un equivalent of turning pale—and replied instantly.

"I do not know—I got the bowl from the kitchen—"

She grabbed Vena's hand and the two of them ran off, with Dick closely behind, still carrying the bowl. When they arrived at the kitchen, Vena and Shivari cornered all the staff while Dick blocked the exit. He had a fair grasp of Lacu'un by now, but Vena and Shivari were talking much too fast for him to get more than two words in four.

Soon enough, though, Vena turned away with anger and dissatisfaction on her face, while Shivari began a blistering harangue worthy of Captain Singh. "There was a new servant that no one recognized on staff this morning," Vena said in disgust. "Obviously they were smart enough to keep him away from the food meant for people, but no one thought anything of letting him open up the cat food into a bowl."

"Well, they know better now," Dick replied grimly.

"I'll put the Embassy on alert—and give me that—" Vena took the bowl from him. "I'll have the Marines run it through an analyzer."

Embassy guards by long tradition were called "Marines," although they were merely another branch of the Patrol. Dick readily surrendered the poisoned food to Vena, knowing that if SCat could smell a poison, the forensic analyzer every Embassy possessed—just in case—would easily be able to find it. Relations with the Lacu'un were important enough that Vena had gone from being merely a trade advisor and titular consul to a full-scale ambassador, with the attendant staff and amenities. It was that promotion that had persuaded her to remain here instead of returning to her former position in the Scouts.

Dick himself went to the storage vault that held the imported cat-food, got a highly compressed cube out, and opened it over a freshly washed bowl. The stuff puffed up to ten times its compressed size once it came into contact with air and humidity; it would be impossible to tamper with the packages without a resulting "explosion" of food. The entire feline family flowed into the kitchen as soon as his fingers touched the package; the kittens swarmed around his legs, mewling piteously, but he offered the bowl for SCat's inspection before allowing them to engulf it.

His mind buzzed with questions, but two were uppermost—who would have tried to poison the kittens? And why?

SCat and SKitty herded their kittens along like a pair of attentive sheepdogs when they'd finished eating, following behind Dick as he left the palace, heading for the Embassy. The Marine at the entrance gave him a brisk nod of recognition, saving her grin for the moving black-furred flock behind him.

A second Marine at a desk just inside, skilled in the Lacu'un tongue, served double-duty as a receptionist. "The Ambassador is expecting you, sir," he said. "She left orders for you to go straight in."

Dick led his parade past the desk—a desk of cast marble reinforced with plastile, which would serve very nicely as a blast-and-projectile-proof bunker at need. The door to Vena's office (a cleverly concealed blast-door) was slightly ajar; it sensed his approach and opened fully for him after a retinal scan.

"Have you ever wondered why our peaceful hosts happen to field a battle-ready army?" Vena asked him, without even a preliminary greeting.

"Ah, no, I hadn't—but now that you mention it, it does seem odd." Dick took a seat, cats pooling around his ankles, as Vena tossed her compuslate aside.

"Our hosts aren't the sole representatives of their race on this dirtball," Vena replied, with no expression that Dick could see. "And *now* they finally get around to telling me this. It seems that there is another nation entirely on this continent—we thought that it was just another fief of the Lacu'ara, and they never disabused us of that impression."

"Let me guess—the other side doesn't like Terrans?" Dick hazarded.

"I wish it was that simple. Unfortunately, the other side worships the *kreshta* as children of their prime deity." Vena couldn't quite repress a snarl. "Kill one, and you've got a holy war on your hands—we've been slaughtering hundreds for better than two years. The attempt on the Octet was just the opening salvo for us heretics. The Chief Minister has been here, telling me all about it and falling all over himself in apology. Here—" She pulled a micro reader out of a drawer in her desk and tossed it to him. "My head of security advises that you commit this to memory."

"What is it?" Dick asked, thumbing it on, and seeing (with some puzzlement) the line drawing of a nude Lacu'un appear on the plate.

"How to kill or disable a Lacu'un in five easy lessons, as written by the Patrol Marines." Her face had gone back to that deadpan expression again. "Lieutenant Reynard thinks you might need it."

The prickling of claws set carefully into his clothing alerted him that one of the cats was swarming up to drape itself over his shoulders, but somewhat to his surprise, it wasn't SKitty, it was SCat. The tom peered at the screen in his hand with every evidence of fascinated concentration, too.

*He was Patrol, after all . . . .* was his second thought, after the initial surprise. And on the heels of that thought, he decided to hold the reader up so that SCat could use the touch screen too.

It was easier to disable a Lacu'un than to kill one, at least in hand-to-hand combat. Their throats were armored with bone plates, their heads with amazingly thick skulls. But there were vulnerable major nerve-points at all joints; concentrated pinpoint pressure would paralyze everything from the joint down when applied there. When Dick figured he had the scanty contents by heart, he tossed the reader back to Vena, though what he was supposed to do with the information was beyond him at the moment. He wasn't exactly trained in anything but the most basic of self-defense—that was more in Erica Makumba's line, and she was several light-years away at the moment.

"The Lacu'un Army has been alerted, the Palace has been put under tight security, and the caretakers of the other cats have been warned about the poisoning attempt. However, the mysterious kitchen-helper got clean away, so we can assume he'll make another attempt. My advisors and I would like to take him alive if we can—we've got some plans that may abort this mess before it gets worse than it already is."

SCat's deep-voiced growl showed what he thought of that idea, and Vena lowered her smoldering, dark eyes from Dick's to the tom's, and smiled grimly.

"I'd like to put a Marine guard on the cats—but I know that's hardly possible," Vena continued, as SCat and SKitty voiced identical snorts of disdain. "But let's walk back over to the Palace and talk about what we *can* do on the way."

SCat looked up at him and made an odd noise, easy enough to interpret. "SCat thinks he and SKitty can guard the kittens well enough," Dick replied, as Vena waved him through the door, a torrent of cats washing around his ankles.

"I'm sure he does," Vena retorted. "But let's remember that he's only a cat, however much his genes have been tweaked. I hardly think he's capable of understanding the danger of the current situation."

"He isn't just a cat, he was a *Patrol* cat," Dick pointed out, but Vena just shook her head at that.

"Dick, we don't even know exactly what we're into—all we know is that there was an attempt to poison the cats by an assassin that got away. We don't know if it was a lone fanatic, someone sent by our hosts' enemies, if there's only one or more than one—" She sighed as they reached the street. "We're doing all the intelligence gathering we can, but it's difficult to manage when you don't look anything like the dominant species on the planet."

The street was empty, which was fairly normal at this time of day when most Lacu'un were inside at their evening meal. The sky of this world seemed a bit greenish to him, but he'd gotten used to it—today, there were some clouds that might mean rain. Or might not, he didn't know very much about planetside weather.

SCat's squall was all the warning Dick got to throw himself out of the way as something dark and fast whizzed through the place where he'd been standing. SKitty and the kittens fairly flew back to the safety of the Embassy, SCat whisked out of sight altogether; a larger, cloaked shape sprang from the shadows of a doorway, and before Dick managed to get halfway to his feet, the gray-cloaked, pale-skinned Lacu'un seized Vena and enveloped her, holding a knife to her throat.

"Be still, blasphemous she-demon!" it grated, holding both of Vena's arms pinned behind her back in a way that had to be excruciatingly painful. She grimaced but said nothing. "And you, father of demons, be still also!" it snapped at Dick. "I am the righteous hand of Kresh'kali, the all-devouring, the purifier! I am the bringer of cleansing, the anointed of God! In His name, and by His mercy, I give you this choice—remove yourselves from our soil, take yourselves back into the sky forever, or you will die, first you and your she-demon and your god-killing pests, then all of those who brought you." Its voice rose, taking on the tones of a hellfire-and-brimstone preacher. "Kresh'kali is the One, the true God, whose word is the only law, and whose minions cleanse the world in His image; His will shall not be flouted, and His servants not denied—"

It sounded like a well-rehearsed speech, and probably would have gone on for some time had it not been interrupted by the speaker's own scream of agony.

And small wonder, for SCat had crept up unseen even by Dick, until the instant he leapt for the assassin's knife-wielding wrist, and fastened his teeth unerringly into those sensitive nerves at the joining of hand and wrist.

The knife clattered to the street, Vena twisted away, and Dick charged, all at the same moment; his shoulder hit the assassin and they both went down on the hard stone paving. But not in a disorderly heap, no; by the time the Marines came piling out of the Embassy, alerted by the frantic herd of cats, Dick had the miscreant face down on the ground with both arms paralyzed from the shoulders down. And, miracle of miracles, this time *he* wasn't the one battered and bruised—in fact, he was intact beyond a few scrapes!

He wasn't taking any chances though; he waited until the Marines had all four limbs of the assassin in stasis-cuffs before he got off his captive and surrendered him.

"Do we turn him over to the locals?" one of the Marines asked Vena diffidently.

"Not a chance," she growled. "Hustle him into the Embassy before anyone asks any questions."

"What are you going to do?" Dick asked *sotto voce,* following the Marines and their cursing burden.

"I told you, we've got some ideas—and a couple of experiments I'd rather try on this dirtbag rather than any Lacu'un volunteers," was all she said, leaving him singularly unsatisfied. All he could be certain of was that she didn't plan to execute the assassin out-of-hand. "*We* caught him, and we've got a chance to try those ideas out."

He continued to follow, and was not prevented, as Vena led the way up the stairs to the Embassy med-lab. The entire entourage of cats followed, and Vena not only *let* them, she waved them all inside before shutting and locking the door. The prisoner was strapped into a dental chair and gagged, which at least put an end to the curses, though not to the glares he cast at them.

But Vena dropped down onto one knee and looked into SKitty's eyes. "I know you're a telepath, SKitty," she said, in Terran. "Can you project to anyone but Dick? Could you project into our prisoner's mind? Put your voice in his head?"

SKitty turned her head to look up at Dick. *:Walls,:* she complained. *:Dick has no walls for SKitty.:*

"She says he's got barriers," Dick interpreted. "I understand that most nontelepathic people have and it's just an accident that the two of us are compatible."

"I may be able to change that," Vena replied, with a tight smile, as she got to her feet. "SKitty, I'm going to do some things to this prisoner, and I want you to tell me when the barriers are gone." She turned to a cabinet and unlocked it; inside were hypospray vials, and she selected one. "We've been cooperating with the Lacu'un Healers; putting together drugs we've been developing for the Lacu'un," she continued. "There are hypnotics that are proven to lower telepathic barriers in humans, and I have a few that may do the same for the Lacu'un. If they don't kill him, that is." She raised an eyebrow at Dick. "You can see why we didn't want to test them even on volunteers."

"But if the drugs kill him—" Dick gulped.

"Then we save the Lacu'ara the cost of an execution, and we apologize that the prisoner expired from fear," she replied smoothly. Dick gulped again; this was a ruthless side of Vena he'd had no notion existed!

She placed the first hypo against the side of the prisoner's neck; the device hissed as it discharged its contents, and the prisoner's eyes widened with fear.

An hour later, there were only two vials left in the cabinet; Vena had administered all the rest, and their antidotes, with sublime disregard for the strain this was probably putting on the prisoner's body. The effects of each had been duly noted, but none of them produced the desired effect of lowering the barriers nontelepaths had against telepathic intrusion.

Vena picked up the first of the last two, and sighed. "If one of these doesn't work, I'll have to make a decision about giving him to the locals," she said with what sounded like disappointment. "I'd really rather not do that."

Dick didn't ask why, but one of the two Marines in the room with them must have seen the question in his eyes. "If the Ambassador turns this fellow over to them, they'll execute him, and that might be enough to send cold war hostilities into a real blaze," the young lieutenant muttered as Vena administered the hypo. "And the word from the Palace is that the other side is as advanced in atomic physics as our lot is. In other words, these are religious fanatics with a nuclear arsenal."

Dick winced; the Terrans would be safe enough in a nuclear exchange, and so would the bulk of city-dwellers, for the Lacu'un had mastered force-shield technology. But in a nuclear exchange there were always accidents and as yet it wasn't possible to encase anything bigger than a city in a shield; he'd seen enough blasted lands never to wish a nuc-war on anyone, and *certainly* not on the decent folk here.

SKitty watched the prisoner as she would a mouse; his eyes unfocused when the drug took hold, and *this* time, she meowed with pleasure. It didn't take Dick's translation for Vena to know that the prisoner's telepathic barriers to SKitty's probing thoughts were gone.

"Excellent!" she exclaimed with relief. "All right, little one—we're going to leave the room until you send one of the kittens to come get us. Let him think we've lost interest in him for the moment, *then* get into his head and convince him that *he* is a very, very bad kitten and *you* are his mother and you're going to punish him unless he says he's sorry and he won't do it again. Make him think that you are so angry that you might kill him if he can't understand how bad he's been. In fact, any of you cats that can get into his head should do that. Then make him promise that he'll always obey everything you tell him to, and don't let up the pressure until he does."

SKitty looked at Vena as if she thought the human had gone crazy, then sighed. :*Stupid*,: she told Dick privately. :*But okay. I do.*:

Dick as baffled as SKitty was, as he followed Vena out into the hall, leaving the cats with the prisoner. "Just what is that going to accomplish?" he demanded.

She chuckled. "I rather doubt he's ever heard anyone speak in his mind before," she pointed out. "Not even his god."

Now Dick saw exactly what she'd had in mind—and stifled his bark of laughter. "He's going to be certain SKitty's more powerful than *his* god if she can do that—and if she treats him like a naughty child rather than an enemy to be destroyed—"

"Exactly," Vena said with satisfaction. "This is what Lieutenant Reynard wanted me to try, though we thought we'd have to add halucinogens and a VR headset, rather than getting right directly into his head. My problem was finding a way to tell her to act like an all-powerful, rebuking god in a way she'd understand. In the drugged state he's in now, he'll accept whatever happens as the truth."

"So *he* won't threaten the cats anymore—but then what?" Dick asked.

"According to Reynard, the worst that will happen is that he'll be convinced that this new god of his enemies is a lot more powerful and real than his own, and that's the story he'll take back home."

"And the best?" Dick inquired.

She shrugged. "He converts."

"Just what will that accomplish?"

She paused, and licked her lips unconsciously. "We ran some simulations, based on what we've learned about Lacu'un psychology and projecting the rest from history. Historically, the most fanatic followers of a new religion are the converts who were just as fanatical in their former religion. In either case, imagine the reaction when he returns home, which he will, and miraculously, because we'll take a stealthed flitter and drop him over the border while he's drugged and unconscious. He'll probably figure out that we brought him, but there won't be any sign of how. Imagine what his superiors will think?"

The Marine lieutenant standing diffidently at her elbow cleared his throat. "Actually, you don't have to guess," he said respectfully. "As the Ambassador mentioned, we've been running a psych-profiles for possible contingencies, and they agree with her educated assessment. No matter what, the fanatics will be too frightened of the power of this new 'god' to hazard either a war or another assassination attempt. And if we send back a convert—there's a seventy-four-point-three-percent chance he'll end up starting his own crusade, or even a holy war *within* their culture. No matter what, they cease to be a problem."

"Now *that*," Dick replied with feeling, "is really a better mousetrap!"

*This is a very old story, dating back at least ten years. Published in a short-lived magazine called* American Fantasy, *I doubt that many people had a chance to see it. It was old enough that I felt it needed a bit of rewriting, so although the general plot is the same, it's undergone a pretty extensive change.*

# The Last of the Season

## Mercedes Lackey

They said on TV that her name was Molly, but Jim already knew that. They also said that she was eight years old, but she didn't look eight, more like six; didn't look old enough to be in school, even. She didn't look anything like the picture they'd put up on the screen, either. The picture was at least a year old, and done by some cut-rate outfit for her school. Her hair was shorter, her face rounder, her expression so stiff she looked like a kid-dummy. There was nothing like the lively spark in her eyes, or the naughty smile she'd worn this afternoon. The kid in the picture was so clean she squeaked; where was the sticky popsicle residue on her face and hands, the dirt smudges on her knees?

Jim lost interest as soon as the station cut away to the national news, and turned the set off.

The remote-controlled TV was the one luxury in his beige box of an apartment. His carpet was the cheapest possible brown industrial crap; the curtains on the picture-window a drab, stiff, cheap polyester stuff, backed with even cheaper vinyl that was seamed with cracks after less than a year. He had one chair (Salvation Army, brown corduroy), one lamp (imitation brass, from K-mart), one vinyl sofa (bright orange, St. Vincent de Paul) that was hard and uncomfortable, and one coffee table (imitation Spanish, Goodwill) where the fancy color TV sat, like a king on a peasant's crude bench.

In the bedroom, just beyond the closed door, was his bedroom, no better furnished than the living room. He stored his clothing in odd chests of folded cardboard, with a clamp-lamp attached to the cardboard table by the king-sized bed. Like the TV, the bed was top-of-the-line, with a satin bedspread. On that bed, sprawled over the royal blue satin, was Molly.

Jim rose, slowly and silently, and tiptoed across the carpet to the bedroom door, cracking it open just an inch or so, peering inside. She looked like a Norman Rockwell picture, lying on her side, so pale against the dark, vivid fabric, her red corduroy jumper rumpled across her stomach where she clutched her teddy bear with one arm. She was still out of it, sleeping off the little knock on the skull he'd given her. Either that, or she was still under the whiff of ether that had followed. When he was close to her, he could still smell the banana-scent of her popsicle, and see a sticky trace of syrup around her lips. The light from the door caught in the eyes of her teddy bear, and made them shine with a feral, red gleam.

She'd been easy, easy—so trusting, especially after all the contact he'd had with her for the past three weeks. He'd had his eye on two or three of the kids at Kennedy Grade School, but she'd been the one he'd really wanted; like the big TV, she was top-of-the-line, and any of the others would have been a disappointment. She was perfect, prime material, best of the season. Those big, chocolate-brown eyes, the golden-brown hair cut in a sweet page-boy, the round dolly-face—she couldn't have been any better.

He savored the moment, watching her at a distance, greedily studying her at his leisure, knowing that he had her all to himself and no one could interfere.

She'd been one of the last kids to leave the school on this warm, golden afternoon—the rest had scattered on down the streets, chasing the fallen leaves by the time she came out. He'd been loitering, waiting to see if he'd missed her, if someone had picked her up after school, or if she'd had a dentist appointment or something—but no one would ever give a second look at the ice cream man loitering outside a grade school. He looked like what everybody expected, a man obviously trying to squeeze every last dime out of the rug-rats that he could.

The pattern while he'd had this area staked out was that Molly only had ice cream money about a third of the time. He'd set her up so carefully—if she came out of the school alone, and started to pass the truck with a wistful look in her eyes, he'd made a big production out of looking around for other kids, then signalling her to come over. The first couple of times, she'd shaken her head and run off, but after she'd bought cones from him a time or two, *he* wasn't a stranger, and to her mind, was no longer in the catagory of people she shouldn't talk to. Then she responded, and he had given her a broken popsicle in her favorite flavor of banana. "Do me a favor and eat this, all right?" he'd said, in his kindest voice. "I can't sell a broken popsicle, and I'd hate for it to go to waste." Then he'd lowered his voice to a whisper and bent over her. "But don't tell the other kids, okay? Let's just keep it a secret."

She nodded, gleefully, and ran off. After that he had no trouble getting her to come over to the truck; after all, why should she be afraid of the friend who gave her ice cream for free, and only asked that she keep it a secret?

Today she'd had money, though, and from the sly gleam in her eyes he would bet she'd filched it from her momma's purse this morning. He'd laid out choices for her like a servant laying out a feast for a princess, and she'd sparkled at him, loving the attention as much as the treat.

She'd dawdled over her choice, her teddy bear clutched under one arm, a toy so much a part of her that it could have been another limb. That indecision bought time for the other kids to clear out of the way, and all the teachers to get to their cars and putt out of the parking lot. His play-acting paid off handsomely, especially after he'd nodded at the truck and winked. She'd wolfed down her cone, and he gave her another broken popsicle; she lingered on, sucking on the yellow ice in a way that made his groin tighten with anticipation. He'd asked her ingenuous questions about her school and her teacher, and she chattered amiably with him between slurps.

Then she'd turned to go at the perfect moment, with not a child, a car, or a teacher in sight. He reached for the sock full of sand inside the freezer door, and in one, smooth move, gave her a little tap in just the right place.

He caught her before she hit the ground. Then it was into the special side of the ice cream truck with her; the side not hooked up to the freezer unit, with ventilation holes bored through the walls in places where no one would find them. He gave her a whiff of ether on a rag, just in case, to make sure she stayed under, then he slid her limp body into the cardboard carton he kept on that side, just in case somebody wanted to look inside. He closed and latched the door, and was back in the driver's seat before two minutes were up, with still no sign of man nor beast. Luck, luck, all the way.

Luck, or pure genius. He couldn't lose; he was invulnerable.

Funny how she'd kept a grip on that toy, though. But that was luck, too; if she'd left it there—

Well, he might have forgotten she'd had it. Then somebody would have found it, and someone might have remembered her standing at the ice cream truck with it beside her.

But it had all gone smoothly, perfectly planned, perfectly executed, ending with a drive through the warm September afternoon, bells tinkling slightly out of tune, no different from any other ice cream man out for the last scores of the season. He'd felt supremely calm and in control of everything the moment he was in his seat; no one would ever suspect him, he'd been a fixture since the beginning of school. Who ever *sees* the ice cream man? He was as much a part of the landscape as the fire hydrant he generally stopped beside.

They'd ask the kids of course, now that Molly was officially missing—and they'd say the same stupid thing they always did. "Did you see any strangers?" they'd ask. "Any strange cars hanging around? Anyone you didn't recognize?"

Stupid; they were just stupid. *He* was the smart one. The kids would answer just like they always did, they'd say "no," they hadn't "seen any strangers."

No, *he* wasn't a stranger, he was the ice cream man. The kids saw him today, and they'd see him tomorrow, he'd make sure of that. He'd be on his route for the next week at least, unless there was a cold snap. He knew how cops thought, and if he disappeared, they might look for him. No way was he going to break his pattern. Eventually the cops would question him—not tomorrow, but probably the day after that. He'd tell them he *had* seen the little girl, that she'd bought a cone from him. He'd cover his tracks there, since the other kids would probably remember that she'd been at the truck. But he'd shrug helplessly, and say that she hadn't been on the street when he drove off. He'd keep strictly to the truth, just not all the truth.

Now Molly was all his, and no one would take her away from him until he was done with her.

He drove home, stopping to sell cones when kids flagged him down, taking his time. It wouldn't do to break his pattern. He took out the box that held Molly and brought it upstairs, then made two more trips, for the leftover frozen treats, all in boxes just like the one that held Molly. The neighbors were used to this; it was another part of his routine. He was the invisible man. Old Jim always brings in the leftovers and puts 'em in his freezer overnight; it's cheaper than running the truck freezer overnight.

He knew what they said about him. That Jim was a good guy— kept to himself mostly, but when it was really hot or he had too much left over to fit in his freezer, he'd pass out freebies. A free ice-cream bar was appreciated in this neighborhood, where there wasn't a lot of money to spare for treats. Yeah, Jim was real quiet, but okay, never gave any trouble to anybody.

If the cops went so far as to look into his background, they wouldn't find anything. He ran a freelance ice cream route in the summer and took odd jobs in the winter; there was no record of his ever getting into trouble.

Of course there was no record. He was smart. Nobody had ever caught him, not when he set fires as a kid, not when he prowled the back alleys looking for stray dogs and cats, and not later, when he went on to the targets he really wanted. He was careful. When he first started on kids, he picked the ones nobody would miss. And he kept up with the literature; he knew everything the cops would look for.

Jim's apartment was a corner unit, under the roof. There was nobody above him, the old man under him was stone-deaf, the guy on one side was a stoner on the nightshift, and the couple on the other side kept their music blasting so loud it was a wonder that *they* weren't deaf. Nobody would ever hear a thing.

Meanwhile, Jim waited, as darkness fell outside, for Molly to sleep off her ether and her bump; it wasn't any fun for him when his trophies were out of it. Jim liked them awake; he liked to see their eyes when they realized that no one was coming to rescue them.

He changed into a pair of old jeans and a tee-shirt in the living-room, hanging his white uniform in the closet, then looked in on her again.

She still had a hold on that teddy bear. It was a really unusual toy; it was one of the many things that had marked her when he'd first looked for targets. Jim was really glad she'd kept such a tight grip on it; it was so different that there was little doubt it would have been spotted as hers if she'd dropped it. The plush was a thick, black fur, extremely realistic; in fact, he wasn't entirely certain that it *was* fake fur. There was no sign of the wear that kids usually put on that kind of beloved plaything. The mouth was half-open, lined with red felt, with white felt teeth and a red felt tongue. Instead of a ribbon bow, this bear had a real leather collar with an odd tag hanging from it; pottery or glass, maybe, or enameled metal, it certainly wasn't plastic. There was a faint, raised pattern on the back, and the word "Tedi" on the front in a childishly printed scrawl. The eyes were oddest of all— whoever had made this toy must have used the same eyes that taxidermists used; they looked real, alive.

It was going to prove a little bit of problem dealing with that bear, after. He was so careful not to leave any fiber or hair evidence; he always washed them when he was through with them, dressing them in fancy party clothing he took straight out of the packages, then wrapping them in plastic once they were dressed, to keep from contaminating them. Once he was through with her and dressed her in that frilly blue party dress he'd bought, he'd cut up her old clothing into tiny pieces and flush them down the john, a few at a time, to keep from clogging the line. That could be fatal.

He'd do the part with the knife in the bathtub, of course, so there wouldn't be any bloodstains. He knew exactly how to get blood-evidence scrubbed out of the bathroom, what chemicals to use and everything. They'd have to swab out the pipes to find anything.

But the bear was a problem. He'd have to figure out a smart way to get rid of it, because it was bound to collect all kinds of evidence.

*Maybe give it to a kid?* Maybe not; there was a chance the kid would remember him. By now it had probably collected fibers . . . .

He had it; the Salvation Army box, the one on Colby, all the way across town. They'd let that thing get stuffed full before they ever emptied it, and by then the bear would have collected so much fiber and hair they'd never get it all sorted out. Then he could take her to MacArthur Park; it was far enough away from the collection box. He'd leave her there like he always did, propped up on a bench like an oversized doll, a bench off in an out-of-the-way spot. He'd used MacArthur Park before, but not recently, and at this time of year it might be days before anyone found her.

But the bear—better get it away from her now, before it collected something more than hair. For one thing, it would be harder to handle her if she kept clinging to it. Something about those eyes bothered him, too, and he wasn't in a mood to be bothered.

He cracked the door open, slipped inside, pried the bear out of her loose grip. He threw it into the bathroom, but Molly didn't stir; he was vaguely disappointed. He'd hoped she show *some* sign of coming around when he took the toy.

Well, he had all night, all weekend, as long as she lasted. He'd have to make the most of this one; she was the last of the season.

Might as well get the stuff out.

He went into the kitchenette and dragged out the plastic step-stool. Standing it in the closet in the living room, he opened up the hatch into the crawl-space. It wasn't tall enough for him to see what was up there, but what he wanted was right by the hatch anyway. He felt across the fiberglass battings; the paper over the insulation crackled under his fingers. He groped until his hand encountered the cardboard box he'd stored up there. Getting both hands around it, straining on tiptoe to do so, he lowered it carefully down through the hatch. He had to bring it through the opening catty-cornered to make it fit. It wasn't heavy, but it was an awkward shape.

He carried it to the center of the living room and placed it on the carpet, kneeling beside it with his stomach tight with anticipation. Slowly, with movements ritualized over time, he undid the twine holding it closed, just so. He coiled up the twine and laid it to the side, exactly five inches from the side of the box. He reached for the lid.

But as he started to open it, he thought he heard a faint sound, as if something moved in the bedroom. Was Molly finally awake?

He got to his feet, and moved softly to the door. But when he applied his eye to the crack, he was disappointed to see that she hadn't moved at all. She lay exactly as he'd left her, head pillowed on one arm, hair scattered across his pillow, lips pursed, breathing softly but regularly. Her red corduroy jumper was still in the same folds it had been when he'd put her down on the bed, rucked up over her hip so that her little pink panties showed the tiniest bit.

Then he saw the bear.

It was back right where it had been before, sitting up in the curve of her stomach. Looking at him.

He shook his head, frowning. Of course it wasn't looking at him, it was his imagination; it was just a toy. He must have been so wrapped up in anticipation that he'd flaked—and *hadn't* thrown it in the bathroom as he'd intended, or else he'd absent-mindedly put it back on the bed.

Easily fixed. He took the few steps into the room, grabbed the bear by one ear, and threw it into the bedroom closet, closing the door on it. Molly didn't stir, and he retired to the living room and his treasure chest.

On the top layer of the box lay a tangle of leather and rubber. He sorted out the straps carefully, laying out all the restraints in their proper order, with the rubber ball for her mouth and the gag to hold it in there first in line. That was one of the most important parts. Whatever sound got past the gag wouldn't get past the neighbors' various deficiencies.

Something was definitely moving in the next room. He heard the closet door opening, then the sounds of shuffling.

He sprinted to the door—

Only to see that Molly was lying in exactly the same position, and the bear was with her.

He shook his head. Damn! He couldn't be going crazy—

Then he chuckled at a sudden memory. The third kid he'd done had pulled something like this—the kid was a sleepwalker, with a knack for lying back down in precisely the same position as before, and it wasn't until he'd stayed in the bedroom instead of going through his collection that he'd proved it to himself. Molly had obviously missed her bear, gotten up, searched blindly for her toy, found it, then lay back down again. Yeah, come to think of it, her jumper was a bit higher on her hip, and she was more on her back than her side, now.

But that bear had to go.

He marched in, grabbed the bear again, and looked around. Now where?

The bathroom, the cabinet under the sink. There was nothing in there but a pair of dead roaches, and it had a child-proof latch on it.

The eyes flashed at him as he flipped on the bathroom light and whipped the cabinet open. For one moment he almost thought the eyes glared at him with a red light of their own before he closed the door on the thing and turned the lock with a satisfying click.

Back to the box.

The next layer was his pictures. They weren't of any of his kids; he wasn't that stupid. Nothing in this box would ever connect him with the guy they were calling the "Sunday-School Killer" because he left them dressed in Sunday best, clean and shining, in places like parks and beaches, looking as if they'd just come from church.

But the pictures were the best the Internet had to offer, and a lot of these kids looked like the ones he'd had. Pretty kids, real pretty.

He took them out in the proper order, starting with the simple ones, letting the excitement build in his groin as he savored each one. First, the nudes—ten of them, he knew them all by heart. Then the nudes with the kids "playing" together, culled from the "My Little Fishie" newsletter of a nut-case religious cult that believed in kid-sex.

Then the good ones.

Halfway through, he slipped his hand into his pants without taking his eyes off the pictures.

This was going to be a good one. Molly looked just like the kid in the best of his pictures. She was going to be perfect; the last of the season, the best of the season.

He was pretty well-occuppied as he got to the last set, though he noted absently that it sounded as if Molly was up and moving around again. This was the bondage-and-snuff set, very hard to get, and the only reason he had them at all was because he'd stolen them from a storage-locker. He wouldn't have taken the risk of getting them personally, but they'd given him some of his best ideas.

Molly must be awake by now. But this wasn't to be hurried— there wouldn't be any Mollys or Jeffreys until next year, next spring, summer, and fall. He had to make this one last.

He savored the emotions in the pictured eyes as he would savor Molly's fear; savored their pleading expressions, their helplessness. Such pretty little things, like her, like all his kids.

They wanted it, anybody knew that. Freud said so—that had been in that psychology course he took by correspondence when he was trying to figure himself out. Look at the way kids played "doctor" the minute you turned your back on them. That religious cult had it right; kids wanted it, needed it, and the only thing getting in the way was the way a bunch of repressed old men felt about it.

He'd show her what it was she wanted, show her good. He'd make it last, take it slow. Then, once she was all his and would do anything he said, he'd make sure nobody else would ever have her again. He'd keep her his, forever. Not even her parents would have her the way he did.

Under the last layer of pictures was the knife, the beautiful, shining filleting knife, the best made. Absolutely stainless, rust-proof, with a pristine black handle. He laid it reverently beside the leather straps, then zipped up his pants and rose to his feet.

No doubt, she was shuffling around on the other side of the door, moving uncertainly back and forth. She should be just dazed enough that he'd get her gagged before she knew enough to scream.

He paused a moment to order his thoughts and his face before putting his hand on the doorknob. Next to the moment when the kid lay trussed-up under him, this was the best moment.

He flung the door wide open. *"Hel*-lo, Mo—"

That was as far as he got.

The screams brought the neighbors to break down the door. There were two sets of screams; his, and those of a terrified little girl pounding on the closet door.

A dozen of them gathered in the hall before they got up the courage to break in, and by then Jim wasn't screaming anymore. What they found in the living room made the first inside run back out the way they had come.

One managed to get as far as the bedroom to release the child, a pale young woman who lived at the other end of the floor, whose maternal instincts overrode her stomach long enough to rescue the weeping child.

Molly fell out of the closet into her arms, sobbing with terror. The young woman recognized her from the news; how could she not? Her picture had been everywhere.

Meanwhile one of the others who had fled the whimpering thing on the living room floor got to a phone and called the cops.

The young woman closed the bedroom door on the horror in the next room, took the hysterical, shivering child into her arms, and waited for help to arrive, absently wondering at her own, hitherto unsuspected courage.

While they were waiting, the thing on the floor mewled, gasped, and died.

Although the young woman hadn't known what to make of the tangle of leather she'd briefly glimpsed on the carpet, the homicide detective knew exactly what it meant. He owed a candle to Saint Jude for the solving of his most hopeless case and another to the Virgin for saving *this* child before anything had happened to her.

And a third to whatever saint had seen to it that there would be no need for a trial.

"You say there was no sign of anything or anyone else?" he asked the young woman. She'd already told him that she was a librarian—that was shortly after she'd taken advantage of their arrival to close herself into the bathroom and throw up. He almost took her to task for possibly destroying evidence, but what was the point? This was one murder he didn't really want to solve.

She was sitting in the only chair in the living room, carefully not looking at the outline on the carpet, or the blood-spattered mess of pictures and leather straps a little distance from her feet. He'd asked the same question at least a dozen times already.

"Nothing, no one." She shook her head. "There's no back door, just the hatches to the crawl-space, in each closet."

He looked where she pointed, at the open closet door with the kitchen stool still inside it. He walked over to the closet and craned his head around sideways, peering upward.

"Not too big, but a skinny guy could get up there," he said, half to himself. "Is that attic divided at all?"

"No, it runs all along the top floor; I never put anything up there because anybody could get into it from any other apartment." She shivered. "And I put locks on all my hatches. Now I'm glad I did. Once a year they fumigate, so they need the hatches to get exhaust fans up there."

"A skinny guy, one real good with a knife—maybe a Nam vet. A SEAL, a Green Beret—" he was talking mostly to himself. "It might not have been a knife; maybe claws, like in the karate rags. Ninja claws. That could be what he used—"

He paced back to the center of the living room. The librarian rubbed her hands along her arms, watching him out of sick blue eyes.

"Okay, he knows what this sicko is up to—maybe he *just* now found out, doesn't want to call the cops for whatever reason. He comes down into the bedroom, locks the kid in the closet to keep her safe—"

"She told me that a bear locked her into the closet," the woman interrupted.

The detective laughed. "Lady, that kid has a knot the size of a baseball on her skull; she could have seen Luke Skywalker lock her in that closet!" He went back to his deductions. "Okay, he locks the kid in, then makes enough noise so joy-boy thinks she finally woke up. Then when the door opens—yeah. It'll fly." He nodded. "Then he gets back out by this hatch." He sighed, regretful that he wouldn't ever get a chance to thank this guy. "Won't be any fingerprints; guy like this would be too smart to leave any."

He stared at the outline on the blood-soaked carpet pensively. The librarian shuddered.

"Look, officer," she said, asserting herself, "If you don't need me anymore—"

"Hey, Pete—" the detective's partner poked his head in through the door. "The kid's parents are here. The kid wants her teddy—she's raising a real howl about it, and the docs at the hospital don't want to sedate her if they don't have to."

"Shit, the kid misses being a statistic by a couple of minutes, and all she can think about is her toy!" He shook his head, and refocused on the librarian. "Go ahead, miss. I don't think you can tell us anything more. You might want to check into the hospital yourself, get checked over for shock. Either that, or pour yourself a stiff one. Call in sick tomorrow."

He smiled, suddenly realizing that she was pretty, in a wilted sort of way—and after what she'd just been through, no wonder she was wilted.

"That was what I had in mind already, Detective," she replied, and made good her escape before he changed his mind.

"Pete, her folks say she won't be able to sleep without it," his partner persisted.

"Yeah, yeah, go ahead and take it," he responded absently. If things had gone differently—they'd be shaking out that toy for hair and fiber samples, if they found it at all.

He handed the bear to his partner.

"Oh—before you give it back—"

"What?"

"There's blood on the paws," he replied, already looking for trace evidence that would support his theories. "Wouldn't want to shake her up any further, so make sure you wash it off first."

*Okay, so I don't always take Diana Tregarde very seriously. When this story appeared in* Marion Zimmer Bradley's Fantasy Magazine, *however, there was a reader (a self-proclaimed romance writer) who took it seriously, and was quite irate at the rather unflattering picture I painted of romance writers. She wrote a long and angry letter about it to the editor.*

*The editor, who like me, has seen romance writers at a romance convention, declined to comment.*

*A note: The character of Robert Harrison and the concept of "whoopie witches" was taken from the excellent supernatural role-playing game,* Stalking the Night Fantastic *by Richard Tucholka and used with the creator's permission. There is also a computer game version,* Bureau Thirteen. *Both are highly recommended!*

# Satanic, Versus . . .

## Mercedes Lackey

"Mrs. Peel," intoned a suave, urbane tenor voice from the hotel doorway behind Di Tregarde, "we're needed."

The accent was faintly French rather than English, but the inflection was dead-on.

Di didn't bother to look in the mirror, although she knew there *would* be a reflection there. Andre LeBrel might be a 200-year-old vampire, but he cast a perfectly good reflection. She was too busy trying to get her false eyelashes to stick.

"In a minute, lover. The glue won't hold. I can't understand it—I bought the stuff last year for that unicorn costume and it was fine then—"

"Allow me." A thin, graceful hand appeared over her shoulder, holding a tiny tube of surgical adhesive. "I had the sinking feeling that you would forget. This glue, *cherie,* it does not age well."

"Piffle. Figure a back-stage haunt would know that." She took the white plastic tube from Andre, and proceeded to attach the pesky lashes properly. This time they obliged by staying put. She finished her preparations with a quick application of liner, and spun around to face her partner. "Here," she said, posing, feeling more than a little smug about how well the black leather jumpsuit fit, "How do I look?"

Andre cocked his bowler to the side and leaned on his umbrella. "Ravishing. And I?" His dark eyes twinkled merrily. Although he looked a great deal more like Timothy Dalton than Patrick Macnee, anyone seeing the two of them together would have no doubt who he was supposed to be costumed as. Di was very glad they had a "pair" costume, and blessed Andre's infatuation with old TV shows.

*And they're damned well going to see us together all the time,* Di told herself firmly. *Why I ever agreed to this fiasco . . .*

"You look altogether too good to make me feel comfortable," she told him, snapping off the light over the mirror. "I hope you realize what you're letting yourself in for. You're going to think you're a drumstick in a pool of piranha."

Andre made a face as he followed her into the hotel room from the dressing alcove. *"Cherie,* these are only romance writers. They—"

"Are for the most part over-imaginative middle-aged *hausfraus,* married to guys that are going thin on top and thick on the bottom, and you're likely going to be one of a handful of males in the room. And the rest are going to be middle-aged copies of their husbands, agents, or gay." She raised an eyebrow at him. "So where do you think that leaves you?"

"Like Old Man Kangaroo, very much run after." He had the audacity to laugh at her. "Have no fear, *cherie.* I shall evade the sharp little piranha teeth."

"I just hope *I* can," she muttered under her breath. Under most circumstances she avoided the Romance-Writers-of-the-World functions like the plague, chucked the newsletter in the garbage without reading it, and paid her dues only because Morrie pointed out that it would look really strange if she didn't belong. The RWW, she had found, was a hotbed of infighting and jealousy, and "my advances are bigger than your advances, so I am writing Deathless Prose and you are writing tripe." The general attitude seemed to be, "the publishers are out to get you, the agents are out to get you and your fellow writers are out to get you." Since Di got along perfectly well with agent and publishers, and really didn't *care* how well or poorly other writers were doing, she didn't see the point.

But somehow Morrie had talked her into attending the RWW Halloween party. And for the life of her, she couldn't remember why or how.

"Why am I doing this?" she asked Andre, as she snatched up her purse from the beige-draped bed, transferred everything really necessary into a black-leather belt-pouch, and slung the latter around her hips, making very sure the belt didn't interfere with the holster on her other hip. "You were the one who talked to Morrie on the phone."

"Because M'sieur Morrie wishes you to give his client Robert Harrison someone to talk to," the vampire reminded her. "M'sieur Harrison agreed to escort Valentine Vervain to the party in a moment of weakness equal to yours."

"Why in Hades did he agree to *that*?" she exclaimed, giving the sable-haired vampire a look of profound astonishment.

"Because Miss Vervain—*cherie,* that is not her *real* name, is it?— is one of Morrie's best clients, is newly divorced and alone and Morrie claims most insecure, and M'sieur Harrison was kind to her," Andre replied.

Di took a quick look around the hotel room, to make sure she hadn't forgotten anything. One thing about combining her annual "make nice with the publishers" trip with Halloween, she had a chance to get together with all her old New York buddies for a *real* Samhain celebration and avoid the Christmas and Thanksgiving crowds and bad weather. "I remember. That was when she did that crossover thing, and the sci-fi people took her apart for trying to claim it was the best thing since Tolkien." She chuckled heartlessly. "The less said about that, the better. Her magic system had holes I could drive a Mack truck through. But Harrison was a gentleman and kept the bloodshed to a minimum. But Morrie doesn't know Valentine—and no, sexy, her name used to be Edith Bowman until she changed it legally—if he thinks she's as insecure as she's acting. Three quarters of what La Valentine does is an act. And everything is in Technicolor and Dolby-enhanced sound. So what's Harrison doing in town?"

She snatched up the key from the desk, and stuffed it into the pouch, as Andre held the door open for her.

"I do not know," he replied, twirling the umbrella once and waving her past. "You should ask him."

"I hope Valentine doesn't eat him alive," she said, striding down the beige hall, and frankly enjoying the appreciative look a hotel room-service clerk gave her as she sauntered by. "I wonder if she's going to wear the outfit from the cover of her last book—if she does, Harrison may decide he wants to spend the rest of the party in the men's room." She reached the end of the hall a fraction of a second before Andre, and punched the button for the elevator.

"I gather that is what we are to save him from, *cherie*," Andre pointed out wryly, as the elevator arrived.

"Oh well," she sighed, stepping into the mirror-walled cubicle. "It's only five hours, and it can't be that bad. How much trouble can a bunch of romance writers get into, anyway?"

There was enough lace, chiffon, and satin to outfit an entire Busby Berkeley musical. Di counted fifteen Harem Girls, nine Vampire Victims, three Southern Belles (the South was Out this year), a round dozen Ravished Maidens of various time periods (none of them peasants), assorted Frills and Furbelows, and one "witch" in a black chiffon outfit clearly purchased from the Frederick's catalog. Aside from the "witch," she and Andre were the only ones dressed in black—and they *were* the only ones covered from neck to toes— though in Di's case, that was problematical; the tight black leather jumpsuit really didn't leave anything to the imagination.

The Avengers outfits had been Andre's idea, when she realized she really *had* agreed to go to this party. She *had* suggested Dracula for him and a witch for her—but he had pointed out, logically, that there was no point in coming as what they really were.

*Besides, I've always wanted a black leather jumpsuit, and this made a good excuse to get it. And since I'm doing this as a favor to Morrie, I might be able to deduct it . . . .*

*And even if I can't, the looks I'm getting are worth twice the price.*

Most of the women here—and as she'd warned Andre, the suite at the Henley Palace that RWW had rented for this bash contained about eighty percent women—were in their forties at best. Most of them demonstrated amply the problems with having a sedentary job. And most of them were wearing outfits that might have been worn by their favorite heroines, though few of them went to the extent that Valentine Vervain did, and copied the exact dress from the front of the latest book. The problem was, their heroines were all no older than twenty-two, and as described, weighed *maybe* ninety-five pounds. Since a great many of the ladies in question weighed *at least* half again that, the results were not what the wearers intended.

The sour looks Di was getting were just as flattering as the wolf-whistle the bellboy had sent her way.

A quick sail through the five rooms of the suite with Andre at her side ascertained that Valentine and her escort had not yet arrived. A quick glance at Andre's face proved that he was having a very difficult time restraining his mirth. She decided then that discretion was definitely the better part of valor, and retired to the balcony with Andre in tow and a couple of glasses of Perrier.

It was a beautiful night; one of those rare, late-October nights that made Di regret—briefly—moving to Connecticut. Clear, cool and crisp, with just enough wind to sweep the effluvium of city life from the streets. Below them, hundreds of lights created a jewelbox effect. If you looked hard, you could even see a few stars beyond the light-haze.

The sliding glass door to the balcony had been opened to vent some of the heat and overwhelming perfume (Di's nose said, nothing under a hundred dollars a bottle), and Di left it that way. She parked her elbows on the balcony railing and looked down, Andre at her side, and sighed.

He chuckled. "You warned me, and I did not believe. I apologize, *cherie*. It is—most remarkable."

"Hmm. Exercise that vampiric hearing of yours, and you'll get an earful," she said, watching the car-lights crawl by, twenty stories below. "When they aren't slaughtering each other and playing little powertrip games, they're picking apart their agents and their editors. If you've ever wondered why I've never bothered going after the big money, it's because to get it I'd have to play by *those* rules."

"Then I devoutly urge you to remain with modest ambitions, *cherie*," he said, fervently. "I—"

"Excuse me?" said a masculine voice from the balcony door. It had a distinct note of desperation in it. "Are you Diana Tregarde?"

Di turned. Behind her, peering around the edge of the doorway, was a harried-looking fellow in a baggy, tweedy sweater and slacks—not a costume—with a shock of prematurely graying, sandy-brown hair, glasses and a moustache. And a look of absolute misery.

"Robert Harrison, I presume?" she said, archly. "Come, join us in the sanctuary. It's too cold out here for chiffon."

"Thank God." Harrison ducked onto the balcony with the agility of a man evading Iraqi borderguards, and threw himself down in an aluminum patio chair out of sight of the windows. "I think the password is, 'Morrie sent me.'"

"Recognized; pass, friend. Give the man credit; he gave you an ally and an escape route," Di chuckled. "Don't tell me; she showed up as the Sacred Priestess Askenazy."

"In a nine-foot chiffon train and see-through harem pants, yes," Harrison groaned. "And let me know I was Out of the Royal Favor for *not* dressing as What's-His-Name."

"Watirion," Di said helpfully. "Do you realize you can pronounce that as 'what-tire-iron'? I encourage the notion."

"But that wasn't the worst of it!" Harrison shook his head, distractedly, as if he was somewhat in a daze. "The worst was the monologue in the cab on the way over here. Every other word was

Crystal this and Vibration that, Past Life Regression, and Mystic Rituals. The woman's a whoopie witch!"

Di blinked. That was a new one on *her*. "A what?"

Harrison looked up, and for the first time, seemed to see her. "Uh—" he hesitated. "Uh, some of what Morrie said—uh, he seemed to think you—well, you've seen things—uh, he said you know things—"

She fished the pentagram out from under the neck of her jumpsuit and flashed it briefly. "My religion is non-traditional, yes, and there are more things in heaven and earth, etcetera. Now what in Tophet is a whoopie witch?"

"It's—uh—a term some friends of mine use. It's kind of hard to explain." Harrison's brow furrowed. "Look, let me give you examples. Real witches have grimorie, sometimes handed down through their families for centuries. Whoopie witches have books they picked up at the supermarket. Usually right at the check-out counter."

"Real witches have carefully researched spells—" Di prompted.

"Whoopie witches draw a baseball diamond in chalk on the living room floor and recite random passages from the *Satanic Bible*."

"When real witches make substitutions, they do so knowing the exact difference the substitute will make—"

"Whoopie witches slop taco sauce in their pentagram because it looks like blood."

"Real witches gather their ingredients by hand—" Di was beginning to enjoy this game.

"Whoopie witches have a credit card, and *lots* of catalogues." Harrison was grinning, and so was Andre.

"Real witches spend hours in meditation—"

"Whoopie witches sit under a pyramid they ordered from a catalogue and watch *Knot's Landing*."

"Real witches cast spells knowing that any change they make in someone's life will come back at them three-fold, for good or ill—"

"Whoopie witches call up the Hideous Slime from Yosotha to eat their neighbor's poodle because the bitch got the last carton of Haagen-Daaz double-chocolate at the Seven-Eleven."

"I think I've got the picture. So dear Val decided to take the so-called research she did for the Great Fantasy Novel seriously?" Di leaned back into the railing and laughed. "Oh, Robert, I pity you! Did she try to tell you that the two of you just *must* have been priestly lovers in a past life in Atlantis?"

"Lemuria," Harrison said, gloomily. "My God, she must be supporting half the crystal miners in Arkansas."

"Don't feel too sorry for her, Robert," Di warned him. "With her advances, she can afford it. And I know some perfectly nice people in Arkansas who should only soak her for every penny they can get. Change the subject; you're safe with us—and if she decides to hit the punch bowl hard enough, you can send her back to her hotel in a cab and she'll never know the difference. What brings you to New York?"

"Morrie wants me to meet the new editors at Berkley; he thinks I've got a shot at selling them that near-space series I've been dying to do. And I had some people here in the City I really needed to see." He sighed. "And, I'll admit it, I'd been thinking about writing bodice-rippers under a pseudonym. When you know they're getting ten times what I am—"

Di shrugged. "I don't think you'd be happy doing it, unless you've written strictly to spec before. There's a lot of things you have to conform to that you might not feel comfortable doing. Listen, Harrison, you seem to know quite a bit about hot-and-cold-running esoterica—how did you—"

Someone in one of the other rooms screamed. Not the angry scream of a woman who has been insulted, but the soul-chilling shriek of pure terror that brands itself on the air and stops all conversation dead.

"What in—" Harrison was on his feet, staring in the direction of the scream. Di ignored him and launched herself at the patio door, pulling the Glock 19 from the holster on her hip, and thankful she'd loaded the silver-tipped bullets in the first clip.

Funny how everybody thought it couldn't be real because it was plastic . . . .

"Andre—the next balcony!" she called over her shoulder, knowing the vampire could easily scramble over the concrete divider and come in through the next patio door, giving them a two-pronged angle of attack.

The scream hadn't been what alerted her—simultaneous with the scream had been the wrenching feeling in her gut that was the signal that someone had breached the fabric of the Otherworld in her presence. She didn't know who, or what—but from the stream of panicked chiffon billowing towards the door at supersonic speed, it probably wasn't nice, and it probably had a great deal to do with one of the party-goers.

Three amply endowed females (one Belle, one Ravished and one Harem) had reached the door to the next room at the same moment, and jammed it, and rather than one of them pulling free, they all three kept shoving harder, shrieking at the tops of their lungs in tones their agents surely recognized.

*You'd think their advances failed to pay out!* Di kept the Glock in her hand, but sprinted for the door. She grabbed the nearest flailing arm (Harem), planted her foot in the midsection of her neighbor (Belle) and shoved and pulled at the same time. The clot of feminine hysteria came loose with a sound of ripping cloth; a crinoline parted company with its wearer. The three women tumbled through the door, giving Di a clear launching path into the next room. She took it, diving for the shelter of a huge wooden coffee table, rolling, and aiming for the door of the last room with the Glock. And her elbow hit someone.

"What are *you* doing here?" asked Harrison, and Di, simultaneously. Harrison cowered—no, *had taken cover*, there was a distinct difference—behind the sofa beside the coffee table, his own huge magnum aimed at the same doorway.

"My *job*," they said—also simultaneously.

"*What?*" (Again in chorus).

"This is all a very amusing study in synchronicity," said Andre, crouching just behind Harrison, bowler tipped and sword from his umbrella out and ready, "but I suggest you both pay attention to that most boorish party-crasher over there—"

Something very large occluded the light for a moment in the next room, then the lights went out, and Di distinctly heard the sound of the chandelier being torn from the ceiling and thrown against the wall. She winced.

*There go my dues up again.*

"I got a glimpse," Andre continued. "It was very large, perhaps ten feet tall, and—*cherie*, looked like nothing so much as a rubber creature from a very bad movie. Except that I do not think it was rubber."

At just that moment, there was a thrashing from the other room, and Valentine Vervain, long red hair liberally beslimed, minus nine-foot train and one of her sleeves, scrambled through the door and plastered herself against the wall, where she promptly passed out.

"Valentine?" Di murmured—and snapped her head towards Harrison when he moaned—"Oh *no*," in a way that made her *sure* he knew something.

"Harrison!" she snapped. "Cough it up!"

There was a sound of things breaking in the other room, as if something was fumbling around in the dark, picking up whatever it encountered, and smashing it in frustration.

"Valentine—she said something about getting some of her 'friends' together tonight and 'calling up her soul mate' so she could 'show that ex of hers.' I gather he appeared at the divorce hearing with a twenty-one-year-old blonde." Harrison gulped. "I figured she was just blowing it off—I never thought she had any power—"

"You'd be amazed what anger will do," Di replied grimly, keeping her eyes on the darkened doorway. "Sometimes it even transcends a total lack of talent. Put that together with the time of year—All Hallow's E'en—Samhain—is tomorrow. The Wall Between the Worlds is especially thin, and power flows are heavy right now. That's a recipe for disaster if I ever heard one."

"And here comes M'sieur Soul Mate," said Andre, warningly.

What shambled in through the door was nothing that Di had ever heard of. It was, indeed, about ten feet tall. It was a very dark brown— It was covered with luxuriant brown hair—all over. Otherwise, it was nude. If there were any eyes, the hair hid them completely. It was built something along the lines of a powerful body-builder, taken to exaggerated lengths, and it drooled. It also stank, a combination of sulfur and musk so strong it would have brought tears to the eyes of a skunk.

"Wah-wen-ine!" it bawled, waving its arms around, as if it were blind. "Wah-wen-ine!"

"Oh goddess," Di groaned, putting two and two together and coming up with—*she called a soul mate, and specified parameters. But she forgot to specify "human."* "Are you thinking what I'm thinking?"

The other writer nodded. "Tall, check. Dark, check. Long hair, check. Handsome—well, I suppose in some circles." Harrison stared at the thing in fascination.

"Some—thing—that will accept her completely as she is, and love her completely. Young, sure, he can't be more than five minutes old." Di watched the thing fumble for the doorframe and cling to it. "Look at that, he can't see. So love *is* blind. Strong and as masculine as you can get. And not too bright, which I bet she also specified. Oh, my ears and whiskers."

Valentine came to, saw the thing, and screamed.

"*Wah-wen-ine!*" it howled, and lunged for her. Reflexively, Di and Harrison both shot. He emptied his cylinder, and one speed-loader; Di gave up after four shots, when it was obvious they *were* hitting the thing, to no effect.

Valentine scrambled on hands and knees over the carpet, still screaming—but crawling in the wrong direction, towards the balcony, not the door.

"*Merde!*" Andre flung himself between the creature's clutching hands and its summoner, before Di could do anything.

And before Di could react to *that*, the thing back-handed Andre into a wall hard enough to put him through the plasterboard.

Valentine passed out again. Andre was already out for the count. There are some things even a vampire has a little trouble recovering from.

"Jesus!" Harrison was on his feet, fumbling for something in his pocket. Di joined him, holstering the Glock, and grabbed his arm.

"Harrison, distract it, make a noise, anything!" She pulled the atheme from her boot sheath and began cutting Sigils in the air with it, getting the Words of Dismissal out as fast as she could without slurring the syllables.

Harrison didn't even hesitate; he grabbed a couple of tin serving trays from the coffee table, shook off their contents, and banged them together.

The thing turned its head toward him, its hands just inches away from its goal. "Wah-wen-ine?" it said.

Harrison banged the trays again. It lunged toward the sound. It was a lot faster than Di thought it was.

Evidently Harrison made the same error in judgment. It missed him by inches, and he scrambled out of the way by the width of a hair, just as Di concluded the Ritual of Dismissal.

To no effect.

"Hurry *up*, will you?" Harrison yelped, as the thing threw the couch into the wall and lunged again.

"I'm *trying!*" she replied through clenched teeth—though not loud enough to distract the thing, which had concluded either (a) Harrison was Valentine or (b) Harrison was keeping it from Valentine. Whichever, it had gone from wailing Valentine's name to simply wailing, and lunging after Harrison, who was dodging with commendable agility in a man of middle age.

*Of course, he has a lot of incentive.*

She tried three more dismissals, still with no effect, the room was trashed, and Harrison was getting winded, and running out of heavy, expensive things to throw . . . .

And the only thing she could think of was the "incantation" she used—as a joke—to make the stoplights change in her favor.

*Oh hell—a cockamamie incantation pulled it up—*

"By the Seven Rings of Zsa Zsa Gabor and the Rock of Elizabeth Taylor I command thee!" she shouted, stepping between the thing and Harrison (who was beginning to stumble). "By the Six Wives of Eddie Fisher and the Words of Karnak the Great I compel thee! *Freeze, buddy!*"

Power rose, through her, crested over her—and hit the thing. And the thing—stopped. It whimpered, and struggled a little against invisible bonds, but seemed unable to move.

Harrison dropped to the carpet, right on top of a spill of guacamole and ground-in tortilla chips, whimpering a little himself.

*I have to get rid of this thing, quick, before it breaks the compulsion*—She closed her eyes and trusted to instinct, and shouted the first thing that came into her mind. The Parking Ritual, with one change . . .

"Great Squat, send him *to* a spot, and I'll send you three nuns—"

Mage energies raged through the room, whirling about her, invisible, intangible to eyes and ears, but she felt them. She was the heart of the whirlwind, she and the other—

There was a *pop* of displaced air; she opened her eyes to see that the creature was gone—but the mage energies continued to whirl—faster—

"Je-*sus*," said Harrison. "How did you—"

She waved him frantically to silence as the energies sensed his presence and began to circle in on him.

"Great Squat, thanks for the spot!" she yelled desperately, trying to complete the incantation before Harrison could be pulled in. "*Your nuns are in the mail!*"

The energies swirled up and away, satisfied. Andre groaned, stirred, and began extracting himself from the powdered sheetrock wall. Harrison stumbled over to give him a hand.

Just then someone pounded on the outer door of the suite.

"Police!" came a muffled voice. "Open the door!"

"It's open!" Di yelled back, unzipping her belt-pouch and pulling out her wallet.

Three people, two uniformed NYPD and one fellow in a suit with an impressive .357 Magnum in his hand, peered cautiously around the doorframe.

"Jee-zus Christ," one said in awe.

"Who?" the dazed Valentine murmured, hand hanging limply over her forehead. "Wha' hap . . ."

Andre appeared beside Di, bowler in hand, umbrella spotless and innocent-looking again.

Di fished her Hartford PD Special OPs ID out of her wallet and handed it to the man in the suit. "This lady," she said angrily, pointing to Valentine, "played a little Halloween joke that got out of hand. Her accomplices went out the back door, then down the fire escape. If you hurry you might be able to catch them."

The two NYPD officers looked around at the destruction, and didn't seem any too inclined to chase after whomever was responsible. Di checked out the corner of her eye; Harrison's own .44 had vanished as mysteriously as it had appeared.

"Are you certain this woman is responsible?" asked the hard-faced, suited individual with a frown, as he holstered his .357. He wasn't paying much attention to the plastic handgrip in the holster at Di's hip, for which she was grateful.

*House detective, I bet. With any luck, he's never seen a Glock.*

Di nodded. "These two gentlemen will back me up as witnesses," she said. "I suspect some of the ladies from the party will be able to do so as well, once you explain that Ms. Vervain was playing a not-very-nice joke on them. Personally, I think she ought to be held accountable for the damages."

*And keep my RWW dues from going through the roof.*

"Well, I think so too, miss." The detective hauled Valentine ungently to her feet. The writer was still confused, and it wasn't an act this time. "Ma'am," he said sternly to the dazed redhead, "I think you'd better come with me. I think we have a few questions to ask you."

Di projected outraged innocence and harmlessness at them as hard as she could. The camouflage trick worked, which after this evening, was more than she expected. The two uniformed officers didn't even look at her weapon; they just followed the detective out without a single backwards glance.

Harrison cleared his throat, audibly. She turned and raised an eyebrow at him.

"You—I thought you were just a writer—"

"And I thought *you* were just a writer," she countered. "So we're even."

"But—" He took a good look at her face, and evidently thought better of prying. "What did you do with that—thing? That was the strangest incantation I've ever heard!"

She shrugged, and began picking her way through the mess of smashed furniture, spilled drinks, and crushed and ground-in refreshments. "I have *no* idea. Valentine brought it in with something screwy, I got rid of it the same way. And that critter has no idea how lucky he was."

"Why?" asked Harrison, as she and Andre reached the door.

"Why?" She turned and smiled sweetly. "Do you have any idea how hard it is to get a parking place in Manhattan at this time of night?"

*This is the very first attempted professional appearance of Diana Tregarde, my occult detective. I've always enjoyed occult detectives, but there is a major problem with them—what are they supposed to do for a living? Ghosts don't get paid very well! So Di writes romances for a living and saves the world on the side. This story was originally rejected by the anthology I submitted it to; it became the basis for* Children of the Night *by Another Company, and was then published in this form by* Marion Zimmer Bradley's Fantasy Magazine.

# Nightside

## Mercedes Lackey

It was early spring, but the wind held no hint of verdancy, not even the promise of it—it was chill and odorless, and there were ghosts of dead leaves skittering before it. A few of them jittered into the pool of weak yellow light cast by the aging streetlamp—a converted gaslight that was a relic of the previous century. It was old and tired, its pea-green paint flaking away; as weary as this neighborhood, which was older still. Across the street loomed an ancient church, its congregation dwindled over the years to a handful of little old women and men who appeared like scrawny blackbirds every Sunday, and then scattered back to the shabby houses that stood to either side of it until Sunday should come again. On the side of the street that the lamp tried (and failed) to illuminate, was the cemetery.

Like the neighborhood, it was very old—in this case, fifty years shy of being classified as "colonial." There were few empty gravesites now, and most of those belonged to the same little old ladies and men that had lived and would die here. It was protected from vandals by a thorny hedge as well as a ten-foot wrought-iron fence. Within its confines, as seen through the leafless branches of the hedge, granite cenotaphs and enormous Victorian monuments bulked shapelessly against the bare sliver of a waning moon.

The church across the street was dark and silent; the houses up and down the block showed few lights, if any. There was no reason for anyone of this neighborhood to be out in the night.

So the young woman waiting beneath the lamppost seemed that much more out of place.

Nor could she be considered a typical resident of this neighborhood by any stretch of the imagination—for one thing, she was young; perhaps in her mid-twenties, but no more. Her clothing was neat but casual, too casual for someone visiting an elderly relative. She wore dark, knee-high boots, old, soft jeans tucked into their tops, and a thin windbreaker open at the front to show a leotard beneath. Her attire was far too light to be any real protection against the bite of the wind, yet she seemed unaware of the cold. Her hair was long, down to her waist, and straight—in the uncertain light of the lamp it was an indeterminate shadow, and it fell down her back like a waterfall. Her eyes were large and oddly slanted, but not Oriental; catlike, rather. Even the way she held herself was feline; poised, expectant—a graceful tension like a dancer's or a hunting predator's. She was not watching for something—no, her eyes were unfocused with concentration. She was *listening*.

A soft whistle, barely audible, carried down the street on the chill wind. The tune was of a piece with the neighborhood—old and timeworn.

Many of the residents would have smiled in recollection to hear "Lili Marlene" again.

The tension left the girl as she swung around the lamppost by one hand to face the direction of the whistle. She waved, and a welcoming smile warmed her eyes.

The whistler stepped into the edge of the circle of light. He, too, was dusky of eye and hair—and heartbreakingly handsome. He wore only dark jeans and a black turtleneck, no coat at all—but like the young woman, he didn't seem to notice the cold. There was an impish glint in his eyes as he finished the tune with a flourish.

"A flair for the dramatic, Diana, *mon cherie*?" he said mockingly. "Would that you were here for the same purpose as the lovely Lili! Alas, I fear my luck cannot be so good . . . ."

She laughed. His eyes warmed at the throaty chuckle. "Andre," she chided, "don't you ever think of anything else?"

"Am I not a son of the City of Light? I must uphold her reputation, *mais non*?" The young woman raised an ironic brow. He shrugged. "Ah well—since it is you who seek me, I fear I must be all business. A pity. Well, what lures you to my side this unseasonable night? What horror has *Mademoiselle* Tregarde unearthed this time?"

Diana Tregarde sobered instantly, the laughter fleeing her eyes. "I'm afraid you picked the right word this time, Andre. It *is* a horror. The trouble is, I don't know what kind."

"Say on. I wait in breathless anticipation." His expression was mocking as he leaned against the lamppost, and he feigned a yawn.

Diana scowled at him and her eyes darkened with anger. He raised an eyebrow of his own. "If this weren't so serious," she threatened, "I'd be tempted to pop you one—Andre, people are dying out there. There's a 'Ripper' loose in New York."

He shrugged, and shifted restlessly from one foot to the other. "So? This is new? Tell me when there is *not*! That sort of criminal is as common to the city as a rat. Let your police earn their salaries and capture him."

Her expression hardened. She folded her arms tightly across the thin nylon of her windbreaker; her lips tightened a little. "Use your head, Andre! If this was an ordinary slasher-killer, would *I* be involved?"

He examined his fingernails with care. "And what is it that makes it *extraordinaire*, eh?"

"The victims had no souls."

"I was not aware," he replied wryly, "that the dead possessed such things anymore."

She growled under her breath, and tossed her head impatiently, and the wind caught her hair and whipped it around her throat. "You are *deliberately* being difficult! I have half a mind—"

It finally seemed to penetrate the young man's mind that she was truly angry—and truly frightened, though she was doing her best to conceal the fact; his expression became contrite. "Forgive me, *cherie*. I *am* being recalcitrant."

"You're being a pain in the ass," she replied acidly. "Would I have come to you if I wasn't already out of my depth?"

"Well—" he admitted. "No. But—this business of souls, *cherie*, how can you determine such a thing? I find it most difficult to believe."

She shivered, and her eyes went brooding. "So did I. Trust me, my friend, I know what I'm talking about. There isn't a shred of doubt in my mind. There are at least six victims who no longer exist in *any* fashion anymore."

The young man finally evidenced alarm. "But—how?" he said, bewildered. "How is such a thing possible?"

She shook her head violently, clenching her hands on the arms of her jacket as if by doing so she could protect herself from an unseen—but not unfelt—danger. "I don't know, I don't know! It seems incredible even now—I keep thinking it's a nightmare, but—Andre, it's real, it's not my imagination—" Her voice rose a little with each word, and Andre's sharp eyes rested for a moment on her trembling hands.

"*Eh bien,*" he sighed, "I believe you. So there is something about that devours souls—and mutilates bodies as well, since you mentioned a 'Ripper' persona?"

She nodded.

"Was the devouring before or after the mutilation?"

"Before, I think—it's not easy to judge." She shivered in a way that had nothing to do with the cold.

"And you came into this how?"

"Whatever it is, it took the friend of a friend; I—happened to be there to see the body afterwards, and I knew immediately there was something wrong. When I unshielded and used the Sight—"

"Bad." He made it a statement.

"Worse. I—I can't describe what it felt like. There were still residual emotions, things left behind when—" Her jaw clenched. "Then when I started checking further I found out about the other five victims—that what I had discovered was no fluke. Andre, whatever it is, it has to be stopped." She laughed again, but this time there was no humor in it. "After all, you could say stopping it is in my job description."

He nodded soberly. "And so you become involved. Well enough, if you must hunt this thing, so must I." He became all business. "Tell me of the history. When, and where, and who does it take?"

She bit her lip. " 'Where'—there's no pattern. 'Who' seems to be mostly a matter of opportunity; the only clue is that the victims were always out on the street and entirely alone, there were no witnesses whatsoever, so the thing needs total privacy and apparently can't strike where it will. And 'when'—is moon-dark."

"Bad." He shook his head. "I have no clue at the moment. The *loup-garou* I know, and others, but I know nothing that hunts beneath the dark moon."

She grimaced. "You think I do? That's why I need your help; you're sensitive enough to feel something out of the ordinary, and you can watch and hunt undetected. I can't. And I'm not sure I *want* to go trolling for this thing alone—without knowing what it is, I could end up as a late-night snack for it. But if that's what I have to do, I will."

Anger blazed up in his face like a cold fire. "You go hunting alone for this creature over my dead body!"

"That's a little redundant, isn't it?" Her smile was weak, but genuine again.

"Pah!" he dismissed her attempt at humor with a wave of his hand. "Tomorrow is the first night of moon-dark; *I* shall go a-hunting. Do *you* remain at home, else I shall be most wroth with you. I know where to find you, should I learn anything of note."

"You ought to—" Diana began, but she spoke to the empty air.

\*\*\*\*

The next night was warmer, and Diana had gone to bed with her windows open to drive out some of the stale odors the long winter had left in her apartment. Not that the air of New York City was exactly fresh—but it was better than what the heating system kept recycling through the building. She didn't particularly like leaving her defenses open while she slept, but the lingering memory of Katy Rourk's fish wafting through the halls as she came in from shopping had decided her. Better exhaust fumes than burned haddock.

She hadn't had an easy time falling asleep, and when she finally managed to do so, tossed restlessly, her dreams uneasy and readily broken—

—as by the sound of someone in the room.

Before the intruder crossed even half the distance between the window and her bed, she was wide awake, and moving. She threw herself out of bed, somersaulted across her bedroom, and wound up crouched beside the door, one hand on the lightswitch, the other holding a polished dagger she'd taken from beneath her pillow.

As the lights came on, she saw Andre standing in the center of the bedroom, blinking in surprise, wearing a sheepish grin.

Relief made her knees go weak. "Andre, you *idiot*!" She tried to control her tone, but her voice was shrill and cracked a little. "You could have been *killed*!"

He spread his hands wide in a placating gesture. "Now, Diana—"

" 'Now Diana' my eye!" she growled. "Even *you* would have a hard time getting around a severed spine!" She stood up slowly, shaking from head to toe with released tension.

"I didn't wish to wake you," he said, crestfallen.

She closed her eyes and took several long, deep, calming breaths; focusing on a mantra, moving herself back into stillness until she knew she would be able to reply without screaming at him.

"Don't," she said carefully. "Ever. Do. That. Again." She punctuated the last word by driving the dagger she held into the doorframe.

"*Certainement, mon petite*," he replied, his eyes widening a little as he began to calculate how fast she'd moved. "The next time I come in your window when you sleep, I shall blow a trumpet first."

"You'd be a *lot* safer. *I'd* be a lot happier," she said crossly, pulling the dagger loose with a snap of her wrist. She palmed the lightswitch and dimmed the lamps down to where they would be comfortable to his light-sensitive eyes, then crossed the room, the plush brown carpet warm and soft under her bare feet. She bent slightly, and put the silver-plated dagger back under her pillow. Then with a sigh she folded her long legs beneath her to sit on her rumpled bed. This was the first time Andre had ever caught her asleep, and she was irritated far beyond what her disturbed dreams warranted. She was somewhat obsessed with her privacy and with keeping her night boundaries unbreached—she and Andre were off-and-on lovers, but she'd never let him stay any length of time.

He approached the antique wooden bed slowly. "*Cherie*, this was no idle visit—"

"I should bloody well hope not!" she interrupted, trying to soothe her jangled nerves by combing the tangles out of her hair with her fingers.

"—I have seen your killer."

She froze.

"It is nothing I have ever seen or heard of before."

She clenched her hands on the strand of hair they held, ignoring the pull. "Go on—"

"It—no, *he*—I could not detect until he made his first kill tonight. I found him then, found him just before he took his hunting-shape, or I never would have discovered him at all; for when he is in that shape there is nothing about him that *I* could sense that marked him as different. So ordinary—a man, an Oriental; Japanese, I think, and like many others—not young, not old; not fat, not thin. So unremarkable as to be invisible. I followed him—he was so normal I found it difficult to believe what my own eyes had seen a moment before; then, not ten minutes later, he found yet another victim and—fed again."

He closed his eyes, his face thoughtful. "As I said, I have never seen or heard of his like, yet—yet there was something familiar about him. I cannot even tell you what it was, and yet it was familiar."

"You said you saw him attack—*how*, Andre?" she leaned forward, her face tight with urgency as the bed creaked a little beneath her.

"The second quarry was—the—is it 'bag lady' you say?" At her nod he continued. "He smiled at her—just smiled, that was all. She froze like the frightened rabbit. Then he—changed—into dark, dark smoke; only smoke, nothing more. The smoke enveloped the old woman until I could see her no longer. Then—he fed. I—I can understand your feelings now, *cherie*. It was—nothing to the eye, but—what I felt *within*—"

"Now you see," she said gravely.

"*Mais oui*, and you have no more argument from me. This thing is abomination, and must be ended."

"The question is—" She grimaced.

"How? I have given some thought to this. One cannot fight smoke. But in his hunting form—I think perhaps he is vulnerable to physical measures. As you say, even *I* would have difficulty in dealing with a severed spine or crushed brain. I think maybe it would be the same for him. Have you the courage to play the wounded bird, *mon petite*?" He sat beside her on the edge of the bed and regarded her with solemn and worried eyes.

She considered that for a moment. "Play bait while you wait for him to move in? It sounds like the best plan to me—it wouldn't be the first time I've done that, and I'm not exactly helpless, you know," she replied, twisting a strand of hair around her fingers.

"I think you have finally proved that to me tonight!" There was a hint of laughter in his eyes again, as well as chagrin. "I shall never again make the mistake of thinking you to be a fragile flower. *Bien*. Is tomorrow night too soon for you?"

"Tonight wouldn't be too soon," she stated flatly.

"Except that he has already gone to lair, having fed twice." He took one of her hands, freeing it from the lock of hair she had twisted about it. "No, we rest—I know where he is to be found, and tomorrow night we face him at full strength." Abruptly he grinned. "*Cherie*, I have read one of your books—"

She winced, and closed her eyes in a grimace. "Oh Lord—I was afraid you'd ferret out one of my pseudonyms. You're as bad as the Elephant's Child when it comes to 'satiable curiosity'."

"It was hardly difficult to guess the author when she used one of my favorite expressions for the title—and then described me so very intimately not three pages from the beginning."

Her expression was woeful. "Oh *no*! Not *that* one!"

He shook an admonishing finger at her. "I do not think it kind, to make me the villain, and all because I told you I spent a good deal of the Regency in London."

"But—but—Andre, these things follow *formulas*, I didn't really have a choice—anybody French in a Regency romance *has* to be either an expatriate aristocrat or a villain—" She bit her lip and looked pleadingly at him. "—I needed a villain and I didn't have a clue—I was in the middle of that phony medium thing *and* I had a deadline—and—" Her words thinned down to a whisper, "—to tell you the truth, I didn't think you'd ever find out. You—you aren't angry, are you?"

He lifted the hair away from her shoulder, cupped his hand beneath her chin and moved close beside her. "I *think* I may possibly be induced to forgive you—"

The near-chuckle in his voice told her she hadn't offended him. Reassured by that, she looked up at him, slyly. "Oh?"

"You could—" He slid her gown off her shoulder a little, and ran an inquisitive finger from the tip of her shoulderblade to just behind her ear "—write another, and let me play the hero—"

"Have you any—suggestions?" she replied, finding it difficult to reply when his mouth followed where his finger had been.

"In that 'Burning Passions' series, perhaps?"

She pushed him away, laughing. "The soft-core porn for housewives? Andre, you can't be serious!"

"Never more." He pulled her back. "Think of how much enjoyable the research would be—"

She grabbed his hand again before it could resume its explorations. "Aren't we supposed to be resting?"

He stopped for a moment, and his face and eyes were deadly serious. "*Cherie*, we must face this thing at strength. You need sleep—and to relax. Can you think of any better way to relax body and spirit than—"

"No," she admitted. "I always sleep like a rock when you get done with me."

"Well then. And I—I have needs; I have not tended to those needs for too long, if I am to have full strength, and I should not care to meet this creature at less than that."

"Excuses, excuses—" She briefly contemplated getting up long enough to take care of the lights—then decided a little waste of energy was worth it, and extinguished them with a thought. "C'mere, you— let's do some research."

He laughed deep in his throat as they reached for one another with the same eager hunger.

She woke late the next morning—so late that in a half-hour it would have been "afternoon"—and lay quietly for a long, contented moment before wriggling out of the tumble of bedclothes and Andre. No fear of waking him—he wouldn't rouse until the sun went down. She arranged him a bit more comfortably and tucked him in, thinking that he looked absurdly young with his hair all rumpled and those long, dark lashes of his lying against his cheek—he looked much better this morning, now that she was in a position to pay attention. Last night he'd been pretty pale and hungry-thin. She shook her head over him. Someday his gallantry was going to get him into trouble. "Idiot—" she whispered, touching his forehead, "—all you ever have to do is *ask*—"

But there were other things to take care of—and to think of. A fight to get ready for; and she had a premonition it wasn't going to be an easy one.

So she showered and changed into a leotard, and took herself into her barren studio at the back of the apartment to run through her *katas* three times—once slow, twice at full speed—and then into some *Tai Chi* exercises to rebalance everything. She followed that with a half-hour of meditation, then cast a circle and charged herself with all of the Power she thought she could safely carry.

Without knowing what it was she was to face, that was all she could do, really—that, and have a really good dinner—

She showered and changed again into a bright red sweatsuit and was just finishing that dinner when the sun set and Andre strolled into the white-painted kitchen, shirtless, and blinking sleepily.

She gulped the last bite of her liver and waggled her fingers at him. "If you want a shower, you'd better get a fast one—I want to get in place before he comes out for the night."

He sighed happily over the prospect of a hot shower. "The perfect way to start one's—day. *Petite,* you may have difficulty in dislodging me now that you have let me stay overnight—"

She showed her teeth. "Don't count your chickens, kiddo. I can be very nasty!"

"*Mon petite—I—*" He suddenly sobered, and looked at her with haunted eyes.

She saw his expression and abruptly stopped teasing. "Andre— please don't say it—I can't give you any better an answer now than I could when you first asked—if I—cared for you as more than a friend."

He sighed again, less happily. "Then I will say no more, because you wish it—but—what of this notion—would you permit me to stay with you? No more than that. I could be of some use to you, I think, and I would take nothing from you that you did not offer first. I do not like it that you are so much alone. It did not matter when we first met, but you are collecting powerful enemies, *cherie.*"

"I—" She wouldn't look at him, but only at her hands, clenched white-knuckled on the table.

"Unless there are others—" he prompted, hesitantly.

"No—no, there isn't anyone but you." She sat in silence for a moment, then glanced back up at him with one eyebrow lifted sardonically. "You *do* rather spoil a girl for anyone else's attentions."

He was genuinely startled. "*Mille pardons, cherie,*" he stuttered, "I—I did not know—"

She managed a feeble chuckle. "Oh Andre, you idiot—I *like* being spoiled! I don't get many things that are just for me—" she sighed, then gave in to his pleading eyes. "All right then, move in if you want—"

"It is what *you* want that concerns me."

"I want," she said, very softly. "Just—the commitment—don't ask for it. I've got responsibilities as well as Power, you know that; I— can't see how to balance them with what you offered before—"

"Enough," he silenced her with a wave of his hand. "The words are unsaid, we will speak of this no more unless you wish it. I seek the embrace of warm water—"

She turned her mind to the dangers ahead, resolutely pushing the dangers *he* represented into the back of her mind. "And I will go bail the car out of the garage."

He waited until he was belted in on the passenger's side of the car to comment on her outfit. "I did not know you planned to race him, Diana," he said with a quirk of one corner of his mouth.

"Urban camouflage," she replied, dodging two taxis and a kamikaze panel truck. "Joggers are everywhere, and they run at night a lot in deserted neighborhoods. Cops won't wonder about me or try to stop me, and our boy won't be surprised to see me alone. One of his other victims was out running. His boyfriend thought he'd had a heart attack. Poor thing. He wasn't one of us, so I didn't enlighten him. There are some things it's better the survivors don't know."

"*Oui.* Left here, *cherie.*"

The traffic thinned down to a trickle, then to nothing. There are odd little islands in New York at night; places as deserted as the loneliest country road. The area where Andre directed her was one such; by day it was small warehouses, one floor factories, an odd store or two. None of them had enough business to warrant running second or third shifts, and the neighborhood had not been gentrified yet, so no one actually lived here. There were a handful of night watchmen, perhaps, but most of these places depended on locks, burglar alarms, and dogs that were released at night to keep out intruders.

"There—" Andre pointed at a building that appeared to be home to several small manufactories. "He took the smoke-form and went to roost in the elevator control house at the top. That is why I did not advise going against him by day."

"Is he there now?" Diana peered up through the glare of sodium-vapor lights, but couldn't make out the top of the building.

Andre closed his eyes, a frown of concentration creasing his forehead. "No," he said after a moment. "I think he has gone hunting."

She repressed a shiver. "Then it's time to play bait."

Diana found a parking space marked dimly with the legend "President"—she thought it unlikely it would be wanted within the next few hours. It was deep in the shadow of the building Andre had pointed out, and her car was dead-black; with any luck, cops coming by wouldn't even notice it was there and start to wonder.

She hopped out, locking her door behind her, looking now exactly like the lone jogger she was pretending to be, and set off at an easy pace. She did not look back.

If absolutely necessary, she knew she'd be able to keep this up for hours. She decided to take all the north-south streets first, then weave back along the east-west. Before the first hour was up she was wishing she'd dared bring a "walk-thing"—every street was like every other street; blank brick walls broken by dusty, barred windows and metal doors, alleys with only the occasional dumpster visible, refuse blowing along the gutters. She was bored; her nervousness had worn off, and she was lonely. She ran from light to darkness, from darkness to light, and saw and heard nothing but the occasional rat.

Then he struck, just when she was beginning to get a little careless. Careless enough not to see him arrive.

One moment there was nothing, the next, he was before her, waiting halfway down the block. She knew it was him—he was exactly as Andre had described him, a nondescript Oriental man in a dark windbreaker and slacks. He was tall for an Oriental—taller than she by several inches. His appearance nearly startled her into stopping—then she remembered that she was supposed to be an innocent jogger, and resumed her steady trot.

She knew he meant her to see him, he was standing directly beneath the streetlight and right in the middle of the sidewalk. She would have to swerve out of her path to avoid him.

She started to do just that, ignoring him as any real jogger would have—when he raised his head and smiled at her.

She was stopped dead in her tracks by the purest terror she had ever felt in her life. She froze, as all of his other victims must have—unable to think, unable to cry out, unable to run. Her legs had gone numb, and nothing existed for her but that terrible smile and those hard, black eyes that had no bottom—

Then the smile vanished, and the eyes flinched away. Diana could move again, and staggered back against the brick wall of the building behind her, her breath coming in harsh pants, the brick rough and comforting in its reality beneath her hands.

"Diana?" It was Andre's voice behind her.

"I'm—all right—" she said, not at all sure that she really was.

Andre strode silently past her, face grim and purposeful. The man seemed to sense his purpose, and smiled again—

But Andre never faltered for even the barest moment.

The smile wavered and faded; the man fell back a step or two, surprised that his weapon had failed him—

Then he scowled, and pulled something out of the sleeve of his windbreaker; and to Diana's surprise, charged straight for Andre, his sneakered feet scuffing on the cement—

And something suddenly blurring about his right hand. As it connected with Andre's upraised left arm, Diana realized what it was—almost too late.

"Andre—he has nunchucks—they're *wood*," she cried out urgently as Andre grunted in unexpected pain. "He can *kill* you with them! Get the *hell* out of here!"

Andre needed no second warning. In the blink of an eye, he was gone.

Leaving Diana to face the creature alone.

She dropped into guard-stance as he regarded her thoughtfully, still making no sound, not even of heavy breathing. In a moment he seemed to make up his mind, and came for her.

At least he didn't smile again in that terrible way—perhaps the weapon was only effective once.

She hoped fervently he wouldn't try again—as an empath, she was doubly vulnerable to a weapon forged of fear.

They circled each other warily, like two cats preparing to fight—then Diana thought she saw an opening—and took it.

And quickly came to the conclusion that she was overmatched, as he sent her tumbling with a badly bruised shin. The next few moments reinforced that conclusion—as he continued scatheless while she picked up injury after painful injury.

She was a brown belt in karate—but he was a black belt in kung fu, and the contest was a pathetically uneven match. She knew before very long that he was toying with her—and while he still swung the wooden nunchucks, Andre did not dare move in close enough to help.

She realized, (as fear dried her mouth, she grew more and more winded, and she searched frantically for a means of escape) that she was as good as dead.

If only she could get those damn 'chucks away from him!

And as she ducked and stumbled against the curb, narrowly avoiding the strike he made at her, an idea came to her. He knew from her moves—as she knew from his—that she was no amateur. He would never expect an amateur's move from her—something truly stupid and suicidal—

So the next time he swung at her, she stood her ground. As the 'chuck came at her she took one step forward, smashing his nose with the heel of her right hand and lifting her left to intercept the flying baton.

As it connected with her left hand with a sickening crunch, she whirled and folded her entire body around hand and weapon, and went limp, carrying it away from him.

She collapsed in a heap at his feet, hand afire with pain, eyes blurring with it, and waited for either death or salvation.

And salvation in the form of Andre rose behind her attacker. With one *savate* kick he broke the man's back; Diana could hear it cracking like green wood—and before her assailant could collapse, a second double-handed blow sent him crashing into the brick wall, head crushed like an eggshell.

Diana struggled to her feet, and waited for some arcane transformation.

Nothing.

She staggered to the corpse, face flat and expressionless—a sign she was suppressing pain and shock with utterly implacable iron will. Andre began to move forward as if to stop her, then backed off again at the look in her eyes.

She bent slightly, just enough to touch the shoulder of the body with her good hand—and released the Power.

Andre pulled her back to safety as the corpse exploded into flame, burning as if it had been soaked in oil. She watched the flames for one moment, wooden-faced; then abruptly collapsed.

Andre caught her easily before she could hurt herself further, lifting her in his arms as if she weighed no more than a kitten. "*Mon pauvre petite*," he murmured, heading back towards the car at a swift but silent run. "It is the hospital for you, I think—"

"Saint—Francis—" she gasped, every step jarring her hand and bringing tears of pain to her eyes, "One of us—is on the night staff—Dr. Crane—"

"*Bien*," he replied. "Now be silent—"

"But—how are you—"

"In your car, foolish one. I have the keys you left in it."

"But—"

"I can drive."

"But—"

"*And* I have a license. Will you be silent?"

"How?" she said, disobeying him.

"Night school," he replied succinctly, reaching the car, putting her briefly on her feet to unlock the passenger-side door, then lifting her into it. "You are not the only one who knows of urban camouflage."

This time she did not reply—mostly because she had fainted from pain.

The emergency room was empty—for which Andre was very grateful. His invocation of Dr. Crane brought a thin, bearded young man around to the tiny examining cubicle in record time.

"Good God Almighty! What did you tangle with, a bus?" he exclaimed, when stripping the sweatsuit jacket and pants revealed that there was little of Diana that was not battered and black-and-blue.

Andre wrinkled his nose at the acrid antiseptic odors around them, and replied shortly. "No. Your 'Ripper.'"

The startled gaze the doctor fastened on him revealed that Andre had scored. "Who—won?" he asked at last.

"We did. I do not think he will prey upon anyone again."

The doctor's eyes closed briefly; Andre read prayerful thankfulness on his face as he sighed with relief. Then he returned to business. "You must be Andre, right? Anything I can supply?"

Andre laughed at the hesitation in his voice. "Fear not, your blood supply is quite safe, and I am unharmed. It is Diana who needs you."

The relief on the doctor's face made Andre laugh again.

Dr. Crane ignored him. "Right," he said, turning to the work *he* knew best.


She was lightheaded and groggy with the Demerol Dr. Crane had given her as Andre deftly stripped her and tucked her into her bed; she'd dozed all the way home in the car.

"I just wish I knew *what* that thing was—" she said inconsequentially, as he arranged her arm in its light Fiberglas cast a little more comfortably. "—I won't be happy until I *know*—"

"Then you are about to be happy, *cherie*, for I have had the brainstorm—" Andre ducked into the living room and emerged with a dusty leather-bound book. "Remember I said there was something familiar about it? Now I think I know what it was." He consulted the index, and turned pages rapidly—found the place he sought, and read for a few moments. "As I thought—listen. 'The *gaki*—also known as the Japanese vampire—also takes its nourishment only from the living. There are many kinds of *gaki*, extracting their sustenance from a wide variety of sources. The most harmless are the *perfume* and *music gaki*—and they are by far the most common. Far deadlier are those that require blood, flesh—or souls.'"

"Souls?"

"Just so. 'To feed, or when at rest, they take their normal form of a dense cloud of dark smoke. At other times, like the *kitsune*, they take on the form of a human being. Unlike the *kitsune*, however, there is no way to distinguish them in this form from any other human. In the smoke form, they are invulnerable—in the human form, however, they can be killed; but to permanently destroy them, the body must be burned—preferably in conjunction with or solely by Power.' I said there was something familiar about it—it seems to have been a kind of distant cousin." Andre's mouth smiled, but his eyes reflected only a long-abiding bitterness.

"There is *no way* you have any relationship with that—thing!" she said forcefully. "It had no more honor, heart or soul than a rabid beast!"

"I—I thank you, *cherie*," he said, slowly, the warmth returning to his eyes. "There are not many who would think as you do."

"Their own closed-minded stupidity."

"To change the subject—what was it that made you burn it as you did? I would have abandoned it. It seemed dead enough."

"I don't know—it just seemed the thing to do," she yawned. "Sometimes my instincts just work . . . right . . . ."

Suddenly her eyes seemed too leaden to keep open.

"Like they did with you . . . ." She fought against exhaustion and the drug, trying to keep both at bay.

But without success. Sleep claimed her for its own.

He watched her for the rest of the night, until the leaden lethargy of his own limbs told him dawn was near. He had already decided not to share her bed, lest any movement on his part cause her pain—instead, he made up a pallet on the floor beside her.

He stood over her broodingly while he in his turn fought slumber, and touched her face gently. "Well—" he whispered, holding off torpor far deeper and heavier than hers could ever be—while she was mortal. "You are not aware to hear, so I may say what I will and you cannot forbid. Dream; sleep and dream—I shall see you safe—my only love."

And he took his place beside her, to lie motionless until night should come again.

*This was originally for a Susan Shwartz anthology,* Sisters of Fantasy 2.

# Wet Wings

## Mercedes Lackey

Katherine watched avidly, chin cradled in her old, arthritic hands, as the chrysalis heaved, and writhed, and finally split up the back. The crinkled, sodden wings of the butterfly emerged first, followed by the bloated body. She breathed a sigh of wonder, as she always did, and the butterfly tried to flap its useless wings in alarm as it caught her movement.

"Silly thing," she chided it affectionately. "You know you can't fly with wet wings!" Then she exerted a little of her magic; just a little, brushing the butterfly with a spark of calm that jumped from her trembling index finger to its quivering antenna.

The butterfly, soothed, went back to its real job, pumping the fluid from its body into the veins of its wings, unfurling them into their full glory. It was not a particularly rare butterfly, certainly not an endangered one; nothing but a common Buckeye, a butterfly so ordinary that no one even commented on seeing them when she was a child. But Katherine had always found the markings exquisite, and she had used this species and the Sulfurs more often than any other to carry her magic.

*Magic.* That was a word hard to find written anymore. No one approved of magic these days. Strange that in a country that gave the Church of Gaia equal rights with the Catholic Church, no one believed in magic.

But magic was not "correct." It was not given equally to all, nor could it be given equally to all. And that which could not be made equal, must be destroyed . . . .

"We always knew that there would be repression and a burning time again," she told the butterfly, as its wings unfolded a little more. "But we never thought that the ones behind the repression would come from our own ranks."

Perhaps she should have realized it would happen. So many people had come to her over the years, drawn by the magic in her books, demanding to be taught. Some had the talent and the will; most had only delusions. How they had cursed her when she told them the truth! They had wanted to be like the heroes and heroines of her stories; *special, powerful.*

She remembered them all; the boy she had told, regretfully, that his "telepathy" was only observation and the ability to read body-language. The girl whose "psychic attacks" had been caused by potassium imbalances. The would-be "bardic mage" who had nothing other than a facility to delude himself. And the many who could not tell a tale, because they would not let themselves see the tales all around them. They were neither powerful nor special, at least not in terms either of the power of magic, nor the magic of storytelling. More often than not, they would go to someone else, demanding to be taught, unwilling to hear the truth.

Eventually, they found someone; in one of the many movements that sprouted on the fringes like parasitic mushrooms. She, like the other mages of her time, had simply shaken her head and sighed for them. But what she had not reckoned on, nor had anyone else, was that these movements had gained strength and a life of their own— and had gone political.

Somehow, although the process had been so gradual she had never noticed when it had become unstoppable, those who cherished their delusions began to legislate some of those delusions. "Politically correct" they called it—and *some* of the things they had done she had welcomed, seeing them as the harbingers of more freedom, not less.

But they had gone from the reasonable to the unreasoning; from demanding and getting a removal of sexism to a denial of sexuality and the differences that should have been celebrated. From legislating the humane treatment of animals to making the possession of any animal or animal product without licenses and yearly inspections a crime. Fewer people bothered with owning a pet these days—no, not a pet, an "Animal Companion," and one did not "own" it, one "nurtured" it. Not when inspectors had the right to come into your home, day or night, to make certain that you were giving your Animal Companion all the rights to which it was entitled. And the rarer the animal, the more onerous the conditions . . . .

"That wouldn't suit you, would it, Horace?" she asked the young crow perched over the window. Horace was completely illegal; there was no way she could have gotten a license for him. She lived in an apartment, not on a farm; she could never give him the four-acre "hunting preserve" he required. Never mind that he had come to her, lured by her magic, and that he was free to come and go through her window, hunting and exercising at will. He also came and went with her little spell packets, providing her with eyes on the world where she could not go, and bringing back the cocoons and chrysalises that she used for her butterfly-magics.

She shook her head, and sighed. They had sucked all the juice of life out of the world, that was what they had done. Outside, the gray overcast day mirrored the gray sameness of the world they had created. There were no bright colors anymore to draw the eye, only pastels. No passion, no fire, nothing to arouse any kind of emotions. They had decreed that everyone *must* be equal, and no one must be offended, ever. And they had begun the burning and the banning . . . .

She had become alarmed when the burning and banning started; she knew that her own world was doomed when it reached things like "Hansel and Gretel"—banned, not because there was a witch in it, but because the witch was evil, and that might offend witches. She had known that her own work was doomed when a book that had been lauded for its portrayal of a young gay hero was banned because the young gay hero was unhappy and suicidal. She had not even bothered to argue. She simply announced her retirement, and went into seclusion, pouring all her energies into the magic of her butterflies.

From the first moment of spring to the last of autumn, Horace brought her caterpillars and cocoons. When the young butterflies emerged, she gave them each a special burden and sent them out into the world again.

*Wonder. Imagination. Joy. Diversity.* Some she sent out to wake the gifts of magic in others. Some she sent to wake simple stubborn will.

*Discontent. Rebellion.* She sowed her seeds, here in this tiny apartment, of what she hoped would be the next revolution. She would not be here to see it—but the day would come, she hoped, when those who *were* different and special would no longer be willing or content with sameness and equality at the expense of diversity.

Her door buzzer sounded, jarring her out of her reverie.

She got up, stiffly, and went to the intercom. But the face there was that of her old friend Piet, the "Environmental Engineer" of the apartment building, and he wore an expression of despair.

"Kathy, the Psi-cops are coming for you," he said, quickly, casting a look over his shoulder to see if there was anyone listening. "They made me let them in—"

The screen darkened abruptly.

*Oh, gods*—She had been so careful! But—in a way, she had expected it. She had been a world-renowned fantasy writer; she had made no secret of her knowledge of real-world magics. The Psi-cops had not made any spectacular arrests lately. Possibly they were running out of victims; she should have known they would start looking at peoples' pasts.

She glanced around at the apartment reflexively—

No. There was no hope. There were too many things she had that were contraband. The shelves full of books, the feathers and bones she used in her magics, the freezer full of meat that she shared with Horace and his predecessors, the wool blankets—

For that matter, they could arrest her on the basis of her jewelry alone, the fetish necklaces she carved and made, the medicine wheels and shields, and the prayer feathers. She was not Native American; she had no right to make these things even for private use.

And she knew what would happen to her. The Psi-cops would take her away, confiscate all her property, and "re-educate" her. *Drugged, brainwashed, wired and probed.* There would be nothing left of her when they finished. They had "re-educated" Jim three years ago, and when he came out, everything, even his magic and his ability to tell a story, was gone. He had not even had the opportunity to gift it to someone else; they had simply crushed it. He had committed suicide less than a week after his release.

She had a few more minutes at most, before they zapped the lock on her door and broke in. She had to save something, anything!

Then her eyes lighted on the butterfly, his wings fully unfurled and waving gently, and she knew what she would do.

First, she freed Horace. He flew off, squawking indignantly at being sent out into the overcast sky. But there was no other choice; if they found him, they would probably cage him up and send him to a forest preserve somewhere. He did not know how to find food in a wilderness—let him at least stay here in the city, where he knew how to steal food from birdfeeders, and where the best dumpsters were.

Then she cupped her hands around the butterfly, and gathered all of her magic. *All* of it this time; a great burden for one tiny insect, but there was no choice.

*Songs and tales, magic and wonder; power, vision, will, strength—* She breathed them into the butterfly's wings, and he trembled as the magic swirled around him, in a vortex of sparkling mist.

*Pride. Poetry. Determination. Love. Hope—*

She heard them at the door, banging on it, ordering her to open in the name of the Equal State. She ignored them. There was at least a minute or so left.

*The gift of words. The gift of difference—*

Finally she took her hands away, spent and exhausted, and feeling as empty as an old paper sack. The butterfly waved his wings, and though she could no longer see it, she knew that a drift of sparkling power followed the movements.

There was a whine behind her as the Psi-cops zapped the lock.

She opened the window, coaxed the butterfly onto her hand, and put him outside. An errant ray of sunshine broke through the overcast, gilding him with a glory that mirrored the magic he carried.

"Go," she breathed. "Find someone worthy."

He spread his wings, tested the breeze, and lifted off her hand, to be carried away.

And she turned, full of dignity and empty of all else, to face her enemies.

*Here is the first Valdemar short story I ever did, largely because I hate to waste a good story idea on something as small as a short story! This first appeared in the anthology,* Horse Fantastic.

# Stolen Silver

## Mercedes Lackey

Silver stamped restively as another horse on the picket-line shifted and blundered into his hindquarters. Alberich clucked to quiet him and patted the stallion's neck; the beast swung his head about to blow softly into the young Captain's hair. Alberich smiled a little, thinking wistfully that the stallion was perhaps the only creature in the entire camp that felt anything like friendship for him.

*And possibly the only creature that isn't waiting for me to fail.*

Amazingly gentle, for a stallion, Silver had caused no problems either in combat or here, on the picket-line. Which was just as well, for if he had, Alberich would have had him gelded or traded off for a more tractable mount, gift of the Voice of Vkandis Sunlord or no. Alberich had enough troubles without worrying about the behavior of his beast.

He wasn't sure where the graceful creature had come from; *Shin'a'in-bred,* they'd told him. Chosen for him out of a string of animals "liberated from the enemy." Which meant war booty, from one of the constant conflicts along the borders. Silver hadn't come from one of the bandit nests, that was sure—the only beasts the bandits owned were as disreputable as their owners. Horses "liberated" from the bandits usually weren't worth keeping. Silver probably came from Menmellith via Rethwellan; the King was rumored to have some kind of connection with the horse-breeding, blood-thirsty Shin'a'in nomads.

Whatever; when Alberich lost his faithful old Smoke a few weeks ago he hadn't expected to get anything better than the obstinate, intractable gelding he'd taken from its bandit-owner.

But fate ruled otherwise; the Voice chose to "honor" him with a superior replacement along with his commission, the letter that accompanied the paper pointing out that Silver was the perfect mount for a Captain of light cavalry. It was also more evidence of favoritism from above, with the implication that he had earned that favoritism outside of performance in the field. Not a gift that was likely to increase his popularity with some of the men under his command, and a beast that was going to make him pretty damned conspicuous in any encounter with the enemy.

*Plus one that's an unlucky color. Those witchy-Heralds of Valdemar ride white horses, and the blue-eyed beasts may be witches too, for all I know.*

The horse nuzzled him again, showing as sweet a temper as any lady's mare. He scratched its nose, and it sighed with content; he wished *he* could be as contented. Things had been bad enough before getting this commission. Now—

There was an uneasy, prickly sensation between his shoulder-blades as he went back to brushing his new mount down. He glanced over his shoulder, to intercept the glare of Leftenant Herdahl; the man dropped his gaze and brushed his horse's flank vigorously, but not quickly enough to prevent Alberich from seeing the hate and anger in the hot blue eyes.

The Voice had done Alberich no favors in rewarding him with the Captaincy and this prize mount, passing over Herdahl and Klaus, both his seniors in years of service, if not in experience. Neither of them had expected that *he* would be promoted over their heads; during the week's wait for word to come from Headquarters, they had saved their rivalry for each other.

*Too bad they didn't murder each other,* he thought resentfully, then suppressed the rest of the thought. It was said that some of the priests of Vkandis could pluck the thoughts from a man's head. It could have been thoughts like that one that had led to Herdahl's being passed over for promotion. But it could also be that this was a test, a way of flinging the ambitious young Leftenant Alberich into deep water, to see if he would survive the experience. If he did, well and good; he was of suitable material to continue to advance, perhaps even to the rank of Commander. If he did not—well, that was too bad. If his ambition undid him, then he wasn't fit enough for the post.

That was the way of things, in the armies of Karse. You rose by watching your back, and (if the occasion arose) sticking careful knives into the backs of your less-cautious fellows, and insuring other enemies took the punishment. All the while, the priests of the Sunlord, who were the ones who were truly in charge, watched and smiled and dispensed favors and punishments with the same dispassionate aloofness displayed by the One God.

But Alberich had given a good account of himself along the border, at the corner where Karse met Menmellith and the witch-nation Valdemar, in the campaign against the bandits there. He'd *earned* his rank, he told himself once again, as Silver stamped and shifted his weight beneath the strokes of Alberich's brush. The spring sun burned down on his head, hotter than he expected without the breeze to cool him.

There was no reason to feel as if he'd cheated to get where he was. He'd led more successful sorties against the bandits in his first year in the field than the other two had achieved in their entire careers together. He'd cleared more territory than anyone of Leftenant rank ever had in that space of time—and when Captain Anberg had met with one too many arrows, the men had seemed willing that the Voice chose him over the other two candidates.

It had been the policy of late to permit the brigands to flourish, provided they confined their attentions to Valdemar and the Menmellith peasantry and left the inhabitants of Karse unmolested. A stupid policy, in Alberich's opinion; you couldn't trust bandits, that was the whole reason why they became bandits in the first place. If they could be trusted, they'd be in the army themselves, or in the Temple Guard, or even have turned mercenary. He'd seen the danger back when he was a youngster in the Academy, in his first tactics classes. He'd even said as much to one of his teachers—phrased as a question, of course—and had been ignored.

But as Alberich had predicted, there had been trouble from the brigands, once they began to multiply; problems that escalated past the point where they were useful. With complete disregard for the unwritten agreements between them and Karse, they struck everyone, and when they finally began attacking villages, the authorities deemed it time they were disposed of.

Alberich had just finished cavalry training as an officer when the troubles broke out; he'd spent most of his young life in the Karsite military schools. The ultimate authority was in the hands of the Voices, of course; the highest anyone not of the priesthood could expect to rise was to Commander. But officers were never taken from the ranks; many of the rank-and-file were conscripts, and although it was never openly stated, the Voices did not trust their continued loyalty if they were given power.

Alberich, and many others like him, had been selected at the age of thirteen by a Voice sent every year to search out young male children, strong of body and quick of mind, to school into officers.

Alberich had both those qualities, developing expertise in many weapons with an ease that was the envy of his classmates, picking up his lessons in academic subjects with what seemed to be equal ease.

It wasn't ease; it was the fact that Alberich studied long and hard, knowing that there was no way for the bastard son of a tavern whore to advance in Karse except in the army. There was no place for him to go, no way to get into a trade, no hope for any but the most menial of jobs. The Voices didn't care about a man's parentage once he was chosen as an officer, they cared only about his abilities and whether or not he would use them in service to his God and country. It was a lonely life, though—his mother had loved and cared for him to the best of her abilities, and he'd had friends among the other children of similar circumstances. When he came to the Academy, he had no friends, and his mother was not permitted to contact him, lest she "distract him," or "contaminate his purity of purpose." Alberich had never seen her again, but both of them had known this was the only way for him to live a better life than she had.

Alberich had no illusions about the purity of the One God's priesthood. There were as many corrupt and venal priests as there were upright, and more fanatic than there were forgiving. He had seen plenty of the venal kind in the tavern; had hidden from one or two that had come seeking pleasures strictly forbidden by the One God's edicts. He had known they were coming, looking for him, and had managed to make himself scarce long before they arrived. Just as, somehow, he had known when the Voice was coming to look for young male children for the Academy, and had made certain he was noticed and questioned—

And that he had known which customers it was safe to cadge for a penny in return for running errands—

Or that he had known that drunk was going to try to set the stable afire.

Somehow. That was Alberich's secret. He knew things were going to happen. That was a witch-power, and forbidden by the Voices of the One God. If anyone knew he had it—

But he had also known, as surely as he had known all the rest, that he had to conceal the fact that he had this power, even before he knew the law against it.

He'd succeeded fairly well over the years, though it was getting harder and harder all the time. The power struggled inside him, wanting to break free, once or twice overwhelming him with visions so intense that for a moment he was blind and deaf to everything else. It was getting harder to concoct reasons for knowing things he had no business knowing, like the hiding places of the bandits they were chasing, the bolt-holes and escape routes. But it was harder still to ignore them, especially when subsequent visions showed him innocent people suffering because he didn't act on what he knew.

He brushed Silver's neck vigorously, the dust tickling his nose and making him want to sneeze—

—and between one brush-stroke and the next, he lost his sense of balance, went light-headed, and the dazzle that heralded a vision-to-come sparkled between his eyes and Silver's neck.

*Not here!* he thought desperately, clinging to Silver's mane and trying to pretend there was nothing wrong. *Not now, not with Herdahl watching*—

But the witch-power would not obey him, not this time.

A flash of blue light, blinding him. The bandits he'd thought were south had slipped behind him, into the north, joining with two more packs of the curs, becoming a group large enough to take on his troops and give them an even fight. But first, they wanted a secure base. They were going to make Alberich meet them on ground of their choosing. Fortified ground.

*That this ground was already occupied was only a minor inconvenience . . . one that would soon be dealt with.*

He fought free of the vision for a moment, clinging to Silver's shoulder like a drowning man, both hands full of the beast's silky mane, while the horse curved his head back and looked at him curiously. The big brown eyes flickered blue, briefly, like a half-hidden flash of lightning, reflecting—

—another burst of sapphire. The bandits' target was a fortified village, a small one, built on the top of a hill, above the farmfields. Ordinarily, these people would have no difficulty in holding off a score of bandits. But there were three times that number ranged against them, and a recent edict from the High Temple decreed that no one but the Temple Guard and the Army could possess anything but the simplest of weapons. Not three weeks ago, a detachment of priests and a Voice had come through here, divesting them of everything but knives, farm implements, and such simple bows and arrows as were suitable for waterfowl and small game. And while they were at it, a third of the able-bodied men had been conscripted for the regular Army.

*These people didn't have a chance.*

*The bandits drew closer, under the cover of a brush-filled ravine.*

Alberich found himself on Silver's back, without knowing how he'd gotten there, without remembering that he'd flung saddle and bridle back on the beast—

No, not bridle; Silver still wore the hackamore he'd had on the picket-line. Alberich's bugle was in his hand; presumably he'd blown the muster, for his men were running towards him, buckling on swords and slinging quivers over their shoulders.

Blinding flash of cerulean—

*The bandits attacked the village walls, overpowering the poor man who was trying to bar the gate against them, and swarming inside.*

It hadn't happened yet, he knew that with the surety with which he knew his own name. It wasn't even going to happen in the next few moments. But it was going to happen *soon*—

*They poured inside, cutting down anyone who resisted them, then throwing off what little restraint they had shown and launching into an orgy of looting and raping. Alberich gagged as one of them grabbed a pregnant woman and with a single slash of his sword, murdered the child that ran to try and protect her, followed through to her—*

The vision released him, and he found himself surrounded by dust and thunder, still on Silver's back—

—but leaning over the stallion's neck as now he led his troops up the road to the village of Sunsdale at full gallop. Hooves pounded the packed earth of the road, making it impossible to hear or speak; the vibration thrummed into his bones as he shifted his weight with the stallion's turns. Silver ran easily, with no sign of distress, though all around him and behind him the other horses streamed saliva from the corners of their mouths, and their flanks ran with sweat and foam, as they strained to keep up.

The lack of a bit didn't seem to make any difference to the stallion; he answered to neck rein and knee so readily he might have been anticipating Alberich's thoughts.

Alberich dismissed the uneasy feelings *that* prompted. Better not to think that he might have a second witch-power along with the first. He'd never shown any ability to control beasts by thought before. There was no reason to think he could now. The stallion was just superbly trained, that was all. And he had more important things to worry about.

They topped the crest of a hill; Sunsdale lay atop the next one, just as he had seen in his vision, and the brush-filled ravine beyond it.

There was no sign of trouble.

*This time it's been a wild hare,* he thought, disgusted at himself for allowing blind panic to overcome him. *And for what? A daytime nightmare? Next time I'll probably see trolls under my bed,* he thought, just about to pull Silver up and bring the rest of his men to a halt—

When a flash of sunlight on metal betrayed the bandits' location.

He grabbed for the bugle dangling from his left wrist instead, and pulled his blade with the right; sounded the charge, and led the entire troop down the hill, an unstoppable torrent of hooves and steel, hitting the brigands' hidden line like an avalanche.

Sword in hand, Alberich limped wearily to another body sprawled amid the rocks and trampled weeds of the ravine, and thrust it through to make death certain. His sword felt heavy and unwieldy, his stomach churned, and there was a sour taste in his mouth. He didn't think he was going to lose control of himself, but he was glad he was almost at the end of the battle-line. He hated this part of the fighting—which wasn't fighting at all; it was nothing more than butchery.

But it was necessary. This scum was just as likely to be feigning death as to actually be dead. Other officers hadn't been that thorough—and hadn't lived long enough to regret it.

Silver was being fed and watered along with the rest of the mounts by the youngsters of Sunsdale; the finest fodder and clearest spring water, and a round dozen young boys to brush and curry them clean. And the men were being fed and made much of by the older villagers. Gratitude had made them forgetful of the loss of their weapons and many of their men. Suddenly the army that had conscripted their relatives was no longer their adversary. Or else, since the troops had arrived out of nowhere like Vengeance of the Sunlord Himself, they assumed the One God had a hand in it, and it would be prudent to resign themselves to the sacrifice. And meanwhile, the instrument of their rescue probably ought to be well-treated . . . .

Except for the Captain, who was doing a dirty job he refused to assign to anyone else.

Alberich made certain of two more corpses and looked dully around for more.

There weren't any, and he saw to his surprise that the sun was hardly more than a finger-breadth from the horizon. Shadows already filled the ravine, the evening breeze had picked up, and it was getting chilly. Last year's weeds tossed in the freshening wind as he gazed around at the long shadows cast by the scrubby trees. More time had passed than he thought—and if he didn't hurry, he was going to be late for SunDescending.

He scrambled over the slippery rocks of the ravine, cursing under his breath as his boots (meant for riding) skidded on the smooth, rounded boulders. The last thing he needed now was to be late for a Holy Service, especially this one. The priest here was bound to ask him for a Thanks Prayer for the victory. If he was late, it would look as if he was arrogantly attributing the victory to his own abilities, and not the Hand of the Sunlord. And with an accusation like that hanging over his head, he'd be in danger not only of being deprived of his current rank, but of being demoted into the ranks, with no chance of promotion, a step up from stablehand, but not a big one.

He fought his way over the edge, and half-ran, half-limped to the village gates, reaching them just as the sun touched the horizon. He put a little more speed into his weary, aching legs, and got to the edge of the crowd in the village square a scant breath before the priest began the First Chant.

He bowed his head with the others, and not until he raised his head at the end of it did he realize that the robes the priest wore were not black, but red. This was no mere village priest—this was a Voice!

He suppressed his start of surprise, and the shiver of fear that followed it. He didn't know what this village meant, or what had happened to require posting a Voice here, but there was little wonder now why they had submitted so tamely to the taking of their men and the confiscation of their weapons. No one sane would contradict a Voice.

The Voice held up his hand, and got instant silence; a silence so profound that the sounds of the horses on the picket-line came clearly over the walls. Horses stamped and whickered a little, and in the distance, a few lonely birds called, and the breeze rustled through the new leaves of the trees in the ravine. Alberich longed suddenly to be able to mount Silver and ride away from here, far away from the machinations of Voices and the omnipresent smell of death and blood. He yearned for somewhere clean, somewhere that he wouldn't have to guard his back from those he should be able to trust . . . .

"Today this village was saved from certain destruction," the Voice said, his words ringing out, but without passion, without any inflection whatsoever. "And for that, we offer thanksgiving to Vkandis Sunlord, Most High, One God, to whom all things are known. The instrument of that salvation was Captain Alberich, who mustered his men in time to catch our attackers in the very act. It seems a miracle—"

During the speech, some of the men had been moving closer to Alberich, grouping themselves around him to bask in the admiration of the villagers.

Or so he thought. Until the Voice's tone hardened, and his next words proved their real intent.

"It *seems* a miracle—but it was not!" he thundered. "You were saved by the power of the One God, whose wrath destroyed the bandits, but Alberich betrayed the Sunlord by using the unholy powers of witchcraft! *Seize him!*"

The men grabbed him as he turned to run, throwing him to the ground and pinning him with superior numbers. He fought them anyway, struggling furiously, until someone brought the hilt of a knife down on the back of his head.

He didn't black out altogether, but he couldn't move or see; his eyes wouldn't focus, and a gray film obscured everything. He felt himself being dragged off by the arms—heaved into darkness—felt himself hitting a hard surface—heard the slamming of a door.

Then heard only confused murmurs as he lay in shadows, trying to regain his senses and his strength. Gradually his sight cleared, and he made out walls on all sides of him, close enough to touch. He raised his aching head cautiously, and made out the dim outline of an ill-fitting door. The floor, clearly, was dirt. And smelled unmistakably of birds.

They must have thrown him into some kind of shed, something that had once held chickens or pigeons. He was under no illusions that this meant his prison would be easy to escape; out here, the chicken sheds were frequently built better than the houses, for chickens were more valuable than children.

Still, once darkness descended, it might be possible to get away. If he could overpower whatever guards the Voice had placed around him. If he could find a way out of the shed . . .

If he could get past the Voice himself. There were stories that the Voices had other powers than plucking the thoughts from a man's head—stories that they commanded the services of demons tamed by the Sunlord—

While he lay there gathering his wits, another smell invaded the shed, overpowering even the stench of old bird droppings. A sharp, thick smell . . . it took a moment for him to recognize it.

But when he did, he clawed his way up the wall he'd been thrown against, to stand wide-eyed in the darkness, nails digging into the wood behind him, heart pounding with stark terror.

Oil. They had poured oil around the foundations, splashed it up against the sides of the shed. And now he heard them out there, bringing piles of dry brush and wood to stack against the walls. The punishment for witchery was burning, and they were taking no chances; they were going to burn him now.

The noises outside stopped; the murmur of voices faded as his captors moved away—

Then the Voice called out, once—a set of three sharp, angry words—

And every crack and crevice in the building was outlined in yellow and red, as the entire shed was engulfed in flames from outside.

Alberich cried out, and staggered away from the wall he'd been leaning against. The shed was bigger than he'd thought—but not big enough to protect him. The oil they'd spread so profligately made the flames burn hotter, and the wood of the shed was old, weathered, probably dry. Within moments, the very air scorched him; he hid his mouth in a fold of his shirt, but his lungs burned with every breath.

His eyes streamed tears of pain as he turned, staggering, searching for an escape that didn't exist.

One of the walls burned through, showing the flames leaping from the wood and brush piled beyond it. He couldn't hear anything but the roar of the flames. At any moment now, the roof would cave in, burying him in burning debris—

:*Look out!*:

How he heard the warning—or how he knew to stagger back as far as he could without being incinerated on the spot—he did not know. But a heartbeat after that warning shout in his mind, a huge, silver-white shadow lofted through the hole in the burning wall, and landed beside him. It was still wearing his saddle and hackamore—

And it turned huge, impossibly *blue* eyes on him as he stood there gaping at it. It? No. *Him.*

:*On!*: the stallion snapped at him. :*The roof's about to go!*:

Whatever fear he had of the beast, he was more afraid of a death by burning. With hands that screamed with pain, he grabbed the saddle-bow and threw himself onto it. He hadn't even found the stirrups when the stallion turned on his hind feet.

There was a crack of collapsing wood, as fire engulfed them. Burning thatch fell before and behind them, sparks showering as the air was sucked into the blaze, hotter . . .

But, amazingly, no fire licked at his flesh once he had mounted . . . .

Alberich sobbed with relief as the cool air surged into his lungs— the stallion's hooves hit the ground beyond the flames, and he gasped with pain as he was flung forward against the saddle-bow.

Then the real pain began, the torture of half-scorched skin, and the broken bones of his capture, jarred into agony by the stallion's head-long gallop into the night. The beast thundered towards the villagers, and they screamed and parted before it; soldiers and Voice alike were caught unawares, and not one of them raised a weapon in time to stop the flight.

:*Stay on,*: the stallion said grimly, into his mind, as the darkness was shattered by the red lightning of his own pain. :*Stay on, stay with me; we have a long way to go before we're safe. Stay with me . . . .*:

*Safe where?* he wanted to ask—but there was no way to ask around the pain. All he could do was to hang on, and hope he could do what the horse wanted.

An eternity later—as dawn rose as red as the flames that had nearly killed him—the stallion had slowed to a walk. Dawn was on their right, which meant that the stallion was heading north, across the border, into the witch-kingdom of Valdemar. Which only made sense, since what he'd thought was a horse had turned out to be one of the blue-eyed witch-beasts . . . .

None of it mattered. Now that the stallion had slowed to a walk, his pain had dulled, but he was exhausted and out of any energy to think or even feel. What could the witches do to him, after all? Kill him? At the moment, that would be a kindness . . . .

The stallion stopped, and he looked up, trying to see through the film that had come over his vision. At first he thought he was seeing double; two white witch-beasts and two white-clad riders blocked the road. But then he realized that there *were* two of them, hastily dismounting, reaching for him.

He let himself slide down into their hands, hearing nothing he could understand, only a babble of strange syllables.

Then, in his mind—

:*Can you hear me?*:

:*I—what?*: he replied, without thinking.

:*Taver says his name's Alberich,*: came a second voice in his head. :*Alberich? Can you stay with us a little longer? We need to get you to a Healer. You're going into shock; fight it for us. Your Companion will help you, if you let him.*:

His what? He shook his head; not in negation, in puzzlement. Where was he? All his life he'd heard that the witches of Valdemar were evil—but—

:*And all our lives we've heard that nothing comes out of Karse but brigands and bad weather,*: said the first voice, full of concern, but with an edge of humor to it. He shook his head again and peered up at the person supporting him on his right. A woman, with many laugh-lines etched around her generous mouth. She seemed to fit that first voice in his head, somehow . . . .

*:So, which are you, Alberich?:* she asked, as he fought to stay awake, feeling the presence of the stallion *(his Companion?)* like a steady shoulder to lean against, deep inside his soul. *:Brigand, or bad weather?:*

*:Neither . . . I hope . . .:* he replied, absently, as he clung to consciousness as she'd asked.

*:Good. I'd hate to think of a Companion Choosing a brigand to be a Herald,:* she said, with her mouth twitching a little, as if she was holding back a grin, *:And a thunderstorm in human guise would make uncomfortable company.:*

*:Choosing?:* he asked. *:What—what do you mean?:*

*:I mean that you're a Herald, my friend,:* she told him. *:Somehow your Companion managed to insinuate himself across the Border to get you, too. That's how Heralds of Valdemar are made; Companions Choose them—:* She looked up and away from him, and relief and satisfaction spread over her face at whatever it was she saw. *:—and the rest of it can wait. Aren's brought the Healer. Go ahead and let go, we'll take over from here.:*

He took her at her word, and let the darkness take him. But her last words followed him down into the shadows, and instead of bringing the fear they *should* have given him, they brought him comfort, and a peace he never expected.

*:It's a hell of a greeting, Herald Alberich, and a hell of a way to get here—but welcome to Valdemar, brother. Welcome . . . :*

*This odd little story was first published in* Marion Zimmer Bradley's Fantasy Magazine. *It's the one I always use as an example when people ask me where I get my ideas. This one literally came as I was driving to work, saw a piece of cardboard skitter across the road in front of me as if it was alive, and thought, "Now what if it was alive?"*

# Roadkill

## Mercedes Lackey

A gust of wind hit the side of George Randal's van and nearly tore the steering wheel out of his hands. He cursed as the vehicle lurched sideways, and wrestled it back into his own lane.

It was a good thing there weren't too many people on the road. It was just a damned good thing that Mingo Road *was* a four-lane at this point, or he'd have been in the ditch. A mile away, it wasn't, but all the shift traffic from the airline maintenance base, the Rockwell plant and the McDonald-Douglas plant where he worked would have put an intolerable strain on a two-lane road.

The stoplight at Mingo and 163rd turned yellow, and rather than push his luck and doing an "Okie caution, he obeyed it." ("Step on the gas, Fred, she's fixin' to turn red"). This was going to be another typical late spring Oklahoma day. Wind gusting up to 60 per, and rain off and on. Used to be, when he was a kid, it'd be dry as old bones by this late in the season, but not anymore. All the

403

flood-control projects and water-management dams had changed the micro-climate, and it was unlikely this part of Oklahoma would ever see another Dust Bowl.

Although with winds like this, he could certainly extrapolate what it had been like, back then during the thirties.

The habit of working a mental simulation was so ingrained it was close to a reflex; once the thought occurred, his mind took over, calculating windspeed, type of dust, carrying capacity of the air. He was so intent on the internal calculations that he hardly noticed when the light turned green, and only the impatient honk of the car behind him jolted him out of his reverie. He pulled the van out into the intersection, and the red sportscar behind roared around him, driver giving him the finger as he passed.

"You son of a—" he noted with satisfaction the MacDac parking permit in the corner of the rear window: the vanity plate was an easy one to remember, "HOTONE." He'd tell a little fib to the guard at the guard shack, and have the jerk cited for reckless driving in the parking lot. That would go on his work record, and serve him right, too.

If it hadn't been for the combination of the wind gust and the fool in the red IROC, he would never have noticed the strange behavior of that piece of cardboard in the median strip.

But because of the gust, he *knew* which direction the wind was coming from. When the IROC screamed right over the center line, heading straight toward a piece of flattened box, and the box skittered just barely out of the way as if the wind had picked it up and moved it in time, something went off in his brain.

As he came up even to where the box had been, he saw what the thing had been covering; roadkill, a dead 'possum. At that exact moment he knew what had been wrong with the scene a second before, when the box had moved. Because it had moved *against* the wind.

He cast a startled glance in his rear-view mirror just in time to see the box skitter back, with the wind this time, and stop just covering the dead animal.

That brought all the little calculations going on in his head to a screeching halt. George was an orderly man, a career engineer, whose one fervent belief was that everything could be explained in terms of physics if you had enough data.

Except that this little incident was completely outside his ordered universe.

He was so preoccupied with trying to think of an explanation for the box's anomalous behavior that he didn't remember to report the kid in the sportscar at the guard shack. He couldn't even get his mind on the new canard specs he'd been so excited about yesterday. Instead he sat at his desk, playing with the CAD/CAM computer, trying to find *some* way for that box to have done what it did.

And coming up dry. It should not, *could* not, have moved that way, and the odds against it moving back to exactly the same place where it had left were unbelievable.

He finally grabbed his gymbag, left his cubicle, and headed for the tiny lockerroom MacDac kept for those employees who had taken up running or jogging on their lunch breaks. Obviously he was not going to get anything done until he checked the site out, and he might just as well combine that with his lunchtime exercise. Today he'd run out on Mingo instead of around the base.

A couple of Air National Guard A-4s cruised by overhead, momentarily distracting him. He'd forgotten exactly where the roadkill had been, and before he was quite ready for it, he was practically on top of it. Suddenly he was no longer quite sure that he wanted to do this. It seemed silly, a fantasy born of too many late-night movies. But as long as he was out here . . .

The box was nowhere in sight. Feeling slightly foolish, he crossed to the median and took a good look at the body.

It was half-eaten, which wasn't particularly amazing. Any roadkill that was relatively fresh was bound to get chewed on.

Except that the last time he'd seen roadkill on the median, it had stayed there until it bloated, untouched. Animals didn't like the traffic; they wouldn't go after carrion in the middle of the road if they could help it.

And there was something wrong with the way the bite marks looked too. Old Boy Scout memories came back, tracking and identifying animals by signs . . . .

The flesh hadn't been bitten off so much as carved off—as if the carcass had been chewed by something with enormous buck teeth, like some kind of carnivorous horse, or beaver. Nothing in his limited experience made marks like that.

As a cold trickle ran down his spine, a rustle in the weeds at the side of the road made him jump. He looked up.

The box was there, in the weeds. He hadn't seen it, half-hidden there, until it had moved. It almost seemed as if the thing was watching him; the way it had a corner poked out of the weeds like a head . . . .

His reaction was stupid and irrational, and he didn't care. He bolted, ran all the way back to the guard shack with a chill in his stomach that all his running couldn't warm.

He didn't stop until he reached the guard shack and the safety of the fenced-in MacDac compound, the sanity and rational universe of steel and measurement where nothing existed that could not be simulated on a computer screen.

He slowed to a gentle jog as he passed the shack; he'd have liked to stop, because his heart was pounding so hard he couldn't hear anything, but if he did, the guards would ask him what was wrong . . . .

He waited until he was just out of sight, and then dropped to a walk. He remembered from somewhere, maybe one of his jogging tapes, that it was a bad idea just to stop, that his muscles would stiffen. Actually he had the feeling if he went to his knees on the verge like he wanted to, he'd never get up again.

He reached the sanctuary of his air-conditioned office and slumped down into his chair, still panting. He waited with his eyes closed for his heart to stop pounding, while the sweat cooled and dried in the gust of metallic-flavored air from the vent over his chair. He tried to summon up laughter at himself, a grown man, for finding a flattened piece of cardboard so frightening, but the laughter wouldn't come.

Instead other memories of those days as a Boy Scout returned, of the year he'd spent at camp where he'd learned those meager tracking skills. One of the counselors had a grandfather who was—or so the boy claimed—a full Cherokee medicine man. He'd persuaded the old man to make a visit to the camp. George had found himself impressed against his will, as had the rest of the Scouts; the old man still wore his hair in two long, iron-gray braids and a bone necklace under his plain work shirt. He had a dignity and self-possession that kept all of the rowdy adolescents in awe of him and silent when he spoke.

He'd condescended to tell stories at their campfire several times. Most of them were tales of what his life had been like as a boy on the reservation at the turn of the century—but once or twice he'd told them bits of odd Indian lore, not all of it Cherokee.

Like the shape-changers. George didn't remember what he'd called them, but he did recall what had started the story. One of the boys had seen *I Was A Teenage Werewolf* before he'd come to camp, and he was regaling all of them with a vivid description of Michael Landon's transformation into the monster. The old man had listened, and scoffed. That was no kind of shape-changer, he'd told them scornfully. Then he had launched into a new story.

George no longer recalled the words, but he remembered the gist of it. How the shape-changers would prey upon the Indians in a peculiar fashion, stealing what they wanted by deception. If one wanted meat, for instance, he would transform himself into a hunter's gamebag and wait for the Indian to stuff the "bag" full, then shift back and carry the game off while the hunter's back was turned. If one wanted a new buffalo robe, he would transform himself into a stretching frame—or if very ambitious, into a tipi, and make off with all of the inhabitant's worldly goods.

"Why didn't they just turn into horses and carry everything off?" he'd wanted to know. The old man had shaken his head. "Because they cannot take a living form," he'd said, "only a dead one. And you do not want to catch them, either. Better for you to pretend it never happened."

But he wouldn't say what would happen if someone *did* catch the thief at work. He only looked, for a brief instant, very frightened, as if he had not intended to say that much.

George felt suddenly sick. What if these things, these shape-changers, *weren't* just legend. What could they be living on now?

They wouldn't be able to sneak into someone's house and counterfeit a refrigerator.

But there was all that roadkill, enough dead animals along Mingo alone each year to keep someone going, if that someone wasn't too fastidious.

And what would be easier to mimic than an old, flattened box?

He wanted to laugh at himself, but the laughter wouldn't come. This was such a stupid fantasy, built out of nothing but a boy's imagination and a box that didn't behave the way it ought to.

Instead, he only felt sicker, and more frightened. Now he could recall the one thing the old man had said about the creatures and their fear of discovery.

"*They do not permit it*," he'd said, as his eyes widened in that strange flicker of fear. "*They do not permit it.*"

Finally he just couldn't sit there anymore. He picked up the phone and mumbled something to his manager about feeling sick, grabbed his car keys and headed for the parking lot. Several of the others on the engineering staff looked at him oddly as he passed their desks; the secretary even stopped him and asked him if he felt all right. He mumbled something at her that didn't change her look of concern, and assured her that he was going straight home.

He told himself that he was going to do just that. He even had his turn signal on for a right-hand turn, fully intending to take the on-ramp at Pine and take the freeway home.

But instead he found himself turning left, where the roadkill was still lying.

He saw it as he came up over the rise; and the box was lying on top of it once again.

Suddenly desperate to prove to himself that this entire fantasy he'd created around a dead 'possum and a piece of cardboard was nothing more than that, he jerked the wheel over and straddled the median, gunning the engine and heading straight for the dingy brown splotch of the flattened box.

There was no wind now; if the thing moved, it would have to do so under its own power.

He floored the accelerator, determined that the thing wasn't going to escape his tires.

It didn't move; he felt a sudden surge of joy—

Then the thing struck.

It leapt up at the last possible second, landing with a *splat,* splayed across his windshield. He had a brief, horrifying impression of some kind of face, flattened and distorted, red eyes and huge, beaverlike teeth as long as his hand—

Then it was gone, and the car was out of control, tires screaming, wheel wrenching under his hands.

He pumped his brakes—once, twice—then the pedal went flat to the floor.

And as the car heeled over on two wheels, beginning a high-speed roll that could have only one ending, that analytical part of his mind that was not screaming in terror was calculating just how easy it would be for a pair of huge, chisellike teeth to shear through a brake-line.

*Larry and I wrote this for the Keith Laumer* Bolo *anthology, but it stands pretty well alone. All you have to know is that Bolos are fairly unstoppable, self-aware, intelligent tanks.*

# Operation Desert Fox

## Mercedes Lackey and Larry Dixon

Siegfried O'Harrigan's name had sometimes caused confusion, although the Service tended to be color-blind. He was black, slight of build and descended from a woman whose African tribal name had been long since lost to her descendants.

He wore both Caucasian names—Siegfried and O'Harrigan—as badges of high honor, however, as had all of that lady's descendants. Many times, although it might have been politically correct to do so, Siegfried's ancestors had resisted changing their name to something more ethnic. Their name was a gift—and not a badge of servitude to anyone. One did not return a gift, especially not one steeped in the love of ancestors . . . .

Siegfried had heard the story many times as a child, and had never tired of it. The tale was the modern equivalent of a fairy-tale, it had been so very unlikely. *O'Harrigan* had been the name of an Irish-born engineer, fresh off the boat himself, who had seen Siegfried's many-times-great grandmother and her infant son being herded down the gangplank and straight to the Richmond Virginia slave market. She had been, perhaps, thirteen years old when the Arab slave traders had stolen her. That she had survived the journey at all was a miracle. And she was the very first thing that O'Harrigan set eyes on as he stepped onto the dock in this new land of freedom.

The irony had not been lost on him. Sick and frightened, the woman had locked eyes with Sean O'Harrigan for a single instant, but that instant had been enough.

They had shared neither language nor race, but perhaps Sean had seen in her eyes the antithesis of everything he had come to America to find. *His* people had suffered virtual slavery at the hands of the English landlords; he knew what slavery felt like. He was outraged, and felt that he had to do *something.* He could not save all the slaves offloaded this day—but he could help these two.

He had followed the traders to the market and bought the woman and her child "off the coffle," paying for them before they could be put up on the auction block, before they could even be warehoused. He fed them, cared for them until they were strong, and then put them on *another* boat, this time as passengers, before the woman could learn much more than his name. The rest the O'Harrigans learned later, from Sean's letters, long after.

The boat was headed back to Africa, to the newly founded nation of Liberia, whose very name meant "land of liberty," a place of hope for freed slaves." Life there would not be easy for them, but it would not be a life spent in chains, suffering at the whims of men who called themselves "Master."

Thereafter, the woman and her children wore the name of O'Harrigan proudly, in memory of the stranger's kindness—as many other citizens of the newly formed nation would wear the names of those who had freed them.

No, the O'Harrigans would not change their name for any turn of politics. Respect earned was infinitely more powerful than any messages beaten into someone by whips or media.

And as for the name "Siegfried"—that was also in memory of a stranger's kindness; this time a member of Rommel's Afrika Korps. Another random act of kindness, this time from a first lieutenant who had seen to it that a captured black man with the name O'Harrigan was correctly identified as Liberian and not as American. He had then seen to it that John O'Harrigan was treated well and released.

John had named his first-born son for that German, because the young lieutenant had no children of his own. The tradition and the story that went with it had continued down the generations, joining that of Sean O'Harrigan. Siegfried's people remembered their debts of honor.

Siegfried O'Harrigan's name was at violent odds with his appearance. He was neither blond and tall, nor short and red-haired—and in fact, he was not Caucasian at all.

In this much, he matched the colonists of Bachman's World, most of whom were of East Indian and Pakistani descent. In every other way, he was totally unlike them.

He had been in the military for most of his life, and had planned to stay in. He was happy in uniform, and for many of the colonists here, that was a totally foreign concept.

Both of those stories of his ancestors were in his mind as he stood, travel-weary and yet excited, before a massive piece of the machinery of war, a glorious hulk of purpose-built design. It was larger than a good many of the buildings of this far-off colony at the edges of human space.

Bachman's World. A poor colony known only for its single export of a medicinal desert plant, it was not a place likely to attract a tourist trade. Those who came here left because life was even harder in the slums of Calcutta, or the perpetually typhoon-swept mud-flats of Bangladesh. They were farmers, who grew vast acreages of the "saje" for export, and irrigated just enough land to feed themselves. A hot, dry wind blew sand into the tight curls of his hair and stirred the short sleeves of his desert-khaki uniform. It occurred to him that he could not have chosen a more appropriate setting for what was likely to prove a life-long exile, considering his hobby—his obsession. And yet, it was an exile he had chosen willingly, even eagerly.

This behemoth, this juggernaut, this mountain of gleaming metal, was a Bolo. Now, it was *his* Bolo, his partner. A partner whose workings he knew intimately . . . and whose thought processes suited his so uniquely that there might not be a similar match in all the Galaxy.

*RML-1138.* Outmoded now, and facing retirement—which, for a Bolo, meant *deactivation.*

Extinction, in other words. Bolos were more than "super tanks," more than war machines, for they were inhabited by some of the finest AIs in human space. When a Bolo was "retired," so was the AI. Permanently.

There were those, even now, who were lobbying for AI rights, who equated deactivation with murder. They were opposed by any number of special-interest groups, beginning with religionists, who objected to the notion than anything housed in a "body" of electronic circuitry could be considered "human" enough to "murder." No matter which side won, nothing would occur soon enough to save this particular Bolo.

Siegfried had also faced retirement, for the same reason. *Outmoded.* He had specialized in weapons-systems repair, the specific, delicate tracking and targeting systems.

Which were now outmoded, out-of-date; *he* had been deemed too old to retrain. He had been facing an uncertain future, relegated to some dead-end job with no chance for promotion, or more likely, given an "early-out" option. He had applied for a transfer, listing, in desperation, everything that might give him an edge somewhere. On the advice of his superiors, he had included his background and his hobby of military strategy of the pre-Atomic period.

And to his utter amazement, it had been that background and hobby that had attracted the attention of someone in the Reserves, someone who had been looking to make a most particular match . . .

The wind died; no one with any sense moved outside during the heat of midday. The port might have been deserted, but for a lone motor running somewhere in the distance.

The Bolo was utterly silent, but Siegfried knew that he—*he,* not *it*—was watching him, examining him with a myriad of sophisticated instruments. By now, he probably even knew how many fillings were in his mouth, how many grommets in his desert boots. He had already passed judgment on Siegfried's service record, but there was this final confrontation to face, before the partnership could be declared a reality.

He cleared his throat, delicately. Now came the moment of truth. It was time to find out if what one administrator in the Reserves—and one human facing early-out and a future of desperate scrabbling for employment—thought was the perfect match really *would* prove to be the salvation of that human and this huge marvel of machinery and circuits.

Siegfried's hobby was the key—desert warfare, tactics, and most of all, the history and thought of one particular desert commander.

*Erwin Rommel.* The "Desert Fox," the man his greatest rival had termed "the last chivalrous knight." Siegfried knew everything there was to know about the great tank commander. He had fought and refought every campaign Rommel had ever commanded, and his admiration for the man whose life had briefly touched on that of his own ancestor's had never faded, nor had his fascination with the man and his genius.

And there was at least one other being in the universe whose fascination with the Desert Fox matched Siegfried's. This being; the intelligence resident in this particular Bolo, the Bolo that called *himself* "Rommel." Most, if not all, Bolos acquired a name or nickname based on their designations—LNE became "Lenny," or "KKR" became "Kicker." Whether this Bolo had been fascinated by the Desert Fox because of his designation, or had noticed the resemblance of "RML" to "Rommel" because of his fascination, it didn't much matter. Rommel was as much an expert on his namesake as Siegfried was.

Like Siegfried, RML-1138 was scheduled for early-out, but unlike Siegfried, the Reserves offered him a reprieve. The Reserves didn't usually take or need Bolos; for one thing, they were dreadfully expensive. A Reserve unit could requisition a great deal of equipment for the cost of one Bolo. For another, the close partnership required between Bolo and operator precluded use of Bolos in situations where the partnerships would not last past the exercise of the moment. Nor were Bolo partners often "retired" to the Reserves.

And not too many Bolos were available to the Reserves. Retirement for both Bolo and operator was usually permanent, and as often as not, was in the front lines.

But luck (good or ill, it remained to be seen) was with Rommel; he had lost his partner to a deadly virus, he had not seen much in the way of combat, and he was in near-new condition.

And Bachman's World wanted a Reserve battalion. They could not field their own—every able-bodied human here was a farmer or engaged in the export trade. A substantial percentage of the population was of some form of pacifistic religion that precluded bearing arms—Janist, Buddhist, some forms of Hindu.

Bachman's World was *entitled* to a Reserve force; it was their right under the law to have an on-planet defense force supplied by the regular military. Just because Bachman's World was back of beyond of nowhere, and even the most conservative of military planners thought their insistence on having such a force in place to be paranoid in the extreme, that did not negate their right to have it. Their charter was clear. The law was on their side.

Sending them a Reserve battalion would be expensive in the extreme, in terms of maintaining that battalion. The soldiers would be full-timers, on full pay. There was no base—it would have to be built. There was no equipment—that would all have to be imported.

That was when one solitary bean-counting accountant at High Command came up with the answer that would satisfy the letter of the law, yet save the military considerable expense.

The law had been written stipulating, not numbers of personnel and equipment, but a monetary amount. That unknown accountant had determined that the amount so stipulated, meant to be the equivalent value of an infantry battalion, exactly equaled the worth of one Bolo and its operator.

The records search was on.

Enter one Reserve officer, searching for a Bolo in good condition, about to be "retired," with no current operator-partner—

—and someone to match him, familiar with at least the rudiments of mech-warfare, the insides of a Bolo, and willing to be exiled for the rest of his life.

Finding RML-1138, called "Rommel," and Siegfried O'Harrigan, hobbyist military historian.

The government of Bachman's World was less than pleased with the response to their demand, but there was little they could do besides protest. Rommel was shipped to Bachman's World first; Siegfried was given a crash course in Bolo operation. He followed on the first regularly scheduled freighter as soon as his training was over. If, for whatever reason, the pairing did not work, he would leave on the same freighter that brought him.

Now, came the moment of truth.

"*Guten tag, Herr Rommel,*" he said, in careful German, the antique German he had learned in order to be able to read first-hand chronicles in the original language. "*Ich bin Siegfried O'Harrigan.*"

A moment of silence—and then, surprisingly, a sound much like a dry chuckle.

"*Wie geht's, Herr O'Harrigan.* I've been expecting you. Aren't you a little dark to be a Storm Trooper?"

The voice was deep, pleasant, and came from a point somewhere above Siegfried's head. And Siegfried knew the question was a trap, of sorts. Or a test, to see just how much he really *did* know, as opposed to what he claimed to know. A good many pre-Atomic historians could be caught by that question themselves.

"Hardly a Storm Trooper," he countered. "Field Marshall Erwin Rommel would not have had one of *those* under his command. And no Nazis, either. Don't think to trap *me* that easily."

The Bolo uttered that same dry chuckle. "Good for you, Siegfried O'Harrigan. *Willkommen.*"

The hatch opened, silently; a ladder descended just as silently, inviting Siegfried to come out of the hot, desert sun and into Rommel's controlled interior. Rommel had replied to Siegfried's response, but had done so with nothing unnecessary in the way of words, in the tradition of his namesake.

Siegfried had passed the test.

Once again, Siegfried stood in the blindingly hot sun, this time at strict attention, watching the departing back of the mayor of Port

City. The interview had not been pleasant, although both parties had been strictly polite; the mayor's back was stiff with anger. He had not cared for what Siegfried had told him.

"They do not much care for us, do they, Siegfried?" Rommel sounded resigned, and Siegfried sighed. It was impossible to hide anything from the Bolo; Rommel had already proven himself to be an adept reader of human body-language, and of course, anything that was broadcast over the airwaves, scrambled or not, Rommel could access and read. Rommel was right; he and his partner were not the most popular of residents at the moment.

What amazed Siegfried, and continued to amaze him, was how *human* the Bolo was. He was used to AIs of course, but Rommel was something special. Rommel cared about what people did and thought; most AIs really didn't take a great interest in the doings and opinions of mere humans.

"No, Rommel, they don't," he replied. "You really can't blame them; they thought they were going to get a battalion of conventional troops, not one very expensive piece of equipment and one single human."

"But we are easily the equivalent of a battalion of conventional troops," Rommel objected, logically. He lowered his ladder, and now that the mayor was well out of sight, Siegfried felt free to climb back into the cool interior of the Bolo.

He waited until he was settled in his customary seat, now worn to the contours of his own figure after a year, before he answered the AI he now consciously considered to be his best friend as well as his assigned partner. Inside the cabin of the Bolo, everything was clean, if a little worn—cool—the light dimmed the way Siegfried liked it. This was, in fact, the most comfortable quarters Siegfried had ever enjoyed. Granted, things were a bit cramped, but he had everything he needed in here, from shower and cooking facilities to multiple kinds of entertainment. And the Bolo did not need to worry about "wasting" energy; his power-plant was geared to supply full-combat needs in any and all climates; what Siegfried needed to keep cool and comfortable was miniscule. Outside, the ever-present desert sand blew everywhere, the heat was enough to drive even the most patient person mad, and the sun bleached everything to a bone-white. Inside was a compact world of Siegfried's own.

Bachman's World had little to recommend it. That was the problem.

"It's a complicated issue, Rommel," he said. "If a battalion of conventional troops had been sent here, there would have been more than the initial expenditure—there would have been an ongoing expenditure to support them."

"Yes—that support money would come into the community. I understand their distress." Rommel would understand, of course; Field Marshal Erwin Rommel had understood the problems of supply only too well, and his namesake could hardly do less. "Could it be they demanded the troops in the first place in order to gain that money?"

Siegfried grimaced, and toyed with the controls on the panel in front of him. "That's what High Command thinks, actually. There never was any real reason to think Bachman's World was under any sort of threat, and after a year, there's even less reason than there was when they made the request. They expected something to bring in money from outside; you and I are hardly bringing in big revenue for them."

Indeed, they weren't bringing in any income at all. Rommel, of course, required no support, since he was not expending anything. His power-plant would supply all his needs for the next hundred years before it needed refueling. If there had been a battalion of men here, it would have been less expensive for High Command to set up a standard mess hall, buying their supplies from the local farmers, rather than shipping in food and other supplies. Further, the men would have been spending their pay locally. In fact, local suppliers would have been found for nearly everything except weaponry.

But with only one man here, it was far less expensive for High Command to arrange for his supplies to come in at regular intervals on scheduled freight-runs. The Bolo ate nothing. They didn't even use "local" water; the Bolo recycled nearly every drop, and distilled the rest from occasional rainfall and dew. Siegfried was not the usual soldier-on-leave; when he spent his pay, it was generally off-planet, ordering things to be shipped in, and not patronizing local merchants. He bought books, not beer; he didn't gamble, his interest in food was minimal and satisfied by the R.E.M.s (Ready-to-Eat-Meals) that were standard field issue and shipped to him by the crateful. And he was far more interested in that four-letter word for "intercourse" that began with a "t" than in intercourse of any other kind. He was an ascetic scholar; such men were not the sort who brought any amount of money into a community. He and his partner, parked as they were at the edge of the spaceport, were a continual reminder of how Bachman's World had been "cheated."

And for that reason, the mayor of Port City had suggested—stiffly, but politely—that his and Rommel's continuing presence so near the main settlement was somewhat disconcerting. He had hinted that the peace-loving citizens found the Bolo frightening (and never mind that they had requested some sort of defense from the military). And if they could not find a way to make themselves useful, perhaps they ought to at least *earn* their pay by pretending to go on maneuvers. It didn't matter that Siegfried and Rommel were perfectly capable of conducting such exercises without moving. That was hardly the point.

"You heard him, my friend," Siegfried sighed. "They'd like us to go away. Not that they have any authority to order us to do so—as I reminded the mayor. But I suspect seeing us constantly is something of an embarrassment to whoever it was that promised a battalion of troops to bring in cash and got us instead."

"In that case, Siegfried," Rommel said gently, "we probably should take the mayor's suggestion. How long do you think we should stay away?"

"When's the next ship due in?" Siegfried replied. "There's no real reason for us to be here until it arrives, and then we only need to stay long enough to pick up my supplies."

"True." With a barely audible rumble, Rommel started his banks of motive engines. "Have you any destination in mind?"

Without prompting, Rommel projected the map of the immediate area on one of Siegfried's control-room screens. Siegfried studied it for a moment, trying to work out the possible repercussions of vanishing into the hills altogether. "I'll tell you what, old man," he said slowly, "we've just been playing at doing our job. Really, that's hardly honorable, when it comes down to it. Even if they don't need us and never did, the fact is that they asked for on-planet protection, and we haven't even planned how to give it to them. How about if we actually go out there in the bush and *do* that planning?"

There was interest in the AI's voice; he did not imagine it. "What do you mean by that?" Rommel asked.

"I mean, let's go out there and scout the territory ourselves; plan defenses and offenses, as if this dustball *was* likely to be invaded. The topographical surveys stink for military purposes; let's get a real war plan in place. What the hell—it can't hurt, right? And if the locals see us actually doing some work, they might not think so badly of us."

Rommel was silent for a moment. "They will still blame High Command, Siegfried. They did not receive what they wanted, even though they received what they were entitled to."

"But they won't blame *us*." He put a little coaxing into his voice. "Look, Rommel, we're going to be here for the rest of our lives, and we really can't afford to have the entire population angry with us forever. I know our standing orders are to stay at Port City, but the mayor just countermanded those orders. So let's have some fun, and show 'em we know our duty at the same time! Let's use Erwin's strategies around here, and see how they work! We can run all kinds of scenarios—let's assume in the event of a real invasion we could get some of these farmers to pick up a weapon; that'll give us additional scenarios to run. Figure troops against you, mechs against you, troops and mechs against you, plus untrained men against troops, men against mechs, you against another Bolo-type AI—"

"It would be entertaining." Rommel sounded very interested. "And as long as we keep our defensive surveillance up, and an eye on Port City, we would not technically be violating orders . . . ."

"Then let's do it," Siegfried said decisively. "Like I said, the maps they gave us stink; let's go make our own, then plot strategy. Let's find every wadi and overhang big enough to hide you. Let's act as if there really *was* going to be an invasion. Let's give them some options, log the plans with the mayor's office. We can plan for evacuations, we can check resources, there's a lot of things we can do. And let's start right now!"

They mapped every dry streambed, every dusty hill, every animal trail. For months, the two of them rumbled across the arid landscape, with Siegfried emerging now and again to carry surveying instruments to the tops of hills too fragile to bear Rommel's weight. And when every inch of territory within a week of Port City had been surveyed and accurately mapped, they began playing a game of "hide and seek" with the locals.

It was surprisingly gratifying. At first, after they had vanished for a while, the local news channel seemed to reflect an attitude of "good riddance." But then, when *no one* spotted them, there was a certain amount of concern—followed by a certain amount of annoyance. After all, Rommel was "their" Bolo—what was Siegfried doing, taking him out for some kind of vacation? As if Bachman's World offered any kind of amusement . . . .

That was when Rommel and Siegfried began stalking farmers.

They would find a good hiding place and get into it well in advance of a farmer's arrival. When he would show up, Rommel would rise up, seemingly from out of the ground, draped in camouflage-net, his weaponry trained on the farmer's vehicle. Then Siegfried would pop up out of the hatch, wave cheerfully, retract the camouflage, and he and Rommel would rumble away.

Talk of "vacations" ceased entirely after that.

They extended their range, once they were certain that the locals were no longer assuming the two of them were "gold-bricking." Rommel tested all of his abilities to the limit, making certain everything was still up to spec. And on the few occasions that it wasn't, Siegfried put in a requisition for parts and spent many long hours making certain that the repairs and replacements *were* bringing Rommel up to like-new condition.

Together they plotted defensive and offensive strategies; Siegfried studied Rommel's manuals as if a time would come when he would have to rebuild Rommel from spare parts. They ran every kind of simulation in the book—and not just on Rommel's computers, but with Rommel himself actually running and dry-firing against plotted enemies. Occasionally one of the newspeople would become curious about their whereabouts, and lie in wait for them when the scheduled supplies arrived. Siegfried would give a formal interview, reporting in general what they had been doing—and then, he would carefully file another set of emergency plans with the mayor's office. Sometimes it even made the evening news. Once, it was even accompanied by a clip someone had shot of Rommel roaring at top speed across a ridge.

Nor was that all they did. As Rommel pointed out, the presumptive "battalion" would have been available in emergencies—there was no reason why *they* shouldn't respond when local emergencies came up.

So—when a flash flood trapped a young woman and three children on the roof of her vehicle, it was Rommel and Siegfried who not only rescued them, but towed the vehicle to safety as well. When a snowfall in the mountains stranded a dozen truckers, Siegfried and Rommel got them out. When a small child was lost while playing in the hills, Rommel found her by having all searchers clear out as soon as the sun went down, and using his heat sensors to locate every source of approximately her size. They put out runaway brushfires by rolling over them; they responded to Maydays from remote locations when they were nearer than any other agency. They even joined in a manhunt for an escaped rapist—who turned himself in, practically soiling himself with fear, when he learned that Rommel was part of the search party.

It didn't hurt. They were of no help for men trapped in a mine collapse; or rather, of no *more* help than Siegfried's two hands could make them. They couldn't rebuild bridges that were washed away, nor construct roads. But what they could do, they did, often before anyone thought to ask them for help.

By the end of their second year on Bachman's World, they were at least no longer the target of resentment. Those few citizens they had aided actually looked on them with gratitude. The local politicians whose careers had suffered because of their presence had found other causes to espouse, other schemes to pursue. Siegfried and Rommel were a dead issue.

But by then, the two of them had established a routine of monitoring emergency channels, running their private war-games, updating their maps, and adding changes in the colony to their defense and offense plans. There was no reason to go back to simply sitting beside the spaceport. Neither of them cared for sitting idle, and what they were doing was the nearest either of them would ever get to actually refighting the battles their idol had lost and won.

When High Command got their reports and sent recommendations for further "readiness" preparations, and *commendations* for their "community service," Siegfried, now wiser in the ways of manipulating public opinion, issued a statement to the press about both.

After that, there were no more rumblings of discontent, and things might have gone on as they were until Siegfried was too old to climb Rommel's ladder.

But the fates had another plan in store for them.

Alarms woke Siegfried out of a sound and dreamless sleep. Not the synthesized pseudo-alarms Rommel used when surprising him for a drill, either, but the real thing—

He launched himself out of his bunk before his eyes were focused, grabbing the back of the comm-chair to steady himself before he flung himself into it and strapped himself down. As soon as he moved, Rommel turned off all the alarms but one; the proximity alert from the single defense satellite in orbit above them.

Interior lighting had gone to full-emergency red. He scrubbed at his eyes with the back of his hand, impatiently; finally they focused on the screens of his console, and he could read what was there. And he swore, fervently and creatively.

One unknown ship sat in geosynch orbit above Port City; a big one, answering no hails from the port, and seeding the skies with what appeared to his sleep-fogged eyes as hundreds of smaller drop-ships.

"The mother-ship has already neutralized the port air-to-ground defenses, Siegfried," Rommel reported grimly. "I don't know what kind of stealthing devices they have, or if they've got some new kind of drive, but they don't match anything in my records. They just appeared out of nowhere and started dumping drop-ships. I think we can assume they're hostiles."

They had a match for just this in their hundreds of plans; unknown ship, unknown attackers, dropping a pattern of offensive troops of some kind—

"What are they landing?" he asked, playing the console board. "You're stealthed, right?"

"To the max," Rommel told him. "I don't detect anything like life-forms on those incoming vessels, but my sensors aren't as sophisticated as they could be. The vessels themselves aren't all that big. My guess is that they're dropping either live troops or clusters of very small mechs, mobile armor, maybe the size of a Panzer."

"Landing pattern?" he asked. He brought up all of Rommel's weaponry; AIs weren't allowed to activate their own weapons. And they weren't allowed to fire on living troops without permission from a human, either. That was the only real reason for a Bolo needing an operator.

"Surrounding Port City, but starting from about where the first farms are." Rommel ran swift readiness tests on the systems as Siegfried brought them up; the screens scrolled too fast for Siegfried to read them.

They had a name for that particular scenario. It was one of the first possibilities they had run when they began plotting invasion and counterinvasion plans.

"Operation Cattle Drive. Right." If the invaders followed the same scheme he and Rommel had anticipated, they planned to drive the populace into Port City, and either capture the civilians, or destroy them at leisure. He checked their current location; it was out beyond the drop-zone. "Is there anything landing close to us?"

"Not yet—but the odds are that something will soon." Rommel sounded confident, as well he should be—his ability to project landing patterns was far better than any human's. "I'd say within the next fifteen minutes."

Siegfried suddenly shivered in a breath of cool air from the ventilators, and was painfully aware suddenly that he was dressed in nothing more than a pair of fatigue shorts. Oh well; some of the Desert Fox's battles had taken place with the men wearing little else. What they could put up with, he could. There certainly wasn't anyone here to complain.

"As soon as you think we can move without detection, close on the nearest craft," he ordered. "I want to see what we're up against. And start scanning the local freqs; if there's anything in the way of organized defense from the civvies, I want to know about it."

A pause, while the ventilators hummed softly, and glowing dots descended on several screens. "They don't seem to have anything, Siegfried," Rommel reported quietly. "Once the ground-to-space defenses were fried, they just collapsed. Right now, they seem to be in a complete state of panic. They don't even seem to remember that *we're* out here—no one's tried to hail us on any of our regular channels."

"Either that—or they think we're out of commission," he muttered absently. "Or just maybe they are giving us credit for knowing what we're doing and are trying *not* to give us away. I hope so. The longer we can go without detection, the better chance we have to pull something out of a hat."

An increase in vibration warned him that Rommel was about to move. A new screen lit up, this one tracking a single vessel. "Got one," the Bolo said shortly. "I'm coming in behind his sensor sweep."

Four more screens lit up; enhanced front, back, top, and side views of the terrain. Only the changing views on the screens showed that Rommel was moving; other than that, there was no way to tell from inside the cabin what was happening. It would be different if Rommel had to execute evasive maneuvers of course, but right now, he might have still been parked. The control cabin and living quarters were heavily shielded and cushioned against the shocks of ordinary movement. Only if Rommel took a direct hit by something impressive would Siegfried feel it . . . .

*And if he takes a direct hit by something more than impressive— we're slag. Bolos are the best, but they can't take everything.*

"The craft is down."

He pushed the thought away from his mind. This was what

Rommel had been built to do—this moment justified Rommel's very existence. And *he* had known from the very beginning that the possibility, however remote, had existed that he too would be in combat one day. That was what being in the military was all about. There was no use in pretending otherwise.

*Get on with the job. That's what they've sent me here to do.* Wasn't there an ancient royal family whose motto was "God, and my Duty?" Then let that be his.

"Have you detected any sensor scans from the mothership?" he asked, his voice a harsh whisper. "Or anything other than a forward scan from the landing craft?" He didn't know why he was whispering—

"Not as yet, Siegfried," Rommel replied, sounding a little surprised. "Apparently, these invaders are confident that there is no one out here at all. Even that forward scan seemed mainly to be a landing aid."

"Nobody here but us chickens," Siegfried muttered. "Are they offloading yet?"

"Wait—yes. The ramp is down. We will be within visual range ourselves in a moment—there—"

More screens came alive; Siegfried read them rapidly—

Then read them again, incredulously.

"Mechs?" he said, astonished. *"Remotely controlled* mechs?"

"So it appears." Rommel sounded just as mystified. "This does not match any known configuration. There is one limited AI in that ship. Data indicates it is hardened against any attack conventional forces at the port could mount. The ship seems to be digging in— look at the seismic reading on 4-B. The limited AI is in control of the mechs it is deploying. I believe that we can assume this will be the case for the other invading ships, at least the ones coming down at the moment, since they all appear to be of the same model."

Siegfried studied the screens; as they had assumed, the mechs were about the size of pre-Atomic Panzers, and seemed to be built along similar lines. "Armored mechs. Good against anything a civilian has. Is that ship hardened against anything *you* can throw?" he asked finally.

There was a certain amount of glee in Rommel's voice. "I think not. Shall we try?"

Siegfried's mouth dried. There was no telling what weaponry that ship packed—or the mother-ship held. The mother-ship might be monitoring the drop-ships, watching for attack. *God and my Duty,* he thought.

"You may fire when ready, Herr Rommel."

They had taken the drop-ship by complete surprise; destroying it before it had a chance to transmit distress or tactical data to the mother-ship. The mechs had stopped in their tracks the moment the AI's direction ceased.

But rather than roll on to the next target, Siegfried had ordered Rommel to stealth again, while he examined the remains of the mechs and the controlling craft. He'd had an idea—the question was, would it work?

He knew weapons systems; knew computer-driven control. There were only a limited number of ways such controls could work. And if he recognized any of those here—

He told himself, as he scrambled into clothing and climbed the ladder out of the cabin, that he would give himself an hour. The situation would not change much in an hour; there was very little that he and Rommel could accomplish in that time in the way of mounting a campaign. As it happened, it took him fifteen minutes more than that to learn all he needed to know. At the end of that time, though, he scrambled back into Rommel's guts with mingled feelings of elation and anger.

The ship and mechs were clearly of human origin, and some of the vanes and protrusions that made them look so unfamiliar had been tacked on purely to make both the drop-ships and armored mechs look alien in nature. Someone, somewhere, had discovered something about Bachman's World that suddenly made it valuable. From the hardware interlocks and the programming modes he had found in what was left of the controlling ship, he suspected that the "someone" was not a government, but a corporation.

And a multiplanet corporation could afford to mount an invasion force fairly easily. The best force for the job would, of course, be something precisely like this—completely mechanized. There would be no troops to "hush up" afterwards; no leaks to the interstellar press. Only a nice clean invasion—and, in all probability, a nice, clean extermination at the end of it, with no humans to protest the slaughter of helpless civilians.

And afterwards, there would be no evidence anywhere to contradict the claim that the civilians had slaughtered each other in some kind of local conflict.

The mechs and the AI itself were from systems he had studied when he first started in this specialty—outmoded even by his standards, but reliable, and when set against farmers with hand weapons, perfectly adequate.

There was one problem with this kind of setup . . . from the enemy's standpoint. It was a problem they didn't know they had.

Yet.

He filled Rommel in on what he had discovered as he raced up the ladder, then slid down the handrails into the command cabin. "Now, here's the thing—I got the access code to command those mechs with a little fiddling in the AI's memory. Nice of them to leave in so many manual overrides for me. I reset the command interface freq to one you have, and hardwired it so they shouldn't be able to change it—"

He jumped into the command chair and strapped in; his hands danced across the keypad, keying in the frequency and the code. Then he saluted the console jauntily. "Congratulations, Herr Rommel," he said, unable to keep the glee out of his voice. "You are now a Field Marshal."

"*Siegfried!*" Yes, there was astonishment in Rommel's synthesized voice. "You just gave me command of an armored mobile strike force!"

"I certainly did. And I freed your command circuits so that you can run them without waiting for my orders to do something." Siegfried couldn't help grinning. "After all, you're not going against living troops, you're going to be attacking AIs and mechs. The next

AI might not be so easy to take over, but if you're running in the middle of a swarm of 'friendlies,' you might not be suspected. And when we knock out *that* one, we'll take over again. I'll even put the next bunch on a different command freq so you can command them separately. Sooner or later they'll figure out what we're doing, but by then I hope we'll have at least an equal force under our command."

"This is good, Siegfried!"

"You bet it's good, *mein Freund*," he retorted. "What's more, we've studied the best—they can't possibly have that advantage. All right— let's show these amateurs how one of the old masters handles armor!"

The second and third takeovers were as easy as the first. By the fourth, however, matters had changed. It might have dawned on either the AIs on the ground or whoever was in command of the overall operation in the mother-ship above that the triple loss of AIs and mechs was not due to simple malfunction, but to an unknown and unsuspected enemy.

In that, the hostiles were following in the mental footsteps of another pre-Atomic commander, who had once stated, "Once is happenstance, twice is circumstance, but three times is enemy action."

So the fourth time their forces advanced on a ship, they met with fierce resistance.

They lost about a dozen mechs, and Siegfried had suffered a bit of a shakeup and a fair amount of bruising, but they managed to destroy the fourth AI without much damage to Rommel's exterior. Despite the danger from unexploded shells and some residual radiation, Siegfried doggedly went out into the wreckage to get that precious access code.

He returned to bad news. "They know we're here, Siegfried," Rommel announced. "That last barrage gave them a silhouette upstairs; they know I'm a Bolo, so now they know what they're up against."

Siegfried swore quietly, as he gave Rommel his fourth contingent of mechs. "Well, have they figured out exactly what we're doing yet? Or can you tell?" Siegfried asked while typing in the fourth unit's access codes.

"I can't—I—can't—Siegfried—" the Bolo replied, suddenly without any inflection at all. "Siegfried. There is a problem. Another. I am stretching my—resources—"

This time Siegfried swore with a lot less creativity. That was something he had not even considered! The AIs they were eliminating were much less sophisticated than Rommel—

"Drop the last batch!" he snapped. To his relief, Rommel sounded like himself again as he released control of the last contingent of mechs.

"That was not a pleasurable experience," Rommel said mildly.

"What happened?" he demanded.

"As I needed to devote more resources to controlling the mechs, I began losing higher functions," the Bolo replied simply. "We should have expected that; so far I am doing the work of three lesser AIs and all the functions you require, *and* maneuvering of the various groups we have captured. As I pick up more groups, I will inevitably lose processing functions."

Siegfried thought, frantically. There were about twenty of these invading ships; their plan absolutely required that Rommel control at least eight of the groups to successfully hold the invasion off Port City. There was no way they'd be anything worse than an annoyance with only three; the other groups could outflank them. "What if you shut down things in here?" he asked. "Run basic life-support, but nothing fancy. And I could drive—run your weapons systems."

"You could. That would help." Rommel pondered for a moment. "My calculations are that we can take the required eight of the groups if you also issue battle orders and I simply carry them out. But there is a further problem."

"Which is?" he asked—although he had the sinking feeling that he knew what the problem was going to be.

"Higher functions. One of the functions I will lose at about the seventh takeover is what you refer to as my personality. A great deal of my ability to maintain a personality is dependent on devoting a substantial percentage of my central processor to that personality. And if it disappears—"

The Bolo paused. Siegfried's hands clenched on the arms of his chair.

"—it may not return. There is a possibility that the records and algorithms which make up my personality will be written over by comparison files during strategic control calculations." Again Rommel paused. "Siegfried, this is our duty. I am willing to take that chance."

Siegfried swallowed, only to find a lump in his throat and his guts in knots. "Are you sure?" he asked gently. "Are you very sure? What you're talking about is—is a kind of deactivation."

"I am sure," Rommel replied firmly. "The Field Marshal would have made the same choice."

Rommel's manuals were all on a handheld reader. He had studied them from front to back—wasn't there something in there? "Hold on a minute—"

He ran through the index, frantically keyword searching. This was a memory function, right? Or at least it was software. The designers didn't encourage operators to go mucking around in the AI functions . . . what would a computer jock call what he was looking for?

Finally he found it; a tiny section in programmerese, not even listed in the index. He scanned it, quickly, and found the warning that had been the thing that had caught his eye in the first place.

*This system has been simulation-proven in expected scenarios, but has never been fully field-tested.*

What the hell did that mean? He had a guess; this was essentially a full-copy backup of the AI's processor. He suspected that they had never tested the backup function on an AI with a full personality. There was no way of knowing if the restoration function would actually "restore" a lost personality.

But the backup memory-module in question had its own power-supply, and was protected in the most hardened areas of Rommel's interior. Nothing was going to destroy it that didn't slag him and Rommel together, and if "personality" was largely a matter of memory—

It might work. It might not. It was worth trying, even if the backup procedure was fiendishly hard to initiate. They really *didn't* want operators mucking around with the AIs.

Twenty command-strings later, a single memory-mod began its

simple task; Rommel was back in charge of the fourth group of mechs, and Siegfried had taken over the driving.

He was not as good as Rommel was, but he was better than he had thought.

They took groups five, and six, and it was horrible—listening to Rommel fade away, lose the vitality behind the synthesized voice. If Siegfried hadn't had his hands full already, literally, it would have been worse.

But with group seven—

That was when he just about lost it, because in reply to one of his voice commands, instead of a, "Got it, Siegfried," what came over the speakers was the metallic, "Affirmative," of a simple voice-activated computer.

All of Rommel's resources were now devoted to self-defense and control of the armored mechs.

*God and my Duty.* Siegfried took a deep breath, and began keying in the commands for mass armor deployment.


The ancient commanders were right; from the ground, there was no way of knowing when the moment of truth came. Siegfried only realized that they had won when the mother-ship suddenly vanished from orbit, and the remaining AIs went dead. Cutting their losses; there was nothing in any of the equipment that would betray *where* it came from. Whoever was in charge of the invasion force must have decided that there was no way they would finish the mission before *someone,* a regularly scheduled freighter or a surprise patrol, discovered what was going on and reported it.

By that time, he had been awake for fifty hours straight; he had put squeeze-bulbs of electrolytic drink near at hand, but he was starving and still thirsty. With the air conditioning cut out, he must have sweated out every ounce of fluid he drank. His hands were shaking and every muscle in his neck and shoulders was cramped from hunching over the boards.

Rommel was battered and had lost several external sensors and one of his guns. But the moment that the mother-ship vanished, he had only one thought.

He manually dropped control of every mech from Rommel's systems, and waited, praying, for his old friend to "come back."

But nothing happened—other than the obvious things that any AI would do, restoring all the comfort-support and life-support functions, and beginning damage checks and some self-repair.

Rommel was gone.

His throat closed; his stomach knotted. But—

*It wasn't tested. That doesn't mean it won't work.*

Once more, his hands moved over the keyboard, with another twenty command-strings, telling that little memory-module in the heart of his Bolo to initiate full restoration. He hadn't thought he had water to spare for tears—yet there they were, burning their way down his cheeks. Two of them.

He ignored them, fiercely, shaking his head to clear his eyes, and continuing the command-sequence.

Damage checks and self-repair aborted. Life-support went on automatic.

And Siegfried put his head down on the console to rest his burning eyes for a moment. Just for a moment—

Just—

"Ahem."

Siegfried jolted out of sleep, cracking his elbow on the console, staring around the cabin with his heart racing wildly.

"I believe we have visitors, Siegfried," said that wonderful, familiar voice. "They seem most impatient."

Screens lit up, showing a small army of civilians approaching, riding in everything from outmoded sandrails to tractors, all of them cheering, all of them heading straight for the Bolo.

"We seem to have their approval at least," Rommel continued.

His heart had stopped racing, but he still trembled. And once again, he seemed to have come up with the moisture for tears. He nodded, knowing Rommel would see it, unable for the moment to get any words out.

"Siegfried—before we become immersed in grateful civilians— how *did* you bring me back?" Rommel asked. "I'm rather curious—I actually seem to remember fading out. An unpleasant experience."

"How did I get you back?" he managed to choke out—and then began laughing.

He held up the manual, laughing, and cried out the famous quote of George Patton—

" 'Rommel, you magnificent bastard, *I read your book!*'"

*Sometimes we write for odd markets; I wrote this piece for a magazine called* Pet Bird Report, *which is bird behaviorist Sally Blanchard's outlet for continuing information on parrot behavior and psychology. It's a terrific magazine, and if you have a bird but haven't subscribed, I suggest you would find it worth your while. With twelve birds, I need all the help I can get! At any rate, Sally asked me for some fiction, and I came up with this.*

# Gray

## Mercedes Lackey

For nine years, Sarah Jane Lyon-White lived happily with her parents in the heart of Africa. Her father was a physician, her mother, a nurse, and they worked at a Protestant mission in the Congo. She was happy there, not the least because her mother and father were far more enlightened than many another mission worker in the days when Victoria was Queen; taking the cause of healing as more sacred than that of conversion, they undertook to work *with* the natives, and made friends instead of enemies among the shamans and medicine-people. Because of this, Sarah was a cherished and protected child, although she was no stranger to the many dangers of life in the Congo.

When she was six, and far older in responsibility than most of her peers, one of the shaman brought her a parrot-chick still in quills;

he taught her how to feed and care for it, and told her that while *it* was a child, she was to protect it, but when it was grown, it would protect and guide *her.* She called the parrot "Gray," and it became her best friend—and indeed, although she never told her parents, it became her protector as well.

But when she was nine, her parents sent her to live in England for the sake of her health. And because her mother feared that the climate of England would not be good for Gray's health, she had to leave her beloved friend behind.

Now, this was quite the usual thing in the days when Victoria was Queen and the great British Empire was so vast that there was never an hour when some part of it was not in sunlight. It was thought that English children were more delicate than their parents, and that the inhospitable humors of hot climes would make them sicken and die. Not that their *parents* didn't sicken and die quite as readily as the children, who were, in fact, far sturdier than they were given credit for—but it was thought, by anxious mothers, that the climate of England would be far kinder to them. So off they were shipped, some as young as two and three, torn away from their anxious mamas and native nurses and sent to live with relatives or even total strangers.

Now, as Mr. Kipling and Mrs. Hope-Hodgson have shown us, many of these total strangers—and no few of the relatives—were bad, wicked people, interested only in the round gold sovereigns that the childrens' parents sent to them for their care. There were many schools where the poor lonely things were neglected or even abused; where their health suffered far more than if they had stayed safely at the sides of their mamas.

But there were good schools too, and kindly people, and Sarah Jane's mama had been both wise and careful in her selection. In fact, Sarah Jane's mama had made a choice that was far wiser than even she had guessed . . . .

Nan—that was her only name, for no one had told her of any other—lurked anxiously about the back gate of the Big House. She was new to this neighborhood, for her slatternly mother had lost yet another job in a gin mill and they had been forced to move all the way across Whitechapel, and this part of London was as foreign to Nan as the wilds of Australia. She had been told by more than one of the children hereabouts that if she hung about the back gate after tea, a strange man with a towel wrapped about his head would come out with a basket of food and give it out to any child who happened to be there. Now, there were not as many children willing to accept this offering as might have been expected, even in this poor neighborhood. They were afraid of the man, afraid of his piercing, black eyes, his swarthy skin, and his way of walking like a great hunting-cat. Some suspected poison in the food, others murmured that he and the woman of the house were foreigners, and intended to kill English children with terrible curses on the food they offered. But Nan was faint with hunger; she hadn't eaten in two days, and was willing to dare poison, curses, and anything else for a bit of bread.

Furthermore, Nan had a secret defense; under duress, she could often sense the intent and even dimly hear the thoughts of others. That was how she avoided her mother when it was most dangerous to approach her, as well as avoiding other dangers in the streets themselves. Nan was certain that if this man had any ill intentions, she would know it.

Still, as tea-time and twilight both approached, she hung back a little from the wrought-iron gate, beginning to wonder if it wouldn't be better to see what, if anything, her mother brought home. If she'd found a job—or a "gen'lmun"—there might be a farthing or two to spare for food before Aggie spent the rest on gin. Behind the high, grimy wall, the Big House loomed dark and ominous against the smoky, lowering sky, and the strange, carved creatures sitting atop every pillar in the wall and every corner of the House fair gave Nan the shivers whenever she looked at them. There were no two alike, and most of them were beasts out of a rummy's worst deliriums. The only one that Nan could see that looked at all normal was a big, gray bird with a fat body and a hooked beak that sat on top of the right-hand gatepost of the back gate.

Nan had no way to tell time, but as she waited, growing colder and hungrier—and more nervous—with each passing moment, she began to think for certain that the other children had been having her on. Tea-time was surely long over; the tale they'd told her was nothing more than that, something to gull the newcomer with. It was getting dark, there were no other children waiting, and after dark it was dangerous even for a child like Nan, wise in the ways of the evil streets, to be abroad. Disappointed, and with her stomach a knot of pain, Nan began to turn away from the gate.

"I think that there is no one here, Missy S'ab," said a low, deep voice, heavily accented, sounding disappointed. Nan hastily turned back, and peering through the gloom, she barely made out a tall, dark form with a smaller one beside it.

"No, Karamjit—look there!" replied the voice of a young girl, and the smaller form pointed at Nan. A little girl ran up to the gate, and waved through the bars. "Hello! I'm Sarah—what's your name? Would you like some tea-bread? We've plenty!"

The girl's voice, also strangely accented, had none of the imperiousness that Nan would have expected coming from the child of a "toff." She sounded only friendly and helpful, and that, more than anything, was what drew Nan back to the wrought-iron gate.

"Indeed, Missy Sarah speaks the truth," the man said; and as Nan drew nearer, she saw that the other children had not exaggerated when they described him. His head was wrapped around in a cloth; he wore a long, high-collared coat of some bright stuff, and white trousers that were tucked into glossy boots. He was as fiercely erect as the iron gate itself; lean and angular as a hunting tiger, with skin so dark she could scarcely make out his features, and eyes that glittered at her like beads of black glass.

But strangest, and perhaps most ominous of all, Nan could sense nothing from the dark man. He might not even have been there; there was a blank wall where his thoughts should have been.

The little girl beside him was perfectly ordinary by comparison; a bright little wren of a thing, not pretty, but sweet, with a trusting smile that went straight to Nan's heart. Nan had a motherly side to her; the younger children of whatever neighborhood she lived in tended to flock to her, look up to her, and follow her lead. She in her turn tried to keep them out of trouble, and whenever there was extra to go around, she fed them out of her own scant stocks.

But the tall fellow frightened her, and made her nervous, especially when further moments revealed no more of his intentions than Nan had sensed before; the girl's bright eyes noted that, and she whispered something to the dark man as Nan withdrew a little. He nodded, and handed her a basket that looked promisingly heavy.

Then he withdrew out of sight, leaving the little girl alone at the gate. The child pushed the gate open enough to hand the basket through. "Please, won't you come and take this? It's awfully heavy."

In spite of the clear and open brightness of the little girl's thoughts, ten years of hard living had made Nan suspicious. The child might know nothing of what the dark man wanted. "Woi're yer givin' food away?" she asked, edging forward a little, but not yet quite willing to take the basket.

The little girl put the basket down on the ground and clasped her hands behind her back. "Well, Mem'sab says that she won't tell Maya and Selim to make less food for tea, because she won't have us going hungry while we're growing. And she says that old, stale toast is fit only for starlings, so people ought to have the good of it before it goes stale. And she says that there's no reason why children outside our gate have to go to bed hungry when we have enough to share, and my Mum and Da say that sharing is charity and Charity is one of the cardinal virtues, so Mem'sab is being virtuous, which is a good thing, because she'll go to heaven and she would make a good angel."

Most of that came out in a rush that quite bewildered Nan, especially the last, about cardinal virtues and heaven and angels. But she did understand that "Mem'sab," whoever that was, must be one of those daft religious creatures that gave away food free for the taking, and Nan's own Mum had told her that there was no point in letting other people take what you could get from people like that. So Nan edged forward and made a snatch at the basket handle.

She tried, that is; it proved a great deal heavier than she'd thought, and she gave an involuntary grunt at the weight of it.

"Be careful," the little girl admonished mischievously. "It's heavy."

"Yer moight'o warned me!" Nan said, a bit indignant, and more than a bit excited. If this wasn't a trick—if there wasn't a brick in the basket—oh, she'd eat well tonight, and tomorrow, too!

"Come back tomorrow!" the little thing called, as she shut the gate and turned and skipped towards the house. "Remember me! I'm Sarah Jane, and I'll bring the basket tomorrow!"

"Thenkee, Sarah Jane," Nan called back, belatedly; then, just in case these strange creatures would think better of their generosity, she made the basket and herself vanish into the night.

She came earlier the next day, bringing back the now-empty basket, and found Sarah Jane waiting at the gate. To her disappointment, there was no basket waiting beside the child, and Nan almost turned back, but Sarah saw her and called to her before she could fade back into the shadows of the streets.

"Karamjit is bringing the basket in a bit," the child said. "There's things Mem'sab wants you to have. And—what am I to call you? It's rude to call you 'girl,' but I don't know your name."

"Nan," Nan replied, feeling as if a cart had run over her. This child, though younger than Nan herself, had a way of taking over a situation that was all out of keeping with Nan's notion of how things were. "Wot kind'o place is this, anyway?"

"It's a school, a boarding-school," Sarah said promptly. "Mem'sab and her husband have it for the children of people who live in India, mostly. Mem'sab can't have children herself, which is very sad, but she says that means she can be a mother to us. Mem'sab came from India, and that's where Karamjit and Selim and Maya and the others are from, too; they came with her."

"Yer mean the black feller?" Nan asked, bewildered. "Yer from In'ju too?"

"No," Sarah said, shaking her head. "Africa. I wish I was back there." Her face paled and her eyes misted, and Nan, moved by an impulse she did not understand, tried to distract her with questions.

"Wot's it loik, then? Izit loik Lunnun?"

"Like London! Oh, no, it couldn't be less like London!" Nan's ploy worked; the child giggled at the idea of comparing the Congo with a metropolis, and she painted a vivid word-picture of the green jungles, teeming with birds and animals of all sorts; of the natives who came to her father and mother for medicines. "Mum and Da don't do what some of the others do—they went and talked to the magic men and showed them they weren't going to interfere in the magic work, and now whenever Mum and Da have a patient who thinks he's cursed, they call the magic man in to help, and when a magic man has someone that his magic can't help right away, he takes the patient to Mum and Da and they all put on feathers and Mum and Da give him White Medicine while the magic man burns his herbs and feathers and makes his chants, and everyone is happy. There haven't been any uprisings at our station for *ever* so long, and our magic men won't let anyone put black chickens at our door. One of them gave me Gray, and I wanted to bring her with me, but Mum said I shouldn't." Now the child sighed, and looked woeful again.

"Wot's a Gray?" Nan asked.

"She's a Polly, a gray parrot with the beautifullest red tail; the medicine man gave her to me when she was all prickles, he showed me how to feed her with mashed-up yams and things. She's *so* smart, she follows me about, and she can say, oh, hundreds of things. The medicine man said that she was to be my guardian and keep me from harm. But Mum was afraid the smoke in London would hurt her, and I couldn't bring her with me." Sarah looked up at the fat, stone bird on the gatepost above her. "That's why Mem'sab gave me *that* gargoyle, to be my guardian instead. We all have them, each child has her own, and that one's mine." She looked down again at Nan, and lowered her voice to a whisper. "Sometimes when I get lonesome, I come here and talk to her, and it's like talking to Gray."

Nan nodded her head, understanding. "Oi useta go an' talk t' a stachew in one'a the yards, 'til we 'adta move. It looked loik me grammum. Felt loik I was talkin' to 'er, I fair did."

A footstep on the gravel path made Nan look up, and she jumped to see the tall man with the head wrap standing there, as if he had come out of the thin air. She had not sensed his presence, and once again, even though he stood materially before her she *could not*. He took no notice of Nan, which she was grateful for; instead, he handed the basket he was carrying to Sarah Jane, and walked off without a word.

Sarah passed the basket to Nan; it was heavier this time, and Nan *thought* she smelled something like roasted meat. Oh, if *only* they'd given her the drippings from their beef! Her mouth watered at the thought.

"I hope you like these," Sarah said shyly, as Nan passed her the much-lighter empty. "Mem'sab says that if you'll keep coming back, I'm to talk to you and ask you about London; she says that's the best way to learn about things. She says otherwise, when I go out, I might get into trouble I don't understand."

Nan's eyes widened at the thought that the head of a school had said anything of the sort—but Sarah Jane hardly seemed like the type of child to lie. "All roit, I s'pose," she said dubiously. "If you'll be 'ere, so'll Oi."

The next day, faithful as the rising sun, Sarah was waiting with her basket, and Nan was invited to come inside the gate. She wouldn't venture any farther in than a bench in the garden, but as Sarah asked questions, she answered them as bluntly and plainly as she would any similar question asked by a child in her own neighborhood. Sarah learned about the dangers of the dark side of London first-hand— and oddly, although she nodded wisely and with clear understanding, they didn't seem to *frighten* her.

"Garn!" Nan said once, when Sarah absorbed the interesting fact that the opium den a few doors from where Nan and her mother had a room had pitched three dead men out into the street the night before. "Yer ain't never seen nothin' loik that!"

"You forget, Mum and Da have a hospital, and it's very dangerous where they are," Sarah replied matter-of-factly. "I've seen dead men, and dead women and even babies. When Nkumba came in clawed up by a lion, I helped bring water and bandages, while Mum and Da sewed him up. When there was a black-water fever, I saw lots of people die. It was horrid and sad, but I didn't fuss, because Nkumba and Da and Mum were worked nearly to bones and needed me to be good."

Nan's eyes widened again. "Wot else y'see?" she whispered, impressed in spite of herself.

After that, the two children traded stories of two very different sorts of jungles. Despite its dangers, Nan thought that Sarah's was the better of the two.

She learned other things as well; that "Mem'sab" was a completely remarkable woman, for she had a Sikh, a Gurkha, two Moslems, two Buddhists, and assorted Hindus working in peace and harmony together—"and Mum said in her letter that it's easier to get leopards to herd sheep than that!" Mem'sab was by no means a fool; the Sikh and the Gurkha shared guard duty, patrolling the walls by day and night. One of the Hindu women was the "ayah," who took care of the smallest children; the rest of the motley assortment were servants and even teachers.

She heard many stories about the remarkable Gray, who really *did* act as Sarah's guardian, if Sarah was to be believed. Sarah described times when she had inadvertently gotten lost; she had called frantically for Gray, who was allowed to fly free, and the bird had come to her, leading her back to familiar paths. Gray had kept her from eating some pretty but poisonous berries by flying at her and nipping her fingers until she dropped them. Gray alerted the servants to the presence of snakes in the nursery, always making a patrol before she allowed Sarah to enter. And once, according to Sarah, when she had encountered a lion on the path, Gray had flown off and made sounds like a young gazelle in distress, attracting the lion's attention before it could scent Sarah. "She led it away, and didn't come back to me until it was too far away to bother coming back," the little girl claimed solemnly. "Gray is *very* clever." Nan didn't know whether to gape at her or laugh; she couldn't imagine how a mere bird could be intelligent enough to talk, much less act with purpose.

Nan had breath to laugh with, nowadays, thanks to baskets that held more than bread. The food she found in there, though distinctly odd, was always good, and she no longer felt out of breath and tired all the time. She had stopped wondering and worrying about why "Mem'sab" took such an interest in her, and simply accepted the gifts without question. They might stop at any moment; she accepted that without question, too.

The only thing she couldn't accept so easily was the manservant's eerie mental silence.

"How is your mother?" Sarah asked, since yesterday Nan had confessed that Aggie been "on a tear" and had consumed, or so Nan feared, something stronger and more dangerous than gin.

Nan shook her head. "I dunno," she replied reluctantly. "Aggie didn' wake up when I went out. Tha's not roight, she us'lly at least waked up t'foind out wha' I got. She don' half loik them baskets, 'cause it means I don' go beggin' as much."

"And if you don't beg money, she can't drink," Sarah observed shrewdly. "You hate begging, don't you?"

"Mostly I don' like gettin' kicked an' cursed at," Nan temporized. "It ain't loik I'm gettin' underfoot . . ."

But Sarah's questions were coming too near the bone, tonight, and Nan didn't want to have to deal with them. She got to her feet and picked up her basket. "I gotter go," she said abruptly.

Sarah rose from her seat on the bench and gave Nan a penetrating look. Nan had the peculiar feeling that the child was looking at *her* thoughts, and deciding whether or not to press her further. "All right," Sarah said. "It *is* getting dark."

It wasn't, but Nan wasn't about to pass up the offer of a graceful exit. "'Tis, that," she said promptly, and squeezed through the narrow opening Karamjit had left in the gate.

But she had not gone four paces when two rough-looking men in shabby tweed jackets blocked her path. "You Nan Killian?" said one hoarsely. Then when Nan stared at him blankly, added, "Aggie Killian's girl?"

The answer was surprised out of her; she hadn't been expecting such a confrontation, and she hadn't yet managed to sort herself out. "Ye—es," she said slowly.

"Good," the first man grunted. "Yer Ma sent us; she's gone t' a new place, an' she wants us t'show y' the way."

Now, several thoughts flew through Nan's mind at that moment. The first was, that as they were paid up on the rent through the end of the week, she could not imagine Aggie ever vacating before the time was up. The second was, that even if Aggie *had* set up somewhere else, she would never have sent a pair of strangers to find Nan.

And third was that Aggie had turned to a more potent intoxicant than gin—which meant she would need a deal more money. And Aggie had only one thing left to sell.

Nan.

Their minds were such a roil that she couldn't "hear" any distinct thoughts, but it was obvious that they meant her no good.

"Wait a minnit—" Nan said, her voice trembling a little as she backed away from the two men, edging around them to get to the street. "Did'jer say Aggie *Killian's* gel? Me Ma ain't called Killian, yer got th' wrong gel—"

It was at that moment that one of the men lunged for her with a curse. He had his hands nearly on her, and would have gotten her, too, except for one bit of interference.

Sarah came shooting out of the gate like a little bullet. She body-slammed the fellow, going into the back of his knees and knocking him right off his feet. She danced out of the way as he fell in the nick of time, ran to Nan, and caught her hand, tugging her towards the street. "Run!" she commanded imperiously, and Nan ran.

The two of them scrabbled through the dark alleys and twisted streets without any idea where they were, only that they had to shake off their pursuers. Unfortunately, the time that Nan would have put into learning her new neighborhood like the back of her grimy little hand had been put into talking with Sarah, and before too long, even Nan was lost in the maze of dark, fetid streets. Then their luck ran out altogether, and they found themselves staring at the blank wall of a building, in a dead-end cul-de-sac.

They whirled around, hoping to escape before they were trapped, but it was already too late. The bulky silhouettes of the two men loomed against the fading light at the end of the street.

"Oo's yer friend, ducky?" the first man purred. "Think she'd loik t'come with?"

To Nan's astonishment, Sarah stood straight and tall, and even stepped forward a pace. "I think you ought to go away and leave us alone," she said clearly. "You're going to find yourselves in a lot of trouble."

The talkative man laughed. "Them's big words from such a little gel," he mocked. "We ain't leavin' wi'out we collect what's ours, an' a bit more fer th' trouble yer caused."

Nan was petrified with fear, shaking in every limb, as Sarah stepped back, putting her back to the damp wall. As the first man touched Sarah's arm, she shrieked out a single word.

"Gray!"

As Sarah cried out the name of her pet, Nan let loose a wordless prayer for something, *anything*, to come to their rescue.

Something screamed behind the man; startled and distracted for a moment, he turned. For a moment, a fluttering shape obscured his face, and *he* screamed in pain. He shook his head, violently.

"Get it off!" he screamed at his partner. "*Get it off!*"

"Get what off?" the man said, bewildered. "There ain't nothin' there!"

The man clawed frantically at the front of his face, but whatever had attacked him had vanished without a trace. But not before leading more substantial help to the rescue.

Out of the dusk and the first wisps of fog, Karamjit and another swarthy man ran on noiseless feet. In their hands were cudgels which they used to good purpose on the two who opposed them. Nor did they waste any effort, clubbing the two senseless with a remarkable economy of motion.

Then, without a single word, each of the men scooped up a girl in his arms, and bore them back to the school. At that point, finding herself safe in the arms of an unlooked-for rescuer, Nan felt secure enough to break down into hysterical tears.

Nor was that the end of it; she found herself bundled up into the sacred precincts of the school itself, plunged into the first hot bath of her life, wrapped in a clean flannel gown, and put into a real bed. Sarah was in a similar bed beside her. As she sat there, numb, a plain-looking woman with beautiful eyes came and sat down on the foot of Sarah's bed, and looked from one to the other of them.

"Well," the lady said at last, "what have you two to say for yourselves?"

Nan couldn't manage anything, but that was all right, since Sarah wasn't about to let her get in a word anyway. The child jabbered like a monkey, a confused speech about Nan's mother, the men she'd sold Nan to, the virtue of Charity, the timely appearance of Gray, and a great deal more besides. The lady listened and nodded, and when Sarah ran down at last, she turned to Nan.

"I believe Sarah is right in one thing," she said gravely. "I believe we will have to keep you. Now, both of you—sleep."

And to Nan's surprise, she fell asleep immediately.

But that was not the end to the story. A month later, Sarah's mother arrived, with Gray in a cage. Nan had, by then, found a place where she could listen to what went on in the best parlor without being found, and she glued her ear to the crack in the pantry to listen when Sarah was taken into that hallowed room.

"—found Gray senseless beside her perch," Sarah's mother was saying. "I thought it was a fit, but the Shaman swore that Sarah was in trouble and the bird had gone to help. Gray awoke none the worse, and I would have thought nothing more of the incident, until your message arrived."

"And so you came, very wisely, bringing this remarkable bird." Mem'sab made chirping noises at the bird, and an odd little voice said, "Hello, bright eyes!"

Mem'sab chuckled. "How much of strangeness are you prepared to believe in, my dear?" she asked gently. "Would you believe me if I told you that I have seen this bird once before—fluttering and pecking at my window, then leading my men to rescue your child?"

"I can only answer with Hamlet," Sarah's mother said after a pause. "That there are more things in heaven and earth than I suspected."

"Good," Mem'sab replied decidedly. "Then I take it you are not here to remove Sarah from our midst."

"No," came the soft reply. "I came only to see that Sarah was well, and to ask if you would permit her pet to be with her."

"Gladly," Mem'sab said. "Though I might question which of the two was the pet!"

"Clever bird!" said Gray.

*I enjoyed the characters in Gray so much that I decided to write another novella for this anthology using the same characters. You might think of Mem'sab Harton as the Victorian version of Diana Tregarde, sans vampire boyfriend. I'm toying with the idea of doing an entire book about the Harton School, Nan, Sarah, and Gray, and I'd be interested to hear if anyone besides parrot-lovers would want to read it.*

# Gray's Ghost

## Mercedes Lackey

When Victoria was the Queen of England, there was a small, unprepossessing school for the children of expatriate Englishmen that had quite an interesting reputation in the shoddy Whitechapel neighborhood on which it bordered, a reputation that kept the students safer than all the bobbies in London.

Once, a young, impoverished beggar-girl named Nan Killian had obtained leftovers at the back gate, and most of the other waifs and gutterrats of the neighborhood shunned the place, though they gladly shared in Nan's bounty when she dared the gate and its guardian.

But now another child picked up food at the back gate of the Harton School For Boys and Girls on the edge of Whitechapel in London, not Nan Killian. Children no longer shunned the back gate of the school, although they treated its inhabitants with extreme caution. Adults—particularly the criminal, disreputable criminals who preyed on children—treated the place and its inhabitants with a great deal more than mere caution. Word had gotten around that two child-pimps had tried to take one of the pupils, and had been found with arms and legs broken, beaten senseless. Word had followed that anyone who threatened another child protected by the school would be found dead—*if* he was found at all.

The two tall, swarthy "black fellas" who served as the school's guards were rumored to have strange powers, or to be members of the *thugee* cult, or worse. It was safer just to pretend the school didn't exist and go about one's unsavory business elsewhere.

Nan Killian was no longer a child of the streets; she was now a pupil at the school herself, a transmutation that astonished her every morning when she awoke. To find herself in a neat little dormitory room, papered with roses, curtained in gingham, made her often feel as if she was dreaming. To then rise with the other girls, dress in clean, fresh clothing, and go off to lessons in the hitherto unreachable realms of reading and writing was more than she had ever dared dream of.

Her best friend was still Sarah, the little girl from Africa who had brought her that first basket of leftovers. But now she slept in the next bed over from Sarah's, and they shared many late-night giggles and confidences, instead of leftover tea-bread.

Nan also had a job; she had discovered, somewhat to her own bemusement, that the littlest children instinctively trusted her and would obey her when they obeyed no one else. So Nan "paid" for her tutoring and keep by helping Nadra or "Ayah," as they all called her, the babies' nurse. Nadra was from India, as were most of the servants, from the formidable guards, the Sikh Karamjit and the Gurkha Selim, to the cook, Maya. Mrs. Helen Harton—or Mem'sab, as everyone called her—and her husband had once been expatriates in India themselves. Master Harton—called, with ultimate respect, Sahib Harton—now worked as an advisor to an import firm; his service in India had left him with a small pension, and a permanent limp. When he and his wife had returned and had learned quite by accident of the terrible conditions children returned to England often lived in, they had resolved that the children of their friends back in the Punjab, at least, would not have that terrible knowledge thrust upon them.

Here the children sent away in bewilderment by anxious parents fearing that they would sicken in the hot foreign lands found, not a cold and alien place with nothing they recognized, but the familiar sounds of Hindustani, the comfort and coddling of a native nanny, and the familiar curries and rice to eat. Their new home, if a little shabby, held furniture made familiar from their years in the bungalows. But most of all, they were not told coldly to "be a man" or "stop being a crybaby"—for here they found friendly shoulders to weep out their homesickness on. If there were no French Masters here, there *was* a great deal of love and care; if the furniture was unfashionable and shabby, the children were well-fed and rosy.

It never ceased to amaze Nan that more parents didn't send their children to the Harton School, but some folks mistakenly trusted relatives to take better care of their precious ones than strangers, and some thought that a school owned and operated by someone with a lofty reputation or a title was a wiser choice for a boy-child who would likely join the Civil Service when he came of age. And as for the girls, there would always be those who felt that lessons by French dancing masters and language teachers, lessons on the harp and in water-color painting, were more valuable than a sound education in the same basics given to a boy.

Sometimes these parents learned their lessons the hard way.

"Ready for m'lesson, Mem'sab," Nan called into the second-best parlor, which was Mem'sab's private domain. It was commonly understood that sometimes Mem'sab had to do odd things— "Important things that we don't need to know about," Sarah said wisely—and she might have to do them at a moment's notice. So it was better to announce oneself at the door before venturing over the threshold.

But today Mem'sab was only reading a book, and looked up at Nan with a smile that transformed her plain face and made her eyes bright and beautiful.

By now Nan had seen plenty of ladies who dressed in finer stuffs than Mem'sab's simple Artistic gown of common stuffs, made bright with embroidery courtesy of Maya. Nan had seen ladies who were acknowledged Beauties like Mrs. Lillie Langtry, ladies who obviously spent many hours in the hands of their dressers and hairdressers rather than pulling their hair up into a simple chignon from which little curling strands of brown-gold were always escaping. Mem'sab's jewelry was not of diamonds and gold, but odd, heavy pieces in silver and semi-precious gems. But in Nan's eyes, not one of those ladies was worth wasting a single glance upon.

Then again, Nan *was* a little prejudiced.

"Come in, Nan," the headmistress said, patting the flowered sofa beside her invitingly. "You're doing much better already, you know. You have a quick ear."

"Thenkee, Mem'sab," Nan replied, flushing with pleasure. She, like any of the servants, would gladly have laid down her life for Mem'sab Harton; they all worshipped her blatantly, and a word of praise from their idol was worth more than a pocketful of sovereigns. Nan sat gingerly down on the chintz-covered sofa and smoothed her clean pinafore with an unconscious gesture of pride.

Mem'sab took a book of etiquette from the table beside her, and opened it, looking at Nan expectantly. "Go ahead, dear."

"Good morning, ma'am. How do you do? I am quite well. I trust your family is fine," Nan began, and waited for Mem'sab's response, which would be her cue for the next polite phrase. The point here was not that Nan needed to learn manners and mannerly speech, but that she needed to *lose* the dreadful cadence of the streets which would doom her to poverty forever, quite literally. Nan spoke the commonplace phrases slowly and with great care, as much care as Sarah took over her French. An accurate analogy, since the King's English, as spoken by the middle and upper classes, was nearly as much a foreign language to Nan as French and Latin were to Sarah.

She had gotten the knack of it by thinking of it exactly as a foreign language, once Mem'sab had proven to her how much better others would treat her if she didn't speak like a guttersnipe. She was still fluent in the language of the streets, and often went out with Karamjit as a translator when he went on errands that took him into the slums or Chinatown. But gradually her tongue became accustomed to the new cadences, and her habitual speech marked her less as "untouchable."

"Beautifully done," Mem'sab said warmly, when Nan finished her recitation. "Your new assignment will be to pick a poem and recite it to me, properly spoken, and memorized."

"I think I'd loike—*like*—to do one uv Mr. Kipling's, Mem'sab," Nan said shyly.

Mem'sab laughed. "I hope you aren't thinking of 'Gunga Din,' you naughty girl!" the woman mock-chided. "It had better be one from the *Jungle Book,* or *Puck of Pook's Hill,* not something written in Cockney dialect!"

"Yes, Mem'sab, I mean, no, Mem'sab," Nan replied quickly. "I'll pick a right 'un. Mebbe the lullaby for the White Seal?" Ever since discovering Rudyard Kipling's stories, Nan had been completely enthralled; Mem'sab often read them to the children as a go-to-bed treat, for the stories often evoked memories of India for the children sent away.

"That will do very well. Are you ready for the other lesson?" Mem'sab asked, so casually that no one but Nan would have known that the "other lesson" was one not taught in any other school in this part of the world.

"I—think so." Nan got up and closed the parlor door, signaling to all the world that she and Mem'sab were not to be disturbed unless someone was dying or the house was burning down.

For the next half-hour, Mem'sab turned over cards, and Nan called out the next card before she turned it over. When the last of the fifty-two lay in the face-up pile before her, Nan waited expectantly for the results.

"Not at all bad; you had almost half of them, and all the colors right," Mem'sab said with content. Nan was disappointed; she knew that Mem'sab could call out all fifty-two without an error, though Sarah could only get the colors correctly.

"Sahib brought me some things from the warehouse for you to try your 'feeling' on," Mem'sab continued. "I truly think that is where you true Gifts lie, dear."

Nan sighed mournfully. "But knowin' the cards would be a lot more *useful,*" she complained.

"What, so you can grow up to cheat foolish young men out of their inheritances?" Now Mem'sab actually laughed out loud. "Try it, dear, and the Gift will desert you at the time you need it most! No, be content with what you have and learn to use it wisely, to help yourself and others."

"But card-sharpin' *would* help me, an' I could use takin's to help others," Nan couldn't resist protesting, but she held out her hand for the first object anyway.

It was a carved beetle; very interesting, Nan thought, as she waited to "feel" what it would tell her. It felt like pottery or stone, and it was of a turquoise-blue, shaded with pale brown. "It's old," she said finally. Then, "*Really* old. Old as—Methusalum! It was made for an important man, but not a king or anything."

She tried for more, but couldn't sense anything else. "That's all," she said, and handed it back to Mem'sab.

"Now this." The carved beetle that Mem'sab gave her was, for all intents and purposes, identical to the one she'd just held, but immediately Nan sensed the difference.

"Piff! That 'un's new!" She also felt something else, something of *intent,* a sensation she readily identified since it was one of the driving forces behind commerce in Whitechapel. "Feller as made it figgers he's put one over on somebody."

"Excellent, dear!" Mem'sab nodded. "They are both *scarabs,* a kind of good-luck carving found with mummies—which are, indeed, often as old as Methuselah. The first one I knew was real, as I helped unwrap the mummy myself. The second, however, was from a shipment that Sahib suspected were fakes."

Nan nodded, interested to learn that this Gift of hers had some practical application after all. "So could be I could tell people when they been gammoned?"

"Very likely, and quite likely that they would pay you for the knowledge, as long as they don't think that *you* are trying to fool them as well. Here, try this." The next object placed in Nan's hand was a bit of jewelry, a simple silver brooch with "gems" of cut iron. Nan dropped it as soon as it touched her hand, overwhelmed by fear and horror.

"Lummy!" she cried, without thinking. "He *killed* her!"

Who "they" were, she had no sense of; that would require more contact, which she did *not* want to have. But Mem'sab didn't seem at all surprised; she just shook her head very sadly and put the brooch back in a little box which she closed without a word.

She held out a child's locket on a worn ribbon. "Don't be afraid, Nan," she coaxed, when Nan was reluctant to accept it. "This one isn't bad, I promise you."

Nan took the locket gingerly, but broke out into a smile when she got a feeling of warmth, contentment, and happiness. She waited for other images to come, and sensed a tired, but exceedingly happy woman, a proud man, and one—no, *two* strong and lively mites with the woman.

Slyly, Nan glanced up at her mentor. "She's 'ad twins, 'asn't she?" Nan asked. "When was it?"

"I just got the letter and the locket today, but it was about two months ago," Mem'sab replied. "The lady is my best friend's daughter, who was given that locket by her mother for luck just before the birth of her children. She sent it to me to have it duplicated, as she would like to present one to each little girl."

"I'd 'ave it taken apart, an' put half of th' old 'un with half of the new 'un," Nan suggested, and Mem'sab brightened at the idea.

"An excellent idea, and I will do just that. Now, dear, are you feeling tired? Have you a headache? We've gone on longer than we did at your last lesson."

Nan nodded, quite ready to admit to both.

Mem'sab gave her still-thin shoulders a little hug, and sent her off to her afternoon lessons.

Figuring came harder to Nan than reading; she'd already had some letters before she had arrived, enough to spell out the signs on shops and stalls and the like and make out a word here and there on a discarded broadsheet. When the full mystery of letters had been disclosed to her, mastery had come as naturally as breathing, and she was already able to read her beloved Kipling stories with minimal prompting. But numbers were a mystery arcane, and she struggled with the youngest of the children to comprehend what they meant. Anything past one hundred baffled her for the moment, and Sarah did her best to help her friend.

After arithmetic came geography, but for a child to whom Kensington Palace was the end of the universe, it was harder to believe in the existence of Arabia than of Fairyland, and Heaven was quite as real and solid as South America, for she reckoned that she had an equal chance of seeing either. As for how all those odd names and shapes fit together . . . well!

History came easier, although she didn't yet grasp that it was as real as yesterday, for to Nan it was just a chain of linking stories. Perhaps that was why she loved the Kipling stories so much, for she often felt as out-of-place as Mowgli when the human tribe tried to reclaim him.

At the end of lessons Nan usually went to help Nadra in the nursery; the children there, ranging in age from two to five, were a handful when it came to getting them bathed and put to bed. They tried to put off bedtime as long as possible; there were a half-dozen of them, which was just enough that when Nadra had finally gotten two of them into a bathtub, the other four had escaped, and were running about the nursery like dripping, naked apes, screaming joyfully at their escape.

But tonight, Karamjit came for Nan and Sarah as soon as the history lesson was over, summoning them with a look and a gesture. As always, the African parrot Gray sat on Sarah's shoulder; she was so well-behaved, even to the point of being housebroken, that she was allowed to be with her from morning to night. The handsome gray parrot with the bright red tail had adapted very well to this new sort of jungle when Sarah's mother brought her to her daughter; Sarah was very careful to keep her warm and out of drafts, and she ate virtually the same food that she did. Mem'sab seemed to understand the kind of diet that let her thrive; she allowed her only a little of the chicken and beef, and made certain that she filled up on carrots and other vegetables before she got any of the curried rice she loved so much. In fact, she often pointed to Gray as an example to the other children who would rather have had sweets than green stuffs, telling them that Gray was smarter than they were, for *she* knew what would make her grow big and strong. Being unfavorably compared to a bird often made the difference with the little boys in particular, who were behaving better at table since the parrot came to live at the school.

So Gray came along when Karamjit brought them to the door of Mem'sab's parlor, cautioning them to wait quietly until Mem'sab called them.

"What do you suppose can be going on?" Sarah asked curiously, while Gray turned her head to look at Nan with her penetrating pale-yellow eyes.

Nan shushed her, pressing her ear to the keyhole to see what she could hear. "There's another lady in there with Mem'sab, and she sounds sad," Nan said at last.

Gray cocked her head to one side, then turned his head upside down as she sometimes did when something puzzled her. "Hurt," she said quietly, and made a little sound like someone crying.

Nan had long since gotten used to the fact that Gray noticed everything that went on around her and occasionally commented on it like a human person. If the wolves in the *Jungle Book* could think and talk, she reasoned, why not a parrot? She accepted Gray's abilities as casually as Sarah, who had raised her herself and had no doubt of the intelligence of her feathered friend.

Had either of them acquired the "wisdom" of their elders, they might have been surprised that Mem'sab accepted those abilities too.

Nan jumped back as footsteps warned her that the visitor had risen and was coming towards the door; she and Sarah pressed themselves back against the wall as the strange woman passed them, her face hidden behind a veil. She took no notice of the children, but turned back to Mem'sab.

"Katherine, I believe going to this woman is a grave mistake on your part," Mem'sab told her quietly. "You and I have been friends since we were in school together; you know that I would never advise you against anything you felt so strongly about unless I thought you might be harmed by it. This woman does you no good."

The woman shook her head. "How could I be harmed by it?" she replied, her voice trembling. "What *possible* ill could come of this?"

"A very great deal, I fear," Mem'sab, her expression some combination of concern and other emotions that Nan couldn't read.

Impulsively, the woman reached out for Mem'sab's hand. "Then come *with* me!" she cried. "If this woman cannot convince *you* that she is genuine, and that she provides me with what I need more than breath, then I will not see her again."

Mem'sab's eyes looked keenly into her friend's, easily defeating the concealment of the veil about her features. "You are willing to risk her unmasking as a fraud, and the pain for you that will follow?"

"I am certain enough of her that I know that you will be convinced, even against your will," the woman replied with certainty.

Mem'sab nodded. "Very well, then. You and I—and these two girls—will see her together."

Only now did the woman notice Sarah and Nan, and her brief glance dismissed them as unimportant. "I see no reason why you wish to have children along, but if you can guarantee they will behave, and that is what it takes you to be convinced to see Madame Varonsky, then so be it. I will have an invitation sent to you for the next seance."

Mem'sab smiled, and patted her friend's hand. "Sometimes children see things more clearly than we adults do," was all she replied. "I will be waiting for that invitation."

The woman squeezed Mem'sab's hand, then turned and left, ushered out by one of the native servants. Mem'sab gestured to the two girls to precede her into the parlor, and shut the door behind them.

"What did you think of the lady, Nan?" asked their teacher, as the two children took their places side-by-side, on the loveseat they generally shared when they were in the parlor together.

Nan assessed the woman as would any street-child; economics came first. "She's in mournin' an' she's gentry," Nan replied automatically. "Silk gowns fer mournin' is somethin' only gentry kin afford. I 'spect she's easy t' gammon, too; paid no attention t'us, an' I was near enough t' get me hand into 'er purse an' her never knowin' till she was home. An' she didn' ask fer a cab t' be brung, so's I reckon she keeps 'er carriage. That's not jest gentry, tha's *quality*."

"Right on all counts, my dear," Mem'sab said, a bit grimly. "Katherine has no more sense than one of the babies, and never had. Her parents didn't spoil her, but they never saw any reason to educate her in practical matters. They counted on her finding a husband who would do all her thinking for her, and as a consequence, she is pliant to any hand that offers mastery. She married into money; her husband has a very high position in the Colonial Government. Nothing but the best school would do for her boy, and a spoiled little lad he was, too."

Gray suddenly began coughing, most realistically, a series of terrible, racking coughs, and Sarah turned her head to look into her eyes. Then she turned back to Mem'sab. "He's dead, isn't he?" the child said, quite matter-of-factly. "He got sick, and died. That's who she's in mourning for."

"Quite right, and as Gray showed us, he caught pneumonia." Mem'sab looked grim. "Poor food, icy rooms, and barbaric treatment—" She threw up her hands, and shook her head. "There's no reason to go on; at least Katherine has decided to trust her twins to us instead of the school her husband wanted. She'll bring them to Nadra tomorrow, Nan, and they'll probably be terrified, so I'm counting on you to help Nadra soothe them."

Nan could well imagine that they would be terrified; not only were they being left with strangers, but they would know, at least dimly, that their brother had come away to school and died. They would be certain that the same was about to happen to them.

"That, however, is not why I sent for you," Mem'sab continued. "Katherine is seeing a medium; do either of you know what that is?"

Sarah and Nan shook their heads, but Gray made a rude noise. Sarah looked shocked, but Nan giggled and Mem'sab laughed.

"I am afraid that Gray is correct in her opinions, for the most part," the woman told them. "A *medium* is a person who claims to speak with the dead, and help the souls of the dead speak to the living." Her mouth compressed, and Nan sensed her carefully controlled anger. "All this is accomplished for a very fine fee, I might add."

"Ho! Like them gypsy palm-readers, an' the conjure-men!" Nan exclaimed in recognition. "Aye, there's a mort'a gammon there, and that's sure. You reckon this lady's been gammoned, then?"

"Yes I do, and I would like you two—*three*—" she amended, with a penetrating look at Gray, "—to help me prove it. Nan, if there is trickery afoot, do you think you could catch it?"

Nan had no doubt. "I bet I could," she said. "Can't be harder'n keepin' a hand out uv yer pocket—or grabbin' the wrist once it's in."

"Good girl—you *must* remember to speak properly, and only when you're spoken to, though," Mem'sab warned her. "If this so-called medium thinks you are anything but a gently reared child, she might find an excuse to dismiss the seance." She turned to Sarah. "Now, if by some incredible chance this woman *is* genuine, could you and Gray tell?"

Sarah's head bobbed so hard her curls tumbled into her eyes. "Yes, Mem'sab," she said, with as much confidence as Nan. "M'luko, the Medicine Man that gave me Gray, said that Gray could tell when the spirits were there, and someday I might, too."

"Did he, now?" Mem'sab gave her a curious look. "How interesting! Well, if Gray can tell us if there are spirits or not, that will be quite useful enough for our purposes. Are either of you afraid to go with me? I expect the invitation will come quite soon." Again, Mem'sab had that grim look. "Katherine is too choice a fish to be allowed to swim free for long; the Madame will want to keep her under her control by 'consulting' with her as often as possible."

Sarah looked to Nan for guidance, and Nan thought that her friend might be a little fearful, despite her brave words. But Nan herself only laughed. "I ain't afraid of nobody's sham ghost," she said, curling her lip scornfully. "An' I ain't sure I'd be afraid uv a *real* one."

"Wisely said, Nan; spirits can only harm us as much as we permit them to." Nan thought that Mem'sab looked relieved, like maybe she hadn't wanted to count on their help until she actually got it. "Thank you, both of you." She reached out and took their hands, giving them a squeeze that said a great deal without words. "Now, both of you get back to whatever it was that I took you from. I will let you know in plenty of time when our excursion will be."

It was past the babies' bedtime, so Sarah and Nan went together to beg Maya for their delayed tea, and carried the tray themselves up to the now-deserted nursery. They set out the tea-things on one of the little tables, feeling a mutual need to discuss Mem'sab's strange proposition.

Gray had her "tea," too; a little bowl of curried rice, carrots, and beans. They set it down on the table and Gray climbed carefully down from Sarah's shoulder to the table-top, where she selected a bean and ate it neatly, holding it in one claw while she took small bites, watching them both.

"Do you think there might be real ghosts?" Sarah asked immediately, shivering a little. "I mean, what if this lady can bring real ghosts up?"

Gray and Nan made the same rude noise at the same time; it was easy to tell where Gray had learned it. "Garn!" Nan said scornfully. "Reckon that Mem'sab only ast if you could tell as an outside bet. *But* the livin' people might be the ones as is dangerous." She ate a bite of bread and butter thoughtfully. "I dunno as Mem'sab's thought that far, but that Missus Katherine's a right easy mark, an' a fat 'un, too. People as is willin' t' gammon the gentry *might* not be real happy about bein' found out."

Sarah nodded. "Should we tell Karamjit?" she asked, showing a great deal more common sense than she would have before Nan came into her life. "Mem'sab's thinking hard about her friend, but she might not think a bit about herself."

"Aye, an' Selim an' mebbe Sahib, too." Nan was a little dubious about that, having only seen the lordly Sahib from a distance.

"I'll ask Selim to tell Sahib, if you'll talk to Karamjit," Sarah said, knowing the surest route to the master from her knowledge of the school and its inhabitants. "But tell me what to look for! Three sets of eyes are better than two."

"Fust thing, whatever they *want* you t' look at is gonna be what makes a fuss—noises or voices or whatever," Nan said after a moment of thought. "I dunno how this *medium* stuff is gonna work, but that's what happens when a purse gets nicked. You gotta get the mark's attention, so he won't be thinkin' of his pocket. So whatever they *want* us to look at, we look away from. That's the main thing. Mebbe Mem'sab can tell us what these things is s'pposed to be like—if I know what's t' happen, I kin guess what tricks they're like t' pull." She finished her bread and butter, and began her own curry; she'd quickly acquired a taste for the spicy Indian dishes that the other children loved. "If there ain't ghosts, I bet they got somebody dressed up t' *look* like one." She grinned slyly at Gray. "An' I betcha a good pinch or a bite would make 'im yell proper!"

"And you couldn't hurt a real ghost with a pinch." Sarah nodded. "I suppose we're just going to have to watch and wait, and see what we can do."

Nan, as always, ate as a street-child would, although her manners had improved considerably since coming to the school; she inhaled her food rapidly, so that no one would have a chance to take it from her. She was already finished, although Sarah hadn't eaten more than half of her tea. She put her plates aside on the tray, and propped her head up on her hands with her elbows on the table. "We got to talk to Karamjit an' Selim, that's the main thing," she said, thinking out loud. "They might know what we should do."

"Selim will come home with Sahib," Sarah answered, "but Karamjit is probably leaving the basket at the back gate right now, and if you run, you can catch him alone."

Taking that as her hint, for Sarah had a way of knowing where most people were at any given time, Nan jumped to her feet and ran out of the nursery and down the back stairs, flying through the kitchen, much to the amusement of the cook, Maya. She burst through the kitchen door, and ran down the path to the back gate, so quickly she hardly felt the cold at all, though she had run outside without a coat. Mustafa swept the garden paths free of snow every day, but so soon after Boxing Day there were mounds of the stuff on either side of the path, snow with a faint tinge of gray from the soot that plagued London in almost every weather.

Nan saw the Sikh, Karamjit, soon enough to avoid bouncing off his legs. The tall, dark, immensely dignified man was bundled up to the eyes in a heavy quilted coat and two mufflers, his head wrapped in a dark brown turban. Nan no longer feared him, though she respected him as only a street-child who has seen a superior fighter in action could. "Karamjit!" she called, as she slowed her headlong pace. "I need t' talk wi' ye!"

There was an amused glint in the Sikh's dark eyes, though only much association with him allowed Nan to see it. "And what does Missy Nan wish to speak of that she comes racing out into the cold like the wind from the mountains?"

"Mem'sab ast us t' help her with somethin'—there's this lady as is a *meedeeyum* that she thinks is gammonin' her friend. We—tha's Sarah an' Gray an' me—we says a'course, but—" Here Nan stopped, because she wasn't entirely certain how to tell an adult that she thought another adult didn't know what she was getting herself into. "I just got a bad feelin'," she ended, lamely.

But Karamjit did not belittle her concerns, nor did he chide her. Instead, his eyes grew even darker, and he nodded. "Come inside, where it is warm," he said. "I wish you to tell me more."

He sat her down at the kitchen table, and gravely and respectfully asked Maya to serve them both tea. He took his with neither sugar nor cream, but saw to it that Nan's was heavily sweetened and at least half milk. "Now," he said. after she had warmed herself with the first sip, "tell me all."

Nan related everything that had happened from the time he came to take both of them to the parlor to when she had left Sarah to find him. He nodded from time to time, as he drank tea and unwound himself from his mufflers and coat.

"I believe this," he said when she had finished. "I believe that Mem'sab is a wise, good, and brave woman. I also believe that *she* does not think that helping her friend will mean any real danger. But the wise, the good, and the brave often do not think as the mean, the bad, and the cowardly do—the jackals that feed on the pain of others will turn to devour those who threaten their meal. And a man can die from the bite of a jackal as easily as that of a tiger."

"So you think my bad feelin' was right?" Nan's relief was total;

not that she didn't trust Mem'sab, but—Mem'sab didn't know the kind of creatures that Nan did.

"Indeed I do—but I believe that it would do no good to try to persuade Mem'sab that she should not try to help her friend." Karamjit smiled slightly, the barest lifting of the corners of his mouth. "Nevertheless, Sahib will know how best to protect her without insulting her great courage." He placed one of his long, brown hands on Nan's shoulder. "You may leave it in our hands, Missy Nan— though we may ask a thing or two of you, that we can do our duty with no harm to Mem'sab's own plans. For now, though, you may simply rely upon us."

"Thenkee, Karamjit," Nan sighed. He patted her shoulder, then unfolded his long legs and rose from his chair with a slight bow to Maya. Then he left the kitchen, allowing Nan to finish her tea and run back up to the nursery, to give Sarah and Gray the welcome news that they would not be the only ones concerned with the protection of Mem'sab from the consequences of her own generous nature.

Sahib took both Nan and Sarah aside just before bedtime, after Karamjit and Selim had been closeted with him for half an hour. "Can I ask you two to come to my study with me for a bit?" he asked quietly. He was often thought to be older than Mem'sab, by those who were deceived by the streaks of gray at each temple, the stiff way that he walked, and the odd expression in his eyes, which seemed to Nan to be the eyes of a man who had seen so much that nothing surprised him anymore. Nan had trusted him the moment that she set eyes on him, although she couldn't have said why.

"So long as Nadra don't fuss," Nan replied for both of them. Sahib smiled, his eyes crinkling at the corners.

"I have already made it right with Nadra," he promised. "Karamjit, Selim, and Mem'sab are waiting for us."

Nan felt better immediately, for she really hadn't wanted to go sneaking around behind Mem'sab's back. From the look that Sarah gave her, Nan reckoned that she felt the same.

"Thank you, sir," Sarah said politely. "We will do just as you say."

Very few of the children had ever been inside the sacred precincts of Sahib's office; the first thing that struck Nan was that it did *not* smell of tobacco, but of sandalwood and cinnamon. That surprised her; most of the men she knew smoked although their womenfolk disapproved of the habit, but evidently Sahib did not, not even in his own private space.

There was a tiger-skin on the carpet in front of the fire, the glass eyes in its head glinting cruelly in a manner unnerving and lifelike. Nan shuddered, and thought of Shere Khan, with his taste for man-cub. Had this been another terrible killer of the jungle? Did tigers leave vengeful ghosts?

Heavy, dark drapes of some indeterminate color shut out the cold night. Hanging on the walls, which had been papered with faded gold arabesque upon a ground of light brown, was a jumble of mementos from Sahib's life in India: crossed spears, curious daggers and swords, embroidered tapestries of strange characters twined with exotic flowers and birds, carved plaques of some heavy, dark wood inlaid with brass, bizarre masks that resembled nothing less than brightly painted demons. On the desk and adorning the shelves between the books were statues of half- and fully-naked gods and goddesses, more bits of carving in wood, stone, and ivory. Bookshelves built floor-to-ceiling held more books than Nan had known existed. Sahib took his place behind his desk, while Mem'sab perched boldly on the edge of it. Selim and Karamjit stood beside the fire like a pair of guardian statues themselves, and Sahib gestured to the children to take their places on the overstuffed chairs on either side of the fireplace. Nan waited tensely, wondering if Mem'sab was going to be angry because they went to others with their concerns. Although it had not fallen out so here, she was far more used to being in trouble over something she had done than in being encouraged for it, and the reflexes were still in place.

"Karamjit tells me that you four share some concern over my planned excursion to the medium, Nan," Mem'sab said, with a smile that told Nan she was *not* in trouble for her meddling, as she had feared. "They went first to Sahib, but as we never keep secrets from one another, he came to me. And I commend all four of you for your concern and caution, for after some discussion, I was forced to agree with it."

"And I would like to commend both of you, Nan, Sarah, for having the wisdom to go to an adult with your concerns," added Sahib, with a kindly nod to both of them that Nan had not expected in the least. "That shows great good sense, and please, continue to do so in the future."

"I thought—I was afeared—" Nan began, then blurted out all that she'd held in check. "Mem'sab is 'bout the smartest, goodest lady there is, but she don't *know* bad people! Me, I know! I seed 'em, an' I figgered that they weren't gonna lay down an' lose their fat mark without a fight!"

"And very wise you were to remind us of that," Sahib said gravely. "I pointed out to Mem'sab that we have no way of knowing *where* this medium is from, and she is just as likely to be a criminal as a lady—more so, in fact. Just because she speaks, acts, and dresses like a lady, and seeks her clients from among the gentry, means nothing; she could easily have a crew of thugs as her accomplices."

"As you say, Sahib," Karamjit said gravely. "For, as it is said, it is a short step from a deception to a lie, from a lie to a cheat, from a cheat to a theft, and from a theft to a murder."

Mem'sab blushed. "I will admit that I was very angry with you at first, but when my anger cooled, it was clear that your reasoning was sound. And after all, am I some Gothic heroine to go wide-eyed into the villain's lair, never suspecting trouble? So, we are here to plan what we *all* shall do to free Katherine of her dangerous obsession."

"Me, I needta know what this see-ants is gonna be like, Mem'sab," Nan put in, sitting on the edge of the chair tensely. "What sorta things happens?"

"Generally, the participants are brought into a room that has a round table with chairs circling it." Mem'sab spoke directly to Nan as if to an adult, which gave Nan a rather pleasant, if shivery, feeling. "The table often has objects upon it that the spirits will supposedly move; often a bell, a tambourine and a megaphone are among them, though why spirits would feel the need to play upon a tambourine when they never had that urge in life is quite beyond me!"

She laughed, as did Sahib; the girls giggled nervously.

"At any rate, the participants are asked to sit down and hold hands. Often the medium is tied to the chair; her hands are secured to the arms, and her feet to the legs." Nan noticed that Mem'sab used the word "legs" rather than the mannerly "limbs," and thought the better of her for that. "The lights are brought down, and the seance begins. Most often objects are moved, including the table, the tambourine is played, the bell is rung, all as a sign that the spirits have arrived. The spirits most often speak by means of raps on the table, but Katherine tells me that the spirit of her little boy spoke directly, through the floating megaphone. Sometimes a spirit will actually appear; in this case, it was just a glowing face of Katherine's son."

Nan thought that over for a moment. "Be simple 'nuff t' tilt the chair an' get yer legs free by slippin the rope down over the chair-feet," she observed. "An' all ye hev t' do is have chair arms as isn't glued t' *their* pegs, an' ye got yer arms free too. Be easy enough to make all kind uv things dance about when ye got arms free. Be easy 'nuff t' make th' table lift if's light enough, an' rap on it, too."

Sahib stared at her in astonishment. "I do believe that you are the most valuable addition to our household in a long time, young lady!" he said with delight that made Nan blush. "I would never have thought of any of that."

"I dunno how ye'd make summat glow, though," Nan admitted.

"Oh, *I* know that," Sarah said casually. "There's stuff that grows in rotten wood that makes a glow; some of the magic-men use it to frighten people at night. It grows in swamps, so it probably grows in England, too."

Karamjit grinned, his teeth very white in his dark face, and Selim nodded with pride. "What is it that the Black Robe's Book says, Sahib? 'Out of the mouths of babes comes wisdom'?"

Mem'sab nodded. "I should have told you more, earlier," she said ruefully. "Well, that's mended in time. Now we all know what to look for."

Gray clicked her beak several times, then exclaimed, "Ouch!"

"Gray is going to try to bite whatever comes near her," Sarah explained.

"I don't want her venturing off your arm," Mem'sab cautioned. "I won't chance her getting hurt." She turned to Sahib. "The chances are, the room we will be in will have very heavy curtains to prevent light from entering or escaping, so if you and our warriors are outside, you won't know what room we are in."

"Then I'd like one of you girls to exercise childish curiosity and go *immediately* to a window and look out," Sahib told them. "At least one of us will be where we can see both the front and the back of the house. Then if there is trouble, one of you signal us and we'll come to the rescue."

"Just like the shining knights you are, all three of you," Mem'sab said warmly, laying her hand over the one Sahib had on the desk. "I think that is as much of a plan as we can lay, since we really don't know what we will find in that house."

"It's enough, I suspect," Sahib replied. "It allows two of us to break into the house if necessary, while one goes for the police." He stroked his chin thoughtfully with his free hand. "Or better yet, I'll take a whistle; that will summon help in no time." He glanced up at Mem'sab. "What time did you say the invitation specified?"

"Seven," she replied promptly. "Well after dark, although Katherine tells me that *her* sessions are usually later, nearer midnight."

"The medium may anticipate some trouble from sleepy children," Sahib speculated. "But that's just a guess." He stood up, still holding his wife's hand, and she slid off her perch on the desk and turned to face them. "Ladies, gentlemen, I think we are as prepared as we can be for trouble. So let us get a good night's sleep, and hope that we will not find any."

Then Sahib did a surprising thing; he came around his desk, limping stiffly, and bent over Nan and took her hand. "Perhaps only I of all of us can realize how brave you were to confide your worry to an adult you have only just come to trust, Nan," he said, very softly, then grinned at her so impishly that she saw the little boy he must have been in the eyes of the mature man. "Ain't no doubt 'uv thet, missy. Yer a cunnin' moit, an' 'ad more blows then pats, Oi reckon," he continued in street cant, shocking the breath out of her. "I came up the same way you are now, dear, thanks to a very kind man with no son of his own. I want you to remember that to us here at this school, there is no such thing as a stupid question, nor will we dismiss *any* worry you have as trivial. Never fear to bring either to an adult."

He straightened up, as Mem'sab came to his side, nodding. "Now both of you try and get some sleep, for every warrior knows that sleep is more important than anything else before a battle."

*Ha,* Nan thought, as she and Sarah followed Karamjit out of the study. *There's gonna be trouble; I kin feel it, an' so can he. He didn' get that tiger by not havin' a nose fer trouble. But—I reckon the trouble's gonna have its hands full with him.*

The medium lived in a modest house just off one of the squares in the part of London that housed those clerks and the like with pretensions to a loftier address than their purses would allow, an area totally unfamiliar to Nan. The house itself had seen better days, though, as had most of the other homes on that dead-end street, and Nan suspected that it was rented. The houses had that peculiarly faded look that came when the owners of a house did not actually live there, and those who did had no reason to care for the property themselves, assuming that was the duty of the landlord.

Mem'sab had chosen her gown carefully, after discarding a walking-suit, a mourning-gown and veil, and a peculiar draped garment she called a *sari,* a souvenir of her time in India. The first, she thought, made her look untrusting, sharp, and suspicious; the second would not be believed had the medium done any research on the backgrounds of these new sitters; and the third smacked of mockery. She chose instead one of the plain, simple gowns she preferred, in the mode called "Artistic Reform"; not particularly stylish, but Nan thought it was a good choice. For one thing, she could move in it; it was looser than the highest mode, and did not require tight corseting. If Mem'sab needed to run, kick, or dodge, she could.

The girls followed her quietly, dressed in their starched pinafores and dark dresses, showing the best possible manners, with Gray tucked under Sarah's coat to stay warm until they got within doors.

It was quite dark as they mounted the steps to the house and rang the bell. It was answered by a sour-faced woman in a plain black dress, who ushered them into a sitting room and took their coats, with a startled glance at Gray as she popped her head out of the front of Sarah's jacket. She said nothing, however, and neither did Gray as she climbed to Sarah's shoulder.

The woman returned a moment later, but not before Nan had heard the faint sounds of surreptitious steps on the floor above them. She knew it had not been the sour woman, for she had clearly heard *those* steps going off to a closet and returning. If the seance room was on this floor, then, there was someone else above.

The sitting room had been decorated in a very odd style. The paintings on the wall were all either religious in nature, or extremely morbid, at least so far as Nan was concerned. There were pictures of women weeping over graves, of angels lifting away the soul of a dead child, of a woman throwing herself to her death over a cliff, of the spirits of three children hovering about a man and woman mourning over pictures held in their listless hands. There was even a picture of a girl crying over a dead bird lying in her hand.

Crystal globes on stands decorated the tables, along with bouquets of funereal lilies whose heavy, sweet scent dominated the chill room. The tables were all draped in fringed cloths of a deep scarlet. The hard, severe furniture was either of wood or upholstered in prickly horsehair. The two lamps had been lit before they entered the room, but their light, hampered as it was by heavy brocade lamp shades, cast more shadows than illumination.

They didn't have to wait long in that uncomfortable room, for the sour servant departed for a moment, then returned, and conducted them into the next room.

This, evidently, was only an antechamber to the room of mysteries; heavy draperies swathed all the walls, and there were straight-backed chairs set against them on all four walls. The lily-scent pervaded this room as well, mixed with another, that Nan recognized as the Hindu incense that Nadra often burned in her own devotions.

There was a single picture in this room, on the wall opposite the door, with a candle placed on a small table beneath it so as to illuminate it properly. This was a portrait in oils of a plump woman swathed in pale draperies, her hands clasped melodramatically before her breast, her eyes cast upwards. Smoke, presumably that of incense, swirled around her, with the suggestion of faces in it. Nan was no judge of art, but Mem'sab walked up to it and examined it with a critical eye.

"Neither good nor bad," she said, measuringly. "I would say it is either the work of an unknown professional or a talented amateur."

"A talented amateur," said the lady that Mem'sab had called "Katherine," as she too was ushered into the chamber. "My dear friend Lady Harrington painted it; it was she who introduced me to Madame Varonsky." Mem'sab turned to meet her, and Katherine glided across the floor to take her hand in greeting. "It is said to be a very speaking likeness," she continued. "I certainly find it so."

Nan studied the woman further, but saw nothing to change her original estimation. Katherine wore yet another mourning gown of expensive silk and mohair, embellished with jet beadwork and fringes that shivered with the slightest movement. A black hat with a full veil perched on her carefully coiffed curls, fair hair too dark to be called golden, but not precisely brown either. Her full lips trembled, even as they uttered words of polite conversation, her eyes threatened to fill at every moment, and Nan thought that her weak chin reflected an overly sentimental and vapid personality. It was an assessment that was confirmed by her conversation with Mem'sab, conversation that Nan ignored in favor of listening for other sounds. Over their heads, the floor creaked softly as someone moved to and fro, trying very hard to be quiet. There were also some odd scratching sounds that didn't sound like mice, and once, a dull thud, as of something heavy being set down a little too hard.

Something was going on up there, and the person doing it didn't want them to notice.

At length the incense-smell grew stronger, and the drapery on the wall to the right of the portrait parted, revealing a door, which opened as if by itself.

Taking that as their invitation, Katherine broke off her small talk to hurry eagerly into the sacred precincts; Mem'sab gestured to the girls to precede her, and followed on their heels. By previous arrangement, Nan and Sarah, rather than moving towards the circular table at which Madame Varonsky waited, went to the two walls likeliest to hold windows behind their heavy draperies before anyone could stop them.

It was Nan's luck to find a corner window overlooking the street, and she made sure that some light from the room within flashed to the watcher on the opposite side before she dropped the drapery.

"Come away from the windows, children," Mem'sab said in a voice that gently chided. Nan and Sarah immediately turned back to the room, and Nan assessed the foe.

Madame Varonsky's portraitist had flattered her; she was decidedly paler than she had been painted, with a complexion unpleasantly like wax. She wore similar draperies, garments which could have concealed anything. The smile on her thin lips did not reach her eyes, and she regarded the parrot on Sarah's shoulder with distinct unease.

"You did not warn me about the bird, Katherine," the woman said, her voice rather reedy.

"The bird will be no trouble, Madame Varonsky," Mem'sab soothed. "It is better behaved than a good many of my pupils."

"Your pupils—I am not altogether clear on why they were brought," Madame Varonsky replied, turning her sharp black eyes on Nan and Sarah.

"Nan is an orphan, and wants to learn what she can of her parents, since she never knew them," Mem'sab said smoothly. "And Sarah lost a little brother to an African fever."

"Ah." Madame Varonsky's suspicions diminished, and she gestured to the chairs around the table. "Please, all of you, do take your seats, and we can begin at once."

As with the antechamber, this room had walls swathed in draperies, which Nan decided could conceal an entire army if Madame Varonsky were so inclined. The only furnishings besides the seance table and chairs were a sinuous statue of a female completely enveloped in draperies on a draped table, with incense burning before it in a small charcoal brazier of brass and cast iron.

The table at which Nan took her place was very much as Mem'sab had described. A surreptitious bump as Nan took her seat on Mem'sab's left hand proved that it was quite light and easy to move; it would be possible to lift it with one hand with no difficulty at all. On the draped surface were some of the objects Mem'sab had described; a tambourine, a megaphone, a little handbell. There were three lit candles in a brass candlestick in the middle of the table, and some objects Nan had not expected—a fiddle and bow, a rattle, and a pair of handkerchiefs.

*This is where we're supposed to look,* Nan realized, as Sarah took her place on Mem'sab's right, next to Madame Varonsky, and Katherine on Nan's left, flanking the medium on the other side. She wished she could look *up*, as Gray was unashamedly doing, her head over to one side as one eye peered upwards at the ceiling above them.

"If you would follow dear Katherine's example, child," said Madame, as Katherine took one of the handkerchiefs and used it to tie the medium's wrist to the arm of her chair. She smiled crookedly. "This is to assure you that I am not employing any trickery." Sarah, behaving with absolute docility, did the same on the other side, but cast Nan a knowing look as she finished. Nan knew what that meant; Sarah had tried the arm of the chair and found it loose.

"Now, if you all will hold hands, we will beseech the spirits to attend on us." The medium turned her attention to Mem'sab as Katherine and Sarah stretched their arms across the table to touch hands, and the rest reached for the hands of their partners. "Pray do not be alarmed when the candles are extinguished; the spirits are shy of light, for they are so delicate that it can destroy them. They will put out the candles themselves."

For several long moments they sat in complete silence, as the incense smoke thickened and curled around. Then although there wasn't a single breath of moving air in the room, the candle-flames began to dim, one by one, and go out!

Nan felt the hair on the back of her neck rising, for this was a phenomena she could not account for—to distract herself, she looked up quickly at the ceiling just in time to see a faint line of light in the form of a square vanish.

She felt better immediately. However the medium had

extinguished the candles, it had to be a trick. If she had any real powers, she wouldn't need a trapdoor in the ceiling of her seance room. As she looked back down, she realized that the objects on the table were all glowing with a dim, greenish light.

"Spirits, are you with us?" Madame Varonsky called. Nan immediately felt the table begin to lift.

Katherine gasped; Mem'sab gave Nan's hand a squeeze; understanding immediately what she wanted, Nan let go of it. Now Mem'sab was free to act as she needed.

"The spirits are strong tonight," Madame murmured, as the table settled again. "Perhaps they will give us a further demonstration of their powers."

Exactly on cue, the tambourine rose into the air, shaking uncertainly; first the megaphone joined it, then the rattle, then the handbell, all floating in midair, or seeming to. But Nan was looking *up,* not at the objects, and saw a very dim square, too dim to be called *light,* above the table. A deeper shadow moved back and forth over that area, and Nan's lip curled with contempt. She had no difficulty in imagining how the objects were "levitating"; one by one, they'd been pulled up by wires or black strings, probably hooked by means of a fishing rod from the room above.

Now rapping began on the table, to further distract their attention. Madame began to ask questions.

"Is there a spirit here for Helen Harton?" she asked. One rap— that was a *no;* not surprising, since the medium probably wouldn't want to chance making a mistake with an adult. "Is there a spirit here for Katherine Boughmont?" Two raps—yes. "Is this the spirit of a child?" Two raps, and already Katherine had begun to weep softly. "Is it the spirit of her son, Edward?" Two raps plus the bell rang and the rattle and tambourine played, and Nan found herself feeling very sorry for the poor, silly woman.

"Are there other spirits here tonight?" Two raps. "Is there a spirit for the child Nan?" Two raps. "Is it her father?" One rap. "Her mother?" Two raps, and Nan had to control her temper, which flared at that moment. She knew very well that her mother was still alive, though at the rate she was going, she probably wouldn't be for long, what with the gin and the opium and the rest of her miserable life. But if she had been a young orphan, her parents dead in some foreign land like one or two of the other pupils, what would she not have given for the barest word from them, however illusory? Would she not have been willing to believe anything that sounded warm and kind?

There appeared to be no spirit for Sarah, which was just as well. Madame Varonsky was ready to pull out the next of her tricks, for the floating objects settled to the table again.

"My spirit-guide was known in life as the great Paganini, the master violinist," Madame Varonsky announced. "As music is the food of the soul, he will employ the same sweet music he made in life to bridge the gap between our world and the next. Listen, and he will play this instrument before us!"

Fiddle music appeared to come from the instrument on the table, although the bow did not actually move across the strings. Katherine gasped.

"Release the child's hand a moment and touch the violin, dear Katherine," the medium said, in a kind, but distant voice. Katherine evidently let go of Sarah's hand, since she still had hold of Nan's, and the shadow of her fingers rested for a moment on the neck of the fiddle.

"The strings!" she cried. "Helen, the strings are vibrating as they are played!"

If this was supposed to be some great, long-dead music master, Nan didn't think much of his ability. If she wasn't mistaken, the tune he was playing was the child's chant of "London Bridge Is Falling Down," but played very, very slowly, turning it into a solemn dirge.

"Touch the strings, Helen!" Katherine urged. "See for yourself!"

Nan felt Mem'sab lean forward, and another hand-shadow fell over the strings. "They are vibrating . . . ." she said, her voice suddenly uncertain.

The music ground to a halt before she took her hand away—and until this moment, Gray had been as silent as a stuffed bird on a lady's hat. Now she did something.

She began to sing. It was a very clever imitation of a fiddle, playing a jig-tune that a street-musician often played at the gate of the school, for the pennies the pupils would throw to him.

She quit almost immediately, but not before Mem'sab took her hand away from the strings, and Nan sensed that somehow Gray had given her the clue she needed to solve that particular trick.

But the medium must have thought that her special spirit was responsible for that scrap of jig-tune, for she didn't say or do anything.

Nan sensed that all of this was building to the main turn, and so it was.

Remembering belatedly that she should be keeping an eye on that suspicious square above. She glanced up just in time to see it disappear. As the medium began to moan and sigh, calling on Paganini, Nan kept her eye on the ceiling. Sure enough, the dim line of light appeared again, forming a grayish square. Then the lines of the square thickened, and Nan guessed that a square platform was being lowered from above.

Pungent incense smoke thickened about them, filling Nan's nose and stinging her eyes so that they watered, and she smothered a sneeze. It was hard to breathe, and there was something strangely, disquietingly familiar about the scent.

The medium's words, spoken in a harsh, accented voice, cut through the smoke. "I, the great Paganini, am here among you!"

Once again, Katherine gasped.

"Harken and be still! Lo, the spirits gather!"

Nan's eyes burned, and for a moment, she felt very dizzy; she thought that the soft glow in front of her was due to nothing more than eyestrain, but the glow strengthened, and she blinked in shock as two vague shapes took form amid the writhing smoke.

For a new brazier, belching forth such thick smoke that the coals were invisible, had "appeared" in the center of the table, just behind the candlestick. It was above this brazier that the glowing shapes hovered, and slowly took on an identifiable form. Nan felt dizzier, sick; the room seemed to turn slowly around her.

The faces of a young woman and a little boy looked vaguely out over Nan's head from the cloud of smoke. Katherine began to weep—

presumably she thought she recognized the child as her own. But the fact that the young woman looked *nothing* like Nan's mother (and in fact, looked quite a bit like the sketch in an advertisement for Bovril in the *Times*) woke Nan out of her mental haze.

And so did Gray.

She heard the flapping of wings as Gray plummeted to the floor. She sneezed urgently, and shouted aloud, "Bad air! Bad air!"

And *that* was the moment when she knew what it was that was so familiar in the incense smoke, and why she felt as tipsy as a sailor on shore leave.

"*Hashish!*" she choked, trying to shout, and not managing very well. She knew this scent; on the rare occasions when her mother could afford it—and before she'd turned to opium—she'd smoked it in preference to drinking. Nan could only think of one thing; that she *must* get fresh air in here before they all passed out!

She shoved her chair back and staggered up and out of it; it fell behind her with a clatter that seemed muffled in the smoke. She groped for the brazier as the two faces continued to stare, unmoved and unmoving, from the thick billows. Her hands felt like a pair of lead-filled mittens; she had to fight to stay upright as she swayed like a drunk. She didn't find it, but her hands closed on the cool, smooth surface of the crystal ball.

That was good enough; before the medium could stop her, she heaved up the heavy ball with a grunt of effort, and staggered to the window. She half-spun and flung the ball at the draperies hiding the unseen window; it hit the drapes and carried them into the glass, crashing through it, taking the drapery with it.

A gush of cold air, as fresh as air in London ever got, streamed in through the broken panes, as bedlam erupted in the room behind Nan.

She dropped to the floor, ignoring everything around her for the moment, as she breathed in the air tainted only with smog, waiting for her head to clear. Gray ran to her and huddled with her rather than joining her beloved mistress in the poisonous smoke.

Katherine shrieked in hysteria, there was a man as well as the medium shouting, and Mem'sab cursed all of them in some strange language. Gray gave a terrible shriek and half-ran, half-flew away. Nan fought her dizziness and disorientation; looked up to see that Mem'sab was struggling in the grip of a stringy fellow she didn't recognize. Katherine had been backed up into one corner by the medium, and Sarah and Gray were pummeling the medium with small fists and wings. Mem'sab kicked at her captor's shins and stamped on his feet with great effect, as his grunts of pain demonstrated.

Nan struggled to her feet, guessing that *she* must have been the one worst affected by the hashish fumes. She wanted to run to Mem'sab's rescue, but she couldn't get her legs to work. In a moment the sour-faced woman would surely break into the room, turning the balance in favor of the enemy—

The door *did* crash open behind her just as she thought that, and she tried to turn to face the new foe—

But it was not the foe.

Sahib charged through the broken door, pushing past Nan to belabor the man holding Mem'sab with his cane; within three blows the man was on the floor, moaning. Before Nan fell, Karamjit caught her and steadied her. More men flooded into the room, and Nan let Karamjit steer her out of the way, concentrating on those steadying breaths of air. She thought perhaps that she passed out of consciousness for a while, for when she next noticed anything, she was sitting bent over in a chair, with Karamjit hovering over her, frowning. At some point the brazier had been extinguished, and a policeman was collecting the ashes and the remains of the drug-laced incense.

Finally her head cleared; by then, the struggle was over. The medium and her fellow tricksters were in the custody of the police, who had come with Sahib when Nan threw the crystal ball through the window. Sahib was talking to a policeman with a sergeant's badge, and Nan guessed that he was explaining what Mem'sab and Katherine were doing here. Katherine wept in a corner, comforted by Mem'sab. The police had brought lamps into the seance-room from the sitting room, showing all too clearly how the medium had achieved her work; a hatch in the ceiling to the room above, through which things could be lowered; a magic lantern behind the drapes, which had cast its image of a woman and boy onto the thick brazier smoke. That, and the disorienting effect of the hashish had made it easy to trick the clients.

Finally the bobbies took their captives away, and Katherine stopped crying. Nan and Sarah sat on the chairs Karamjit had set up, watching the adults, Gray on her usual perch on Sarah's shoulder. A cushion stuffed in the broken window cut off most of the cold air from outside.

"I can't believe I was so foolish!" Katherine moaned. "But—I wanted to see Edward so very much—"

"I hardly think that falling for a clever deception backed by drugs makes you foolish, ma'am," Sahib said gravely. "But you are to count yourself fortunate in the loyalty of your friends, who were willing to place themselves in danger for you. I do not think that these people would have been willing to stop at mere fraud, and neither do the police."

His last words made no impression on Katherine, at least none that Nan saw—but she did turn to Mem'sab and clasp her hand fervently. "I thought so ill of you, that you would not believe in Madame," she said tearfully. "Can you forgive me?"

Mem'sab smiled. "Always, my dear," she said, in the voice she used to soothe a frightened child. "Since your motive was to enlighten me, not to harm me—and your motive in seeking your poor child's spirit—"

A chill passed over Nan at that moment that had nothing to do with the outside air. She looked sharply at Sarah, and saw a very curious thing.

There was a very vague and shimmery shape standing in front of Sarah's chair; Sarah looked at it with an intense and thoughtful gaze, as if she was listening to it. More than that, Gray was doing the same. Nan got the distinct impression that it was asking her friend for a favor.

Gray and Sarah exchanged a glance, and the parrot nodded once, as grave and sober as a parson, then spread her wings as if sheltering Sarah like a chick.

The shimmering form melted into Sarah; her features took on a mischievous expression that Nan had never seen her wear before, and she got up and went directly to Katherine.

The woman looked up at her, startled at the intrusion of a child into an adult discussion, then paled at something she saw in Sarah's face.

"Oh, Mummy, you don't have to be so sad," Sarah said in a curiously hollow, piping soprano. "I'm all right, really, and it wasn't your fault anyway, it was that horrid Lord Babbington that made you and Papa send me to Overton. But you *must* stop crying, please! Laurie is already scared of being left, and you're scaring her more."

Now, Nan knew very well that Mem'sab had not said anything about a Lord Babbington, nor did she and Sarah know what school the poor little boy had been sent to. Yet, she wasn't frightened; in fact, the protective but calm look in Gray's eye made her feel rather good, as if something inside her told her that everything was going wonderfully well.

The effect on Katherine was not what Nan had expected, either.

She reached out tentatively, as if to touch Sarah's face, but stopped short. "This *is* you, isn't it, darling?" she asked in a whisper.

Sarah nodded—or was it Edward who nodded? "Now, I've *got* to go, Mummy, and I can't come back. So don't look for me, and don't cry anymore."

The shimmering withdrew, forming into a brilliant ball of light at about Sarah's heart, then shot off, so fast that Nan couldn't follow it. Gray pulled in her wings, and Sarah shook her head a little, then regarded Katherine with a particularly measuring expression before coming back to her chair and sitting down.

"Out of the mouths of babes, Katherine," Mem'sab said quietly, then looked up at Karamjit. "I think you and Selim should take the girls home now; they've had more than enough excitement for one night."

Karamjit bowed silently, and Gray added her own vote. "Wan' go back," she said in a decidedly firm tone. When Selim brought their coats and helped them to put them on, Gray climbed right back inside Sarah's, and didn't even put her head back out again.

They didn't have to go home in a cab, either; Katherine sent them back to the school in her own carriage, which was quite a treat for Nan, who'd had no notion that a private carriage would come equipped with such comforts as heated bricks for the feet and fur robes to bundle in. Nan didn't say anything to Sarah about the aftermath of the seance until they were alone together in their shared dormitory room.

Only then, as Gray took her accustomed perch on the headboard of Sarah's bed, did Nan look at her friend and ask—

"That last—was that—?"

Sarah nodded. "I could see him, clear as clear, too." She smiled a little. "He must've been a horrid brat at times, but he really wasn't bad, just spoiled enough to be a bit selfish, and he's been—learning better manners, since."

All that Nan could think of to say was—"Ah."

"Still; I think it was a *bit* rude of him to have been so impatient with his mother," she continued, a little irritated.

"I 'spose that magic-man friend of yours is right," Nan replied, finally. "About what you c'n do, I mean."

"Oh! You're right!" Sarah exclaimed. "But you know, I don't think I could have done it if Gray hadn't been there. I thought if I ever saw a spirit I'd be too scared to do anything, but I wasn't afraid, since she wasn't."

The parrot took a little piece of Sarah's hair in her beak and preened it.

"*Wise* bird," replied Gray.

# PART
## ✷ II ✷
# Tales of the Secret World Chronicles

**Strories Never Previously in Print**

┿══✷✷✷══┿

These are stories from our superhero series,
*The Secret World Chronicles,* from Baen Books.
Never previously in print, some are prequel stories
set during World War II, and two, co-written
with Dennis Lee and Cody Martin, are set between
*Book One, Invasion!* and
*Book Two, World Divided.*

# For Those About To Rock

## Mercedes Lackey and Dennis Lee

I drink a lot of coffee and tea; I have a minifreezer just for the coffee, 'cause I order it bulk, delivered. Today was a day I was glad I had a lot of backstock, because I was going to need a lot of coffee. Djinni was out on another solo job and Bell had ordered me to keep tabs on him with Overwatch. Keeping track of the Djinni on solo is a lot like keeping track of a flea on a hot griddle; it taxes even my considerable capabilities. Though that's mostly because he hates magic so much.

Jeebus. Hates magic. We were not exactly talking right now. We'd had this . . . explosion.

Actually, he'd snapped at me and jabbed me in the proverbial gut, right when and where I was most vulnerable. It's as if he has radar for that kind of thing.

This was how it happened. The explosion, I mean. He'd been on another solo job, right after the Goldman Catacombs. Not a surprise, since he recovers faster than anyone I had ever seen. There'd been a news story just before he went out, courtesy of Spin Doctor. We'd both caught it. He thought it was hilarious.

I was in the Overwatch room, he was on the system. ". . . and for those curious about last night's specTACular lightshow over the Nevada desert," he'd mimicked, "rest assured, those were your own, your brave, your heroic boys and girls of ECHO on some routine training maneuvers. ECHO, training to keep you, your loved ones and America safe!" He'd snorted. "Training maneuvers. Gotta love that friendly fire then. Feels good to be out of the infirmary. Was getting tired of Scope's retching anytime a new layer of skin grew back."

I'd been raw, still trying to get over Herb. "Remind me again why this thing of yours is supposed to be a *super* power?" But I had a job to do, Overwatch on the Bad Boy.

He'd been surprisingly civil. "Hey Victrix. You better?"

I'd toyed with being honest, decided on a white lie. "If I say 'no,' Spin Doctor will read me the riot act for 'negative impact on morale.' I'm fine, thanks for asking." I just hadn't wanted to open myself up to him.

"Oh screw him." He sounded gruffly sympathetic. "He was pushing me to reveal my real face, for the sake of good press."

I tried to sound light. Probably hadn't succeeded. "It would be, if you look like Brad Pitt. If you look like Emo Phillips, not so much." I couldn't help it. It slipped out. After all Djinni was the only person besides Bella that . . . knew. Knew that what I'd called up hadn't been just this giant rock Elemental, but a very dear friend. "I miss Herb."

There was a moment of hesitation. Then something unexpected. "Yeah . . . listen, I'm sorry about what happened to him."

I don't know why I said it . . . except that it was true. And maybe he needed to hear that I *knew* this. "Magic has a price. Always does. Always will."

He sounded surprised. "Hey, that's my line."

Finally I asked. "That why you hate it? Everything has a price, you just don't always know about it." I guess maybe I was trying to figure a way to make him understand not just where I was coming from, but about how seriously I took magic. How it was so much a part of me that magic and me couldn't be separated, and I understood the risks I was taking, dancing on the edge of quantum physics as I was.

He'd paused, a long pause on the freq. "That sums it up, I'd say. Professional habit. I like knowing the odds before going in, and magic complicates that. It's hard to give estimates to a client when the potential pitfalls of a job range from 'papercut' to 'complete and utter obliteration of everything in existence.'"

I'd raised an eyebrow over that. What the hell had he—or someone he knew—been tinkering with in his deep, dark past? "Hmm. I take it you've never worked with a properly trained mage before. Odds of the latter are pretty insignificant most of the time."

The reply I'd gotten was not anything like I wanted. I'd intended it as an opening. I got dissed. "Fine, whatever."

Well one of the advantages of being Overwatch is they can't turn you off. Not without taking out the earpiece, and he didn't dare, not on a job. "Hey. Look I'm not trying to blow smoke up your ass here. Yeah, things can get nasty, yeah, there's a price, and yeah, there is a quantum uncertainty thing going on, but a properly trained mage has the equivalent of a PhD in Nuclear Physics. Sure, the odds of turning on a linear accelerator and blowing up the universe are there, but they're pretty small. Most of the time. A trained mage knows the risks and the costs and knows when to back down on the bad ones. Unless, of course, you're trying to *prevent* the blowing up of the universe, in which case, the risk you take is probably worth it."

The anger in his voice was very real. "And what gives you the right, any of you, to mess with shit like that?"

Where the hell had *that* come from? I was just as angry, how *dared* he? What did he know? And how about all those perfectly ordinary people out there who took horrible risks using nothing more but their hands and their brains? Or all the metas who took risks that *always* endangered the innocent? Wasn't that why ECHO had the DCOs in the first place? "What gives you metas the right to do what you do? And you—what about you? You weren't exactly fighting the good fight until you got dragooned into ECHO."

His voice dripped with contempt, as if I was some stupid teenager who'd been playing games with the DoD computers in Iron Mountain. "Christ, get some perspective, lady. I'll admit I've never been a boy scout, but I wasn't messing with primal forces. You want to argue the relative morality of what I did with trying to control the fabric of reality? Good luck."

The arrogant, judgemental son of a—oh he'd pushed my buttons but good. "Arthur C. Clarke: 'Sufficiently advanced technology is indistinguishable from magic.' From where I sit there are plenty of people besides mages messing with the fabric of reality. Including plenty of metas."

He had an answer for that, too. "So? I'm hardly defending any of those douchebags. Magic, science, anything and anyone with the audacity to mess with crap on that scale is an asshole."

I'd snorted my own contempt. "So you'd prefer it if everyone went back to living in caves? You can't pick and choose."

Now his voice just dripped scorn. "You're big with the absolutes, aren't you? Someone who invents the wheel? Good job. Someone who tries to ignite a new sun in Kansas? Douchebag."

So who had died and appointed *him* Lord High Everything Else? "Look, brainiac, on some level everyone with strong enough willpower messes with the fabric of reality. That's what luck is! You want something bad enough, if there's not enough force opposing you, by damn, you get it! That's why one of the Prime Laws is 'Be careful what you wish for'! Even YOU. Bet you have done just that, and gotten it. Bet you any amount of money you have."

Evidently I had pushed one of his buttons right back. If words were weapons, he'd skewered me with them then. "Right, 'cause you know so much about me! Victoria Victrix, the lady with ALL the answers! Tell me you've got it all down, that you have it all figured out, that you knew what would happen to Herbert!"

I froze. The hurt—it felt like a heart attack for a minute. Finally I managed to say something. "Transmitting your requested info. Overwatch out."

I still heard him, of course, heard the sudden guilt, the contrition, the instant before I shut the comm down. "Shit . . . Victrix! I'm sorry dammit!"

But it was too late.

So now it was two days later, and I was settling in with the closest thing I could get to Tim Horton's coffee (dark roast, pinch of salt on the grounds, double cream, double sugar) and wondering if I could stand to listen to his voice. If he'd skewer me again. Of course I was feeling much, much better now, since Herb was back. In fact, the now-little Elemental was perched on one of the desks, watching the monitors curiously.

Bella had been all over me to kiss and make up. I guess she'd been at him . . . more directly, because when I put on the headset and opened the feed the first thing I heard was, "Word to the wise—when Bella knocks on your door, get ready to duck, she's got a mean suckerpunch. Ow."

I couldn't help it. I felt a smirk coming on. "Jaw hurt?" I asked sweetly.

"Would that make you happy?" His tone was quite neutral.

Honesty, or not? I opted for prevarication. "Yes and no. I'd be lying if I gave an unqualified no. But hey, schadenfreude. You have a solo job. I'm supposed to inform you because you haven't been checking your email, phone or PDA. There. You've been informed. You're also on Overwatch at Bell's insistence."

"Thanks." A very long pause. "Victrix?"

I was bringing up my camera feeds. And I was not at all inclined to be anything other than chill and civil. "Yes, Red Djinni?"

"I really am sorry."

I don't often explode. That's Bella's thing. I'm usually . . . ok; face it I am usually huddling in a corner shaking in every limb rather than dealing with anger and confrontation. But this time I exploded. "You're an unmitigated cream-faced spleeny unwashed bugbear. A pustulant boor. A ham-handed, toad-spotted malcontent. A beslubbering, pickle-brained pigeon egg. A lumpish folly-fallen apple-john. A qualling ill-breeding malcontent. A clouted common-kissing wagtail. A . . . " I groped for words. They weren't there. "Damn. I'm running out of Shakespearian insults."

"S'ok. Thanks for putting in the effort." That kind of floored me. What the hell did that mean?

Well at least I wouldn't have to talk to him for long. "We're supposed to keep radio silence on this one. We only break it if you're in too deep to get out alone." Or alive, but he would know that was what I meant.

"No constant Overwatch?" He sounded surprised.

Well of course I *could*. But . . . him and magic. Again. "Nothing you'd accept."

Then he floored me a second time. "What about a magic line?"

The hell? I nearly inhaled my coffee. "I thought you were against me messing with the fabric of the universe."

"I think the universe will hold up to one arcane phone call." When he said that, I almost went to the window to see if there were pigs flying in attack formation over the Varsity.

OK. OK. Let's make this the littlest and least intrusive thing I could. "Safest and smallest would be a light charm to link the PDAs and text." Why text? Cause the spell to make what appeared on his screen also appear on mine was . . . well it was easy, small, and used less magic than lighting a candle.

Which, by the way, is the single most cliched way to show you are a mage in the entire universe. So don't do it, OK? Just don't. It only impresses the rubes. It makes the rest of us sigh and roll our eyes.

I couldn't read his voice, but his words were clear enough. "All right, make it happen."

I did. A few moments later I was typing. *Testing.*

*Agh! My testicles!* This is what passes for Djinni humor.

OK, it was funny.

*Dr. Ruth has a pill for that,* I replied. *You want 2027 West Catalpa. Surveillance. Possible Doppelganger sighting. Definite explosives, hence radio silence. They know there's a bomb maker in there and they know he's using a radio transmitter to detonate, but they don't know what freqs he has his detonators set for. I can't find out magically because I don't know who he is, I don't have anything of his to use as a target. And I can't find out by computer because I don't know his IP address and there's nothing around there I can hack to find it. Which makes the technomancy out on both counts.* I was babbling, overexplaining. Why was I doing this? What about this man made me double-think myself, made me think I had to explain anything to him? I couldn't help it. It was like scratching at a scab. *Rules. There are rules to this magic stuff. Lots of rules. Unless, of course, you don't mind killing and hurting a lot of people, including random strangers and yourself.*

His reply was . . . well . . . right on. *Christ, even texting you talk a lot. Alright, objective?*

That was simpler, and required no overexplanation. *Determine if DG is in there or not. If not, get Bomb Boy out without him setting off anything. If so, let me know and wait for backup.*

*K. I should be at destination in 15 minutes.*

Now . . . let me get this straight, here. When I say I have the magic equivalent of a Ph.D. in Astrophysics, I am not kidding. Yes, there are instinctive mages. And some of them, a very few, are very good. Those few are the equivalent of natural athletes, or people who sing opera well with no training. The rest? They're like every yahoo who says, "Hold my beer" and thinks he can drive like Mario Andretti or Paul Newman. Not. Gonna. Happen. Oh, they can get where they are going, most of the time, but there's a lot of flailing and flogging and very often, very, very often, there is collateral damage.

And yes, there are the old "Fam-Trad" mages, trained in the traditional manner, by a family or coven member. Things mostly work. They mostly never stray out of the family recipe book. They honestly do not know what they are working with, in the same sense that people drive cars every day and have no idea of the mechanics and physics of an internal combustion engine.

Then there are the people like me, trained in very small, very special schools. I won't tell you where. I *will* tell you that every day from the time I was seven years old, I went to the regular P.S. 17 grade school, then came home, and spent another four hours in a very different school far, far from my home. It was not Hogwarts, let me tell you. It was more like Kiddie CalTech. I did that every day of my life, including weekends, right up to college. And then I went to college. *That* college, one that was *in* a university but . . . and I'll tell you what it is. Merlin College, Oxford University. Good luck finding it. You can look at Magdalene College in the north corner of First Court by the Chapel all you like; if you aren't in Merlin College, you'll never see the door.

So, yeah, it was like that. I did this because my parents determined that I had a double dose of the family knack for the power, and knew it was either train me early and hard, or burn it out before I killed someone. Now, don't get me wrong; I *wanted* this. There were very few times I rebelled, and the rebellion never lasted more than a day or two. You know how prodigies always are, math, science, letters, dance, music—it's not our parents driving us into it, it's us, charging in on our own, sometimes *against* the will of our parents. You punish us by taking away the music, the math books, the magic.

It was in high school that this magic school figured out I was one *rara avis* indeed, a technomage, as well as a geomancer. In short, I could magic machines, the more complicated and computerized the better. I had an affinity for them. Most mages . . . don't. Catastrophically don't. Some I know can't even live in a place with electricity without starting electrical fires. The fact that *I* could use them the way most mages use an atheme and chants blew people out of the water. Now, actually I had known this for some time, I just figured it was no big deal, everyone else could too, and eventually we'd get to technomancy in the classes. When *I* realized that no, I was the only one and *they* realized what I could do—well—let's just say I ended up with a bit of an ego which bit me in the ass . . . but that's another story.

This only intensified my education. I'm a math whiz. And I do technomancy. Which means I can make shit up and know it's going to work. Or to be precise, I know the exact odds of getting it to work. I can improvise *way* outside of the normal things that modern mages do—substituting components and the like. If I don't have what I need for a spell, since I know the math and can deconstruct the original, I can make up a whole *new* spell on the spot that will use what I've got. I can, and do, run calculus in my head, though I always double check on the computer. This is because, at its root, magic is the ability to move energy in a way that gets things done that you want to get done. The tool for moving it is your will, reinforced by the energies of the stuff you use to make up the spell. Usually mathemagical diagrams in my case; I don't need to use many components these days. That magical energy is all around you; conventional science just hasn't discovered it yet. The energy *you* use to move that energy comes from inside you.

Yes, if you've made the intuitive leap already, I'll confirm it for you. Luck is magic. Energy responding to will, changing reality to suit you.

But there's always a price. *Always* a price. Part of my price to become the technomancer that I am was to have a mere sliver of a childhood. I understood, bone deep, very early in my life, that I was potentially juggling with nuclear bombs. I also understood, bone deep, what the consequences of failure were, because my parents took me on a visit to a ward full of people who had slipped while juggling.

Trust me, you never want to go there.

This is why, when I do the things that have less-than-perfect odds, they're set up so I am the meat-shield between catastrophe and anyone else around.

There is no free lunch. *Most* of the time, the price is sheer, physical exhaustion. Sometimes you end up with a higher price than that. I did once. That is why I am a mass of aching, burning scarred tissue from my collarbone to my soles. Yet another story.

But I can no more give it up than I can give up breathing. It's me. It defines me. I *need* it like I need air. I never realized how much until ECHO came knocking on my door post-Invasion, and I built Overwatch, and was operating at the height of my powers again.

I say, without false modesty, I am a Robert Oppenheimer of magic. And just as he, I understand the math, and the consequences of not understanding the math completely. He did not embark on the creation of the A-bomb in a spirit of anything other than full understanding of the consequences of failure. I do not embark on spellcasting in a spirit of anything other than a righteous dread of what might go wrong. Ever.

So this is why I see red—pun not intended—when the Djinni acts as if I was some street witch trying to hex her boyfriend's ex with a supermarket spellbook.

Then we get into the fact that not only am I an exquisitely trained mage, I am a mage steeped in magical ethics until it oozes from every pore. Ethical magic is *hard*. You can do nothing without consent. You clean every speck up after yourself. You *think*, a lot, about all the possible ramifications that your alteration to the universe might have.

But I digress.

While I was thinking this over, my screen lit up. *Reading me, Overwatch?*

*That's a roger.* Something occurred to me. I knew he had headed out without a lot of warning, and that he'd be there a while. *Jeet yet? Yontoo?*

*Mwha?*

*That's southern for, "Did you eat yet? Want to?"* I glanced at Herb, who was peering at the screen in a way that suggested he was very eager. He had come back to me, just hours after Red's words had sent me reeling. He was a mere pebble of what he once was, but he had clung to life. He was still with us and he liked Djinni, and . . . well, if Djinni was feeling guilt or remorse over what he thought had happened to Herb, it wasn't fair to let him continue to feel bad.

Herb is an interesting barometer for bullshit. I have no idea how he does it, but he always *knows* if somebody is a basically good guy hiding behind the facade of an asshat, or scumbag hiding behind the mask of someone you can trust. He's never been wrong. Not even when I thought he was.

And he liked Djinni. Go figure.

*Yeah, I suppose I could do with something to munch on, why?*

*You're likely going to be there a while. I've mapped you in the alley and it's not paved.* Which meant, of course, that Herb could sneak in through the ground after I gave him a magical shortcut to a spot I knew nearby.

*I think sending some Chinese delivery my way might be counter-productive to the nature of this stake-out.*

*I had something more discreet in mind. Provided you're good with a little visitor of the arcane kind.* Herb was jumping up and down and clapping his hands.

*Chinese . . . elves?* I took that as a yes. I went to the kitchen and packed up a small, hardened "lunchbox" of mil-spec steel. It was going to have to survive being hauled behind Herb through the dirt. Coffee in a thermos and a sandwich Bella brought me from the deli. She thinks I don't eat enough. I used a little magic to make it hot and fresh—"go back to the way you were an hour and a half ago" basically. Reverse entropy. Normally I'd use the microwave, but I think Djinni's taste buds are better than mine.

I gave the box to Herb. I had little arcane "landing zones" plotted all over the city these days, in case I needed to send someone—or something—there in a hurry. Without a landing pad, whatever you apport has 85% odds of ending up a smear on the ground. Or worse, embedded *in* the ground. Herb and the lunch were small, it wouldn't take much out of me. Even better, Herb was magic in nature. Magic critters are easier to apport. He stepped into the diagram I drew on the counter with the box strapped to his back like a backpack. I'd ask Djinni to bring him home, later, unless he wanted me to apport him back, or to take the long way back. Sometimes he does. I think he's exploring Atlanta underground. Literally underground.

I ran through the math, sketched more diagrams in the air, said the right sounds, and with a *pop* of displaced air, he was gone.

I went back to the keyboard. *OK, you hearing something nearby that sounds like digging? Check there.*

*You're not sending gnomes at me, are ya?*

*What do you think I am, a travel agency? Naw, just a Philly cheesesteak and some coffee.*

*That works.* There was another long pause. I wondered what he was thinking as Herb pushed the box up out of the ground. Finally: *What the hell is that?*

*Take a good look. I know it looks like a walking lunchbucket, look who's carrying it.*

Another long pause, and I swear to you, the text looked angry. *That's messed up, Victrix. Herb was your friend, wasn't he? What is this? Some animated chew-toy look-alike?*

Simpler was better. *Hold your horses. It's Herb. It really is. Hell, go take your lunch and talk to him, you'll see.*

Another long pause. *The hell you say. How?*

Well, now that was a tricky question. *Not sure, really. My guess? It wasn't his time.* Simplistic and not my best guess. I don't believe in fate; I've personally changed "fate" too often. Closer to say that Elementals don't work like us. They have different rules. *He used up everything of himself for you guys, but something's kept him here.* Like maybe his will. Earth Elementals have the most powerful will of all of the Elements. Herb just could have made up his mind that he was *not* going, and imposed that on the universe. Of course, there had to be a reason why he would have decided that—

*Like what?*

*I dunno, our friendship maybe? Or maybe he just wants to see what shit you'll get into next.* Could have been either. Could have been both. Could have been a reason I hadn't even guessed at.

Captain Sarcastic had to put in his two cents on it, of course. *So now . . . what . . . he's your delivery boy?*

I didn't rise to the bait. *He wanted to say hi in person. Other than that . . . he hangs out with Gray and does what he wants to do. Right now, that seems to be MMORPGs. He's with the Horde.*

Evidently I said the right thing. *Just shook his hand. Now he's dancing.*

I found myself reluctantly smiling. *He likes you.*

I did not expect the response I got. *Yeah, everybody makes that mistake at the beginning.*

Say what? *Bitter much?* I replied.

Again, a response I did not expect; not from a guy who, from everything I had seen, had an ego that almost left enough space in the room for some air to breathe. *Many hours of expensive psychotherapy have classed it as "acceptance," thank you very much.* Yeah, right. As if the Djinni would ever come within a nautical mile of a shrink if he could avoid it.

I decided it was a good idea to switch subjects. *How's action at the target? All quiet on the Western Front?*

Immediate reply. *Nothing, I'm getting extremely cold vibes here. How solid is your intel on this one?*

That part, I was sure of. *The DG sighting was a definite maybe. The bomb lab is a hard yes. But our little Nazi sympathizer might not be home.*

Evidently his patience had been stretched thin. *Okay, I'm heading in. Breaking contact for a bit, keep Herb around, he might need to get back to you with a report if I don't come out. Give me ten minutes.*

What could I say? It was his op. The building was all artificial, I couldn't even scry in there clearly. *Roger. Be as safe as you can.*

*And thanks, the coffee was good.*

It was a very long ten minutes. My only comfort was that Herb was there. If the excrement really did hit the rotating blades, Herb could get through to me quickly. Though small, he still had enough power to do that.

And he did. Before I got a text, I got a message from Herb, as a bloodstone apported to my desktop. Not good.

I opened Bella's freq. "Bell! Djinni's hurt."

"How bad?" was the instant reply. "I'm at ECHO Medical, I can add myself to any team that goes out after him."

"Don't know yet—"

I was about to open Djinni's radio freq in defiance of the orders when I got another text.

*Area's secure, Overwatch. Send in the cleaners.*

I pulled my little smoke-and-mirrors thing, and called ECHO dispatch using a CCCP freq. "Comrades, this is Upyr, of CCCP. You are to be havink man down, Comrade Krasny Djinni. He is to be sendink me at safe distance, and is to be tellink me to be havink cleaners and medic sent." ECHO proper did not know about Overwatch. ECHO proper was not going to learn about it until Tesla gave it the official blessing.

"Roger that, CCCP Upyr." They didn't ask what a CCCP op was doing out of their neighborhood, and I broke the freq. When ECHO Medical got the buzz Bell would handle it.

All this took seconds. I texted back. *Herb says you need a Band-Aid. Scrambled ECHO Cleaners with Bell in tow.*

*Wouldn't mind if they rushed a bit.*

My heart jumped into my throat. OK, I knew he was able to heal himself crazy well, and I was still kinda annoyed with him but—*You okay?* I responded immediately.

The reply did not comfort me. *Not really, the guy knew how to use that machete.*

My heart nearly stopped. *Shit Red! How bad?*

*Pretty bad, I can see . . . well, parts that I shouldn't be able to see.*

I wanted to swear and didn't have time. Instead, I got on Bella's

CCCP comm. When she answered the thing, I could hear the siren in the background. "This is beink Upyr, Comrade Blue. Your man down is nyet good. Is being cut half open." This was for the benefit of the others in the response vehicle.

"Roger. Spasiba, Upyr." Off-mic I heard, "You heard the woman! Floor it!" then the comm clicked off.

I got back on the keyboard. *Got the pedal to the metal. You should be able to hear the sirens soon. Stay with me, keep typing. What about the mark?* I didn't want him to pass out. He was experienced. He knew what to keep pressure on, how to make his body help him, and he would as long as he could. He was his own best aid at the moment.

*Oh, HIS parts are all over the place now. He didn't leave me much choice.*

I was going to type anything to keep him alert. *And DG?*

*No sign of him. Hope the cleaners pick up his scent.*

A pause, and I was about to try and prod him when more text came. *Herb's not dancing anymore. He just keeps looking at me.*

*You made him sad. I'll explain it to him later.* Now . . . that was way, way oversimplifying. Herb was an Elemental. He might be childlike, but he was no child. He understood very well what Djinni had just done, and—although I do not know this for certain, I am quite sure that either an Elemental Herb knew, or even Herb himself, had killed in the past when someone had tried to coerce him magically. They did that. That was what Red had been afraid of. You'd fight to the death, too, if someone tried to enslave you. And Herb was an *Elemental.* They are nature spirits. As in "Nature, red in tooth and claw." They are well-acquainted with innocent violence. These are not happy peaceful little stone Buddhists.

So Herb was not sad that Red had killed someone. He was sad that Red had been hurt, and sad that Red had been forced to kill someone and that—which the text "he didn't leave me much choice" told me—had made Red feel guilty. What I would explain was why all of this had happened, why it had been needful, and that humans felt guilt even when we did needful things.

He might act with the open emotions of a toddler, but his

understanding was completely adult.

Another message from Herb. A roughly truck-shaped rock apported to my keyboard with a click. I breathed a sigh of relief.

But Red . . . Red didn't know what I knew, or what I meant. And the last text I got from him as Bell and the crew reached him made my heart ache.

*Guess he likes me less now. Told ya. Everyone makes that mistake in the beginning . . .*

# Haunt You

## Mercedes Lackey and Cody Martin

This might have been the best motel John had ever stayed in in his entire life.

Vickie had guided him to it, after having him leave the beater rental van, pick up a newer rental van, and visit a mega-mart. It wasn't just a room, it was a whole two-story suite, one of those "extended stay" places. Three bedrooms and a bath up, one bedroom and bath, a living-room-thing and a real kitchen down. The fridge even came stocked. With beer. And other things, but the beer was what interested John most after that little adventure in the missile silo. He'd been listening to the radio on the way back to KC, and the explosion had made the news, which meant that John had been very eager to not make himself available in the immediate area. Someone might have noticed an athletically built fellow with some interesting bags and a beater van in that no-tell motel. *Can you say "terrorist profile"? I knew you could.* So now he was an athletically built fellow in newish clean athletic gear, athletic bags and a name-brand rental van, with the story that he was waiting for his sports team—sport unspecified—to arrive, and they were all going to be living here in a fancy suite motel. Now someone just had to think of a sport that would have a lot of Russians on the team. Pavel might be part of it. He didn't think Pavel was going to go unnoticed.

John closed the door behind him, noted that Vickie had gotten a suite that was as secure as a motel could be, and let his guard down, a little. He chose the downstairs bedroom, which had a king-sized bed, dropping his bags on the floor. "Nice digs. Still with me, blondie?"

"Five by five, tall, dark and waterproof." The voice in his ear sounded relaxed, almost cheerful. "It's easier to hack their stuff than the Roach Hotel, oddly enough. I'm on channel 99."

"A-ffirmative." John retrieved a cold beer from the fridge—local swill, but he wasn't about to complain—and plopped down on his bed with the remote in hand. A smart-remote, so this TV was equipped to surf, which meant he could treat it like a computer of sorts. "An' we're up. Start feedin' me whatcha got."

"Tesla and Marconi got me a translation program, so all that stuff we downloaded is cooking at a rapid rate. There definitely is a big staging area somewhere there in KC. Saviour is sending you a team, hence, the suite."

"How big are we talkin' 'bout here?" He took a long draught from the beer, looking up to the TV.

"Well, this is where the trucks are coming from for this area. So big enough to load the trucks. More staff than the silo. Staff to repair the armor and maybe the Robo-Wolves and Robo-Eagles. Didn't seem to have anything for Death Machines."

John had read briefings on the mechanical horrors that the Thulians fielded, but he never had had the unpleasant opportunity to fight against them. "Nasty customers, their Robo-whatsits?"

"Pretty damn. Uh, look, I can do something called 'retro-scrying' if I have a piece of stuff that came from where I want to look. I was gonna call up the fight that the Misfits had down in the Catacombs after I lost their feed and before I got it back. I could do that now and you could watch it while I burn it to memory. Want?"

"Certainly." He retrieved a fresh beer while Vickie did whatever mumbo-jumbo she did to make this stuff happen. "Got any relevant AARs an' dossiers I could browse in a sidebar?"

"Yep, got the analysis ECHO did on the downed eagles from the

Slycke caper. Use the scroll-down and page-down buttons on your remote, this hotel rig is set up for reading email." The screen split into two windows, one with text popping up and the other with some . . . interesting patterns at the moment.

"You're a peach."

"I can't do a lot in the field, Johnny. I kinda gotta make it up with what I can do in here." She was muttering something too quietly for him to hear, but it didn't sound like English, so he didn't pay a lot of attention to it. "Did I ever tell you that magic on the computer level is basically math and physics?" She didn't wait for him to answer. "All that high-level physics stuff running around these days says that pretty much everything in time and space is connected, you just have to bend things around the connections and you're looking at what you want to."

"Y'know, this all sounds like it's a helluva lot higher than my pay grade. Hey, I'm still gettin' paid in things other than beer, right?"

She chuckled. "Right now you're getting one meeeeeeellion Polish zlotys a day."

"By my math, I might be able to buy a few popsicles with that. If I find someone that's nearsighted."

"And you call yourself a Marxist!"

"Not in the slightest, cupcake." He leaned back, propping his head up with a pillow so he could still drink and watch the television. "Anyways, keep goin.'"

"I do have something of interest for you besides your wallet and the intel. KC is a beef-packing town. There's some very nice T-bones in the meat drawer if you can cook. Aha." The patterns on the screen resolved into a static image. "And here we go. Connection between now and then, my rig and the Catacombs established. And rolling."

At first, there wasn't much of interest to see—except for the rank upon rank of power-armor down in that enormous vault, and the Misfits wandering around among the silent giants like kids in a museum. He was getting an overhead view, which was interesting, and probably better than the original camera feed would have been. "So, why are they called the Misfits again?"

"We," she corrected. "I'm part of the team." She sighed. "No one else will have us but Bulwark. He makes a habit of trying to save people. Particularly the ones no one else believes in."

"Huh. Kind've a raggedy-looking bunch. And y'all have that Djinni guy with you?" John had heard about "the" Red Djinni during his time on the run; the criminal element and people like John seemed to intermingle regularly.

"Red . . . has his moments."

"Don't we all—" John was cut off when the doors in the Vault slammed shut. A structure smack dab in the middle of the room seemed to change, and very quickly the Misfits were fighting Robo-Wolves and Robo-Eagles. They got split up immediately; the three girls, Bella, Harmony, and Scope, were under attack by the birds, while one wolf chased Djinni and one chased Acrobat. "Jesus, those things are mean. Besides blowin' them to hell an' softenin' them up with fire, what weaknesses do they have?" John was already looking for joints, ammunition magazines, power cells, anything that could be exploited. It was becoming increasingly hard with the flurry of action on the screen.

"There's a pretty good AI in there, and we think that the wolves had an uplink somewhere. The wolves are fangs and claws, the eagles are beak, claws and an energy gun in their mouth that uses a different mechanism from the arm-cannon. They've got IR and UV vision, night vision of course, the usual ability to camera-zoom in tight on a target. Bella found out that if you shoot that area in the eagle's mouth where the gun is, you have a good chance at making whatever they use as ammo explode the head. The eagles DON'T seem to have radar; when Scope shoots out their eyes later, they collide."

"All the sensors located in the head? Whatever they use for a processor?"

"From the wreckage, the processor is buried deep inside the body, the sensors are all in the head."

"Well, that's a pain. But, y'knock out the head, ought to be easier to pry the bastard apart."

Right about then, Bulwark, who had raised his force-field, was driven to his knees with a grunt as the wolf on him pounded the outside of the field. "Yeah, that looks harsh. Bull's power isn't like a sci-fi field; energy applied outside gets some transferred inside."

"Jesus! Any casualties on this op? I hate surprises."

"Thanks to the powers that watch over fools, no. Bull was pretty messed up with a lot of internal injury, Scope nearly ruptured her eyes, and Bell was drained down to just about nothing. And Djinni looked like one of those carcasses hanging on a hook over in the stockyards. But everybody lived. Oh, watch this, this is how Djinni takes out his wolf." Red was looking a little worse for wear—and naked—but certainly not as bad as Vickie had made out to be. John saw how he ended up matching her description. The meta paused, measuring up the Robo-Wolf, and then pounced on its neck. His hands dug into a seam that had formed where the contraption had taken a beating, and then his hands seemed to distend and harden into grotesque claws, while his body somehow grew a kind of encasement that was part insect carapace and part rhino hide. The wolf did *not* like this turn of events, and started to buck and turn to try to dislodge Djinni. It was vicious and fast, but finally a shower of sparks erupted from the seam, and the wolf slumped to the floor.

"Well, I've gotta say, I've seen some eight-second rodeo riders that would've had a helluva time stayin' on for that ride."

There was silence for a moment on the other end. Then, "Holy Jeebus Cluny Frog on a pogo stick. I—wow. Uh, OK, this is where I got the feed back."

This version was one-sided; John couldn't hear what Vickie was probably saying, but as the weird protection sloughed off, leaving the Djinni raw and bruised but looking reasonably like a human again, if a skinned one, Red said something in Russian.

"OK rewind. I'll show you Bull and Acrobat taking out theirs." This was a little more straightforward. Acrobat teased the wolf into chasing him, returned on Bulwark's signal, and the two of them working together got the wolf impaled on the gigantic sword of one of the more primitive suits of toppled armor.

"Those damned things were carrying swords? I never really thought I'd dislike Nazis more than I already did, but I'm learnin' new things every day."

"We are pretty sure that's something like Version 1.5. They hadn't figured out how to make energy cannon yet, or maybe how to get the stuff small enough to fit in an arm. So since these things were supposed to be terror weapons, they just gave them honking big swords to mow people down like a John Deere harvester."

John shook his head and finished his beer. "If they had come out with those things a couple of decades earlier, they could've still done some nasty damage."

"Rewind to Scope taking out the two birds with a couple good shots."

This was even more straightforward. Despite being under fire, despite a lot of hysterical screaming and shouting, and with Bella finally pouring enough of herself into Scope that she went the color of skim milk and passed out, Scope managed to take out the "eyes" of both birds in mid-dive. Unable to see or correct, they crashed into each other.

"So. Dat's dat. More shit went down with a Death Sphere that was probably operating on AI, but you already know how to take those out, and I have the camera feed on on that. I'm not looking forward to when they figure out what we're doing and make improvements."

"Tough customers. Remind me never to play 'Raiders of the Lost Ark' with you, though."

"Trust me, this was *not* my idea, nor would I have sent in one small team." The second window closed, leaving John with the report on the downed eagle from outside Atlanta. "On one level, I am glad Alex Tesla is gone. He made some piss-poor decisions." Her voice sounded curiously hard, even a little angry. "I know they say not to bad-mouth the dead, but those were my teammates he put on a suicide mission down there."

"Ain't this grand adventure we're all on just one big potential suicide mission, though? We all gotta die sometime, kiddo. An' sometimes . . . we gotta let some folks die to save others." John looked away from the TV, finishing his beer in a long draught.

"And I don't have to like it, and I aim to prevent it where and when I can."

"Y'know somethin' that just struck me 'bout those damned Eagles and Wolves? They aren't nearly as effective as the rest of Thulian arsenal, 'cept for one task."

"Bet I can guess, but tell me."

"Terror weapons. Power armor suits, flying death orbs an' whatnot are frightenin' enough. But those robots are just goddamned scary on a primordial, primitive level." He shook his head, taking another swig of his beer. "Imagine a pack or a flight of those things bearin' down on ya."

"That was my thought when I saw them. And think of the intimidation factor in a parade, or standing bodyguard over a leader." He could hear Vickie typing over the link. A second later, in a little window, was a photoshopped image of Hitler with a wolf at either hand and an eagle above him.

*Got to hand it to the Kriegers, they know 'bout presentation.*

Another window opened and dossiers of CCCP members appeared in tabs across the top. "Your team. Saviour has you on command on this one."

"Oh? She couldn't have been too happy 'bout that one. You an' Blue blackmail 'er or somethin'?"

"Unter pointed out how no one else could pass as a Murkan. So I hear."

"Giorgi must be goin' soft in his old age. I'll get caught up on all of 'em in a bit. I'd offer ya a beer, 'cept I don't think y'can work teleportation—wait, can you?"

"Yes, within reason. Only in my case there's no 'tele' about it. It's magic and not psionic, it's called 'apporting' and I need a landing strip. In other words, I need a prepared area where I'm sending things or they tend to end up as a smear on the floor. I can bring stuff *to* me safely enough, it's sending them off that's hard." She chuckled. "But I don't need your beer, thanks. Sorry about the generic brand, it was all I could get the hotel to stock. But I found a package store that makes deliveries, so say when you want one and I'll have 'em bring up a case of Guinness and some wodka for the comrades later."

"Much obliged." John continued to scan the files and information that Vickie was sending him, but his mind was elsewhere. *She really is a friggin' witch. If she can do all of this, just with a computer and some hand waving and chanting . . . what does she know about me, without even breaking a sweat?*

"You do realize that in magic, it's TANSTAFL, right?"

"There Ain't No Such Thing As a Free Lunch?" *Girl knows her Heinlein.*

"Da tovarisch. I go through a lot of calories. I build up a bunch of magical batteries to use in an emergency."

"Kind of the same thing that happens with Blueberry with her meta-healin', right? All the energy has to come from somewhere."

"Exact-a-mundo. Very big bad stuff means I better have reserves. VERY big bad stuff means I may need backup." She sighed. "So far, that is what makes the computer stuff work so well. Don't need a lot of energy to move electrons around. It's amazing what you can do when you know the math. Like . . . OK, look at this—"

A new window opened; it was a DoD document with about ninety percent of it blacked out. "You can get that via Freedom of Information. Real useful, right?" The sarcasm was thick.

"Only math I was ever really good at involved calculating bullet weight and drop, but I think I follow what you're sayin.'" He scanned through the large blocks of black, only picking out some inconsequential words and bits that gave nothing away. "Yeah, right. There's a 'but' here, right?"

"You bet. Oh, this is the doc on our dear departed friend the 'Echo Janitor.' Now what I can do, since I know the math, is I can tell the image I have in my computer, 'Become what you used to look like before they blacked out all that stuff.' Watch and learn." Slowly, letters, words, resolved out of the black, as if the ink was dissolving away. "I can do this with a real document too, but on the computer image it costs less in energy because I am moving a few electrons, not actual ink."

"So, the image and the original hard-copy are connected, then? I'm still confused by this crazy stuff."

"Laws of Similarity and Contagion. The Law of Similarity says 'If A looks like B, I can make it act like B'; Law of Contagion says 'If A was ever in contact with B, I can make either one look like the other and affect the other.' Both of those are what make voudoun dolls work."

"Christ, voodoo is real, too?"

"One of the more effective real-world magics. Djinni, Bull and I just recruited a voudoun houngan from New Orleans."

"I don't know what that is, but anyways. With the effects of these two laws, you can get into a lot of places and see a lot of things that folks don't want others to see. Corporate espionage made easy, research files, government dossiers . . ."

"Very true, o wolves. Howsomever, there are not too many people who do what I do. I only know of me for certain, actually. At least, on the good-guy side. Most magicians make tech go all wonky." There were more typing sounds. "Even my folks don't do this for the FBI. Mom is a standard witch and glitches probability, Dad is a werewolf, which makes him great for passing as a guard dog."

*Werewolves, too? Hell, an' here I thought I had a decent handle on how the world was, even with Kriegers blowin' it to hell.*

"There just aren't a lot of magicians around, way fewer than people with powers. But we've been around a long, long time. Anyway . . ." The window with the document closed. "That's part of what I can do." There was a long . . . a very long . . . pause. "I have mentioned a time or two that I am paranoid right?"

"You? Never!" John imagined Vickie wishing for a few busts of The Heroes of the War of Northern Aggression to throw at his head right then. "Paranoia is just heightened awareness of danger, t'me. I assume Blue gave you enough of a rundown on how much runnin' around I've done the past few years."

"Ah . . . er . . . uh . . ." Another long pause. Then, in a very small voice, "I've got more. On you."

John's blood turned to ice in his veins, but he did his best to sound casual. "Oh? Well, all the good stuff is fabrications and all the bad rumors are true." He took a sip of his beer, hardly tasting it as he waited for her to continue.

"So, you really turned down the head cheerleader for the Senior Prom?" A note on the page of his senior yearbook opened in a new window. "You made a good-looking sergeant." What looked like his entire Army file took its place.

"I still would."

"And then there was the 'little accident' they arranged for your squad in Panama."

Another redacted file replaced the Army file, and the black dissolved away from the words.

"So that was how they got you into that secret program of theirs. I dunno why they picked you out of the rest for that . . . but I can prolly find out if I keep digging. There's a block on a lot of stuff." She sounded a little annoyed, maybe disconcerted. "I'm better than their blocker, it's pretty brute-force stuff, I just need to be careful and sneaky and finesse it. I can get past it if I work at it long enough, but I kinda have had a lot on my plate."

"I would've thought you'd know already. Seems like the rest of my history is an open book to ya, kiddo."

"Well . . . it could be. It took me a long time to dig out this file. That blocker again." The cursor hovered over the window she had just brought up. "A lot of stuff isn't in computers, or is in computers it's harder for me to crack. I only just got this one before Tesla was murdered." Another sigh. "How angry at me are you?"

"Not very. Can't blame ya for lookin' in on someone that you're doin' Overwatch for. Much."

"Knowledge is a shield. The more I know . . . the more I can shield myself. Or you." The cursor continued to hover. "You want to read this? You want me to stop digging, or keep going?"

John shook his head. "Don't need to read it. I went through it, one day at a time. Keep diggin'. Never know, might find something I can use."

"That's a good part of why I'd do it, Johnny. If they get hold of you again, I want to know how to crack you out."

"So, have you told me everythin' y'know 'bout . . . well, shit, me?"

"I can send a full file copy with the Commies. Or you can read it onscreen."

"Don't send it with the team."

A folder icon popped up in the corner. "At your leisure. But once you close this connection if you want to look at it again you'll have to ping me. That's a link, not a copy. None of the things I'm passing to you are actually on the hotel net."

John scanned the beginning of the first file. It was an operational report; the status listed it as a failure. It was dated for five years ago, and the location was Albuquerque—

*Retrieval: Subject 371 Project Metamorphosis. John Murdock. Status: Failure. Subject neutralized agents and escaped . . .*

—New Mexico. John was lost in the desert, somewhere in New Mexico. He had no supplies, no water, and didn't know how far away from civilization he was. His clothes were tattered and burned; it was night time, and the temperature had plunged as soon as the sun went down. He was trained to survive in extreme situations, but between the drugs coursing through his system and the state of shock he was in, he could hardly think. *I think I might die out here. That's a laugh. Get away, and turn into buzzard food. The Invisible Man in the Sky has a helluva sense of humor for someone who doesn't exist. If I do die, at least I won't do it at the hands of those murdering bastards.* John felt the bile rise in his throat, dizzied by the sudden flare of emotion. After what seemed like hours, the sensation passed. Everything was blurring together. The chattering of his teeth, the pain in his shoeless and bleeding feet, even the cuts and burns that covered most of his exposed skin.

There was a moon, a full moon. It rose, fat and cold, over the mountains. It stared blankly down on him, as indifferent as the eyes of those "doctors" that had done such terrible things to him, to all of them.

More blurred time. The moon was higher. And he heard the sound of a motor. An engine.

The crazy impulse surged through him to bash his head out on a rock, to immolate himself, to do anything to kill himself. Suicide was a better option than being taken *back*. And they would surely want him back. He was too expensive to just let die. After what he'd done? More than ever. He was too tired to fight, and too tired to try to kill himself. Instead, he just collapsed onto his hands and knees, silhouetted by the sudden flash of a vehicle's headlights.

He expected to hear barked orders, see the glint of the moonlight or the glaring headlights off the barrels of weapons. Instead he heard a stream of profanity. Then "Buddy—are you from Alpha Centauri?"

John craned his head upwards with an effort to see the driver. It was a man, late 50s to early 60s. He had a crazy beard, with hair flowing out from a straw hat all the way down to his shoulders. A Hawaiian shirt, cargo shorts, and sandals completed the picture. "Oh man . . . you look like hell, what'd they do to ya? They been interrogatin' ya? Torturin' ya?"

"Somethin' like that," was all that John could manage to croak out. He lifted a hand up towards the driver.

The fellow grasped it, then took him by the elbow, and helped him to his feet. "We gotta get ya outa here. The MIBs'll be here any minute. Dontcha worry, I won't let 'em take ya back." The man half-carried John to the passenger side of the vehicle; it was an old Jeep, and despite its age was in fairly good condition with almost no rust. "You know, you're lucky I found you when I did. This desert can swallow people whole, especially this far out. Only reason why I came around this part was the big fire to the east. Big ol' jets of fire, huge columns of it shooting up into the sky like volcanoes erupting! Was that you?"

John shook his head wearily, pointing to a canteen on the dash. "I don't know what it was. I just remember guys in suits and them takin' me somewhere."

The man handed him the canteen without a moment of hesitation. "It's electrolyte solution, you prolly need it. Black suits and black shades, right? What'd they pick ya up for?"

John drank greedily from the canteen, gasping for breath long enough to say, "My good looks."

The man cackled, and shoved the 4-by in gear. He turned off his headlights. "You musta seen somethin'. UFO?" He pronounced it "you-foe." "Landing? Close encounter? Third kind? Lizard men? Or the Grays? You gotta watch them Grays, man, the lizard men'll only dissect ya, the Grays . . . they got . . . probes."

"I don't know the why, pal. Just that I don't wanna go back." John did his best to keep his seat as the Jeep rolled over the bumps and rocks. "What's your name?"

"We don't use names, man. Safer. Ya can call me Sandman."

"Right. I owe ya, 'Sandman'. I was as good as dead out here."

"You ain't lyin'. MIBs count on the desert t'kill anything that tries to get close or get away. Ya gotta have good survival trainin' t'be out here."

"In my condition, I don't think there's much that trainin' could have done." He shook his head, then changed the subject. "Where are we headed? Anywhere but here is good enough for right now, but I'm the curious sort." His wits were starting to come back to him now that he had hydrated and was at least momentarily safe.

"Ya done with that canteen? There's 'nother under your seat, an' a baggie fulla meal bars. We're headin' fer Albuquerque, but I'm gonna drop ya at the edge. Well, first we're gonna make a stop where the Black Helicopters can't spot us, I'm gonna get the kit, and you're gonna patch yerself up and take a spare shirt an' pair of pants. An' shoes. Then I'm gonna loan ya one-a my spare bikes an' ya can pedal yer way into town."

"You're a saint, Sandman. I don't know how I can repay ya. In fact, you helpin' me might've been the start of some trouble for ya. The worst kind."

Sandman cackled again. "Put yer hand on the outside of the Jeep door."

John did. The surface felt . . . odd.

"Stealth paint. I don't show up on radar, man. 'Struth. Mighty Wing's gotta Corvette he stealthed with the stuff, he makes runs at a hunnert-ten an' the cops never tag him. An' I ain't gonna say nothin' about this on the net, man. Two peeps can share a secret, three, and it ain't a secret no more. Right?" Sandman cast him a sly look. "Yer my secret. I helped one-a the MIBs, prisoners! I bin hopin' fer somethin' like this fer twenty years!" His grin showed white in the moonlight.

For the first time in what felt like years, John smiled, and then slept. He woke only briefly, when the Sandman stopped somewhere dark and gave him old, clean clothing and loaded a bicycle into the back. Then he slept again.

It felt like John slept for years; entirely too long, and not long enough at the same time. The only thing he saw was fire and blood in his dreams; he woke up to Sandman shaking him awake.

"OK, brother. I took the route 'round Robin Hood's barn, just, ya know, to be sure. We were south of ABQ in case ya didn't know, I went west and north and around and we're on the south side of 40 right now, on Central." He cackled a little. "They call this the 'war zone.' You can prolly tell."

Tattoo parlor, Vietnamese restaurant, pawn shop, beauty parlor, all in the same tiny strip mall, all burglar-grilled except for the tattoo parlor, which was open. Gas station with bars on the cash box. Burger joint, taco joint, Mexican grocery, all closed at this late an hour, all with cages.

"I can drop you about anywhere along here with the bike, you can bike straight up Central to the Uni, and get public transport there."

"This is pretty close to where I need to be. I still can't tell ya how much I owe ya, Sandman. You're doin' me a solid." John looked at the bike in the backseat. "Don't think I'll have a chance to get your bike back to ya, unfortunately."

"I get 'em cheap at cop auctions. There's always another twenty-buck bike out there." Sandman shrugged.

"Let's pull off into an alley. Better if I get out that way than out here in the open."

Sandman took a right at the next corner and pulled into—well it wasn't an alley; it appeared that Albuquerque didn't exactly have alleys, but it was behind another strip mall where dumpsters were lined up, smelling of things best forgotten.

"Here's as good as it gets, brother," Sandman said, a little wistfully. "I kinda wish you could tell me more, but hey, probable deniablity right?"

"Safer this way, compadre." John hefted the bicycle out of the back of the vehicle, then held out his hand to Sandman. "Time for me to go."

Sandman shook it heartily. He had a good handshake. "Safe journeys, brother."

"I like that. Safe journeys to you, Sandman." John grinned lopsidedly. He wished that he could do more to show his appreciation, but time was against them both.

Sandman reached into his back pocket and stuffed something into the breast pocket of the vest John was wearing. "Stopped on the way, you were out and didn't wake up. Figure you can use this."

Without waiting for an answer, he waved, gunned the engine, and drove off. John reached into his pocket, and was surprised to find a wad of hundreds in his hand. There was a small bit of metal sandwiched in the cash, about as big as a large button. It was a scorched and tarnished badge in the shape of a star, red with a golden hammer and sickle in the middle. *Now what in the hell would he give me this for?*

It didn't take long for John to pedal to where he'd rented a long-term storage shed. Inside was everything that he'd need to get clear of the trouble that he was in. Forged documents, extra cash, disguises, some basic necessities, and an unregistered pistol. He'd paid for the rental for several years in advance, in cash, upfront, with a few extra bills slipped to the manager to make sure that things weren't disturbed. In this part of town, that wasn't that unusual. After doing what John had done the past few years, he'd learned that being prepared was a reward in and of itself. Readying everything into a single backpack, John closed and locked the shed for a final time. *Time for the hard part: getting away.*

The thing about a university is that an abandoned bicycle will get snatched up before the seat has a chance to get cold—and the public transportation will generally take you to the train station if there is one, and the bus depot. Since universities are full of students who know nothing about an area, the public transportation stops are generally plastered with route maps. John sat in the back of the bus, and tried to look as relaxed as possible. He was still partially dehydrated, burnt and cut worse than a piece of roadkill, and coming off a laundry list of drugs that the doctors had pumped into him. He was a bundle of nerves, but did his best to appear disinterested in everything. There were maybe eight people on this thing, and most of them looked almost as beat up as he did. The only two who didn't were a couple of teenagers more concerned with eating each other's faces than anything around them. Despite everything, John almost allowed himself to feel good again. Just being around people, normal people, after what he'd been through . . .

He shook himself out of it. The bus was approaching the train station's stop. No one else was getting off at the stop with him. He shrugged on his backpack and pulled his cap lower over his eyes. Taking a deep breath, he made his way off the bus and into the main building. The building had a vaguely Pueblo vibe, like many public buildings in this part of the country. The inside was institutionally clean, but still had the rundown feeling of a place that no one wanted to spend too much time in. John located the ticket counter, and paid for the earliest train that would take him to Kansas. It was scheduled to leave in about two hours. He'd worked out his "grand escape" on the bus ride over. He'd get into Kansas on the train. From there, he'd either hitchhike into Oklahoma, or just stow away on a semi going in the right direction. Same would go for Texas after Oklahoma. From there, John would cross the border into Mexico, and do his best to disappear in South America after that. If anyone was looking for him, they'd figure he'd take the direct route, bus straight down to Las Cruces and from there to Juarez. Juarez really *was* a war zone, and it would be easy for him to get lost there, so . . . if there was pursuit, his picture would be all over the border guard post by then. The more twists and turns he could put between himself and any pursuit, the better.

After purchasing his ticket, John found a dark corner seat in the waiting room. The seats next to it were either broken or covered in vomit; luckily, the owner of the vomit had probably already been shuffled off. John kept his head low, but made sure that he kept his eyes on everyone. It wasn't very hard; this early in the morning, there were few people occupying the terminal. Just some custodial staff and a couple of fellow transients. John wanted nothing more than to sleep again, but he was still too keyed up. One thing he did need though, was water. Lots of it. He spent his time waiting by getting water from a machine, and then filling the empty bottle at a nearby water fountain. No telling when he'd get a chance to rehydrate again.

That's where everything went to hell.

"Hey buddy."

John turned, slowly. There was a transit cop standing behind him. "Look, buddy, I've been watching you for a while. You've probably drunk close to a half a gallon of water." The cop actually looked concerned. "That's not good, you know?"

"Honestly, I'm fine, officer. If it's alright with you, I'm just gonna sit and rest for awhile until my train comes in." John made a show of holding his ticket up, slowly; transit cops at terminals spent a lot of time clearing out drunks and the homeless who would take up space trying to sleep under a roof.

But the cop was shaking his head. "Look, you obviously aren't from around here. You're probably sick and don't know it. Heat exhaustion . . . swine flu . . . diabetes . . . all those things will make you drink like that and the last thing I need is to have to clear you out when you have a seizure or pass out or start vomiting like the Exorcist. Look, come with me to the aid station and we can get you checked out. There's plenty of time before the train. If you're ok, no blood, no foul, and if you're not, we find out before you become a problem."

John was stuck. If he argued with the cop and made an issue of it, the cop would *force* the issue. If he ran, he would need to find a new way to get clear of New Mexico. And he certainly was *not* at the point where he'd kill a cop in cold blood just to save his own hide. "Alright, officer, if ya say so."

The cop kept up a running monologue about some college kids who'd gotten heat stroke and put the whole station into an uproar. John really wasn't listening. He was trying to keep track of where possible exits were. His eyes were darting to cameras, exits, obstacles, anything that could be used as a distraction or a weapon.

"Alrighty, here we are. I'm just going to finish a quick check at the front desk, and then we'll get you sorted out. Just sit tight in here for a few minutes." The cop smiled, showing John to a seat in front of his desk. John sat quietly, running over his options mentally, looking for a different one. He could still slip out, quiet-like, if he did it now . . .

Four of them came into the room at once, from both doors. They slowly walked in, locking the doors behind them. Four men in identical black suits and sunglasses, all of them in their mid-30s. Walking cliches. *Sandman would die to see these guys.* John immediately tensed, but stayed seated. The men were all very casual in approaching him, self-assured. *Goddamnit! How the hell did they find me so quickly?* John was the first to speak. "So."

"So, John. You left quite a mess, you know. Some very important people spent a lot of time and money on you and the others, and now most of that has gone up in flames. Literally!" It was the shortest of the four men who spoke, a redhead with a severe jaw. He chuckled to himself. "You're going to come back with us. You suddenly became much more valuable, with the destruction of the Facility. More than valuable enough to overlook everything that happened back there. And, as they say, 'The Program must go on.'"

"I don't want any part of it. Not anymore. I'm *done*, goddamnit." John stood out of his chair, backing up to the wall. Three of the "suits" thrust a hand into their jackets, obviously going for pistols. The redhead was the only one who didn't, instead motioning for the others to hold off. "It don't matter what you offer me, it ain't enough, and it ain't ever gonna be enough."

"John, you're talking like you have some choice in this matter. You most assuredly don't. Despite your recent . . . changes, you can't kill all of us before we kill you." He walked over in front of John until his face was mere inches in front of John's. "I've read your dossier. You're good, or you were. Losing it over a skirt? You've lost that edge, that focus. Besides, even if you were still good . . . I don't think you have it in you to kill us." That same self-assured smirk.

John leaned forward the barest few centimeters, his face betraying no emotion. "I just escaped from the Facility. To do that, I had to kill several hundred people. While tied to a table, waiting to be executed. And right now I don't have a goddamn thing to lose but my life, which you're gonna have one way or another. Do you really think I don't have what it takes to end you?" The redhead's expression broke, and John saw the man's eyes go wide as he fully appreciated the situation. There was still a chance . . . still a chance that these goons would back down.

But then he saw the redhead reach for his pistol and all bets were off. John immediately clamped his hand around the bulge in the redhead's jacket. John squeezed—hard—and the weapon fired. The round passed through the suit jacket and hit one of the government goons, wounding him. John had been unconsciously breathing quickly as soon as the suits came into the office. He felt as if his body was a tuning fork that had just been struck the right way. Putting all of his might into it, John shoved the redhead away from him. Somehow he flung the man far too quickly into one of the suits behind him. They both violently crumpled into a heap as they crashed into and dented a large metal filing cabinet, sending papers flying. John and the others were momentarily stunned, and John could practically hear his whole body humming. It was the closest he'd ever had to being high on something like coke or meth—like being drunk, but with everything operating with full clarity and at high speed. Amped up. *Jesus . . . these 'enhancements' are more than the docs ever promised.*

The other two suits reacted before John had snapped out of his daze. One ran towards him with a blackjack raised. It looked like he was moving a little slower than he should have been. John quickly raised his left arm to block the overhand strike, but his timing was off; he moved too fast and was out of position when the blow landed. John staggered backwards, and his opponent pressed his advantage, raining blows on John's head and shoulders. Every counter John tried, he overextended himself, punching or kicking too hard, blocking too fast and early, which basically amounted to him missing the block every time. John's left eye had closed up, and he could feel blood flowing freely from his scalp. He was backed up against the wall, and the suit that had been shot had joined in trying to subdue him. John roared and grabbed the blackjack-wielder in a tackle suddenly and carried him into the opposite wall. Somewhere in the back of his mind, he noticed that the cinder-block wall of the office cracked and deformed when they impacted. John started pounding the man's midsection, still shouting. He immediately stopped both after looking up to see the man's vacant eyes; the back of his head was—flat. And blood was splattered all over the wall around it. John gasped, stepping back and away from the body; it slid messily to the floor.

The injured suit behind him got his attention, shocking him back to the present out of his self-horror. "Bastard!" He raised a pistol at John, leveling it with his chest. Moving faster than he knew he could,

John was upon the suit almost instantly. He spun the man around, and then twisted his pistol arm behind his back, jamming the gun into his spine. There were popping and snapping sounds as sinew and bone gave way to John's brute strength. The man started—well it wasn't screaming, exactly, it was more like a high-pitched whine through clenched teeth. *I've already killed one. First one's expensive, the rest are cheap. Screw it.* John forced the man to fire the pistol repeatedly, emptying the magazine. Since the muzzle was pressed deeply into the man's back, the shots were muffled.

The redhead made the mistake of getting up, instead of playing dead. The suit he had landed on didn't need to play; he was most certainly dead, neck broken by the impact. "You . . . fucking . . . asshole!" Redhead was cradling a broken left arm, his pistol still in his right hand. "We gave you a way back in! You could've been made! Helped us stay on top . . . but you threw it away! Any one of us would've killed to have the opportunity you had, to be what you've become!" He then swung the pistol towards John. Still moving with blinding speed, John drew his 1911 from his waistband, lined the front sight up with the redhead's chest, and fired four times in rapid succession. The man crumpled, whimpering, without ever getting a shot off. John slowly walked over to the man, picking up and shouldering his backpack.

"You wanted to be like me? Wish granted, shithead. Now we're both dead men." John fired the pistol a final time at the man's face, finishing him. He reholstered the pistol in his waistband, moving the jacket to cover the exposed grip.

*Is this what it's going to be like? Is this what I have to do? Is this what I might become?*

*No time for that shit now.*

John heard and *felt* the suit with the broken neck get up. Slowly, he turned around. The man's neck was still at an odd angle. That is, until he used his hands and snapped it back into place with a sickening pop. "What? You thought they'd only send chumps to bring one of *us* back?" The man didn't wait for a reply; he simply charged, wordlessly and without expression, moving just as fast as John could. John caught him just in time, locking his hands onto the man's shoulders. They were equally matched for strength and speed. John brought his knee up between them, and then flexed his leg as hard as he could. The man was kicked out less than a foot—damn he was strong!—but it was enough to break the grip that they had on each other.

Time slowed down for John again. *He's like me. That's what they want from me. Some sort of obedient, Frankensteinian bastard.* Everything that John had been through in the last two days blurred through his mind in a tumble of jumbled images, all out of sequence. The training, the fighting, the running, the drugs, his escape . . . *her* . . . All the rage came swimming back to the surface, surging through him, overwhelming him. He didn't notice the fire forming in his hands, crawling up his arms and shoulders. He was still too amped up from his enchancements, from all the fighting. He saw the man through a red haze, someone not unlike him. That only made him hate the suit even more, their similarities. John screamed once, and reached for the man. He knew he wanted the bastard dead, but he didn't know how he was going to make it happen. The wanting was all it took, though. A giant stream of fire erupted from John's hand; it engulfed the man, fanning over him and splaying against the wall behind him. Before John could even think to stop, the entire room was on fire. The man was a charred cinder on the ground, still twitching. The enhancements . . . they seemed to make it harder for John to control himself when he was amped up.

The scene around him resembled the Facility far too much for his liking. *I need to get out of here.* Less than two minutes had passed since the men had walked into the room. It felt like a lifetime. John opened the door that he had first entered to get into the office . . . and came face to face with the transit cop. John was faster on the draw, however; more practice, and more opportunity to put that practice to use. He had a bead on the cop's center of mass before the cop had even cleared his holster. Behind him the office was on fire, flames licking across the ceiling tiles.

John slowly raised his aim from the cop's chest to his forehead. "Just let me go. This isn't a great day for either of us, right?"

They both had to choose. John desperately did not want to shoot.

This wasn't some Program goon, this was just a regular joe, an honest cop. The guy wasn't in on the score. Hell he had wanted to *help* him. But, right now, he was an obstacle. The cop had to choose, between a dangerous man and the fire behind him. He couldn't deal with both. And if he chose wrong, he might end up dead and able to deal with neither.

The fire alarms went off, and so did the sprinkler system, which didn't seem to be doing anything to the fire in the office. "So? What's your call? You're decent. You tried to help an asshole like me, and that's a lot more than most would've thought 'bout doing. I'm just tryin' to get clear." You could still see that there were bodies in the office, even through the flames. The cop's eyes widened, shocked. Had he known the goons were in there? John had the feeling that he hadn't. "Trust me," he added impulsively, "this was way, way past yer pay-grade."

There was another of those moments, when time got slower, or John got faster, and he could practically see thoughts flashing behind the cop's eyes. Then the man reached out with an empty, open hand; John kept from reacting. The cop grabbed his shoulder and pulled him into the corridor, then shoved him towards the exit. "Get! And grab anybody you run into and get them out too!"

John nodded. There wasn't anything that he could say. He'd had two decent people go above and beyond to help him in less than a day. There just weren't words for something like that. So, without another word, John disappeared into the station, and out, pulling a couple of random strangers who were reacting to the alarm with bewilderment out with him. Looked like he'd have to find another way out of town.

"YO! Daydreamer!" Vickie's voice in his ear kicked him out of memory. "I've got incoming CCCP in less than an hour. Uh . . . just to remind you, one of 'em's The Bear. I have a food delivery service showing at your door in fifteen, booze in thirty."

John shook his head to clear it. "Christ. I'm not sure that there's enough vodka in this dry little town. Not to mention Chef Boyardee." He thought for a moment. "If you can get some diesel and noodles with ketchup delivered, I think it'll suffice; not sure Ol' Pavel could tell the difference twixt any of 'em."

Vickie chuckled. "Hell if I know . . . but you're the one that's gonna have to stow the case of cans."

John sobered. "Hey, Vic?"

"Roger?"

"You know everything in that file. An', I suppose any other files you've dug up on me. Are we still cool? This Overwatch only works if we're both in on it, after all."

Vickie's voice softened. "Cool as a cucumber, bonehead. It's not just what's in your file. It's what you *are*."

" . . . and what am I?" John's voice had the barest hint of pain in it, longing to be understood. Save for Sera, no one knew him the way Vick did.

"A helluva man, and my friend. The guy I trust at my back. More, the guy I trust at Bell's. Now get ready for incoming food and universit, in that order."

"Roger, dodger. And . . . thanks, Vic."

He heard unaccustomed warmth in her voice. "Da nada, big guy." There was a buzz of a doorbell at the door of the unit. "Huh. Early. Twenty-buck tip. Don't be a cheapskate."

"Oh, don't worry. This is comin' outta the 'operational budget.' Just another thing for Nat to yell at me for. I'm pretty sure she has a list, by now."

Vicke laughed in his ear all the way to the door.

# Valse Triste

## Mercedes Lackey

*My name is Triste Steinmann. I am fifteen years old. I have been a prisoner for two years, three days, and six hours. I have been an orphan for two years, two days, and twelve hours.*

Triste always began her journal entries with the record of her imprisonment. It amused Gruppenführer Bruenner when he read it. And he did read it. She had to leave her journal in a drawer in a little desk in his big office, and she had to write in it every day. She had thought he would be angry the first time, but he laughed uproariously. He would never say why, but by this point she knew. Gruppenführer Bruenner was a sadist, like all of the SS, and a narcissist like many of them. She knew what both of these things were, because she had read about them in the works of Herr Doktor Sigmund Freud, which were in French translation in the library of this stolen mansion. Gruppenführer Bruenner did not know this, because he never bothered to read anything that was not related to the war, much less anything in French. His lover did not bother to read at all. As for Frau Gruppenführer Bruenner, well, she was back in Munich, with the half-dozen little Bruenners, so Triste did not know what she did, other than produce babies nine months after Der Gruppenführer made a visit.

*Today I began the piano works of Schumann. Gruppenführer Bruenner wishes me to particularly learn the Lieder, since the Ubermensch—though perhaps that should be Uberfräulein—Brunnhilde is to perform a concert here tonight. There was a piece of Jan Sibelius mixed in with the others, a "Valse Triste," and I learned it quite by accident. I think I will play it when the Gruppenführer requires music for his guests to mingle by. It . . . speaks to me.*

Triste closed her journal and put it in the drawer of the desk where, of course, the Gruppenführer would find it and laugh. There was a little time before the party, a few hours. She would go upstairs to her room, eat when food was brought to her, and wait until she was told to put on the black gown and come down to entertain. She would not need to look at the scores she had studied today. They were in her head, in her fingers, already.

As soon as Triste had been old enough to walk, she had played—first on the little toy piano, to her parents' bewildered astonishment, then on the piano in her teacher's studio, where she could not even reach the pedals. As soon as she had connected the black notes on the page with the keys on the keyboard, she had only to read a score through once, and it was in her fingers. At first, she had been a mere prodigy, a freak, a kind of player-piano in child form. It had been her teacher who had taught her to make her music sing. Her teacher, who was now dead, or in a concentration camp, along with the other Jews of the Lorraine.

Triste had escaped that fate, because of Gruppenführer Bruenner. Not because he was kind. Not because he particularly cared for music, even. But because the music of the German Reich was displayed at every occasion, like draping a beautiful pall over a rotting corpse, and it was easy and cheap to keep her about. She did not argue, did not disobey, was fundamentally invisible; she was nearly as good as a music-playing robot, and rather better than a gramophone. She would be relatively safe, she hoped, as long as she was amusing and useful. She really did not want to die.

She reached her little attic room, which had once been the provenance of one of the housemaids. There was a bed with many worn blankets and a bright white coverlet, a white-painted wardrobe, a white-painted wash-stand. Her gown for the evening hung on the back of the door, newly cleaned and perfumed with lavender. It was plain and black, made of heavy, dull satin, with the yellow *magen David* discreetly embroidered like a brooch on the left side. She did not touch it. She went instead to the white-painted, wooden wardrobe, and made sure that her coat was still there, still untouched. She ran her hands over the inside. The tough little packets of franc-notes were still there, sewn into the false lining she had hung between the wool outside and the real lining. The hair she had tied across the front of the coat, from button to button, was intact. No one had touched her coat. She, and it, were still safe from discovery.

Whenever she got a chance, she stole money from Didi, Bruenner's lover. Didi had been a nude at the Folies Bergere. Didi never kept track of the money the Gruppenführer gave her; she tipped lavishly, bought whatever she cared to, sent money accidentally down in the clothing to be laundered, and when she ran out of money, the Gruppenführer gave her more. Triste was often in Didi's rooms, especially when she was tipsy; that was part of her job too, to amuse Didi, playing popular tunes, sentimental German songs, and pieces from operettas, while Didi drank or danced or sang to them. All she had to do was play and tell Didi how beautiful she was. This was easy. Didi did not have a bad temper, even when drunk. Didi had a magnificent body, long, wavy hair that was really, truly golden blond without any help, and the face of a goddess. The Gruppenführer never allowed Didi out except to shop with one of his men, and Didi was exceptionally stupid as well as exceptionally beautiful; she didn't know what else to do with her time but drink and dance alone, and sing. When Didi finally slept, Triste would prowl briefly about the room, steal money, and slip back to her own room to sew another packet into oilcloth, and then into the lining of her coat. She prayed nightly that God would send her a chance to escape—perhaps when the Gruppenführer was away, or perhaps the English would even bomb Paris.

She knew where she would go. She could see it from her window. Montmartre, the artist's quarter. There had been musicians from there who had visited with her before the war and made a pet of her. If any of them were still alive, and still there, perhaps for enough money they could help her escape France altogether. Triste no longer believed in the kindness of people—but money, especially now, when the only place you could get anything good was on the black market, meant you didn't have to trust to anyone's kindness or lack of it.

She sat back in the little window seat, her fingers moving restlessly against the sill as she gazed out at the Basilique du Sacre-Coeur on the top of the hill. Her fingers played the notes she had learned today, and she let them move without thinking about it. They always did this; it was as if her hands had a mind of their own. When she was not doing something with her hands, they played, and played and played. Unless she clasped them, they played on top of the bedcovers at night. Sometimes she wondered if they would keep playing when she was dead. She hoped this idea never occurred to Gruppenführer Bruenner. He might try the experiment. He would find it terribly amusing to have a couple of disembodied, piano-playing hands he could keep in a box. But of course, without her head, they could never learn anything new, so perhaps that would not be as amusing as he would like.

Then, suddenly, her hands paused. This was unusual enough that she broke out of her reverie to look at them. It was as if they were waiting for her to look at them; they lifted gently off the sill, and the fingers came down, slowly, and she knew what they were playing.

The piece by Sibelius. It had had her name. And it had spoken to her in a way no other piece of music had until this moment. It had called to her. There had been a power in it—she had almost run to the piano to *hear* it, but fear and caution had kept her at her task. Brunnhilde would decide what *Lieder* to sing on the spur of the moment, and Triste had been told in no uncertain terms that she must learn them all.

But she had never seen a piece that she had desired to hear more, never in her entire life. It had been so strong, that she had studied the entire score, hungry to know more. Luckily, there had been notes on the score, telling what it was about.

*It is night. The son, who has been watching beside the bedside of his sick mother, has fallen asleep from sheer weariness. Gradually a ruddy light is diffused through the room: there is a sound of distant music: the glow and the music steal nearer until the strains of a valse melody float distantly to our ears. The sleeping mother awakens, rises from her bed and, in her long white garment, which takes the semblance of a ball dress, begins to move silently and slowly to and fro. She waves her hands and beckons in time to the music, as though she were summoning a crowd of invisible guests. And now they appear, these strange visionary couples, turning and gliding to an unearthly valse rhythm. The dying woman mingles with the dancers; she strives to make them look into her eyes, but the shadowy guests one and all avoid her glance. Then she seems to sink exhausted on her bed and the music breaks off. Presently she gathers all her strength and invokes the dance once more, with more energetic gestures than before. Back come the shadowy dancers, gyrating in a wild, mad rhythm. The weird gaiety reaches a climax; there is a knock at the door, which flies wide open; the mother utters a despairing cry; the spectral guests vanish; the music dies away. Death stands on the threshold.*

She had almost cried, had crumpled the music in her hand, reminded so sharply of her own dying mother. Her mother had not risen from her sickbed to dance with spectral visitors, but she had kept asking for Triste to play so often in her last illness that Triste had sometimes fallen asleep at the piano.

"Triste," her mother had named her. "Sorrow." An odd name for a child, but her mother had insisted. Sometimes Triste wondered if her mother had somehow known what was coming, the war, the SS, the camps. Triste knew all about the camps, although they were still a secret to many, if not most. Bruenner made sure she knew about them. The woman with the cruel eyes had shown her pictures and a film before she brought Triste to Bruenner, properly schooled and obedient. *"You will obey. You will do everything the Gruppenführer wishes. Or you will go here."* Sometimes those scenes of horror played behind her eyes at night, while her fingers danced on the bedclothes.

*Now* Triste was glad that her mother had died when she had, for two months later the *boches* had come marching in, and two months after that, they had come for the Jews. The last she had seen of her father, as Gruppenführer Bruenner's men carried her away screaming, was his body sprawled in front of the door in a pool of too much blood, his eyes staring sightlessly, his head caved in by the butt of a rifle. That was when she came to be part of Gruppenführer Bruenner's household, and that two-week session with the cold woman with evil eyes convinced her to do and be everything the Gruppenführer wanted of her. It had not taken much. She was a timid child by nature. And despite all that had happened, she wanted very much to live.

There was a tap at the door. Triste opened it and accepted the tray from the maid. The servants here were contemptuous of her; she was always polite to them, and never gave them a reason to torment her. The Gruppenführer saw to it that the servants kept her fed; he wanted his music machine healthy. Tonight it was fish, with a little salad, vegetables, some fruit, bread. Coffee, to make sure she stayed awake. She ate it methodically, and put the tray outside the door. She went back to the window, to watch the sun set on the Basilique, and waited. She watched as the cloudless sky behind the Basilique turned a deep and translucent blue, and the white building became pink, then rose, then red. This was her favorite time of the day, and her favorite sight. Her fingers danced on the windowsill, the Basilique turned to ashes of roses, then a ghost floating over the city, against a sky spangled with stars. There were no lights, of course, nothing but what the stars and moon provided. No lights to guide the bombs of the English, for which she prayed nightly.

She was not provided a light in this room. It was not thought that she needed one.

Finally came the tap at her door, the brusque order, "Get ready." She left the seat at the window, took off her plain dress, slipped on the black dress, brushed her hair and bound it at the back of her neck by touch, pulled on the satin slippers that went with the dress, and went downstairs.

By the servants' stairs, of course. She must be unobtrusive, go like a shadow to the ballroom, slip into place at the piano and begin to play in such a way that no one would notice her coming. It was not hard; the piano stood at one end, in a kind of bulge in the room with windows all around it, and since she needed no light, no light was provided there. All the windows had been covered with thick, blue velvet drapes, and blackout covers behind them. The cover had already been lifted from the keys; she took her place at the bench and began to play, a mere whisper of sound, gradually increasing it as more and more people came into the room. Outside her bubble of shadow, the ballroom was brilliantly lit, the parquet floor shining, the chandeliers glowing with light and sparkling with crystal. There was a fountain of wine on a table, and white-gloved waiters with crystal goblets waiting to serve it. There was fruit, cheese, bonbons, little crystal plates and linen napkins on another table. At a third, waiters with boxes of cigarettes, cigars, and lighters. More and more people arrived, most of the men in the uniforms of the occupying army, the women like exotic birds in form-fitting gowns, spangled with beadwork, jewels at throat and ears. None—or very few—of these women were wives, of course. No respectable wife would be seen at a soiree presided over by a mistress, especially not one who had been a Folies Bergère nude.

Though Didi did make a very good hostess. She had an instinct for when to laugh, when to smile, and when to be silent and merely look attentive. Triste watched them all, as her hands played inconsequential, tinkling music, mostly Bach exercises that would disturb no one, or lullabies, or popular songs. They moved about the floor like elegant, dangerous beasts on their best behavior at the waterhole. They were sated now, and had the luxury of being playful with one another.

The servants began to bring in chairs, and she knew the concert was about to begin. Two of Bruenner's men brought in a pair of electric spotlights on tall poles, focusing their light on a spot in front of Triste's alcove. The crowd began to take seats.

She had wondered which of the guests was Brunnhilde, but she should have realized that someone like the Uberfräulein would not be inclined to mingle, at least not before the concert. The servants dimmed the lights, and lit up the electric spotlights. The guests took the hint and the few who were still standing took the remaining seats. Then the diva made her entrance from the rear, the two servants manning the spotlights illuminating her as she paused in the doorway. Everyone began to clap as she made her way to the front of the gathering.

She looked—well, she looked like a very Germanic version of Didi. Taller, built more squarely and robustly, extremely blond; she wore a gown made entirely of silver beads that looked as if it had been molded to her body. A silver belt clasped her waist, with a long piece hanging down in the front, almost to the floor. There was a heavy silver collar around her neck, and a silver diadem around her head. She did not look at Triste, but Triste did not expect her to. She only looked at the audience. When they stopped applauding, she nodded her head graciously, and said, "Zwielicht." Triste obediently began to play.

She had to admit Brunnhilde's voice was glorious, full and rich. She had an enormous range, too, from contralto all the way to coloratura, with no break-point. If Brunnhilde had expected to catch her out, she was to be disappointed; Triste had done her job well, and there was no song that Brunnhilde asked for that she could not play.

Finally the Gruppenführer stepped up into the spotlight as servants began to raise silver balls on ropes to the ceiling. Triste wondered what on earth they could be doing, and why.

"Our gracious and beloved guest has agreed to display for us tonight a little of the power that makes her one of the Führer's chosen Ubermenschen," said Bruenner, with a little smirk. "I know that you will be impressed; I know you will be even more impressed when I tell you that this little display will require no more than a fraction of the power she possesses." He bowed to Brunnhilde, who bowed back, then glanced into the shadows where Triste sat at the piano. "Ride of the Valkyries," he ordered.

Triste began.

For the first part of the aria, the spotlights remained on Brunnhilde, but there was something about the tone of her singing that was giving Triste uneasy shivers and making her stomach knot. Then as she reached the thundering conclusion, and the final "to-yo, to-ho" calls, the spotlights swiveled up to illuminate those silver metal balls.

And that was when Brunnhilde showed her power.

With each "to-yo to-ho!" she somehow directed her voice *at* one of the balls, and the ball literally shredded into a silver metal flower.

You could see from where Triste sat that these were no flimsy little foil balls, either; the metal plating was a good quarter-inch thick, and it just peeled back the way a child would peel the foil from a chocolate. In her mind's eye, Triste could almost see this happening to the front of a tank . . . of an airplane . . . to a man . . . and her insides twisted with horror. Her hands continued to do their job, however, and brought the aria to its thunderous conclusion.

All the guests leapt to their feet, applauding wildly, as Brunnhilde smirked and took bow after bow after bow.

Finally the party began again, with Brunnhilde now circulating among the guests, taking their congratulations. Triste feared that Didi might sulk, but her instincts must have warned her against any such thing; she stood back and smiled, and nodded, and said nothing at all. Finally the chairs were all cleared away, the tables moved back, and Triste knew this was the signal that she was to begin dance music.

Dance music must always begin with a few Strauss waltzes; the Gruppenführer led Brunnhilde out for the first one. Brunnhilde was a competent dancer, and Bruenner was good, if mechanical; there were no mishaps. Meanwhile, Triste played in a sort of daze, still numb with the horror of what this blond creature could do, what a terrible weapon she was. Why, she could be anything from a weapon on the battlefield to an assassin! Who would suspect that music could kill until it was too late?

But there was nothing she could do about it . . .

Her hands began to play the fourth waltz, and her attention snapped back to the keyboard. Those soft little notes . . . that sad melody . . . this was not Strauss.

This was the *Valse Triste*. The Sibelius.

No one seemed to notice. They were all still vying for the attention of Brunnhilde. But the music woke Triste out of her horror, and carried her straight into grief.

She had not wept since her mother died. Not for her father, not for all the people she knew had, must have, gone to the camps, and who were probably dead by now. Not for herself. Her tears seemed to have dried and gone until this moment. But now, as her hands played, the floodgates opened, and the tears flowed, silently; she sobbed silently, weeping for her mother, her father, the sweet, sweet pair of men who loved each other and had unfailingly brought her chocolates, for her teacher . . . their sad, gray spirits rose up before her and she wept for them and for all the others she did not even know. Her grief poured out of her in a torrent—

And out on the dance floor, a strange mist began to rise.

The dancers did not notice it at first, and when one or two did, they must have thought it was some clever effect that the Gruppenführer had arranged. It rose to their knees . . . and then to their waists . . . and then it was too late.

The mist seized them, caught them as the Wilis of legend would catch unwary young men who dared their graves after dark. It caught them; Triste looked up, something telling her that there was something different out there, and saw the moment it caught them, saw the moment the mist formed into human shapes, separated the dancing partners until each of them had a partner made of mist, and whirled them off into a dance of terror. Brunnhilde spun past, her mouth in a soundless "O" of fear. The Gruppenführer, his pupils dilated. Even the servants.

And Triste's hands played on, driving them into the frenzied conclusion of the *Valse,* their faces, their eyes now contorted with horror.

And then, as she brought her hands down on the keys in the final crashing chords, the mist rose up over each dancer like a wave, and engulfed them.

Then there was only silence. The mist vanished, leaving behind a room strewn with the dead.

Triste could not think, but her body, it seemed, had already decided what to do. She got up from the piano, and went to the body of one of the servant girls who was sprawled beside a table. Her hands stripped the girl of her maid's uniform, and redressed her in Triste's gown. Now wearing only her underwear and barefoot, Triste found herself going back upstairs. She left the maid's uniform in one of the rooms, took armfuls of clothing, and the maid's papers. When her arms were full, she took everything to her room. She went down to

Didi's room, and took a suitcase from a closet, and the pair of expensive and hard-to-get rubber-soled shoes Didi wore to go shopping. When she was done, she dressed in some of what she had taken, put on the rubber-soled shoes and her coat full of money, picked up the suitcase, and went back down into the silent house.

The mist was gathering again, following along behind her. But rather than feeling threatened by it, she felt comforted, as if it was protecting her.

At the music room she stopped. Her senses were coming back to her, it seemed; she found herself able to think again. She looked back at the billows of mist.

"I could escape to England," she said, tentatively.

The shadows in the mist seemed to agree. But sadly. As if she were obscurely disappointing them.

"But . . . maybe I can . . . do something . . . " she continued, groping her way through unfamiliar territory. Was this what courage felt like? "If I stay. If you help me. Will you help me?"

There was no doubt. She felt the surge of fierce assent.

She made up her mind. She would stay. And she would need an instrument . . .

She knew exactly what to get. The music room was full of instruments the Gruppenführer had confiscated, but there was one her hands would know what to do with, that was easy and portable to take—and would not be missed. She dashed inside and came out with the concertina in its case. Now she would have her disguise—a means of moving around Montmarte almost invisibly—and her weapon.

"Now we go," she told the shadows, and headed for the door, and freedom. It would be a long walk to Montmarte, but her shoes would make no sound, and she could hide in shadows with the mist's help when patrols came by. She had the maid's papers, and no one would be looking for *her* now. She would find a little garret or basement room, begin playing in the cafes, and eventually, she knew, she would find the Resistance. And then her real work would begin.

She hurried out of the mansion driveway, into the streets of Paris, with the shadows gathering behind her like dark wings.

# White Bird

## Mercedes Lackey

White bird
In a golden cage
On a winter's day
In the rain
White bird
In a golden cage
Alone

Jeanne Blanchette guided her Spitfire through the low-hanging winter clouds, ducking below the ceiling only now and again to confirm her heading. This was no kind of weather to be flying in, but the Armée de l'Air needed their planes, and as soon as one was fit to fly, one of the ferry pilots would be called from the barracks to take it out to its destination. British Spitfires and some P-51s were replacing the Dewoitine D.520s, despite much anguish on the part of the French pilots. Still, it could not be denied that the Spitfire was, in every way, superior to her French counterpart. Jeanne loved the way they handled, and whenever she had to turn her charge over at the end of a flight a part of her mourned at giving it up. They called to her soul, these lovely creatures of war. They called to her heart.

They told her that it was she who should be guiding them against the filthy Boche, and not . . . whoever would get them.

It wasn't as if she wanted to be a ferry pilot. She was as good as the best of the Frenchmen flying now, and better than most. She had thousands of hours in air races under her belt, and she knew this countryside from the air as most folk knew the roads and lanes around their little villages. Most of the poor boys in these airplanes hadn't a fraction of her air-time. She had been racing over this land since she had been old enough to beg, bribe, and browbeat those around her into letting her into a cockpit. Most little girls were horse-mad, and grew out of it. Jeanne was airplane-mad and never would. Unlike the vast majority of those horse-mad little girls, Jeanne had the wherewithal to satisfy her craving, and the stubborn temper to persist in the face of the most adamant opposition.

She dropped below the clouds again, just verifying that she was where she thought she should be. The war-torn landscape was a hell of shattered trees, shattered villages and cratered fields, but the wretched Boche tried to refrain from shelling the village churches directly. Not because they were any kind of religious, the opposite in fact, since they went out of their way to defile the places and murder and torment priests and nuns. No, it was because the tall steeples gave them landmarks to fly by to, as well as marking points to shell or bomb.

She spotted the tipsy little shell of Saint Marie au Fleur below her, and corrected her course a trifle, then eased back up into the shelter of the clouds.

No, she did not want to be here, in a plane she must give over into the hands of some clumsy recruit, a plan with empty six guns, an easy target for Eisenfaust's Messerschmitts. She wanted to be fighting. How not? She was raised in Orleans, she was named Jeanne, and like every little French girl, she was fed the tales of Saint Jeanne d'Arc the way American children were fed the tales of Mickey Mouse.

A broadside wind buffeted the little plane, and again, she dropped below the cloud cover to check her bearings. The storm was worsening. She remembered another day, another storm.

The leaves blow
Cross the long black road
To the darkened skies
In its rage
But the white bird
Just sits in her cage
Unknown.

White bird must fly
Or she will die

Jeanne played in the opulent nursery of her parents' chateau outside Orleans, with her birthday presents. Or, to be precise, with one of her birthday presents, the only thing she had specifically requested that she had gotten. The lovely dolls, porcelain beauties all, sat on a shelf with the rest of her dolls, pristine and untouched. The beautiful dollhouse, a miniature of the chateau itself, served only one purpose: to house the wood and paper, the glue and thread that she used to make her air fleet. And now she played quietly with the pride of her air fleet, an exact model of a real plane. But she did not play with it as another child would, soaring it over her own head as she ran, and making it do all the aerobatics she had seen the stunting pilots and fairs and shows do. No, she was studying it, so that she might make more. Only her Grandmere, who understood her, had given her the model airplane she had asked for.

Her Papa should have understood her. Her Papa was mad for motorcars, for speed, and raced as often as he could escape from the business of his wine and vineyards. But he did not. Perhaps because he seldom saw her, and then, never looked at her. She knew why. He did not want to see her, he wanted to see the boy that she should have been; instead, she was the disappointing girl who had cost her Maman her life. She understood all these things dimly, for eventually Grandmere had explained them patiently to her. Still, too many times, she retreated to her room in abject misery, after facing his cold rejection of even a simple greeting. Papa was Grandmere's son, and it made her sad to see how he neglected Jeanne, so it was Grandmere who tried to take the place of both Maman and Papa.

And it was Grandmere who was there when, with a clap of thunder that seemed to herald the end of the world, the doors to the chateau burst open, and the building erupted with screams and wailing; Grandmere who held her and tried to comfort her, when the body of the chateau's master, killed by the speed he worshipped, was carried in on the raging wings of the storm.

> White bird
> Dreams of the aspen trees
> With their dying leaves
> Turning gold
> But the white bird
> Just sits in her cage
> Growing old.
>
> White bird must fly
> Or she will die
> White bird must fly
> Or she will die

Jeanne might have been like a hundred other rich little girls, if it had not been for Grandmere. But Grandmere would not let her give up her need to fly. It was Grandmere to whom she told the dreams she had, of soaring, arms outstretched, through blue skies and stormy, without need for a plane. It was Grandmere who bought her books on aviation, took her unfailingly to aviation displays and shows. It was Grandmere who persuaded a pilot who gave lessons that teaching the little girl could do no harm, for after all, what would she do with the lessons? Everyone knew that girls did not fly. Of course, the fat wad of francs did a great deal of persuasion too.

But girls did fly, were flying, in increasing numbers. Jeanne got her lessons. Then Jeanne got her airstrip where the unused tennis courts had been. Then Jeanne got her racing plane. And before she died, Grandmere got to see Jeanne win her first race. She did not weep at Grandmere's funeral. People whispered, she knew. But she had had a dream that night, of flying free beside a startlingly youthful Grandmere, who told her, "The sky is your home, and your lover, cherie. Never let anyone make you give it up."

"But what about you?" she asked, crying then, as she had not at the funeral.

"Ah, my home is the stars now!" Grandmere had said, with a brilliant smile. "I am going on such a journey!"

And with that, she had shot ahead of Jeanne, soaring into the night sky, until Jeanne lost sight of her altogether and she was gone.

> The sunsets come
> The sunsets go
> The clouds float by
> And the Earth turns slow
> And the young bird's eyes
> Do always know
> And she must fly
> She must fly
> She must fly

The wind buffeted the plane again, slewing it sideways. Jeanne did not fight the controls, she caressed them, eased them over, making the plane fly with the storm and not against it. No one really understood how she was able to feel so at one with machinery. Not even Henri, who lovingly worked on these beauties, who crooned to them and talked to them and coaxed them back to life after grievous injuries.

It was hard for a woman like Jeanne to find a lover. Fellow pilots did not hold the women in great esteem. Some regarded them with anger, as interlopers. Some regarded them as an affront to nature. Some laughed at them, as if this need that they shared was something in a female that was nothing more than a childish whim, soon grown out of. And last of all, some men regarded them as something to be conquered and cured of their affliction, so that they could display their trophy before all the other men as proof of their prowess.

But Henri Dubois, engineer and mechanic, shared her love of the planes without sharing the love of flying. He did not understand it, but he did understand how it was an all-consuming passion. He of all the men she had ever met was willing to share her with that passion. He had given her the nickname of "White Bird," a pun on her name of Blanchette.

But perhaps even that would not have happened had the war not come. The war, and the Boche, and their hideous supermen . . . which she must, at all costs, avoid, every time she delivered an airplane to the airfields of Belgium.

She dropped below the clouds again, into lashing curtains of rain. And a tiny, tiny thread of alarm thrilled along her nerves.

This storm was stronger than it should have been. Much. Not only had there been no prediction of such a storm, but it felt wrong. Jeanne had always had a kind of sixth sense for the weather, as she did for her planes. And this storm felt *wrong*.

There was one of Eisenfaust's hellish squadron who was said to fly in on storms like this one.

Valkeyria—

—that sixth sense was all that saved Jeanne at that moment, when the clouds tore open, and lightning slashed through on either side of the golden Messerschmitt with its distinctive snarling-horse nose painting. As bullets from the Messerschmitt's guns tore through the place where she had been, Jeanne had sideslipped the Spitfire out of the way, and sent her into a steep, diving turn.

The forces of gravity and centripetal force shoved her back and sideways into the seat; she felt the skin of her cheeks stretching back over her bared teeth. She squeezed her insides as hard as she could to keep from blacking out and felt the tell-tale juddering in her hands wrapped around the stick, as the Spitfire warned her that she was reaching the limit of what the plane could take.

At the last possible moment, she pulled up, mere feet from the churned-up earth of the field below her. The Spitfire soared, and she glanced down and sideways, hoping without much hope to see the smoke and crater where Valkeyria's own craft had plowed into the ground.

Instead, she felt, as if in her own body, the bullets stitching across her right wing.

She had no weapons of her own. All she could do was try to outfly the German bitch. And Valkeyria was one of the super-humans. She could take more g-stress, she had better, faster reactions—and should Jeanne somehow make her crash, she would walk away from it.

*No!* thought Jeanne, as she did a wing-over that turned into a hammer-fall. *I will not let you take my sky!*

They did not fight their way across the sky, with lightning arcing all around them, even striking the planes themselves. There was no fight here, for Jeanne could not fight. She could only try to run, tiny silvery-white falcon pursued by the cruel golden eagle, losing a little more ground with every line of bullets that stitched across some part of the plane.

And then, Jeanne felt it. Felt the moment when the damage reached the critical level. Felt the weakened wings start to part from the body, the tail-empennage bending and about to snap under the stress of the turn. And felt, rather than saw, the massive bolt of lightning that enveloped plane and Jeanne and all in a moment of searing whiteness and a mental shriek of outrage and denial.

There was a single moment of unbelievable pain, as if her entire body was taken apart in an instant, and instantly reformed in a whole new shape.

And then—

She was flying.

She was not in the plane. She *was* the plane. Wings were at her back, her arms stretched out beneath them, both swept back like a V. She felt—something—something strange and alien. It felt like a second set of lungs, except it was above her, and it sucked in air and squirted it out so that she was propelled as she had once seen a squid propelled. She vaguely remembered something Henri had been obsessed with. Something—a rocket? A jet?

She felt the armor, a part of her, a silver-white metal skin covering every part of her, but especially heavy on her visored head.

Visor?

Yes, she had a visor, a glass visor, protecting her eyes. And she sensed the inches-thick plating on her hands, and her head. And she saw Valkeyria's plane below her, and she knew what it was she had to do.

She would knock that Teutonic bitch out of her sky.

She went into a steep dive, and only the German's own sixth sense and lightning reflexes saved her. Now the shoe was on the other foot. She was faster than the Messerschmitt, and more maneuverable. But that speed was her undoing, for she overshot Valkeyria time and time again, and had to turn and make up the distance before she could try to close.

And finally, she was defeated in her attempt to get to the German by the only weapon Valkeyria could bring to bear to cover her retreat.

The storm.

Suddenly, Jeanne herself was all but knocked out of the sky by the torrent of rain that poured out of the clouds. She couldn't see. She could barely stay aloft. She certainly could not find the German.

It was over in a moment, not even a supernatural storm could sustain itself at that level for long. But when the rain subsided, Valkeyria was gone.

And now, too weary to think, Jeanne only turned herself towards the distant airfield that she had flown out of. Home. She wanted to go home . . .

> White bird
> In a golden cage
> On a winter's day
> In the rain
> White bird
> In a golden cage
> Alone

It was a shock to the airfield command to hear Jeanne's voice on the radio reporting an encounter with Valkeyria.

It was a greater shock to see what landed. A strange construction, some frankensteinian creation, as if pulled from a science fiction serial, half woman, half silvery white airplane. It was not much larger than a woman, if that woman could bear carrying swept-back metal wings on her back, and enough armor to make a medieval knight go to his knees.

They only heard snatches of the encounter out there on the tarmac, between what had been Jeanne Blanchette and the engineer they all knew had been her lover, Henri Dubois. Mostly it was drowned in the static on the radio, static that sounded like electricity weeping. " . . . it does not come off . . . but . . . I cannot . . . *it was not my fault! Would you rather I had died?*"

But they did hear Henri's shouted reply to that question, which rang across the airfield like the bullet from an executioner's rifle.

*"Yes!"*

The man made a gesture in which horror and revulsion were equally mixed, turned, and walked away without looking back, as the terrible static sobbed over the airwaves and the men in the control tower fell utterly silent.

They sensed that, had the rigid skin allowed it, the strange figure on the runway would have sagged in despair.

And then, as the static faded and the silence stretched as tight as an over-wound violin string, the figure raised her head, and—from the posture—looked into the sky.

"Clear the runway," said the voice, like Jeanne's but with a hardness in it they had never heard before. "There are Boche in my sky. When I am finished with my patrol, there will be fewer of them."

"But Jeanne—" someone ventured.

"Jeanne Blanchette is dead," the voice replied, hard and dead. "I am La Faucon Blanc, and the skies are mine."

> White bird must fly
> Or she will die
> White bird must fly
> Or she will die
> White bird must fly
> Or she will die
> White bird must fly*

*Lyrics: "White Bird" by It's A Beautiful Day

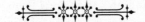

# Sgian Dubh

## Mercedes Lackey

Not for the first time, Roddy MacSgian wished he hadn't been born a bloody metahuman.

It wasn't that he was unhappy with being dragooned into MI6 . . . the good gods knew that every man jack and plenty of woman jills were needed in this war. The bloody damned Nazis had run over everything in their path and had eaten most of France by now. About the time they took all of the Netherlands, they had started bombing the hell out of London . . . not just the damned Luftwaffe but the Luftwaffe Übermenschen too. The "Superior Men," like Eisenfaust and his squad. Blitzkrieg, they called it, and it looked like a lightning storm every night. Not that Roddy had seen it when it first started, no, he'd been where the Auld Woman said he belonged, right on the farm, tending the shaggy, sleepy-eyed cattle, like his father, and his father's father, and so on back to the first of his line to hold that particular piece of Highland land. Not that he wouldn't have volunteered if the Auld Woman hadn't strictly forbade it, on account of his being the only male left of his clan, the oddly named clan, "Son of the Knife." But even so, they wouldn't have taken him. Not on account of his being the only male left of his clan, but on account of his size. He knew jockeys who were taller than he was. The Auld Woman said it was the Pharisee blood in him; once he'd gotten his marching orders, the learned fellows at MI6 looked interested and said that it might well be he was almost pure Pictish. Whatever the case was, it was a fact that Roddy topped out at four feet tall, and they didn't make uniforms in his size, nor boots, nor rifles that weren't taller than he was.

So when the whole bleeding War started, and the Nazis began wrapping up other countries and taking them home, and Tommys started joining the Frogs at the border of Lorraine, well, the Auld Woman wanted him to stay. He saw no reason not to; the Army had no bleeding use for him.

That was true through the months and weeks that followed right up to the point where three things happened. The Blitz began and Spitfire, and then the rest of Wing Alpha, suddenly proved that the Nazis weren't the only ones that could spawn what the authorities decided primly to call "metahumans"; The Yanks didn't sit around on their hands the way some people had predicted, as newsreel footage of the Ubermenschen in action was enough to convince even a pacifist that the Germans weren't going to stop at the Channel.

And he, Roderick MacSgian, woke up to find himself in a bed that was not his own.

The lady already in the bed, Deidre of the grass-green eyes and flaming hair, of the tiny foot and the winsome smile, of the breasts of a goddess and skin like newly skimmed cream, who he had in fact been dreaming about before he woke up, was not anyone he'd have had a ghost of a chance with. She proved it by screaming her fiery head off.

And Roddy, panicked, did . . . something.

And found himself back in his own bedroom, though he missed his bed by about a foot and landed on his arse on the cold stone floor.

It was that bruising that convinced him he hadn't been dreaming.

Now, even the Auld Woman would admit that Roddy had a knack for thinking quickly, especially when things went badly wrong, and the first thing that flashed into his head was that he had better be able to prove he was in his cottage and not in Deidre MacFarland's bed ten miles away, which meant he'd better get himself one or more sober witnesses to this at some point in the next five minutes.

He pulled on a pair of pants with naught on beneath, because he slept with naught on, shoved his feet into boots, and ran out into the street. "Didja hear that?" he shouted to his neighbor, who was just feeding his hutch of rabbits, doing his best to look wild-eyed.

"Roddy, ye wee bastard, I heerd nowt!" the neighbor laughed. "Ye bin dreamin' again."

Then the neighbor sobered, for it was known that the Old Blood was thick in the MacSgian family, and although the Auld Woman swore that not a bit of the magic had made its way into him, there was always the chance it was late in coming. The neighbor knew this, because it was his wife it was that stood for the East in the Auld Woman's monthly Gathers. "It wasna that sort of dream, now?"

Roddy shook his head, rubbed the back of his neck and looked sheepish. "Och nay," he said, and forbore to say what kind of a dream it was.

Now Deidre MacFarland was a canny lass, and before she went accusing a man of being where no man should have been at six in the morning, and especially not a man she did not know, and did not care to know, she made certain inquiries in that man's neighborhood. And being not wanting to be made a fool of, when she found witnesses that he'd been standing in his own back garden at six-oh-one, she kept her mouth tight shut.

And being no fool, and a month later, sober reflection on Roddy's ability to keep his own mouth shut, and a good memory telling her that not everything about Roddy MacSgian was less than a proper man's size, when a general, no less, came and took him up by special draft, Miss Deidre MacFarland gave him a proper patriotic farewell which bid fair to match that dream. And even at this moment, his ability to be ten miles (or more) awa' in seconds was known only to her, him and MI6.

By the time the general came for him the village and most of the district knew of his other talent, for it had manifested in front of most of them.

Roddy could turn invisible.

He'd done it in full view, in front of a young host of people, in the middle of market-day, when he was in the public house when he was *supposed* to be making rabbit hutches for the Auld Woman.

Now the way that came about was this. The Auld Woman was as tightfisted as any six Scots put together, which is saying a fair bit, and the wood and nails she had given Roddy to build those hutches with were all scavenged from every scrap of an abandoned structure that the Auld Woman's sturdy boots could carry her to. Before he could even use the nails, he had to straighten them, and after having banged his fingers and thumbs to flinders doing so, he reckoned he needed a dram or two or three to take the ache out. As to why the Auld Woman wanted rabbit hutches, well, she and every other person in the village remembered the Great War, and the meat all going to the soldiers, as well it should. That was rationing, and it was understood as something that had to be done. There was War again, and the young men marching off, and there was no doubt the little fellow that looked like Charlie Chaplin and sounded like a madman needed to be put down. Even the Auld Woman, though she would not let Roddy go, said that Hitler was doing some wicked bad things and needed to be put down. But it was a hard thing to be sending the cattle off and getting no meat for yourself.

Ah, but there were plenty alive who remembered the last dust-up. And remembered rabbits now . . . the last time the rabbits had been poached, mostly, but you needed a more reliable system than poaching for a war that looked as black as the inside of a widow's hat. The last time, no one had been making tinned rabbit, and the chances of rabbit-rationing were pretty slim. So hutches were being put up all over the village, and rabbits, after all, could be fed on hay and grass and cabbage leaves and such-like that was easily come by in the country.

So the Auld Woman was to have her hutches too, and no shilly-shallying about the work, for all that she had given him shite to build with. And he was just lifting his second dram to his lips when he heard someone sitting at the window of the pub exclaim, "Ach! 'Tis the Auld Woman a coomin' this way!"

And the men that had been standing shoulder to shoulder with him at the bar cursed, and looked through him, no more did the Auld Woman see him when she poked her head in through the door.

When he went visible again, there was a great old to-do, the Auld Woman boxed his ears and checked him for magic and still found none, and he wasn't at all surprised when the general turned up looking for him. Likely so, and rightly done. With talents like his, there was a lot even a little fellow could do.

By then, of course, the Auld Woman had cast his Weird, and had summoned him, and looked at him in the way that made him go hot and cold together, and told him soberly that though he hadn't a smidge of the Old Magic in him, he had something else, and he had best go to use it for to save a great many lives.

So that was why he was in a tiny little fisherman's smack on the English Channel, one among hundreds, maybe thousands even, of more tiny little boats and not so tiny boats and great huge troopships and all manner of craft, all rushing towards a place called Dunkirk. *They* were going to evacuate troops off the beaches, the troops of the Allies that had been trapped there by German troops and a tank division, and three Ubermenschen—Panzer-Wolf, Panzer-Loewe, and Panzer-Tiger. *He* was going to save, if he could, the pride of the USA, the first two metahumans to come from the United States to fight at the side of the British and French—Dixie Bell and Yankee Doodle.

And here he was, one lone, little man, crouched in the bottom of one lone, little boat, trying not to be sick, with the weight of the Alliance on his back and the blessing of the Auld Woman on his head. Not Young Roddy anymore. Now he was something else entirely. He was, by fiat of MI6, Sgian Dubh, the "little black knife," the last, hidden, and most desperate of the weapons of a Scot.

In the chaos that was the evacuation of the Allied forces from the beachheads up and down the coast of France on either side of the seacoast town of Dunkirk, it was easy for one small man, going the wrong way, to make himself lost without ever going invisible. In fact, going invisible was probably ill-advised; he'd have been trampled.

It was unbelievable, probably horrible, and Roddy was right glad that the darkness hid most of it from him. The fear was so thick you could cut it. The smell of cordite and smoke mingled with the smell of blood and death and the smell of the sea. The men crowded onto the beaches were in despair, seeing escape from the meat-grinder that was the Nazi Blitzkrieg, and yet fearing that they would be cut down before reaching safety. The noise was incredible. The beaches were being shelled, and the edges of the evacuation harried by Nazi storm-troopers. If there was a hell on earth, this was it.

And yet it was not as bad as it could have been, and he knew why. The tank division had halted far short of here. The commanders on the ground expected it to arrive at any moment and were harrying their men into the hundreds of tiny shallow-drafted boats coming right up to the sand that would take the evacuees out to the larger ships.

It was not going to come. In fact, it would not arrive until the beaches were deserted and every last man that could be got off, had been.

That was the Auld Woman's doing, her and her Gathering, and Gatherings and Moots and Meets wherever they had been alerted as to the need for a Great Work tonight. Roddy was entirely vague as to what they were doing, but he had no question as to how it was being done.

Magic.

Magic that ran in Roddy's ancestry, but that he did not share. Not that he was terribly unhappy about this. There were all manner of rules about using magic, and he was pretty sure he would run afoul of them. And the wizards and witches and sorcerers and what-all generally seemed to always be having some sort of quarrel with each other, which made it all the more rare that they ever could get together long enough for a Great Work, like chasing off the Spanish Armada or stopping a German Panzer division.

But the men here didn't know that was happening, and wouldn't believe him if he told them, so they were vibrating between panic and apathy, though they tried to show neither. And Roddy couldn't blame them, seeing as he was steadily making his way *towards* the enemy lines rather than away.

In an hour, he had cleared the jam-up. That was when he went invisible.

Immediately he felt a rush of relief. Every moment since he'd waded ashore, he'd felt terrified. It had all sounded so simple, back in that briefing room. Get onto the beach, under cover of the evacuation; ghost his way to his contact, find out where Dixie Belle and Yankee Doodle were being held, free them, or more likely, help them to free themselves. They were infinitely more powerful than he was. Both of them could fly without needing an airplane; Yankee Doodle shot some sort of energy blasts from his eyes and Dixie Belle was unbelievably strong. He'd seen footage of Belle punching holes in airplanes and picking up cars. Freeing them seemed almost trivial; two people like that, probably all he had to do was go invisible, meet his contact, go invisibly to wherever they were being kept, unlock a door or some such, and they would do the rest.

But of course, he hadn't been able to take on his invisibility, and he had felt as if there was a target painted on his back the whole time he had been scrambling through that mess—short as he was, he stood out as something unusual, and the Nazis *knew* the Alliance had its own metahumans now, and why would there be someone as short as he was on that beach unless he had something to make up for what he lacked in size?

But now, now in the safety of a copse of shattered trees, he faded into nothingness and drew a deep, relieved breath. Now he had only to get through the enemy lines and find his contact. From here on in it should be smooth sailing.

Roddy was coming to the conclusion that nothing was ever as simple as it seemed. He had found his contact easily enough, and the first complication set in right there. His contact was a woman—a girl really—and one who carried a rifle on her back as casually as Deidre MacFarland carried a tennis racket.

They huddled just outside the high brick wall—with broken glass or other nastiness atop it, no doubt—where she said Belle and Yank were being kept. "Eet ees some sort of laboratory," she had explained. "It was so before zee Boche came, and zay took it ovair. So, you *poof* yourself within, *mon ami,* free zem and—"

"Ah, it doesna worrrk that way, lassie," he whispered apologetically.

"I canna go where I havena been before, or at least—" he amended hastily "—where I know some'un that's there." He flushed, thinking of Miss Deidre. The Auld Woman would have been scandalized to know how little she slept in . . .

"*Nom du nom! Sacre merde* . . ." The young woman swore vehemently under her breath. "You can at least *poof* out again, no?"

He thought about that, and flushed again. "Ah . . . I dinna think so," he admitted. "I canna see where we are, ye ken. It bein' dark an' all. I mean, I could likely go *home,* but not out here. It'll haveta be the harrrd way."

The woman tossed her head, and unslung her rifle. "It is not to be helped, then," she said with resignation. "I will to remain here. Someone must report if you do not succeed."

For a moment he felt a surge of resentment, but in the next moment he realized she was right. "Right," he said with resignation. "I'm off."

He might be invisible but that did not mean he was undetectable. Dogs could smell him, for instance. He could leave footprints. People could bump into him and he could bump into things. In fact, he had to be twice as careful in tight quarters, as he couldn't see where his feet and arms were.

So the first step was to get past the dogs. Prowling carefully about downwind told him that there were two with their handlers at the gate, and at least two more patrolling the area between the walls and the building. He considered this carefully. He couldn't slip past the ones at the gate; there wasn't enough room between them, and they would surely smell him. He could go over the wall, perhaps, but then he would still have to contend with the dogs and handlers inside.

On the other hand . . . he looked up at the top of the wall. If he could get up there, and didn't get slashed up on whatever was up there . . . .

He prowled around the outside until he found a section in shadow. The wall itself was no challenge for a lad who had been scampering about the Highlands most of his life. It was the glass and added razor-wire atop it that made it a challenge, and if he got too cut up, he'd bleed, and a trail of blood was not invisible.

Finally he balanced precariously atop the support and peered at the roof of the building itself. This was going to be very tricky—because he couldn't teleport himself and stay invisible at the same time.

*Oh, oh, let there be no lads with sharp eyes at those windows.*

He waited until the dog and handler were out of sight. Waited until everything seemed quiet. Fixed his eyes on a shadowed nook where the chimney met the slippery slate roof, took a deep breath and—

—found himself sliding momentarily down the slates until he lodged against the chimney, cast frantically about himself to make sure he hadn't been seen, made the little twist of his mind that made him invisible again and—

—clung to the tiles and tried to catch his breath. No turning back now.

It took careful climbing and hunting, spread-eagled on the roof-pitch, to find the entrance to the roof that he knew must be there. A building like this one, with over a dozen chimney-pots and three or four times as many fireplaces would have needed the attentions of a chimney sweep regularly, and people who put walls with glass atop them around their buildings did not want sweeps leaning ladders against their walls, so there had to be a roof access. By now, of course, the fireplaces were disused and probably boarded up, but the roof access was still there.

He paused and listened with every fiber, but heard nothing. Cautiously, he tried the hatch.

It was locked, but he could tell it was a simple slip-catch. A bit of knife-work, and it wasn't locked anymore. It opened up on complete blackness. There was no way of telling if the attic was clear or crammed with rubbish, or full of snoring soldiers.

Well maybe not the latter, not unless they could sleep without breathing. He glanced up; he didn't dare risk a match. Not with the air above full of the drone of planes.

Breathing a prayer, he lowered himself down until he was hanging on by his fingertips, then let go.

It was just about a four-foot drop; he hit as "softly" as he could, and remained crouched in place, frozen, listening. Had anyone heard him? Was anyone coming?

Nothing. Feeling his way inch by inch, he moved away from the open hatch and took a chance with a match.

Except for some crates piled up in half the attic, the low-ceilinged room was empty. And there was another hatch in the floor. He let the match burn almost down to his fingers, memorizing the room, then blew it out.

Once again, he listened with everything he had at the hatch, and heard nothing. If luck was with him, this building, now labs, had once been a stately old home, and this hatch gave out into the little rooms that had once been the servants' quarters. Provided they hadn't been gutted to make more lab space.

He raised the hatch open a hair.

There was light, but it was dim, and seemed to come from some distant point. There was no one he could see immediately. He raised it a little more and took a better look. It looked like the hall of servants' quarters. They were probably used for storage, being more convenient than the attic. Moving as quickly as he could and still be quiet, he slid through the hatch and let it down.

Again, he sighed. *Now* he was safer. The soldiers would notice doors and hatches opening and shutting, but they could not see him, and the dogs were all outside.

Halfway down the hallway, he heard the tramp of boots on stairs and the sound of voices speaking what he assumed was German. For a moment, he froze—then slipped quickly to the end of the hall and the blacked-out window there. He squeezed himself in next to it as four soldiers, smelling slightly of wine and sausages, clumped their way past him and separated, two to a room. So the guards on duty here were using these rooms as their quarters . . . so much for using the roof as an escape route if he was spotted and pursued.

Pressing his back to the wall, he inched his way down the stairs to the second floor.

This one was lit, much better, and he realized that now he had another problem.

He didn't know where, exactly, Belle and Yank were being held.

Which essentially meant that he was going to have to check every room—wouldn't he?

It was a big building. Why, there must be twenty rooms on this floor alone!

His moment of hesitation was cut through by the sound of a child screaming.

The sound sent a rush of electricity fueled by fury across his nerves. As the child continued to cry out, screams fading into a pitiful whimpering that was worse than the screams, he raced down the hallway, following his ears. And he was just about to break down the door that the cries led him to when his good sense kicked in, and instead of crashing through it, he placed his hand on the knob and opened it just a crack. Just enough to see inside.

He saw the back of someone dressed in a surgeon's gown, as pristine and white as bleach and scrubbing could make such a garment. The man leaned over something or someone, utterly preoccupied, muttering to himself. Silently, Roddy slipped inside, closing and locking the door behind him.

At this point the contents of the room were in full view. There were four beds here, if you could call something with straps and harnesses like a torture device a "bed." Only one was occupied, by a frail-looking girl who could not have been more than thirteen or fourteen years old, dark-skinned, black-haired; without thinking twice about it, Roddy knew what she was. A gypsy—one of the Travelers.

The man turned away from the little table he had been fussing with, and back to the girl strapped down to the bed. There was a wicked sharp scalpel in his hand, and at the sight of it, the girl's whimpers turned to screams again.

Less than a second later, the man was on the floor, with his own scalpel sticking out of his eye. He was quite dead. Roddy was no stranger to killing, although this was the first human being he had killed. Then again, anyone that would do what that man had been doing to that poor little girl—her body was a mass of scars, healing wounds, and fresh ones. Even as he fought with the straps to get her undone, one of the fresh wounds began to heal before his eyes. It was pretty clear what had been happening here; the wee thing was a metahuman too, one that could heal herself, and this butcher had been cutting on her, trying to find out how she was doing it.

Now, she watched him silently, looking remarkably calm for someone who had just been rescued from torture by a man who had been invisible. But when he got her right hand free, the first thing she did was to reach for him, and rest her fingers lightly on his forehead.

He froze, as a picture formed in his mind, which pretty much confirmed what he had guessed. The Auld Woman had quite a bit to do with the Travelers, or the Romany, as they liked to call themselves. There was a lot of Magic in some of their bloodlines, and when one magician entered the territory of another, it was only polite to come calling, unless you planned on open warfare. And no one in his right mind would go to war against the Auld Woman. So he knew a bit of the lingo, and he struggled to make himself plain. *"I didn't come here to fetch you, but I'll get you out anyway, lass."*

Her eyes widened and filled with tears, and another picture came into his mind . . .

It fair made him sick to his stomach and infused him with an energy he hadn't known he had. Fired by it, he gathered the girl in his arms and—

—landed heavily on the painfully clean stone floor of the Auld Woman's cottage. As he knew she would be, the Auld Woman and her Gathering were convened in their Circle, one small cog in the Great Work going on that was keeping the worst of the German menace from falling on the heads of the evacuation at Dunkirk. And because they were only one small cog, it did no harm for the Auld Woman to rise from her place, and take the fainting girl out of Roddy's arms.

"Her people be dead, I got no time. Take care of her!" he said, the first time he had ever issued an order to the Auld Woman. He barely had time to register her nod before he gathered himself again and—

—landed back on the corridor, outside the door to the room of horror.

He made himself invisible again, then knelt where he had landed, exhausted, and unable to move. That was the longest he had ever jumped before. He wasn't sure he could ever do it again . . . .

Fortunately, it seemed that the sick bastard that had been torturing the girl was not exactly popular with the rest of his lot. The rest of the floor was empty, and there was not even so much as a single soldier guarding the area. Roddy was left undisturbed while he waited for the weakness to pass.

And it was while he was kneeling there with his head down that he realized that, no, he was *not* going to have to hunt through every room in the building to find the American metahumans.

He was only going to have to look for the room with all the guards on it.

That room was on the ground floor, and whatever its purpose had been when this was a house, it had been heavily reinforced with a banklike vault door. The purpose of such a thing puzzled Roddy for a moment, as did the symbol on a sign beside the door; a small red dot with five red lightening bolts radiating outwards from it. Whatever it was that the former owners of this place thought needed such protection, it must have been dangerous.

But not nearly so dangerous—at least to the Nazis—as what was in there now, judging by all the guards.

But Germans were nothing if not precise. And that very precision made it possible for Roddy, moving slowly and carefully, to ease his way past them and into the room beyond just in time to hear a resonant voice say in heavily accented English—

" . . . I think that there is no more need for a mask to hide behind, little white dove—*Gott im Himmel! Du bist ein Schwarze!*" He jumped back, giving Roddy a clear view of the female captive, her arms and legs encased in what looked like layer upon layer of anchor chains.

"Watch who you're calling *white,* you Ku Klux Klan reject!" spat Dixie Belle, her dark, handsome face contorted with contempt as she looked up at the chiseled features of Eisenfaust. Roddy recognized both of them from photographs, although he was probably the only person outside of the select circle of enlisted metahumans that knew Dixie Belle was not, in fact, the blond-haired, blue-eyed girl on the American recruitment posters. Then again, the ongoing romance she had with Yankee Doodle—assuming there really was a romance and not that it too was a complete fabrication—was illegal in several states. Or so this had been explained to him as the reason why the rescue had to be kept secret.

"Dieses ist unmoeglich," the German muttered, the back of his neck going red. Then he straightened. "I was going to offer you the opportunity to join us," he said, his voice so cold as to freeze the very air in the room. "But—"

"Oh, don't I fit in with your Master Race?" Belle replied, the sweet sarcasm in her voice as palpable as the ice.

"I guess you don't, sugar," said a second voice. "Not that we would have accepted, of course. Beer gives me gas, and that tinpot despot of yours gives me worse gas."

Eisenfaust pulled back and slapped Yank with the back of his hand so hard that the *crack* sounded like a gunshot. Belle screamed an obscenity and Eisenfaust raised his hand to slap her too—then thought better of it.

"I will not contaminate my flesh with touching you," he said contemptuously. "Contemplate your fates. When Herr Doktor Herbsten is finished with his subject upstairs, he will come to study you. Most of his subjects have not lived too long. Perhaps you will be the exception."

With that, Eisenfaust turned abruptly and marched out the door, which swung ponderously shut behind him.

Now Roddy could see that, like Belle, Yankee Doodle was tied hand and foot to a chair that had been bolted to the floor. But the top half of his head was encased in a kind of helmet with an opaque visor. That visor, Roddy realized immediately, must be mirrored on the inside, so that anything Yank tried would just get shot back into his own face.

But the important thing was not what their captors had intended to do to them. The important thing was that he and the prisoners had the entire room to themselves.

He allowed himself to become visible; Belle reacted with a startled, smothered squeak.

"Marie? Baby?" Yank reacted with alarm, turning his head blindly from side to side. "What is it? What—"

"'Tis all right, laddie," Roddy assured him as he stepped forward to take the helmet from Yank's head. "I'm Sgian Dubh of MI6, and I'm here t' help."

With a little puff of displaced air, the Scotsman landed beside his French Resistance guide, falling wearily to the ground as she bit back a scream that turned only into a swift intake of breath. "*Sacre merde!*" she whispered harshly. "Do not—what happened? Were zey not zere? Could you not free zem? What—"

Roddy tiredly held up one hand for silence, forgetting that in the dark she couldn't see it. But it hardly mattered as in the next moment the old stone mansion literally erupted with the sound of the pride of the USA metahuman forces as they began the grimly joyful task of kicking and blasting their way out of imprisonment. Holes began to appear in the slate roof as Yankee Doodle's energy blasts reached for the heavens.

Under cover of the ruckus, Roddy and his contact slipped away. He looked back only once, just in time to see the two figures, illuminated by the flames licking up from the ravaged building beneath them, shooting off into the sky.

Roddy smiled. The Auld Woman couldn't have done it better herself.